EX LIBRIS

VINTAGE CLASSICS

ROBERTO BOLAÑO

Roberto Bolaño was born in Santiago, Chile, in 1953. He grew up in Chile and Mexico City, where he was a founder of the Infrarealism poetry movement. Described by the *New York Times* as 'the most significant Latin American literary voice of his generation', he was the author of over twenty works, including *The Savage Detectives*, which received the Herralde Prize and the Rómulo Gallegos Prize when it appeared in 1998, and *2666*, which posthumously won the 2008 National Book Critics Circle Award for Fiction. Bolaño died in Blanes, Spain, at the age of fifty, just as his writing found global recognition.

ALSO BY ROBERTO BOLAÑO

NOVELS

The Savage Detectives

2666

Nazi Literature in the Americas

The Skating Rink

The Third Reich

Woes of the True Policeman

The Spirit of Science Fiction

NOVELLAS

By Night in Chile

Distant Star

Amulet

Antwerp

Monsieur Pain

A Little Lumpen Novelita

Cowboy Graves

POETRY

The Romantic Dogs

Tres

The Unknown University

ROBERTO BOLAÑO

THE COLLECTED SHORT STORIES

TRANSLATED FROM THE SPANISH BY
Chris Andrews and Natasha Wimmer

WITH AN INTRODUCTION BY
Chris Power

VINTAGE CLASSICS

3 5 7 9 10 8 6 4 2

Vintage Classics is part of the Penguin Random House group
of companies whose addresses can be found at global.penguinrandomhouse.com

First published as *The Collected Short Stories* in Vintage Classics in 2024

The stories in *Last Evenings on Earth* were first published in Spain as *Llamadas telefónicas* and *Putas asesinas* by Editorial Anagrama in 1997 and 2001 respectively
First published in Great Britain with the title *Last Evenings on Earth* by Harvill Secker in 2007
Copyright © Estate of Roberto Bolaño 1997, 2001
Translation copyright © Chris Andrews 2007

The stories in *The Return* were first published in Spain as *Llamadas telefónicas* and *Putas asesinas* by Editorial Anagrama in 1997 and 2001 respectively
First published in the United States of America with the title *The Return* by New Directions Books in 2010
Copyright © Roberto Bolaño 1997, 2001
Translation copyright © Chris Andrews 2010

The Insufferable Gaucho was first published in Spain with the title *El gaucho insufrible* by Editorial Anagrama in 2003
First published in the United States of America with the title *The Insufferable Gaucho* by New Directions Books in 2010
Copyright © the heirs of Roberto Bolaño 2003
Translation copyright © Chris Andrews 2010

The stories in *Posthumous Stories* were first published in Spain with the title *El secreto del mal* by Editorial Anagrama in 2007
First published in the United States of America with the title *The Secret of Evil* by New Directions Books in 2012
Copyright © the heirs of Roberto Bolaño and Editorial Anagrama 2007
Translation copyright © Chris Andrews 2012
Translation copyright © Natasha Wimmer 2011

Introduction copyright © Chris Power 2024

Roberto Bolaño has asserted his right to be identified as the author of this
Work in accordance with the Copyright, Designs and Patents Act 1988

The permissions on pages 719 are an extension of this copyright page

penguin.co.uk/vintage-classics

Typeset in 12/14.75pt Bembo Book MT Pro by Jouve (UK), Milton Keynes
Printed and bound in Great Britain by Clays Ltd, Elcograf S.p.A.

The authorised representative in the EEA is Penguin Random House Ireland,
Morrison Chambers, 32 Nassau Street, Dublin D02 YH68

A CIP catalogue record for this book is available from the British Library

ISBN 9781784879488

Penguin Random House is committed to a sustainable future
for our business, our readers and our planet. This book is made from
Forest Stewardship Council® certified paper.

Contents

Introduction — xi

PART I: LAST EVENINGS ON EARTH

Sensini	3
Henri Simon Leprince	22
Enrique Martín	30
A Literary Adventure	47
Phone Calls	60
The Grub	66
Anne Moore's Life	80
Mauricio 'The Eye' Silva	113
Gómez Palacio	129
Last Evenings on Earth	140
Days of 1978	169
Vagabond in France and Belgium	184
Dentist	201
Dance Card	225

Contents

PART II: THE RETURN

Snow	237
Another Russian Tale	256
William Burns	261
Detectives	271
Cell Mates	294
Clara	307
Joanna Silvestri	319
Prefiguration of Lalo Cura	336
Murdering Whores	354
The Return	371
Buba	389
Photos	417
Meeting with Enrique Lihn	427

PART III: THE INSUFFERABLE GAUCHO

Jim	439
The Insufferable Gaucho	442
Police Rat	474
Álvaro Rousselot's Journey	502
Two Catholic Tales	525
Literature + Illness = Illness	542
The Myths of Cthulhu	563

Contents

PART IV: POSTHUMOUS STORIES

Colonia Lindavista	581
The Secret of Evil	588
The Old Man of the Mountain	591
The Colonel's Son	595
Scholars of Sodom	611
The Room Next Door	618
Labyrinth	622
The Vagaries of The Literature of Doom	643
Crimes	652
I Can't Read	660
Beach	668
Muscles	673
The Tour	688
Daniela	692
Suntan	695
Death of Ulises	700
The Troublemaker	709
Sevilla Kills Me	713
The Days of Chaos	717
Permissions	719

Introduction

*The Third Man: On the Short Fiction of Roberto Bolaño**

In *2666*, the novel Roberto Bolaño was working on when he died in 2003, aged just fifty, the melancholy Professor Óscar Amalfitano lets his mind wander while teaching a class. Mention of the Austrian poet Georg Trakl, who worked as a pharmacist in Vienna, has reminded Amalfitano of a pharmacist he once knew in Barcelona. One night, the professor asked this young man what he liked to read:

> Without turning, the pharmacist answered that he liked books like *The Metamorphosis*, *Bartleby*, *A Simple Heart*, *A Christmas Carol*. And then he said that he was reading Capote's *Breakfast at Tiffany's*. Leaving aside the fact that *A Simple Heart* and *A Christmas Carol* were stories, not books, there was something revelatory about the taste of this bookish young pharmacist, who in another life might have been Trakl or who in this life might still be writing poems as desperate as those of his distant Austrian counterpart, and who clearly and inarguably preferred minor works to major ones. He chose *The Metamorphosis* over *The Trial*, he chose *Bartleby* over *Moby-Dick*, he chose *A Simple Heart* over *Bouvard and Pécuchet*,

---

* All translations are by Chris Andrews unless otherwise stated.

Introduction

and *A Christmas Carol* over *A Tale of Two Cities* or *The Pickwick Papers*. What a sad paradox, thought Amalfitano. Now even bookish pharmacists are afraid to take on the great, imperfect, torrential works, books that blaze paths into the unknown. They choose the perfect exercises of the great masters. Or what amounts to the same thing: they want to watch the great masters spar, but they have no interest in real combat, when the great masters struggle against that something, that something that terrifies us all, that cows us and spurs us on, amid blood and mortal wounds and stench.*

Yet in Bolaño's own case this division, between the perfectly wrought but bloodless miniature and the messy profundities of larger-scale work, is a false one. In part because his own longest, 'torrential' novels, *The Savage Detectives* and *2666* itself, both consist of a profusion of nested stories; and because his short fiction – in fact his fiction of whatever length – is characterised by the same dizzying ambition, and establishes itself in the same arena of 'blood and mortal wounds and stench', as all the rest.

On the level of subject matter, his short fiction also occupies itself with the same obsessions that run through the novels and novellas: failed or failing writers, the unpredictable pathways that a life can take, sex and love, madness and violence, intimations of evil, the Latin American diaspora, the Second World War. The stories are peopled by poets, detectives, porn stars, journalists and killers, as well as by those who are drifting through life not yet having discovered what it is they want to do. Or, as is the case with the most

---

* Translated by Natasha Wimmer.

Introduction

tragic of Bolaño's characters, those who know but aren't good enough to succeed.

Bolaño's short fiction consists of four collections. Two, *Phone Calls* (1997) and *Murdering Whores* (2001), were published in his lifetime. At the time of his death he had already prepared *The Insufferable Gaucho* (2003) for publication (it appeared four months later). A collection of posthumous stories, many of them incomplete, followed in 2007. In English, selections from the first two collections appeared in *Last Evenings on Earth* (2006), its title chosen by Bolaño. The stories omitted from that volume were later collected in *The Return* (2010). Where appropriate I might specify a particular collection in which a story is included, but for the most part this introduction will consider the short fiction as an entire body of work, not least because that is how Bolaño wanted all his work – so rich in recurring characters and other forms of interconnection – to be treated.

The majority of these stories belong to the extraordinary creative period that ran from 1996, which saw the publication of *Nazi Literature in the Americas*, to Bolaño's death. During this time he wrote three novels, four novellas and those aforementioned short-story collections, as well as seeing two older works come into print. Having worked in obscurity for many years, first as a poet and latterly as a prose writer, the award of the 1999 Rómulo Gallegos International Novel Prize, for *The Savage Detectives*, made Bolaño a literary star throughout the Spanish-speaking world. The posthumous publication of *2666*, in Spanish in 2004 and in Natasha Wimmer's English translation in 2008, made his one of the most prominent names in world literature.

Born in Santiago, Chile, in 1953, Bolaño grew up in the

Introduction

south of the country, in the city of Los Ángeles. In 1968, when he was fifteen, his family relocated to Mexico City. Attracted by the possibilities raised by the election of Salvador Allende's socialist government, Bolaño returned to Chile in 1973 and was there when General Pinochet's right-wing coup took place in September of that year. Imprisoned, he was fortuitously freed when a policeman and former schoolmate recognised him – an experience that fed into several short stories, particularly 'Dance Card' and 'Detectives', and which he describes in another as '[a]n episode from the chronicle of Latin America's doomed revolutions'. Returning to Mexico, Bolaño met Mario Santiago, with whom he founded the Infrarealists, 'a group of adolescent poets who have no respect for anyone. Anyone at all', as he describes them in the posthumous story 'The Old Man and the Mountain'. Santiago was reborn in Bolaño's fiction as Ulises Lima, and in *The Savage Detectives* the Infrarealists became the Visceral Realists. In 1977 Bolaño left Mexico for Europe, where he drifted for a period before ending up in the town of Blanes on Spain's Costa Brava. He married and had his first child, a son, in 1990, and it was this that prompted his move from poetry to prose, which he saw as being more likely to provide money for his family. He was diagnosed with a progressive autoimmune disease of the liver in 1993 and died of liver failure ten years later while awaiting a transplant.

That the majority of Bolaño's prose work, and all his greatest books, were written in the shadow of death, alongside his perennial obsession with evil in numerous forms and his own experience of one of the darkest chapters in Latin American history, is what is perhaps responsible for the vein of menace that runs very nearly unbroken through his work.

Introduction

As 'Mauricio "The Eye" Silva' begins, 'violence, real violence, is unavoidable, at least for those of us who were born in Latin America during the fifties and were about twenty years old at the time of Salvador Allende's death'. This sense of humanity's darker drives being in some way inescapable infuses many of his stories with a compelling narrative tension, even when – as is often the case – they are apparently desultory in structure, or even plotless. Bolaño generates this tension from spare, and sometimes perplexing, sources; it can be difficult to say from precisely where the menace issues. Return to a story looking for clues, like a detective – that favoured Bolaño archetype – revisiting a crime scene, and you discover his methods are accumulative: small, disturbing details that begin to build from its opening lines.

The menace of Bolaño's fiction is amplified by his willingness to leave his stories open, like doorways beyond which gapes an impenetrable darkness. This embrace of irresolution is a trait he might well have inherited from Franz Kafka, whom he considered the greatest writer of the twentieth century. If a story's menacing atmosphere is unresolved, if the source of terror is never located, then it lingers even as you finish one and begin the next. Reading Bolaño triggers all sorts of questions in the reader, whether it's to wonder if the French surrealist poet he is writing about is real or invented or whether, for example, the evil that appears to emanate from a painting in 'Dentist' is merely an expression of the narrator's psychological instability. Surrealist poets, such as Gui Rosey, in the story 'Last Evenings on Earth', can be looked up easily enough, but questions about malignant paintings are left for the reader to interpret alone.

Bolaño's stories teem with such moments. Consider 'A

Introduction

Literary Adventure', in which B, in a chapter of his debut book, caricatures A, a writer of similar background to B but who is considerably more famous, and whom B finds unbearably pompous. Unexpectedly A gives the book a rave review in a national newspaper. Two months later A praises the book again, in an interview this time, and now B begins to grow suspicious. Did A not recognise the insulting portrait B drew of him? Or is he laying some kind of trap? B wants to confront A, but they live in different cities, and A's telephone 'is almost always engaged or the answering-machine is on, in which case B hangs up immediately because he is terrified of answering-machines'.

After a while B tells himself to forget the whole thing 'and almost succeeds'. But when his next book is published, the very first review is by A, 'a long review, at least five pages of typescript, considered and insightful too, a lucid, illuminating reading, even for B, to whom it reveals aspects of the book that had escaped his notice'. He is flattered, but then becomes frightened. He goes out to dinner and reads the review again. Straightforwardly positive, it nevertheless sends him into a spiral: 'I have to see A, he thinks. I have to tell him I'm sorry, I should never have started this game.' But what game has he started? And is it one both men are playing, or only him? Perhaps all of this is just a story B is telling himself. In the world that Bolaño's fiction describes, storytelling is shown to be a thing of undeniable, if unpredictable, power: it shapes reality and can drag our lives in unexpected, even calamitous directions.

But the eerie and inexplicable don't always reside only in the minds of Bolaño's characters. B eventually convinces himself that his behaviour has been ludicrous. Perhaps, he

Introduction

thinks, 'it was a delusion spawned by his secret fears, or a symptom of nervous exhaustion after so many years of hard labour and obscurity'. But when he is invited to a writers' conference in Madrid, where A lives, he stays on in the city after it ends, moves to a cheaper hotel and 'devotes the whole afternoon to ringing A's home number'. He gets the answering machine every time. Eventually, at ten o'clock that night, a woman picks up. B recognises her as A's partner, having so often heard the message on their machine. She asks who it is, but B can't speak. She repeats her question and, met by further silence, hangs up. Half an hour later:

> B calls again, from a telephone booth. Again it is the woman who picks up the phone, asks who it is and waits for an answer. I want to see A, says B. He should have said: I want to *speak* to A. Or at least that is what the woman assumes he meant, and she says so. After a moment of silence, B says sorry, but what he wants is to *see* A. And who may I say is calling? It's B, says B. The woman hesitates for a few seconds, as if she were wondering who B is, then says: very well, wait a moment. Her tone of voice hasn't changed, thinks B, not the slightest hint of fear or aggression. B can hear voices; she must have left the receiver on a table or a chair, or hanging from the wall in the kitchen. Although what they are saying is completely unintelligible, he can distinguish the voices of a man and a woman: A and his young partner, thinks B, but then a third voice joins in, a man's voice, much deeper. At first it seems they are engaged in a conversation of such riveting interest that A cannot tear himself away from it, even for a moment. Then B thinks it sounds more like they are arguing. Or trying to reach agreement on an urgent question that

must be settled before A can pick up the phone. And in this suspense or uncertainty someone shouts, maybe A. Suddenly there is silence on the line, as if the woman had sealed B's ears with wax. And then (several five-peseta coins later), quietly, gently, someone hangs up.

Who is the third man? What is he doing in A's flat and what do they discuss with such urgency while B stands in a telephone booth, straining to hear? The story has a few pages left to run, but we never learn the answers to these questions. In this way the third man is emblematic of the gulf of the unknowable at the edge of which Bolaño's fiction establishes itself.

These enigmatic presences and atmospheres can sometimes give narratives that are in no other way supernatural the feel of a horror story, such as when, in 'Dentist', the narrator's friend describes his theory of empty buildings:

> Later, when I was trying to explain what I had felt in the waiting room (apprehension, anxiety, fear mounting uncontrollably), my friend declared that something similar often happened to him in buildings that seemed to be empty. Basically, I knew, he meant well. I tried to put it out of my mind. But once my friend got talking there was no stopping him, and during the meal, which lasted from three till six in the evening, he kept coming back to the subject of seemingly empty buildings, that is, buildings that you think are empty, because you can't hear a sound, but in fact they're not, and somehow you can tell, although your senses, your ears, your eyes, are telling you they are. So it's not that you feel anxious or afraid because you're in an empty building, or even because you might be trapped or locked inside an empty building,

Introduction

which is not beyond the realm of possibility, no, the reason you're anxious or afraid is that you know, deep down, that there is *no such thing* as an empty building; in every so-called empty building, someone is hiding, keeping quiet, and that's the terrifying thing: the fact that you are *not* alone, said my dentist friend, even when everything indicates that you are.

The unknown voice coming down the telephone line, the unlocatable presence in an empty building – a similar sensation was described by Fernando Pessoa in *The Book of Disquiet* (in Richard Zenith's translation):

> Every day things happen in the world that can't be explained by any law of things we know. Every day they're mentioned and forgotten, and the same mystery that brought them takes them away, transforming their secret into oblivion. Such is the law by which things that can't be explained must be forgotten. The visible world goes on as usual in the broad daylight. Otherness watches us from the shadows.

Here Pessoa, the great Portuguese modernist – who, like so many of the writers in Bolaño's fiction, worked in obscurity for much of his life – invokes an atmosphere most readily associated with the cosmic horror of H. P. Lovecraft, which Bolaño enjoyed and sometimes drew from. As we explore Bolaño's fictional world we constantly cross these fault lines between the everyday and the eerily other, whether in the motel 'beside a highway leading nowhere' in 'Gómez Palacio', in the unidentifiable something that seems to be lurking in the 'hermetically black' shadows of a Parisian parking garage in 'Labyrinth', in the dead sewers – 'places that have been forgotten for one reason or another' – of 'Police Rat', or in the 'house of solitude, which was later to become the house of crime, out there on its own, among clumps of trees and blackberry bushes', in 'Prefiguration of Lalo Cura'. In these places and numerous others we encounter the sense that, as Bolaño writes in his autobiographical story 'The Grub', 'sooner or later something bad is going to happen, some dislocation of reality'.

For all their intimations of horror, all the voids and abysses their protagonists uncover or disappear into, the presiding mood of Bolaño's stories is often one of melancholy. They are elegies to lost youth and its unrealised aspirations, studies of decaying lives, relationships, literary careers. Their strong resistance to traditional narrative resolution ensures this sense of decomposition is expressed in the way the stories are told – often stopping, more than ending – as well as by what they are about.

Yet even if Bolaño's stories can seem wilfully inconclusive (after all its twists and turns, 'A Literary Adventure' ends just as B finally meets A, the two men standing at the threshold of A's flat and about to embark on the conversation that we, as readers, have been waiting for, almost since the story began), they are full of departures of one kind or another, which gives them an organic sense of completion, even if it isn't one that satisfies the readerly curiosity Bolaño so often provokes. 'I never saw him again' ('Jim'); 'Then I left and I never saw her again' ('Anne Moore's Life'); 'Two days later I went to his boarding-house to look for him and they told me he had gone up north. I never saw him again' ('The Grub'); 'It is clear to B now that he will never travel with his father again' ('Last Evenings on Earth'); 'We said goodbye at the door of the station,

Introduction

and that was the last time I saw her' ('Clara'); 'at best they gave off a dingy kind of resignation, which stained the things around them or the way I remember those things now that they've all disappeared' ('Colonia Lindavista'). If Bolaño's stories can be said (with admiration or frustration, depending on the reader) to lack endings, they are nevertheless also filled with them.

They are filled too with writers from the past: the eponymous Henri Simon Leprince, a French poet who, as a member of the Resistance, helps escort to freedom those who, 'perhaps with good reason', poured scorn on his literary efforts before the war; Gui Rosey, a surrealist who disappeared while trying to escape Occupied Europe ('Last Evenings on Earth'); a group of writers associated with the avant-garde literary magazine *Tel Quel* ('Labyrinth').

Most of the poets and writers in Bolaño's fiction have either been forgotten or never had any attention paid to them in the first place. The Argentinian novelist at the heart of the story 'Sensini' lives in genteel poverty in Spain, scraping a living by entering stories into provincial writing contests (an activity Bolaño himself pursued with some vigour in the early 1990s, with the quixotic goal of providing financial security for his family). Sensini's masterpiece is *Ugarte*, dismissed by some critics as 'Kafka in the colonies', but which has over the years 'recruited a small group of devoted readers, scattered around Latin America and Spain'. Another Argentinian writer, Alvaro Rousselot, writes a novel, *Solitude*, which received one or two good reviews before it 'vanished into the limbo of remote shelves and overloaded tables in second-hand bookstores'. Bolaño seems to admire Sensini and Rousselot – just as he admires Henri Simon Leprince, whose

Introduction

'place, his natural habitat, is among the hacks, the embittered, the third-rate' – precisely because they are largely ignored, or derided by their peers. Nevertheless they abandon themselves, as Robert Walser wrote of Heinrich von Kleist, 'to the entire catastrophe of being a poet', marking them out as heroic figures in Bolaño's work, even if that heroism is cut with an amount of their creator's wry humour. It is the successful professionals he detests, those he attacks in his essay 'The Myths of Cthulhu', which is included in *The Insufferable Gaucho*:

> Writers today, as [the Spanish poet, translator and novelist] Pere Gimferrer would be quick to point out, are no longer young men of means unafraid to inveigh against the norms of respectable society, much less a bunch of misfits, but products of the middle and working classes determined to scale the Everest of respectability, hungry for respectability. Blond- and dark-haired children of Madrid, born into the lower-middle class and hoping to end their days on the next rung up. They don't reject respectability. They pursue it desperately. And in order to attain it they really have to sweat. They have to sign books, smile, travel to unfamiliar places, smile, make fools of themselves on celebrity talk shows, keep on smiling, never, never bite the hand that feeds them, participate in literary festivals and reply good-humoredly to the most moronic questions, smile in the most appalling situations, look intelligent, control population growth, and always say thank you.

One of the most memorable, and certainly tragic, of Bolaño's writer characters is Enrique Martín, from the story of the same name. He has a loose friendship, and strange rivalry,

Introduction

with Arturo Belano – Bolaño's recurring alter ego (more on whom later). Enrique, who writes poetry in Castilian and Catalan, is, according to Belano, bad in both. The story describes their intermittent meetings, the vagaries of their writing careers, and the tricky line one must navigate between politeness and honesty when asked to give feedback on an acquaintance's poems ('I realised that if I said they were bad, I would never see him again, as well as getting myself into an argument that could easily continue into the small hours').

Enrique gets nowhere with his poems. The magazine he starts runs for only one issue. He puts on a play at a Barcelona arts centre that is 'greeted with boos and jeers'. The next time they see each other, a year or two later, he tells Belano he has stopped writing poetry. '[W]hen I looked up he was smiling as if to say, I've grown up, I've realised you can enjoy art without making a fool of yourself, without keeping up some pathetic pretence of being a writer.' Belano tells Enrique he's made the right decision, but thinks the other man 'didn't believe me'.

Enrique and his girlfriend get involved in the world of the paranormal, reporting for a magazine called *Questions & Answers*. Belano reads a couple of their articles and finds them 'badly written, dull, pseudo-scientific – the word *science*, in any case, was used several times – and insufferably arrogant'. Some time later, after Belano has moved to the fringes of a village outside Barcelona, he receives an envelope containing a map and several mysterious sequences of numbers, like a code, written on the back of two invitations to the launch of his own first novel ('a party', Belano notes, showing the disdain for the professional side of literature discussed earlier, 'which I did not attend'). The following week another letter

Introduction

comes, which extends the map. He is convinced the sender is Enrique, but soon forgets about them.

A few months later he hears a car pull up outside his house late at night, and a scene unfolds that contains all the elements that are central to Bolaño's craft. It begins tensely, the car's motor running and its lights preventing Belano from seeing who, or how many people, it contains. Eventually Enrique steps out. He asks if Belano received his letters, and if they looked as though they had been tampered with. He asks about the lights and noises from a nearby quarry, and Belano explains that 'at least once a year, I had no idea why, they kept working till after midnight. That's strange, said Enrique.' When a series of explosions come from the quarry, the noise seems to panic Enrique, and although Belano says, 'It's nothing', he too is unsettled: 'in fact it was the first time I had heard explosions at that time of night' – one more inexplicable mystery of the Bolañoverse. Enrique is keen to leave, but first asks Belano to look after a package for him. Belano thinks, 'He's gone back to writing poetry', but Enrique, seeming to read Belano's mind, or perhaps just the expression on his face, says, 'It isn't poetry', with a smile 'that was at once forlorn and brave'.

And then something extraordinary happens. Amid this compelling scene, soundtracked by mysterious explosions and humming with Enrique's paranoia, which contrasts with Belano's grudging tolerance of the situation, the former poet asks, 'Can I give you a hug?' Of course, Belano replies. It is an intensely emotional moment, all the more touching for how unexpected it is, and the simplicity with which it is described. Such moments are rare in Bolaño's fiction – which is one of the reasons they possess such power – but considered together,

Introduction

they represent a counterweight to the darkness that seethes around his work, like the nights of the American continent he describes in 'The Insufferable Gaucho', 'which are dark like a void, where there's nothing to hold on to, no shelter from the elements, just empty, storm-whipped space, above and below'.

In 'Last Evenings on Earth', the story of a disastrous father-and-son holiday to Acapulco, the story's palpable sense of menace – perhaps the most relentlessly constructed, line by line, in all Bolaño's short fiction – is nevertheless underpinned by a sense of filial love, even if it is in its terminal stages. Watching his father return to their hotel late at night, B considers the older man's white moccasins. Normally he finds them 'profoundly disgusting, but the feeling they provoke in him now is something like tenderness'. They have a brief conversation about the horse B's father bought him when he was a child, before they moved from Chile to Mexico, and the son watches his father swim in a rough sea, despite a fisherman's warnings. 'He shuts his eyes and doesn't open them again until he feels a large wet hand grip his shoulder and hears his father's voice proposing they go and eat turtle eggs.' While much of the story describes two men who are – or are on the way to being – entirely separate people ('It is clear to B now that he will never travel with his father again') – these moments speak to the web of feeling, the complicated love, that exists between a father and son.

Bolaño's story 'The Return' adopts a very different take on male relationships, describing that which forms between the ghost of a man who dies early one morning in a Parisian discotheque and the man who rents his corpse from a couple of morgue orderlies in order to have sex with it. Its opening

Introduction

lines are among Bolaño's most playful: 'I have good news and bad news. The good news is that there is life (of a kind) after this life. The bad news is that Jean-Claude Villeneuve is a necrophiliac.' But Bolaño defies our expectation that the narrator's ghost might exact some kind of revenge on his abuser, opening the story out instead into a portrait of male loneliness and companionship. The two men talk, and when the narrator's corpse is collected by the orderlies and returned to the morgue, the ghost elects to remain at Villefranche's mansion as the new day arrives: 'I sat on a chair in front of him, a chair of carved wood with a satin backrest, facing the window and the garden and the beautiful morning light, and I let him go on talking as long as he liked.'

Another graceful act of forgiveness occurs in 'Álvaro Rousselot's Journey', from *The Insufferable Gaucho*. Rousselot, a relatively obscure Argentinian writer, is in the unusual position of having a French film director, Morini, plagiarise several of his novels. His friends in Buenos Aires tell him that he should sue, but despite his sense of outrage, he declines to undertake any such action. When he is invited to a German literary festival, he takes the opportunity to travel on to Paris to meet Morini. He eventually tracks the man down to a Normandy hotel, closed for the off-season, where the director's parents work as caretakers. When Rousselot tells Morini who he is, the man flees the room in terror. The writer finds him in the attic, gazing out into the garden. He pats Morini on the back, writes the address of his hotel in Paris and leaves, feeling he 'had committed a reprehensible act, executed a reprehensible gesture'. The truth is, he feels that Morini's films, while they plagiarised his books, also improved them, and that the man was possibly his best reader – 'the reader for whom he had really been writing, the only one who was capable of fully responding to his work'. (In an act of metafictional homage to a writer he greatly admired, Bolaño commits his own act of plagiarism in the story: the plot of one of Rousselot's novels sharing similarities with that of *The Buenos Aires Affair* by Manuel Puig.)

And then there is the emotion that permeates 'Anne Moore's Life', Bolaño's longest short story (in the words of his translator, Chris Andrews, it 'might be more aptly described as an accelerated novel'). Despite being filled with disastrous relationships, the tragic outcomes of emotional damage and repeated failures to learn from one's mistakes, it is telling that Bolaño should choose to end the story with an act of care by Anne, who, despite the chaotic nature of her life, has somehow managed to remain in touch with an old neighbour from her days living in Girona in Spain. The narrator, Anne's sometime lover who has been searching for traces of her, finds this elderly Russian and reads the postcards she has sent him, in which she tells him 'to look after himself and eat every day, if only a little'. A few pages earlier, while reading the extensive diaries that span fifty years of Anne's tumultuous life, the narrator admits that it 'could be painful, plunging into that writing in the presence of the author (sometimes I wanted to throw the notebook aside and go and hug her)'.

The unexpected request for a hug in 'Enrique Martín' positions it among this constellation of moments from Bolaño's short fiction, but it isn't just that which makes the story one of his most moving pieces of writing. After Enrique's latenight visit, Belano doesn't see him for two years. He hears that Enrique has opened a bookshop in Barcelona. He receives

Introduction

a letter 'from the man himself, signed this time', filled with talk of hyperdimensional tunnels and the thought police. It is their last contact. After learning of Enrique's suicide – he hanged himself in the back room of the bookshop, the walls covered in a baffling array of numbers – Belano opens the package that had been entrusted to him. It contains not maps and cryptographic number sequences, 'just poems, mainly in the style of Miguel Hernández, but there were also some imitations of León Felipe, Blas de Otero, and Gabriel Celaya'.

Flipping the story in this way – the closest thing to a twist in Bolaño's fiction – has an alchemical effect, transforming its paranoid energies into tragedy. Enrique was a man who had to traduce his great passion as a 'pathetic pretence' because he knew he wasn't good enough, and yet he kept creating in secret. By the story's end, he is no longer risible in Belano's eyes, but a figure to admire and a warning to heed. 'That night I couldn't get to sleep,' the story ends. 'Now it was my turn to escape.'

It's possible to track the course of Belano's escape beyond the final page of 'Enrique Martín' and on into other stories and books. As well as being Bolaño's alter ego, Belano is his creator's most regularly recurring character, wandering through his work as he wanders – between the 1960s and the early 2000s – across the globe. Besides 'Enrique Martín', he is the narrator, the protagonist or a prominent character in 'The Grub', 'Photos', 'Detectives', 'The Old Man and the Mountain', 'Death of Ulises' and 'The Days of Chaos'. He might also be the 'I' narrator of another twelve stories, all of which more or less fit Belano's personal history. He could also, in theory, be the character simply called 'B' who features in the stories 'A Literary Adventure', 'Phone Calls', 'Last Evenings

Introduction

on Earth', 'Days of 1978' and 'Vagabond in France and Belgium', but I think if this were the case, Bolaño would have been more explicit. Indeed, there is no sense even that the B in any one of these stories is the same as that in another. If they are linked, it is in the way that Josef K of *The Trial* and K the surveyor in *The Castle* are linked: not by blood, but by their shared embattled positions in Kafka's inimical universe. The Belano stories, by contrast, really do amount to a life story, spread across the full spectrum of Bolaño's fiction, albeit one with many blank spaces along its length. For example, we know that some years after making his escape at the end of 'Enrique Martín', Belano turns up as a war reporter in the midst of the First Liberian Civil War, as described by the photographer Jacobo Urenda in *The Savage Detectives*, in which book Belano is one of the main characters. But what happened in the years between? That's less certain. As well as the stories mentioned above, Belano is also the narrator of *Distant Star* and plays a part in *Amulet*. And in the papers left with the manuscript of *2666*, Bolaño's literary executor discovered a note suggesting Belano was the novel's narrator, although it seems Bolaño died before he had time to weave this idea into the texture of the book.

But it isn't only the Arturo Belano stories that interconnect within the larger body of Bolaño's work. All of it, from *Nazi Literature in the Americas* onwards at least, can be seen as a network, each story unfolding within a single, vast fictional world in which a character or location from one book or story might be encountered again in another. As Bolaño told an interviewer in 1998, 'in a very humble way, I think of all my prose works and even a part of my poetry as a whole. Not just in stylistic terms, but in terms of plot as well: there is a continual dialogue among the characters and they keep appearing and disappearing.'

Discovering these connections is one of the great excitements offered by Bolaño's work, so I will give only a flavour. 'Another Russian Tale' is recounted by Óscar Amalfitano, a significant character in *2666*. The title character of 'The Grub', whom Arturo Belano meets in Mexico City as a teenager, comes from Villaviciosa, the fictional Sonoran town that Belano will visit years later in *The Savage Detectives*, and where he will possibly father a prominent character from *2666*. 'Joanna Silvestri' centres on the eponymous porn actress and is, for the most part, a richly melancholy story about a trip she takes to Los Angeles, where she tracks down and spends time with a retired porn star, Jack Holmes, who is dying – presumably like his real-life homonym John Holmes – of AIDS. But the frame story involves a Chilean detective visiting Joanna in a clinic in the south of France. He asks her about an assistant cameraman who worked on some of her films and who might be a murderer. This same interview is recounted to Belano by the detective in Bolaño's novella *Distant Star*, and finding the counterpart, whichever way round you experience them, feels like uncovering secret knowledge.

Sometimes, however, the trail can be a false one. 'Prefiguration of Lalo Cura' has as its main character a hit man who shares his name with a bodyguard-turned-policeman in *2666*. In that novel, however, Cura comes (like the Grub) from Villaviciosa, whereas in the short story he grew up in Medellín, Colombia. Taken together, the two Curas present a blurred image, both alike and unalike in fundamental ways. And then there are the connections that we ourselves identify, but have no way of proving. Chris Andrews has written about the way

Introduction

in which Bolaño 'trains us in suspicion', and to seek connections throughout his work. He cites his own reading of the suspenseful late story 'Crimes', in which a female journalist discusses the murder of a woman with a man claiming to be a sock salesman, who has wandered into her newspaper's empty offices after hours. 'But when I wonder,' Andrews writes, 'whether the unnamed Chilean sock salesman in "Crimes" is Carlos Wieder [the murderous poet in *Distant Star*], whom some claim to have seen selling socks and ties in Valparaíso, I may have crossed over into paranoid reading.' My own experience of this is wondering about the relationship between the 'mysterious car, a black Impala' that Belano is told ran down his old friend Ulises Lima in 'Death of Ulises', and the menacing black cars that move like vultures through the streets of Santa Teresa in *2666*. Add it to the list of questions without answers, the unknown third men, in Bolaño's work.

The uncertainties seeded by Bolaño's writing strategies spilled over, on occasion, into his own life. His story 'Beach', which immediately establishes a strong confessional tone – 'I gave up heroin and went home and began the methadone treatment administered at the outpatient clinic and I didn't have much else to do except get up each morning and watch TV and try to sleep at night' – was first published in the Spanish newspaper *El Mundo* as part of a series in which writers were asked to submit pieces about the worst summer of their lives. Most of the responses were non-fiction, and many took 'Beach' to be autobiographical. From there the fallacious story grew that Bolaño had at one time been a heroin addict, and that his liver disease was hepatitis C contracted from sharing dirty needles.

Introduction

But even these aberrant elements – contradictory characters, false trails, misclassifications, paranoid readings – feel appropriate to the world into which Bolaño plunges us, with its treacherous currents and repeated warnings of life's uncertainty and inconclusiveness. The foreshortened span of Bolaño's own life was testament to that, despite it ending (in literary terms at least) with the capstone that is *2666*. And there is one inconsistency in the fiction that should certainly be celebrated. In 'Days of Chaos', a story left unfinished at the time of Bolaño's death, Belano – by now a writer of note who 'thought that all his adventures were over and done with' – travels to Berlin to find his son, who has gone missing amid an episode of civil disorder. We do not discover what happens in Berlin, or where Belano goes afterwards, but we know it is 2005, a fact stated twice as if to underline it: two years after Roberto Bolaño's death. Arturo Belano, one of so many fictional writers in his creator's work, but the one he most closely resembled, has slipped through death's fingers, made off for parts unknown, and perhaps lives and writes there still.

Chris Power, London, 2024

Part I
Last Evenings on Earth

Sensini

The way in which my friendship with Sensini developed was somewhat unusual. At the time I was twenty-something and poorer than a church mouse. I was living on the outskirts of Girona, in a dilapidated house that my sister and brother-in-law had left me when they moved to Mexico, and I had just lost my job as a night watchman in a Barcelona campsite, a job that had exacerbated my tendency not to sleep at night. I had practically no friends and all I did was write and go for long walks, starting at seven in the evening, just after getting up, with a feeling like jet lag: an odd sensation of fragility, of being there and not there, somehow distant from my surroundings. I was living on what I had saved during the summer, and although I spent very little, my savings dwindled as autumn drew on. Perhaps that was what prompted me to enter the Alcoy National Literature Competition, open to writers in Spanish, whatever their nationality or place of residence. There were three categories: for poems, stories, and essays. First I thought about going in for the poetry prize, but I felt it would be demeaning to send what I did best into the ring with the lions (or hyenas). Then I thought about the essay, but when they sent me the conditions, I discovered that it had to be about Alcoy, its environs, its history, its eminent sons, its future prospects, and I couldn't face it. So I decided to enter for the story prize, sent off three copies of the best one I had (not that I had many), and sat down to wait.

When the winners were announced I was working as a vendor in a handicrafts market where absolutely no one was selling anything hand-crafted. I won fourth prize and 10 000 pesetas, which the Alcoy Council paid with scrupulous promptitude. Shortly afterwards I received the anthology, with the winning story and those of the six finalists, liberally peppered with typographical errors. Naturally my story was better than the winner's, so I cursed the judges and told myself, Well, what can you expect? But the real surprise was coming across the name Luis Antonio Sensini, the Argentine writer, who had won third prize with a story in which the narrator went away to the countryside where his son had died, or went to the country because his son had died in the city – it was hard to tell – in any case, out there in the countryside, on the bare plains, the narrator's son went on dying, that much was clear. It was a claustrophobic story, very much in Sensini's manner, set in a world where vast geographical spaces could suddenly shrink to the dimensions of a coffin, and it was better than the winning story and the one that came second, as well as those that came fourth, fifth, and sixth.

I don't know what moved me to ask the Alcoy Council for Sensini's address. I had read one of his novels and some of his stories in Latin American magazines. The novel was the kind of book that circulates by word of mouth. Entitled *Ugarte,* it was about a series of moments in the life of Juan de Ugarte, a bureaucrat in the Viceroyalty of the Río de la Plata at the end of the eighteenth century. Some (mainly Spanish) critics had dismissed it as Kafka in the colonies, but gradually the novel had made its way, and by the time I came across Sensini's name in the Alcoy anthology, *Ugarte* had recruited a small group of devoted readers, scattered around Latin America and Spain, most of whom knew each other, either as friends or as gratuitously bitter enemies. He had published other books, of course, in Argentina, and with Spanish publishers who had since gone to the wall, and he belonged to that intermediate generation of Argentine writers, born in the twenties, after Cortázar, Bioy Casares, Sábato, and Mujica Láinez, a generation whose best known representative (to me, back then, at any rate) was Haroldo Conti, who disappeared in one of the special camps set up by Videla and his henchmen during the dictatorship. It was a generation (although perhaps I am using the word too loosely) that hadn't come to much, but not for want of brilliance or talent: followers of Roberto Arlt, journalists, teachers and translators; in a sense they foreshadowed what was to come, in their own sad and sceptical way, which led them one by one to the abyss.

I had a soft spot for those writers. In years gone by, I had read Abelardo Castillo's plays and the stories of Daniel Moyano and Rodolfo Walsh (who was killed under the dictatorship, like Conti). I read their work piecemeal, whatever I could find in Argentine, Mexican, or Cuban magazines, or the second-hand bookshops of Mexico City: pirated anthologies of Buenos Aires writing, probably the best writing in Spanish of the twentieth century. They were part of that tradition, and although, of course, they didn't have the stature of Borges or Cortázar, and were soon overtaken by Manuel Puig and Osvaldo Soriano, their concise, intelligent texts were a constant source of complicit delight. Needless to say, my favourite was Sensini, and the fact that I had been his fellow runner-up in a provincial literary competition – an association that I found at once flattering and profoundly depressing – encouraged me to make contact with him, to pay my respects and tell him how much his work meant to me.

The Alcoy Council sent me his address without delay – he lived in Madrid – and one night, after dinner or a light meal or just a snack, I wrote him a long letter, which rambled from *Ugarte* and the stories of his that I had read in magazines to myself, my house on the outskirts of Girona, the competition (I made fun of the winner), the political situation in Chile and in Argentina (both dictatorships were still firmly in place), Walsh's stories (along with Sensini, Walsh was my other favourite in that generation), life in Spain, and life in general. To my surprise, I received a reply barely a week later. He began by thanking me for my letter; he said that the Alcoy Council had sent him the anthology too but that, unlike me, he hadn't found time to look at the winning story or those of the other finalists (later on, in a passing reference, he admitted that it wasn't so much a lack of time as a lack of 'fortitude'), although he had just read mine and thought it well done, 'a first-rate story', he said (I kept the letter), and he urged me to persevere, not, as I thought at first, to persevere with my writing, but to persevere with the competitions, as he intended to do himself, so he assured me. He went on to ask me which competitions were 'looming on the horizon', imploring me to notify him as soon as I heard of one. In exchange he sent me the conditions of entry for two short-story competitions, one in Plasencia and the other in Écija, with prizes of 25,000 and 30,000 pesetas respectively. He had tracked these down, as I later discovered, in

Madrid newspapers or magazines whose mere existence was a crime or a miracle, depending on your point of view. There was still time for me to enter both competitions, and Sensini finished his letter on a curiously enthusiastic note, as if the pair of us were on our marks for a race that, as well as being hard and meaningless, would have no end. 'Pen to paper now, no shirking!' he wrote.

I remember thinking, What a strange letter. I remember reading a few chapters of *Ugarte*. Around that time the book dealers came to Girona to set up their stalls in the square where the cinemas are, displaying their mostly unsaleable stock: remaindered books published by firms that had recently gone bankrupt, books printed during the Second World War, romantic fiction and wild west novels, collections of postcards. At one of the stalls I found a book of stories by Sensini and bought it. It was as good as new – in fact it *was* new, one of those titles that publishers sell off to the book dealers when no one else can move it, when there's not a bookshop or a distributor left who's willing to take it on – and for the following week I lived and breathed Sensini. I read his letter over and over, leafed through *Ugarte*, and when I wanted a little action, something new, I turned to the stories. Although the themes and situations varied, the settings were usually rural, and the protagonists were the fabled horsemen of the pampas, that is to say armed and generally unfortunate individuals, either loners or men endowed with a peculiar notion of sociability. Whereas *Ugarte* was a cold book, written with neurosurgical precision, the collection of stories was all warmth: brave and aimless characters adrift in landscapes that seemed to be gradually drawing away from the reader (and sometimes taking the reader with them).

I didn't manage to submit an entry for the Plasencia competition, but I did for the Écija one. As soon as I had posted off the copies of my story (under the pseudonym Aloysius Acker), I realised that sitting around waiting for the results could only make things worse. So I decided to look for more competitions; that way at least I'd be able to comply with Sensini's request. Over the next few days, when I went down to Girona, I spent hours looking through back copies of newspapers in search of announcements. Some papers put them in a column next to the society news; in others, they came after the crime reports and before the sports section; the most serious paper had them wedged between the weather and the obituaries. They were never in the book pages, of course. In my search I discovered a magazine put out by the Catalonian government, which, along with advertisements for scholarships, exchanges, jobs, and postgraduate courses, published announcements of literary competitions, mostly for Catalans writing in Catalan, but there were some exceptions. I soon found three for which Sensini and I were eligible, and they were still open, so I wrote him a letter.

As before, I received a reply by return of post. Sensini's letter was short. He answered some of my questions, mainly about the book of stories I had recently bought, and included photocopies of the details for three more short-story competitions, one of which was sponsored by the National Railway Company, with a tidy sum for the winner and 50,000 pesetas per head (as he put it) for the ten finalists: no prize for dreaming, you have to be in it to win it. I wrote back saying I didn't have enough stories for all six competitions, but most of my letter was about other things (in fact I got rather carried away): travel, lost love, Walsh, Conti, Francisco Urondo . . .

I asked him about Gelman, whom he was bound to have known, gave him a summary of my life story, and somehow ended up going on about the tango and labyrinths, as I always do with Argentines (it's something Chileans are prone to).

Sensini's reply was prompt and extensive, at least as far as writing and competitions were concerned. On one sheet, recto and verso, single-spaced, he set out a kind of general strategy for the pursuit of provincial literary prizes. I speak from experience, he wrote. The letter began with a blessing on the prizes (whether in earnest or in jest, I have never been able to tell), those precious supplements to the writer's modest income. He referred to the sponsors – local councils and savings banks – as 'those good people with their touching faith in literature' and 'those disinterested and dutiful readers'. He entertained no illusions, however, about the erudition of the 'good people' in question, who presumably exercised their touching faith on these ephemeral anthologies (or not). He told me I should compete for as many prizes as possible, although he suggested I take the precaution of changing a story's title if I was entering it for, say, three competitions that were due to be judged around the same time. He cited the example of his story 'At Dawn', a story I didn't know, which he had used to test his method, as a guinea pig is used to test the effects of a new vaccine. For the first competition, with the biggest prize, 'At Dawn' was entered as 'At Dawn'; for the second, he changed the title to 'The Gauchos'; for the third, it was called 'The Other Pampa'; and for the last, 'No Regrets'. Of these four competitions, it won the second and the fourth, and with the money from the prizes he was able to pay a month and a half's rent (in Madrid the rents had gone through the roof).

Of course, no one realised that 'The Gauchos' and 'No Regrets' were the same story with different titles, although there was always the risk that one of the judges might have read the story in another competition (in Spain the peculiar occupation of judging literary prizes was obstinately monopolised by a clique of minor poets and novelists, as well as former laureates). The little world of letters is terrible as well as ridiculous, he wrote. And he added that even if one's story did come before the same judge twice, the danger was minimal, since they generally didn't read the entries or only skimmed through them. Furthermore, who was to say that 'The Gauchos' and 'No Regrets' were not two different stories whose singularity resided precisely in their respective titles? Similar, very similar even, but different. Towards the end of the letter he said that of course, in a perfect world, he would be otherwise occupied, living and writing in Buenos Aires, for example, but the way things were, he had to earn a crust somehow (I'm not sure they say that in Argentina; we do in Chile) and, for the time being, the competitions were helping him to get by. It's like a lesson in Spanish geography, he wrote. At the end, or maybe in a post-script, he declared: I'm getting on for sixty, but I feel as if I were twenty-five. At first this struck me as very sad, but when I read it for the second or third time I realised it was his way of asking me: How old are you, kid? I remember I replied immediately. I told him I was twenty-eight, three years older than him. That morning I felt not exactly happy again, but more alive, as if an infusion of energy were reanimating my sense of humour and my memory.

Although I didn't follow Sensini's advice and become a full-time prize-hunter, I did enter for the competitions he and I had recently discovered, without success. Sensini pulled off another double in Don Benito and in Écija, with a story originally called 'The Sabre', renamed 'Two Swords' for Écija and 'The Deepest Cut' for Don Benito. And in the competition sponsored by the Railways he was one of the finalists. As well as a cash sum, he won a ticket that entitled him to travel free on Spanish trains for a year.

Little by little I learnt more about him. He lived in a flat in Madrid with his wife and his daughter, Miranda, who was seventeen years old. He had a son, from his first marriage, who had gone to ground somewhere in Latin America, or that was what he wanted to believe. The son's name was Gregorio; he was thirty-five and had worked as a journalist. Sometimes Sensini would tell me about the enquiries he was making through human rights organisations and the European Union in an attempt to determine Gregorio's whereabouts. When he got on to this subject, his prose became heavy and monotonous, as if he were trying to exorcise his ghosts by describing the bureaucratic labyrinth. I haven't lived with Gregorio, he once told me, since he was five years old, just a kid. He didn't elaborate, but I imagined a five-year-old boy and Sensini typing in a newspaper office: even then it was already too late. I also wondered about the boy's name and somehow came to the conclusion that it must have been an unconscious homage to Gregor Samsa. Of course I never mentioned this to Sensini. When he got on to the subject of Miranda, he cheered up. Miranda was young and ready to take on the world, insatiably curious, pretty too, and kind. She looks like Gregorio, he wrote, except that (obviously) she's a girl and she has been spared what my son had to go through.

Gradually, Sensini's letters grew longer. The district where he lived in Madrid was run down; his flat had two bedrooms, a dining room-cum-living room, a kitchen and a bathroom. At first I was surprised to discover that his place was smaller than mine; then I felt ashamed. It seemed unfair. Sensini wrote in the dining room, at night, 'when the wife and the girl are asleep', and he was a heavy smoker. He earned his living doing some kind of work for a publisher (I think he edited translations) and by sending his stories out to do battle in the provinces. Every now and then he received a royalty cheque for one of his many books, but most of the publishers were chronically forgetful or had gone broke. The only book that went on selling well was *Ugarte*, which had been published by a firm in Barcelona. It didn't take me long to realise that he was living in poverty: not destitution, but the genteel poverty of a middle-class family fallen on hard times. His wife (her name was Carmela Zadjman, a story in itself) did freelance work for publishers and gave English, French, and Hebrew lessons, although she had occasionally been obliged to take on cleaning jobs. The daughter was busy with her studies and would soon be going to university. In one of my letters I asked Sensini whether Miranda wanted to be a writer too. He wrote back: No, thank God, she's going to study medicine.

One night I wrote and asked for a photo of his family. Only after putting the letter in the post did I realise that what I really wanted was to see what Miranda looked like. A week later I received a photo, no doubt taken in the Retiro, which showed an old man and a middle-aged woman next to a tall, slim adolescent girl with straight hair and very large breasts. The old man was smiling happily, the middle-aged woman

Sensini

was looking at her daughter, as if saying something to her, and Miranda was facing the photographer with a serious expression that I found both moving and disturbing. Sensini also sent me a photocopy of another photo, showing a young man more or less my age, with sharp features, very thin lips, prominent cheekbones and a broad forehead. He was strongly built and probably tall, and he was gazing at the camera (it was a studio photo) with a confident and perhaps slightly impatient air. It was Gregorio Sensini, at the age of twenty-two, before he disappeared, quite a bit younger than me, in fact, but he had an air of experience that made him seem older.

The photo and the photocopy lived on my desk for a long time. I would sit there staring at them or take them to the bedroom and look at them until I fell asleep. Sensini had asked me to send a photograph of myself. I didn't have a recent one, so I decided to go to the photo booth in the station, which at the time was the only photo booth in the whole of Girona. But I didn't like the way the photos came out. I thought I looked ugly and skinny and scruffy-haired. So I kept putting off sending any of them and went back to spend more money at the photo booth. Finally I chose one at random, put it in an envelope with a postcard, and sent it to him. It was a while before I received a reply. In the meantime I remember I wrote a very long, very bad poem, full of voices and faces that seemed different at first, but all belonging to Miranda Sensini, and when, in the poem, I finally realised this and could put it into words, when I could say to her, Miranda it's me, your father's friend and correspondent, she turned around and ran off in search of her brother, Gregorio Samsa, in search of Gregorio Samsa's eyes, shining at the end of a dim corridor in which the shadowy masses of Latin America's terror were shifting imperceptibly.

The reply, when it came, was long and friendly. Sensini and Carmela's verdict on my photo was positive: they thought I looked nice, as they imagined me, a bit on the skinny side maybe, but fit and well, and they liked the postcard of Girona cathedral, which they hoped to see for themselves in the near future, as soon as they had sorted out a few financial and household problems. It was clear that they were hoping to stay at my place when they came. In return they offered to put me up whenever I wanted to go to Madrid. It's a modest flat, and it isn't clean either, wrote Sensini, imitating a comic-strip gaucho who was famous in South America at the beginning of the seventies. He didn't say anything about his literary projects. Nor did he mention the competitions.

At first I thought of sending Miranda my poem, but after much hesitation and soul-searching I decided not to. I must be going mad, I thought, if I sent her that poem, there'd be no more letters from Sensini, and who could blame him? So I didn't send it. For a while I applied myself to the search for new literary prizes. In one of his letters Sensini said he was worried that he might have run his race. I misunderstood; I thought he meant he was running out of competitions to enter.

I wrote back to say they must come to Girona; he and Carmela were most welcome to stay at my house. I even spent several days cleaning, sweeping, mopping, and dusting, having convinced myself (quite unreasonably) that they might turn up at any moment, with Miranda. Since they had one free pass they would only have to buy two tickets, and Catalonia, I stressed, was full of wonderful

Sensini

things to see and do. I mentioned Barcelona, Olot, the Costa Brava, talked about the happy days we could spend together. In a long reply, thanking me for my invitation, Sensini said that for the moment they couldn't leave Madrid. Unlike any of the preceding letters, this one was rather confused, although in the middle he returned to the theme of prizes (I think he had won one again) and encouraged me not to give up, to keep on trying. He also said something about the writer's trade or profession, and I had the impression that his words were meant partly for me and partly for himself, as a kind of reminder. The rest, as I said, was a muddle. When I got to the end I had the feeling that someone in his family wasn't well.

Two or three months later Sensini wrote to tell me that one of the bodies in a recently discovered mass grave was probably Gregorio's. His letter was restrained. There was no outpouring of grief; all he said was that on a certain day, at a certain time, a group of forensic pathologists and members of human rights organisations had opened a mass grave containing the bodies of more than fifty young people, etc. For the first time, I didn't want to reply in writing. I would have liked to ring him, but I don't think he had a telephone, and if he did I didn't know his number. My letter was brief. I said I was sorry, and ventured to point out that they still didn't know for sure that the body was Gregorio's.

Summer came and I took a job working in a hotel on the coast. In Madrid that summer there were numerous lectures, courses and all sorts of cultural activities, but Sensini didn't participate in any of them, or if he did, it wasn't mentioned in the newspaper I was reading.

At the end of August I sent him a card. I said that maybe

when the season was over I would visit him. That was all. When I got back to Girona, in the middle of September, among the small pile of letters that had been slipped under the door, I found one from Sensini dated August 7. He had written to say goodbye. He was going back to Argentina; with the return of democracy he would be safe now, so there was no point staying away any longer. And it was the only way he would be able to find out for sure what had happened to Gregorio. Carmela, of course, is returning with me, he said, but Miranda will stay. I wrote to him immediately, at the only address I had, but received no reply.

Gradually I came to accept that Sensini had gone back to Argentina for good and that, unless he wrote to me again, our correspondence had come to an end. I waited a long time for a letter from him, or so it seems to me now, looking back. The letter, of course, never came. I tried to tell myself that life in Buenos Aires must be hectic, an explosion of activity, hardly time to breathe or blink. I wrote to him again at the Madrid address, hoping that the letter would be sent on to Miranda, but a month later it was returned to me marked 'not known at this address'. So I gave up and let the days go by and gradually forgot about Sensini, although on my rare visits to Barcelona I would sometimes spend whole afternoons in second-hand bookshops looking for his other books, the ones I knew by their titles but was destined never to read. All I could find in the shops were old copies of *Ugarte* and the collection of stories published in Barcelona by a company that had recently gone into receivership, almost as if a message were being sent to Sensini (and to me).

One or two years later I discovered that he had died. I think I read it in a newspaper, I don't know which one. Or maybe I didn't read it; maybe someone told me, but I can't remember talking to anyone who knew him around that time, so I probably did read the obituary somewhere. It was brief, as I remember it: the Argentinian writer Luis Antonio Sensini, who lived for several years in exile in Spain, had died in Buenos Aires. I think there was also a mention of *Ugarte* at the end. I don't know why, but it didn't come as a surprise. I don't know why, but it seemed logical that Sensini would go back to Buenos Aires to die.

Some time later, when the photo of Sensini, Carmela and Miranda, and the photocopied image of Gregorio were packed away with my other memories in a cardboard box that I still haven't committed to the flames for reasons I prefer not to expand upon here, there was a knock at the door of my house. It must have been about midnight, but I was awake. It gave me a shock all the same. I knew only a few people in Girona and none of them would have turned up like that unless something out of the ordinary had happened. When I opened the door there was a woman with long hair, wearing a big black overcoat. It was Miranda Sensini, although she had changed a good deal in the years since her father had sent me the photo. Next to her was a tall young man with long blond hair and an aquiline nose. I'm Miranda Sensini, she said to me with a smile. I know, I said, and invited them in. They were on their way to Italy; after that they planned to cross the Adriatic to Greece. Since they didn't have much money they were hitch-hiking. They slept in my house that night. I made them something to eat. The young man was called Sebastian Cohen and he had been born in Argentina too, although he had lived in Madrid since he was a child. He helped me prepare the meal while Miranda looked around the house. Have you known her for long? he asked. Until a moment ago, I'd only seen her in a photo, I replied.

After dinner, I prepared one of the rooms for them and said they could go to bed whenever they wanted. I thought about going to bed myself, but realised it would be hard, if not impossible, to sleep, so I gave them a while to get settled, then went downstairs, put on the television with the volume down low, and sat there thinking about Sensini.

Soon I heard someone on the stairs. It was Miranda. She couldn't get to sleep either. She sat down beside me and asked for a cigarette. At first we talked about their trip, about Girona (they had been in the city all day, but I didn't ask why they had come to my house so late), and the cities they were planning to visit in Italy. Then we talked about her father and her brother. According to Miranda, Sensini never got over Gregorio's death. He went back to look for him, although we all knew he was dead. Carmela too? I asked. He was the only one who hadn't accepted it, she said. I asked her how things had gone in Argentina. Same as here, same as in Madrid, said Miranda, same as everywhere. But he was well known and loved in Argentina, I said. Same as here, she said. I got a bottle of cognac from the kitchen and offered her a drink. You're crying, she said. When I looked at her she turned away. Were you writing? she asked. No, I was watching TV. No, I mean when we arrived. Yes, I said. Stories? No, poems. Ah, said Miranda. For a long time we sat there drinking in silence, watching the black and white images on the television screen. Tell me something, I said, Why did your father choose the name Gregorio? Because of Kafka, of course, said Miranda. Gregor Samsa? Of course, she said. I thought so, I said. Then

Sensini

Miranda told me the story of Sensini's last months in Buenos Aires.

He was already sick when he left Madrid, against the advice of various Argentine doctors, who never billed him and had even arranged hospital treatment on the National Health a couple of times. Returning to Buenos Aires was a painful and happy experience. In the first week he started taking steps to locate Gregorio. He wanted to go back to his job at the university, but what with the bureaucracy and the inevitable jealousies and bitterness, it wasn't going to happen, so he had to make do with translating for a couple of publishing houses. Carmela, however, got a teaching position and towards the end they lived exclusively on her earnings. Each week Sensini wrote to Miranda. He knew he didn't have long to live, she said, and sometimes he seemed to be impatient, as if he wanted to use up the last of his strength and get it over with. As for Gregorio, there was nothing conclusive. Some of the pathologists thought his bones might have been in the pile exhumed from the mass grave, but they would of course have to do a DNA test, and the government didn't have the money or didn't really want the tests done, so they kept being postponed. Sensini also went searching for a girl who had probably been Greg's girlfriend when he was in hiding, but he couldn't find her either. Then his health deteriorated and he had to go into hospital. He didn't even write after that, said Miranda. It had always been very important to him, writing every day, whatever else was happening. Yes, I said, that's the way he was. I asked her if he'd found any literary competitions to enter in Buenos Aires. Miranda looked at me and smiled. Of course! You were the one he used to enter the competitions with; he met you through a competition. Then it struck me: the reason she had my address was simply that she had all her father's addresses, and she had only just realised who I was. That's me, I said. Miranda poured me out some more cognac and said there was a year when her father used to talk about me quite a lot. I noticed she was looking at me differently. I must have annoyed him so much, I said. Annoyed him? You're joking; he loved your letters. He always read them to Mum and me. I hope they were funny, I said, without much conviction. They were really funny, said Miranda, my mother even gave you guys a name. A name? Which guys? Dad and you. She called you the gunslingers or the bounty hunters, I can't remember now, something like that, or the buccaneers. I see, I said, but the real bounty hunter was your father. I just passed on some information. Yes, he was a professional, said Miranda, suddenly serious. How many prizes did he win all told? I asked her. About fifteen, she said with an absent look. And you? So far just the one, I said. A short-listed place in the Alcoy competition, that's how I got to know your father. Did you know that Borges once wrote to him in Madrid, to say how much he liked one of his stories? No, I didn't know, I said. And Cortázar wrote about him, and Mujica Láinez too. Well, he was a very good writer, I said. Jesus! said Miranda, then got up and went out on to the terrace as if I had said something to offend her. I let a few seconds go by, picked up the bottle of cognac and followed her. Miranda was leaning on the balustrade, looking at the lights of Girona. You have a good view, she said. I filled her glass, then my own, and we stood there for a while looking at the moonlit city. Suddenly I realised that we were at peace, that for some mysterious reason the two of us had reached a state of peace, and that from now on, imperceptibly, things would begin to change. As if the world really was shifting. I asked her how old she was. Twenty-two, she said. I must be over thirty then, I said, and even my voice sounded different.

Henri Simon Leprince

The events recounted here took place in France shortly before, during, and shortly after the Second World War. The protagonist, whose name, Leprince, is oddly appropriate, although he is quite the opposite of a prince (middle-class, well educated, respectable friends, but downwardly mobile and short of money) – is a writer.

Naturally, he is a failed writer, barely scraping a living in the Paris gutter press, and his stories and poems (which the bad poets regard as bad and the good poets don't even read) are published in provincial magazines. Publishing houses and their accredited readers (that execrable sub-caste) seem for some mysterious reason to detest him. His manuscripts are invariably rejected. He is middle-aged, single, and accustomed to failure. In his own way, he is a stoic. He reads Stendhal with a kind of defiant pride. He reads certain surrealists whom deep down he utterly despises (or envies). He reads the balsamic prose of Alphonse Daudet, and out of fidelity to the father he also reads the deplorable Léon Daudet, a stylist of some distinction.

1940: France capitulates, and in the aftermath of the storm, the writers, who until then have been divided into scores of pullulating schools, gather to form two bands opposed by a mortal enmity: on the one hand, those who are prepared to resist, including the few partisans of active resistance and the advocates of passive resistance (the majority) as well as mere sympathisers and others who resist by omission, or are moved by suicidal urges, or the lure of transgression or by a sense of fair play or decency, and so on, and, on the other hand, those who are prepared to collaborate, similarly subdivided into various categories, all of them under the gravitational sway of the seven deadly sins. For many, the political reprisals provide an opportunity to settle literary scores. The collaborationists take control of various publishing houses, magazines, and newspapers. Leprince would seem to be stranded in a no-man's-land, or so he thinks until it dawns on him that his place, his natural habitat, is among the hacks, the embittered, the third-rate.

In due course he is approached by the collaborationists, who regard him, justifiably, as one of their kind. It is a friendly and no doubt generous gesture on their part. The recently appointed editor of the newspaper that he works for calls him, explains the new editorial policy, in line with the new direction that Europe is taking, offers him a better position, more money, prestige: minimal rewards that Leprince has never enjoyed.

That morning he finally comes to a realisation. Never before has he fully grasped the abjection of his place in the pyramidal hierarchy of literature. Never before has he felt so important. After a night of soul-searching and exaltation, he rejects the offer.

The following days are a test. Leprince tries to go on with his life and his work as if nothing had happened, knowing all the while that the attempt is vain. He tries to write but nothing comes. He tries to return to his favourite authors, but the pages seem to have gone blank, or to conceal mysterious signals that spring out from every paragraph. He tries new books but, unable to concentrate, he can find no instruction or enjoyment in reading. He has nightmares; sometimes he talks to himself without realising. Whenever he can, he goes for long walks through familiar parts of the city, which, to his amazement, look just the same, impervious to the occupation and the changes. Shortly afterwards he makes contact with a number of malcontents, people who listen to the BBC broadcasts from London and believe that conflict is unavoidable.

At first his participation in the Resistance is minimal; he is simply present at its birth. A discreet and calm figure (although opinions differ as to his calmness), he generally goes unnoticed. Nevertheless, those to whom responsibilities have fallen (none belong to the guild of writers) soon single him out and place their trust in him, perhaps because there are so few willing to take risks. In any case, Leprince joins the Resistance, and his diligence and composure soon qualify him for increasingly delicate missions (although these short errands and minor skirmishes are of little significance beyond literary circles).

For the writers, however, Leprince is something of an enigma and a surprise. Those who enjoyed a certain notoriety before the capitulation and never deigned to notice Leprince find themselves running into him everywhere they go, and worse, depending on him for protection and safe passage. Leprince seems to have emerged from limbo; he helps them, puts the meagre sum of his possessions at their disposal; he is cooperative and diligent. The writers talk to him. The conversations take place at night, in dark rooms or corridors, and are always conducted in whispers. One writer suggests he try his hand at composing stories, verse or essays. Leprince assures him that he has been doing precisely that since 1933. The nights of waiting are long and anxious, and some of the writers are talkative; they ask where he has published his works. Leprince mentions mouldering magazines and newspapers whose mere names provoke nausea or sadness. These conversations generally end at daybreak: Leprince leaves his charge in a safe house, with a hearty handshake or a brisk hug followed by a few words of thanks. And the words are sincere, but once the episode is over the writers avoid Leprince and he fades from their minds like an unpleasant but forgettable dream.

There is something elusive, something indefinable about him that people find repellent. They know he is there to help, but deep down they simply cannot warm to him. Perhaps they sense that Leprince is tainted by the years he has spent in the underworld of sad magazines and the gutter press, from which no man or beast escapes, except the exceedingly strong, brilliant, and bestial.

Needless to say, Leprince has none of these qualities. He is not a fascist, or a card-carrying Party member, nor does he belong to any society of authors. The authors with whom he is in contact regard him, perhaps, as a paradoxical *parvenu* or reverse opportunist (since for him the obvious thing would be to denounce and insult them, to help the police in their interrogations and devote himself heart and soul to the collaborationist cause) who, in one of those fits of madness to which the literary journalist is prone, happened to choose the right side, as unconsciously as bacteria infecting a host.

The flamboyant novelist from Languedoc, Monsieur D., for example, notes in his diary that Leprince reminds him of a Chinese shadow puppet, but does not elaborate. The others ignore him, with one or two exceptions; there is the odd mention of Leprince the man, but nothing about his writing. Nobody can be bothered to look up the works of the writer who saved their life.

Utterly detached, Leprince goes on working at the newspaper office (where he is regarded with increasing suspicion) and drafting poems. The daily risks he runs are considerably superior to the minimum required for the preservation of self-respect. He is often courageous to the point of recklessness. One night he shelters a surrealist poet hunted by the Gestapo, who is destined to end his days (through no fault of Leprince's) in a German concentration camp. The poet leaves without a word of thanks; for him, Leprince is simply a comrade doing what he himself would do in the same situation, not a colleague (to use that appalling term) or a fellow member of his demanding profession. One weekend Leprince escorts a critic to a village near the Spanish border. The critic once poured scorn (perhaps with good reason) on a book penned by his guide, a book which, at this crucial moment, he has completely forgotten, so negligible, so insubstantial is Leprince's work and public stature.

Sometimes Leprince suspects that his face, his education, his attitude or the books he has read are to blame for this rejection. Between articles for the newspaper and clandestine missions, he throws himself into the composition of a long poem: over 600 lines exploring the mystery and the martyrdom of minor poets. When the poem is finished, after three months of strenuous and painful effort, he realises, to his astonishment, that he is not a minor poet. Any other writer would have pursued his investigations, but Leprince is devoid of curiosity about himself. He burns the poem.

In April 1943 he loses his job. In the months that follow he lives from hand to mouth, on the run, pursued by the police, informers, and destitution. One night, as chance would have it, he is given shelter by a young lady novelist. Leprince is anxious and the novelist is an insomniac, so they stay up talking for hours.

That night, deep inside Leprince, a mechanism is released; he openly confesses all his frustrations, all his dreams and ambitions. The young novelist, who frequents literary circles as only a Frenchwoman can, recognises Leprince or thinks she does. Over the previous months she has seen him on hundreds of occasions, always in the shadow of some famous writer wanted by the authorities, or waiting outside the room of a playwright involved in the Resistance, always in the role of messenger, secretary, or valet. You were the only one I didn't know, says the young novelist, and I kept wondering what you were doing there. You were like the invisible man, she adds, always waiting silently, ready to help.

Encouraged by the young woman's frankness, he opens his heart. He talks about his work and she is hugely surprised. Naturally, they broach the subject of Leprince's obscurity. After some hours of conversation, the young woman believes that she has identified the problem and its solution. She speaks bluntly: there is something about him, she says, something in his face, his way of speaking, his gaze, that most people find repellent. The solution is obvious: he has to disappear, go under cover, try not to let his face show in his writing. The solution is so childishly simple, it is bound to work. Leprince listens in amazement and agrees. He knows he is not going to follow the young novelist's advice; he feels surprised and perhaps slightly offended, but he also knows it is the first time that someone has listened to him and understood him.

The following morning a Resistance car comes to pick him up. Before he leaves, the young novelist shakes him by the hand and wishes him luck. Then she kisses him on the lips and starts to cry. Leprince doesn't understand what is happening. Confused, he mumbles a few words of thanks and walks away. The novelist watches him from the window: Leprince gets into the car without looking back. She spends the rest of that morning thinking of him (as Leprince will somehow sense or dream, perhaps in a passage of his uneven work), fantasising about him, telling herself she is in love with him, until weariness finally overcomes her and she falls asleep on the sofa.

They will never see each other again.

Modest and repellent, Leprince survives the war, and in 1946 retires to a small village in Picardy where he takes a job as a teacher. His contributions to the press and certain literary magazines are regular if not numerous. In his heart, Leprince has finally accepted his lot as a bad writer, but he has also come to understand and accept that good writers need bad writers if only to serve as readers and stewards. He also knows that by saving (or helping) several good writers he has earned the right to sully clean sheets of paper and make mistakes. He has also earned the right to publish in two or maybe three magazines. At some point, of course, he tries to locate the young novelist, to find out about her. But when he goes back to her house, other people are living there and nobody knows where she has gone. Leprince, of course, searches for her, but that is another story. In any case he never sees her again.

He does, however, see the Parisian writers. Not as often as he would really like to, but he sees them, and talks to them and they know who he is (vaguely in most cases); there are even one or two who have read a couple of his prose poems. For some, his presence, his fragility, his terrifying sovereignty serve as a spur or reminder.

Enrique Martín

for Enrique Vila-Matas

A poet can endure anything. Which amounts to saying that a human being can endure anything. Except that it's not true: there are obviously limits to what a human being can endure. Really endure. A poet, on the other hand, *can* endure anything. We grew up with this conviction. The opening assertion is true, but that way lie ruin, madness, and death.

I met Enrique Martín a few months after arriving in Barcelona. He was born in 1953, like me, and he was a poet. He wrote in Castilian and Catalan with results that were fundamentally similar, though formally different. His Castilian poetry was well meaning, affected, and quite often clumsy, without the slightest glimmer of originality. His model (in Castilian) was Miguel Hernández, a good poet whom, for some reason, bad poets seem to adore (my explanation, though it's probably simplistic, is that Hernández writes about pain, impelled by pain, and bad poets generally suffer like laboratory animals, especially during their protracted youths). Enrique's Catalan poetry, by contrast, was about real things and daily life, and only his friends ever read or heard it (although to be perfectly frank, the same is probably true of what he wrote in Castilian; the only difference, in terms of audience, was that he published the Castilian poems in magazines with tiny circulations, seen only, I suspect, by his friends, if at all, while he read the Catalan poems to us in bars or when he came round to visit). Enrique's Catalan, however, was bad (how he managed to write better poems in a language he hadn't mastered than he did in his mother tongue must, I suppose, be numbered among the mysteries of youth). In any case Enrique had a very shaky grasp of the rudiments of Catalan grammar and it has to be said that he wrote badly, whether in Castilian or in Catalan, but I still remember some of his poems with a certain emotion, coloured no doubt by nostalgia for my own youth. Enrique *wanted* to be a poet, and he threw himself into this endeavour with all his energy and willpower. He was tenacious in a blind, uncritical way, like the bad guys in westerns, falling like flies but persevering, determined to take the hero's bullets, and in the end there was something likable about this tenacity; it gave him an aura, a kind of literary sanctity that only young poets and old whores can appreciate.

At the time I was twenty-five and thought I had seen everything. Enrique was the opposite: there were so many things he wanted to do, and, in his own way, he was preparing to take on the world. His first step was to bring out a literary magazine, or fanzine, really, which he financed with his savings (he had been working in some obscure office near the port since he was fifteen). At the last minute, Enrique's friends (and one of mine among them) decided not to include my poems in the first issue, an incident which, I am ashamed to admit, led to an interruption of our friendship. According to Enrique, it was the fault of another Chilean, an old friend of his, who had opined that two Chileans was one Chilean too many for the first issue of a little magazine devoted to Spanish writing. I was in Portugal at the time, and when I got back, I decided that was it: I would have nothing more to do with the magazine and it would have nothing more to do with me. I refused to listen to Enrique's explanations, partly because I couldn't be bothered, partly to assuage my wounded pride, and I washed my hands of the whole business.

We didn't see each other for a while. But in the bars of the Gothic Quarter I would sometimes run into mutual acquaintances, and they kept me laconically informed of Enrique's latest adventures. That's how I found out that the magazine (prophetically named *White Rope*, although I'm sure it wasn't his idea) had folded after the first issue, that the first performance of a play he had tried to put on at a cultural centre in the Nou Barris district had been greeted with boos and jeers, and that he was planning to launch another magazine.

One night he turned up at my flat. He was carrying a folder full of poems and he wanted me to read them. We went out to dinner at a restaurant in the Calle Costa and over coffee he read me a few of the poems. He awaited my judgement with a mixture of self-satisfaction and fear. I realised that if I said they were bad, I would never see him again, as well as getting myself into an argument that could easily continue into the small hours. I said I thought they were well written. I wasn't overly enthusiastic, but carefully avoided the slightest criticism. I even said I thought one of them was very good, in the manner of León Felipe, a nostalgic poem about the landscapes of Extremadura, where Enrique had never lived. I don't know if he believed me. He knew I was reading Sanguineti at the time and subscribed (though not exclusively) to the Italian's views on modern poetry, so I could hardly be expected to admire his verses about Extremadura. But he pretended to believe me; he pretended to be glad he had read me the poems and then, revealingly, he started talking about the magazine that had perished after the first issue, and that's when I realised that he didn't believe me but wasn't going to say so.

That was it. We talked a while longer, about Sanguineti and Frank O'Hara (I still like Frank O'Hara but I haven't read Sanguineti for ages), about the new magazine he was planning to launch (he didn't invite me to contribute), and then we said goodbye in the street, near my house. It must have been a year or two before I saw him again.

At the time I was living with a Mexican woman and it looked as if the relationship would be the death of her, and me, and the neighbours, and sometimes even the people who ventured to pay us a visit. Once was enough for our unfortunate visitors, and soon we were hardly seeing anyone. We were poor (although the woman came from a well-off family in Mexico City, she absolutely refused all their offers of financial assistance); our battles were Homeric and a dark cloud seemed to be looming over us day and night.

That's how things were when Enrique Martín reappeared. As he crossed the threshold with a bottle of wine and some French pâté, I had the impression he had come as a spectator, to watch the final act of a major crisis in my life (although in fact I felt fine, it was my girlfriend who was feeling rotten), but later, when he invited us to dinner at his flat, and was so keen to introduce us to his girlfriend, I realised that he hadn't come to observe but, probably, to be observed, or possibly even because, in a sense, my opinion still mattered to him. I know I didn't appreciate this at the time. For a start, I was annoyed by his sudden appearance, and tried to make my greeting sound ironic or cynical, though it probably just sounded apathetic. To be honest, I wasn't fit company for anyone in those days. This was common knowledge: people avoided me or fled my presence. But Enrique wanted to see me and, for some mysterious reason, the Mexican woman liked Enrique and his girlfriend, so we ended up having a series of meals together, five in all.

Naturally, by the time we resumed our friendship – though the term is no doubt excessive – we disagreed about almost everything. My first surprise came when I saw his flat (when our ways had parted he was still living with his parents and although I later heard that he was sharing a place with three friends, for one reason or another I never went there). Now he had a loft in the Barrio de Gràcia, full of books, records and paintings, a large though perhaps rather dim dwelling that his girlfriend had decorated with eclectic taste, and they had some interesting things: objects picked up on recent trips to Bulgaria, Turkey, Israel, and Egypt, some of which were more than tourist souvenirs or imitations. My second surprise came when he told me that he had stopped writing poetry. He said this after dinner, in the presence of my girlfriend and his, although in fact the confession was directed specifically at me (I was playing with an enormous Arab dagger, with ornamental working on both sides of the blade; it can't have been very practical to use), and when I looked up he was smiling as if to say, I've grown up, I've realised you can enjoy art without making a fool of yourself, without keeping up some pathetic pretence of being a writer.

The Mexican woman (who was forthright to a fault) thought it was a shame he had given up; she made him tell the

Enrique Martín

story of the magazine in which my poems hadn't appeared, and in the end she judged the arguments that Enrique had marshalled in defence of his renunciation to be sound and sensible, predicting that before too long he would be writing again with renewed vigour. Enrique's girlfriend agreed with her completely, or almost. Both women seemed to think (although Enrique's girlfriend, for obvious reasons, held this opinion more strongly than mine) that his decision to concentrate on his job – he'd been promoted, which meant he had to travel to Cartagena and Málaga for reasons I didn't care to ascertain – and spend his spare time looking after his record collection, his flat, and his car was far more poetic than wasting his time imitating León Felipe or at best (so to speak) Sanguineti. I was totally non-committal when Enrique asked my opinion (as if it might be an irreparable loss for lyric poetry in Spanish or Catalan, for God's sake). I told him I was sure he had made the right decision. He didn't believe me.

That night, or at one of the other four dinners, the conversation turned to children. It was inevitable: poetry and children. I remember (and this I remember with absolute clarity) Enrique confessing that he would like to have a child. The experience of childbirth, those were his words. Not to share it with a woman, no, he wanted it for himself: carrying the child for nine months inside him and then giving birth. I remember, as he said this, I felt a chill in my blood. The two women looked at him tenderly, but I had an intimation, and this was what chilled me, of what would happen years later, and not many years, unfortunately. When the feeling faded – it was brief, just a twinge – Enrique's declaration struck me as a quip, unworthy of reply. Predictably, the others all wanted to have children, and I, predictably, didn't, and in the end, of the four who were present at that dinner, I am the only one who has a child. Life is mysterious as well as vulgar.

It was during the last dinner, when my relationship with the Mexican woman was on the point of exploding, that Enrique told us about a magazine that he contributed to. Here we go, I thought. He corrected himself immediately: That *we* contribute to. The plural puzzled me momentarily, but then the penny dropped: he and his girlfriend. For once (and for the last time) the Mexican woman and I were in agreement: we asked to see the magazine straight away. It turned out to be one of the numerous periodicals sold at newsstands, with stories on subjects ranging from UFOs and ghosts to apparitions of the Virgin, little known pre-Columbian civilisations and, generally, any kind of paranormal event. It was called *Questions & Answers*, and I think it's still being published. I asked – we asked – how exactly they contributed. Enrique (his girlfriend said practically nothing during this last dinner) explained: on weekends they went to places where there had been sightings of flying saucers; they interviewed the people who had seen them, examined the surroundings, looked for caves (that night Enrique affirmed that many mountains in Catalonia and the rest of Spain were hollow); they stayed up all night, snug in their sleeping bags, with a camera at the ready, sometimes just the two of them, more often in a group of four, five, or six. It was a nice way to spend the night, out in the open, and when it was over, they wrote a report, part of which was published (so what happened to the rest of it?) with photos in *Questions & Answers*.

That night, after dinner, I read a couple of the articles that Enrique and his girlfriend had contributed to the magazine.

They were badly written, dull, pseudo-scientific – the word *science*, in any case, was used several times – and insufferably arrogant. He wanted to know what I thought of them. I realised that my opinion no longer mattered to him in the least, so, for the first time, I was absolutely frank. I suggested changes; I told him he should learn how to write. I asked him if they had editors at the magazine.

Once we got out of the flat, the Mexican woman and I burst into uncontrollable laughter. I think it was later that week that we split up. She went to Rome; I stayed on in Barcelona for another year.

For a long time I had no news of Enrique. In fact I think I forgot all about him. I went to live on the outskirts of a village near Girona with five cats and a dog (a bitch, actually). I rarely saw my old friends and acquaintances, although from time to time one of them would drop in and stay with me, never for more than a couple of days. Whoever the visitor happened to be, we would end up talking about friends from Barcelona or Mexico, but I can't remember any of them mentioning Enrique Martín. I only went down to the village once a day, with the dog, to buy food and rummage through my post office box, where I would often find a letter from my sister in Mexico City, which seemed to have changed beyond recognition. The other letters, few and far between, were from South American poets adrift somewhere in South America, with whom I engaged in desultory exchanges, tetchy and melancholic by turns, just like me and my correspondents, coming to the end of youth, coming to accept the end of our dreams.

One day, however, I received a different sort of letter. Actually, it wasn't, strictly speaking, a letter. On the backs of two cards – invitations to a kind of cocktail party thrown by a Barcelona publisher to launch my first novel, a party which I did not attend – someone had sketched a rather rudimentary map, next to which were written the following numbers:

3860 + 429777 – 469993? + 51179 –
588904 + 966 – 39146 + 498207856

Unsurprisingly, this missive was not signed. The anonymous sender had evidently attended the launch. I made no attempt to decipher the numbers, although I guessed it was an eight-word sentence, no doubt dreamt up by one of my friends. There was nothing particularly mysterious about it, except, perhaps, for the sketched map. It showed a winding path, a tree beside a house, a river dividing into two, a bridge, a mountain or a hill, a cave. On one side, a simple compass rose indicated north and south. Beside the path, in the opposite direction to the mountain (in the end I decided it must be a mountain), an arrow pointed the way to a village in Ampurdán.

That night, back at my house, while I was preparing dinner, it struck me that it must have been sent by Enrique Martín. I imagined him at the launch, talking to some of my friends (one of whom must have given him the number of my post office box), making scathing remarks about the book, working the room with a glass of wine in his hand, saying hello to everyone, loudly enquiring whether or not I would put in an appearance. I think I felt something like contempt. I think I remembered my exclusion from *White Rope,* which was ancient history by then.

A week later I received another anonymous letter. Again it

was written on one of the invitations to my book launch (he must have picked up several), but this time I noticed some differences. Under my name he had written out a line by Miguel Hernández, about happiness and work. And on the other side, the same numbers and a map, radically different from the first one. To begin with, I thought it was just scribble: tangled, intersecting, broken, dotted lines, exclamation marks, drawings rubbed out and superimposed. Finally, after scrutinising it for the umpteenth time and comparing it with the original cards, I cottoned on: the new map was a continuation of the first one; it was a map of the cave.

I remember thinking we were too old for this sort of joke. One afternoon I leafed through an issue of *Questions & Answers* at a newsstand. I didn't see Enrique's name among the contributors. After a few days I forgot all about him and his letters.

Some months went by, three, maybe four. One night I heard the sound of a car pulling up outside my house. I thought it must have been someone who had got lost. I went out with the dog to see who it was. The car had stopped next to some brambles, with the motor running and the lights on. For a while, nothing happened. From where I was standing I couldn't see how many people were in the car, but I wasn't scared; with that dog at my side I was hardly ever scared. She was growling, keen to hurl herself at the strangers. Then the lights went off, the motor stopped, and the car's single occupant opened the door and greeted me like an old friend. It was Enrique Martín. I'm afraid I didn't reciprocate. The first thing he asked me was whether I had received his letters. I said yes. No one had interfered with the envelopes? The envelopes were still properly sealed? I replied in the affirmative and asked him what was going on. Problems, he said, looking back at the lights of the village and the curving road, beyond which there was a stone quarry. Let's go inside, I said, but he didn't budge. What's that? he asked, meaning the lights and the noises from the quarry. I told him what it was and explained that at least once a year, I had no idea why, they kept working till after midnight. That's strange, said Enrique. Again I said, let's go in, but either he didn't hear me or he pretended not to. I don't want to bother you, he said, after my dog had sniffed him. Come in, we'll have a drink, I said. I don't drink alcohol, said Enrique. I was at your book launch, he added. I imagined you'd come. No, I didn't go, I said. Now he's going to start criticising my book, I thought. I was hoping you could look after something for me, he said. That was when I realised that he was holding a kind of package in his right hand; it looked like a bundle of A4 sheets. He's gone back to writing poetry, I thought. He seemed to guess what I was thinking. It isn't poetry, he said with a smile that was at once forlorn and brave, a smile I hadn't seen for many years, not on his face, at any rate. What is it, I asked? Nothing, just some stuff. I don't want you to read it; I only want you to look after it. All right, let's go inside, I said. No, I don't want to bother you, and anyway I haven't got time; I have to get going straight away. How did you know where I live? I asked. Enrique named a mutual friend, the Chilean who had decided that one Chilean was enough for the first issue of *White Rope*. He's got a nerve, giving out my address, I said. You're not friends any more? asked Enrique. I guess we are, I said, but we don't see each other much. Anyway I'm glad he did; it's been really nice to see you, said Enrique. I should have said: and to see you, but I just stood there. Well,

I'm off, said Enrique. Then there was a series of very loud noises, like explosions, coming from the quarry, which made him jumpy. I reassured him. It's nothing, I said, but in fact it was the first time I had heard explosions at that time of night. Well, I'm off, he said. Take care, I said. Can I give you a hug? he asked. Of course, I said. What about the dog, he won't bite me? It's a she, I said, and no, she won't.

For the next two years, while I lived in that house outside the village, I complied with Enrique's request and kept his packet of papers intact, fastened with sticky tape and string, among old magazines and my own papers, which, it doesn't go without saying, multiplied at an alarming rate during that period. The only news I had of Enrique was supplied by the Chilean from *White Rope*; one day we talked about the magazine and the old days, and he clarified his role in the elimination of my poems, which was non-existent, so he said, and so I concluded after listening to his account, not that it mattered to me by then. He told me that Enrique had a bookshop in the Barrio de Gràcia, near his old flat, which, years before, I had visited five times with the Mexican woman. He told me that Enrique and his wife had split up and no longer contributed to *Questions & Answers*, and that his ex was working with him in the bookshop. They weren't living together any more, he said, they were just friends, and Enrique gave her the job because she was out of work. And how's his bookshop going? I asked. Really well, said the Chilean, apparently he got good severance pay from the company where he'd been working since he was a teenager. He lives on the premises, he said. Behind the bookshop, in two smallish rooms. The rooms, I later found out, gave on to an interior courtyard, where Enrique grew geraniums, ficus, forget-me-nots and lilies.

There were two doors in the shopfront and a metal screen that he pulled down every night and locked, as well as a little door that opened on to the building's entrance hall. I didn't feel like asking the Chilean for the address. I didn't ask him whether or not Enrique was writing either. But shortly afterwards I received a long letter from the man himself, signed this time, informing me that he had been in Madrid (I think he was writing from Madrid, but I'm not sure any more) for the famous International Science Fiction Writers' Convention. No, he wasn't writing science fiction (I think he used the expression SF); he had been sent as a special correspondent by *Questions & Answers*. The rest of the letter was muddled. He talked about some French writer whose name didn't ring a bell, according to whom we are all aliens, 'we' meaning every living creature on planet earth; exiles, all of us, wrote Enrique, or outcasts. Then he explained just how it was that the French writer had reached this hare-brained conclusion. But that part was incomprehensible. He mentioned the 'thought police', speculated about 'hyper-dimensional tunnels', and went gabbling on in the way he used to in his poems. The letter ended with an enigmatic sentence: 'all who know are saved'. Then there were the conventional closing formulae. It was the last letter he wrote to me.

Again it was our mutual Chilean friend who filled me in and told me the latest news. We were having a meal together, during one of my increasingly frequent trips to Barcelona, and in the course of the conversation he let it drop, casually, without dramatising the facts.

Enrique had been dead for two weeks. It had happened more or less like this: one morning his ex-wife, now his employee at the bookshop, arrived and found the premises still locked. This surprised her, but she was not alarmed, because Enrique sometimes slept in. For such occasions she had her own key, with which she proceeded to unlock the metal screen and then the glass door in the shopfront. She went straight to the flat at the back, and there she found Enrique hanging from a rafter in his bedroom. The sight almost gave her a heart attack, but she pulled herself together, called the police, shut the shop and waited outside, sitting on the curb, crying, I suppose, until the first patrol car pulled up. When she went back inside, she was surprised to find Enrique still hanging from the rafter. While the police were asking her questions, she noticed that the walls of the room were covered with numbers, big and small, some painted with a stencil, others with a spray-can. She remembered the policemen taking photos of the numbers (659983 + 779511 − 336922, that sort of thing: incomprehensible) and Enrique looking down at them dismissively. The ex-wife turned employee thought the numbers represented debts he had run up. Yes, Enrique was in debt, not much, not enough for anyone to want to kill him, but he did have debts. The policemen asked her whether the numbers had been on the walls the previous day. She said no. Then she said she didn't know. She didn't think so. She hadn't been into that room for a while.

They checked the doors. The one that opened on to the entrance hall was locked from the inside. They found no indication that any of the doors had been forced. There were only two sets of keys: she had one, and they found the other next to the cash register. When the magistrate arrived, they took Enrique's body down and removed it from the premises. The findings of the autopsy were conclusive: he had died almost instantly, by his own hand, another one of Barcelona's frequent suicides.

Night after night, in the solitude of my house in Ampurdán, which I would soon be leaving, I thought about Enrique's suicide. I found it hard to believe that the man who had wanted to have a child, who had wanted to give birth to it himself, could have been so thoughtless as to let his employee and ex-wife find his body hanging – naked? clothed? in pyjamas? – and possibly still swinging from a rafter in the middle of the room. The business with the numbers was more believable. I had no trouble imagining Enrique busy at his cryptography all night long, from eight o'clock, when he shut the bookshop, until four in the morning, a good time to die. Naturally I elaborated various hypotheses in an attempt to explain the manner of his death. The first was directly related to the last letter I had received from him: suicide as a ticket home to the planet of his birth. According to the second hypothesis, he had been murdered in one of two ways. But both strained credibility. I remembered our last meeting, in front of my house, how nervous he had been, as if he were being followed, or hunted.

On my subsequent visits to Barcelona, I compared notes with Enrique's other friends. No one had noticed any significant change in him; he hadn't given sketch maps or sealed packets to anyone else. Concerning one aspect of his life, however, the information was contradictory or incomplete: his work for *Questions & Answers*. Some said that his association with the magazine had come to an end long ago. According to others, he had been a regular contributor up to his death.

One afternoon when I had nothing to do, after sorting out

Enrique Martín

a few things in Barcelona, I went to the office of *Questions & Answers*. The editor received me. Had I been expecting a shady character, I would have been disappointed. He could have been an insurance salesman, pretty much like any magazine editor. I told him Enrique Martín was dead. He didn't know, said he was sorry to hear it, and waited. I asked if Enrique had been a regular contributor to the magazine and, as I expected, he replied in the negative. I mentioned the International Science Fiction Writers' Conference, which had been held recently in Madrid. He told me that his magazine had not sent anyone to cover the event. Fiction, he explained, was not their domain; they were investigative journalists. Although personally, he added, he was a science fiction fan. So Enrique went on his own account, I thought aloud. He must have, said the editor, in any case he wasn't working for us.

Before everyone forgot about Enrique, before his friends grew accustomed to his definitive absence, I obtained his ex-wife and ex-employee's phone number and called her. She didn't remember me at first.

'It's me,' I said, 'Arturo Belano. I went to your flat five times; I was living with a Mexican woman.'

'Ah yes,' she said.

Then there was a silence and I thought there was a problem with the line. But she was still there.

'I rang to say how sorry I was to hear what happened.'

'Enrique went to your book launch.'

'I know, I know.'

'He wanted to see you.'

'We did see each other.'

'I don't know why he wanted to see you.'

'I'd also like to know.'
'Well it's too late now, isn't it?'
'I guess so.'

We talked for a while more, about her nerves, I think, and the state she was in, then I ran out of coins (I was calling from Girona) and we got cut off.

A few months later I left the house. I took the dog with me. I gave the cats to some neighbours. The night before leaving I opened the package that Enrique had given me to look after. I thought I'd find numbers and maps, maybe some sign that might explain his death. There were fifty A4 sheets, neatly bound. There were no maps or coded messages on any of them, just poems, mainly in the style of Miguel Hernández, but there were also some imitations of León Felipe, Blas de Otero, and Gabriel Celaya. That night I couldn't get to sleep. Now it was my turn to escape.

A Literary Adventure

B writes a book in which he makes fun of certain writers, variously disguised, or, to be more precise, certain *types* of writers. In one of his stories there is a character not unlike A, a writer of about B's age, but who, unlike B, is famous, well-off and has a large readership; in other words he has achieved the three highest goals (in that order) to which a man of letters can aspire. B is not famous, he has no money and his poems are published in little magazines. Yet A and B are not entirely dissimilar. They both come from lower-middle-class or upwardly mobile working-class families. Politically, both are left wing; they have in common a keen intellectual curiosity and a deficient formal education. With A's meteoric rise, however, a sanctimonious tone has crept into his writing, and B, who is a slave to print, finds this particularly irritating. In his newspaper articles, and with increasing frequency in his books, A has taken to pontificating on all things great and small, human or divine, with a leaden pedantry, like a man who, having used literature as a ladder to social status and respectability, now safely ensconced in his nouveau-riche ivory tower, snipes at anything that might tarnish the mirror in which he contemplates himself and the world. For B, in short, A has become a prig.

B, as I said, writes a book, and in one of the chapters he makes fun of A. The portrait is not especially cruel (and it is confined to one chapter of a sizeable volume). He creates a character, Álvaro Medina Mena, a successful writer, who happens to express the same opinions as A. The contexts are transposed: where A rails against pornography, Medina Mena attacks violence; where A criticises the commercialism of contemporary art, Medina Mena marshals his arguments against pornography. The story of Medina Mena doesn't stand out from the others in the book, most of which are better (in terms of composition, though perhaps no better written). B's book is published – it is the first time he has been taken on by a major publishing house – and reviews begin to appear. Very slowly at first. Then, in one of the country's leading newspapers, A publishes a review positively glowing with enthusiasm, which convinces the remaining critics and turns B's book into a minor bestseller. Naturally, B feels uncomfortable. Initially, at least. Then, as is often the way, it strikes him as natural (or at least logical) that A should praise his book; after all, it is an interesting book in a number of ways, and A is not a bad critic, after all.

But two months later, in an interview published in another (less prestigious) newspaper, A mentions B's book again, in extremely laudatory terms, wholeheartedly giving it his stamp of approval: 'an untarnished mirror'. There is something about A's tone, however, that makes B wary, as if there were a message to be read between the lines, as if the famous writer were saying to him, Don't think you've fooled me; I know you put me in your book; I know you made fun of me. He's praising my book to the skies, thinks B, so he can let it drop back to earth later on. Or he's praising my book to make sure no one will identify him with Medina Mena. Or he hasn't even realised, and it was a case of genuine appreciation, a simple meeting of minds. None of these possibilities seems to bode well. B doesn't believe that minds can meet in a simple (or innocent) way and he resolves to do all he can to make A's acquaintance. Deep down he knows that A has recognised himself in Medina Mena. He is at least reasonably sure that A has read his book in its entirety with due attention. So why would he refer to it like this? Why praise a book that makes fun of you? (By now B is beginning to think that the caricature was not only exaggerated but also perhaps a little unfair.) He can't figure it out. The only half-plausible explanation is that A hasn't, in fact, identified himself, which, given his advancing cretinism, might just be the case (B reads his articles systematically; he has read every one since the glowing review, and some mornings he longs to plant his fist in A's increasingly prudish face, oozing self-assurance and righteous anger, as if he thought he were the reincarnation of Unamuno or something).

So B does everything he can to meet A face to face, but does not succeed. They live in different cities. A travels a good deal and B can't be sure of finding him at home. His telephone is almost always engaged or the answering-machine is on, in which case B hangs up immediately because he is terrified of answering-machines.

After a while B gives up the idea of contacting A. He tries to forget the whole business and almost succeeds. He writes another book. When it is published, the first review to appear is by A. So soon does it appear in fact that B cannot see how even the most assiduous reader could have finished the book so quickly. It was sent out to the critics on a Thursday and A's review was published the following Saturday; a long review, at least five pages of typescript, considered and insightful too, a lucid, illuminating reading, even for B, to whom it reveals aspects of the book that had escaped his notice. At first B is grateful and flattered. Then he is frightened. It strikes him that A could not possibly have read the book between the day the publisher sent it out and the review's publication date. The way the post works in Spain, if a book is sent on Thursday, you'd be lucky to receive it the following Monday. The first explanation that occurs to B is that A wrote the review without reading the book, but that is untenable. A has obviously read the book and read it carefully. There is, however, a more credible explanation: A obtained the book directly from the publishing house. B phones the marketing manager. He asks how it is possible that A has already read his book. The marketing manager has no idea (although he has read the review and is very pleased). He promises to look into it. B almost gets down on his knees (in so far as one can transmit such a posture via the telephone) and begs him to ring back that night. Predictably enough, he spends the rest of the day coming up with increasingly absurd scenarios. At nine that evening he rings the marketing manager from home. There is, of course, a perfectly logical explanation: A happened to visit the publishing house some days before the copies were sent out; he took one with him, and so was able to read it at his leisure and write the review. Having heard this, B calms down. He tries to put a meal together but there's nothing in the fridge so he decides to go out for dinner. He takes along the newspaper with the review in it. At first he walks aimlessly through the empty streets. Then he finds a little restaurant that he has never patronised and goes in. All the

A Literary Adventure

tables are empty. B sits down next to the window, in a corner away from the fireplace, which is feebly warming the room. A girl asks him what he would like. B says he would like to have dinner. The girl is very pretty. Her hair is long and messy, as if she just got out of bed. B orders soup, and a meat and vegetable dish to follow. While he is waiting he reads the review again. I have to see A, he thinks. I have to tell him I'm sorry, I should never have started this game. There is, however, absolutely nothing offensive about the review: the other reviewers will end up saying all the same things, though perhaps not as well (A does know how to write, thinks B reluctantly or perhaps resignedly). The food tastes like earth, decay, and blood. The chill in the restaurant is seeping into his bones. That night he has serious stomach trouble and the next morning he staggers to the outpatients' department of the nearest hospital. The doctor who sees him prescribes antibiotics and bland food for a week. Lying in bed, and inclined to stay there, B decides to ring a friend; he needs to tell someone the whole story. But he can't decide who to ring. What if I rang A and told him, pretending it was all about someone else, he wonders. But no, at best, A would think it was a coincidence; he would go back and read B's books in a different light, then tear him to shreds in public. At worst, A would pretend not to have understood him. In the end, B doesn't ring anyone and soon another kind of fear begins to grow in him: what if someone, some anonymous reader, has realised that Álvaro Medina Mena is A in disguise? The situation is already horrible; if someone else found out, he reflects, it could become intolerable. But who would be able to identify the model for Álvaro Medina Mena? In theory, any of the 3,500 readers of the novel's first edition; in practice, a handful of individuals: A's devoted fans, literary sleuths or people like B who are exasperated by the rising tide of millennial moralising and pontification. What can B do to keep the secret? He doesn't know. He runs through various possibilities, from enthusiastically reviewing A's next opus or even writing a book-length study of his work to date (including the unfortunate newspaper articles) to ringing him up and laying his cards (whatever they might be) on the table, or paying him a visit one night, cornering him in the hallway of his flat and forcing him to confess why he is doing this, why he has fastened on to B's work like a limpet, what kind of redress he is seeking in this roundabout way.

In the end, B doesn't do anything.

His new book is favourably reviewed but sells poorly. No one is surprised that A has endorsed it. Except when he is judging Spanish letters (and politics) from his high horse, like Cato the Censor, A is reasonably generous in his treatment of newcomers to the literary scene. After a while, B forgets the whole business. Perhaps, he tells himself, it was all a figment of his feverish imagination, overexcited by having two books come out with major publishers; perhaps it was a delusion spawned by his secret fears, or a symptom of nervous exhaustion after so many years of hard labour and obscurity. So he puts it out of his mind and after a while the incident begins to fade, like any other memory, though perhaps it remains more vivid than most. Then, one day, he is invited to a conference on new writing to be held in Madrid.

B is delighted to attend. He is about to finish another book and the conference, he thinks, will serve as a platform for prepublicity. The trip and the hotel have been paid for, of course, and B wants to take advantage of his time in the capital to visit galleries and relax. The conference will last two days; B is participating in the first day's proceedings and will be a member of the audience on the second day. When it is all over, the writers are to be transported *en masse* to the residence of the Countess of Bahamontes, woman of letters and patron of various cultural programmes and organisations, including a writer's fellowship bearing her name and a poetry magazine, probably the best of those published in the capital. B, who knows no one in Madrid, joins the group going to round off the evening at the Countess's house. After a light but delicious supper, liberally washed down with wines from the family vineyards, the party continues into the small hours. At the start there are no more than fifteen people present, but as the hours go by, the festivities are enlivened by the arrival of a variegated array of arts personalities, including several writers, but also film makers, actors, painters, television presenters, and bullfighters.

At one point, B has the privilege of being introduced to the Countess and the honour of being taken aside by her, and led to a corner of the terrace, where there is a view over the garden. There's a friend waiting for you down there, says the smiling Countess, gesturing with her chin towards a wooden arbour surrounded by palms, pines, and plane trees. B looks at her uncomprehendingly. Once, he thinks, long ago, she must have been pretty, but now she is a jumble of flesh and twitchy sinews. B doesn't dare ask who the 'friend' is. He nods, assures her he will go down immediately, but doesn't move. The Countess doesn't move either and for a moment they both stand there in silence, looking into each other's eyes as if they had known each other (or loved and hated each other) in another life. Then other guests commandeer the

Countess and B is left alone, fearfully gazing at the garden and the arbour, in which, after a while, he is sure he can see someone, or the fleeting movement of a shadow. It must be A, he thinks, from which he immediately deduces: he must be armed.

B's first thought is to flee. But then he realises that the only way out, as far as he knows, is past the arbour, so the best escape plan would be to stay in one of the mansion's innumerable rooms and wait for dawn. But maybe it's not A, thinks B, maybe it's the editor of some magazine, or a publisher, or a writer who would like to meet me. Barely conscious of what he is doing, B withdraws from the terrace, picks up a drink, goes down the stairs and out into the garden. There he lights a cigarette and approaches the arbour, taking his time. When he gets there, he finds it empty, but he is sure he saw someone, so he decides to wait. An hour later, bored and tired, he returns to the house. He asks the few remaining guests, who are wandering about like sleepwalkers or actors in a terribly slow play, where the Countess is, but none of them can give him a coherent answer. A waiter (who could just as well be a guest) tells him that the lady of the house has no doubt retired for the night, as it is past her usual bed-time; you know what old people are like. B nods and thinks: fair enough, at her age she can't afford to overdo things. Then he says goodbye to the waiter, they shake hands and he walks back to his hotel. It takes him more than two hours to get there.

The next day, instead of catching the plane back to the city where he lives, B spends the morning moving to a cheaper hotel and settling in, as if he intended to spend a long time in the capital, and then devotes the whole afternoon to ringing

A Literary Adventure

A's home number. To begin with, he keeps getting the answering-machine. A's voice and the voice of a woman, saying, one after another, in cheerful tones, that they aren't in, but will be back soon, so leave a message, and if it's important, leave a number so we can ring back. By the time he has listened to this invitation several times, without leaving a message, B has formed some hypotheses about A and his partner and the mysterious entity they constitute. First, the woman's voice. She is young, much younger than A and B, energetic by the sound of it, determined to carve out her place in A's life and make sure that place is respected. Poor fool, thinks B. Then A's voice. Supremely serene, the voice of Cato. This guy is a year younger than me, thinks B, but he sounds fifteen or twenty years older. Finally, the message: why the joyful tone? Why do they suppose that if it's important the caller is going to stop trying and be content to leave his or her number? Why do they take turns, as if they were reading out a play? To make it clear that two people live there? Or to show the world what a wonderful couple they make? All these questions remain unanswered, of course. But B keeps calling, roughly once every half-hour, and finally, at ten that night, ringing from a pay phone in a cheap restaurant, he gets through and a woman's voice answers. B is so surprised that at first he doesn't know what to say. Who is it? asks the woman. She asks several times, then remains silent, without hanging up, as if she were giving B time to gather his courage and speak. Then, slowly and thoughtfully (so he imagines), the woman hangs up. Half an hour later, B calls again, from a telephone booth. Again it is the woman who picks up the phone, asks who it is and waits for an answer. I want to see A, says B. He should have said: I want to *speak* to

A. Or at least that is what the woman assumes he meant, and she says so. After a moment of silence, B says sorry, but what he wants is to *see* A. And who may I say is calling? It's B, says B. The woman hesitates for a few seconds, as if she were wondering who B is, then says: very well, wait a moment. Her tone of voice hasn't changed, thinks B, not the slightest hint of fear or aggression. B can hear voices; she must have left the receiver on a table or a chair, or hanging from the wall in the kitchen. Although what they are saying is completely unintelligible, he can distinguish the voices of a man and a woman: A and his young partner, thinks B, but then a third voice joins in, a man's voice, much deeper. At first it seems they are engaged in a conversation of such riveting interest that A cannot tear himself away from it, even for a moment. Then B thinks it sounds more like they are arguing. Or trying to reach agreement on an urgent question that must be settled before A can pick up the phone. And in this suspense or uncertainty someone shouts, maybe A. Suddenly there is silence on the line, as if the woman had sealed B's ears with wax. And then (several five-peseta coins later), quietly, gently, someone hangs up.

B doesn't sleep that night. He plans to call again, but, impelled by superstition, decides to change booths. The next two phones he tries are out of order (surprising how run down and dirty the capital is) and when he finally finds one that is working and goes to put the coins in the slot, his hands start shaking as if he were having some kind of attack. The sight of his shaking hands distresses him so much he almost bursts into tears. The best thing to do, he thinks sensibly, would be to calm down and collect himself, and for that, what better place than a bar. So he starts walking and after a

A Literary Adventure

while, having rejected several bars for various and sometimes contradictory reasons, he enters a small establishment with excessively bright lighting, into which more than thirty people are packed. The atmosphere, as he promptly realises, is one of unrestrained and noisy camaraderie. He soon finds himself talking to perfect strangers who, in normal circumstances (back home, in his day-to-day life), he would avoid. They are celebrating someone's last night as a bachelor, or the victory of a local football team. He returns to his hotel at dawn, feeling vaguely ashamed and cursing himself for not having persisted with his calls.

The next day, instead of looking for somewhere to eat (he is not particularly surprised to discover that his appetite has disappeared), B goes into the first phone booth he can find, in a fairly noisy street, and calls A. Once again, the woman answers. He doesn't expect her to recognise him straight away, but she does. A's not in, says the woman, but he wants to see you. And after a silence: we're very sorry about what happened yesterday. What happened yesterday? asks B in all sincerity. We kept you waiting, and then we hung up. I mean, I hung up. A wanted to talk to you, but I didn't think it was a good time. Why not? asks B, who has now cast aside all semblance of discretion. For a number of reasons, says the woman... A hasn't been well lately... When he talks on the phone he tends to get overexcited... He was working, and I don't like to interrupt him... She doesn't sound as young as she did before. She is definitely lying and not even taking the trouble to come up with convincing lies, on top of which she hasn't mentioned the man with the deep voice. But in spite of all this, B is charmed. She's lying like a spoilt little girl, secure in the knowledge that I will forgive her lies, he thinks. And the way she is protecting A makes her all the more irresistible. How long are you going to be in the city? asks the woman. Just until I see A, then I'll go, says B. Uh huh, says the woman (sending a shiver down B's spine), then she thinks for a while in silence. During those seconds or minutes B imagines her face. The image is vague but haunting. The best thing would be for you to come tonight, says the woman. Do you have the address? Yes, says B. Good, we'll expect you for dinner at eight. All right, says B in a faltering voice and hangs up.

B spends the rest of the day wandering around like a vagabond or a lunatic. He doesn't visit a single gallery, of course, although he does go into a couple of bookshops, in one of which he buys A's latest book. He finds a spot in a park and sits down to read it. The book is fascinating, although every page is steeped in sadness. He is such a good writer, thinks B. He considers his own work, blemished by satire and rage, and compares it unfavourably to A's. Then he falls asleep in the sun, and when he wakes up the park is full of beggars and junkies who seem, at first glance, to be moving around, but are not, in fact, although to say they are still would also be inaccurate.

B goes back to his hotel, takes a shower, shaves, puts on his cleanest set of clothes, the ones he wore on his first day in Madrid, and sets off. A lives in the centre of the city, in an old five-storey building. B presses the intercom button and a woman's voice asks who it is. It's B, he says. Come in, says the woman, and the buzzing noise that the security door makes when it is unlocked continues until B reaches the lift. B even thinks he can hear it as he goes up to A's flat, as if the lift were dragging a long tail, like that of a lizard or a snake.

A is waiting for him on the landing, by the open door. He

A Literary Adventure

is tall, pale, and slightly fatter than in the photos. There is a certain shyness in his smile. For a moment B feels as if the energy that brought him to A's door has suddenly drained away. He pulls himself together, tries to smile, holds out his hand. If I can just get through this without violence or melodrama, he thinks. At last, says A. How are you? Very well, says B.

Phone Calls

B is in love with X. Unhappily, of course. There was a time in his life when B would have done anything for X, as people generally say and think when they are in love. X breaks up with him. She breaks up with him over the phone. At first, of course, B suffers, but eventually he gets over it, as people generally do. Life, as they say in the soap operas, goes on. The years pass.

One night when he has nothing to do, B manages to get through to X after ringing a couple of times. Neither of them is young any more and age is audible in their voices transmitted from one side of Spain to the other. They renew their friendship and after a few days decide to meet again. Both have been through divorces, suffered new illnesses and frustrations. When B gets on the train and sets off for the city where X lives, he is not yet in love. They spend the first day holed up in X's flat, talking about their lives (in fact X does all the talking, B listens and asks a question now and then). That night X invites him to share her bed. B doesn't really want to sleep with X, but he accepts. When he wakes up in the morning, he is in love again. But is he in love with X or with the idea of being in love? The relationship is difficult and intense: X is on the brink of suicide every day; she is having psychiatric treatment (pills, lots of pills, but they don't seem to be helping at all), she often bursts into tears for no apparent reason. So B looks after X. His attentions are loving and diligent, but awkward too. They mimic the attentions of a man who is truly in love, as B soon comes to realise. He tries to show X a way out of her depression, but all he does is steer her into a dead end, or what she considers a dead end. Sometimes, when he is on his own or watching X sleep, he thinks it is a dead end too. As a kind of antidote, he tries to remember his former loves, he tries to convince himself that he can live without X, that he can survive on his own. One night X asks him to go away, so B takes a train and leaves the city. X goes to the station to see him off. Their farewell is tender and hopeless. B has booked a sleeper but he can't get to sleep until very late. When he finally falls asleep, he dreams of a snowman walking through the desert. The snowman is following a border, and probably headed for disaster. But he presses on regardless, arming his will with cunning: he walks at night, when freezing starlight sweeps the desert. When B wakes up (the train has already arrived at the Sants Station in Barcelona), he thinks he understands the meaning of the dream (if it has a meaning) and finds some degree of solace in it as he makes his way home. That night he rings X and tells her the dream. X says nothing. The next day he rings X again. And the day after. X's attitude is increasingly cold, as if B were receding further into the past with each phone call. I'm disappearing, thinks B. She's rubbing me out and she knows just what she's doing and why she's doing it. One night B threatens to catch a train and turn up at X's flat the next day. Don't even think about it, says X. I'm coming, says B, I can't stand these phone calls any more, I want to see your face when I'm talking to you. I won't open the door, says X, and then hangs up. B simply can't understand. For a long time he wonders how it is possible for the feelings and desires of a human being to swing from one extreme to the other like that. Then he gets drunk or tries to lose himself in a book. The days go by.

One night, six months later, B calls X. X recognises his voice immediately. Ah, it's you, she says. Her lack of warmth is positively chilling. Yet B senses that X wants to tell him something. She's listening to me as if no time had passed, he thinks, as if we had spoken yesterday. How are you? asks B. What's new? After a few monosyllabic replies, X hangs up. Perplexed, B dials her number again. When he gets through, however, he decides to remain silent. At the other end X's voice says: Well, who is it? Silence. Then she says: I'm listening, and waits. The telephone line is transmitting time – the time that came between B and X, that B could not understand – compressing and stretching it, revealing a part of its nature. Without realising, B starts to cry. He knows that X knows who is calling. Then, silently, he hangs up.

Up to this point the story is banal; unfortunate, but banal. It is clear to B that he should never ring X again. One day there is a knock at the door; it is A and Z. They are policemen and they want to ask him some questions. In connection with what, B would like to know. A is reluctant to say; but Z, after clumsily beating around the bush, comes out with it. Three days ago, on the other side of Spain, someone killed X. At first B is shattered; then he realises that he is a suspect and his instinct for survival puts him on his guard. The policemen ask him about his movements on two days in particular. B can't remember what he did or whom he saw on those days. Naturally he knows that he didn't leave Barcelona – in fact he didn't leave his neighbourhood or even his flat – but he can't prove it. The policemen take him away. B spends the night at the police station. At one point during the questioning he thinks they are going to take him to the city where X used to live and, strangely, this prospect appeals to him, but in the end it doesn't happen. They take his fingerprints and ask if he will agree to a blood test. He agrees. The next morning they let him go home. Officially, B has not been under arrest; he has only been helping the police in a murder inquiry. When he gets back to his flat, he collapses on his bed and falls asleep immediately. He dreams of a desert and of X's face. Shortly before waking, he realises that they are one and the same. From which it is fairly simple for him to infer that he is lost in the desert.

That night he puts some clothes in a bag, goes to the station and takes a train to the city where X used to live. The journey, from one side of Spain to the other, lasts the entire night. Unable to sleep, he thinks about all the things he could have done, but didn't do; all the things he could have given X, but didn't. He also thinks: If I had died, X wouldn't be travelling right across Spain in the other direction. Then he thinks: and that is precisely why I am the one who is still alive. For the first time, during that sleepless trip, he sees X's true worth; he feels love for her again, and, for the last time, half-heartedly, he despises himself. When he arrives, very early in the morning, he goes straight to X's brother's flat. X's brother is surprised and confused, but invites him in and offers him a coffee. He is half dressed and his face is wet. B notices that he hasn't had a shower; he has only washed his face and wet his hair a bit. B accepts the offer of coffee, then says that he just found out about the murder of X, explains that he has been questioned by the police, and asks what happened. The whole thing's been awful, says X's brother, making coffee in the kitchen, but I can't see what you've got to do with it. The police think I might be the killer, says B. X's brother laughs. You've always been unlucky, haven't you, he says. Odd you should say that, thinks B, when I'm the one who's still alive. But he is also grateful not to have his innocence doubted. Then X's brother goes to work, leaving B in the flat. Exhausted, B soon falls into a deep sleep. Unsurprisingly, X appears in his dreams.

When he wakes, he thinks he knows who the killer is. He has seen his face. That night he goes out with X's brother. They go to various bars and talk about this and that and although they do their best to get drunk, they can't. Walking back to the flat through the empty streets, B says he once rang X but didn't speak. What the fuck for? says X's brother. I only did it once, says B, but I realised that X got lots of calls like that. And she thought they were from me, you see? says B. You mean the murderer is the anonymous caller? Exactly, says B, and X thought it was me. X's brother frowns. I think it was one of her exes; there were quite a few of them, you know. B says nothing in reply (it's as if X's brother hadn't understood at all) and they continue in silence until they reach the flat.

In the lift B thinks he is going to throw up. He says: I'm going to throw up. Hold on, says X's brother. They walk quickly down the passage, X's brother unlocks the door and B rushes in looking for the bathroom. But when he gets there, his nausea has subsided. He is sweating and his stomach aches, but he can't throw up. The toilet with the lid up looks like a toothless mouth laughing at him. Or laughing at someone, anyway. After washing his face, he looks at himself in the mirror: his face is white as a sheet. He spends what is left of the night dozing fitfully, trying to read and listening to X's brother snore. The next day they say goodbye and B returns to Barcelona. I'll never go back to that city again, thinks B, because X doesn't live there any more.

A week later, X's brother calls to tell him that the police have caught the killer. The guy was harassing her with anonymous phone calls, he says. B doesn't answer. An ex, says X's brother. Well, it's good to know, says B. Thanks for calling. Then X's brother hangs up and B is alone.

The Grub

He looked like a white grub, with his straw hat and a Bali cigarette hanging from his bottom lip. Each morning when I went to the Librería de Cristal to browse I would see him sitting on a bench in the Alameda. The bookshop, as its name suggests, was glass-fronted, and when I looked up, there he was, sitting still among the trees, staring into nothingness.

I guess we got used to each other's presence. I would arrive at eight-thirty in the morning, and he would already be there, sitting on a bench, doing nothing except smoking and keeping his eyes open. I never saw him with a newspaper or a sandwich, a beer or a book. I never saw him speak to anyone. Once, noticing him there as I glanced up from the French literature shelves, I thought he must sleep in the Alameda, on a bench, or in a doorway in one of the neighbouring streets, but then I realised he was too clean and tidy to be sleeping in the street and must have a room in some boarding-house nearby. He was, I noticed, a creature of habit, like myself. My routine consisted of getting up early, having breakfast with my mother, father, and sister, pretending to go to school, then catching a bus to the centre of the city, where I would devote the first part of my morning to books and walking around, and the second part to movies and, more surreptitiously, to sex.

I generally bought my books at the Librería de Cristal or the Librería del Sótano. If I was short of cash, I'd pick over the special offers table at the Cristal, but if I was sufficiently solvent, I'd go to the Sótano for the new titles. If I had no money at all, which was often the case, I would steal from one or the other, indiscriminately. But in any case, I would invariably pay a visit to both the Librería de Cristal and the Librería del Sótano (located, as the name suggests, in a basement, across from the Alameda). If I arrived before the shops opened, I'd look for a street vendor, buy myself a ham sandwich and a mango juice and wait. Sometimes I'd sit on a bench in the Alameda, tucked away in the shrubbery, and write. All this lasted until about ten in the morning, which is when the cinemas began to open up for their first screenings. I preferred European films, though if I was feeling particularly inspired, I wasn't averse to New Mexican Erotic or New Mexican Horror, which were pretty much the same thing, anyway.

The film I saw most often was French, I think. It was about two girls who live alone in a house outside town. One is blonde and the other's a redhead. The blonde's boyfriend has left her, and as well as having to deal with that, she is going through a personality crisis: she thinks she is falling in love with her housemate. The redhead is younger, more innocent, more irresponsible; in other words, she's happier (although, when I saw this film, I was young, irresponsible, and innocent and believed myself to be deeply wretched). One day a criminal on the run sneaks into their house and holds them hostage. By an odd coincidence this happens on the very night the blonde, after making love with the redhead, has decided to commit suicide. The fugitive climbs in through a window, creeps around the house, knife in hand, goes into the redhead's room, overpowers her, ties her up, interrogates her, asks her how many other people live there (just her and the blonde, she replies), then he gags her. But the blonde is not in her room and the fugitive goes searching through the house, getting more and more nervous, until finally he finds her lying unconscious on the floor of the cellar, having obviously swallowed the contents of the medicine cabinet. The fugitive, who is not a killer (he wouldn't kill a woman, anyway) saves the blonde: he makes her vomit, brews a litre of coffee, makes her drink milk, etc.

As the days go by, the women and the fugitive start to get to know one another. The fugitive tells them his story: he is an ex-bank robber, who has escaped from jail, and his former associates have killed his wife. The women are cabaret artists, and one afternoon or one night (it's hard to tell since they keep the curtains closed the whole time) they put on a show for him: the blonde slips into a magnificent bear skin and the redhead pretends to be the trainer. At first the bear is obedient, but then he rebels and claws at the redhead's clothes, tearing them off piece by piece. Finally, naked, she collapses in defeat and the bear leaps on to her. No, he doesn't kill her; he makes love to her. And the strangest thing of all is that, having watched this performance, the fugitive falls in love not with the redhead but with the blonde, that is, with the bear.

The ending is predictable but not without a certain poetry: one rainy night, after killing his two former associates, the fugitive flees with the blonde to an unknown destination leaving the redhead sitting in an armchair, reading, giving them time before she calls the police. The book she is reading – I realised this the third time I saw the film – is *The Fall* by Camus. I also saw some Mexican films more or less in the same style: women kidnapped by villains who turn out to have hearts of gold; fugitives who take rich young ladies hostage and get themselves shot to pieces after a night of passion; beautiful servants who, starting from nothing, climb the tall ladder of crime to reach the pinnacle of wealth and power. In those days most of the films produced by the Churubusco studios were erotic thrillers, although there were quite a few erotic horror films and erotic comedies too. The horror films basically followed the pattern set by Mexican Horror in the fifties, which is as much a part of the national culture as the mural painting of Rivera, Siqueiros, and company. The innovations were limited to supplementing the stock of timeless icons – Saint, Mad Scientist, Cowboy Vampire, Ingénue – with contemporary nudes, preferably played by unknown North American, European, or occasionally Argentine actresses, slipping in scenes of a more or less overtly sexual nature, and treading a line between the laughable and the intolerable in the depiction of violence. I wasn't so keen on the erotic comedies.

One morning, while I was looking for a book in the Librería del Sótano, I noticed that a film was being shot in the middle of the Alameda and I went over to see what I could see. I recognised Jacqueline Andere straight away. She was on her own, gazing at a row of trees to her left, hardly moving, as if waiting for a signal. Spotlights had been set up around her. I don't know what possessed me to ask for her autograph; I've never been interested in autographs. I waited till they had finished shooting. A man approached her and they talked (was it Ignacio López Tarso?). He gesticulated irritably, then walked off, and after a few moments of hesitation Jacqueline Andere chose a different path. She was coming directly towards me. I started walking too and we met halfway. It was one of the simplest things that has ever happened to me: no one stopped me, or said anything, or came between Jacqueline and me. No one asked me what I was doing there. Before our paths crossed, Jacqueline stopped and turned back to look at the crew, as if she were listening to something, although none of them had spoken. Then she kept walking with the same carefree air towards the Palacio de Bellas Artes, and all I had to do was stop, greet her, ask for an autograph, and hide my surprise at how short she was, even wearing high heels. For a moment we were alone together and it struck me that if I had wanted to kidnap her, I could have. The mere thought made the hair stand up on the back of my neck. She looked at me from head to toe, with her ash-blonde hair (I didn't remember it being that colour – maybe she had dyed it), her big brown almond eyes, so soft, no, soft is not the word, calm, astonishingly calm, as if she were sedated or brain dead or an alien, and she said something to me, but I didn't catch it at first.

A pen, she said, a pen to sign with. I found a biro in the pocket of my jacket and got her to sign the first page of *The Fall*. She took the book from me and looked at it for a few seconds. Her hands were small and very delicate. How would you like me to sign? As Albert Camus or Jacqueline Andere? Whichever you prefer, I said. Although she didn't look up from the book I could tell she was smiling. Are you a student? she asked. I replied in the affirmative. So how come you're here instead of in class? I don't think I'll ever go back to school, I said. How old are you? she asked. Seventeen, I said. And do your parents know you're not going to class? No, of course not, I said. You still haven't answered my question, she said, looking up and into my eyes. Which question? I asked. What are you doing here? When I was young, kids used to hang out in pool halls or bowling alleys when they skipped classes. Well, I read books and go to the movies, I said. Anyway, I'm not skipping a class. No, you leave that to the amateurs, she said. Now it was my turn to smile. And what movies can you see at this time of the day? All sorts, I said, some of yours. She didn't seem to like that; she looked at the book again, bit her bottom lip, looked at me and blinked as if her eyes were hurting. Then she asked my name. Well, let's get this signed, she said. She was left-handed. Her handwriting was large and hard to read. I have to go, she said, handing me the book and the biro. She held out her hand, shook mine and went back across the Alameda towards the film crew. I stood still, watching her. When she was about fifty metres away two women approached her, dressed as missionary nuns, two Mexican missionary nuns who escorted Jacqueline to the shade of an ahuehuete tree. Then a man went over to her, they talked, and the four of them walked away down one of the paths that lead out of the Alameda.

On the first page of *The Fall*, she had written: 'For Arturo Belano, student at large, with a kiss from Jacqueline Andere.'

Suddenly I had no desire to browse in a bookshop, walk around, read, or least of all go to a matinée session. The prow of an enormous cloud appeared over the centre of Mexico City, while to the north the first thunderclaps resounded. I realised that the shooting of Jacqueline's film had been suspended because of the imminent rain and I felt lonely. For a few seconds I didn't know what to do, where to go. Then the

Grub said hello to me. Having seen me so many times, I suppose he had begun to recognise me too. I turned around and there he was, sitting on the same bench as always, a clear-cut presence, absolutely real, with his straw hat and his white shirt. The scene, as I was troubled to discover, had undergone a subtle but decisive transformation with the departure of the film crew: it was as if the waters had parted to reveal the sea floor. The empty Alameda was the sea floor, and the Grub its most precious treasure. I said hello, probably made some banal remark, and it began to pour. We left the Alameda together and headed for the Avenida Hidalgo; then we walked down Lázaro Cárdenas to the corner with Perú.

What happened next is hazy, as if seen through the rain that was lashing the streets, yet perfectly natural. The bar was called Las Camelias and it was full of mariachis and chorus girls. I ordered enchiladas and a beer, the Grub ordered a Coke and a bit later on he bought three turtle eggs from a vendor. He wanted to talk about Jacqueline Andere. I soon realised, to my astonishment, that he didn't know she was a film star. I pointed out that she was there for a film shoot, but he simply didn't remember the crew or the equipment they had set up. Jacqueline's apparition on his path, near his bench, had obliterated all the rest. When it stopped raining, the Grub pulled a bunch of notes from his back pocket, paid, and left.

We saw each other again the next day. From the expression on his face when he saw me I thought he couldn't remember who I was or didn't want to say hello. I went over to him anyway. He seemed to be asleep, although his eyes were open. He was thin, but his flesh, except on his arms and legs, gave the impression of being soft, even flaccid, like the flesh of an athlete no longer in training. His flaccidity, however, was not

The Grub

so much physical as psychological. His bones were small and strong. I soon discovered that he was from the north, or had lived there a long time, which comes to the same thing. I'm from Sonora, he said. By coincidence, that was where my grandfather came from. This intrigued the Grub and he wanted to know what part of Sonora. From Santa Teresa, I said. I'm from Villaviciosa, said the Grub. One night I asked my father if he knew Villaviciosa. Of course I do, said my father, it's a few kilometres from Santa Teresa. I asked him to describe it for me. It's a very small town, said my father, wouldn't be more than a thousand people (later I found out there weren't even five hundred), pretty poor, not many jobs, and no industry at all. It'll disappear sooner or later, he said. How do you mean disappear? I asked him. Emigration, he said, the people will leave and to go to Santa Teresa or Hermosillo or the United States. When I reported this to the Grub he didn't agree, although it would be an exaggeration to say that he ever agreed or disagreed with anything. The Grub never argued or expressed opinions, but not out of any particular respect for others; he simply listened and stored things away, or maybe he just listened and forgot it all, off in a world of his own. His speech was soft and monotonous, although occasionally he would raise his voice, and then he sounded like a madman imitating a madman. I never knew whether those outbursts were intentional, part of some private game, or beyond his control, cries from hell. His conviction that Villaviciosa would endure was founded on the town's long history, but also (though I only came to understand this later) on the tenuous nature of its existence, threatened from all quarters, which is precisely what doomed it to extinction, according to my father.

Although the Grub was not a curious man, few things escaped his notice. He once examined the books I was carrying, one by one, as if he could barely read or couldn't read at all. After that he never showed the slightest interest in my books, although I had a new one every morning. Sometimes, perhaps because he considered me a fellow countryman of sorts, we talked about Sonora, which I hardly knew: I had been there only once, for my grandfather's funeral. He would speak of towns like Nacozari, Bacoache, Fronteras, Villa Hidalgo, Bacerac, Bavispe, Agua Prieta, Naco, names that were pure gold to my imagination. He would mention forsaken villages in the districts of Nácori Chico and Bacadéhuachi, near the border with Chihuahua state, and then, I don't know why, he would cover his mouth as if he were about to sneeze or yawn. He seemed to have roamed over all the mountain ranges, on foot, camping out: the Sierra Las Palomas and the Sierra La Cieneguita, the Sierra Guijas and the Sierra La Madera, the Sierra San Antonio and the Sierra Cibuta, the Sierra Tumacacori and the Sierra Sierrita right up into Arizona, the Sierra Cuevas and the Sierra Ochitahueca in the northeast, near Chihuahua, the Sierra La Pola and the Sierra Las Tablas in the south, towards Sinaloa, the Sierra La Gloria and the Sierra El Pinacate, up in the north-east, on the way to Baja California. He knew the whole of Sonora, from Huatabampo and Empalme on the Gulf coast to the remote one-horse towns in the desert. He could speak Yaqui and Pápago (a language that straddles the Sonora–Arizona border) and he understood Seri, Pima, Mayo, and English. His Spanish was dry, with a slightly oratorical tone from time to time, undercut by the look in his eye. Like a soul in torment, I have wandered all over your grandfather's country, may he rest in peace, he said to me once.

We met each morning. Sometimes I tried not to notice him and go back to my solitary walks and matinées, but he was always there, sitting on the same bench in the Alameda, very still, with a Bali cigarette hanging from his lip, and his straw hat half covering his grub-like forehead; and inevitably, looking up from the books in the Librería de Cristal, I would see him, watch him for a while, and end up going over to sit beside him.

I soon discovered that he always carried a gun. At first I thought maybe he was a policeman or someone was out to get him, but he couldn't have been a policeman (or not any more, if he ever had been) and I have rarely seen anyone so unconcerned by the presence of others; he never looked behind him, or to the side, and he hardly ever looked down. When I asked him why he carried a gun, the Grub said, Habit, and I didn't doubt him for a moment. He carried it in the back of his trousers. Have you used it much? I asked him. Yes, lots of times, he said, as if in a dream. For several days I was obsessed with the Grub's gun. Sometimes he would take it out, remove the clip and hand it to me so I could inspect it. It looked old and felt heavy. Generally I gave it back to him after a few seconds and asked him to put it away. Sometimes it made me nervous to be sitting on a bench in the Alameda talking to (or at) a man with a gun, not because of what he might have done to me – I knew from the start that the Grub and I would always be friends – but because I was worried the Mexico City police might see us there, search us, find the Grub's gun, and dump us both in some dark prison cell.

One morning he was unwell and that was when he told me about Villaviciosa. I saw him from the Librería del Cristal and he looked the same as ever, but when I went over to him, I noticed that his shirt was crumpled, as if he had slept in it. When I sat down beside him I could see that he was trembling. Soon he began to tremble more violently. You've got a fever, I said, you should go to bed. I accompanied him to the boarding-house where he lived, although he insisted there was no need. Lie down, I said. The Grub took off his shirt, put the pistol under his pillow, and seemed to fall asleep immediately, though with his eyes open and fixed on the ceiling. In the room there was a narrow bed, a bedside table and a decrepit wardrobe. Inside the wardrobe I found three perfectly folded white shirts like the one he had just taken off and two pairs of matching trousers on hangers. Under the bed I noticed a very classy leather suitcase, the sort that has a lock like a safe. I couldn't see a single newspaper or magazine. The room smelt of disinfectant, like the boarding-house stairs. Give me some money so I can go to the chemist and buy you something, I said. He pulled a bundle of notes from his trouser pocket, gave it to me, and lay still again. Every now and then a shudder ran down his body from head to foot as if he were about to die. But only every now and then. For a moment I thought I really should call a doctor, but then I realised that the Grub wouldn't like that. By the time I returned, bearing medicine and bottles of Coke, he really had fallen asleep. I gave him a hefty dose of antibiotics and pills to bring his temperature down. Then I made him drink half a litre of Coke. I had also bought a pasty, which I left on the bedside table in case he got hungry later on. As I was

The Grub

getting ready to go, he opened his eyes and started talking about Villaviciosa.

For a man of so few words, it was a detailed description. He said the village had seventy houses, no more, two bars and a general store. He said the houses were made of adobe and some had cement patios. He said the patios gave off a bad and sometimes unbearable smell. Unbearable, he said, for anyone with a soul, or even without a soul, even without senses. He said that was why some of the patios had been cemented. He said the village was between two and three thousand years old and its native sons worked as hired killers or security guards. He said a killer never hunted a killer, how could he, it would be like a snake biting its own tail. He said that snakes had been known to bite their own tails. He said that snakes had even been known to swallow themselves whole and if you see a snake in the process of swallowing itself you better run because sooner or later something bad is going to happen, some dislocation of reality. He said the village was near a river, called Río Negro because its water was black, and as it flowed past the cemetery it spread out in a delta and sank into the dry earth. He said that sometimes the people would stare for hours at the horizon and the sun setting behind a mountain called El Lagarto, and the horizon was the colour of flesh, like the back of a dying man. And what do they expect to see? I asked. The sound of my own voice frightened me. I don't know, he said. Then he said: a shaft. And then: wind and dust, maybe. Then he calmed down and after a while he seemed to be asleep. I'll come back tomorrow, I murmured, take the medicines and don't get out of bed.

I left quietly.

The next morning, before going to the Grub's boarding-house, I spent a while as usual at the Librería de Cristal. When I was about to leave, I looked out through the shop window and saw him. He was sitting on the same bench, wearing a clean, loose white shirt and a pair of perfectly white trousers, his face half covered by his straw hat, and a Bali cigarette hanging from his lower lip. He was gazing straight ahead, as normal, and he seemed well. At noon, as we were about to say goodbye, he held out several notes with a sullen expression on his face and said something about the trouble he'd caused me the previous day. It was a lot of money. I told him he didn't owe me anything, I would have done the same for any friend. The Grub insisted I take the money. You can use it to buy some books, he said. I've got lots, I replied. Well you can stop stealing them for a while, he said. In the end I took the money. It's a long time ago and I can't remember exactly how much it was, the Mexican peso has been devalued over and over again, but I remember it was enough to buy twenty books and two Doors records, and for me that was a fortune. The Grub wasn't short of cash.

He never talked to me again about Villaviciosa. For a month and a half, or maybe two months, we met each morning and at midday went our separate ways, when it was time for me to catch a bus back home to La Villa for lunch. Once I invited the Grub to see a movie, but he didn't want to. He liked to talk to me, either sitting on his bench in the Alameda or wandering around the neighbouring streets, and every now and then he deigned to go into a bar, where he would always look for the turtle-egg vendor. I never saw him touch alcohol. A few days before he disappeared for good he got me to talk about Jacqueline Andere for some reason. I realised it was his way of remembering her. I talked about her ash-blonde hair and compared it favourably or unfavourably to the honey-blonde colour it was in her films, and the Grub nodded almost imperceptibly, looking straight ahead as if the image of Jacqueline Andere were imprinted on his retinas or as if he were seeing her for the first time. Once I asked him what kind of women he liked. It was a stupid question, asked by an adolescent looking for something to say. But the Grub took it seriously and considered his reply for a long time. Finally he said, Calm women. And then he added, But only the dead are really calm. And after a while, Not even the dead, come to think of it.

One morning he gave me a knife. On the bone handle the word 'Caborca' had been inscribed in fine letters of nickel silver. I remember thanking him effusively. That morning, as we talked in the Alameda or walked through the busy streets of the city centre, I kept opening the blade and shutting it again, admiring the handle, feeling its weight in the palm of my hand, marvelling at its perfect proportions. Otherwise, that day was identical to all the others. The next morning the Grub was gone.

Two days later I went to his boarding-house to look for him and they told me he had gone up north. I never saw him again.

Anne Moore's Life

Anne Moore's father served his country and the free world aboard a hospital ship in the Pacific from 1943 to 1945. His first daughter, Susan, was born while he was at sea off the Philippines, just before the end of the Second World War. Soon after, he returned to Chicago, where Anne was born in 1948. But Dr Moore didn't like Chicago, so three years later, he and his family moved to Great Falls, in the state of Montana.

That is where Anne grew up. Her childhood was peaceful, but it was also strange. In 1958, when she was ten years old, she glimpsed for the first time what she would later call the ashen (or the dirty) face of reality. Her sister had a boyfriend called Fred, who was fifteen. One Friday Fred came to the Moores' house and said that his parents had gone on a trip. Anne's mother said it wasn't right, he was just a boy, he shouldn't be left alone in the house like that. Anne's father reckoned that Fred was old enough to look after himself. That night Fred had dinner at the Moores' house, then sat on the porch chatting to Susan and Anne until ten. Before leaving he said goodbye to Mrs Moore. Dr Moore had already gone to bed.

The next day Fred took Susan and Anne for a drive

around the park in his parents' car. According to what Anne told me, Fred's state of mind was noticeably different from the night before. He was preoccupied and hardly spoke, as if he and Susan had argued. For a while they just sat there in the car, in silence, Fred and Susan in the front and Anne in the back, then Fred proposed that they go to his house. Susan didn't answer. Fred started the car and drove to a poor neighbourhood where Anne had never been; it was as if he was lost or, deep down, didn't really want to take them to his house, even though he was the one who had suggested it. Anne remembers that as they drove around Susan didn't look at Fred once; she spent the whole time looking out of the window, as if the houses and the streets slowly filing past were part of a never to be repeated show. And Fred, gazing fixedly straight ahead, didn't once look at Susan. Neither of them said a word or turned to look at the young girl in the back seat, although at one point, momentarily, she caught Fred's eye in the rear-view mirror, staring at her, hard and bright.

When they finally arrived at Fred's house, neither Fred nor Susan made a move to get out. Even the way Fred parked the car in the street instead of in the garage seemed provisional, a way of breaking the flow. As if by parking like that, he was giving us and himself extra time to think, says Anne in hindsight.

After a while (Anne doesn't remember how long) Susan got out of the car, ordered her sister to do the same, took her by the hand, and they walked away without saying goodbye. When they were several yards away, Anne turned and saw the back of Fred's neck; he hadn't moved, he was still at the wheel, as if still driving, staring straight ahead, says Anne, although by then he may have closed or half-closed his eyes; he may have been looking down, or crying.

They walked back home and Susan refused to explain her behaviour, in spite of Anne's questions. She wouldn't have been surprised to find Fred in the garden that afternoon. It wasn't the first time he and her sister had fought, and they always made up soon afterwards. But Fred didn't come round that Saturday, or on Sunday, and he wasn't in class on Monday, as Susan was later to confess. On Wednesday the police arrested Fred for drunken driving in a poor neighbourhood of Great Falls. After questioning him, they went to his house and found the bodies of his parents: his mother's in the bathroom and his father's in the garage. His father's body was partly wrapped in blankets and cardboard, as if Fred had been intending to dispose of it in the coming days.

As a result of this crime, Susan, who seemed at first to be coping remarkably well, had a mental breakdown and was in therapy for several years with a series of psychologists. Anne, by contrast, was unaffected, although the incident, or the shadow it cast, would revisit her intermittently in later years. But at the time she didn't even dream about Fred, or if she did, she sensibly forgot the dreams as soon as she emerged from sleep.

At the age of seventeen, Anne went to college in San Francisco. Susan had gone there two years earlier, to study medicine at Berkeley, and was sharing an apartment with two other students in the southern part of Oakland, near San Leandro. Her letters home were infrequent. When Anne arrived she found her sister in a terrible state. Susan was not studying; she slept during the day, disappeared at night and wouldn't come back until well into the next morning. Anne began a degree in English Literature and took a course in Impressionist Painting. She found an afternoon job at a cafeteria in Berkeley. To begin with she lived in the same room as her sister. In fact they could have gone on like that indefinitely. During the day, while Anne was at college, Susan was at home sleeping, and since she was hardly ever there at night, they could make do with one bed. But after a month Anne moved to a place in Hackett Street, near the café where she was working, and stopped seeing her sister, although she would sometimes call her (it was always one of her housemates who answered the phone) to see how she was, pass on news about Great Falls and find out if she needed anything. Susan was drunk the few times Anne got through to her. One morning they told her that Susan had moved out. For two weeks she searched all over Berkeley but couldn't find her. Finally, one night she rang her parents in Great Falls, and it was her sister Susan who answered the phone. Anne couldn't believe it. She felt somehow cheated and betrayed. Susan had given up her studies for good and now she wanted to start all over again in a nice, quiet town, she said. If that's what you want to do, I'm sure that's best, said Anne, although in fact she felt her sister was in a mess and was throwing her life away.

Not long after this, Anne met Paul, a painter, grandson of Russian-Jewish anarchists, and moved in with him. Paul had a little two-storey house. His studio, full of large, permanently unfinished pictures, occupied the ground floor, and on the first floor there was a big space that served as bedroom, living room and dining room, as well as a tiny kitchen and bathroom. Of course he wasn't the first man she had slept with. She had gone out with a classmate from the

Impressionist Painting course – he was the one who introduced her to Paul – and back in Great Falls she had had two boyfriends: a basketball player and a boy who worked in a bakery. For a while she thought she was in love with the boy from the bakery. His name was Raymond and the bakery belonged to his father. In fact, Raymond came from a long line of bakers, going back several generations. He was studying and working at the same time, but when he graduated he decided to become a full-time baker. He wasn't an outstanding student, according to Anne, but he wasn't bad either. And what she especially remembered about Raymond, in those years, was how proud he was of his trade, the family trade, in a place where people pride themselves on all sorts of things, but not, as a rule, on baking bread for a living.

Anne and Paul's relationship was unusual. Anne was seventeen going on eighteen and Paul was twenty-six. They had problems in bed from the start. In summer Paul was often impotent, in winter he was prone to premature ejaculation, and in spring and autumn he wasn't interested in sex. That's according to Anne; she also says that he was the most intelligent person she had ever met. Paul knew about everything: painting, art history, literature, music. Sometimes he was insufferable, but he could tell when it was coming on and knew to shut himself up in his studio and paint until he had stopped being insufferable and reverted to his normal self – charming, chatty, and loving – at which point he would stop painting and take Anne to the movies, or the theatre, or one of the many talks and readings that were happening at Berkeley, preparing people's minds for the decisive years to come. At first they lived off Anne's wages from the cafeteria and a scholarship that Paul had. Then one day they decided to travel to Mexico and Anne quit her job.

They went to Tijuana, Hermosillo, Guaymas, Culiacán, and Mazatlán, where they rented a beach house. They went swimming every morning; in the afternoon Paul painted while Anne read, and at night they went to a North American bar, the only one in town, called The Frog, frequented by tourists and Californian students. They stayed there late into the night, drinking and talking to people they would normally have ignored. Outside The Frog they bought marijuana from a thin Mexican guy who always wore white and wasn't allowed into the bar. He waited for clients in his car, parked opposite, next to a dead tree.

The thin guy was called Rubén, and sometimes he would exchange marijuana for cassettes, which he played straight away in the car. They soon made friends with him. One afternoon, while Paul was painting, Rubén turned up at the beach house and Paul asked him to pose. From that day on, they never had to pay for their marijuana. But Rubén would sometimes arrive in the morning and stay well into the night, which annoyed Anne, not just because she had to cook for an extra person, but also because, the way she saw it, the Mexican was intruding on the idyllic life they had planned to lead, just the two of them.

At first Rubén talked only to Paul, as if he could tell that Anne resented his presence, but as the days went by they became friends. Rubén spoke a little English and Paul and Anne practised their rudimentary Spanish with him. One afternoon, while they were swimming, Anne felt Rubén touching her legs under the water. Paul was on the beach, watching them. When Rubén came up to the surface he looked her in the eyes and said he was in love with her. That day, as they later found out, someone drowned: a boy who used to go to The Frog; they had chatted with him a couple of times.

Shortly afterwards they went back to San Francisco. It was a good time for Paul. He had two exhibitions, sold some paintings, and his relationship with Anne was steadier than ever. At the end of the year they both travelled to Great Falls and spent Christmas with Anne's parents. Paul didn't like Anne's mother and father, but he got on well with Susan. One night Anne woke up alone in bed. She went looking for Paul and heard voices in the kitchen. When she went downstairs she found Paul and Susan talking about Fred. Paul was listening and asking questions, and Susan was telling him about the last day she had spent with Fred, driving around the poorest neighbourhoods of Great Falls. She told the story over and over, from different points of view. Anne remembers that there was something oddly artificial about this conversation between her lover and her sister, as if they were assessing the plot of a film, not something that had happened in real life.

The following year Anne quit her studies and devoted herself to looking after Paul. She bought his canvases, stretchers, and paint; she cooked, washed, swept, mopped the floors, did the washing-up, and generally tried to make their home a haven of peace and creativity. But their relationship was far from perfect. As a lover Paul kept getting worse. Sex with him did nothing for Anne and she began to wonder if she might be a lesbian. Around that time they met Linda and Marc. Linda sold drugs for a living, like Rubén in Mazatlán, and occasionally she wrote children's stories, which kept getting rejected by publishers. Marc was a poet, or at least that was what Linda said. At that stage he usually spent most of the day shut up in his apartment, listening to the radio or watching television. In the morning he would go out and buy three or four newspapers, and on rare occasions he went to the university, where he met up with old friends or attended the classes of some famous poet who was doing a stint as a visiting professor at Berkeley. But, according to Anne, the rest of the time, he stayed in his apartment, or in his room if Linda had visitors, listening to the radio, watching television and waiting for the declaration of the Third World War.

It came as a surprise to Anne when Paul's career suddenly stalled. Everything happened too quickly. First he lost his scholarship, then the galleries in the Bay area stopped exhibiting his work, and in the end he gave up painting and started studying literature. In the afternoons, Paul and Anne would go to Linda and Marc's apartment and talk for hours about the Vietnam war and about travel. Although Paul and Marc were never really close, they could spend hours on end reading each other poems and drinking (around that time, Anne remembers, Paul began to write poems in the style of William Carlos Williams and Kenneth Rexroth, whom they had once heard give a reading in Palo Alto). Anne's friendship with Linda, on the other hand, deepened imperceptibly but surely, although it seemed to lack a firm base. Anne liked Linda's self-assurance, her independence, her eclectic way of life, the way she flouted certain social conventions while respecting others.

When Linda got pregnant, her relationship with Marc

came to a sudden end. She went to live in an apartment in Donaldson Street and kept working until a few days or maybe (Anne can't remember) a few hours before the birth. Marc stayed on in the old apartment and became even more reclusive. At first Paul continued to visit Marc, but he soon realised they had nothing to say to each other, so he stopped. The two women, however, grew closer, and Anne would sometimes even sleep over at Linda's apartment, mainly at weekends, to help her look after the baby when she was busy with her clients.

A year after their first trip to Mexico, Paul and Anne went back to Mazatlán. This time it was different. Paul wanted to rent the beach house, but it was taken, so they had to make do with a sort of bungalow three blocks away. As soon as they arrived in Mazatlán, Anne fell ill. She had diarrhoea and a fever and couldn't get out of bed for three days. The first day Paul stayed in the bungalow and looked after her, but then he started disappearing for hours, and once he stayed out all night. Rubén, however, came to see her. Anne realised that Paul had been out on the town with Rubén and at first she hated the Mexican. But on the third night, when she was starting to feel a bit better, Rubén turned up at the bungalow at two in the morning to enquire about the state of her health. They talked until five and then made love. Anne was still feeling weak. The door was ajar, and at one point she was sure that Paul was behind it, watching them, or looking through the window, but Rubén was so tender and it went on so long that she forgot about everything else, she says.

When Paul appeared the next day, Anne told him what had happened. Paul said 'Shit!' but didn't elaborate. For a couple of days he tried to write something in a notebook with a black cover that Anne was never allowed to read, but he soon gave up and applied himself to sleeping on the beach and drinking. Sometimes he went out with Rubén as if nothing had happened; other nights he stayed at the bungalow and twice they tried to make love, with less than satisfactory results. She slept with Rubén again. Once, at night, on the beach, and another time in the bedroom at the bungalow, while Paul was sleeping on the sofa next door. As the days went by, Anne noticed that Rubén was becoming jealous of Paul. But this only happened when the three of them were together, or when Anne and Rubén were alone, not when Paul and Rubén went out at night to visit the bars of Mazatlán. They were like brothers then, Anne remembers.

When the day came to leave, Anne decided to stay in Mexico. Paul understood and said nothing. It was a sad goodbye. She and Rubén helped Paul pack his bags and put them in the car and then they gave him presents: an old book of photos from Anne and a bottle of tequila from Rubén. Paul didn't have any presents for them, but he gave Anne half the money he had left. When Paul was gone, Anne and Rubén shut themselves in the bungalow and spent three days in a row making love. Anne's money soon ran out and Rubén went back to selling drugs outside The Frog. Anne left the bungalow and went to live at Rubén's house in a suburb from which you couldn't see the ocean. The house belonged to Rubén's grandmother, who lived there with her eldest son, Rubén's uncle, an unmarried fisherman, about forty years old. Things soon took a turn for the worse. Rubén's grandmother didn't like the way Anne walked around the house half-naked. One afternoon, when Anne was in the bathroom, Rubén's uncle came in and propositioned her. He offered her money. Anne, of course, refused the offer, but not firmly enough (she didn't want to offend him, she remembers) and the next day Rubén's uncle offered her money again in return for her favours.

Without realising what she was about to unleash, Anne told Rubén. That night Rubén took a knife from the kitchen and tried to kill his uncle. The shouting was loud enough to wake the whole neighbourhood, Anne remembers, but strangely nobody seemed to hear. Luckily, Rubén's uncle, who was a stronger and more experienced fighter, soon disarmed him. But Rubén wasn't about to give in, and threw a vase at his uncle's head. As bad luck would have it, just at that moment his grandmother was coming out of her room, wearing a very bright red nightdress, the likes of which Anne had never seen. Rubén's uncle ducked and the vase struck his grandmother on the chest. The uncle gave Rubén a beating, then took his mother to hospital. When they returned, the uncle and the grandmother marched straight into the room where Anne and Rubén were sleeping and gave them two hours to get out of the house. Rubén had bruises all over his body and could hardly move, but he was so scared of his uncle that before the two hours were up, they had packed all their gear into the car.

Rubén had relatives in Guadalajara, so that's where they went. They ended up staying only four days. The first night they slept in Rubén's sister's house, which was small, stiflingly hot, and crowded. They shared a room with three small children and the next day Anne decided to find a hotel. They had no money, but Rubén still had some marijuana and acid tablets he could sell, or so he thought. His first attempt was a failure. He didn't know Guadalajara well; he didn't know where to deal, and he came back to the hotel tired and empty-handed. That night they talked until very late and in a moment of frustration Rubén asked Anne what they would do if they couldn't get money to pay for the hotel or buy petrol for the car. Anne said (she was joking, of course) that she could sell her body. Rubén didn't get the joke and slapped her. It was the first time a man had ever hit her. I'd rob a bank before I let you do that, he said, and threw himself on her. Anne remembers what followed as some of the weirdest sex of her life. It was as if the walls of the hotel room were made of meat. Raw meat and grilled meat, bits of both. And while they were fucking she looked at the walls and she could see things moving, scurrying over that irregular surface, like something from a John Carpenter horror movie, though I can't remember that actually happening in any of his films.

The next day Rubén sold the drugs and they headed for Mexico City. They lived with Rubén's mother, in a suburb near La Villa, pretty close to where I was living at the time. If I'd seen you then, I would have fallen in love with you, I told Anne many years later. Who knows, said Anne. Then she added: If I'd been a teenage boy, I wouldn't have fallen in love with me.

For some time, two or three months, Anne thought she was in love with Rubén and envisaged spending the rest of her life in Mexico. But one day she rang her parents, asked them for money to buy an air ticket, said goodbye to Rubén and went back to San Francisco. She moved into Linda's apartment and found a job as a waitress. Sometimes when she came home from work, Linda was still up and they would talk until late. Some nights they talked about Paul and Marc. Paul was living on his own and had started painting again, though much less than before, and with no prospect of exhibiting. According to Linda the problem with Paul's paintings was that they were very bad. Marc was living like a recluse in his apartment, listening to the radio and watching all the news broadcasts on television. He had hardly any friends left. Anne remembers that a few years later, Marc published a book of poems, which was something of a success in the Berkeley student community, and he gave readings and took part in some conferences. It seemed like the ideal moment for him to start a new relationship and share his life with someone, but after the initial buzz, he retreated to his apartment and she never heard anything more about him.

When a guy called Larry moved in with Linda, Anne rented a little apartment in Berkeley, near the café. Things seemed to be going well, but Anne knew they were about to fall apart. She could tell from her dreams, which were increasingly strange, from her state of mind, drifting towards melancholy, from her unpredictable mood swings. She went out with a couple of guys, but in both cases it was a disappointment. Sometimes she went to see Paul, but she soon stopped, because although the visits would begin well enough they almost always ended in tears, self-reproach, and sadness, or in violent outbursts (Paul would tear up sketches, even destroy paintings). Sometimes she thought about Rubén and laughed at how naïve she had been. One day she met a guy called Charles and they became lovers.

Charles seemed to be the opposite of Paul, Anne remembers, although deep down they were very similar. He was black and had no source of income. He liked to talk and he knew how to listen. Sometimes they spent the whole night making love and talking. Charles liked talking about his childhood and his adolescence, as if he sensed there was a secret there that he had overlooked. Anne, on the other hand, preferred to talk about what was happening to her at that precise moment in her life. She would also talk about her fears, the catastrophe looming ahead, lurking in some apparently normal day. In bed, Anne remembers, things were as unsatisfactory as ever. For a little while, maybe because of the novelty, it was pleasant, maybe even magical on occasions, but then it went back to being like it always was. And that was when Anne made what, from a certain point of view at least, she regards as a monumental error. She told Charles what it was like for her in bed, with all the men she had slept with, including him. At first Charles didn't know what to say, but several days later he suggested that since she didn't feel anything, she might as well use the situation to her advantage. It took Anne a few days to realise that Charles was talking about prostitution.

Maybe she accepted because at the time she was fond of him. Or because it seemed an exciting thing to try. Or because she thought it would bring on the catastrophe. Charles bought her a red dress and matching high-heeled shoes, and he bought himself a gun, because, as he said to Anne, no one respects a pimp without a gun. Anne first saw the gun when they were driving from San Francisco to Berkeley and she opened the glove box to look for something, cigarettes maybe. She got a fright. Charles assured her there was no reason to be frightened; the gun was like an insurance policy, for her and for him. Then he showed her the hotel where she was to take the clients, drove around the neighbourhood a couple of times and dropped her at the entrance to a bar where guys used to go looking for women. He went off, possibly to another bar, to hang out with his friends, although he told Anne he was going to be on the lookout the whole time.

Never in her life had she felt so ashamed, Anne remembers, as when she went in and sat down on a bar stool, knowing she was there to pick up her first client, knowing that everyone else in the bar could tell. She hated the red dress, the red shoes; she hated Charles's gun and the catastrophe that was always about to happen but never did. And yet she managed to collect herself, order a double martini and begin a conversation with the barman. They talked about boredom. The barman seemed to be an expert on the subject. Soon they were joined by a man of about fifty, who looked like her father, but shorter and fatter, whose name Anne has forgotten or maybe she never knew it; in any case I will call him Jack. Jack paid for Anne's drink and proposed they continue their conversation elsewhere. As Anne was about to get down from her stool, the barman came over and said he had something important to tell her. She thought maybe it was a reflection on boredom, for her ears only. The barman leant across the bar and whispered in her ear, Don't you ever set foot in this bar again. When he had resumed his normal posture, he and Anne looked each other in the eye and Anne said, OK and left. The man who looked like her father was waiting on the sidewalk. They got into his car and went to the hotel Charles had pointed out. For the duration of the short trip, Anne stared out at the streets as if she were a tourist. She vaguely hoped to catch a glimpse of Charles in a doorway or an alley, but there was no sign of him and she thought, I bet he's in some bar.

Anne's contact with the man who looked like her father

was brief, though not devoid of tenderness, surprisingly for her. When he left, Anne took a taxi home. The next day she told Charles it was all over, she didn't want to see him again. Charles was very young, Anne remembers, and his fondest dream, apparently, was to have a whore, but he took it well, although he nearly burst into tears. Some time later, when Anne was working nights in another café in Berkeley, she saw him again. He was with friends and they laughed at her. This hurt Anne much more than all their fights. Charles was wearing cheap clothes, so perhaps he hadn't made his way in the world of prostitution, though Anne preferred not to think about that.

The following years, as Anne remembers them, were fairly restless. For a while she lived with some friends in a cabin near Lake Martis; she slept with Paul again; she took a course in creative writing at the university. Sometimes she would ring her parents in Great Falls. Sometimes her parents would come to San Francisco and spend two or three days with her. Susan had married a pharmacist and was living in Seattle. Paul had become a computer salesman. Sometimes Anne asked why he didn't start painting again, but Paul wouldn't answer that question. She travelled outside the United States. She went to Mexico a couple of times. With some friends, she drove a station wagon down to Guatemala, where she was held overnight by the police, and one of her friends was beaten up. She went to Canada about five times to stay with a friend who wrote children's stories, like Linda, and had bought a house in the country near Vancouver to get away from it all. But she always came back to San Francisco and that was where she met Tony.

Tony was Korean, from South Korea, and he worked in a

clothing factory where most of the employees were illegal immigrants. He was friends with Paul, or Linda, or one of her workmates from the café at Berkeley, Anne can't remember, all she remembers is that it was love at first sight. Tony was very gentle and very sincere, the first truly sincere man Anne had met, so sincere that, the first time they went to the movies together (to see an Antonioni film), as they came out of the cinema he confessed without the slightest embarrassment that he had found the film boring and that he was a virgin. When they slept together for the first time, however, Anne was surprised by Tony's sexual know-how; he was far better than any of her previous lovers.

Before long they got married. Anne had never really thought about marriage, but she did it so Tony could get a green card. Instead of getting married in California, they went all the way to Taiwan, where Tony had relatives, and held the wedding there. Then Tony went to Korea to see his family and Anne travelled to the Philippines to visit a friend from college who was married to a successful Filipino lawyer and had been living in Manila for two years. When they went back to the United States they settled down in Seattle (Tony had relatives there too) and with his savings, and Anne's, and money from his parents, Tony set up a fruit shop.

Living with Tony, Anne remembers, was like living in a protective cocoon. Outside, storms raged every day, people lived in constant fear of a private earthquake, everyone was talking about collective catharsis, but she and Tony had found a refuge where they could be at peace. And we were, says Anne, though not for long.

A curious aside: Tony loved pornographic films and he used to take Anne to watch them, something she would, of course, never have thought of doing on her own. She was shocked by the fact that in the films the men always ejaculated on to, rather than in, their partners: on their breasts, buttocks, or face. Going to those cinemas made her feel ashamed, unlike Tony, who couldn't see what there was to be ashamed of, given that the films were legal. In the end she decided not to go with him, so Tony went on his own. Another aside: Tony was very hard working; he worked harder (by far) than any of Anne's previous lovers. And another: Tony never got angry, never argued, as if he could see absolutely no point in trying to make someone else agree with him, as if, for him, everyone was lost, so how could one lost person presume to show another the way. Especially since the way, as well as being hidden from everyone, probably didn't even exist.

One day Anne's love for Tony ran out and she left Seattle. She went back to San Francisco, where she slept with Paul again and with other men. For a while she stayed in Linda's apartment. Tony was devastated. Night after night he called her, trying to find out why she had left him. Night after night Anne explained it to him: that was just the way things had turned out, love comes to an end, maybe it hadn't even been love that had brought them together in the first place, she needed a change. For several months Tony went on calling her and asking what it was that had made her break off their marriage. One night, Anne remembers, one of Tony's sisters telephoned and begged her to give him a second chance. She told Anne she had rung her parents in Great Falls and didn't know what else she could do. Anne was taken aback by this, yet it struck her as extraordinarily caring. In the end Tony's sister started crying, apologised for having called (it was after midnight) and hung up.

Tony travelled to San Francisco twice in the hope of convincing Anne to come back. They had countless phone conversations. Finally, Tony seemed to accept the inevitable, but still he kept calling her. He liked talking about their trip to Taiwan, their marriage, the things they had seen; he asked Anne what it was like in the Philippines and he told her about South Korea. Sometimes he was sorry he hadn't gone to the Philippines with her and Anne had to remind him that she had wanted to go alone. When Anne asked about the fruit shop, how the business was going, Tony replied in monosyllables and quickly changed the subject. One night Tony's sister rang again. At first all Anne could hear was a murmur and she asked to her speak up. Tony's sister raised her voice, but only a little, and said that Tony had committed suicide that morning. Then, without a trace of bitterness in her voice, she asked if Anne would be attending the funeral. Anne said yes. But the next morning, instead of catching a plane to Seattle, she took one that landed a couple of hours later in Mexico City. Tony had died at the age of twenty-two.

During the days Anne spent in Mexico City, our paths might have crossed again; again I might have fallen in love with her, although Anne doubts it. She remembers those days as unreal and dreamlike, yet in spite of everything she had time for sight-seeing. She went to visit the city's museums and almost all of the pre-Columbian ruins still standing among the buildings and the traffic. She tried to find Rubén, but couldn't. After two months, she took a plane to Seattle and visited Tony's grave. She almost fainted in the cemetery.

The following years went by too quickly. There were too many men, too many jobs; there was too much of everything. One night, working in a cafeteria, she made friends with two brothers, Ralph and Bill. That night she went to bed with both of them, though while she was making love to Ralph, she looked into his brother's eyes, and when she made love to Bill, she shut her eyes but could still see his. The next night Bill came round, on his own this time. They slept together, but spent longer talking than making love. Bill was a construction worker and his outlook on life was brave and melancholic, more or less the same as Anne's. Both of them had one older sibling, both had been born in 1948 and they were even physically alike. Within a month they had decided to live together. Around that time Anne received a letter from Susan; she had got divorced and was having treatment for her alcoholism. She said in her letter that once a week, sometimes more often, she went to an Alcoholics Anonymous meeting and it was opening up a new world for her. Anne replied on the back of a tourist postcard of San Francisco, saying things she didn't really feel, but when she finished writing the card she thought of Bill and herself and felt that she had finally found something in life, her own private Alcoholics Anonymous, something solid, something she could hold on to, like a high branch she could swing from and balance on.

The only thing she didn't like about her relationship with Bill was his brother. Sometimes Ralph would turn up at midnight, completely drunk, and get Bill out of bed to talk about the strangest things. They talked about a town in North Dakota where they had been when they were teenagers. They talked about death and what comes after death: nothing according to Ralph, less than nothing according to Bill. They talked about how a man's life consists of learning, working, and dying. Sometimes, but less and less often,

Anne participated in these conversations, and she had to admit she was impressed by Ralph's intelligence or his aptitude for finding the weak points in other people's arguments. But one night Ralph tried to sleep with her and from then on she kept her distance, until he finally stopped coming around.

After living together for six months Anne and Bill moved to Seattle. Anne found a job in a company that distributed electrical appliances and Bill went to work on a thirty-floor building that was under construction. For once, they had money to spare and Bill suggested they buy a house and settle down in Seattle for good, but Anne didn't feel ready, so for the time being they rented one floor of a big house occupied by three families, with a wonderful garden they all shared. In the garden, Anne remembers, there was an oak tree, a beech, and a creeper that covered the walls of the house.

Those were perhaps the calmest years of her life in the United States, says Anne, but one day she fell ill and the doctors diagnosed a serious condition. She became irritable and couldn't stand Bill's conversation, or his friends, or even the sight of him coming home each day from the construction site in his overalls. She couldn't stand her own job either, so one day she quit, put some clothes in a suitcase and went to Seattle airport without a clear idea of where she was heading. She had thought about going home to Great Falls and talking to her father, asking his advice as a doctor, but by the time she got to the airport, it all seemed so pointless. She spent five hours sitting there thinking about her life and her illness, and both seemed empty, like a horror film with a subtle twist, one of those films that doesn't seem scary at first, but by the end you're either screaming or shutting your eyes. She would have liked to cry, but couldn't. She turned around, went back to her house in Seattle and waited for Bill to come home. When he arrived, she told him everything that had happened that day and asked him what he thought. Bill said he really couldn't understand, but she could count on his support.

After a week, however, things started going wrong again. She and Bill got drunk, argued, made love, and drove around neighbourhoods they didn't know, but which somehow seemed vaguely familiar to Anne. They came close to having an accident several times that night, Anne remembers. From then on it only got worse. A few months later Anne had an operation but the result was not conclusive. For the moment the illness was in remission, but Anne had to stay on medication and have frequent checkups. A relapse was possible and could have been fatal, according to Anne.

Not much else worthy of note happened during those months. Anne and Bill went to Great Falls for Christmas. Susan started drinking again. Linda kept selling drugs in San Francisco and her finances were sound although her love-life was unstable. Paul bought a house and sold it shortly afterwards. Sometimes, mainly at night, he and Anne would talk on the phone, like two strangers, coldly, without ever mentioning what, for Anne, were the really important things. One night, while they were making love, Bill suggested they have a child. Anne's reply was brief and calm, she simply said no, she was still too young, but inside she could feel herself starting to scream, or rather, she could feel, and see, the dividing line between not-screaming and screaming. It was like opening your eyes in a cave bigger than the earth, Anne remembers. It was around then that she had a relapse and the doctors decided to operate again. Her spirits fell, and Bill's too; they were like a pair of zombies some days. The only activity that gave Anne any pleasure was reading; she read anything she could get her hands on, mostly North American novels and essays, but also poetry and history. She couldn't sleep at night and would usually stay awake until six or seven in the morning. When she did sleep, it was on the sofa; she couldn't bear to get into bed with Bill. Not that she wanted to reject him, or found him repulsive, not at all – Anne even remembers going into the bedroom sometimes and staying there a while to watch him sleep – she just couldn't feel calm lying beside him.

After the second operation Anne put her clothes and books in a pair of suitcases, and this time she did leave Seattle. First she went to San Francisco and then she took a plane to Europe.

When she arrived in Spain she had barely enough money to last two weeks. She spent three days in Madrid, then went to Barcelona, where one of Paul's friends lived. She had his address and phone number, but when she rang there was no answer. She stayed in Barcelona for a week, ringing Paul's friend morning, afternoon, and night, going for long walks around the city, always on her own, or sitting on a bench in the Parque de la Ciudadela and reading. She slept in a hotel on the Ramblas and ate, irregularly, in cheap restaurants in the old part of the city. Little by little, her insomnia relented. One afternoon she tried to make a reverse charge call to Bill, but he wasn't there. Then she rang her parents, who were out too. After leaving the long-distance office, she stopped at a telephone booth and rang Paul's friend: no answer. It occurred to her that maybe she was dead, but she dismissed the thought immediately. Solitude is one thing, death is quite another.

That night, Anne remembers, she tried to stay up late reading a book about the life of Willa Cather that Linda had given her before she left, but sleep overcame her.

The following day she rang Paul reverse charges and he was in. She told him she hadn't been able to get in touch with his friend in Barcelona, but didn't mention her financial situation. Paul thought for a few seconds and then had an idea: she could try ringing another friend, or at least an acquaintance of his, a woman who lived in Mallorca but also had a house near Girona. Gloria was her name; she had started studying music at the age of forty-something, and now she was playing with the Palma Symphony Orchestra, or something like that. You probably won't get her either, said Paul, or that is what Anne remembers anyway. Next she rang Susan in Great Falls and asked her to send money to Barcelona. Susan promised she would do it that same day. Her voice sounded strange, as if she had been asleep or was drunk. The second possibility worried Anne, because it might mean that Susan would forget to send the money.

That night she rang Gloria twice from a telephone booth in the Ramblas. She reached her the second time and explained her situation in detail. They talked for fifteen minutes, and then Gloria told Anne that she could go and live in her house in Vilademuls, a village near Banyoles, where the famous lake is; no need to worry about money, she could pay later when she got a job. Anne asked how she would be able to get into the house, and Gloria said she would be sharing the house with two other Americans, one of whom was bound to be there when she arrived. There was no warmth in Gloria's voice, Anne remembers, but no pretence either. She had a slight New England accent, although Anne knew straight away she wasn't from New England; it was an objective voice, like Linda's (though less nasal), the voice of a woman who walks alone, which sounds like something from a Western, though very few women in Westerns walk alone; in any case that was the image that occurred to Anne.

So she spent two more days in Barcelona until Susan's money arrived, paid the bill at the hotel and went to Vilademuls, a village with no more than fifty inhabitants in winter and two hundred and something in summer. As Gloria had assured her, one of the Americans was there at the house, waiting for her. He was called Dan and he taught English in Barcelona, but every weekend he went up to Vilademuls to work on his detective novels. The only time Anne left the village that winter was to see a doctor in Barcelona. Dan and sometimes Christine, the other American, would arrive on Friday night. Very occasionally they brought friends, Americans too for the most part, but as a rule they came to the house to be alone: Dan worked on his drafts and Christine wove at her loom. Anne spent the weekdays writing letters, reading (she found a large collection of books in English in Gloria's room), cleaning, or doing the minor repairs that the ancient house often required. When spring came, Christine found her a job teaching in a language school in Girona, and, to begin with, Anne shared a flat with an English and an American woman; but then, since she had a steady income, she decided to rent a flat of her own, although she still spent the weekends at Vilademuls.

Around that time Bill came to visit her. It was the first time he had been out of the States and he spent a month travelling around Europe. He didn't like it. Nor did he like the atmosphere at Vilademuls, Anne remembers, although Dan and

Christine were straightforward people, and in fact Dan was not unlike Bill: he had worked in construction for a while and had similar experiences; he also liked to think of himself, wrongly, as a tough guy. But Bill didn't like Dan and Dan probably didn't like Bill either, although he took care not to let it show. According to Anne, seeing Bill again was beautiful and sad, though the words hardly begin to convey something deeper and indefinable. It was around then that I saw her for the first time. I was in a bar called La Arcada, on the Rambla de Girona. I saw Bill walk in and she came in after him. Bill was tall, his skin was tanned and his hair was completely white. Anne was tall and slim, with high cheekbones and very straight brown hair. They sat at the bar and I could hardly take my eyes off them. I hadn't seen such a beautiful man and woman for a long time. They were so sure of themselves. So distant and disconcerting. I thought all the other people in the bar should have knelt before them.

Shortly afterwards I saw Bill again. He was walking along a street in Girona and this time, not surprisingly, he didn't seem quite so beautiful. In fact he seemed tired and flustered. A few days later, as I was coming down the hill from my house in La Pedrera, I saw Anne. She was going the other way and for a second or two we looked at each other. At that stage, Anne remembers, she had left the language school and was giving private English lessons and making a fair bit of money. Bill had left and she was living in the old part of Girona, opposite a bar called Freaks and a cinema called the Opera.

From then on our paths began to cross quite often, as I remember. And although we didn't talk, we recognised each other. I guess at some point we started to say hello, as people do in smaller cities.

One morning I was in the Rambla chatting with Pep Colomer, an old painter who lives in Girona, when Anne stopped and talked to me for the first time. I can't remember what we said, maybe our names and where we came from. At the end of the conversation I invited her to dinner at my house that evening. It was Christmas time, or nearly, and I made a pizza and bought a bottle of wine. We talked until very late. That was when Anne told me she'd been to Mexico several times. Overall, her adventures were very similar to mine. Anne thought this was because the lives or the youths of any two individuals would always be fundamentally alike, in spite of the obvious or even glaring differences. I preferred to think that somehow she and I had both explored the same map, fought the same doomed campaigns, received a common sentimental education. At five in the morning, or perhaps later, we went to bed and made love.

Anne immediately became an important part of my life. After the first two weeks I realised that sex was a pretext; what really drew us together was friendship. I got into the habit of going to her flat at about eight at night, when she had finished her last lesson, and we would talk until one or two in the morning. At some point, she would make sandwiches and we'd open a bottle of wine. We'd listen to some music or go down to Freaks to continue drinking and talking. A fair few of Girona's junkies used to gather outside that bar, and the local toughs were often to be seen cruising around, but Anne would reminisce about the toughs of San Francisco, who were seriously tough, and I would reminisce about the toughs of Mexico City, and we'd laugh and laugh, although now, to be honest, I can't remember what was so funny, perhaps just the fact that we were alive. At two in the morning we'd say

Anne Moore's Life

goodnight and I would go back to my house in La Pedrera, up on the hill.

Once I went with her to the doctor, at the Dexeus Clinic in Barcelona. By then I was going out with another girl and she was going out with an architect from Girona, but I wasn't surprised (in fact I was flattered) when, as we entered the waiting room, she whispered, They'll probably think you're my husband. Once we went to Vilademuls together. Anne wanted me to meet Gloria, but Gloria didn't turn up that weekend. At Vilademuls, however, I discovered something that up until then I had only suspected: Anne could be different; she could be another person. It was a terrible weekend. Anne drank non-stop. Dan would occasionally emerge from his room and promptly disappear again (he was writing) and I had to endure the presence of one of Christine or Dan's ex-students, a brainless Catalan girl from Barcelona or Girona, the sort who's more American than the Americans.

The following year Anne travelled to the States. She was going to Great Falls to see her parents and her sister, then on to Seattle to see Bill. I got a postcard from New York, and another from Montana, but nothing from Seattle. Later on I got a letter from San Francisco in which she told me that her time with Bill had been a disaster. I imagined her writing the letter in Linda's flat, or Paul's, drinking and maybe crying, although Anne rarely cried.

When she came back from the States she brought some packages with her. One afternoon she showed me: they were the diaries she had kept from shortly after her arrival in San Francisco up until her first meeting with Bill and Ralph. Thirty-four notebooks in all, just under a hundred pages each, each page covered with small, hurried writing, and quotations, drawings, and plans scattered throughout (plans of what? I asked her the first time I saw them: dream houses, imaginary cities or suburbs, the paths a woman's life should follow, though hers had not).

The diaries were kept in a box in the living room. I began to browse through them, in Anne's presence, and gradually my visits fell into a new and very peculiar pattern: I would arrive and sit down in the living room; Anne would put on some music or start drinking, while I resumed my perusal of her diaries. We hardly talked, except when I asked her about something I didn't understand, turns of phrase or words I didn't know. It could be painful, plunging into that writing in the presence of the author (sometimes I wanted to throw the notebook aside and go and hug her), but mostly it was stimulating, although I couldn't say exactly what it stimulated. It was like a fever rising imperceptibly. It made you want to scream or shut your eyes, but Anne's handwriting had the power to sew your lips shut and prop your eyes open, so you had no choice but to go on reading.

One of the early notebooks was entirely devoted to Susan, and the words 'horror' and 'sisterly love' give only the vaguest idea of its content. Two notebooks had been written after Tony's suicide; in these Anne reflected and discoursed on youth, love, death, the dimly recollected landscapes of Taiwan and the Philippines (where she had gone without Tony), the streets and cinemas of Seattle, and perfect evenings in Mexico. One notebook covered the early days of her relationship with Bill, but I couldn't bring myself to read it. My verdict was predictably uninspired. You should publish them, I said, and then I think I shrugged my shoulders.

At the time Anne had become preoccupied by her age,

time slipping away, the few years left before she turned forty. At first I thought this was just a kind of coquetry (how could a woman like Anne Moore be worried about turning forty?), but soon I realised that her fear was real. Her parents came once, but I wasn't in Girona and when I got back Anne and her parents had gone off to travel in Italy, Greece, and Turkey.

Not long after this Anne and the architect parted on the best of terms, and she started going out with one of her ex-students, a technician who worked for a company that imported machinery. He was a quiet sort of guy, and short, too short for Anne; the difference was not only physical, but also, to put it preciously, metaphysical, though I didn't tell her that – I felt it would have been rude. I think at this stage Anne was thirty-eight and the technician was forty, and that was the main thing he had going for him: being older than her. One day I moved away from Girona, and when I came back Anne was no longer living in the flat opposite the Opera cinema. I wasn't particularly worried; she had my new address, but I didn't hear from her for a long time.

During the months when I didn't see her, Anne went travelling in Europe and Africa, had a car accident, left the technician from the machinery-importing firm, saw Paul and Linda who came to visit her, started sleeping with an Algerian, developed a skin complaint on her hands and arms caused by nervous tension, read several books by Willa Cather, Eudora Welty, and Carson McCullers.

One day she finally turned up at my house. I was on the patio, pulling up weeds when suddenly I heard steps, turned around and there was Anne.

That afternoon we made love to hide the sheer joy of seeing each other again. Some days later I went to see her in

Girona. She had moved to the new part of town and was living in a tiny attic room. She told me that her neighbour was an old Russian man, a guy called Alexei, the sweetest, most polite person she had ever met. Her hair was cut very short and she had done nothing to disguise the grey. I asked her what had happened to her beautiful hair. I looked like an old hippy, she said.

She was about to go to the States. This time the Algerian was going with her and I think they had problems getting him a visa at the consulate in Barcelona. So it's serious with him, I said. She didn't reply. She said that at the consulate they thought he wanted to go and live in the States for good. And doesn't he? I asked. No, he doesn't, she said.

I don't know where the rest of the time went. I can't remember what we said to each other, the stories we told, nothing important, anyway. Then I left and I never saw her again. A while later I got a letter from her, written in Spanish, from Great Falls. She told me that her sister Susan had killed herself with an overdose of barbiturates. Her parents and her sister's partner, a carpenter from Missoula, were devastated and simply couldn't understand why. I prefer not to say anything, she wrote, there's no point adding to the pain, or adding our own little mysteries to it. As if the pain itself were not enough of a mystery, as if the pain were not the (mysterious) answer to all mysteries. Shortly before leaving Spain, she added (having finished with the topic of Susan's death), Bill had called her several times.

According to Anne, Bill would ring her at all hours of the day and night, and he almost always ended up insulting her. They almost always ended up insulting one another. The last few times, Bill had threatened to come to Girona and kill her.

Anne Moore's Life

The funny thing, she said, was that she was saving him the trip, although she had hardly any friends left to visit in Seattle. She didn't mention the Algerian, but he must have been there with her, or so I preferred to assume, for my own peace of mind.

After that I had no more news of her.

Several months went by. I moved house. I went to live by the sea in a village that has acquired a legendary aura since Juan Marsé wrote about it in the seventies. I was too busy working and dealing with my own problems to do anything about Anne Moore. I think I even got married.

Finally, one day I caught a train, returned to grey Girona and climbed up to Anne's little attic room. As I had anticipated, a stranger opened the door. Of course she knew nothing about the previous tenant. Before turning to go I asked if there was a Russian gentleman living in the building, an elderly man, and the stranger said yes, and told me which door to knock at on the second floor.

A very old man came to the door, walking with great difficulty and the aid of a spectacular oak stick, which looked rather as if it had been designed for ceremonial occasions or combat. He remembered Anne Moore. In fact he remembered almost all of the twentieth century, but that, he admitted, was beside the point. I explained that I hadn't heard from her in a long time and had come to see if he had any news. Not much news, he said, just a few letters from America, a great country where I should have liked to stay longer. He took the opportunity to tell me briefly about the years he had spent in New York and his adventures as a croupier in Atlantic City. Then he remembered the letters, made me a cup of tea and went off to look for them. Finally he appeared with three postcards. All from America, he said. I don't know exactly when I realised he was completely mad. It seemed logical, all things considered. It seemed appropriate, so I sat back and waited for the ending.

The Russian handed me the three cards over the steaming tea. They were arranged in order of arrival and written in English. The first was from New York. I recognised Anne's handwriting. She said the usual things and at the end she told him to take care of himself and to eat every day. She said she was thinking of him, with love. There was a photo of Fifth Avenue on the other side. The second postcard was from Seattle. A view of the port from the air. It was much briefer than the first, and harder to understand. There was something about exile and crime. The third postcard was from Berkeley: a quiet street in bohemian Berkeley, read the caption. I'm seeing my old friends and making new ones, said Anne's clear handwriting. And it ended like the first card, advising dear Alexei to look after himself and eat every day, if only a little.

Sadly, curiously, I looked at the Russian. He looked back at me kindly. Have you been following her advice? I asked. Of course, he replied, I always follow a lady's advice.

Mauricio 'The Eye' Silva

*for Rodrigo Pinto
and María and Andrés Braithwaite*

Mauricio Silva, also known as 'The Eye', always tried to avoid violence, even at the risk of being considered a coward, but violence, real violence, is unavoidable, at least for those of us who were born in Latin America during the fifties and were about twenty years old at the time of Salvador Allende's death. That's just the way it goes.

The case of The Eye is paradigmatic and exemplary, and it may well be worth recalling, especially now that so many years have passed.

In January 1974, four months after the military coup, The Eye left Chile. First he went to Buenos Aires, but then the ill winds blowing in the neighbouring republic sent him to Mexico, where he lived for a couple of years. That is where I met him.

He wasn't like most of the Chileans living in Mexico City at the time: he didn't brag about his role in the largely phantasmal resistance; he didn't frequent the various groups of Chileans in exile.

We became friends and used to meet at least once a week at the Café La Habana in the Avenida Bucareli or at my house in the Calle Versalles, where I lived with my mother and sister. For the first few months, The Eye scraped by doing odd jobs, before finding work as a photographer for a newspaper. I can't remember which one it was, maybe *El Sol*, if such a newspaper ever existed in Mexico, or *El Universal*; I would like to think it was *El Nacional*, whose cultural supplement was edited by the old Spanish poet Juan Rejano, but it can't have been, because I worked there and I never saw him at the office. Anyway, he worked for one of the Mexico City papers, I'm quite sure of that, and his financial situation improved, imperceptibly to start with, because The Eye had grown accustomed to a spartan way of life, but if you looked carefully, you could detect unequivocal signs of an economic upturn.

For example, during the early months I remember him wearing sweatshirts. Towards the end of his time in Mexico City he had bought himself a pair of shirts with collars and once I even saw him in a tie, an item of apparel quite foreign to me and my poet friends. In fact the only person wearing a tie who ever sat down at our table in the Café La Habana was Mauricio (The Eye) Silva.

At the time, The Eye was reputed to be homosexual. By which I mean that a rumour to that effect was circulating in the various groups of Chileans in exile, who made it their business partly for the sheer pleasure of denigration and partly to add a little spice to their rather boring lives. In spite of their left-wing convictions, when it came to sexuality, they reacted just like their enemies on the right, who had become the new masters of Chile.

The Eye came to dinner at my house once. My mother liked him and The Eye returned her affection by taking family photos from time to time: my mother and one of her friends, my sister and me. Everyone likes to be photographed, he once told me. At the time I thought, I don't care one way or the other, but on reflection I decided he was right. The only people who don't like it are certain Indians, he said. My mother thought he was talking about the Mapuche, but in fact he meant Indians from India, a country that was to play a major part in his life.

One night I ran into him in the Café La Habana. There was hardly anyone else there and The Eye was sitting by the windows that look out on to the Avenida Bucareli, with a white coffee in one of those big, thick glasses they used to have at La Habana (I've never come across them in any other café or restaurant). I sat down next to him and we talked for a while. He seemed translucent. That was the impression I had. The Eye seemed to be made of some vitreous material. His face and the glass of white coffee in front of him seemed to be exchanging signals: two incomprehensible phenomena whose paths had just crossed at that point in the vast universe, making valiant but probably vain attempts to find a common language.

That night he confessed to me that he was homosexual, just as the exiled Chileans had been whispering, and that he was leaving Mexico. For a moment I thought he was leaving *because* he was homosexual. But no, a friend had found him a job with a photographic agency in Paris, the sort of work he had always dreamed of. He was in the mood for talking and I listened. He said that for years he had felt guilty and hidden his sexuality, mainly because he considered himself a socialist and there was a certain degree of prejudice among his friends on the left. We talked about the antiquated word 'invert', which conjured up desolate landscapes, and the term 'ponce', which I would have written with a 'c', while The Eye thought it was spelt with an 's'.

I remember we ended up railing against the Chilean left, and at one point I proposed a toast to the 'wandering warriors of Chile', a substantial subset of the 'wandering warriors of Latin America', a legion of orphans, who, as the name suggests, wander the face of the earth offering their services to the highest bidder, who is almost always the lowest as well. But when we finished laughing, The Eye said violence wasn't for him. I'm not like you, he said, with a sadness I didn't understand at the time, I hate violence. I assured him that I did too. Then we started talking about other things: books and films, and after that we didn't see each other again.

One day I heard that The Eye had left Mexico. One of his former colleagues from the newspaper told me. I wasn't surprised that he hadn't said goodbye. The Eye never said goodbye to anyone. I never said goodbye to anyone either. None of my Mexican friends ever did. For my mother, however, it was a clear case of bad manners.

Two or three years later, I left Mexico, too. I went to Paris, where I tried (not very hard, admittedly) to find The Eye, without success. As time went by I began to forget what he looked like, although I still had a vague sense of his bearing and his manner. There was a certain way of expressing opinions, as if from a distance, sadly but gently, that I went on associating with The Eye, and even when his face had disappeared or receded into shadow, that essence lingered in my memory: a way of moving, an almost abstract entity in which there was no place for calm.

Years went by. Many years. Some friends died. I got married, had a child, published some books.

Mauricio 'The Eye' Silva

At one point I had to go to Berlin. On my last night there, after dinner with Heinrich von Berenberg and his family, I took a taxi to my hotel (as a rule Heinrich drove me back at night) and told the driver to stop before we got there, because I felt like a walk. The driver (an elderly Asian man who was listening to Beethoven) dropped me about five blocks from the hotel. It wasn't very late, but there was hardly anyone about. I walked across a square. The Eye was sitting on a bench. I didn't recognise him until he spoke to me. He called my name and asked me how I was. I turned around and looked at him for a few moments without realising who it was. He remained seated on the bench, looking at me, then he glanced down at the ground or to the side, at the huge trees crowding that little square in Berlin and at the shadows that surrounded him more densely than me (or so I thought). I took two steps towards him and asked who he was. It's me, Mauricio Silva, he said. The Eye, I asked, from Chile? He nodded, and only then did I see him smile.

That night we talked almost until dawn. The Eye had been living in Berlin for some years and knew where to find the bars that stayed open all night. I asked him about his life. He gave me a general idea of the freelance photographer's lot. He had lived in Paris, Milan, and now Berlin, in small flats, where his books kept each other company much of the year. It was only when we went into the first bar that I could tell how much he had changed. He was a lot thinner, his hair was going grey, and wrinkles had creased his face. I also noticed that he drank much more than he used to in Mexico. He wanted to know about me. Our meeting had not been a coincidence, of course. My name had been in the newspapers, and The Eye had seen it, or someone had told him that one of his compatriots was giving a reading or a talk, which he couldn't attend, but he rang the organisers and found out where I was staying. He told me he'd been sitting there in the square thinking while he waited for me to turn up.

I laughed. I was very glad to have met him again. The Eye was the same as ever: an odd person, but good-natured and unassuming. You felt you could say goodbye to him at any time of the night and he would simply say goodbye, without reproach or ill feeling. He was the ideal Chilean, stoic and amiable, a type that has never been very numerous in Chile but cannot be found anywhere else.

Reading over the previous sentence I realise that it is not strictly true. The Eye would never have made such a sweeping generalisation. In any case, the conversation we had, sitting in various bars, he with his whisky and I with my non-alcoholic beer, was made up essentially of recollections; it was, in other words, a confessional and melancholic dialogue. But the most interesting part for me, which was more like a monologue, came as we were returning to my hotel, around two in the morning, and coincidentally it began just as we were crossing the square in which we had met a few hours before. I remember that it was cold and that suddenly The Eye started talking, saying he wanted to tell me something he had never told anyone else. I looked at him. His gaze was fixed on the paved path winding across the square. I asked him what he wanted to tell me about. A trip, he replied immediately. And what happened on this trip? I asked. Then The Eye stopped and for a few moments nothing seemed to exist for him except the tops of the tall German trees and, above them, the fragments of sky and silently seething clouds.

Something terrible, said The Eye. Do you remember a

conversation we had in the Café La Habana before I left Mexico? Yes, I said. Did I tell you I was gay? asked The Eye. You said you were homosexual, I said. Let's sit down, said The Eye.

He sat down on the very same bench as before, I swear, as if I still hadn't arrived, as if I hadn't yet started to cross the square and he was still waiting for me and thinking about his life and the story that he was compelled, by history or destiny or chance, to tell me. He turned up the collar of his coat and began to talk. I remained standing and lit a cigarette. The Eye's story was set in India. He had gone there for work, not as a tourist, and he had two assignments. The first was typical third world photo-journalism, a mixture of Marguerite Duras and Hermann Hesse (we smiled); there are people who like to imagine India as a cross between *India Song* and *Siddhartha*, he said, and we have to give the editors what they want. So the first assignment consisted of photos of colonial houses, derelict gardens, all sorts of restaurants, especially the seedier kind (or rather restaurants that looked seedy but were in fact normal Indian family restaurants); photos of the city outskirts, the really poor areas, then the country and the transport system: roads, railway junctions, buses and trains arriving and departing; and nature of course, in a dormant state quite unlike Western hibernation, trees that were clearly non-European, rivers and streams, bare fields and fields sown with crops, the Land of Holy Men, said The Eye.

The second assignment took him to the prostitutes' district in an Indian city whose name I will never know.

And that was where The Eye's story really began. He was still living in Paris at the time and had been commissioned to take photos to illustrate a text written by a well-known

French writer who had become a specialist in the underworld of prostitution. In fact, the assignment was only the first of a series, which would cover red-light districts around the world, each one shot by a different photographer, but all described by the same writer.

I don't know which city The Eye flew into, Bombay maybe, or Calcutta, perhaps Benares or Madras; I remember I asked him, but he ignored my question. Anyway, he arrived in India on his own, because the Frenchman had already written his text and he simply had to illustrate it, so he went to the districts mentioned in the text and started taking photographs. According to his plans — and the plans of his publisher — the work, and consequently his visit to India, shouldn't have lasted more than a week. He stayed in a hotel in a quiet part of town. His room was air-conditioned and the window looked on to a garden that didn't belong to the hotel, where he could see two trees on either side of a fountain and part of a terrace on which two women would sometimes appear, followed or preceded by several little boys. The women were dressed in what The Eye took to be traditional Indian style, but not the boys; once he even saw them wearing ties. In the afternoons he went to the red-light district, took photos and talked to the prostitutes, some of whom were very young and beautiful, while others were older or more faded, with the air of sceptical, laconic matrons. He came to like the smell, which had bothered him at first. The pimps (whom he rarely saw) were friendly and carried themselves like Western pimps or perhaps (but this thought only occurred to him later, in his air-conditioned hotel room) it was the other way around: Western pimps had adopted the body language of their Indian counterparts.

One afternoon he was invited to have sexual intercourse with one of the prostitutes. He refused politely. The pimp understood immediately that The Eye was homosexual and the next night took him to a brothel where there were young male prostitutes. That night The Eye fell sick. It was only then, he said, examining the shadows in that Berlin square, that I really knew I was in India. What did you do? I asked. Nothing. I looked and smiled. And did nothing. Then it occurred to one of the boys that perhaps their guest would like to visit another kind of establishment. Or that is what The Eye supposed, because they didn't speak English amongst themselves. So they left the brothel and walked through narrow, filthy streets until they came to a building with a small façade, behind which lay a labyrinth of dim passages and tiny rooms, with altars and shrines emerging here and there from the gloom.

It is customary in some parts of India, said The Eye, looking at the ground, to offer a young boy to a deity whose name I can't remember. I regret to say that here I interrupted to point out that as well as having forgotten the name of the deity, he couldn't remember the name of the city or any of the people in his story. The Eye looked at me and smiled. I've tried to forget, he said.

At that point I started to fear the worst. I sat down beside him and for a while we remained there in silence with our coat collars turned up. After looking around the square as if he were afraid a stranger might be lurking in the shadows, he resumed his story. They make an offering of this boy and he becomes the incarnation of the god, for a time, I couldn't say how long. Maybe only as long as the procession lasts, maybe a week, a month, a year, I don't know. It's a barbaric ceremony, forbidden by Indian law, but that doesn't stop it happening. During the festival the boy is showered with gifts, which his parents, who are generally poor, are only too glad to accept. When the festival is over the boy is sent back to his house, or the filthy hovel he lives in, and in a year's time it all begins again.

Outwardly the ceremony is like a Latin American pilgrimage, but perhaps more joyful, more turbulent, and for the participants, those who know what they're participating in, the experience is probably more intense. But there is one major difference. A few days before the festivities begin, they castrate the boy. The god whose incarnation he is to be during the festival requires a male body – although the boys are usually no more than seven years old – purified of the male sexual organs. So the parents hand him over to the festival doctors, or barbers, or priests, and they emasculate him, and when the boy has recovered from the operation, the festival begins. Weeks or months later, when it is all over, the boy goes home, but now he is a eunuch and his parents reject him. So he ends up in a brothel. These brothels vary; there are all sorts, said The Eye with a sigh. That night, they took me to the very worst.

For a while we said nothing. I lit a cigarette. Then The Eye described the brothel for me and it was as if he were describing a church. Covered interior courtyards. Open galleries. Cells from which hidden eyes watch your every move. They brought him a eunuch who couldn't have been more than ten years old. He looked like a terrified little girl, said The Eye. Terrified and taunting at the same time. Do you understand what I'm saying? Sort of, I said. We fell silent again. When I was finally able to speak I said, No, I have no idea. Neither do

I, said The Eye. No one can have any idea. Not the victim. Not the people who did it to him. Not the people who watched. Only a photo . . .

You took a photo of him? I asked. A shiver seemed to run down The Eye's spine. I got out my camera, he said, and I took a photo of him. I knew I was condemning myself for all eternity, but I did it.

I don't know how long we sat there in silence after that. I know it was cold and at one point I began to shiver. Once or twice I heard The Eye sob beside me, but I didn't want to look at him. I saw the headlights of a car driving down one side of the square. Through the foliage I saw a light come on in a window.

Then The Eye went on with his story. He said the boy smiled, then quietly slipped away down one of the passages of that baffling edifice. At some point a pimp suggested that if none of the boys took his fancy, he should go. But The Eye said no. He couldn't leave. That's what he said to him: I can't leave yet. And it was true, though he didn't know what was stopping him from walking straight out of that lair. The pimp, however, seemed to understand and ordered tea or some such beverage. The Eye remembers that they sat down on the floor, on mats or worn-out rugs. The room was lit by a pair of candles. A poster of the god hung on a wall.

For a while The Eye looked at the god and at first he felt fear, but then he felt something like rage, or perhaps hate.

I have never hated anyone, he said, lighting a cigarette and blowing the first breath of smoke out into the Berlin night.

At one point, while The Eye was staring at the image of the god, the others disappeared, leaving him alone with a male prostitute about twenty years old, who spoke English.

Then, summoned by a couple of claps, the eunuch reappeared. I was crying, or thought I was, said The Eye, or maybe that's what the prostitute thought, poor kid, but none of it was true. I tried to keep a smile on my face (although it wasn't *my* face any more, I could feel it drifting away from me like a leaf on the wind), and all this time, underneath, I was scheming. Not that I had a plan, or any idea of redress, just a blind determination.

The Eye, the prostitute, and the eunuch stood up and walked down a dimly lit corridor, then another more dimly lit still (the eunuch at The Eye's side, watching him and smiling, the prostitute smiling at him too, as The Eye nodded and emptied the money from his pockets into their hands) until they reached a room in which the doctor was dozing beside a boy who was younger than the eunuch, maybe six or seven years old, and had darker skin, and The Eye listened to the doctor's long-winded explanations, invoking tradition, ritual, privilege, communion, elation, and saintliness, and he could see the surgical instruments with which the child would be castrated the following morning or the morning after, in any case the child had come to the temple or the brothel that day, he gathered – a preventive or hygienic measure – and had eaten well, as if he were already the god's incarnation, although what The Eye saw was a drowsy, tearful child, and the eunuch, who was still at his side, with a half-amused half-terrified look on his face. Then The Eye was transformed into something else, although the expression he used was not 'something else' but 'mother'.

Mother, he said and sighed. At last. Mother.

What happened next is all too familiar: the violence from which there is no escape. The lot of Latin Americans born in the fifties. Naturally, The Eye tried to negotiate, bribe, and threaten, without much hope of success. All I know for certain is that there was violence and soon he was out of there, leaving the streets of that district behind, as if in a dream, drenched with sweat. He vividly remembers the feeling of exaltation welling up inside him, stronger and stronger, a joy that felt dangerously like lucidity, but wasn't (couldn't have been). Also, the shadows they cast on to the peeling walls, he and the two boys he was leading by the hand. Anywhere else he would have attracted attention. There, at that time of night, no one took any notice of him.

The rest is more an itinerary than a story or a plot. The Eye went back to the hotel, packed his suitcase and left with the boys. First they took a taxi to a town or a suburb on the outskirts. Then a bus to another town, where they caught a second bus that took them to yet another town. At some point in their flight they boarded a train and travelled all night and part of the following day. The Eye remembered the faces of the boys looking out at a landscape frayed by the morning light, as if all that had ever really existed were the stately and humble scenes framed by the window of that mysterious train.

Then they took another bus, a taxi, a bus again, another train; they even hitch-hiked, said The Eye, gazing at the silhouettes of the German trees but seeing, beyond them, the silhouettes of other trees, countless and incomprehensible. Finally they came to rest in a village somewhere in India, where they rented a house.

After two months The Eye's money ran out and he walked to a neighbouring village, where he sent a letter to the friend he had left behind in Paris. A fortnight later he received a bank draft. To cash it he had to go to a town bigger than the village where he had gone to send the letter and much bigger than the one where he lived. The boys were well. They played with other children but did not go to school, and sometimes they came back to the house with food: vegetables the neighbours had given them. Instead of calling him father, he had the boys call him The Eye, as we used to; he thought it safer, less likely to attract the attention of the curious. He did, however, tell the villagers that they were his sons. His story was that the boy's mother, an Indian woman, had recently died, and he didn't want to go back to Europe. It was believable. Yet The Eye had nightmares about the Indian police coming to arrest him, making shameful accusations. He would wake up trembling. He would go over to the mats where the boys were sleeping, and the sight of them gave him the strength to carry on, to sleep, get up and face another day.

He became a farmer. He tended a small orchard and occasionally worked for the richer farmers in the village. They too were poor, of course, but not as poor as the others. He spent the rest of his time teaching the boys English and a little maths, and watching them play. He could not understand a word of the language they spoke to each other. Sometimes, when he was watching them play, they would stop and wander off across the fields like sleepwalkers. He would call out to them. Sometimes the boys pretended not to hear and kept walking until they disappeared. Other times they turned back and smiled at him.

How long were you in India? I asked, getting worried.

About a year and a half, said The Eye, I'm not exactly sure.

Once his friend from Paris came to the village. He still loved me, said The Eye, although in my absence he had set up house with an Algerian mechanic who worked for Renault.

Telling me this, he laughed. So did I. It was all so sad, said The Eye. His friend arriving in the village in a taxi covered with red dust, the boys chasing after an insect in the dry scrub, the wind, it seemed, bearing good news and bad.

In spite of his friend's entreaties, he did not return to Paris. Months later a letter arrived from France informing him that he was not wanted by the Indian police. Apparently no one had reported the incident at the brothel. This news did not put an end to The Eye's nightmares. The characters who came to arrest and brutalise him simply changed their clothes: instead of policemen, now they were thugs from the sect of the castrated god. Which turned out to be even more horrifying, The Eye confessed, although by then he was used to the nightmares and at some level always knew that he was dreaming, that it wasn't real.

Then the disease came to the village and the boys died. I wanted to die too, said The Eye, but I wasn't that lucky.

After convalescing in a hut that was steadily being destroyed by the rain, The Eye left the village and returned to the city where he had met his children. He was somewhat surprised to discover that it was not nearly as far away as he had thought; his flight had followed a spiral path and the return journey was relatively short. On the afternoon of his return, he went to see the brothel where boys used to be castrated. Its rooms had been converted into lodgings for entire families. The corridors he remembered as lonely and funereal were now swarming with life, from toddling children to old men and women who could barely drag themselves along. To him it was an image of paradise.

That night when he went back to his hotel, he wept for his dead children and all the other castrated boys, for his own lost youth, for those who were young no longer and those who died young, for those who fought for Salvador Allende and those who were too scared to fight. Unable to stop crying, he called his French friend, who was now living with a former weightlifter from Bulgaria, and asked him to send an air ticket and some money for the hotel.

And his friend said yes, of course he would, straight away, and then: What's that sound? Are you crying? And The Eye said yes, he couldn't stop crying, he didn't know what was happening to him, he had been crying for hours. His French friend told him to calm down. At this The Eye, still crying, laughed, said he would do that and hung up. But he went on crying, and couldn't stop.

Gómez Palacio

I went to Gómez Palacio during one of the worst phases of my life. I was twenty-three years old and I knew that my days in Mexico were numbered.

My friend Montero, who worked for the Arts Council, had found me a job teaching a writing workshop in that town, with its hideous name. First, to warm up, so to speak, I had to do a tour of the writing workshops the Arts Council had established in various places throughout the region. A bit of a holiday in the north to start off, said Montero, then you can get down to work in Gómez Palacio and forget all your problems. I don't know why I accepted. I knew that under no circumstances would I settle down in Gómez Palacio. I knew I wouldn't stay long running a writing workshop in some godforsaken town in northern Mexico.

One morning I left Mexico City in a bus packed to capacity and began my tour. I went to San Luis Potosí, Aguascalientes, Guanajuato, León – not necessarily in that order; I can't remember which town came first or how long I spent in each. Then Torreón and Saltillo. I went to Durango as well.

Finally I arrived in Gómez Palacio and visited the Arts Council offices, where I met my future students. I couldn't stop shivering in spite of the heat. The director, a plump, middle-aged woman with bulging eyes, wearing a large dress of printed fabric featuring almost all of the state's native flowers, took me to my lodgings: a frightful motel on the edge of town, beside a highway leading nowhere.

She used to come and pick me up herself mid-morning. She had an enormous, sky-blue car, which she drove perhaps rather too boldly, although generally speaking she wasn't a bad driver. It was an automatic and her feet hardly reached the pedals. Invariably, the first thing we did was to stop at a roadside restaurant that was visible in the distance from the motel, a reddish bump on the blue and yellow horizon. There we breakfasted on orange juice and Mexican-style eggs, followed by several cups of coffee, all paid for (I presume) with Arts Council vouchers — not cash, in any case.

Then she would lean back on her chair and start talking about her life in that northern town, her poetry, which had been published by a small local press subsidised by the Arts Council, and her husband, who didn't understand the poet's calling or the suffering it entailed. Meanwhile I chain-smoked Bali cigarettes, looking out of the window at the highway and thinking about the disaster that was my life. Then we'd get back into her car and head off to the main office of the Arts Council in Gómez Palacio, a two-storey building whose only redeeming feature was an unpaved yard with a grand total of three trees and an abandoned or unfinished garden, swarming with zombie-like adolescents who were studying painting, music, or literature. The first time I hardly noticed the yard. The second time it made me shudder. None of this makes any sense, I thought, but deep down I knew it did make sense and that was what I found unbearably sad, to use a rather hyperbolic expression, though it seemed perfectly accurate at the time. Maybe I was confusing sense with necessity. Maybe I was just a nervous wreck.

I found it hard to get to sleep at night. I had nightmares. Before going to bed, I would make sure the door and windows of my room were securely and tightly shut. My throat kept feeling dry and the only solution was to drink water. I was continually getting up and going to the bathroom to refill my glass. Since I was up, I would check the door and windows again to see that they were properly shut. Sometimes I forgot my fears and stayed by the window, looking out at the desert stretching away into the dark. Then I went back to bed and closed my eyes, but having drunk so much water I soon had to get up again to urinate. And since I was up, I would check all the locks and then stand still listening to the distant sounds of the desert (the muffled hum of cars heading north or south) or looking out of the window at the night. And so on until dawn, when I could finally get some unbroken sleep, two or three hours at most.

One morning while we were having breakfast, the director asked about my eyes. It's because I don't sleep much, I said. Yes, they're bloodshot, she said, and changed the subject. That afternoon, as she was taking me back to the motel, she asked if I would like to drive for a bit. I don't know how to drive, I said. She burst out laughing and pulled up on the shoulder. A white refrigerated truck went past. I managed to read what was written on the side in large blue letters: THE WIDOW PADILLA'S MEAT. The truck had Monterrey number plates and the driver stared at us with a curiosity that struck me as excessive. The director opened her door and got out. Get in the driver's seat, she said. I obeyed. As I gripped the wheel I saw her walk around the back of the car. Then she got into the passenger seat and ordered me to get going.

For a long time I drove along the grey strip connecting Gómez Palacio and the motel. When I reached the motel I didn't stop. I looked at the director; she was smiling, she didn't mind me driving a bit further. To begin with, both of us had stared at the highway in silence. But when we passed the motel she started talking about her poetry, her work, and her insensitive husband. When she had said her piece, she put a cassette into the player and turned it on: a woman singing *rancheras*. She had a sad voice that was always a couple of notes ahead of the orchestra. I'm her friend, said the director. I didn't understand. What? I said. She's a close friend of mine, said the director. Ah. She's from Durango, she said. You've been there, haven't you? Yes, I've been to Durango, I said. And what were the writing workshops like? Worse than the ones here, I replied, meaning it as a compliment, although she didn't seem to take it that way. She's from Durango, but she lives in Ciudad Juárez, she said. Sometimes, when she's going back home to see her mother, she rings me and I reorganise things so I can go to Durango and spend a few days with her. That's nice, I said, keeping my eyes on the road. I stay at her house – her mother's house, actually, said the director. The two of us sleep in her room, and spend hours talking and listening to records. Every now and then one of us goes to the kitchen to make coffee. I usually take biscuits with me, La Regalada biscuits, her favourite. And we drink coffee and eat biscuits. We've known each other since we were fifteen. She's my best friend.

On the horizon I could see the highway disappearing into a range of hills. The night was beginning to approach from the east. Days before, at the motel, I had asked myself, What colour is the desert at night? A stupid rhetorical question, yet somehow I felt it held the key to my future, or perhaps not so much my future as my capacity for suffering. One afternoon, at the writing workshop in Gómez Palacio, a boy asked me how I came to start writing poetry and how long I thought I would go on doing it. The director wasn't present. There were five other people in the workshop, the five students: four boys and a girl. You could tell from the way they dressed that two of them were very poor. The girl was short and thin and her clothes were rather garish. The boy who asked the question should have been studying at a university; instead of which he was working in a factory, the biggest and probably the only soap factory in the state. Another boy was a waiter in an Italian restaurant, the remaining two were at college, and the girl was neither studying nor working.

By chance, I replied. For a while none of us said anything. I considered the possibility of taking a job in Gómez Palacio and staying there for the rest of my life. I had noticed a couple of pretty girls among the painting students in the yard. With a bit of luck I might have been able to marry one of them. The prettier one also seemed to be the more conventional. I imagined a long, complicated engagement. I imagined a dark, cool house and a garden full of plants. And how long do you think you'll go on writing? asked the boy who worked in the soap factory. I could have said anything, but opted for simplicity: I don't know, I said. What about you? I started writing because poetry sets me free, sir, and I'm never going to stop, he said with a smile that barely hid his pride and determination. As an answer it was too vague and declamatory to be convincing, yet somehow it gave me a glimpse of the factory worker's life, not as it was then, but the life he had led at the age of fifteen, or maybe twelve. I saw him running or walking through the outskirts of Gómez Palacio, under a sky that looked like a rockslide. I saw his friends and wondered how they could possibly survive. Yet, one way or another, they probably had.

Then we read some poems. The only one who had any talent was the girl. But by then I wasn't sure of anything. When we came out of the room, the director was waiting with two guys who turned out to be civil servants employed by the state of Durango. For some reason my first thought was, They're policemen, here to arrest me. The kids said goodbye and off they went, the skinny girl with one of the boys, and the other three on their own. I watched them walk down the hallway with its peeling walls. I followed, as if I had forgotten to say something to one of them. And from the door I saw them disappear at opposite ends of that street in Gómez Palacio.

The director said: She's my best friend. That was all. The highway was no longer a straight line. In the rear-view mirror I could see an enormous wall rising beyond the town. It took me a while to realise it was the night. The singer on the cassette began to warble another song. The lyrics were about a remote village in the north of Mexico where everyone was happy, except her. I had the impression the director was crying. Silent, dignified, unstoppable tears. But I couldn't confirm this impression. I had to keep my eyes on the road. The director took out a handkerchief and blew her nose. Switch the headlights on, I heard her say in a barely audible voice. I kept on driving.

Switch on the headlights, she repeated, and without waiting for an answer she leant forward and did so herself. Slow down, she said after a while, her voice stronger now, as the singer reached the final notes of her song. What a sad song, I said, just for something to say.

The car came to a halt by the side of the road. I opened the door and got out. It wasn't yet completely dark, but it was no longer day. The land all around us and the hills into which the highway went winding were a deep, intense shade of yellow that I have never seen anywhere else. As if the light (though it seemed to me not so much light as pure colour) were charged with something, I didn't know what, but it could well have been eternity. I was immediately embarrassed to have had such a thought. I stretched my legs. A car whizzed past honking its horn. I told him where to go with a gesture. Maybe it wasn't just a gesture. Maybe I yelled, Go fuck yourself, and the driver saw or heard me. But it's unlikely, like most things in this story. In any case, when I think about the driver, all I can see is my own image frozen in his rear-view mirror: my hair is still long; I'm thin, wearing a denim jacket and a pair of awful, oversize glasses.

The car pulled up several metres in front of us. The driver didn't get out, or reverse, or honk the horn again, but his mere presence seemed to distend the space that we were now, in some sense, sharing with him. Cautiously, I walked around to the director's side of the car. She wound down her window and asked me what had happened. Her eyes were bulging more than ever. I said I didn't know. It's a man, she said, and slid across into the driver's seat. I got into the seat she had left empty. It was hot and moist, as if the director had a fever. Through the windscreen I could see the man's silhouette, the nape of his neck; like us he was looking ahead, at the line of the highway beginning to wind its way towards the hills.

It's my husband, said the director, her eyes fixed on the stationary car, as if she were talking to herself. Then she flipped the cassette over and turned up the volume. Sometimes my friend rings me up, she said, when she's touring in towns she doesn't know. Once she rang from Ciudad Madero. She'd been singing all night at the Oil Workers' Union building and she rang me at four in the morning. Another time she rang from Reinosa. That's nice, I said. Not especially, said the director. She just rings. Sometimes she needs to talk. If my husband answers, she hangs up.

For a while neither of us said anything. I imagined the director's husband with the telephone in his hand. He picks up the telephone, says, Hello, who is it? Then he hears someone hang up at the other end and he hangs up too, almost by reflex. I asked the director if she wanted me to get out and say something to the driver of the other car. There's no need, she said. Which seemed a reasonable answer to me, although in fact it was mad. I asked her what her husband was going to do, if it was really her husband. He'll stay there until we go, said the director. Then we'd better go straight away, I said. The director seemed to be lost in thought, although much later I surmised that, in fact, all she was doing was shutting her eyes and listening to her friend from Durango, drinking that song down to the very last drop. Then she switched on the ignition, pulled out slowly and passed the car parked several metres ahead. I looked through the window as we went past, but the driver turned his back to us and I couldn't see his face.

Are you sure it was your husband? I asked as we sped off again towards the hills. No, said the director, and started laughing. I don't think it was. I started laughing too. The car was like his, she said, almost choking with laughter, but it probably wasn't him. So it might have been? I said. Not unless he's changed his number plates, said the director. At which point I understood that the whole thing had been a joke. I shut my eyes. Then we came out of the hills and into the desert: a plain swept by the headlights of cars heading north or back towards Gómez Palacio. It was already night.

Now we're coming to a very special place, said the director. Those were her words. Very special.

I wanted you to see this, she said proudly, this is one of my favourite things. She pulled over and stopped in a sort of rest area, although it was really no more than a patch of ground big enough for trucks to park on. Lights were sparkling in the distance: a town or a restaurant. We didn't get out. The director pointed in the direction of something. A stretch of highway that must have been about five kilometres from where we were, maybe less, maybe more. She even wiped the inside of the windscreen with a cloth so I could see better. I looked: I saw the headlights of cars. From the way the beams of light were swivelling, there must have been a bend in the highway. And then I saw some green shapes in the desert. Did you see? asked the director. Yes, lights, I replied. The director looked at me: her bulging eyes gleamed, as do, no doubt, the eyes of the small mammals native to the inhospitable environs of Gómez Palacio in the state of Durango. Then I looked again in the direction she had indicated: at first I couldn't see anything, only darkness, the sparkling lights of that restaurant or town, then some cars went past and the beams of their headlights carved the space in two.

Their progress was exasperatingly slow, but we were beyond exasperation.

And then I saw how the light, seconds after the car or truck had passed that spot, turned back on itself and hung in the air, a green light that seemed to breathe, alive and aware for a fraction of a second in the middle of the desert, set free, a marine light, moving like the sea but with all the fragility of earth, a green, prodigious, solitary light, that must have been produced by something near that curve in the road – a sign, the roof of an abandoned shed, huge sheets of plastic spread on the ground – but that, to us, seeing it from a distance, appeared to be a dream or a miracle, which comes to the same thing, in the end.

Then the director started the car, turned it around and drove back to the motel.

I was to leave for Mexico City the next day. When we arrived at the motel, the director got out of the car and came with me part of the way. Before we reached my room she held out her hand and said goodbye. I know you'll forgive my eccentricities, she said, after all we both read poetry. I was grateful she hadn't said we were both poets. When I got to my room I switched on the light, took off my jacket, and drank some water straight from the tap. Then I went to the window. Her car was still in the parking lot. I opened the door and was hit in the face by a gust of desert air. The car was empty. A little further off, beside the highway, I saw the director, who looked as if she were contemplating a river or the landscape of another planet. From the way she was standing with her arms slightly raised, she might have been talking to the air or reciting, or playing statues like a young girl.

I didn't sleep well. At dawn the director herself came to fetch me. She took me to the bus station and told me that if eventually I accepted the job, I would be very welcome at the workshop. I said I would have to think about it. She said that was fine, best to think things over. Then she said, A hug. I bent down and hugged her. The seat I had been given was on the other side of the bus, so I didn't see her leave. The last thing I remember, vaguely, is her standing there, looking at the bus or perhaps at her watch. Then I had to sit down so the other passengers could get past or settle into their seats, and when I looked again she was gone.

Last Evenings on Earth

This is the situation: B and his father are going to Acapulco on holiday. They are planning to leave very early, at six in the morning. B sleeps the previous night at his father's house. He doesn't dream or if he does he forgets his dreams as soon as he opens his eyes. He hears his father in the bathroom. He looks out of the window; it is still dark. He gets dressed without switching on the light. When he comes out of his room, his father is sitting at the table, reading the sports news from the day before, and breakfast is ready. Coffee and ranch-style eggs. B says hello to his father and goes into the bathroom.

His father's car is a 1970 Ford Mustang. At six-thirty in the morning they get into the car and head out of the city. The city is Mexico City, and the year in which B and his father leave Mexico City for a short holiday is 1975.

Overall, the trip goes smoothly. Leaving the city both father and son feel cold, but as they leave the high valley behind and begin to descend into the state of Guerrero, the temperature rises and they have to take off their sweaters and open the windows. B, who is inclined to melancholy (or so he likes to think), is at first completely absorbed in contemplating the landscape, but after a few hours the mountains and forests become monotonous and he starts reading a book instead.

Before they get to Acapulco, B's father pulls up in front of a roadside café. The café serves iguana. Shall we try it? he suggests. The iguanas are alive and they hardly move when B's father goes over to look at them. B leans against the mudguard of the Mustang, watching him. Without waiting for an answer, B's father orders a portion of iguana for himself and one for his son. Only then does B move away from the car. He approaches the open-air eating area — four tables under a canvas shade that is swaying slightly in the gentle breeze — and sits down at the table furthest from the highway. B's father orders two beers. Father and son have rolled up their sleeves and unbuttoned their shirts. Both are wearing light-coloured shirts. The waiter, by contrast, is wearing a black, long-sleeved shirt and doesn't seem bothered by the heat.

Going to Acapulco? asks the waiter. B's father nods. They are the only customers at the café. Cars whiz past on the bright highway. B's father gets up and goes out the back. For a moment B thinks his father is going to the toilet, but then he realises he has gone to the kitchen to see how they cook the iguanas. The waiter follows him without a word. Then B hears them talking. First his father, then the man's voice, and finally the voice of a woman B can't see. B's forehead is beaded with sweat. His glasses are misted and dirty. He takes them off and cleans them with the corner of his shirt. When he puts them back on he notices his father watching him from the kitchen. He can see only his father's face and part of his shoulder, the rest is hidden by a red curtain with black dots, and B has the intermittent impression that this curtain separates not only the kitchen from the eating area but also one time from another.

Then B looks away and his gaze returns to the book lying on the table. It is a book of poetry. An anthology of French surrealist poets translated into Spanish by the Argentine surrealist Aldo Pellegrini. B has been reading this book for two days. He likes it. He likes the photos of the poets. The photo of Unik, the one of Desnos, the photos of Artaud and Crevel. The book is thick and covered with transparent plastic. It wasn't covered by B (who never covers his books), but by a particularly fastidious friend. So B looks away from his father, opens the book at random and comes face to face with Gui Rosey, the photo of Gui Rosey and his poems, and when he looks up again his father's head has disappeared.

The heat is stifling. B would be more than happy to go back to Mexico City, but he isn't going back, at least not yet, he knows that. Soon his father is sitting next to him and they are both eating iguana with chilli sauce and drinking more beer. The waiter in the black shirt has turned on a transistor radio, and now some vaguely tropical music is blending with the noises of the jungle and the noise of the cars passing on the highway. The iguana tastes like chicken. It's tougher than chicken, says B, not entirely convinced. It's tasty, says his father, and orders another portion. They have cinnamon coffee. The man in the black shirt serves the iguana, but the woman from the kitchen brings out the coffee. She is young, almost as young as B; she is wearing white shorts and a yellow blouse with white flowers printed on it, flowers B doesn't recognise, perhaps because they don't exist. As they drink their coffee, B feels nauseous, but he says nothing. He smokes and looks at the canvas shade, barely moving, as if weighed down by a narrow puddle of rainwater from the last storm. But it can't be that, thinks B. What are you looking at? asks his father. The shade, says B. It's like a vein. But he doesn't say the bit about the vein, he only thinks it.

They arrive in Acapulco as night is falling. For a while they drive up and down the avenues by the sea with the windows wide open and the breeze ruffling their hair. They stop at a bar and go in for a drink. This time B's father orders tequila. B thinks for a moment. Then he orders tequila too. The bar is modern and has air-conditioning. B's father talks to the waiter and asks him about hotels near the beach. By the time they get back to the Mustang a few stars are visible and for the first time that day B's father looks tired. Even so, they visit a couple of hotels, which for one reason or another are unsatisfactory, before finding one that will do. The hotel is called La Brisa: it's small, a stone's throw from the beach, and has a swimming-pool. B's father likes the hotel. So does B. It's the off season, so the hotel is almost empty and the prices are reasonable. The room they are given has two single beds and a small bathroom with a shower. The only window looks on to the terrace, where the swimming-pool is. B's father would have preferred a sea view. The air-conditioning, they soon discover, is out of order. But the room is fairly cool, so they don't complain. They make themselves at home: each opens up his suitcase and puts his clothes in the wardrobe. B leaves his books on the bedside table. They change their shirts. B's father takes a cold shower while B just washes his face, and when they are ready they go out to dinner.

The reception desk is manned by a short guy with teeth like a rabbit. He's young and seems friendly. He recommends a restaurant near the hotel. B's father asks if there's somewhere lively nearby. B understands what his father means. The receptionist doesn't. A place with a bit of action, says B's father. A place where you can find girls, says B. Ah, says the receptionist. For a moment B and his father stand there, without speaking. The receptionist crouches down, disappearing behind the counter, and reappears with a card, which he holds out. B's father looks at the card, asks if the establishment is reliable, then extracts a note from his wallet, which the receptionist is quick to intercept.

But after dinner, they go straight back to the hotel.

The next day, B wakes up very early. As quietly as possible he takes a shower, brushes his teeth, puts on his bathing suit, and leaves the room. There is no one in the hotel dining room, so B decides to go out for breakfast. The hotel is on a street that runs straight down to the beach, which is empty except for a boy hiring out paddle boards. B asks him how much it costs for an hour. The boy quotes a price that sounds acceptable, so B hires a board and pushes off into the sea. Opposite the beach is a little island, towards which he steers his craft. At first he has some trouble, but soon he gets the hang of it. At this time of day the sea is crystal clear and B thinks he can see red fishes under the board, about a foot and a half long, swimming towards the beach as he paddles towards the island.

It takes exactly fifteen minutes for him to get from the beach to the island. B doesn't know this, because he is not wearing a watch, and for him time slows down. The crossing seems to last an eternity. At the last minute, waves rear unexpectedly, impeding his approach. The sand is noticeably different from that of the hotel beach; back there it was a golden, tawny colour, perhaps because of the time of day (though B doesn't think so), while here it is a dazzling white, so bright it hurts your eyes to look at it.

B stops paddling and just sits there, at the mercy of the waves, which begin to carry him slowly away from the island. By the time he finally reacts, the board has drifted halfway back. Having ascertained this, B decides to turn around. The return is calm and uneventful. When he gets to the beach, the boy who hires out the boards comes up and asks if he had a problem. Not at all, says B. An hour later B returns to the hotel without having had breakfast and finds his father sitting in the dining room with a cup of coffee and a plate in front of him on which are scattered the remains of toast and eggs.

The following hours are hazy. They drive around aimlessly, watching people from the car. Sometimes they get out to have a cold drink or an ice cream. In the afternoon, on the beach, while his father is stretched out asleep in a deck chair, B rereads Gui Rosey's poems and the brief story of his life or his death.

One day a group of surrealists arrives in the south of France. They try to get visas for the United States. The north and the west of the country are occupied by the Germans. The south is under the aegis of Pétain. Day after day, the US Consulate delays its decision. Among the members of the group are Breton, Tristan Tzara, and Péret, but there are also less famous figures. Gui Rosey is one of them. In the photo he has the look of a minor poet, thinks B. He is ugly, he is impeccably dressed, he looks like an unimportant public servant or a bank clerk. Up to this point, a few disagreements, but nothing out of the ordinary, thinks B. The surrealists gather every afternoon at a café by the port. They make plans and chat; Rosey is always there. But one day (one afternoon, B imagines), he fails to appear. At first, he isn't missed. He is a minor poet and no one pays much attention to minor poets. After a few days, however, the others start to worry. At the *pension* where he is staying, no one knows what has happened; his suitcases and books are there, undisturbed, so he clearly hasn't tried to leave without paying (as guests at certain *pensions* on the Côte d'Azur are prone to do). His friends try to find him. They visit all the hospitals and police stations in the area. No one can tell them anything. One morning the visas arrive. Most of them board a ship and set off for the United States. Those who remain, who will never get visas, soon forget about Rosey and his disappearance; people are disappearing all the time, in large numbers, and they have to look out for themselves.

That night, after dinner at the hotel, B's father suggests they go and find a bit of action. B looks at his father. He is blond (B is dark), his eyes are grey, and he is still in good shape. He looks happy and ready to have a good time. What sort of action? asks B, who knows perfectly well what his father is referring to. The usual kind, says B's father. Drinking and women. For a while B says nothing, as if he were pondering a reply. His father looks at him. The look might seem inquisitive, but in fact it is only affectionate. Finally B says he's not in the mood for sex. It's not just about getting laid, says his father, we'll go and see, have a few drinks, and enjoy ourselves with some friends. What friends, says B, we don't know anyone here. You always make friends when you're out for a ride. The expression 'out for a ride' makes B think of horses. When he was seven his father bought him a horse. Where did my horse come from? asks B. This takes his father completely by surprise. What horse? he asks. The one you bought me when I was a kid, says B, in Chile. Ah, Hullabaloo, says his father, smiling. He was from the island of Chiloé, he says, then after a moment's reflection he starts talking about brothels again. The way he talks about them, they could be dance halls, thinks B. Then they both fall silent.

That night they don't go anywhere.

While his father is sleeping, B goes out on to the terrace to read by the swimming-pool. There is no one there apart from him. The terrace is clean and empty. From his table B can see part of the reception area, where the receptionist from the night before is standing at the counter reading something or doing the accounts. B reads the French surrealists, he reads Gui Rosey. To tell the truth, Gui Rosey doesn't interest him much. He is far more interested in Desnos and Éluard, and yet he always ends up coming back to Rosey's poems and looking at his photo, a studio portrait, in which he has the air of a solitary, wretched soul, with his large, glassy eyes and a dark tie that seems to be strangling him.

He must have committed suicide, thinks B. He knew he was never going to get a visa for the States or Mexico, so he decided to end his days there and then. B imagines or tries to imagine a town on the Mediterranean coast of France. He still hasn't been to Europe. He has been all over Latin America, or almost, but he still hasn't set foot in Europe. So his image of a Mediterranean town is derived from his image of Acapulco. Heat, a small, cheap hotel, beaches of golden sand and beaches of white sand. And the distant sound of music. B doesn't realise that there is a crucial element missing from the soundtrack of this scene: the rigging of the small boats that throng the ports of all the towns on the Mediterranean coast, especially the smaller ones. The sound of the rigging at night, when the sea is as still as a mill pond.

Suddenly someone comes on to the terrace. The silhouette of a woman. She sits down at the farthest table, in a corner, near two large urns. A moment later the receptionist appears, bringing her a drink. Then, instead of going back to the counter, he comes over to B, who is sitting by the edge of the pool, and asks if he and his father are having a good time. Very good, says B. Do you like Acapulco? asks the receptionist. Very much, says B. How was the San Diego? asks the receptionist. B doesn't understand the question. The San Diego? For a moment he thinks the receptionist is referring to the hotel, but then he remembers that the hotel is called something else. Which San Diego? asks B. The receptionist smiles. The club with the hookers. Then B remembers the card the receptionist gave his father. We still haven't been, he says. It's a reliable place, says the receptionist. B moves his head in a way that could mean almost anything. It's on Constituyentes, says the receptionist. There's another club on the avenue, the Ramada, but I wouldn't recommend it. The Ramada, says B, watching the woman's motionless figure in the corner of the terrace and the apparently untouched glass in front of her, between the enormous urns, whose shadows stretch and taper off under the neighbouring tables. Best to steer clear of the Ramada, says the receptionist. Why? asks B, for something to say, although he has no intention of visiting either club. It's not reliable, says the receptionist, and his bright little rabbit-like teeth shine in the semi-darkness that has suddenly submerged the terrace, as if someone at reception had switched off half the lights.

When the receptionist goes away, B opens his book of

poetry again, but the words are illegible now, so he leaves the book open on the table, shuts his eyes and, instead of the faint chimes of rigging, he hears an atmospheric sound, the sound of enormous layers of hot air descending on the hotel and the surrounding trees. He feels like getting into the pool. For a moment he thinks he might.

Then the woman in the corner stands up and begins to walk towards the stairs that lead from the terrace to the reception area, but she stops midway, as if she felt ill, resting one hand on the edge of a raised bed in which there are no longer flowers, only weeds.

B watches her. The woman is wearing a loose, light-coloured summer dress, cut low, leaving her shoulders bare. He expects her to start walking again, but she stands still, her hand still gripping the edge of the raised bed, looking down, so B gets up with the book in his hand and goes over to her. The first thing that surprises him is her face. She must be about sixty years old, B guesses, although from a distance, he wouldn't have said she was more than thirty. She is North American, and when B approaches she looks up and smiles at him. Good night, she says, rather incongruously, in Spanish. Are you all right? asks B. The woman doesn't understand and B has to ask again, in English. I'm just thinking, says the woman, smiling at him fixedly. For a few seconds B considers what she has said to him. Thinking, thinking, thinking. And suddenly it seems to him that this declaration conceals a threat. Something approaching over the sea. Something advancing in the wake of the dark clouds invisibly crossing the Bay of Acapulco. But he doesn't move or make any attempt to break the spell that seems to be holding him captive. Then the woman looks at the book in B's left hand and asks him what he is reading, and B says: poetry. I'm reading poems. The woman looks him in the eye, with the same smile on her face (a smile at once bright and faded, thinks B, feeling more uneasy by the moment), and says that she used to like poetry, once. Which poets? asks B, keeping absolutely still. I can't remember them now, says the woman, and again she seems to lose herself in the contemplation of something visible only to her. B assumes she is making an effort to remember and waits in silence. After a while she looks at him again and says: Longfellow. And straight away she starts reciting lines with a monotonous rhythm that sound to B like a nursery rhyme, a far cry, in any case, from the poets he is reading. Do you know Longfellow? asks the woman. B shakes his head, although in fact he has read some Longfellow. We did it at school, says the woman, with her immutable smile. And then she adds: It's too hot, don't you think? It is very hot, whispers B. There could be a storm coming, says the woman. There is something very definite about her tone. At this point B looks up: he can't see a single star. But he can see lights in the hotel. And, at the window of his room, a silhouette watching them, which makes him start, as if struck by the first, sudden drops of a tropical downpour.

For a moment he is bewildered.

It's his father, on the other side of the glass, wrapped in a blue dressing-gown that he must have brought with him (B hasn't seen it before and it certainly doesn't belong to the hotel), staring at them, although when B notices him, he steps back, recoiling as if bitten by a snake, lifts his hand in a shy wave, and disappears behind the curtains.

The Song of Hiawatha, says the woman. B looks at her.

The Song of Hiawatha, the poem by Longfellow. Ah, yes, says B.

Then the woman says good night and makes a gradual exit: first she goes up the stairs to reception, where she spends a few moments chatting with someone B can't see, then, in silence, she sets off across the hotel lobby, her slim figure framed by successive windows, until she turns into the corridor that leads to the inside stairs.

Half an hour later, B goes back to the room and finds his father asleep. For a few seconds, before going to the bathroom to brush his teeth, B stands very straight at the foot of the bed, gazing at him, as if steeling himself for a fight. Good night, dad, he says. His father gives not the slightest indication that he has heard.

On the second day of their stay in Acapulco, B and his father go to see the cliff divers. They have two options: they can watch the show from an open-air platform or go to the bar-restaurant of the hotel overlooking the precipice. B's father asks about the prices. The first person he asks doesn't know. He persists. Finally an old ex-diver who is hanging around doing nothing tells him what it costs: six times more to watch from the hotel bar. Let's go to the bar, says B's father without hesitating. We'll be more comfortable. B follows him. The other people in the bar are North American or Mexican tourists wearing what are obviously holiday clothes; B and his father stand out. They are dressed as people dress in Mexico City, in clothes that seem to belong to some endless dream. The waiters notice. They know the sort, no chance of a big tip, so they make no effort to serve them promptly. To top it off, B and his father can hardly see the show from where they are sitting. We would have been better off on the platform, says B's father. Although it's not bad here either, he adds. B nods. When the diving is over, having drunk two highballs each, they go outside and start making plans for the rest of the day. Hardly anyone is left on the platform, but B's father recognises the old ex-diver sitting on a buttress and goes over to him.

The ex-diver is short and has a very broad back. He is reading a cowboy novel and doesn't look up until B and his father are at his side. He recognises them and asks what they thought of the show. Not bad, says B's father, although in precision sports you need experience to be able to judge properly. Would I be right in guessing you were a sportsman yourself? asks the ex-diver. B's father looks at him for a few moments and then says, You could say that. The ex-diver gets to his feet with an energetic movement as if he were back on the edge of the cliff. He must be about fifty, thinks B, so he's not much older than my father, but the wrinkles on his face, like scars, make him look much older. Are you gentlemen on holiday? asks the ex-diver. B's father nods and smiles. And what was your sport, sir, if I might ask? Boxing, says B's father. How about that, says the ex-diver, so you must have been a heavyweight? B's father smiles broadly and says yes.

Before he knows what is going on, B finds himself walking with his father and the ex-diver towards the Mustang, and then all three get into the car and B hears the directions the ex-diver is giving his father as if they were coming from the radio. For a while the car glides along the Avenida Miguel Alemán, but then it turns and heads inland and soon the tourist hotels and restaurants give way to an ordinary cityscape with tropical touches. The car keeps climbing, heading away from the golden horseshoe of Acapulco, along badly paved or unpaved roads, until it pulls up beside the dusty pavement in front of a cheap restaurant, a fixed-menu place (although, thinks B, it's really too big for that). The ex-diver and B's father get out of the car immediately. They have been talking all the way and while they wait for him on the pavement, they continue their conversation gesturing incomprehensibly. B takes his time getting out of the car. We're going to eat, says his father. So it seems, says B.

The place is dark inside and only a quarter of the space is occupied by tables. The rest looks like a dance floor, with a stage for the band, surrounded by a long balustrade made of rough wood. At first, B can't see a thing, until his eyes adjust to the darkness. Then he sees a man coming over to the ex-diver. They look alike. The stranger listens attentively to an introduction that B doesn't catch, shakes hands with his father and a few seconds later turns to B. B reaches out to shake his hand. The stranger says a name and his handshake, which is no doubt meant to be friendly, is not so much firm as violent. He does not smile. B decides not to smile either. B's father and the ex-diver are already sitting at a table. B sits down next to them. The stranger, who looks like the ex-diver and turns out to be his younger brother, stands beside them, waiting for instructions. The gentleman here, says the ex-diver, was heavyweight champion of his country. So you're foreigners? asks his brother. Chileans, says B's father. Do you have red snapper? asks the ex-diver. We do, says his brother. Bring us one, then, a red snapper Guerrero-style, says the ex-diver. And beers all round, says B's father, for you too. Thank you, murmurs the brother, taking a notebook from his pocket and painstakingly writing down an order that, in B's opinion, a child could easily remember.

Along with the beers, the ex-diver's brother brings them some savoury crackers to nibble and three rather small plates of oysters. They're fresh, says the ex-diver, putting chilli sauce on all three. Funny, isn't it. This stuff's called chilli and so's your country, says the ex-diver, pointing to the bottle full of bright red chilli sauce. Yes, intriguing, isn't it, admits B's father. Like the way the sauce is the opposite of chilly, he adds. B looks at his father with barely veiled incredulity. The conversation revolves around boxing and diving until the red snapper arrives.

Later, B and his father leave the premises. The hours have flown without them noticing and by the time they climb into the Mustang, it is already seven in the evening. The ex-diver comes with them. For a moment, B thinks they'll never get rid of him, but when they reach the centre of Acapulco the ex-diver gets out in front of a billiard hall. When he has gone, B's father comments favourably on the service at the restaurant and the price they paid for the red snapper. If we'd had it here, he says, pointing to the hotels along the beachfront boulevard, it would have cost an arm and a leg. When they get back to their room, B puts on his bathing suit and goes to the beach. He swims for a while and then tries to read in the fading light. He reads the surrealist poets and is completely bewildered. A peaceful, solitary man, on the brink of death. Images, wounds. That is all he can see. And the images are dissolving little by little, like the setting sun, leaving only the wounds. A minor poet disappears while waiting for a visa to admit him to the New World. A minor poet disappears without leaving a trace, hopelessly stranded in some town on the

Mediterranean coast of France. There is no investigation. There is no corpse. By the time B turns to Daumal, night has already fallen on the beach; he shuts the book and slowly makes his way back to the hotel.

After dinner, his father proposes they go out and have some fun. B declines this invitation. He suggests to his father that he go on his own, says he's not in the mood for having fun, he'd prefer to stay in the room and watch a film on TV. I can't believe it, says his father, you're behaving like an old man, at your age! B looks at his father, who is putting on clean clothes after a shower, and laughs.

Before his father goes out, B tells him to take care. His father looks at him from the doorway and says he's only going to have a couple of drinks. You take care yourself, he says, and gently shuts the door.

Once he's on his own, B takes off his shoes, looks for his cigarettes, switches on the TV, and collapses on to the bed again. Without intending to, he falls asleep. He dreams that he is living in (or visiting) the city of the Titans. All there is in the dream is an endless wandering through vast dark streets that recall other dreams. And in the dream his attitude is one that he knows he doesn't have in waking life. Faced with buildings whose voluminous shadows seem to be knocking against each other, he is, if not exactly courageous, unworried or indifferent.

A while later, just after the end of the programme, B wakes up with a jolt, and, as if responding to a summons, switches off the TV and goes to the window. On the terrace, half-hidden in the same corner as the night before, the North American woman is sitting with a cocktail or a glass of fruit juice in front of her. B observes her indifferently, then walks away from the window, sits on the bed, opens his book of surrealist poets, and tries to read. But he can't. So he tries to think, and to that end he lies down on the bed again, with his arms outstretched, and shuts his eyes. For a moment he thinks he is on the point of falling asleep. He even catches an oblique glimpse of a street from the dream city. But soon he realises that he is only remembering the dream, opens his eyes and lies there for a while contemplating the ceiling. Then he switches off the bedside lamp and goes back over to the window.

The North American woman is still there, motionless. The shadows of the urns stretch out and touch the shadows of the neighbouring tables. The reception area, fully lit, unlike the terrace, is reflected in the swimming-pool. Suddenly a car pulls up a few yards from the entrance of the hotel. His father's Mustang, thinks B. But no one appears at the hotel gate for a very long time and B begins to think he must have been mistaken. Then he makes out his father's silhouette climbing the stairs. First his head, then his broad shoulders, then the rest of his body, and finally the shoes, a pair of white moccasins that B, as a rule, finds profoundly disgusting, but the feeling they provoke in him now is something like tenderness. The way he came into the hotel, he thinks, it was like he was dancing. The way he made his entrance, it was as if he had come back from a wake, unconsciously glad to be alive. But the strangest thing is that, after appearing briefly in the reception area, his father turns around and heads towards the terrace: he goes down the stairs, walks around the pool and sits at a table near the North American woman. And when the guy from reception finally appears with a glass, his father pays and, without even waiting for him to be gone, gets up, glass in hand, goes over to the table where the North American woman is sitting and stands there for a while, gesticulating and drinking, until, at the woman's invitation, he takes a seat beside her.

She's too old for him, thinks B. Then he goes back to the bed, lies down, and soon realises that all the sleepiness weighing him down earlier has evaporated. But he doesn't want to turn on the light (although he feels like reading); he doesn't want his father to think (even for a moment) that he is spying on him. He thinks about women; he thinks about travel. Finally he goes to sleep.

Twice during the night he wakes up with a start and his father's bed is empty. The third time, day is already dawning and he sees his father's back: he is sleeping deeply. B switches on the light and stays in bed for a while, smoking and reading.

Later that morning B goes to the beach and hires a paddle board. This time he has no trouble reaching the island opposite. There he has a mango juice and swims for a while in the sea, alone. Then he goes back to the hotel beach, returns the board to the boy, who smiles at him, and takes a roundabout way back to the hotel. He finds his father in the restaurant drinking coffee. He sits down beside him. His father has just shaved and is giving off an odour of cheap aftershave that B finds pleasant. On his right cheek there is a scratch from ear to chin. B considers asking him what happened last night, but in the end decides not to.

The rest of the day goes by in a blur. At some point B and his father walk along a beach near the airport. The beach is vast, and it is lined with numerous wattle-roofed shacks where the fishermen keep their gear. The sea is choppy; for a while B and his father watch the waves breaking in the bay of Puerto Marqués. A fisherman tells them it's not a good day for swimming. You're right, says B. His father goes in for a swim anyway. B sits down on the sand, with his knees up, and watches him advance to meet the waves. The fisherman shades his eyes and says something that B doesn't catch. For a moment the head and arms of his father swimming out to sea vanish from his visual field. Now there are two children with the fisherman. They are all standing, looking out to sea, except for B, who is still sitting down. A passenger plane appears in the sky, curiously inaudible. B stops looking at the sea and watches the plane until it disappears behind a rounded hill covered with vegetation. He remembers waking up, exactly a year ago, in Acapulco airport. He was returning from Chile, on his own, and the plane stopped in Acapulco. He remembers opening his eyes and seeing an orange light with blue and pink overtones, like the fading colours of an old film, and knowing then that he was back in Mexico and safe at last, in a sense. That was in 1974 and B had not yet turned twenty-one. Now he is twenty-two and his father must be about forty-nine. B closes his eyes. Because of the wind, the fisherman's and the boys' cries of alarm are almost unintelligible. The sand is cold. When he opens his eyes he sees his father coming out of the sea. He shuts his eyes and doesn't open them again until he feels a large wet hand grip his shoulder and hears his father's voice proposing they go and eat turtle eggs.

There are things you can tell people and things you just can't, thinks B disconsolately. From this moment on he knows the disaster is approaching.

In spite of which the next forty-eight hours go by in a placid sort of daze that B's father associates with 'The Idea of the Holiday' (B can't tell whether his father is serious or pulling his leg). They go to the beach, they eat at the hotel or at a reasonably priced restaurant on the Avenida López Mateos. One afternoon they hire a boat, a tiny plastic rowing-boat, and follow the coastline near their hotel, along with the trinket vendors who peddle their wares from beach to beach, upright on paddle boards or in very shallow-bottomed boats, like tightrope walkers or the ghosts of drowned sailors. On the way back they even have an accident.

B's father takes the boat too close to the rocks and it overturns. In itself, this is not dramatic. Both of them can swim quite well and the boat is built to float when overturned; it isn't hard to right it and climb in again. And that is what B and his father do. Not the slightest danger at any point, thinks B. But then, when both of them have climbed back into the boat, B's father realises that he has lost his wallet. Tapping his chest, he says: My wallet, and without a moment's hesitation he dives back into the water. B can't help laughing, but then, stretched out in the boat, he looks down, sees no sign of his father, and for a moment imagines him diving, or worse, sinking like a stone, but with his eyes open, into a deep trench, over which, on the surface, in a rocking boat, his son has stopped laughing and begun to worry. Then B sits up and, having looked over the other side of the boat and seen no sign of his father there either, jumps into the water, and this is what happens: as B goes down with his eyes open, his father, open-eyed too, is coming up (they almost touch), holding his wallet in his right hand. They look at each other as they pass, but can't alter their trajectories, or at least not straight away, so B's father keeps ascending silently while B continues his silent descent.

For sharks, for most fish in fact (flying fish excepted), hell is the surface of the sea. For B (and many, perhaps most, young men of his age) it sometimes takes the form of the sea bed. As he follows in his father's wake, but heading in the opposite direction, the situation strikes him as particularly ridiculous. On the bottom there is no sand, as he had for some reason imagined there would be, only rocks, piled on top of each other, as if this part of the coast were a submerged mountain range and he were near the top, having hardly begun the descent. Then he starts to rise again, and looks up at the boat, which seems to be levitating one moment and about to sink the next, and in it he finds his father sitting right in the middle, attempting to smoke a wet cigarette.

Then the lull comes to an end, the forty-eight hours of grace in the course of which B and his father have visited various bars in Acapulco, lain on the beach and slept, eaten, even laughed, and an icy phase begins, a phase which appears to be normal but is ruled by deities of ice (who do not, however, offer any relief from the heat that reigns in Acapulco), hours of what, in former days, when he was an adolescent perhaps, B would have called *boredom*, although he would certainly not use that word now, *disaster* he would say, a private disaster whose main effect is to drive a wedge between B and his father: part of the price they must pay for existing.

It all begins with the appearance of the ex-diver, who, as B realises straight away, has come looking for his father, and not the family unit, so to speak, constituted by father and son. B's father invites the ex-diver to have a drink on the hotel terrace. The ex-diver says he knows a better place. B's father looks at him, smiles, and says OK. As they go out into the street, the light is beginning to fade. B feels an inexplicable stab of pain and thinks that perhaps it would have been better to stay at the hotel and leave his father to his own devices. But it's already too late. The Mustang is heading up the Avenida Constituyentes and from his pocket B's father takes the card that the receptionist gave him days ago. The nightspot is called the San Diego, he says. In the ex-diver's opinion, it's too expensive. I've got money, says B's father; I've been living in Mexico since 1968, and this is the first time I've taken a holiday. B, who is sitting next to his father, tries to see the ex-diver's face in the rear-view mirror, but can't. So first they go to the San Diego and for a while they drink and dance with the girls. For each dance they have to give the girl a ticket bought beforehand from the bar. To begin with, B's father buys only three tickets. There's something unreal about this system, he says to the ex-diver. But then he starts enjoying himself and buys a whole bundle. B dances too. His first dance partner is a slim girl with Indian features. The second is a woman with big breasts who, for a reason that B will never discover, seems to be preoccupied or cross. The third is fat and happy, and after dancing for a little while, she whispers into B's ear that she's high. What did you take? asks B. Magic mushrooms, says the woman, and B laughs. Meanwhile B's father is dancing with a girl who looks like an Indian and B is glancing across at him from time to time. Actually, all the girls look like Indians. The one dancing with his father has a pretty smile. They are talking (they haven't stopped talking, in fact) although B can't hear what they are saying. Then his father disappears and B goes to the bar with the ex-diver.

They start talking too. About the old days. About courage. About the narrow coves where the ocean waves break. About women. Subjects that don't interest B, or at least not at the moment. But they talk anyway.

Half an hour later his father comes back to the bar. His blond hair is wet and freshly combed (B's father combs his hair back) and his face is red. He smiles and says nothing; B observes him and says nothing. Time for dinner, says B's father. B and the ex-diver follow him to the Mustang. They eat an assortment of shellfish in a place that's long and narrow, like a coffin. As they eat, B's father watches B as if he were searching for an answer. B looks back at him. He is sending a telepathic message: There is no answer because it's not a valid question. It's an idiotic question. Then, before he knows what is going on, B is back in the car with his father and the ex-diver, who talk about boxing all the way to a place in the suburbs of Acapulco. It's a brick and wood building with no windows and inside there's a juke-box with songs by Lucha Villa and Lola Beltrán. Suddenly B feels nauseous. He leaves his father and the ex-diver and looks for the toilet or the back yard, or the door to the street, belatedly realising that he has had too much to drink. He also realises that apparently well-meaning hands have prevented him from going out into the street. They don't want me to get away, thinks B. Then he vomits several times in the yard, among piles of beer boxes, under the eye of a chained dog, and having relieved himself, gazes up at the stars. A woman soon appears beside him. Her shadow is darker than the darkness of the night. Were it not for her white dress, B could hardly make her out. You want a blow-job? she asks. Her voice is young and husky. B looks at her, uncomprehending. The whore kneels down beside him and undoes his fly. Then B understands and lets her proceed. When it's over he feels cold. The whore stands up and B hugs her. Together they gaze at the night sky. When B says he's going back to his father's table, the woman doesn't follow him. Let's go, says B, but she resists. Then B realises that he has hardly seen her face. It's better that way. I hugged her, he thinks, but I don't even know what she looks like. Before he goes in he turns around and sees her walking over to pat the dog.

Inside, his father is sitting at a table with the ex-diver and two other guys. B comes up to him from behind and whispers in his ear: Let's go. His father is playing cards. I'm winning, he says, I can't leave now. They're going to steal all our money, thinks B. Then he looks at the women, who are looking at him and his father with pity in their eyes. They know what's going to happen to us, thinks B. Are you drunk? his father asks him, taking a card. No, says B, not any more. Have you taken any drugs? asks his father. No, says B. Then his father smiles and orders a tequila. B gets up and goes to the bar, and from there he surveys the scene of the crime with manic eyes. It is clear to B now that he will never travel with his father again. He shuts his eyes; he opens his eyes. The whores watch him curiously; one offers him a drink, which B declines with a gesture. When he shuts his eyes, he keeps seeing his father with a pistol in each hand, entering through an impossibly situated door. In he comes, impossibly, urgently, with his grey eyes shining and his hair ruffled. This is the last time we're travelling together, thinks B. That's all there is to it. The jukebox is playing a Lucha Villa song and B thinks of Gui Rosey, a minor poet who disappeared in the south of France. His father deals the cards, laughs, tells stories, and listens to those of his companions, each more sordid than the last. B remembers going to his father's house when he returned from Chile in 1974. His father had broken his foot and was in bed reading a sports magazine. What was it like? he asked, and B recounted his adventures. An episode from the chronicle of Latin America's doomed revolutions. I almost got killed, he said. His father looked at him and smiled. How many times? he asked. Twice, at least, B replied. Now B's father is roaring with laughter and B is trying to think clearly. Gui Rosey committed suicide, he thinks, or got killed. His corpse is at the bottom of the sea.

A tequila, says B. A woman hands him a half-full glass. Don't get drunk again, kid, she says. No, I'm all right now, says B, feeling perfectly lucid. Then two other women approach him. What would you like to drink? asks B. Your father's really nice, says the younger one, who has long, black hair. Maybe she's the one who gave me the blow-job, thinks B. And he remembers (or tries to remember) apparently disconnected scenes: the first time he smoked in front of his father; he was fourteen, it was a Viceroy cigarette, they were sitting in his father's truck waiting for a goods train to arrive, and it was a very cold morning. Guns and knives, family stories. The whores are drinking tequila with Coca-Cola. How long was I outside vomiting? wonders B. You were kind of jumpy before, says one of the whores. You want some? Some what? says B. He is shaking and his skin is cold as ice. Some weed, says the woman, who is about thirty years old and has long hair like the other one, but dyed blonde. Acapulco Gold? asks B, taking a gulp of tequila, while the two women come a little closer and start stroking his back and his legs. Yep, calms you down, says the blonde. B nods and the next thing he knows there is a cloud of smoke between him and his father. You really love your dad, don't you, says one of the women. Well, I wouldn't go that far, says B. What do you mean? says the dark woman. The woman serving at the bar laughs. Through the smoke B sees his father turn his head and look at him for a moment. A deadly serious look, he thinks. Do you like Acapulco? asks the blonde. Only at this point does he realise that the bar is almost empty. At one table there are two men drinking in silence, at another, his father, the ex-diver, and the two strangers playing cards. All the other tables are empty.

The door to the patio opens and a woman in a white dress appears. She's the one who gave me the blow-job, thinks B. She looks about twenty-five, but is probably much younger, maybe sixteen or seventeen. Like almost all the others, she has long hair, and is wearing shoes with very high heels. As she walks across the bar (towards the bathroom) B looks carefully at her shoes: they are white and smeared with mud on the sides. His father also looks up and examines her for a moment. B watches the whore opening the bathroom door, then he looks at his father. He shuts his eyes and when he opens them again the whore is gone and his father has turned his attention back to the game. The best thing for you to do would be to get your father out of this place, one of the women whispers in his ear. B orders another tequila. I can't, he says. The woman slides her hand up under his loose-fitting Hawaiian shirt. She's checking to see if I have a weapon, thinks B. The woman's fingers climb up his chest and close on his left nipple. She squeezes it. Hey, says B. Don't you believe me? asks the woman. What's going to happen? asks B. Something bad, says the woman. How bad? I don't know, but if I was you, I'd get out of here. B smiles and looks into her eyes for the first time: Come with us, he says, taking a gulp of tequila. Not in a million years, says the woman. Then B remembers his father saying to him, before he left for Chile: 'You're an artist and I'm a worker.' What did he mean by that? he wonders. The bathroom door opens and the whore in the white dress comes out again, her shoes immaculate now, goes across to the table where the card game is happening, and stands there next to one of the strangers. Why do we have to go? asks B. The woman looks at him out of the corner of her eye and says nothing. There are things you can tell people, thinks B, and things you just can't. He shuts his eyes.

As if in a dream, he goes back out to the patio. The woman with the dyed-blonde hair leads him by the hand. I have already done this, thinks B, I'm drunk, I'll never get out of here. Certain gestures are repeated: the woman sits on a rickety chair and opens his fly, the night seems to float like a lethal gas among the empty beer boxes. But some things are missing: the dog has gone, for one, and in the sky, to the east, where the moon hung before, a few filaments of light herald dawn. When they finish, the dog appears, perhaps attracted by B's groans. He doesn't bite, says the woman, while the dog stands a few yards away, baring its teeth. The woman gets up and smoothes her dress. The fur on the dog's back is standing up and a string of translucent saliva hangs from his muzzle. Stay, Fang, stay, says the woman. He's going to bite us, thinks B as they retreat towards the door. What happens next is confused: at his father's table, all the card players are standing up. One of the strangers is shouting at the top of his voice. B soon realises that he is insulting his father. As a precaution he orders a bottle of beer at the bar, which he drinks in long gulps, almost choking, before going over to the table. His father seems calm. In front of him are a considerable number of banknotes, which he is picking up one by one and putting into his pocket. You're not leaving here with that money, shouts the stranger. B looks at the ex-diver, trying to tell from his face which side he will take. The stranger's probably, thinks B. The beer runs down his neck and only then does he realise he is burning hot.

B's father finishes counting his money and looks at the three men standing in front of him and the woman in white. Well, gentlemen, we're leaving, he says. Come over here, son, he says. B pours what is left of his beer on to the floor and grips the bottle by the neck. What are you doing, son? says B's father. B can hear the tone of reproach in his voice. We're going to leave calmly, says B's father, then he turns around and asks the women how much they owe. The woman at the bar looks at a piece of paper and reads out a sizeable sum. The blonde woman, who is standing halfway between the table and bar, says another figure. B's father adds them up, takes out the money and hands it to the blonde: What we owe you and the drinks. Then he gives her a couple more bills: the tip. Now we're going to leave, thinks B. The two strangers block their exit. B doesn't want to look at her, but he does: the woman in white has sat down on one of the vacant chairs and is examining the cards scattered on the table, touching them with her fingertips. Don't get in my way, whispers his father, and it takes a while for B to realise that he is speaking to him. The ex-diver puts his hands in his pockets. The one who was shouting before starts insulting B's father again, telling him to come back to the table and keep playing. The game's over, says B's father. For a moment, looking at the woman in white (who strikes him now, for the first time, as very beautiful), B thinks of Gui Rosey, who disappeared off the face of the earth, quiet as a lamb, without a trace, while the Nazi hymns rose into a blood-red sky, and he sees himself as Gui Rosey, a Gui Rosey buried in some vacant lot in Acapulco, vanished for ever, but then he hears his father, who is accusing the ex-diver of something, and he realises that unlike Gui Rosey he is not alone.

Then his father walks towards the door, stooping slightly, and B stands aside to give him room to move. Tomorrow we'll leave, tomorrow we'll go back to Mexico City, thinks B joyfully. And then the fight begins.

Days of 1978

One day B goes to a party organised by a group of Chileans exiled in Europe. He has recently arrived from Mexico and knows very few of the people there. He is surprised to discover that it is a family gathering: the guests are united by blood ties as well as ties of friendship. Brothers dance with cousins, aunts with nephews, and wine flows in abundance.

At one point, possibly at dawn, a young man starts quarrelling with B on some pretext or other. The argument is regrettable and predictable. The young man, U, shows off his crackpot erudition: he confuses Marx with Feuerbach, Che Guevara with Frantz Fanon, Rodó with Mariátegui and Mariátegui with Gramsci. It is not a good time to start an argument, to say the least: in Barcelona the light of dawn can drive people mad if they've been up all night, or turn them cold and hard like executioners. That's not my comment; that's what B thinks, and consequently his replies are icy and sarcastic, more than enough provocation for U, who is positively spoiling for a fight. But when the fight seems imminent, B stands up and refuses to have it out. U insults and challenges him, hits the table (or maybe the wall) with his fist. All in vain.

B ignores him and leaves.

The story could end there. B hates the Chilean exiles who live in Barcelona, although he is one of them and there's not a thing he can do about it. The poorest and probably the loneliest of them all. Or so he believes. The way he remembers the incident, it was really like a schoolboys' scrap. But U's violence is bitterly disappointing to B, because U was, and possibly still is, an active member of the left-wing party to which he himself, at this point in his life, is most sympathetic. Once again reality has proven that no particular group has a monopoly over demagogy, dogmatism, and ignorance.

But B forgets the incident, or tries to, and gets on with his life.

Periodically he hears U mentioned, in a vague sort of way, as if he were dead. B would really prefer not to know, but when you associate with certain people, you can't avoid hearing what has happened in their circle of friends, or what they think has happened. In this way, B discovers that U has become a Spanish citizen or that U was seen with his wife at a concert given by a Chilean folk group. For a moment, B even imagines U and U's wife sitting in a theatre as it gradually fills with people, waiting for the curtain to go up revealing the folk group, guys with long hair and beards, more or less like U, and he imagines U's wife, whom he has seen only once and remembers as beautiful but with something odd about her, a woman who is absent, elsewhere, who says hello (as she said hello to B at that party) from elsewhere; he imagines her looking at the curtain, which still hasn't been raised, and looking at her husband from elsewhere, from a shapeless place dimly visible in her large, calm eyes. But how, wonders B, could that woman possibly have calm eyes? There is no answer.

Days of 1978

One night, however, the answer presents itself, though it is not the answer that B was expecting. Over dinner with a Chilean couple, B discovers that U has been interned in a psychiatric hospital after having tried to kill his wife.

Perhaps B has had too much to drink that night. Perhaps the Chilean couple's version of the events is grossly exaggerated. In any case B listens to the story of U's misfortunes with considerable pleasure, which imperceptibly gives way to a feeling of triumph, an irrational, small-minded triumph, hailed by all the shadows of his bitterness and disenchantment. He imagines U running down a vaguely Chilean, vaguely Latin American street, howling or shouting, while smoke begins to emerge steadily from the buildings on either side, although at no point can any flames be seen.

From then on, whenever B sees the Chilean couple, he makes a point of asking about U and that is how he discovers, little by little, as if the news were being served up to him once a fortnight or once a month for his secret delectation, that U has left the psychiatric hospital, that U is out of work, that U's wife has not left him (which strikes B as truly heroic on her part), that sometimes U and his wife talk about returning to Chile. Naturally, the Chilean couple find the idea of returning to Chile attractive. B finds it horrific. But wasn't U a revolutionary? he asks. Wasn't U a member of the MIR?

Although he doesn't say so, B feels sorry for U's wife. How could a woman like her fall in love with a guy like that? At some point he even imagines them making love. U is tall and blond and his arms are strong. If we had fought that night, he thinks, I would have lost. U's wife is slim; she has narrow hips and black hair. What colour are her eyes? B wonders. Green. Very pretty eyes. Sometimes it infuriates B to think of U and his wife, and if only he could, he would forget them for ever (after all, he has only seen them once!), but the image of the couple against the background of that awful party has a mysterious purchase on his memory, as if it held some meaning for him, an important meaning, but one that B, though he keeps coming back to it, cannot decipher.

One night as he is walking down the Ramblas, he happens to run into his Chilean friends. They are with U and his wife. U's wife smiles and greets him in what could be described as an effusive manner. U, by contrast, barely says a word to him. For a moment B thinks that U is pretending to be shy or distracted. Yet nothing in his behaviour indicates the slightest hostility. In fact, it is as if U were seeing him for the first time. Is it an act? Is this disinterest natural or a result of the psychotic episode? U's wife talks about a book she has just bought at one of the newspaper stands in the Ramblas, as if she were trying to attract B's attention. She takes out the book, shows it to him, asks what he thinks of the author. B is obliged to confess that he has not read the author in question. You have to, says U's wife, adding: If you like, when I finish it, I'll lend it to you. B doesn't know what to say. He shrugs his shoulders. He mumbles a non-committal yes.

When they say goodbye, U's wife kisses him on the cheek. U gives him a firm handshake. See you soon, he says.

When they are gone, it strikes B that U is not as tall or as strong as he remembered from the party; in fact he is only slightly taller than B. His wife, by contrast, has grown and taken on a singular radiance in B's imagination. For reasons unrelated to this encounter, B has trouble getting to sleep that night and at some point his insomniac ruminations return to U.

Days of 1978

He imagines him in the Sant Boi psychiatric hospital; he sees him tied to a chair, writhing in fury while doctors (or the shadows of doctors) attach electrodes to his head. Maybe that sort of treatment can make a tall person shorter, he thinks. It all seems absurd. Before falling asleep he realises that he has settled his score with U.

But that is not the end of the story.

And B knows it. He also knows that the story of his relationship with U is not the story of a banal grudge.

The days go by. At first, impelled by a somewhat self-destructive urge, B tries to find U and his wife, and to that end he starts visiting the Chilean exiles he knows in Barcelona far more assiduously than before, and listens to their problems and commentaries on daily life with a mixture of horror and indifference, but U and his wife are never there; no one has seen them, although everyone, of course, has an anecdote to recount or an opinion about their dreadful situation, which can only get worse. After a string of such visits and monologues, B is obliged to conclude that U and his wife are avoiding the company of their compatriots. B's urge to see them wanes and dies, and he goes back to his old ways.

One day, however, he runs into U's wife in the Boquería market. He sees her from a distance. She is with a young woman he doesn't know. They have stopped in front of a stall selling tropical fruit. As he approaches them, B notices that there is something different about U's wife, a new depth to her face. She is not just a pretty woman any more; now she is interesting as well. He says hello to them. U's wife responds rather coldly, as if she didn't recognise him. Which is what B thinks has happened at first, so he proceeds to explain who he is. He reminds her of the last time they saw each other, the book she recommended; he even mentions the ill-fated party at which they first met. U's wife keeps nodding, but it is clear that she is increasingly ill at ease, as if she were wishing she could somehow make him vanish. Although he is disconcerted, and knows deep down that the best thing to do would be to say goodbye immediately and go, he stays. What he is really waiting for is something – a signal, a word – to make it quite clear that his presence is unwelcome. But no such signal is forthcoming. U's wife is simply trying not to see him. Her friend, by contrast, is observing him carefully, and B clings to her gaze as if it were a lifeline. Her name is K and she is Danish, not Chilean. Her Spanish is bad but comprehensible. She hasn't been living in Barcelona for long and hardly knows the city. B offers to show her around. K accepts.

So that night B meets the Danish woman and they walk around the Gothic quarter (Why am I doing this? he wonders, while she is happy and slightly drunk – they have already visited a couple of old taverns), and they talk and K points out the shadows their bodies are throwing on the old walls and the paving stones. These shadows have a life of their own, says K. At first B thinks nothing of her remark. But then he observes his shadow, or perhaps it is hers, and for a moment that elongated silhouette seems to be looking askance at him. It gives him a start. Then all three or four of them are swallowed up by shapeless darkness.

That night he sleeps with K. She is studying anthropology with U's wife and although they are not what you would call close friends (in fact they are only classmates), as dawn begins to break, K starts talking about her, perhaps because she is their only mutual acquaintance. B can't make much sense of what she says; it is full of commonplaces. U's wife is a good person, always ready to do you a favour, a bright student (What does that mean? wonders B, who has never been to university), although — and this she states without any evidence, relying solely on her female intuition — she has lots of problems. What kind of problems? asks B. I don't know, says K, all sorts.

The days go by. B has stopped visiting Barcelona's Chilean exiles in the hope of finding U and his wife. Every two or three days he sees K and they make love, but they don't talk about U's wife, or if, occasionally, K mentions her, B pretends not to notice or listens in a deliberately distant, indifferent manner, trying to be objective (and succeeding without too much effort), as if K were talking about social anthropology or the little mermaid of Copenhagen. He returns to his old routines, that is, to his own madness or his own boredom. His relationship with K involves no socialising, so he is spared any unwelcome or chance encounters.

One day, long after his last visit, he happens to drop in on his friends the Chilean couple.

B is not expecting them to have company. B is expecting to have dinner with them, so he comes bearing a bottle of wine. But on arrival he finds the house virtually overrun. His friends are at home, but there is also another Chilean woman, about fifty years old, a tarot reader by trade, and a pale, surly girl, about seventeen, who has a reputation (undeserved, as it will turn out) among the exiled Chileans as something of a prodigy (she is the daughter of a union leader killed under the dictatorship), along with her boyfriend, a Catalan Communist Party official at least twenty years older than she is, together with U's wife, who has been crying, to judge from her eyes and the colour of her cheeks, while in the living room, apparently oblivious to what is going on around him, U sits in an armchair.

B's first impulse is to take his bottle of wine and leave immediately. But he reconsiders, and although he is unable to come up with a single good reason to stay, he does.

The atmosphere at his friends' house is funereal. The mood and the observable activity suggest a secret meeting, but not just one inclusive affair, rather a series of mini- or splinter-meetings, as if a conversation involving everyone were prohibited by an unstated but universally respected rule. The tarot reader and the hostess shut themselves in the host's study. The pale girl, the host, and U's wife shut themselves in the kitchen. The pale girl's boyfriend and the hostess shut themselves in the bedroom. U's wife and the pale girl shut themselves in the bathroom. The tarot reader and the host shut themselves in the corridor, which is no mean feat. With all the coming and going, B even finds himself shut in the guest room with the hostess and the pale girl, listening through the wall to the high-pitched voice of the tarot reader addressing or solemnly admonishing U's wife, the pair having shut themselves in the rear courtyard.

Meanwhile, the only person to remain quite still, as if the agitation had nothing to do with him or were taking place in a world of illusions is U in his armchair in the living room. Which is where B goes after being subjected to a flood of vague if not contradictory reports, from which only one thing emerges clearly: that U tried to kill himself that morning.

In the living room, U greets him with an expression that could hardly be called friendly, but is not aggressive. B sits down in an armchair opposite U. For a while, they both remain silent, looking at the floor or watching the others come and go, until B realises that U has the television on, with no sound, and seems to be interested in the programme.

Nothing in U's face indicates suicidal tendencies, thinks B. On the contrary, there are signs of what could reasonably be interpreted as a new calm, new to B in any case. When he thinks of U, he sees his face as it was at the party: flushed, caught between fear and malice; or the day they met in the Ramblas: an expressionless mask (although it is hardly more expressive now) behind which lurked monsters of fear and malice. The new face has a freshly washed look. As if U had spent hours or maybe days submerged in the waters of a strongly flowing river. Were it not for the soundless television and U's dry eyes carefully following every movement on the screen (while the house is alive with the whispers of the Chileans, engaged in pointless discussions about the possibility of having him committed to Sant Boi again) B might not feel that something extraordinary is going on.

And then what appears at first to be an insignificant movement begins (or rather emerges), a kind of ebbing or backwash: without budging from his armchair, B watches as all the guests (who up to a moment before were conferring or confabulating in little groups) file towards the hosts' bedroom, all except the pale girl, the daughter of the assassinated union leader, who comes into the living room (is it rebellion or boredom, he wonders, or is she just keeping an eye on us?) and sits herself down on a chair not far from the armchair in which U is ensconced, watching television. The bedroom door closes. The muffled sounds cease.

This might be a good moment to leave, thinks B. But

instead he opens the bottle and offers them a glass of wine, which the pale girl accepts without batting an eyelid, as does U, although he seems unwilling or unable to drink and takes only a sip, as if not to offend B. And as they drink, or pretend to drink, the pale girl starts talking, telling them about the last film she saw; it was awful, she says, and then she asks them if they have seen anything good, anything they could recommend. The question is, in fact, rhetorical. By posing it the pale girl is tacitly establishing a hierarchy in which she occupies a position of supremacy. Yet she observes a certain queenly decorum, for the question also implies a disposition (on her part, but also on the part of a higher agency, moved by its own sovereign will) to grant both B and U places in the hierarchy, which is a clear indication of her desire to be inclusive, even in circumstances such as these.

U opens his mouth for the first time and says it's a long while since he went to the cinema. To B's surprise, his voice sounds perfectly normal. A well-modulated voice, with a tone that betrays a certain sadness, a Chilean, bottom-heavy tone, which the pale girl does not find unpleasant, nor would the people shut in the bedroom, were they there to hear it. Not even B finds it unpleasant, although for him that tone of voice has strange associations: it conjures up a silent black-and-white film in which, all of a sudden, the characters start shouting incomprehensibly at the top of their voices, while a red line appears in the middle of the screen and begins to widen and spread. This vision, or premonition, perhaps, makes B so nervous that in spite of himself he opens his mouth and says he has seen a film recently and it was a very good film.

And straight away (though what he would really like to do

is extract himself from that armchair, and put the room, the house, and that part of town behind him) he begins to tell the story of the film. He speaks to the pale girl, who listens with an expression of disgust and interest on her face (as if disgust and interest were inextricable), but he is really talking to U, or that, at least, is what he believes as he rushes through his summary.

The film is scored into his memory. Even today he can remember it in detail. At the time he had just seen it, so his account must have been vivid if not elegant. The film tells the story of a monk who paints icons in medieval Russia. B's words conjure up feudal lords, Orthodox priests, peasants, burnt churches, envy and ignorance, festivals and a river at night, doubt and time, the certainty of art and the irreparable spilling of blood. Three characters emerge as central, if not in the film itself, in the version of this Russian film recounted by a Chilean in the house of his Chilean friends, sitting opposite a frustrated Chilean suicide, one beautiful spring evening in Barcelona: the first of these characters is the monk and painter, who unintentionally brings about the arrest, by soldiers, of the second character, a satirical poet, a goliard, a medieval beatnik, poor and half-educated, a fool, a sort of Villon wandering the vast steppes of Russia; the third character is a boy, the son of a bell caster, who, after an epidemic, claims to have inherited the secrets of his father's difficult art. The monk represents the Artist wholly devoted to his art. The wandering poet is a Fool, with all the fragility and pain of the world written on his face. The adolescent caster of bells is Rimbaud, in other words the Orphan.

The ending of the film, drawn out like a birth, shows the process of casting the bell. The feudal lord wants a new bell, but a plague has decimated the population and the old caster has died. The lord's men go looking for him but all they find is a house in ruins and the sole survivor, the caster's adolescent son. He tries to convince them that he knows how to cast a bell. The lord's henchmen are dubious at first, but finally take him with them, having warned that he will pay with his life if there is anything wrong with the bell.

From time to time, the monk, who has renounced painting and sworn a vow of silence, walks through the countryside, past the place where workers are building a mould for the bell. Sometimes the boy makes fun of him (as he makes fun of everything). He taunts the monk by asking him questions and laughs at him. Outside the city walls, as the construction of the mould progresses, a kind of festival springs up in the shadow of the scaffolding. One afternoon, as he is walking past with some other monks, the former painter stops to listen to a poet, who turns out to be the beatnik, the one he unwittingly sent to prison many years ago. The poet recognises the monk and confronts him with his past action, tells him, in brutal, childish language, about the hardships he had to bear, how close he came to dying, day after day. Faithful to his vow of silence, the monk does not reply, although by the way he gazes at the poet you can tell he is taking responsibility for it all, including what was not his fault, and asking forgiveness. The people look at the poet and the monk and are completely bewildered, but they ask the poet to go on telling them stories, to leave the monk alone, and make them laugh again. The poet is crying, but when he turns back to his audience he recovers his spirits.

And so the days go by. Sometimes the feudal lord and his nobles visit the makeshift foundry to see how work on the

Days of 1978

bell is progressing. They do not talk to the boy, but to one of the lord's henchmen, who serves as intermediary. The monk keeps walking past, watching the work with growing interest. He doesn't know himself why he is so interested. Meanwhile, the tradesmen who are working under the boy's orders are worried about their young master. They make sure he eats. They joke with him. Over the weeks they have become fond of him. And finally the big day arrives. They hoist up the bell. Everyone gathers around the wooden scaffolding from which the bell hangs to hear it ring for the first time. Everyone has come out of the walled city: the feudal lord and his nobles and even a young Italian ambassador, for whom the Russians are barbarians. Everyone is waiting. Lost in the multitude, the monk is waiting too. They ring the bell. The chime is perfect. The bell does not break, nor does the sound die away. Everyone congratulates the feudal lord, including the Italian.

The celebrations begin. When they are over, in what had seemed a fairground and is now a wasteland scattered with debris, only two people remain beside the abandoned foundry: the boy and the monk. The boy is sitting on the ground crying his eyes out. The monk is standing beside him, watching. The boy looks at the monk and says that his father, drunken pig that he was, never taught him the art of casting bells and would have taken his secrets to the grave; he taught himself, by watching. And he goes on crying. Then the monk crouches down and, breaking what was to be a lifelong vow of silence, says, Come with me to the monastery. I'll start painting again and you can make bells for the churches. Don't cry.

And that is where the film ends.

When B stops talking, U is crying.

The pale girl is sitting on her chair looking at something out the window, perhaps just the night. Sounds like a good film, she says, and keeps looking at something that B can't see. U drinks his glass of wine in a single gulp and smiles at the pale girl, then at B, and hides his head in his hands. Silently, the pale girl gets up, leaves the room, and comes back with U's wife and the hostess. U's wife kneels down beside him and strokes his hair. The host and the tarot reader appear in the corridor and stand there in silence, until the tarot reader sees the bottle of wine left on the table and goes to pour herself a glass.

This has the effect of a starting gun. They all proceed to help themselves to the wine. The tarot reader proposes a toast. The host proposes a toast. The pale girl proposes a toast. When B goes to refill his glass there is no wine left. Goodbye, he says to his hosts. And off he goes.

It is only when he reaches the entrance hall (the dark entrance hall and the street awaiting him beyond) that he realises he didn't recount the film for U's benefit but for his own.

This is where the story should end, but life is not as kind as literature.

B does not see U or his wife again. In fact, B no longer needs U or the radiant ghost he used to imagine when he thought of U's life in ruins. One day, however, he hears of U's trip to Paris to visit an old friend from the MIR. U travels with another Chilean. They take a train. Shortly before arriving in Paris, U gets up, leaves the compartment without saying anything, and doesn't come back. His friend wakes up as the train begins to move again. He looks for U but can't find him. After talking to the ticket inspector he concludes that U has got off at the station they have just left. At the same moment, in the early hours of the morning, the telephone rings in U's house. By the time his wife has woken up, got out of bed, and walked to the living room, the phone has stopped ringing. Shortly afterwards, the telephone rings in the house of a friend, who does pick up the receiver in time and is able to speak to U. U says that he is in some French village, that he was going to Paris, but suddenly, inexplicably, changed his mind, and is now on his way back to Barcelona. The friend asks him if he has enough money. U replies in the affirmative. According to the friend, U seems calm and even relieved to have made this decision. So the train in which U was travelling continues on its way north to Paris, while U starts walking through the village, southwards, as if he had fallen asleep and set off sleepwalking back to Barcelona.

He makes no more telephone calls.

Beside the village there is a wood. At some point during the night U leaves the path and enters the wood. The next day a farmer finds him: he has hanged himself from a tree with his own belt, not as simple a task as it might seem at first. The gendarmes find U's passport and his other papers, his driver's licence and social security card, scattered far from the corpse, as if U had thrown them away as he walked through the wood, or tried to hide them.

Vagabond in France and Belgium

B has crossed the border into France. In five months of wandering he will spend all the money he has. Ritual sacrifice, gratuitous act, boredom. Sometimes he takes notes, but as a rule he limits himself to reading. What does he read? Detective novels in French, a language he hardly understands, which makes the novels more interesting. Even so, before the last page he always guesses who the murderer is. France is not as dangerous as Spain and B needs to feel that he is in a low-danger zone. B has crossed the border with money to spend because he has received an advance from his publisher and, after putting sixty per cent of the sum in his son's bank account, he has gone to France because he likes France. Simple as that. He took the train from Barcelona to Perpignan, spent half an hour walking around Perpignan station, until he felt he had understood what there was to understand; he ate in a restaurant in the city, saw an English film at a cinema, and then, as night was falling, took another train, direct to Paris.

In Paris, B stays in a little hotel in the rue Saint-Jacques. The first day he visits the Luxembourg Gardens, sits on a park bench and reads, then goes back to the rue Saint-Jacques, finds a cheap restaurant and eats there.

The second day, after finishing a novel in which the killer

lives in an old people's home (which resembles the world beyond Lewis Carroll's looking glass), he sets off in search of second-hand bookshops and finds one in the rue du Vieux-Colombier, where he discovers an old copy of the magazine *Luna Park*, number 2, a special issue on writing and graphics, with texts or drawings (the texts are drawings and vice versa) by Roberto Altmann, Frédéric Baal, Roland Barthes, Jacques Calonne, Carlfriedrich Claus, Mirtha Dermisache, Christian Dotremont, Pierre Guyotat, Brion Gysin, Henri Lefebvre and Sophie Podolski.

The magazine, edited by Marc Dachy, which comes out or used to come out three times a year, was published in Brussels by TRANSédITION, and has or had its registered office at number 59, rue Henry van Zuylen. At one time Roberto Altmann was a famous artist. Who remembers Roberto Altmann now? wonders B. The same goes for Carlfriedrich Claus. Pierre Guyotat was a notable author. But there is a difference between notable and memorable. In fact, B once thought he wanted to be like Guyotat, in days gone by, when as a young man he was reading Guyotat's work. That bald, massive individual, Pierre Guyotat, ready to take on all comers and eat them alive in the darkness of a mansard room. He doesn't know who Mirtha Dermisache was, but her name rings a bell: possibly a beautiful woman, and almost certainly elegant. Sophie Podolski was a poet whom he and his friend L admired (adored even) back in Mexico, when they were little more than twenty years old. Roland Barthes, well, everyone knows who he is. B has seen Dotremont's name somewhere else, perhaps he once read some of his poems, in a forgotten anthology. Brion Gysin was a friend of Burroughs, the one who gave him the idea for his cutups. And that leaves Henri

Lefebvre. The name means nothing to B. And suddenly, in the second-hand bookshop, that name, the only one that means nothing to B, lights up like a match struck in a dark room. Or that is how it feels to B. He would have preferred it to light up like a lamp. And in a cave rather than a dark room, but the fact is that Lefebvre, the name Lefebvre, flares briefly like a match.

So B buys the magazine and loses himself in the streets of Paris, where he has gone precisely to lose himself, to watch the days slip away, and although he'd been imagining the lost days as sunny, as he walks along with the issue of *Luna Park* in a plastic bag dangling lazily from his hand, that sunny image is cast into shade, as if the old magazine (which is beautifully produced, by the way, and in almost perfect condition in spite of the years and the dust that builds up in second-hand bookshops) had triggered or provoked an eclipse. The eclipse, as B knows, is Henri Lefebvre. It is Henri Lefebvre's relationship with literature. Or more precisely: his relationship with *writing*.

After walking aimlessly for many hours, B arrives at his hotel. He feels well. He is relaxed and feels like reading. Earlier, on a bench in the square Louis XVI, he tried to decipher Lefebvre's graphic script. A difficult undertaking. Lefebvre draws his words as if the letters were blades of grass. The words seem to be shifting in the wind, an easterly wind; a field, grass of uneven height, a cone unravelling. As he watches the words (because the first thing he has to do is to *watch* them) B remembers — as if he were seeing it all on a cinema screen — faraway fields in the southern hemisphere where his adolescent self is searching desultorily for a four-leafed clover. Then it occurs to him that this memory may actually come from a film and not his real life. The real life of Henri Lefebvre, it seems, was touchingly simple: he was born in Masnuy Saint-Jean in 1925. He died in Brussels in 1973. In other words he died in the year of the military coup in Chile. B tries to remember the year 1973. It is no use. He has walked too far and although he feels relaxed, in fact he is tired, and what he needs is food or sleep. But B can't sleep so he goes out to eat. He gets dressed (he is naked though he can't remember taking off his clothes), combs his hair, and goes down to the street. He eats in a restaurant in the rue des Écoles.

At the next table is a woman who is also eating on her own. They smile at each other and leave the restaurant together. He invites her up to his room. The woman accepts spontaneously. They talk and B observes her as if through a curtain. Although he is listening carefully, he cannot understand much. The woman refers to unrelated events: children playing on swings in a park, an old woman knitting, moving clouds, the silence that reigns, so the physicists tell us, in outer space. A world without noises, she says, in which even death is silent. At some point, just to keep the conversation going, B asks her what her job is, and she replies that she is a prostitute. Ah, good, says B. But just for something to say. In fact he doesn't mind one way or the other. When the woman finally falls asleep, he looks for *Luna Park*, which is lying on the floor, almost under the bed. He reads that Henri Lefebvre, who was born in 1925 and died in 1973, spent his childhood and adolescence in the country. In the deep green fields of Belgium. Then his father died. His mother, Julia Nys, remarried when he was eighteen. His stepfather, a jovial fellow, used to call him Van Gogh. Not because he liked Van Gogh, of course, but to make fun of his stepson. Lefebvre moved out to live on his own. But he soon came back to his mother's house and there he stayed until she died in June 1973.

Two or three days after the death of his mother, Henri's body was found beside his desk. Cause of death: a massive overdose of prescribed drugs. B gets out of bed, opens the window and looks at the street. After Lefebvre's death, fifteen kilos of manuscripts and drawings were discovered. 'Very few publishable texts,' says the brief note on the author. In fact, the only thing that Lefebvre published in his lifetime was a critical essay entitled 'Phases de la poésie d'André du Bouchet', under the pseudonym Henri Demasnuy, in *Synthèses*, number 190, March 1962. B imagines Lefebvre in his home town of Masnuy Saint-Jean. He imagines him at the age of sixteen, looking at a German army truck, in which there are only two German soldiers, smoking and reading letters. Henri Demasnuy, Henri of Masnuy. When he turns around, the woman is leafing through the magazine. I have to go, she says, without looking at him, still flicking the pages. You can stay here, says B, knowing it's not likely. The woman says neither yes nor no, but after a while she stands up and starts getting dressed.

B spends the following days wandering around the streets of Paris. Sometimes he comes to the entrance of a museum, but he never goes in. Sometimes he comes to a cinema and stands there examining the photos at length, then walks on. He buys books, which he browses through but never reads to the end. He eats in a different restaurant every time and lingers after his meals, as if he were not in Paris but out in the country and had nothing better to do than smoke and drink camomile tea.

Vagabond in France and Belgium

One morning, after a couple of hours' sleep, B takes a train to Brussels. He has a friend there, a black girl, the daughter of a Chilean exile and a Ugandan woman, but he can't bring himself to ring her. He walks around central Brussels for hours and then into the northern suburbs until he finds a little hotel in a street where there is virtually nothing else. Next to it is a fenced-off vacant lot where grass and garbage are thriving. Opposite is a row of mostly unoccupied houses that look as if they have been bombed. Some have broken windows and shutters hanging precariously as if the wind had unhinged them, but there is practically no wind in this street, thinks B, looking out of the window of his room. He also thinks: I should hire a car. And: I don't know how to drive. The next day he goes to see his friend. Her name is M and she is living on her own now. He finds her at home, wearing jeans and a T-shirt. She is barefoot. When she sees him, for the first few seconds she can't remember who he is. She speaks to him in French and looks at him as if she knows that he is going to do her harm, but doesn't care.

After a moment's hesitation, B says his name. He speaks in Spanish. I'm B, he says. Then M remembers him and smiles, though not because she is particularly happy to see him; it is more that B's sudden appearance, something she hadn't even considered as a possibility, comes as an amusing if perplexing surprise. In any case, she invites him in and offers him a drink. They talk for a while, seated opposite each other. B asks about her mother (her father died a while ago), her studies, her life in Belgium. M replies obliquely and asks about B's health, his books, his life in Spain.

Finally they run out of things to say and sit there in silence. Silence suits M. She is tall, slim, and about twenty-five. Her eyes are green, the same colour as her father's. Even the rings under her eyes, which are very pronounced, remind B of the exiled Chilean he met many years ago (he can't remember how many years, nor does it matter) when M was a little girl, about two, and her parents (her mother was studying politics, though she didn't finish the degree) were travelling through France and Spain on a shoestring, staying with friends.

For a moment he imagines the three of them, M's father, her mother, and M at the age of two or three, with her green eyes, surrounded by precarious suspension bridges. Her father was never really a close friend of mine, thinks B. There were never really any bridges, not even precarious ones.

Before leaving, he gives her the name and the telephone number of his hotel. When night comes he walks through the centre of Brussels in search of a woman, but all he can see are ghostly figures; it's as if the bureaucrats and bank clerks had all worked late and were just leaving their offices. When he returns to his hotel he has to wait a long time before someone comes to the door. The porter is a haggard young man. B gives him a tip and climbs the dark staircase to his room.

The next morning he is woken by a phone call from M. She invites him to breakfast. Where? asks B. Wherever, says M. I'll come and pick you up and then we can go somewhere. As he is getting dressed, B thinks of Julia Nys, Lefebvre's mother, who illustrated some of her son's last texts. They lived here, he thinks, in Brussels, in a house somewhere in this part of the city. A gust of wind is blowing in his memory, blurring the houses he has seen. After shaving, B looks out of the window at the façades of the neighbouring houses. Everything is the same as yesterday. A middle-aged woman, perhaps only a few years older than B, is walking down the street, dragging an empty shopping trolley. A few yards in front of her, a dog has stopped, with his muzzle raised and his eyes, like slots in a money box, fixed on one of the hotel's windows, perhaps the one from which B is looking out. Everything is the same as yesterday, thinks B as he puts on a white shirt, a black jacket, and a pair of black trousers. Then he goes downstairs to wait for M in the lobby.

What do you make of this? B asks M, once they are in the car, showing her Lefebvre's pages in *Luna Park*. It looks like bunches of grapes, says M. Can you read the writing? No, says M. Then she looks at Lefebvre's scribbles again and says that maybe he is talking about existence . . . maybe. But in fact she is the one who talks about existence that morning. She says her life is one error after another; she tells him that she has been very ill (what with, she doesn't say) and describes a trip to New York that sounds more like a descent into hell. M's Spanish is larded with French and her face remains expressionless throughout the monologue, except when she allows herself a smile to underline the farcical nature of this or that situation, as she sees it, although nothing, thinks B, could be further from farce.

They have breakfast together in a café on the rue de l'Orient, near the church of Notre-Dame l'Immaculée, a church M seems to know well, as if she had recently converted to Catholicism. Then she says she's going to take him to the Natural History Museum, next to Leopold Park and the European Parliament, a location that strikes B as paradoxical – though he can't say why when pressed to explain – but first, M informs him, she has to go home and get changed. B has no desire to visit a museum of any sort. And he can't see why M needs to change her clothes. He says so. M bursts out laughing. I look like a junkie, she says.

While M gets changed, B sits in an armchair and starts leafing through *Luna Park*, but soon he gets bored, as if *Luna Park* and M's small flat were incompatible, so he gets up and starts looking at the photos and pictures on the wall, and then the single, sparsely laden bookshelf and the few Spanish books on it, among which he recognises the works of M's father, which M, in all likelihood, has never read: political essays, a history of the coup, a book about the Mapuche communities, and B smiles, taken aback, feeling a slight twinge of emotion, though what it is he doesn't know, tenderness perhaps or disgust or simply a warning that something is wrong. Then suddenly M appears in the room, or rather she walks across it from her bedroom to what must be the bathroom door, unless it's the laundry where her clothes are hanging, and B watches her cross the room half naked or half clothed, a sight which along with her dead father's old books seems to constitute a sign. A sign of what? He doesn't know. An ominous sign, in any case.

   When they leave the flat M is wearing a dark, close-fitting, knee-length skirt, a white shirt with the top buttons undone, showing some cleavage, and high-heeled shoes that make her at least two centimetres taller than B. As they head towards the museum, M talks about her mother and points to a building, which they pass without stopping. B doesn't understand until the building is five blocks behind them: M's mother, the widow of the exiled Chilean, lives there, in one of the flats. Instead of asking about her, as he would like to, he says he really doesn't feel like visiting a museum, and especially not some awful Natural History Museum, of all things. But his feeble resistance is no match for M, who has suddenly become energetic while retaining a certain frosty air, and he lets himself be dragged along.

Another surprise is waiting for him. When they reach the museum, M pays for the tickets, then sits down to wait for him in the café with a newspaper and a cappuccino, her legs crossed in a pose that is at once elegant and solitary, and the sight makes B (who has turned back to look at her) feel old, in a rather abstract way. Then B walks from room to room until he comes to one in which he finds several curvilinear machines. What is going to happen to M? he wonders as he sits down, resting his hands on his knees, with a slight twinge of pain in his chest. He feels like a cigarette, but smoking is prohibited. The pain grows stronger. B shuts his eyes but can still see the silhouettes of the machines, persisting like the pain in his chest, although perhaps they are not machines but bewildering figures, the human race suffering and laughing as it marches towards the void.

When he returns to the museum café M is still sitting there with her legs crossed, underlining something in the newspaper with a silver ballpoint pen, probably an ad for a job. As soon as B appears she discreetly folds the paper away. They eat at a restaurant in the rue des Béguines. M hardly touches her food. She hardly talks either, and when she does, it is to suggest they visit the cemetery together. I often come down this way, she says. B looks at her and makes it clear that he has no desire at all to visit a cemetery. On the way out of the restaurant, however, he asks where the cemetery is. M does not reply. They get into the car and less than three minutes later her hand (a slender and elegant hand, thinks B) is pointing out Du Karreveld castle, Molenbeek cemetery, and a sports complex with tennis courts. B laughs. M's face, by contrast, remains hieratic and impassive. But underneath, thinks B, she is laughing too.

What are you going to do tonight? she asks as she drops him off at his hotel. I don't know, says B, read maybe. For a moment B thinks that M has something to say to him, but she says nothing. That night B does in fact lie down and try to read one of the novels he didn't leave behind in Paris, but after a few pages he gives up and tosses it to the floor. He leaves the hotel. After walking aimlessly for a long time he comes to a part of the city in which there are many coloured people. That is what he thinks, that is how he articulates his thought as he sees himself walking through those streets. He has never liked the expression 'coloured people'. So why did that form of words cross his mind? Black people, Asians, North Africans, yes, but not coloured people, he thinks. Soon after, he goes into a topless bar. He orders camomile tea. The waitress looks at him and laughs. She is pretty, about thirty years old, tall and blonde. B laughs too. I'm not well, he says, still laughing. The waitress makes his camomile tea. B spends the night with a black girl who talks in her sleep. Her voice, which B remembers as soft and musical, has become hoarse and querulous, as if at some point during the night, unbeknownst to B, her vocal cords had undergone a transformation. It is, in fact, her voice that wakes him, with the effect of a hammer blow, and then, once he is over the shock, he lies there propped up on one elbow listening for a while, until he decides to wake her up. What were you dreaming about? he asks her. The girl replies that she was dreaming about her mother, who died not long ago. The dead are at peace, thinks B, stretching out in the bed. As if she had read his mind, the girl says that no one who has passed through this world is at peace. Not any more, not ever, she says with total conviction. B feels like crying, but instead he falls asleep. When he wakes up the following morning, he is alone. He does not have breakfast. He stays in his room reading until the cleaning lady asks if she can make the bed. While he is waiting in the lobby, M rings for him. She asks him what he is planning to do. Before he knows it, M has arranged to come and pick him up.

That day, they visit another museum, as B suspected they might, and then they eat at a restaurant next to a park in which a crowd of children and adolescents are skating. How long are you going to stay here? asks M. B says he is thinking of leaving the next day. And going to Masnuy Saint-Jean, he adds, anticipating M's question. M has no idea what part of Belgium the village is in. Nor do I, says B. If it isn't too far I could take you in my car, says M. Do you have friends there? B replies in the negative. When they finally go their separate ways outside the hotel, B walks around the district until he finds a pharmacy. He buys condoms. Then he heads towards the topless bar where he went the night before, but although he searches street after street (and gets lost several times in the process) he cannot find it. The next day he has breakfast with M in a roadside restaurant. M tells him that sometimes when she is sad she gets into her car and drives, without having a clear idea where she is going, just for the pleasure of being on the move. Once, she says, I got to Bremen and I didn't know where I was. All I knew was that I was in Germany, that I had left Brussels that morning and now it was night. And what did you do? asks B, who can guess the answer. I turned around and came back, says M.

In Masnuy Saint-Jean they see cows. Trees. Fallow fields. A pre-fab shed. Three-storey houses. At B's request, M asks an old woman who is selling vegetables and postcards how to get to Julia Nys's house. The old woman shrugs her shoulders, but then starts laughing and launches into a long speech, which B can hear from the car. M and the old woman are both gesturing, as if they were talking about the rain or the weather, thinks B. The house is in the rue Colombier; it has a sizeable, neglected garden and a shed that has been turned into a garage. The walls of the house are yellow and the windowless left half is shaded by a large tree that has not been pruned for a long time. She was mad, that old bat, says M, it could be this house or any other house in the village. B rings the doorbell. Which sounds like a real bell with a clapper. After a while a girl appears, wearing jeans, with wet hair; she's about fifteen. M asks her if this is the house where Julia Nys and her son Henri used to live. The girl says Monsieur and Madame Marteau live here. Since when? asks B. Since always, says the girl. Were you washing your hair? asks M. I was dyeing it, says the girl. A short conversation follows, which B does not understand, and yet, for a moment, M with her high heels on one side of the fence and the girl in her tight jeans on the other seem to be the principal figures in a painting, which initially gives an impression of peace and balance, but then strikes him as deeply disturbing. Later, after exploring the village from north to south and south to north, they go into what seems to be the library. Is this where Henri of Masnuy came to read? It can't be. The library is new and Lefebvre must have frequented the old one, the one that was here before the war. There must have been at least two libraries between Henri's and this one, says M, who is better acquainted with her country's public institutions. For lunch, B has a steak and M a salad, half of which she leaves. I wasn't even born when your friend died, says M nostalgically. He wasn't my friend, says B. But *you* were alive, says M, with a gently mocking smile. I was travelling when he died, says B.

Later, when all the other customers have left the restaurant, and they are alone at their table by the window, M reads *Luna Park* 2 and stops at the last page, which announces the forthcoming contributions for *Luna Park* 3 or *Luna Park* 4, if the fourth number ever saw the light of day. She reads out the list of future contributors: Jean-Jacques Abrahams, Pierrette Berthoud, Sylvano Bussotti, William Burroughs, John Cage, and so on up to Julia Nys, Henri Lefebvre and Sophie Podolski. An all-star cast, says M with a mocking smile.

They're all dead, thinks B.

And then: What a pity M doesn't smile more often.

You have a beautiful smile, he says. She looks him in the eyes. Are you trying to seduce me? No, no, God forbid, murmurs B.

Late in the afternoon they leave the restaurant and go back to the car. Where to? asks M. Brussels, says B. M sits there pensively for a while, then says she doesn't think it's a good idea. All the same, she switches on the ignition. There's nothing more for me to do here, says B. This sentence will pursue him throughout the return journey like the headlights of a phantom car.

When they arrive in Brussels B wants to go back to his hotel. M thinks it's ridiculous to waste money on a couple of hours in a hotel when she has a sofa bed he can use. They sit talking in the car outside M's flat for a while. Finally B accepts her offer to put him up for the night. He is planning to leave very early the next day to catch the first train to Paris. They have dinner at a vegetarian restaurant run by a couple of Brazilians, which is open till three in the morning. Once again they are the last customers to leave the premises.

Over dinner M talks about her life. For a moment B is under the impression that she is analysing her life as a whole. But he is mistaken: M talks about her adolescence, her trips to New York and back, her sleepless nights. She doesn't mention boyfriends, or work, or madness. M drinks wine and B smokes one cigarette after another. Sometimes they look away from each other and watch a car go past outside the window. When they get back to M's flat she helps him open out the sofa bed, then goes into her bedroom and shuts the door. Still dressed, B falls asleep reading a novel that seems to be written in the language of another planet. He is woken by M's voice. Like the prostitute the other night, thinks B, the one who talked in her sleep. But before he can muster the willpower to get up, go into M's room, and wake her from her nightmare, he falls asleep again.

The following morning he takes a train to Paris.

He stays at the same hotel in the rue Saint-Jacques, but in a different room, and spends the first few days looking for something by André du Bouchet in the second-hand bookshops. He can't find anything. Like Henri of Masnuy, du Bouchet has disappeared from the map. On the fourth day he does not leave the hotel. He orders meals from room service, but hardly touches them. He finishes reading the last novel he bought and tosses it into the waste-paper basket. He sleeps and has nightmares, but when he wakes up he is sure he has not spoken in his sleep. The next day, after a long shower, he goes for a walk in the Luxembourg Gardens. Then he catches

Vagabond in France and Belgium

the métro and gets off at Pigalle. He eats at a restaurant on the rue La Bruyère and sleeps with a prostitute in a little hotel on the rue de Navarin. Her hair is shaved at the back but very long on top of her head. She tells him she lives on the fourth floor. There is no lift. And it is clear that nobody lives there. It is just a room she uses for work, she and her friends.

While they make love the prostitute tells him jokes. B laughs. In his pidgin French he tries to tell her a joke too, but she doesn't understand. When they are finished, the prostitute goes to the bathroom and asks B if he wants a shower. B says no, he had a shower that morning, but all the same he goes into the bathroom to smoke a cigarette and watch her shower.

He is not surprised (or at least he doesn't let it show) when she takes off her wig and leaves it on the toilet lid. Her head is clean-shaven and he can see two relatively recent scars on her scalp. He lights a cigarette and asks how she got them. But the prostitute is already in the shower and doesn't hear him. B doesn't repeat his question. Nor does he leave the bathroom. On the contrary, he makes himself at home; he lies down on the white tiles, feeling placid and relaxed, contemplating the steam billowing out from behind the shower curtain until he can no longer see the wig, or the toilet, or the cigarette in his hand.

By the time they leave, night has fallen, and after saying goodbye he walks unhurriedly but almost without stopping from the Montmartre cemetery to the Pont Royal, by a vaguely familiar route, via the Gare Saint-Lazare. When he gets back to his hotel he looks at himself in a mirror. He is expecting a hangdog look, but what he sees is a thinnish, middle-aged man, sweating slightly from the walk, who seeks, finds, and flees his own gaze, all in a fraction of a second. The next morning he rings M in Brussels. He is not expecting her to be there. He is not expecting anyone to be there. But someone picks up the phone. It's me, says B. How are you? asks M. Well, says B. Have you found Henri Lefebvre? asks M. She must be still half asleep, thinks B. Then he says no. M laughs. She has a pretty laugh. Why are you so interested in him? she asks, still laughing. Because nobody else is, says B. And because he was good. Straight away he thinks: I shouldn't have said that. And he thinks: M is going to hang up. He clenches his teeth and an involuntary grimace tenses his face. But M doesn't hang up.

Dentist

He wasn't Rimbaud, he was just an Indian boy.

I met him in 1986. That year, for reasons that are neither particularly germane to this story nor, it strikes me now, particularly interesting, I spent a few days in Irapuato, the strawberry capital, where I stayed with a dentist friend who was going through a rough patch. I thought I was in a mess (my girlfriend had recently decided to put an end to our long-term relationship), but when I arrived in Irapuato, intending to take some time out, recover my peace of mind and think about my future, I found my dentist friend, normally so discreet and composed, in a state bordering on desperation.

Ten minutes after I arrived he told me he had killed a patient. Since I didn't see how a dentist could possibly kill anyone, I begged him to calm down and tell me the whole story. The story was simple, in as much as a story of this sort can be, and from his rather disjointed telling of it I deduced that in no way could he be held responsible for anybody's death.

The story also struck me as strange. On top of his day job in a private dental clinic, which provided a more than comfortable living, my friend worked for a kind of medical cooperative for the poor and needy, categories that might appear to be synonymous, but for my friend, and above all for the ideologues who had established the charitable organisation in question, there was, it seems, some kind of difference. Only two dentists had volunteered their services and there was a great deal to do. As the cooperative did not possess a dental surgery, the dentists saw patients at their respective clinics, outside business hours (as my friend put it), mainly at night, when they were assisted by volunteers: dentistry students with a social conscience, keen to refine their skills.

The patient who had died was an old Indian woman who had turned up one night with an abscessed gum. The operation on the abscess had not been performed by my friend but by a student working at his clinic. The woman passed out and the student panicked. Another student rang my friend. When he arrived at the clinic and tried to find out what was going on, he was confronted with a cancerous gum, clumsily incised, and soon realised there was nothing to be done. They sent the woman to the Irapuato General Hospital, where she died a week later.

Such cases were, he told me, quite rare, roughly one in a hundred thousand, and a dentist could reasonably expect never to encounter one in the course of his career. I said I understood, although in fact I didn't understand at all, and that night we went out drinking. As we proceeded from bar to bar (they were more or less middle-class bars) I kept thinking about the old Indian woman and the cancer gnawing at her gums.

My friend told me the story again, with a number of significant changes, which I attributed to the quantity of alcohol we had absorbed by that stage, after which we got into his Volkswagen and went to eat at a cheap restaurant on the outskirts of Irapuato. It was a striking change of scene. Before we had been rubbing shoulders with professional people, public servants, and businessmen, now we were surrounded by labourers, the unemployed, and beggars.

Meanwhile, my friend's melancholy was becoming more pronounced. At midnight he began railing against Cavernas. The painter. A few years before, my friend had bought two of his engravings, which had pride of place on his living room wall. One day, at a party thrown by one of his colleagues, a dentist who lived in the Zona Rosa and, if I remember the story rightly, devoted his talents to repairing the smiles of Mexico's screen idols, my friend had tried to engage the prolific artist, who happened to be present, in conversation.

At first, Cavernas had been willing not only to converse but also to confide, revealing, without any prompting from my friend, certain intimate details of his life. At one point Cavernas proposed they share the favours of a young girl who, inexplicably, seemed to fancy the dentist rather than the painter. My friend made it clear that he didn't give a damn about the girl. He wasn't interested in a threesome; what he wanted was to buy another engraving, directly, without middle men; he didn't mind which one, and the artist could name his price, as long as it was personally dedicated: 'For Pancho, in memory of a wild night' or something along those lines.

From that point on, Cavernas's attitude changed. He started to look askance at me, my friend recalled. What the fuck do dentists know about art? he said. He asked if I was an out-and-out faggot or if it was just a phase I was going through. Naturally it took my friend a while to realise he was being insulted. Before he could react and explain that what he felt for Cavernas was simply the admiration of an art lover for the work of a misunderstood genius, one of the world's truly great painters, the genius had made himself scarce.

It was a while before my friend found him again. As he searched, he rehearsed in his head what he would say. Finally, he spotted the painter on the balcony, with two guys who looked like gangsters. Cavernas saw him coming and said something to his companions. My friend the dentist smiled. Cavernas's companions smiled too. My friend was probably rather more drunk than he realised, or than he cared to remember. In any case the painter greeted him with an insult and the two heavies grabbed him by his arms and his waist and dangled him over the balcony. My friend passed out.

He vaguely remembered Cavernas calling him a faggot again, and the men laughing as they dangled him, cars parked in the sky, a grey sky like the Calle Sevilla. Knowing for certain that he was going to die, and for nothing, or something completely stupid; knowing that his life, the life he was about to lose, had been one long series of stupidities – in other words, nothing. And there was not even any dignity in that certain knowledge.

He told me all this as we drank tequila in that cheap restaurant in one of the poor suburbs of Irapuato, which, needless to say, didn't have a licence to sell alcoholic beverages. Then he launched into an argument whose principal objective was to discredit art. Cavernas's engravings, I knew, were still hanging in my friend's living room and I had no reason to suspect that he had taken any steps to sell them. When I tried to point out that what had happened between him and Cavernas was an incident in his life story, not an episode in art history, so that it might be used to discredit certain persons, but not artists in general and certainly not art itself, my friend hit the roof.

But that's where art comes from, he said: life stories. Art history comes along only much later. That's what art *is*, he said, the story of a life in all its particularity. It's the only thing that really is particular and personal. It's the expression of and, at the same time, the fabric of the particular. And what do you mean by the fabric of the particular? I asked, supposing he would answer: Art. I was also thinking, indulgently, that we were pretty drunk already and that it was time to go home. But my friend said: What I mean is the secret story.

He stared at me for a moment, a gleam in his eye. The death of the Indian woman from gum cancer had obviously affected him more than I had realised at first.

So now you're wondering what I mean by the secret story? asked my friend. Well, the secret story is the one we'll never know, although we're living it from day to day, thinking we're alive, thinking we've got it all under control and the stuff we overlook doesn't matter. But every damn thing matters! It's just that we don't realise. We tell ourselves that art runs on one track and life, our lives, on another, we don't even realise it's a lie.

And what separates one track from the other? he asked me. I must have said something, although I can't remember what; in any case, at that point my friend saw someone he knew, turned away from me and started waving. I remember that the restaurant had been gradually filling up with people. I remember that there were green tiles on the walls, like a public urinal, and that the bar, deserted before, was now thronged with weary, jovial, or sinister-looking characters. I remember a blind man singing a song in the corner of the room or maybe the song was *about* a blind man. A cloud of smoke had accumulated over our heads. Then the object of my friend's attention approached our table.

He can't have been more than sixteen years old. He looked younger. He was rather short, and could have been strongly built, but he was filling out and losing definition. His clothes were cheap, yet there was something vaguely incongruent about them, as if they were sending an incomprehensible message from various places at once, and he was wearing a pair of worn-out tennis shoes, shoes that my friends and I, or rather the children of some of my friends, would have laid to rest long ago in a wardrobe or dispatched to the rubbish dump.

He sat down at our table and my friend told him to order whatever he liked. It was then that he smiled for the first time. It wasn't what you would call a pleasant smile; on the contrary, it was wary and suspicious, the smile of someone who expects little from others and all of it bad. Then, as the boy sat down with us and exhibited his wintry smile, it occurred to me that perhaps my friend, a confirmed bachelor who could have chosen to live in Mexico City years ago but had preferred to stay in his home town, Irapuato, had become, or had always been, a homosexual, and that for some obscure reason this fact, kept secret for years, had emerged in the course of our conversation that night about the Indian woman and her cancerous gum. But I soon discarded this idea and concentrated on the newcomer, or perhaps what happened was that his eyes, which I hadn't noticed until then, compelled me to put aside my fears (since in those days, even the remote possibility that my friend might be homosexual frightened me) and turn my full attention to the boy, who seemed to be suspended between adolescence and an appalling childhood.

His eyes were — I don't know how else to put it — forceful. That was the adjective that occurred to me at the time, and clearly it fell far short of capturing the palpable effect they had on the air, the impression they made when you met his gaze, like an ache between the eyebrows — but I still can't come up with a better word. Though his body, as I said, was filling out towards the ampler forms of years to come, his eyes were all sharpness, sharpness in movement.

My friend introduced him with undisguised pleasure. His name was José Ramírez. I held out my hand (I don't know why; I'm not normally so formal, at least not in bars, at night) and he hesitated for a moment. His handshake took me completely by surprise. His right hand, which I had expected to be smooth and indecisive, like that of a typical adolescent, was so covered in calluses it felt like iron. It was quite a small hand, and now that I think back to that night in the suburbs of Irapuato, the hand I see in my mind's eye is small, a small outstretched hand against a background of darkness and the bar's feeble gleams, a hand emerging from parts unknown, like the tentacle of a storm, but hard as iron, a hand forged in a smithy.

My friend was smiling. For the first time that day I saw a glimmer of happiness in his face, as if the physical presence of José Ramírez (with his round face, sharp eyes and hard hands) had dispelled both his guilt about the Indian woman with her cancerous mouth and the recurrent malaise caused by his memory of the painter Cavernas. As if in reply to a question that elementary good manners forbade me to ask, although I was tempted, my friend said that he had met José Ramírez through his work.

It took me a moment to realise that he was referring to his dental practice. Free treatment, said the boy, with a voice that, like his eyes and hands, was at odds with the rest of his body. At the cooperative, said my friend. Six fillings I did for him: a work of art. José Ramírez nodded and lowered his eyes. It was as if he had reassumed his true identity, that of a sixteen-year-old boy. Later on, I remember, we ordered more drinks and José Ramírez ate a helping of corn tortillas with chilli sauce (he didn't want anything more, although my friend kept saying, Order whatever you like, it's my treat).

Throughout the time we spent in the restaurant, they talked to each other; I didn't join in. Now and then I caught a few words of their conversation; it was about art. My friend had gone back to his story about Cavernas, which for some reason he seemed to be mixing up with the story of the Indian woman dying in a hospital bed, in terrible pain, or perhaps not, perhaps she had been anaesthetised, perhaps someone had given her regular doses of morphine, anyway that was the image I had: the Indian woman, a little bundle abandoned in a hospital bed in Irapuato, Cavernas laughing, and his impeccably framed engravings hanging in the dentist's living room, a room that the young José Ramírez, so I gathered from what my friend was saying, had visited (along with the rest of the house no doubt) and in which he had seen, and appreciated, the engravings, the pride of the dentist's art collection.

Eventually we left that restaurant. My friend paid and led the march towards the exit. He wasn't as drunk as I thought and there was no need to suggest that he let me drive. I vaguely remember some other places, where we didn't stay very long, and finally an enormous vacant lot, on a dirt road running out into the country, where José Ramírez got out of the car and said good night without shaking hands.

I said it seemed funny to drop him off there, with no houses in sight, only darkness and the contours of a hill in the background, dimly lit by the moon. I said we should go with him part of the way. Without turning to look at me, my friend (his hands on the wheel, tired but calm) replied that we couldn't go with him, there was no need to worry, the kid knew the way perfectly well. Then he started the engine, switched the headlights to full beam and, before the car started to reverse, I glimpsed an unreal landscape, in black and white, made up of stunted trees, weeds, a cart trail – a cross between a rubbish dump and an idyllic picture postcard of the Mexican countryside.

The boy had disappeared without a trace.

Back at the dentist's house, I had trouble getting to sleep. In the guest room there was a painting by a local artist: an impressionist landscape in which there seemed to be a city and a valley, rendered almost exclusively in a range of yellow tones. I believe there was something evil in that picture. I remember tossing and turning, exhausted but unable to sleep, while a feeble light from the window spread a rippling fire through the landscape. It was not a good picture. It wasn't the picture that was troubling me, stopping me from getting to sleep, filling me with a vague and irreparable sadness, although I was tempted to get up, take it down and turn it to the wall. I was tempted to go back to Mexico City that night.

The next day I got up late and didn't see my friend until lunchtime. I was alone in the house with the woman who came every day to clean, so I thought it would be best to go out for a walk. Irapuato is not a beautiful city, but there is, undeniably, a charm to its streets and the calm central district, where the locals busy themselves conspicuously with what in Mexico City would be considered mere distractions. Since I had nothing to do, after breakfast in a café (orange juice) I sat down on a bench to read the newspaper, while high school students and public servants strolled past, exercising their talents for leisure and idle chat.

For the first time since I had set out for Irapuato, my troubled love-life back in Mexico City seemed remote. There were even birds in the square where I was sitting. Later on I visited a bookshop (it took a while to find one), where I bought a book with illustrations by Emilio Carranza, a landscape painter born in El Hospital, a village or farming cooperative near Irapuato. I was planning to give it to my friend the dentist; I thought he would like it.

We were to meet at two in the afternoon. I went to his clinic. The secretary politely asked me to wait: at the last minute someone had turned up unannounced, but my friend would be free shortly. I sat down in the waiting room and started reading a magazine. I was alone in the room. The silence in my friend's clinic, indeed in the whole building, was almost absolute. For a moment I thought the secretary had lied to me: my friend wasn't there, something bad had happened and he had rushed off, leaving express instructions not to give me any cause for alarm. I stood up and started to walk back and forth in the waiting room; naturally I felt ridiculous.

The secretary had left the reception desk. I went to pick up the phone and make a call, but it was an absurd reflex, since I

Dentist

didn't know anyone to call in that city. I bitterly regretted having come to Irapuato, cursed my emotional susceptibility, swore that as soon as I got back to Mexico City I would find an intelligent, beautiful, and above all sensible woman, whom I would marry after a brief and drama-free engagement. I sat in the secretary's chair and tried to calm down. For a while I stared at the typewriter, the appointments book, a wooden container full of pencils, paperclips, and erasers, arranged in what seemed to be perfect order, which was incomprehensible to me, since no one in their right mind arranges paperclips (pencils and erasers, yes, but not paperclips), until I noticed my hands trembling over the typewriter keys, which made me jump to my feet and set off resolutely in search of my friend with my heart thumping in my chest.

Even in the grip of a sudden panic attack, manners can sometimes prevail. While opening doors and barging through the clinic, calling out to my friend, I was, I remember, trying to think of a way to explain my behaviour when I found him, if I did. I still don't know what came over me that afternoon. It was probably the last outward manifestation of the anxiety or sadness I had brought with me from Mexico City and was to leave behind in Irapuato.

My friend, of course, was in his consulting room, and I found him with a patient, a distinguished-looking woman of about thirty, and his nurse, a short girl with mestizo features, whom I hadn't seen before. None of them seemed surprised by my sudden appearance. My friend smiled at me and said, I'll be finished in a minute.

Later, when I was trying to explain what I had felt in the waiting room (apprehension, anxiety, fear mounting uncontrollably), my friend declared that something similar often happened to him in buildings that seemed to be empty. Basically, I knew, he meant well. I tried to put it out of my mind. But once my friend got talking there was no stopping him, and during the meal, which lasted from three till six in the evening, he kept coming back to the subject of seemingly empty buildings, that is, buildings that you think are empty, because you can't hear a sound, but in fact they're not, and somehow you can tell, although your senses, your ears, your eyes, are telling you they are. So it's not that you feel anxious or afraid because you're in an empty building, or even because you might be trapped or locked inside an empty building, which is not beyond the realm of possibility, no, the reason you're anxious or afraid is that you know, deep down, that there is *no such thing* as an empty building; in every so-called empty building, someone is hiding, keeping quiet, and that's the terrifying thing: the fact that you are *not* alone, said my dentist friend, even when everything indicates that you are.

And then he said: You know when you really are alone? In a crowd, I said, thinking I was following his train of thought, but no, it wasn't in a crowd. I should have been able to guess the answer: When you die. Death: the only real solitude there is in Mexico; the only solitude in Irapuato.

That night we got drunk. I gave him my present. He said he didn't know Carranza's work. We went out to dinner and got drunk.

We started in the bars of the central district and then we returned to the outskirts, where we had been the night before, where we had met young Ramírez. I remember that at one point in our erratic journey I had the impression that my friend was looking for Ramírez. I said so. He said I was mistaken. I told him he could speak freely to me, anything he said would remain between us. He said he had always spoken freely to me and after a while he looked me in the eyes and added that he had nothing to hide. I believed him. But I still had the impression that he was looking for the boy. That night we didn't go to bed until around six in the morning. At one point the dentist started reminiscing about the old days, when we were both students at the UNAM and unconditional admirers of Elizondo. I was enrolled in the Faculty of Philosophy and Literature and he was studying dentistry. We met at a discussion organised by the university film society, after the screening of a film by a Bolivian director, who I guess must have been Sanjinés.

During the discussion my friend got up, and I don't know if he was the only one, but he was certainly the first to say he didn't like the film, and why. I didn't like it either, but at the time I would never have admitted it. We became friends immediately. That night I discovered that he shared my admiration for Elizondo, and during the second summer of our friendship, we attempted to emulate the characters in *Narda or Summer* by renting a shack by the sea in Mazatlán, not exactly the Italian coast, but, with a little imagination and goodwill, it was close enough.

Then we grew up and, looking back, our youthful adventures seemed rather contemptible. Young middle-class Mexicans are condemned to imitate Salvador Elizondo, who in turn imitated the inimitable Klossowski, or fatten slowly in business or bureaucratic suits, or flail around ineffectually in vaguely leftist, vaguely charitable organisations. Between them, Elizondo (whom I had stopped rereading) and the painter Cavernas just about sated our insatiable appetite for Culture, and each mouthful left us poorer, thinner, uglier, and more ridiculous than before. My friend went back to Irapuato and I stayed on in Mexico City and we both, in different ways, tried to distract ourselves from the gradual devastation of our lives, of the ethics and aesthetics we'd professed, the Mexican nation and our useless bloody dreams.

But we still had friendship and that was the main thing. So there we were, passably drunk by this stage, reminiscing about our youth, when suddenly my friend referred to the old Indian woman who had died of gum cancer and our conversation about art history and the particular; he mentioned the 'two tracks' (though I could barely remember what they were supposed to represent), and finally he started talking about the restaurant where we had met José Ramírez (all the rest had been a preamble) and he asked me what I thought of him, although from the way he put it I couldn't really tell if he was referring to the Indian boy or to himself, so to play safe, I said, Nothing much, or maybe I shrugged in a non-committal way. My friend immediately asked me if I thought, if the thought had crossed my mind, that there might be something between him and José Ramírez (it was one of those awful, typically Mexican roundabout questions), and I said, No, of course not, mate . . . How could you think that? Come on, don't worry . . . Perhaps I'm exaggerating or my memory is playing tricks, but perhaps not – the real chasm may have opened at that moment, the chasm I had sensed in the seemingly empty building, the one I had glimpsed as the Indian boy walked over to us for the first time, just as my friend, as it happened, was talking or ranting about the Indian woman and her corpse that seemed to keep shrinking, and then, perhaps because I was drunk, it all swirled together in my mind: the memories of our youth, the books we read, *Narda or Summer* by Elizondo, a living national treasure, our aspiring, make-believe summer in Mazatlán, my girlfriend, who had decided out of the blue to make a new start, guided by her own sweet will, the years, Cavernas, my friend's art collection, the trip to Irapuato, its calm streets, my friend's mysterious decision to settle down and work there, in his home town, when the normal thing to do would have been . . .

And then he said: You have to get to know José. He stressed the verb *know*. You have to get to *know* him. And: I'm not . . . I'm not that way . . . you know . . . inclined. And then he talked about the dead Indian woman and the work of the cooperative. And he said: I'm not . . . you didn't think I was, did you? Of course not, I said. And then we went to a different bar, and on the way there he said: Tomorrow. And I knew it wasn't the drink talking; tomorrow he would remember because a promise is a promise, isn't it? Of course it is. Then, trying to change the subject, I started talking about something that had happened to me when I was a child: I got stuck in the lift of the building where we lived. Then I really *was* alone, I said. And my friend listened to me with a smile, as if he were thinking, What a jerk you've become, all those years in Mexico City, the stacks of books you've read and studied and taught, wherever it is you teach. But I went on: I was alone. For a long time. Sometimes (not often, to be perfectly honest) I still feel what I felt in that lift. And do you know why I felt like that? My friend shrugged as if to say he couldn't care less. But I told him anyway: Because I was a child. I remember his reaction. He turned away from me, trying to see where he had parked the car. Bullshit, he said. Tomorrow you're going to see the real thing.

And the next day he hadn't forgotten. On the contrary, he remembered more than I did. He talked about José Ramírez as if he were the boy's guardian. That night, I remember, we dressed as if we were going out to a singles bar or a brothel; my friend wore a brown corduroy jacket and I wore a leather jacket I had brought in case we went for a day trip into the country.

We began our tour with a couple of whiskies in a dim place near the centre that smelt of aftershave. Then we went straight to the suburb where José Ramírez hung out. We visited a pair of run-down cafés, the restaurant (where we tried to eat, although neither of us was hungry) and a bar called El Cielo. Not a trace of the Indian boy.

When it was starting to look as if we had wasted the night, a curious night in the course of which we had hardly exchanged a word, we saw him, or thought we did, walking down a dimly lit footpath. My friend tooted the horn and executed a reckless U-turn. Ramírez was waiting for us quietly on a corner. I wound down the window and said hello. My friend leaned over in front of me and invited him to get in. The boy climbed into the car without a word. I remember the rest of the night as festive. Irrationally festive. It was as if we were celebrating the birthday of the young man in the back seat. As if we were his parents. As if we were his pimps. Or his minders: two sad white Mexicans protecting an enigmatic Indian compatriot. We laughed. We drank and laughed and everyone left us alone, sensing that to make fun of us would have been to risk life and limb.

We heard the story of José Ramírez, or fragments of it; my friend thought it was wonderful, and, after a moment of puzzlement, so did I, though later, as we approached the unknown slopes of the night, to quote Poe, the story began to blur, as if the Indian boy's words could find nowhere to settle in our memories, which must be why I can hardly remember a thing he said. I do remember him telling us that he had attended a poetry workshop, a free poetry workshop, the literary version of the medical cooperative, although he didn't write a single poem, and at this my friend burst out laughing, but I didn't understand; I couldn't see what was so funny, until they explained that Ramírez wrote fiction. Stories, not poems. Then I asked why he hadn't signed up for a fiction workshop. And my dentist friend said, Because there aren't any fiction workshops. Don't you see? In this shit-hole of a town the only thing they teach for free is poetry. Don't you see?

And then Ramírez started talking about his family, or maybe it was the dentist who told me about his family, but in any case there was nothing to say. Don't you see? Nothing. And I didn't really see, so just for something to say, I started talking about empty buildings and deception, but my friend silenced me with a gesture. There was *nothing* to say about them. Farmers. Dirt poor. Not the slightest indication. Don't you see? I nodded compliantly, but in fact I didn't see at all. And then my friend declared that there were very few writers alive on a par with the boy sitting there before us. I swear to God: Very few. At which point he launched into an explication of Ramírez's work that chilled me.

Better than the lot of them, he said. Mexico's famous writers were like babes in arms compared to this rather fat, inexpressive adolescent with his hands hardened by work in the fields. What fields? I asked. The fields all around us, said the dentist, moving his hand in a circular gesture, as if

Irapuato were an outpost in the wilderness, a fort in the middle of Apache territory. I took a fearful, sidelong glance at the boy and saw that he was smiling. Then my friend began to tell me about one of Ramírez's stories, a story about a child who had to look after his numerous younger brothers and sisters, that was the gist of it, the first part anyway, because then the plot swung around and smashed itself to pieces, and it became a story about the ghost of a schoolmaster trapped in a bottle, and about individual freedom, and new characters appeared: a pair of shady faith-healers, a twenty-year-old girl on drugs, a guy reading a book by de Sade and living in a wrecked car beside the highway. All this in one story, said my friend.

And although the good-mannered thing to say would have been Mmm, sounds interesting, I said I couldn't really express an opinion without reading it for myself. That's how I let myself in for it, when good manners could have saved me. My friend stood up and said to Ramírez, Let's go and get the stories. I remember Ramírez looked up at him, then across at me, and finally stood up without a word. I could have protested. I could have said there was no need. But by then I was already chilled through and nothing mattered to me any more, although from somewhere deep inside I was watching our movements, which seemed to be orchestrated with an almost supernatural precision, and although I knew that those movements were not leading us towards any physical risk, I was also aware that in another sense we were venturing into dangerous territory, from which we would not be allowed to return without having paid a toll of pain or estrangement, a toll that we would eventually come to regret.

But I said nothing. We left the bar, got into my friend's car, and proceeded to lose our way among the streets on the outskirts of Irapuato, where the only other vehicles were police cars and the odd bus, streets that young Ramírez walked, so my friend told me as he drove on in a state of rapture, every night or every morning, returning from his forays into the city. I chose not to make any further comment and looked out at the feebly lit streets and the shadow of the car, intermittently projected on to the high walls of factories or abandoned warehouses, vestiges of a former time, already consigned to oblivion, when attempts had been made to industrialise the city. Then we emerged into a kind of suburb attached to that jumble of obsolete buildings. The street narrowed. There were no street lamps. I heard dogs barking. Like something from *The Children of Sánchez*, isn't it, said the dentist. I didn't reply. Behind me I heard Ramírez's voice saying to turn right, then keep going straight ahead.

The headlights swept across a dirt road and lit up two wretched shacks behind a fence made of wood and wire, and then we emerged suddenly into what seemed to be open country, although it could equally have been a rubbish dump. From there we continued on foot, Indian file, Ramírez leading the way, followed by the dentist and me. In the distance I could see headlights gliding along a highway: another world, and yet I felt those distant moving lights were somehow – horribly – emblematic of our destiny. I saw the silhouette of a hill. I sensed a movement in the darkness, among the bushes, and immediately assumed it was rats, although it could just as well have been birds. Then the moon came out and I saw little houses scattered over the lower slopes of the hill and, further off, a dark, ploughed field, stretching away to a bend in the highway, where a wood jutted up like a construction.

Suddenly I heard the boy's voice saying something to my friend and we stopped. His house had appeared from nowhere; the walls were yellow and white, and it had a low roof, like all the other wretched houses holding out against the night on the outskirts of Irapuato.

For a moment the three of us stood there in silence, spellbound, contemplating the moon or looking sadly at the boy's cramped dwelling or trying to make sense of the objects piled up in the yard: the only thing I could identify with any certainty was a crate. Then we went into a room with a low ceiling that smelt of smoke and Ramírez switched on a light. I saw a table, farm tools leaning against the wall, and a child asleep in an armchair.

The dentist looked at me. His eyes were gleaming with excitement. But I felt we should have been ashamed of what we were doing: rounding off a night on the town with a bit of schadenfreude. Except that we would be contemplating our own misfortune as well, I thought. Ramírez brought over two wooden chairs before disappearing through a doorway that seemed to have been hacked out with an axe. I soon realised that the room in which we were standing was a new addition to the house. We sat down and waited. When Ramírez reappeared he was carrying a stack of papers more than five centimetres thick. With an intent expression he sat down and handed it to us. Read whatever you like, he whispered. I looked at my friend. He had already taken a story from the pile and was carefully arranging the pages. I said I thought the best thing to do would be to borrow the stories, take them back to my friend's house and read them at our leisure. Or maybe I didn't actually say that, probably not. But thinking about it now, I can't imagine the scene any other way: me saying, Let's take them back and read them later, we'll be more receptive, and the dentist looking at me with something hard in his gaze, like a man condemned to death, ordering me to pick a story at random and read it, for Christ's sake.

So I did. I lowered my eyes, ashamed, chose a story and began to read. The story was four pages long; maybe that's why I chose it, because it was short, but when I got to the end, I felt as if I had read a novel. I glanced across at Ramírez. He was sitting in front of us, nodding off. My friend followed my gaze and told me in a whisper that the young writer got up very early in the morning. I nodded and chose another story. When I looked at Ramírez again he was slumped forward, sleeping with his head on his arms. Earlier, I had been almost falling asleep myself, but now I felt wide awake and absolutely sober. My friend passed me another story. Read this one, he whispered. I put it aside and finished the one I was reading before starting it.

As I was coming to the end of the third story, the other door opened and a man appeared who must have been about our age, but seemed much older. He smiled at us before walking quietly out into the yard. José's father, said my friend. Outside I heard tin cans knocking, quickening steps, and the sound of someone urinating on to the ground. In a different situation, this would have been enough to put me on my guard; I would have been straining to interpret those noises, preparing to avert a potential danger, but instead I went on reading.

We never stop reading, although every book comes to an end, just as we never stop living, although death is certain. But, to put it in plain terms and make myself clear, at a certain point I decided that I had read enough. My friend had stopped a while before. He was visibly tired. I suggested we leave. Before standing up, both of us looked at Ramírez, who was sleeping peacefully. When we went outside, day was dawning. There was no one in the yard and the fields all around seemed barren. I wondered where the father had gone. My friend pointed to his car and remarked how strange it was that the car didn't seem strange in those surroundings. Some surroundings! he added, no longer whispering. His voice sounded odd to me: hoarse, as if he had spent the night shouting. Let's go and have some breakfast, he said. I nodded. He said, We can talk about what's happened to us.

But as we left that godforsaken place I realised there was very little we could say about the events of the previous night. Both of us felt happy, but we knew, without a shadow of doubt, and without having to put it into words, that we would not be able to ascertain or reflect on the nature of what we had experienced.

When we got back to the house I poured us out a whisky each, as a nightcap, and my friend lapsed into silent contemplation of the engravings by Cavernas hanging on the wall. I put his glass on the table and stretched out in an armchair without saying a word. The dentist scrutinised his engravings, first with his hands on his hips, then resting his chin on one hand and finally ruffling his hair. I laughed. So did he. For a moment I thought he was going to take one of the pictures down and proceed to destroy it methodically. But instead he sat next to me and drank his whisky. Then we turned in.

We didn't get much sleep. About five hours. I dreamt of

young Ramírez's house. I saw it standing in the middle of Mexico's wastelands, plains and rubbish dumps, exactly as it was, bare of all ornamentation. Just as I had seen it, a few hours before, at the end of that supremely literary night. And for barely a second I understood the mystery of art and its secret nature. But then somehow the corpse of the old Indian woman who had died of gum cancer came into the dream, and that's the last thing I can remember. I think her wake was being held in Ramírez's house.

When I woke up I told the dentist about my dream, or what I could remember of it. You're not looking too good, he said. He wasn't looking too good himself, although I chose not to point this out. I soon realised that he needed some time on his own. When I announced that I was going for a walk around the city, I saw the relief on his face. That afternoon I went to the cinema and fell asleep halfway through the film. I dreamed that we were committing suicide or forcing others to commit suicide. When I got back to my friend's house, he was waiting for me. We went out to dinner and tried to talk about what had happened the night before. It was useless. We ended up talking about some friends from Mexico City, people we had thought we knew but who had in fact turned out to be perfect strangers. Surprisingly, it was a pleasant evening.

The next day, Saturday, I went with him to his clinic, where he had a couple of hours' work to do for the cooperative. Community service, he said in a resigned sort of way as we got into his car. I was thinking of returning to Mexico City on Sunday and my conscience was telling me I should spend as much time as possible with my friend because I didn't know how long it would be before I would see him again.

For a long time (I couldn't even hazard a guess at how long now) we waited for a patient to turn up, my friend the dentist, a dentistry student, and I, but no one came.

Dance Card

1. My Mother read Neruda to us in Quilpué, Cauquenes and Los Ángeles. **2.** A single book: *Veinte poemas de amor y una canción desesperada* (*Twenty Love Poems and a Song of Desperation*), Editorial Losada, Buenos Aires, 1961. On the title page, a drawing of Neruda and a note explaining that this edition commemorated the printing of the millionth copy. Had a million copies of *Veinte poemas* already been printed in 1961? Or did the note refer to all of Neruda's published works? The first, I fear, although both possibilities are disturbing, and unimaginable now. **3.** My mother's name is written on the second page of the book: María Victoria Ávalos Flores. A somewhat hasty examination of the handwriting leads me to the improbable conclusion that someone else wrote her name there. It is not my father's handwriting, or that of anyone I know. Whose is it then? After closely scrutinising the signature blurred by the years, I am obliged to admit, albeit sceptically, that it is my mother's. **4.** In 1961 and 1962, my mother was not as old as I am now; she hadn't turned thirty-five, and was working in a hospital. She was young and full of life. **5.** This copy of *Veinte poemas*, my copy, has travelled a long way. From town to town in southern Chile, from house to house in Mexico City, and then to three cities in

Spain. **6.** The book didn't always belong to me, of course. First it was my mother's. She gave it to my sister, and when my sister left Girona and went to Mexico, she passed it on to me. Of the books my sister left me, my favourites were the science fiction and the complete works (up to that point) of Manuel Puig, which I had given her, and reread after she went. **7.** By that stage I didn't like Neruda any more. Especially not *Veinte poemas de amor*! **8.** In 1968, my family moved to Mexico City. Two years later, in 1970, I met Alejandro Jodorowski, who, for me, was the Archetype of the Artist. I waited for him outside a theatre (he was directing a production of *Zarathustra*, with Isela Varga) and said I wanted him to teach me how to make films. I then became a frequent visitor at his house. I don't think I was a good student. Jodorowski asked me how much I spent a week on cigarettes. Quite a bit, I said (I've always smoked like a chimney). He told me to stop smoking and spend the money on Zen meditation classes with Ejo Takata. All right, I said. I went along for a few days, but during the third session I decided it wasn't for me. **9.** I parted company with Ejo Takata in the middle of a Zen meditation session. When I tried to slip away he came at me brandishing a wooden stick, the one he used on the students. What he would do was hold out the stick; the students would say yes or no, and if the response was affirmative, he'd let them have a couple of whacks, and the sound would echo in the dim room hazy with incense. **10.** On this occasion, however, he didn't ask me first. His attack was precipitate and stentorian. I was sitting next to a girl, near the door, and Ejo was at the back of the room. I thought he had his eyes shut and wouldn't hear me leaving. But the bastard heard and threw himself at me shouting the Zen equivalent of *banzai*.

Dance Card

11. My father was a heavyweight amateur boxing champion. His unchallenged reign was restricted to southern Chile. I never liked boxing, but had been taught since I was a kid; there was always a pair of boxing gloves in the house, whether in Chile or in Mexico. **12.** When Master Ejo Takata threw himself at me shouting, he probably didn't mean to do me any harm, or expect me to defend myself automatically. Normally when he whacked his followers with that stick it was to dissipate their nervous tension. But I wasn't suffering from nervous tension; I just wanted to get out of there once and for all. **13.** If you think you're being attacked, you defend yourself; it's only natural, especially when you're seventeen, especially in Mexico City. Ejo Takata was Nerudian in his ingenuity. **14.** Jodorowski was to thank for Ejo Takata's presence in Mexico, so he said. At one stage Takata used to go looking for drug addicts in the jungles of Oaxaca, mostly North Americans who had gone tripping and never found their way back. **15.** My experience with Takata, however, didn't make me give up smoking. **16.** One of the things I liked about Jodorowski was the way, whenever he talked about Chilean intellectuals (usually in critical terms), he would include me among them. That was a big boost to my confidence, although naturally I had no intention whatsoever of resembling the said intellectuals. **17.** One afternoon, I can't remember how, we got on to the topic of Chilean poetry. He said that the greatest Chilean poet was Nicanor Parra. He recited one of Nicanor's poems straightaway, and another, and then one more. Jodorowski recited well, but I wasn't impressed by the poems. At that stage I was a highly sensitive young man, as well as being ridiculous and full of myself, and I declared that Chile's finest poet was, without any doubt,

Pablo Neruda. All the rest, I added, are midgets. The discussion must have lasted about half an hour. Jodorowski brandished arguments from Gurdjieff, Krishnamurti, and Madame Blavatsky, went on to talk about Kierkegaard and Wittgenstein, then Topor, Arrabal, and himself. I remember him saying that Nicanor, on his way somewhere, had stayed at his house. In this statement I glimpsed a childlike pride which I have since noticed again and again in the majority of writers. **18.** In one of his books Bataille says that tears are the ultimate form of communication. I started crying, not in a normal, ordinary way, letting the tears roll smoothly down my cheeks, but wildly, in spurts, more or less like Alice in Wonderland, wetting everything. **19.** As I left Jodorowski's house I realised I would never return, which hurt as much as what he had said, and I went on crying in the street. More dimly, I also realised that never again would I have a master as charming as that gentleman thief and consummate con-man. **20.** But what dismayed me most of all was my poorly argued, rather pathetic defence (a defence it was, nevertheless) of Pablo Neruda, when all I had read of his were the *Veinte poemas de amor* (which by that stage struck me as unintentionally funny) and *Crepusculario (Twilight)*, including the poem 'Farewell', to which I remain unshakeably faithful, though even then I saw it as the ultimate in schmaltz. **21.** In 1971 I read Vallejo, Huidobro, Martín Adán, Borges, Oquendo de Amat, Pablo de Rokha, Gilberto Owen, López Velarde, Oliverio Girondo. I even read Nicanor Parra. I even read Pablo Neruda! **22.** The Mexican poets I was hanging out and swapping books with at the time belonged for the most part to one of two camps: the Nerudians and the Vallejians. I was, unquestionably, Parrian in my isolation. **23.** But the fathers must be killed; poets are born orphans. **24.** In 1973 I went back to Chile: a long journey over land and sea, repeatedly delayed by hospitality. I met with revolutionaries of various stripes. The whirlwind of fire that would soon engulf Central America could already be glimpsed in the eyes of my friends, who spoke of death as if they were talking about a film. **25.** I reached Chile in August 1973. I wanted to help build socialism. The first book of poems I bought was Parra's *Obra Gruesa (Construction Work)*. The second was *Artefactos (Artifacts)*, also by Parra. **26.** I had less than a month in which to enjoy building socialism. At the time, of course, I didn't know that. I was Parrian in my ingenuity. **27.** I went to an exhibition and saw various Chilean poets; it was awful. **28.** On the eleventh of September I turned up at the only functioning party cell in the suburb where I was living and volunteered. The man in charge was a communist factory worker, chubby and perplexed, but willing to fight. His wife seemed to be more courageous than he was. We all piled into their little wooden-floored dining room. While the man in charge was speaking, I examined the books on the sideboard. There weren't many, mostly cowboy novels like the ones my father used to read. **29.** For me, the eleventh of September was a comic as well as a bloody spectacle. **30.** I kept watch in an empty street. I forgot my password. My comrades were fifteen years old, retired, or out of work. **31.** When Neruda died, I was already in Mulchén, with my uncles, aunts, and cousins. In November, while travelling from Los Ángeles to Concepción, I was arrested during a road check and taken prisoner. I was the only one they took from the bus. I thought they were going to kill me there and then. From the cell I could hear the officer in charge of the patrol, a fresh-faced policeman who looked like an arsehole (an arsehole wriggling around in a sack of flour) talking with his superiors in Concepción. He was saying he had captured a Mexican terrorist. Then he retracted and said: a foreign terrorist. He mentioned my accent, the dollars I was carrying, the brand of my shirt and trousers. **32.** My great-grandparents, the Flores and the Grañas, vainly attempted to tame the wilds of Araucanía (when they couldn't even tame themselves), so they were probably Nerudian in their excess. My grandfather, Roberto Avalos Martí, was a colonel, stationed at various forts in the south until his mysteriously early retirement, which leads me to suspect that he was Nerudian in his sympathy for the blue and white. My paternal grandparents came from Galicia and Catalonia, gave their lives to the province of Bío-Bío and were Nerudian in their landscape and laborious slowness. **33.** I was imprisoned in Concepción for a few days and then released. They didn't torture me, as I had feared; they didn't even rob me. But they didn't give me anything to eat either, or any kind of covering for the night, so I had to rely on the goodwill of the other prisoners, who shared their food with me. In the small hours I could hear them torturing others; I couldn't sleep and there was nothing to read except a magazine in English that someone had left behind. The only interesting article in it was about a house that had once belonged to Dylan Thomas. **34.** I got out of that hole thanks to a pair of detectives who knew me from high school in Los Ángeles, and my friend Fernando Fernández, who was twenty-one, just a year older than me, but possessed of a composure comparable to that of the idealised Englishman on whom Chileans were desperately and vainly trying to model themselves. **35.** In January 1974 I left Chile. I have never been back. **36.** Were the Chileans of my generation courageous? Yes, they were. **37.** In Mexico I heard the story of a young woman from the MIR who had been tortured by having live rats put into her vagina. This woman managed to get out of the country and went to Mexico City. There she lived, but each day she grew sadder, until one day the sadness killed her. That's what I heard. I didn't know her personally. **38.** The story isn't exceptional. We are told of peasant women in Guatemala being subjected to unspeakable humiliations. The amazing thing about the story is its ubiquity. In Paris I heard of a Chilean woman who had been tortured in the same way before emigrating to France. She too had been a member of the MIR; she was the same age as the woman in Mexico and, like her, had died of sadness. **39.** Some time later, I was told of a Chilean woman in Stockholm: she was young, a member or ex-member of the MIR; in November 1973 she had been tortured, using rats, and she had died, to the astonishment of the doctors who were treating her, of sadness, *morbus melancholicus*. **40.** Is it possible to die of sadness? Yes, it is. It is possible (though painful) to die of hunger. It is even possible to die of spleen. **41.** Was this anonymous Chilean, repeatedly subjected to torture and death, a single woman, or three different women who happened to share the same political affiliation and the same kind of beauty? According to a friend, it was one woman, who, as in Vallejo's poem 'Masa' multiplied in death without in any way surviving. (Actually, in Vallejo's poem, it is not the dead man who multiplies but the supplicants begging him not to die.) **42.** Once upon a time there was a Belgian poet called Sophie Podolski. She was born in 1953 and committed suicide in 1974. She published only one book, called *Le pays où tout est permis* (*The Country* *where Everything is Allowed*), Montfaucon Research Centre, 1970, 280 facsimile pages. **43.** Germain Nouveau (1852–1920), a friend of Rimbaud's, spent the last years of his life as a vagabond and beggar. He went by the name of Humilis (in 1910 he published *Les poèmes d'Humilis*) and lived on church porches. **44.** Everything is possible. Every poet *ought* to know that. **45.** I was once asked who were my favourite young Chilean poets. Maybe they didn't say 'young' but 'contemporary'. I said I liked Rodrigo Lira, although he can't really be called contemporary any more (though he is young, younger than any of us) because he's dead. **46.** Dance partners for the new Chilean poetry: the mathematical scions of Neruda and the cruel progeny of Huidobro, the comic followers of Mistral and the humble disciples of De Rokha, the heirs to Parra's bones and to Lihn's eyes. **47.** A confession: I cannot read Neruda's memoirs without feeling seriously ill. What a mass of contradictions. All that effort to hide and beautify a thing with a disfigured face. So little generosity, so little sense of humour. **48.** During a period of my life, thankfully behind me now, I used to see Adolf Hitler in the corridor of my house. All Hitler did was walk up and down the corridor, without even looking at me when he passed the open door of my bedroom. At first I thought it was the devil (who else could it have been?) and feared I had gone irreversibly mad. **49.** After two weeks, Hitler disappeared, and I was expecting him to be replaced by Stalin. But Stalin didn't show. **50.** It was Neruda who took up residence in my corridor. Not for two weeks, like Hitler, but three days – the shorter stay seemed to indicate that my depression was easing. **51.** Neruda, however, made noises (Hitler had been as quiet as a block of drifting ice); he complained, murmuring incomprehensible

Dance Card

words; his hands reached out and his lungs absorbed the air (the air of that cold European corridor) with relish. The pained gestures and beggar-like manner of the first night changed progressively, so that in the end the ghost seemed to have reconstituted himself as a grave and dignified courtier poet. **52.** On the third and final night, as he was going past my door, he stopped and looked at me (Hitler had never done that) and, this is the strangest part, he tried to speak but could not, expressed his impotence with gestures and finally, before disappearing with the first light of dawn, smiled at me (as if to say that communication is impossible, but one should still make an attempt?). **53.** Some time ago I met three Argentine brothers who later gave their lives for revolutionary causes in different Latin American countries. The mutual betrayal of the two elder brothers accidentally implicated the younger one, who hadn't betrayed anyone, and died, so I heard, calling out to them, although it is more likely that he died in silence. **54.** The children of the Spanish lion, said Rubén Darío, a born optimist. The children of Walt Whitman, José Martí, and Violeta Parra; torn apart, forgotten, in mass graves, at the bottom of the sea, the Trojan destiny of their mingled bones terrifying the survivors. **55.** I think of them this week as the veterans of the International Brigades visit Spain: little old men climbing down from the buses, brandishing their fists. There were 40,000 of them, and 350 or so have come back to Spain. **56.** I think of Beltrán Morales, I think of Rodrigo Lira, I think of Mario Santiago, I think of Reinaldo Arenas. I think of the poets who died under torture, who died of AIDS, or overdosed, all those who believed in a Latin American paradise and died in a Latin American hell. I think of their works, which may, perhaps, show the Left a way out of the pit of shame and futility. **57.** I think of our useless pointy heads and the abominable death of Isaac Babel. **58.** When I grow up I want to be Nerudian in my synergy. **59.** Questions to ponder before going to sleep. Why didn't Neruda like Kafka? Why didn't Neruda like Rilke? Why didn't Neruda like De Rokha? **60.** Did he like Barbusse? Everything seems to suggest that he did. And Sholokhov. And Alberti. And Octavio Paz. Odd companions for a voyage through Purgatory. **61.** But he also liked Éluard, who wrote love poems. **62.** If Neruda had been addicted to cocaine or heroin, if he had been killed by a piece of rubble during the siege of Madrid in 1936, if he had been Lorca's lover and committed suicide after Lorca was killed, it would be quite a different story. If Neruda had been the mystery that, deep down, he really is! **63.** In the basement of the edifice known as 'The Works of Pablo Neruda', is Ugolino lurking, waiting to devour his children? **64.** Without the slightest remorse! Innocently! Simply because he's hungry and doesn't want to die! **65.** He didn't have children, but the people loved him. **66.** Do we have to come back to Neruda as we do to the Cross, on bleeding knees, with punctured lungs and eyes full of tears? **67.** When our names no longer mean a thing, his will go on shining, his will go on soaring over an imaginary domain called *Chilean Literature*. **68.** By then all poets will live in artistic communities called jails or asylums. **69.** Our imaginary home, the home we share.

Part II
The Return

Snow

I met him in a bar on Calle Tallers, in Barcelona, it must be about five years ago now. When he found out I was Chilean, he came over to say hello; he too had been born in that far-away place.

He was more or less the same age as me, thirty-odd, and he drank quite a bit, though I never saw him drunk. His name was Rogelio Estrada. He was thin, shortish, and dark. His smile seemed to be permanently poised between wonder and mischief, but after a while I discovered that he was far more innocent than he made out. One night I went to the bar with a group of Catalan friends. We got talking about books. Rogelio came over to our table and said that the greatest writer of the century was, without a doubt, Mikhail Bulgakov. One of the Catalans had read *The Master and Margarita* and *A Theatrical Novel,* but Rogelio mentioned other works by the distinguished novelist, more than ten of them, if I remember correctly, and he gave their titles in Russian. My friends and I thought he was joking, and soon the talk moved on. One night he invited me back to his place and I went, I don't know why. He lived in a street nearby, a few yards from a very decrepit movie theatre known to the local kids as the Ghost Cinema. The apartment was old and full of furniture that wasn't his. We sat down in the living room, Rogelio put on a record – some awful, emphatic music with an unrelenting crescendo – and then he filled two glasses with vodka. On a shelf, presiding over the room, was a silver-framed photo of a girl. The rest of the decor was nothing special: postcards from various European countries and some very old shabby-looking soccer pennants: Colo-Colo, University of Chile and Santiago Morning. Pretty, isn't she? said Rogelio, pointing at the girl in the silver frame. Yes, very pretty, I replied. Then we sat down again and drank for a while in silence. When Rogelio eventually spoke, the bottle was almost empty. First you have to empty the bottle, he said, then your soul. I shrugged. Though, of course, I don't believe in the soul, he added. It all comes down to time, though, doesn't it? Do you have time to listen to my story? Depends on the story, I said, but I think so. It won't take very long, said Rogelio. Then he stood up, took the silver-framed photo, sat down in front of me cradling it in his left arm while holding the glass of vodka in his right hand, and began:

My childhood was happy; it had nothing to do with the way my life turned out later. Things started going wrong when I was a teenager. I was living in Santiago with my family and according to my father I was well on the way to becoming a juvenile delinquent. My father, in case you don't know (and I can't see why you would), was José Estrada Martínez, aka Chubby Estrada, one of the big wheels in the Chilean Communist Party. And we were a proudly proletarian family, fighting the good fight, upstanding and righteous. At the age of thirteen I stole a bicycle. You can imagine, I don't need to spell it out. I was caught two days later and got one hell of a thrashing. At fourteen I started smoking dope – some of my friends in the neighbourhood used to grow it in the foothills of the Andes. At the time my father had a senior position in Allende's government, and his biggest fear, poor old dad, was that the right-wing press would reveal the misdemeanors of his eldest son. At fifteen I stole a car. I wasn't caught (though now I know that with a bit more time, the cops would have found me) because a few days later the coup happened and my whole family took refuge in the Soviet Embassy. I don't need to tell you what the days I spent in there were like. It was awful. I slept in the corridor and kept trying to hit on the daughter of one of my father's comrades, but all they did, that bunch, was sing *The International* or *No pasarán*. You get the picture, it was dismal, like party time at the Bible Hall.

We arrived in Moscow at the beginning of 1974. Personally, to be honest, I was glad to be going: a new city, blonde blue-eyed Russian girls, the plane trip, Europe, a new culture. The reality turned out quite differently. Moscow was like Santiago, but quieter, bigger and brutally cold in winter. At first they put me in a school where it was Spanish half the time, Russian the other half. Two years later I was at a regular school, speaking okay Russian, and bored out of my wits. I guess some strings were pulled to get me into the University, because I really didn't study much. I enrolled in medicine, but dropped out after a semester; it wasn't for me. Still, I have good memories of my time there: it's where I made my first friend, I mean the first friend who wasn't an exiled Chilean like me. His name was Jimmy Fodeba and he came from the Central African Republic, which as the name suggests, is in the middle of Africa. Jimmy's father was a communist, like mine, and like my father, he'd been forced into exile. Jimmy was pretty smart, but underneath he was just like me. I mean, he liked to stay up late, he liked to drink and smoke the occasional joint, and he liked women. Before long we were joined at the hip. The best friend I've ever had, except for the gang back in Santiago, the guys who stayed – I'll probably never see them again, but who knows? Anyway, what happened was that Jimmy and I combined our forces, and our desires, and, while we were at it, our needs as well, and from then on, instead of being two separate exiles, feeling lost and lonely, we were a pair of wolves roaming the streets of Moscow, and whenever one of us was scared, the other one dared, and so, little by little (because sometimes Jimmy had to study, he was a good student, unlike me), we started to get a general idea of the city where both of us would probably be living for a fair while. I won't go on about our youthful adventures, all I'll say is that after a year we knew where to find a bit of weed, which may not seem like much of a feat now, in Barcelona, but in Moscow, back in those days, it was truly heroic. By then I'd tried studying Latin American literature, Russian literature, radio broadcasting, food science, just about everything really, and whether it was because I got bored, or didn't pay attention in class, or just didn't turn up, which is basically what happened most of the time, I failed everything, and eventually my father threatened to send me to work in a factory in Siberia, poor old guy, that's the way he was.

And that was how I came to enroll in the School of Physical Education, which some optimistic Russians used to call the Advanced School of Physical Education, and this time I managed to keep it together until I got my diploma. That's right, my friend, you're looking at a qualified gymnastics instructor. Not a good one, of course, especially not compared with some of the Russians, but qualified all the same. When I handed my father the diploma, the old man was moved to tears. I'd say that's when my adolescence came to an end.

At the time I used to call myself Roger Strada. I was always getting into trouble; my friends weren't what you'd call good, upstanding citizens and I was thoroughly bad. It was like I was full of rage and didn't know how to get it out of my system. I worked as a trainer's assistant for a man of dubious and disconcerting moral character (it was a true meeting of minds); he specialised in recruiting new athletes from secondary schools, and I spent most of my time at parties, making deals and doing shady business to supplement my salary. My boss was called Pultakov. He was divorced and lived in a tiny apartment in Leliushenko Street, near Rogachev Square. As I said, I was a bad boy and Jimmy Fodeba was bad too, and anyone who knew us well knew that we were bad (I think I chose to call myself Roger, at least for a start, because it went with Jimmy, and because I secretly thought of myself as a kind of Italian-American gangster), but Pultakov was *seriously* bad and working with him every day, I gradually came to discover all his tricks, depravities and vices. My father lived in a Moscow of papers and memoranda, a bureaucrats' Moscow, with its commands and countermands, its current issues, its factions and infighting: an ideal Moscow. I lived in a Moscow of drugs and prostitution, black marketeering and living it up, threats and crimes. In certain circles the two Moscows would occasionally come into contact and even intermingle, but as a rule they were two distinct cities, each unaware of the other's existence. Pultakov initiated me into the world of sports betting. We gambled with other people's money of course, but also with our own. Soccer, hockey, basketball, boxing, even championship skiing, a sport I've never really seen the attraction of: we dabbled in everything. I met people. All sorts of people. Nice enough guys, in general, small-time crooks like me, though sometimes I did come across real criminals, the sort who'd stop at nothing, or at least you could tell that *in certain circumstances* they'd stop at nothing. An instinct for survival prevented me from getting too close to those people. Prison-fodder, sewer-food. People who could intimidate Pultakov and terrify me and Jimmy. With one exception, a guy our age, who for some reason took a shine to me. His name was Misha Semionovich Pavlov and he was like the whiz kid of the Moscow underworld. Pultakov and I provided him with information about various sports for his gambling, and from time to time this Misha Pavlov invited us to his apartment, or one of his apartments, never the same one, all of them dingier than Pultakov's or mine, usually out in the old northeastern suburbs, where the workers lived: Poluboyarov, Viktoria and Old Market. Pultakov didn't like Pavlov (he didn't like anyone much) and tried to keep his dealings with him to a minimum, but I've always been naïve; Pavlov's reputation as the underworld's child prodigy and the thoughtful way he treated me – occasionally giving me a chicken or a bottle of vodka or a pair of shoes – finally won me over, and I succumbed completely, body and soul, as they say.

The years went by and my family returned to Chile, except for my younger sister, who married a Russian; my father died in Santiago and had a beautiful funeral, or so they told me in the letters; Jimmy Fodeba went on living in

Snow

Moscow and working in a hospital (his father went back to the Central African Republic, where he was killed), while Pultakov and I went scurrying like a pair of rats around the gyms and sports complexes. With the arrival of democracy and the end of the Soviet Union (not that I've ever been interested in politics) came freedom and the mafias. Moscow became a charming, exuberant city, buzzing with that fierce, typically Russian sort of exuberance. I can't explain it, you have to understand the Slavic soul, and I don't think you do, however many books you've read. Suddenly it all got too big for us. Pultakov, who was a Stalinist at heart (I still don't get that, because under Stalin he would have ended up in Siberia for sure), was nostalgic for the old days. But I adapted to the new situation, and decided to save some money, now that it was possible, so I could get out of there for good and start exploring the world, Europe to begin with, then Africa, which, in spite of my age — by then I was over thirty and old enough to know better — I imagined as the kingdom of adventure, an endless frontier, a new story book where I could begin again, be happy, and find myself, as we used to say when we were kids back in Santiago in 1973. And that was how I joined Misha Pavlov's staff, almost without realising it. At the time his nickname was Billy the Kid. Don't ask me why. Billy the Kid was quick on the draw; Misha never did anything quickly, not even pulling out his credit card. Billy the Kid was brave and, at least in the movies I've seen, agile and thin; Misha was brave too, but built like a Buddha, obese even by Russian standards, and allergic to all forms of physical exercise. I went on being a bookmaker, but soon I began to do other kinds of work for him. Sometimes he'd give me a bundle of cash and send me to see a player I knew to get him to throw a game. On one occasion I managed to bribe half a soccer team, one by one, flattering the more cooperative players and using veiled threats on the others. Sometimes he sent me to persuade other gamblers to withdraw their bets or not to make waves. But most of the time my work consisted of providing reports on athletes, one after another, without any evident rhyme or reason, which Pavlov's IT expert would tirelessly key into his computer.

There was, however, something else I used to do for him. Most of the Moscow gangsters' girls were nightclub hostesses or striptease artists, actresses or wannabes. No surprises there; that's the way it's always been. But Pavlov's taste in women was for athletes: long jumpers, sprinters, middle-distance runners, triple jumpers . . . he fell in love with the occasional javelin thrower, but his real favourites were the high jumpers. He said they were like gazelles, ideal women, and he wasn't wrong. I was the one who organised it all. I went to the training camps and set up dates for him. Some of the girls were delighted at the prospect of spending a weekend with Misha Pavlov, poor things, but others, most of them, weren't. Still, I always got him the girls he wanted, even if it meant spending my own money or resorting to threats. And so it happened that one afternoon he told me he wanted Natalia Mijailovna Chuikova, an eighteen-year-old from the Volgograd region, who had just arrived n Moscow, hoping to get a place on the Olympic team. I don't know what it was exactly, but right from the start I realised that there was something different in the way Pavlov was talking about this Chuikova girl. When he told me to get her, he was with two of his buddies, and they winked at me as if to say: Make sure you do exactly

Snow

what he's telling you, Roger Strada, because this time Billy the Kid is serious.

Two days later I got to talk to Natalia Chuikova. It was at the Spartanovka indoor track, on the Boulevard of Sport, at nine a.m., and I'm definitely not a morning person, but it was the only time I could meet her there. First I saw her in the distance: she was about to start running to the high jump, and she was concentrating, clenching her fists and looking up, as if she was praying or watching for an angel. Then I went over to her and introduced myself. Roger Strada? she said, So you must be Italian. I didn't have the courage to destroy her illusions altogether: I said I was Chilean and that there were lots of Italians in Chile. She was five-foot-ten and can't have weighed more than 120 pounds. She had long brown hair, and her simple ponytail gathered all the grace in the world. Her eyes were almost jet black and she had, I swear, the longest, most beautiful legs I have ever seen.

I couldn't bring myself to tell her the reason for my visit. I bought her a Pepsi, told her I liked her technique and left. That night I didn't know what I was going to say to Pavlov, what lie I was going to invent. In the end I decided to keep it simple. I said we'd have to give Natalia Chuikova a little time, she wasn't like his usual kind of girl. Misha looked at me with that face of his, somewhere between a seal and a spoiled child, and said OK, I'll give you three days. When Misha gave you three days, you had to fix it in three days, not one day more. So I spent a few hours thinking it over, asking myself what my problem was, what was holding me back, and eventually I decided to settle the matter as quickly as possible. Very early the next morning, I saw Natalia again. I was one of the first to arrive at the track. I spent a long time watching the athletes coming and going, all half asleep like me, chatting and arguing, though all I could hear of their voices was a senseless murmur, or shouts in an incomprehensible Russian, as if I'd forgotten the language, until Natalia appeared in the group and started doing warm-up exercises. Her trainer was taking notes in a little book. There were two other high jumpers talking with her. Sometimes they laughed. Sometimes, after jumping, they'd sit down and put on blue and red tracksuits, which they soon took off again. Sometimes they drank water. After half an hour of happiness I realised I was in love. It was the first time it had happened to me. Before that, I'd loved a couple of whores. I'd treated them wrong, or right, it didn't matter. Now I was really in love. I spoke to her. I explained the situation with Misha Pavlov, who he was, what he wanted. Natalia was shocked, then she thought it was funny. She agreed to see him, against my advice. I made the date for as late as I could. In the meantime, I took her to see a Bruce Willis movie – he was one of her favourite actors – and then to dinner at a good restaurant. We talked and talked. Her life, with its hardships and disappointments, was a model of perseverance and willpower, just the opposite of mine. Her tastes were simple; it was happiness she wanted, not wealth. Her attitude to sex, which is what I was really hoping to get out of her, was broad-minded. That depressed me at first: I thought Natalia would be easy game for Pavlov, I imagined her sleeping with all his bodyguards, one by one, and I couldn't bear the thought of it. But then I understood that Natalia was talking about a kind of sexuality that I just didn't understand (and still don't), and it didn't mean she had to go to bed with all the gang. I also understood that in spite of everything, I had to protect her.

Snow

A week later Pavlov sent me back to the indoor track with a big bunch of red and white carnations that must have cost him an arm and a leg. Natalia took the flowers and asked me to wait for her. We spent the whole day together, downtown for a start (where I bought two novels by Bulgakov, her favourite writer, from a stall in Staraya Basmannaya Street) and then in the little room where she lived. I asked her if she'd had a good time. Her reply completely stunned me, I swear. She said the flowers were self-explanatory. It was just so hard, so cold, you know what I mean: she was Russian and I was Chilean, it was like a chasm was opening in front of me, and I burst into tears right there and then. I often think about that afternoon of crying and how it changed my life. I don't know how to explain it; all I know is I felt like a child, and I felt all the cold of Moscow for the first time, and it seemed unbearable. That afternoon we made love.

From then on my life was in Natalia's hands and her life was in the hands of Misha Pavlov. The situation, in itself, seemed simple enough, but knowing Pavlov I knew that by sleeping with Natalia I was risking my neck. Also, as the days went by, the certitude that Natalia was sleeping with Pavlov – and I knew exactly when she was – progressively embittered and depressed me, and led me to take a fatalistic view of my life, and of life in general. I would have liked to talk it over with a friend and get it off my chest. But no way could I tell Pultakov, and Jimmy Fodeba was always really busy; we weren't seeing each other as often as before. All I could do was put up with it and wait.

And so a year went by.

Life with Pavlov was strange. His life was divided into at least three parts and I had the honour or the misfortune of being acquainted with all three: the life of Pavlov the businessman, continually surrounded by his bodyguards, which gave off a subtle odour of money and blood that unsettled the senses; the life of Pavlov the serial romantic, or letch, as we used to say in Santiago, which tormented me in particular and inflamed my imagination; and the life of Pavlov the private man, with his enquiring mind, a man who spent or wanted to spend his spare time, his 'moments of inner repose' as he said, exploring literature and the arts, because Pavlov, though it's hard to believe, was a keen reader, and, of course, he liked to talk about what he was reading. That was why he used to call on the three people who made up what you might call the cultural or cosmopolitan arm of his gang: Fedor Petrovich Semionov, a novelist; Paulo Ripellino, a genuine Italian, who was studying Russian on a scholarship from the Moscow School of Languages; and me, who he always introduced as his friend Roger Strada, though he sometimes treated me like a dog. Two Russians and two Italians, Pavlov would say, with a little smile on his lips. He did it to slight me in front of Ripellino, but Ripellino was always respectful to me. They were actually fun, those meetings, but sometimes we'd be summoned at midnight; the phone would ring and we'd have to get ourselves pronto to one of the many apartments Pavlov owned around Moscow, and endure the boss's rants, when all we wanted to do was to go to bed. Pavlov's tastes were eclectic – that's the word, isn't it? The only author I've read, to be honest, is Bulgakov, and that was only because I was in love with Natalia; as for the others, I've got no idea, I'm not much of a reader, that's pretty obvious. Semionov, as far as I know, wrote pornographic novels, and Ripellino had a film script that he wanted Pavlov to back for him, something about martial arts and the mafia. The only one who really knew about literature was our host. So Pavlov would start talking about Dostoyevsky, for example, and the rest of us would tag along. The next day I'd take myself to the library and look up information about Dostoyevsky, summaries of his works and his life, so I'd have something to say the next time, but Pavlov hardly ever repeated himself; one week he'd talk about Dostoyevsky, the next about Boris Pilniak, the week after that, Chekhov (who he said was a faggot, I don't know why), then he'd be onto Gogol or Semionov himself, raving about his pornographic novels. Semionov was quite a character. He must have been my age, maybe a bit older, and he was one of Pavlov's protégés. I once heard that he'd arranged for his wife to disappear. I didn't know what to think about that rumour. Semionov seemed capable of anything, except biting the hand that fed him. Ripellino was different, a good kid, and the only one who openly confessed that he hadn't read a single one of the novelists that our boss used to hold forth about, although he'd read some poetry (Russian poetry, with proper rhymes, easy to remember), which he'd sometimes recite by heart, usually when we were drunk. And who wrote that? Semionov would ask in a booming voice. Pushkin, who else? Ripellino would reply. Then I'd seize the opportunity to say my piece about Dostoyevsky, and Pavlov and Ripellino would recite Pushkin's poem in unison, and Semionov would get out a little book and pretend to be taking notes for his next novel. Or we'd talk about the Slavic soul and the Latin soul, and once we got on to that subject, of course, Ripellino and I were bound to come off badly. You can't imagine how long Pavlov could go on about the Slavic soul, how profound and sad he could get. Semionov usually ended up crying, and Ripellino and I backed down at the first sign of trouble. It wasn't always just the four of us, of course. Sometimes Pavlov sent out for some whores. Sometimes there'd be one or two unfamiliar faces: the editor of a little magazine, an out-of-work actor, a retired army officer who actually knew the complete works of Alexei Tolstoy. Pleasant or unpleasant company, people who were doing deals with Pavlov or hoping for a favour from him. Sometimes the night even turned out to be enjoyable. But it could go the other way too. I'll never understand the Slavic soul. One night Pavlov showed his guests some photos of what he called his 'women's high-jumping team'. At first I didn't want to look, but they called me over and I couldn't refuse. There were photos of the four or five high-jumpers I'd got for him. Natalia Chuikova was one of them. I felt ill and I think Pavlov realised; he put his massive arms around me and started singing a drinking song in my ear, something about death and love, the only two things in life that are real. I remember laughing or trying to laugh at Pavlov's little joke, like I always did, but the laughter died in my throat. Later, when the others were sleeping it off, or had gone, I sat down by the window and looked at the photos again, taking my time. Funny how it is: right then, everything seemed OK, all in order (as my father used to say), I was breathing deeply, calm, free. It also seemed to me that the Slavic soul was not so different from the Latin soul, in fact they were the same, and the same as the African soul, which presumably illuminated the nights of my friend Jimmy Fodeba. Maybe the Slavic soul could withstand more alcohol, but that was the only difference.

So time went by.

Natalia was dropped from the Olympic team because she

never managed to jump the required height. She competed in the national trials and wasn't highly ranked. It was clear that she wouldn't be breaking any records. Although she didn't want to admit it, her career was over, and sometimes we talked about the future with a mixture of fear and anticipation. Her relationship with Pavlov had its ups and downs; there were days when he seemed to love her more than anyone in the world and days when he treated her badly. One night when we met her face was covered with bruises. She told me it had happened at training, but I knew it was Pavlov. Sometimes we talked late into the night about travel and other countries. I told her stuff about Chile, a Chile of my own invention, I guess, which sounded a lot like Russia to her, so she couldn't get excited about it, but she was curious. Once she travelled to Italy and Spain with Pavlov. They didn't invite me to the send-off, but I was one of the people who went to the airport to welcome them home. Natalia returned looking very tanned and pretty. I gave her a bunch of white roses (the night before, Pavlov had called from Spain and told me to buy them). Thanks, Roger, she said. You're welcome, Natalia Mijailovna, I said, instead of confessing that it was all thanks to a long-distance phone call from our mutual boss. Right then he was talking with some heavies and didn't notice the tenderness in my eyes (which have often been compared to the eyes of a rat, even by my mother, God rest her soul). But the fact is that Natalia and I were letting our guard down.

One winter night Pavlov called me at home. He sounded furious. He ordered me to come and see him immediately. I'd heard through the grapevine that some of his business operations weren't going so well. I tried to suggest that maybe it could wait, given the time and the temperature outside, but

Misha wasn't in a waiting mood: Either you get here in half an hour, he said, or tomorrow morning I cut your balls off. I got dressed as fast as I could and before going out I put a knife in my pocket, a knife I'd bought when I was a medical student. The streets of Moscow, at four in the morning, are not exactly safe, as I guess you know. The trip was like the continuation of the nightmare I'd been having when I was woken by Pavlov's call. The streets were covered with snow, the temperature must have been about five or ten degrees and for quite a while I didn't see another human being. At first I was walking ten yards and then trotting the next ten to warm myself up. After fifteen minutes, my body resigned itself to plodding on, step by step, clenched against the cold. Twice I saw patrol cars coming, and hid. Twice I saw taxis, but neither of them stopped for me. Apart from that, I came across drunks, who ignored me, and shadows, which, as I passed, disappeared into the enormous entrances along Medveditsa Avenue. The apartment where I was to meet Pavlov was in Nemetskaya Street; normally, on foot, it would have taken thirty or thirty-five minutes to get there, but that hellish night it took almost an hour and when I arrived four toes on my left foot were frozen.

Pavlov was waiting for me by the fireplace, reading and drinking cognac. Before I could say anything he smashed his fist into my nose. I hardly felt the blow but I let myself fall anyway. Don't stain my carpet, I heard him say. He proceeded to kick me about five times in the ribs, but since he was wearing slippers, that didn't hurt too much either. Then he took a seat, picked up his book and his glass and seemed to calm down. I got up, went to the bathroom to wash away the blood that was running from my nose, and then returned to the living room. What are you reading? I asked him. Bulgakov, said Pavlov. You know his work, don't you? Ah, Bulgakov, I said as my stomach tied itself in a knot. You mention Natalia, I thought, and I'll kill you. I slipped my hand into my coat pocket, feeling for the little knife. I like sincere people, said Pavlov, honourable people, who aren't underhanded; when I place my trust in someone, I want to be able to trust that person implicitly. My foot is frozen, I said, you should drop me at the hospital. Pavlov didn't listen, so I decided to stop complaining, anyway it wasn't that bad, I could already move my toes. For a while both of us were silent: Pavlov looked at the book by Bulgakov (*The Fateful Eggs*, I think it was), while I watched the flames in the fireplace. Natalia told me you've been seeing her, said Pavlov. I didn't say anything but I nodded. Are you sleeping with that whore? No, I lied. Another silence. Suddenly I was convinced that Pavlov had murdered Natalia and was going to murder me the same night. Without weighing up the consequences I threw myself at him and slashed his throat. I spent the next half hour covering my tracks. Then I went home and got drunk.

A week later the police arrested me and took me to the Ilininkov police station where I was questioned for an hour. A pure formality. Pavlov's replacement was called Igor Borisovich Protopopov, also known as the Sardine. He wasn't interested in athletes, but he kept me on as a bettor and match-fixer. I served him for six months before leaving Russia. What about Natalia, you must be wondering. I saw her the day after killing Pavlov, very early, at the sports centre where she trained. She didn't like the look of me. She said I looked like I was dead. I detected a note of scorn in her voice, but also a note of familiarity, even affection. I laughed and said I'd drunk a lot the night before, that was all. Then I took myself to the hospital where Jimmy Fodeba worked to get my frozen toes checked out. It wasn't really a serious problem, but by greasing a few palms we got them to keep me there for three days; then Jimmy fiddled the admission forms so it turned out that when Pavlov was killed, I had been flat on my back, warmly tucked up and happy as could be.

Like I told you, six months later I left Russia. Natalia came with me. First we lived in Paris and we even talked about getting married. It was the happiest time in my life. So happy that when I think back to it now, it makes me feel ashamed. Then we spent a while in Frankfurt and in Stuttgart, where Natalia had friends and hoped to find a good job. The friends weren't so friendly in the end, and poor Natalia couldn't find steady employment, though she even tried working as a cook in a Russian restaurant. But she was no good at cooking. We hardly ever talked about Pavlov's death. Unlike the police, Natalia thought his own men had done away with him, specifically the Sardine, but I said it must have been a rival gang. Funnily enough, she remembered Pavlov as a gentleman and always spoke warmly of his generosity. I let her go on and laughed to myself. Once I asked her if she was related to General Chuikov, the man who defended Stalingrad, now known as Volgograd. The things you come up with, Roger, she said, of course not. When we'd been living together for a year she left me for a German, by the name of Kurt something or other. She told me she was in love and then she cried, because she felt sorry for me or just because she was happy, I don't know. Come on, that's enough, *mala mujer,* I said to her. She started laughing like she always did when I spoke my language. I started laughing too. We shared a bottle of vodka and said goodbye. After that, when I realised there was nothing to keep me in that German city, I came to Barcelona. I'm working as a gymnastics instructor in a private school. Things aren't going too badly; I sleep with whores and there are two bars where I hang out and have a circle, as they say here. But sometimes, especially at night, I miss Russia, I miss Moscow. It's pretty good here but it's not the same, though if you asked me, I wouldn't be able to say exactly what it is I miss. The joy of just being alive? I don't know. One of these days I'm going to get on a plane and go back to Chile.

Another Russian Tale

for Anselmo Sanjuán

Once, after a conversation with a friend about the mercurial nature of art, Amalfitano told a story he'd heard in Barcelona. The story was about a *sorche*, a rookie, in the Spanish Blue Division, which fought in the Second World War, on the Russian Front, with the German Northern Army Group to be precise, in the vicinity of Novgorod.

The rookie was a little guy from Seville, blue-eyed and thin as a rake, and more or less by accident (he was no Dionisio Ridruejo, not even a Tomás Salvador; when he had to give the Roman salute, he did, but he wasn't really a fascist or a Falangist at heart) he ended up in Russia. And there, for some reason, someone started calling him *sorche* for short: Over here, *sorche*, or: Sorche, do this, Sorche, do that, so the word lodged itself in the guy's head, but in the dark part of his head, and in that capacious and desolate place, with passing time and the daily panicking, it was somehow transformed into *chantre*, cantor. How this happened I don't know, let's just say that some connection dormant since childhood was reactivated, some pleasant memory that had been waiting for its chance to return.

So the Andalusian came to think of himself as being a

cantor and having a cantor's duties, although he had no conscious idea of what the word meant, and couldn't have said that it referred to the leader of a church or cathedral choir. And yet, and this is the remarkable thing, by thinking of himself as a cantor, he somehow turned himself into one. During the terrible winter of '41, he took charge of the choir that sang carols while the Russians were hammering the 250th Regiment. He remembered those days as full of noise (muffled, constant noises) and an underground, slightly unfocused joy. They sang, but it was as if the voices were lagging behind or even anticipating the movements of the singers' lips, throats and eyes, which in their own brief but peculiar journeys often slipped into a kind of silent crevice.

The Andalusian carried out his other duties with courage and resignation, although over time, he did become embittered.

He soon paid his dues in blood. One afternoon he was wounded, more or less accidentally, and spent two weeks in the military hospital in Riga, under the care of robust, smiling German women, nursing for the Reich, who couldn't believe the color of his eyes, and some extremely ugly volunteer nurses from Spain, probably sisters or sisters-in-law or distant cousins of José Antonio.

When he was discharged, a confusion occurred that was to have grave consequences for the Andalusian: instead of giving him a ticket to the right destination, they shunted him off to the barracks of an SS battalion two hundred miles from his regiment. There, among Germans, Austrians, Latvians, Lithuanians, Danes, Norwegians and Swedes, all much taller and stronger than him, he tried to explain the confusion in his rudimentary German, but the SS officers brushed him off, and while it was being sorted out, they gave him a broom and made him sweep the barracks, then a bucket and a rag to clean the floor of the enormous rectangular wooden building in which they held, interrogated and tortured prisoners of all sorts.

Not entirely resigned to his lot, but performing his new tasks conscientiously, the Andalusian watched the time go by in his new barracks, where he ate much better than before and was not exposed to any new dangers, since the SS battalion had been stationed well behind the lines, to combat what they called 'outlaws'. Then, in the dark part of his head, the word *sorche* became legible again. I'm a *sorche*, he said, a rookie, and I should accept my fate. Little by little, the word *chantre* disappeared, although some afternoons, under a limitless sky that filled him with nostalgia for Seville, it resonated still, somewhere, lost in the beyond. Once he heard some German soldiers singing, and he remembered the word; another time there was a boy singing behind a thicket, and again he remembered it, more clearly this time, but when he went around to the other side of the bushes, the boy was gone.

One fine day, what was bound to happen happened. The barracks of the SS battalion came under attack and were captured, some say by a Russian cavalry regiment, though others claim it was a group of partisans. The fighting was brief and the Germans were at a disadvantage from the start. After an hour the Russians found the Andalusian hidden in the rectangular building, wearing the uniform of an SS auxiliary and surrounded by evidence of the atrocities committed there not so long ago. Caught red-handed, so to speak. They attached him to one of the chairs that the SS used for interrogations, with straps on the legs and the armrests, and to every question from the Russians he replied in Spanish that he didn't understand and was just a dogsbody there. He also tried to say it in German, but he barely knew four words of that language and his interrogators knew none at all. After a quick session of slapping and kicking, they went to get a guy who could speak German and was questioning prisoners in another of the rectangular building's cells. Before they came back, the Andalusian heard shots, and knew they were killing some of the SS, which put an end to any hopes he might have had of getting out of there unharmed. And yet, when the shooting stopped, he clung to life again with every fibre of his being. The Russian who knew German asked him what he was doing there, what his job was and his rank. The Andalusian tried to explain, in German, but it was no use. Then the Russians opened his mouth, and with a pair of pincers, which the Germans had used on other body parts, they started pulling and squeezing his tongue. The pain made his eyes water, and he said, or rather shouted, the word *coño*, cunt. The pincers in his mouth distorted the expletive which came out, in his howling voice, as *Kunst*.

The Russian who knew German looked at him in puzzlement. The Andalusian was yelling *Kunst, Kunst* and crying with pain. In German, the word *Kunst* means art, and that was what the bilingual soldier was hearing, and he said, This son of a bitch must be an artist or something. The guys who were torturing the Andalusian removed the pincers along with a little piece of tongue and waited, momentarily hypnotised by the revelation. The word *art*. Art, which soothes the savage beast. And so, like soothed beasts, the Russians took a breather and waited for some kind of signal while the rookie bled from the mouth and swallowed his blood liberally mixed with saliva, and choked. The word *coño* transformed into the word *Kunst*, had saved his life. When he came out of the rectangular building, it was dusk, but the light stabbed at his eyes like midday sun.

They took him away along with the few remaining prisoners, and before long he was able to tell his story to a Russian who knew some Spanish, and he ended up in a prison camp in Siberia while his accidental partners in iniquity were executed. He was in Siberia until well into the fifties. In 1957 he settled in Barcelona. Sometimes he'd open his mouth and cheerfully tell his tales of war. Sometimes he'd open his mouth and show whoever wanted a look the place where a chunk was missing from his tongue. You could hardly see it. The Andalusian explained that over the years it had grown back. Amalfitano didn't know him personally. But when he heard the story, the guy was still living in a janitor's apartment in Barcelona.

William Burns

William Burns, from Ventura, California, told this story to my friend Pancho Monge, a policeman in Santa Teresa, Sonora, who passed it on to me. According to Monge, the North American was a laid-back guy who never lost his cool, a description that seems to be at odds with the following account of the events. In Burns's own words:

It was a dreary time in my life. I was going through a rough patch at work. I was supremely bored, though up till then I'd always been immune to boredom. I was going out with two women. That I do remember clearly. One of them was getting on a bit – she must have been about my age – and the other wasn't much more than a girl. Some days, though, they seemed like two ailing, crotchety old women, and other days like two little girls who just wanted to play. The age difference wasn't so big you'd mistake them for mother and daughter, but almost. Though that's the kind of thing a man can only guess at; you never really know for sure. Anyway, these women had two dogs, a big one and a little one. And I never knew which dog belonged to which woman. They were sharing a house on the outskirts of a town in the mountains where people went for summer vacation. When I mentioned to someone, some friend or acquaintance, that I was going up there for the summer, he told me I should take my fishing rod. But I didn't have a fishing rod. Someone else told me about the stores and the cabins, taking it easy, clearing the mind. But I wasn't going there with the women for a vacation; I was going there to take care of them. Why did they ask me to take care of them? What they told me was that some guy was out to harm them. They called him the killer. When I asked what his motive was, they didn't have an answer, or maybe they preferred to keep me in the dark. So I tried to work it out for myself. They were afraid, they believed they were in danger, and maybe it was all a false alarm. But why should I tell people what to think, especially when they've hired me, and anyway I figured that after a week they'd come around to my point of view. So I went up into the mountains with them and their dogs, and we moved into a little stone-and-timber house full of windows, more windows than I think I've ever seen in the one house, all different sizes and scattered haphazardly. From the outside, the windows gave you the impression that the house had three floors, but in fact there were only two. Inside, especially in the living room and some of the bedrooms on the first floor, they produced a dizzying, exhilarating, maddening effect. In the bedroom I was given there were only two windows, both quite small, one above the other, the top one almost reaching the ceiling, the lower one just over a foot from the floor. Anyway, life up there was pleasant. The older woman wrote every morning, but she didn't shut herself away, like they say writers usually do; she set up her laptop on the living room table. The younger woman spent her time gardening or playing with the dogs or talking with me. I did most of the cooking, and although I'm no chef, the women praised the meals I prepared. I could have gone on living like that for the rest of my life. But one day the dogs ran away and I went out to look for them. I remember searching through a wood nearby, armed only with a flashlight, and peering into the gardens of empty houses. I couldn't find them anywhere. When I got back to the house, the women looked at me as if I was to blame for the dogs' disappearance. Then they mentioned a name, the killer's name. They were the ones who'd been calling him the killer right from the start. I was sceptical, but I listened to what they had to say. They talked about high school romances, money trouble, grudges. I couldn't get my head around how both of them could have had relationships with the same guy in high school, given the age difference between them. But they didn't want to say any more. That night, in spite of the reproaches, one of them came to my room. I didn't switch on the light, I was half asleep, and I never found out which one it was. When I woke up, with the first light of dawn, I was alone. That day I decided to go into town and pay a visit to the guy they were scared of. I asked them for his address and told them to shut themselves in the house and not to move until I got back. I drove down in the older woman's pickup. Just before I got to town, I saw the dogs in the yard of an old canning plant. They came over to me looking abashed and wagging their tails. I put them in the cab of the pickup and drove around the town for a while, laughing at how worried I'd been the previous night. Predictably, I found myself approaching the address the women had given me. Let's say the guy was called Bedloe. He had a store in the middle of town, a store for vacationers, where he sold everything from fishing rods to checked shirts and chocolate bars. For a while I just browsed the shelves. The man looked like a movie actor; he can't have been more than thirty-five. He was strongly built, had dark hair, and was reading a newspaper spread out on the counter. He was wearing canvas pants and a T-shirt. The store must have been doing good business; it was on one of the main streets, which had trams running down it as well as cars. Bedloe's stuff was expensive. For a while I checked out the prices and the stock. As I was leaving, for some reason I had the impression that the poor guy was lost. I hadn't gone more than ten yards when I realised that his dog was following me. I hadn't even seen it in the store: a big black dog, maybe a German shepherd crossed with something else. I've never owned a dog, I've got no idea what makes the damn things tick, but for whatever reason, Bedloe's dog followed me. I tried to get it to go back to the store, of course, but it paid no attention. So I kept walking towards the pickup, with the dog at my side, and then I heard the whistle. The storekeeper was whistling his dog back. I didn't turn around, but I knew that he had come out looking for us. My reaction was automatic and unthinking: I tried to make sure he didn't see me, or didn't see us. I remember hiding behind a dark red tram, the colour of dried blood, with the dog pressed against my legs. Just when I was feeling safely hidden, the tram moved off and the storekeeper saw me from the opposite sidewalk and moved his hands in a gesture that could have meant Grab the dog or Hang the dog or Stay right there till I come over. Which is exactly what I didn't do; I turned around and disappeared into the crowd, while he shouted something like Stop, my dog! Hey buddy, my dog! Why did I behave like that? I don't know. Anyway, the storekeeper's dog followed me submissively to where I'd parked the pickup and as soon as I opened the door, before I had time to react, he jumped in and refused to budge. When they saw me arrive with three dogs, the women said nothing and started playing with all three. The storekeeper's dog seemed to know them from way back. That afternoon, we talked about all sorts of things. I started by telling them about what had happened to me in town, then they talked about their past lives and their work: one had been a teacher, the other a hairdresser, and both had quit their jobs, although from time to time, they said, they looked after kids with problems. At some point, I found myself talking about how the house should be guarded around the clock. The women looked at me and agreed with a smile. I regretted having put it like that. Then we ate. I hadn't prepared the meal that night. The conversation lapsed into silence broken only by the sound of our jaws and teeth working, and the scuffling of the dogs outside as they raced around the house. Later, we started drinking. One of the women, I don't remember which, talked about the roundness of the earth and protection and doctor's voices. My mind was elsewhere, I wasn't following. I guess she was referring to the Indians who had once inhabited those mountain slopes. After a while I couldn't stand it any more, so I got up, cleared the table and shut myself in the kitchen to wash the dishes, but I could hear them even there. When I went back to the living room, the younger woman was lying on the sofa, half covered with a blanket, and the other one was talking about a big city; it was as if she were talking up some big city, saying what a great place it was to live, but in fact she was running it down; I could tell, because every now and then both of them would start sniggering. That was something I never got with those two: their humour. I found them attractive, I liked them, but something about their sense of humour always seemed false and forced. The bottle of whisky I'd opened after dinner was half empty. That bothered me; I had no intention of getting drunk, and I didn't want them to get drunk and leave me out. So I sat down with them and said that we had to talk a few things over. What things? they asked, pretending to be surprised, or maybe they weren't just pretending. This house has too many weak points, I said. We've got to do something about it. What are they? asked one of the women. OK, I said, and I started by reminding them how far it was from town, how exposed it was, but I soon realised they weren't listening. If I was a dog, I thought resentfully, these women would show me a bit more consideration. Later, after I realised that none of us were feeling sleepy, they started talking about children and their voices made my heart recoil. I have seen terrible, evil things, sights to make a hard man flinch, but listening to the women that night, my heart recoiled so violently it almost disappeared. I tried to butt in, I tried to find out if they were recalling scenes from childhood or talking about real children in the present, but I couldn't. My throat felt like it was full of bandages and cotton swabs. Suddenly, in the middle of that conversation or double monologue, I had a premonition and I started moving stealthily towards one of the windows in the living room, a ridiculous little bull's-eye window, in a corner, too close to the main window to serve any useful purpose. I know that at the last moment the women looked at me and realised that something was happening; all I had time to do was put my finger to my lips, before pulling back the curtain and seeing Bedloe's head, the killer's head, outside. What happened next is hazy. And it's hazy because panic is contagious. The killer, I realised immediately, had started running around the outside of the house. The women and I started running around inside. Two circles: he was looking for a way in, trying to find a window left open, while the women and I went around checking the doors and shutting the windows. I know I didn't do what I should have done: gone to my room, got my gun, gone outside and made him surrender. Instead I found myself thinking that the dogs were still out there, and hoping nothing bad would happen to them; one of the dogs was pregnant, I think, I'm not sure – there'd been some talk about it. Anyway, just at that moment, while I was still running around, I heard one of the women say, Jesus, the dog, the dog, and I thought of telepathy, I thought of happiness, and I was afraid that the woman who had spoken, whichever one it was, would go out to look for the dog. Luckily, neither of them made any move to leave the house. Just as well. Just as well, I thought. And then (I'll never forget this) I went into a room on the first floor where I'd never been before. It was long, narrow and dark, illuminated only by the moon and by a faint glow coming from the porch lights. And at that moment I knew, with a terror-driven certitude, that destiny (or misfortune – the same thing in this case) had brought me to that room. At the far end, outside a window, I saw the storekeeper's silhouette. I crouched down, barely able to contain my shaking (my whole body was shaking, the sweat was pouring off me) and waited. The killer opened the window with bewildering ease and slipped quietly into the room. There were three narrow wooden beds each with a bedside table. On the wall, inches above the beds I could see three framed prints. The killer stopped for a moment. I felt him breathe; the air made a healthy sound as it went into his lungs. Then he groped his way forward, between the wall and the feet of the beds, directly towards where I was crouched, waiting for him. Although it was hard to believe, I knew he hadn't seen me: I thanked my lucky stars, and, when he got close enough, I grabbed him by the feet and pulled him down. Once he was on the floor I started kicking him with the aim of doing as much damage as possible. He's here, he's here, I shouted, but the women didn't respond (I couldn't hear them running around either), and the unfamiliar room was like a projection of my brain, the only home, the only shelter. I don't know how long I was in there, kicking that fallen body, I only remember someone opening the door behind me, words I couldn't understand, a hand on my shoulder. Then I was alone again and I stopped kicking him. For a few moments I didn't know what to do; I felt dazed and tired. Eventually, I snapped out of it and dragged the body to the living room. There I found the women, sitting very close together on the sofa, almost hugging each other. I don't know why, but something about the scene made me think of a birthday party. I could see the anxiety in their eyes, and a fading trace of the fear caused not by the episode as a whole but by the sight of Bedloe's body after the beating I'd given him. And it was the look in their eyes that made me lose my grip and let his body drop onto the carpet. Bedloe's face was a blood-spattered mask, garish in the light of the living room. Where his nose had been there was just a bleeding pulp. I checked to see if his heart was beating. The women were watching me without making the slightest movement. He's dead, I said. Before I went out onto the porch, I heard one of them sigh. I smoked a cigarette looking at the stars, thinking about how I'd explain it to the authorities in town. When I went back inside, the women were down on all fours stripping the body and I couldn't stifle a cry. They didn't even look at me. I think I drank a glass of whisky and then went out again, taking the bottle, I think. I don't know how long I was out there, smoking and drinking, giving the women time to finish their task. I went back over the events, piecing them together. I remembered the man looking in through the window, I remembered the look in his eyes, and now I recognised the fear, I remembered when he lost his dog, and finally I remembered him reading a newspaper at the back of the store. I also remembered the light the previous day, the light inside the store and the porch light seen from the room where I'd killed him. Then I started watching the dogs, who weren't sleeping, either, but running from one end of the yard to the other. The wooden fence was broken in places; someone would have to fix it some day, but it wasn't going to be me. Day began to dawn on the other side of the mountains. The dogs came up onto the porch looking for a pat, probably tired after a long night of playing. Just the usual two. I whistled for the other one, but he didn't come. The revelation struck me with the first shiver of cold. The dead man was no killer. We'd been tricked by the real killer, hidden somewhere far away, or, more likely, by fate. Bedloe didn't want to kill anyone – he was just looking for his dog. Poor bastard, I thought. The dogs went back to chasing each other around the yard. I opened the door and looked at the women, unable to bring myself to go into the living room. Bedloe's body was clothed again. Better dressed than before. I was going to say something, but there was no point, so I went back to the porch. One of the women followed me out. Now we have to get rid of the body, she said behind me. Yes, I said. Later I helped to put Bedloe into the back of the pickup. We drove into the mountains. Life is meaningless, said the older woman. I didn't answer; I dug a grave. When we got back, while they were taking a shower, I washed the pickup and got my stuff together. What will you do now? they asked while we were having breakfast on the porch, watching the clouds. I'll go back to the city, I said, and I'll pick up the investigation exactly where I got off track.

And the end of the story, as Pancho Monge tells it, is that six months later William Burns was killed by unidentified assailants.

Detectives

'What kind of weapons do you like?'

'Any kind, except for blades.'

'You mean knives, razors, daggers, *corvos*, switchblades, penknives, that sort of thing?'

'Yeah, more or less.'

'What do you mean, more or less?'

'It's just a figure of speech, asshole. I don't like any of that stuff.'

'You sure?'

'Yes, I'm sure.'

'But how can you not like *corvos*?'

'I just don't, that's all.'

'But you're talking about our national weapon.'

'So the *corvo* is Chile's national weapon?'

'Knives in general, I mean.'

'Come off it, compadre.'

'I swear to God, I read it in an article the other day. Chileans don't like firearms, it must be because of the noise; we're silent by nature.'

'That must be because of the sea.'

'How do you mean? What sea?'

'The Pacific, of course.'

'Oh, you mean the *ocean*. And what's the Pacific Ocean got to do with silence?'

'They say it absorbs noises, useless noises, I mean. I don't know whether there's anything to it.'

'So what about the Argentinians?'

'What have they got to do with the Pacific?'

'Well, they've got the Atlantic and they're pretty noisy.'

'But there's no comparison.'

'You're right about that, there's no comparison – but Argentinians like knives as well.'

'That's exactly why I don't. Even if they're the national weapon. I could make an exception, maybe, for penknives, especially Swiss Army knives, but the rest are just a curse.'

'And why's that, compadre? Come on, explain.'

'I don't have an explanation, compadre, sorry. That's just how it is, period; it's a gut feeling.'

'OK, I see where you're going with this.'

'Do you? Better tell me then, because I don't know myself.'

'Well, I know, but I don't know how to explain it.'

'Mind you, the knife thing does have its advantages.'

'Like what, for example?'

'Well, imagine a gang of thieves armed with automatic rifles. Just an example. Or pimps with Uzis.'

'OK, I'm following you.'

'So you see the advantage?'

'Absolutely, for us. But that's an insult to Chile, you know, that argument.'

'An insult to Chile! What?'

'It's an insult to the Chilean character, the way we are, our collective dreams. It's like being told that all we're good for is suffering. I don't know if you follow me, but I feel like I just saw the light.'

'I follow you, but that's not it.'

'What do you mean, that's not it?'

'That's not what I was talking about. I just don't like knives, period. It's not some big philosophical question.'

'But you'd like guns to be more popular in Chile. Which doesn't mean you'd like there to be more of them.'

'I don't care one way or the other.'

'Anyway, who doesn't like guns?'

'That's true, everyone likes guns.'

'Do you want me to explain what I meant about the silence?'

'Sure, as long as you don't put me to sleep.'

'I won't, and if you start feeling sleepy, we can stop and I'll drive.'

'So tell me about the silence then.'

'I read it in an article in *El Mercurio*.'

'When did you start reading *El Mercurio*?'

'Sometimes there's a copy lying round at headquarters, and the shifts are long. Anyway, the article said we're a Latin people, and Latin people are fixated on knives. Anglo-Saxons, on the other hand, live and die by the gun.'

'It all depends.'

'Exactly what I thought.'

'Until the moment of truth, you never know.'

'Exactly what I thought.'

'We're slower, you have to admit.'

'How do you mean, slower?'

'Slower in every respect. Old-fashioned in a way.'

'You call that being slow?'

'We're still using knives, it's like we're stuck in the Bronze Age, while the gringos have moved on to the Iron Age.'
'I never liked history.'
'Remember when we arrested Chubby Loayza?'
'How could I forget?'
'There, you see – the guy just gave himself up.'
'Yeah, and he had an arsenal in that house.'
'There, you see.'
'So he should have put up a fight.'
'There were only four of us, and five of them. We just had standard issue weapons and Chubby had an arsenal, including a bazooka.'
'It wasn't a bazooka, compadre.'
'It was a Franchi SPAS-15! And he had a pair of sawn-off shotguns. But Loayza gave himself up without firing a shot.'
'So you were disappointed, were you?'
'Or course not. But if he'd been called McCurly instead of Loayza, Chubby would have greeted us with a hail of bullets, and maybe he wouldn't be in jail now.'
'Maybe he'd be dead.'
'Or free, if you get my drift.'
'McCurly? . . . the name rings a bell; wasn't he in a cowboy movie?'
'I think he was, I think we even saw it together.'
'We haven't been to the movies together for ages.'
'Well, this would have been ages ago.'
'The arsenal he had, Chubby Loayza; remember how he greeted us?'
'Laughing his head off.'
'I think it was nerves. One of his gang started crying. I don't think that kid was even seventeen.'

'But Chubby Loayza was over forty and he made himself out to be a tough guy. Though if we're going to be brutally honest, there aren't any tough guys in this country.'

'What do you mean there aren't any tough guys, I've seen really tough guys.'

'Crazies, for sure, you've seen plenty of them, but tough guys? Very few, or none.'

'And what about Raulito Sánchez? Remember Raulito Sánchez, with his Manurhin?'

'How could I forget him?'

'What about him then?'

'Well, he should have got rid of the revolver straightaway. That was his downfall. Nothing's easier to trace than a Magnum.'

'The Manurhin is a Magnum?'

'Of course it's a Magnum.'

'I thought it was a French gun.'

'It's a .357 French Magnum. That's why he didn't get rid of it. It's an expensive piece and he'd got fond of it; there aren't many in Chile.'

'You learn something new every day.'

'Poor Raulito Sánchez.'

'They say he died in jail.'

'No, he died just after getting out, in a boarding house in Arica.'

'They say his lungs were ruined.'

'He'd been spitting blood since he was a kid, but he was brave, he never complained.'

'I remember he was very quiet.'

'Quiet and hard-working, but a bit too attached to material possessions. That Manurhin was his downfall.'

'Whores were his downfall.'
'Come on, Raulito Sánchez was a faggot.'
'You're kidding! I had no idea. Nothing's sacred. Time levels even the tallest towers.'
'Give me a break, what's it got to do with towers?'
'It's just that I remember him as really manly, if you know what I mean.'
'What's it got to do with manliness?'
'But he was a man, in his way, though, wasn't he?'
'I don't really know what to say to that.'
'I saw him with whores at least once. He didn't turn up his nose at whores.'
'He didn't turn up his nose at anyone or anything, but I'm certain he never slept with a woman.'
'That's a very definite assertion, compadre, careful what you say. The dead are always watching us.'
'The dead aren't watching anyone. They're minding their own business. The dead are shit.'
'What do you mean they're shit?'
'All they do is fuck stuff up for the living.'
'I'm afraid I can't agree there, compadre, I have the greatest respect for the departed.'
'Except you never go to the cemetery.'
'What do you mean I never go to the cemetery?'
'All right, then, when's the Day of the Dead?'
'OK, you got me, I go when I feel like it.'
'Do you believe in ghosts?'
'I'm not sure, but I know there are experiences that make your hair stand on end.'
'That's what I was coming to.'
'You're thinking of Raulito Sánchez?'

'That's right. Before he died for real, he pretended to be dead at least twice. One time in a hooker's bar. Remember Doris Villalón? She spent a whole night with him in the cemetery, under the same blanket and, according to Doris, nothing happened all night.'

'Except that Doris's hair turned white.'

'It depends who you talk to.'

'The fact is her hair went white in a single night, like Marie Antoinette's.'

'What I know from a reliable source is that she was cold and they climbed into an empty niche; after that it's not so clear. According to one of Doris's friends, she tried to give Raulito a hand job, but he wasn't really up for it, and in the end he fell asleep.'

'There was a man who never lost his cool.'

'It happened later, when the dogs had stopped barking and Doris was climbing down from the niche; that's when the ghost appeared.'

'So her hair went white because of a ghost?'

'That's what they said.'

'Maybe it was just plaster dust from the cemetery.'

'It's not easy to believe in ghosts.'

'And meanwhile Raulito went on sleeping?'

'Without even having touched the poor woman.'

'And what was his hair like the next morning?'

'Black as ever, but it couldn't be used to prove the point, because he'd upped and left.'

'So the plaster dust might have had nothing to do with it.'

'It might have been the scare she got.'

'The scare she got at the police station.'

'Or maybe her hair dye faded.'

'Such are the mysteries of the human condition. In any case, Raulito never tried it with a girl.'

'But he seemed like a real man.'

'There are no men left in Chile, compadre.'

'You're scaring me now. Careful how you drive. Don't get jumpy on me.'

'I think it was a rabbit, I must have run over it.'

'What do you mean there are no men left?'

'We killed them all.'

'What do you mean we killed them? I haven't killed anyone in my life. And you were just doing your duty.'

'My duty?'

'Duty, obligation, keeping the peace, it's our job, it's what we do. Or would you rather get paid for just sitting around?'

'I've never liked sitting around, I've always had ants in my pants, but that's exactly why I should have left.'

'That just would have helped with the shortage of men in Chile.'

'Don't start making fun of me, compadre, especially when I'm driving.'

'You keep calm and watch where you're going. Anyway, what's Chile got to do with it?'

'Everything, and when I say everything . . .'

'OK, I see where you're going.'

'Do you remember '73?'

'That's what I was thinking of.'

'That's when we killed them all.'

'Maybe you should go easy on the gas, at least while you explain what you mean.'

'There's not a lot to explain. Plenty to cry over, but not to explain.'

'But since it's a long trip, we might as well talk. Who did we kill in '73?'

'The real men we had in this country.'

'No need to exaggerate, compadre. Anyway, we went first; don't forget we were prisoners too.'

'But only for three days.'

'But those were the first three days, and honestly I was scared shitless.'

'Some were never released, like Inspector Tovar, Hick Tovar, remember him? He had guts, that guy.'

'Didn't they drown him on Quiriquina Island?'

'That's what we told his widow, but the real story never came out.'

'That's what I can't stand sometimes.'

'No point getting cut up about it.'

'The dead turn up in my dreams, and I get them mixed up with the ones who are neither dead nor alive.'

'How do you mean neither dead nor alive?'

'I mean the people who've changed, who've grown up, like us, for instance.'

'Now I get you – we're not children any more, if that's what you mean.'

'And sometimes I feel like I'm never going to wake up, like I've gone and fucked it up for good.'

'You just worry too much, compadre.'

'And sometimes it makes me so angry I have to find someone to blame, you know what I'm like, those mornings when I turn up in a rotten mood, looking for someone to blame, but I can't find anyone, or I find the wrong person, which is worse, and then I go to pieces.'

'Yeah, yeah, I know.'

'And I blame Chile, and call it a country of faggots and killers.'

'And why are the faggots to blame, can you tell me that?'

'Well, they're not, but everyone's fair game.'

'I can't agree with you there; life's hard enough as it is.'

'Then I think this country went to hell years ago, and the reason we're here, those of us who stayed, is to have nightmares, just because someone had to stay and face up to them.'

'Watch it, there's a hill coming up. Don't look at me, I'm not arguing with you – watch where you're going.'

'And that's when I think there are no men left in this country. It's like a revelation. There are no men left, just sleepwalkers.'

'And what about the women?'

'You can be thick sometimes, compadre; I'm talking about the human condition, in general, and that includes women.'

'I'm not sure I understand.'

'Well, I was perfectly clear.'

'So you're saying there are no men in Chile and no women who are men either.'

'Not exactly, but almost.'

'I think the women of Chile deserve a bit more respect.'

'Who's disrespecting Chilean women?'

'You are, compadre, for a start.'

'But how could I disrespect Chilean women? They're the only women I know.'

'That's what you say, but it's lip-service, isn't it?'

'How come you're so touchy all of a sudden?'

'I'm not touchy.'

'You know, I kind of feel like stopping and smashing your face in.'

'We'll have to see about that.'
'Jesus, what a beautiful night.'
'Don't beautiful night me. What's the night got to do with anything?'
'It must be because of the full moon.'
'Don't talk in riddles. I'm Chilean, remember, I don't believe in beating around the bush.'
'That's where you're wrong. We're all Chileans here and all we ever do is beat around one great big fucking nightmare of a bush.'
'You're a pessimist, that's what you are.'
'What do you expect?'
'Even in the darkest hours there is a light that shines. I think it was Pezoa who said that.'
'Pezoa Véliz.'
'Even in the blackest moments a little hope remains.'
'Hope has gone to shit.'
'Hope is the only thing that doesn't go to shit.'
'Pezoa Véliz. You know what I just remembered?'
'And how am I supposed to know that, compadre?'
'When we started in Criminal Investigations.'
'At the station in Concepción?'
'At the station in Calle del Temple.'
'All I remember about that station is the whores.'
'I never fucked them.'
'How can you say that, compadre?'
'I mean at the start, the first months; later on it was different, I started picking up bad habits.'
'Anyway it was free, and when you fuck a whore and don't pay, it's like you're not fucking a whore.'
'A whore is always a whore.'

'Sometimes I think you don't like women.'
'What do you mean I don't like women?'
'It's the way you talk about them, with contempt.'
'That's because, in my experience, when you get mixed up with whores it always goes sour.'
'Come on, nothing in the world is sweeter.'
'Yeah, sure, that's why we used to rape them.'
'Are you talking about the station in Calle del Temple?'
'That's exactly what I'm talking about.'
'Come on, we didn't rape them, that was an exchange of favours. It was a way of killing time. The next morning they went off perfectly happy after giving us a bit of relief. Don't you remember?'
'I remember lots of things.'
'The interrogations were worse. I never volunteered.'
'But you'd have done it if you'd been asked.'
'I don't know what I would have done.'
'You remember our classmate from high school who was a prisoner?'
'Of course I do, what was his name?'
'I was the one who realised he was there, though I still hadn't seen him myself. You'd seen him, but you didn't recognise him.'
'We were twenty years old, compadre, and we hadn't seen the guy for at least five years. Arturo I think he was called. He didn't recognise me either.'
'Yeah, Arturo. He left Chile when he was fifteen and came back when he was twenty.'
'Bad timing, eh?'
'Good too, in a way, though, ending up at our station, of all the places he could have been taken . . .'

'Well, that's all ancient history now, we're all living in peace now.'

'As soon as I saw his name on the list of political prisoners, I knew it was him. It's not a very common name.'

'Watch where you're going; we can swap if you like.'

'And the first thing I thought was, It's our old classmate Arturo, crazy Arturo, who went to Mexico when he was fifteen.'

'Well, I reckon he was happy to find us there too.'

'Of course he was happy! When you saw him he was incommunicado and the other prisoners had to feed him.'

'He really was happy.'

'It's like I'm seeing it now.'

'But you weren't even there.'

'No, but you told me. You said, You're Arturo Belano, aren't you, from Los Ángeles, Bio-Bio. And he replied, Yes sir, I am.'

'That's funny, I'd forgotten that.'

'And then you said, Don't you remember me, Arturo? Don't you know who I am, asshole? And he looked at you as if he was thinking, Now it's my turn to get tortured or What does this son of a bitch want with me?'

'There was fear in his eyes, it's true.'

'And he said, No, sir, I've got no idea, but he'd already started to look at you differently, peering through the fecal waters of the past, as the poet might say.'

'There was fear in his eyes, that's all.'

'And then you said, It's me, asshole, your classmate from high school in Los Ángeles, five years ago. Don't you recognise me? Arancibia! And it was like he was making a huge effort, because five years is a long time and a lot of things had happened to him since he'd left Chile, plus what was happening now he'd come back, and he just couldn't place you, he could remember the faces of fifteen-year-olds, not twenty-year-olds, and anyway you were never one of his close friends.'

'He was friends with everyone, but he used to hang out with the tough kids.'

'You were never one of his close friends.'

'I would've liked to be, though, I have to admit.'

'And then he said, Arancibia, yeah, of course, Arancibia, and this is the funny bit, isn't it?'

'It depends. My partner wasn't amused at all.'

'He grabbed you by the shoulders and gave you a thump in the chest that sent you flying back at least three yards.'

'A yard and a half, just like the old days.'

'And your partner jumped on him, of course, thinking the poor jerk had gone crazy.'

'Or was trying to escape. We were so cocky back then we didn't take our guns off to do the roll call.'

'In other words, your partner thought he was after your gun, so he jumped on him.'

'And he would have laid into him, but I said he was a friend.'

'And then you started slapping Belano on the back and said relax and told him what a good time we were having.'

'I only told him about the whores; Jesus, we were green.'

'You said, I get to screw a whore in the cells every night.'

'No, I said we organised raids and then fucked until the sun came up, but only when we were on duty, of course.'

'And he must have said, Fantastic, Arancibia, fantastic, glad to see you're keeping up the good work.'

'Something like that; watch this curve.'

'And you said to him, What are you doing here, Belano? Didn't you go to live in Mexico? And he told you he'd come back, and, of course, he said he was as innocent as the next man in the street.'

'He asked me to do him a favour and let him make a phone call.'

'And you let him use the phone.'

'The same afternoon.'

'And you told him about me.'

'I said: Contreras is here, too. And he thought you were a prisoner.'

'Shut up in a cell, screaming at three in the morning, like Chubby Martinazzo.'

'Who was Martinazzo? I can't remember now.'

'We had him there for a while. Belano would have heard him yelling every night, unless he was a heavy sleeper.'

'But I said, No, compadre, Contreras is a detective too, and I whispered in his ear: But he's left-wing, don't go telling.'

'That was bad; you shouldn't have said that.'

'I wasn't going to hang you out to dry.'

'And what did Belano say?'

'He looked like he didn't believe me. He looked like he didn't know who the hell Contreras was. He looked like he thought this fucking cop is going to take me to the slaughterhouse.'

'Though he was a trusting sort of kid.'

'Everyone's trusting at fifteen.'

'I didn't even trust my own mother.'

'What do you mean you didn't trust your own mother? You can't fool your mother.'

'Exactly, that's why.'

'And then I said to him: You'll see Contreras this morning, when they take you to the john, watch out for him, he'll give you a signal. And Belano said OK, but he wanted me to set up the phone call. That was all he cared about.'

'So he could get someone to bring him food.'

'Anyway, he was happy when I left him. Sometimes I think if we'd met in the street he mightn't even have said hello. It's a funny world.'

'He wouldn't have recognised you. You weren't one of his friends at high school.'

'Neither were you.'

'But he did recognise me. When they took them out around eleven, all the political prisoners in single file, I went over near the corridor that led to the bathroom and gave him a nod. He was the youngest of the prisoners and he wasn't looking too good.'

'But did he recognise you or not?'

'Of course he recognised me. We smiled at each other from a distance and then he believed the stuff you'd told him.'

'And what had I told him? Come on, let's hear it.'

'A whole heap of lies, as I found out when I went to see him.'

'You went to see him?'

'That night, after they transferred the other prisoners. Belano was left all on his own, with hours to go before the new lot arrived, and his spirits were about as low as they could get.'

'Even the toughest guys lose it inside.'

'Well, he hadn't broken down, either, if that's what you mean.'

'No, but nearly.'

'Nearly, that's true. Also, a really weird thing happened to him. I think that's why I remembered him tonight.'

'So what was this weird thing?'

'Well, it happened when he was incommunicado – you know how it was in that station: all it meant was that you starved, because you could send as many messages as you liked to people on the outside. Anyway, Belano was incommunicado, which meant that no one was bringing him any food, and he had no soap, no toothbrush, and no blanket to wrap himself in at night. And after a few days, of course, he was dirty, unshaven, his clothes stank, you know, the usual. The thing is, once a day we used to take all the prisoners to the bathroom, remember?'

'How could I forget?'

'And on the way to the bathroom there was a mirror, not in the bathroom itself, but in a corridor that ran between the bathroom and the gym where the political prisoners were kept, a tiny little mirror, near the records office, you remember, don't you?'

'I don't remember that, compadre.'

'Well, there was this mirror, and all the political prisoners would look at themselves in it. We'd taken down the mirror in the showers, so no one would get any stupid ideas, and this was the only chance they got to see how well they'd shaved or how straight their part was, so they all had a look in it, especially when they'd been allowed to shave or the one day of the week when they got to take a shower.'

'OK, I get you, and since Belano was incommunicado he couldn't even shave or take a shower or anything.'

'Exactly, he didn't have a razor, or a towel, or soap, or clean clothes, and he never got to take a shower.'

'But I can't remember him smelling really bad.'

'Everyone stank. You could wash every day and still stink. You stank, too.'

'You leave me out of it, compadre, and watch that embankment.'

'Well, the thing is, when Belano was in the line with the prisoners, he always avoided looking at himself in the mirror. You see? He turned away. Whether he was going from the gym to the bathroom or from the bathroom back to the gym, when he got to the corridor with the mirror, he looked the other way.'

'He was afraid to look at himself.'

'Until one day, after finding out that his old schoolmates were there to get him out of that fix, he felt up to it. He'd been thinking about it all night and all morning. His luck had changed, so he decided to face the mirror and see how he looked.'

'And what happened?'

'He didn't recognise himself.'

'That's all?'

'That's all; he didn't recognise himself. He told me so the night I got a chance to talk with him. I really wasn't expecting him to come out with that. I'd gone to tell him not to get me wrong, I was really left-wing, I had nothing to do with all the shit that was happening, but he came out with this crap about the mirror and I didn't know what to say.'

'And what did you say about me?'

'I didn't say anything at all. He did all the talking. He said it was a simple thing, it didn't come as a shock at all, if you see what I mean. He was in the line, on the way to the bathroom, and as he passed the mirror, he turned suddenly, looked at his face and saw someone else, but he wasn't frightened, he didn't start shaking or get hysterical. I guess you could say that by then, knowing we were there at the station, he had no reason to get hysterical. Anyway, he did what he needed to do in the bathroom, quietly, thinking about the person he'd seen, thinking it over, but not making a big deal of it. And when they went back to the gym, he looked in the mirror again, and sure enough, he said, it wasn't him, it was someone else, and I said to him, What are you saying, asshole? What do you mean someone else?'

'That's what I would have said, too. What *did* he mean?'

'He said, Someone else. And I said, Explain it to me. And he said, A different person, that's all.'

'And then you thought he'd gone crazy.'

'I don't know what I thought, but to be honest, I was scared.'

'A Chilean? Scared?'

'You think that's so unusual?'

'Well, I wouldn't say it's usual for you.'

'Whatever you say. I realised straightaway that he wasn't trying to kid me. I'd taken him to the little room beside the gym, and he started talking about the mirror and the way they had to file past it every morning, and suddenly I realised that all of it was true: him, me, our conversation. And since we weren't in the gym, and since he'd been a student at our grand old alma mater, it occurred to me that I could take him to the corridor where the mirror was and say, Take another look, with me here beside you this time, take a good calm look, and tell me if it isn't the same old crazy Belano you see.'

'And did you say that?'

'Of course I did, but to be honest, the thought came a long time before the words. As if an eternity had passed between the idea popping into my head and coming out in a comprehensible form. A little eternity, to make things worse. Because if it had been a big or just a regular eternity, I wouldn't have realised, if you follow me, but as it was, I did realise, and that intensified my fear.'

'But you went ahead anyway.'

'Of course I did; by then it was too late to turn back. I said, We're going to do a test; let's see if the same thing happens with me beside you, and he looked at me warily, but he said, All right, if you insist, like he was doing me a favour, when in fact I was the one doing him a favour, as usual.'

'So you went to the mirror?'

'We went to the mirror. I was taking a big risk because you know what would have happened if they'd caught me walking around the station with a political prisoner at midnight. And to help him calm down and be as objective as possible, I offered him a smoke, so we stood there puffing away and it was only when we'd crushed the butts on the ground that we headed off towards the bathroom, and he was relaxed, I guess he was thinking it couldn't get any worse (which was bullshit, it could have been much, much worse), and I was kind of on edge, listening for the slightest noise, the sound of a door shutting, but I was careful not to let it show, and when we got to the mirror I said, Look at yourself, and he looked at himself, he stood in front of the mirror and looked at his face, he even ran a hand through his hair, which was really long, you know, the way people wore it in '73, and then he glanced aside, stepped away from the mirror and looked at the ground for a while.'

'And?'

'That's what I said, And? Is it you or isn't it? And he looked into my eyes and said: It's someone else, compadre, that's all there is to it. I could feel something inside me like a muscle or a nerve, I don't know what it was, I swear, but it was saying: Smile, asshole, smile, and yet however much the muscle strained, I couldn't smile, the best I could do was twitch, a spasm jerked my cheek up, anyway, he noticed and stood there looking at me, and I ran a hand over my face and gulped, because I was afraid again.'

'We're almost there.'

'And then I had this idea. I said to him: Listen, I'm going to look in the mirror, and when I look at myself, you're going to look at me then you're going to look at my reflection, and you're going to realise it's the same, the problem is this filthy mirror and this filthy station and the bad lighting in this corridor. And he didn't say anything, but I took that as a yes – he could have objected – and I came up to the mirror and leaned forward with my eyes shut.'

'You can see the lights already, compadre, we're just about there, take it easy.'

'Are you playing deaf, or what? Didn't you hear me?'

'Of course I heard you. You had your eyes shut.'

'I stood in front of the mirror with my eyes shut. And then I opened them. Maybe that's normal for you: standing in front of a mirror with your eyes shut.'

'Nothing seems normal to me any more, compadre.'

'Then I opened them, suddenly, I opened my eyes right

up and looked at myself and saw someone staring back at me wide-eyed, like he was scared shitless, and behind him I saw a guy about twenty years old, but he looked at least ten years older, a skinny guy with a beard and bags under his eyes, looking at us over my shoulder, and to tell the truth, I couldn't be sure, I saw a swarm of faces, as if the mirror was broken, though I knew perfectly well it wasn't, and then Belano said, very softly, it was barely more than a whisper, he said: Hey, Contreras, is there some kind of room behind that wall?'

'The fuckhead! He'd seen too many movies!'

'And when I heard his voice it was like I woke up, but in reverse, and instead of coming back to this side, I'd come out on the other side, where even my own voice sounded strange. No, I said, as far as I know, behind it there's just the yard. The yard where the cells are? he asked me. Yes, I said, where the regular prisoners are. And then the son of a bitch said: Now I understand. And that completely flummoxed me, because, I mean, what was there to understand? And I said the first thing that came into my head: What the flying fuck do you understand now? But I said it softly, without raising my voice, so softly he didn't hear me, and I didn't have the strength to repeat the question. So I looked in the mirror again and saw two old classmates, a twenty-year-old cop with a loose tie, and a dirty-looking guy with long hair and a beard, all skin and bone, and I thought: Jesus, we really have fucked up, haven't we, Contreras. Then I put my hands on Belano's shoulders and led him back to the gym. When we came to the door a thought crossed my mind: I could take out my gun and shoot him right here; it would have been so easy, all I had to do was aim and put a bullet through his head, I've always been a good shot, even in the dark. Then I could have come up with any old explanation. But of course I didn't do it.'

'Of course you didn't. We don't do that sort of thing, compadre.'

'No, we don't do that sort of thing.'

Cell Mates

We happened to be in prison in the same month of the same year, although the prisons were thousands of miles apart. Sofia was born in 1950 in Bilbao. She was dark, small and very pretty. In November 1973, while I was a prisoner in Chile, she was sent to jail in Aragon.

At the time she was getting her degree in science at the University of Zaragoza, biology or chemistry, one or the other, and she went to jail with almost all of her classmates. On the fourth or fifth night we slept together, as I was adopting a new position, she told me there was no point tiring myself out. I like variety, I said. If I fuck in the same position two nights in a row, I become impotent. Well, don't do it for my sake, she said. The room had a very high ceiling, and the walls were painted red, the colour of a desert at sunset. She had painted them herself a few days after moving in. It looked awful. I've made love every way there is, she said. I don't believe you, I replied. Every way there is? That's right, she said, and I was at a loss for words (maybe I was embarrassed) but I believed her.

Later she told me, but this was quite a few days later, that she was losing her mind. She ate hardly anything, only instant mashed potatoes. Once I went into the kitchen and saw a plastic bag beside the refrigerator. It was a twenty-kilo bag of mashed potato flakes. Is that all you eat? I asked. She smiled and said yes — sometimes she ate other things, but mostly when she went out to a bar or a restaurant. At home it's simpler just to have mashed potatoes, she said. That way there's always something to eat. She didn't put milk in it, only water, and she didn't even wait for the water to boil. She mixed the flakes with warm water, she told me, because she hated milk. I never saw her consume any milk products; she said it was probably some kind of psychological problem that went back to her childhood, something to do with her mother. So when we were both in the apartment at night, she would have her mashed potatoes, and sometimes she would sit up late with me watching movies on TV. We hardly talked. She never argued. At the time there was a Communist living in the apartment; he was in his twenties, like us, and he and I used to get into long, pointless arguments, but she never joined in, although I knew she was more on my side than on his. One day the Communist told me Sofia was hot and he was planning to fuck her at the first opportunity. Go ahead, I said. Two or three nights later, while I was watching a Bardem movie, I heard him go out into the passage and knock discreetly on Sofia's door. They talked for a while and then the door closed and the Communist was in there for a good two hours.

Sofia had been married, though I didn't find out until much later. Her husband had been a student at the University of Zaragoza too, and gone to prison with the rest of them in November 1973. When they finished their degrees they moved to Barcelona and after a while they split up. He was called Emilio and they were still good friends. Did you make love every way there is with Emilio? No, but nearly, said Sofia. She also said she was losing her mind and it was a worry, especially if she was driving. The other night it happened in Diagonal, luckily there wasn't much traffic. Are you taking something? Valium. Lots and lots of Valium. Before we slept together, we went to the movies a couple of times. French movies, I think. One was about a woman pirate; she goes to this island where another woman pirate lives and they have a duel to the death with swords. The other one was set during World War Two; there was a guy who worked for the Germans and for the Resistance at the same time. After we started sleeping together we kept going to the movies and, strangely, I can remember the titles of the films we saw and the names of the directors, but nothing else about them. From the very first night Sofia made it perfectly clear that our relationship wasn't going to be serious. I'm in love with someone else, she said. Our Communist comrade? No, you don't know him; he's a teacher, like me. She didn't want to tell me his name just then. Sometimes she spent the night with him, but not very often, about once a fortnight. We made love every night. At first I tried to tire her out. We would start at eleven and keep going until four in the morning, but soon I realised there was no way of tiring out Sofia.

At the time I used to hang out with anarchists and radical feminists and the books I read were more or less influenced by the company I was keeping. There was one by an Italian feminist, Carla something, called *Let's Spit on Hegel*. One afternoon I lent it to Sofia. Read it, I said, I thought it was really good. (Maybe I said she would get a lot out of it.) The next day Sofia was in a very good mood; she gave me back the book and said that as science fiction it wasn't bad, but otherwise it sucked. Only an Italian woman could have written it, she declared. What have you got against Italian women? I asked. Did one abuse you when you were little or something? She said no, but if she was going to read that sort of thing, she preferred Valerie Solanas. I was surprised to learn that her favourite author was not a woman but an Englishman, David Cooper, one of R. D. Laing's associates. I ended up reading Valerie Solanas and David Cooper and even Laing (his sonnets). One of the things that impressed me most about Cooper was that during his time in Argentina (although I'm not sure now whether Cooper was ever really in Argentina, maybe I'm getting mixed up) he used hallucinogenic drugs to treat left-wing activists. These were people who were cracking up because they knew they could die at any moment, people who might not have the experience of growing old in real life, but they could have it with the drugs, and they got better. Sofía used drugs too, sometimes. She took LSD and amphetamines and Rohypnol, pills to speed up and pills to slow down and pills to steady her hands on the steering wheel. I rarely accepted the offer of a lift in her car. We didn't go out much, in fact. I went on with my life, she went on with hers, and at night, in her room or in mine, our bodies locked in a relentless struggle that lasted till daybreak and left us wrung out.

One afternoon Emilio came to see her and she introduced me to him. He was tall, he had a wonderful smile, and you could tell he was fond of Sofía. His girlfriend was called Nuria; she was Catalan and worked as a high school teacher, like Emilio and Sofía. You couldn't have imagined two women more different. Nuria was blonde, blue-eyed, tall and rather plump. Sofía had dark hair and brown eyes so dark they seemed black; she was short and slim as a marathon runner. In spite of everything they seemed to be good friends. As I found out later on, it was Emilio who had ended the marriage, although the separation had been amicable. Sometimes, when we'd been sitting there for a long time without talking, Nuria looked North American to me and Sofía looked Vietnamese. But Emilio just looked like Emilio, a chemistry or biology teacher from Aragon, who'd been an anti-Franco activist and a political prisoner, a decent sort of guy though not very interesting. One night Sofía told me about the man she was in love with. He was called Juan and he was a member of the Communist Party like our comrade. He worked in the same school as her, so they saw each other every day. He was married and had a son. So where do you do it? In my car, said Sofía, or his. We go out in our cars and follow each other through the streets of Barcelona, sometimes all the way to Tibidabo or Sant Cugat. Sometimes we just park in a dark street and he gets into my car or I get into his. Not long after she told me this, Sofía got sick and had to stay in bed. At that stage there were only three of us in the apartment: Sofía, the Communist and me. The Communist was only around at night so I had to look after Sofía and go to the pharmacy. One night she said we should go travelling. Where? I asked. Portugal, she said. I liked the idea, so one morning we set off for Portugal, hitchhiking. (I thought we would go in her car but Sofía was scared of driving.) It was a long and complicated trip. We stopped in Zaragoza, where Sofía still had her best friends, then at her sister's place in Madrid, then in Extremadura . . .

    I got the feeling Sofía was visiting all her ex-lovers. I got the feeling she was saying goodbye to them one by one, but not in a calm or resigned sort of way. When we made love she seemed absent at first, as if it had nothing to do with her, but after a while she let herself go and ended up coming over and over. Then she started crying and I asked her why. Because I'm such an animal; even though I'm miles away, I can't help coming. Don't be so hard on yourself, I said, and we went on making love. Her face wet with tears was delicious to kiss. Her whole body burned and flexed like a red-hot piece of metal, but her tears were only lukewarm and, as they ran down her neck, as I spread them on her nipples, they turned ice-cold. A month later we were back in Barcelona. Sofia hardly ate a thing all day. She went back to her diet of instant mashed potatoes and decided not to leave the apartment. One night I came home and found her with a girl I didn't know; another time it was Emilio and Nuria, who looked at me as if I were to blame for the state she was in. I felt bad but said nothing and shut myself in my room. I tried to read, but I could hear them. Shocked exclamations, reprimands, advice. Sofia didn't say a thing. A week later she was given four months' sick leave. The government doctor was an old friend from Zaragoza. I thought we'd be able to spend more time together, but little by little we drifted apart. Some nights she didn't come home. I remember staying up very late, watching TV and waiting for her. Sometimes the Communist kept me company. I had nothing to do, so I set about tidying up the apartment: sweeping, mopping, dusting. The Communist was very impressed, but one day he had to go too and I was left all on my own.

By then Sofia had become a ghost; she appeared without a sound, shut herself in her room or the bathroom and disappeared again after a few hours. One night we ran into each other on the stairs, I was going up and she was coming down, and the only thing I could think of asking was if she had a new lover. I regretted it straightaway, but it was too late. I can't remember what she said. In the good old days, five of us had lived in that huge apartment; now it was just me and the mice. Sometimes I imagined Sofia in a prison cell in Zaragoza, back in November 1973, and me, in the southern hemisphere, locked up too, for a few decisive days, and though I realised that this fact or coincidence had to be significant, I couldn't work out what it meant. I've never been any good at analogies. One night, when I came home, I found a note saying goodbye and some money on the kitchen table. At first I went on living as if Sofia was still there. I can't remember exactly how long I waited for her. I think the electricity got cut off. After that I moved to another apartment.

It was a long time before I saw her again. She was walking down Las Ramblas, looking lost. We stood there, the cold seeping into our bones, talking about things that meant nothing to her or to me. Walk me home, she said. She was living near El Borne, in a building that was falling down it was so old. The staircase was narrow and creaked with every step we took. We climbed up to the door of her apartment, on the top floor. To my surprise, she didn't let me in. I should have asked her what was going on, but I left without saying anything; if that's what she wanted, it was up to her.

A week later I went back to her apartment. The bell wasn't working and I had to knock several times. I thought there was no one there. Then I thought there was no one *living* there. Just as I was about to go, the door opened. It was Sofia. The apartment was dark and the light on the landing went off automatically after twenty seconds. At first, because of the darkness, I didn't realise she was naked. You're going to freeze, I said when the landing light came on again and showed her standing there, very straight, thinner than before. Her stomach and legs, which I had kissed so many times, looked terribly helpless, and instead of feeling drawn towards her, I was chilled at the sight, as if I were the one without clothes. Can I come in? Sofia shook her head. I assumed her nakedness meant that she was not alone. I said as much, and smiling stupidly, assured her that I didn't mean to be indiscreet. I was about to go back down the stairs when she said she was alone. I stopped and looked at her, more carefully this time, trying to read her expression, but her face was indecipherable. I also looked over her shoulder. Nothing had stirred in the utter silence and darkness of the apartment, but my instinct told me that someone was hiding there, listening to us, waiting. Are you feeling all right? Fine, she said very quietly. Have you taken something? No, nothing, I haven't taken any drugs, she whispered. Are you going to let me in? Can I make you some tea? No, said Sofia. Since I was asking questions, I thought I might as well try one more: Why won't you let me see your apartment, Sofia? Her answer surprised me. My boyfriend will be back soon and he doesn't like it if there's anyone here with me, especially a man. I didn't know whether to be angry or treat it as a joke. Sounds like this boyfriend of yours is a vampire, I said. Sofia smiled for the first time, although it was a weak, distant smile. I've told him about you, she said. He'd recognise you. And what would he do? Hit me? No, he'd just get angry, she said. And kick me out? (Now I was starting to get indignant. For a moment I hoped he did turn up, this boyfriend Sofia was waiting for, naked in the dark, just to see what would happen, what he would do.) He wouldn't kick you out, she said. He'd just get angry; he wouldn't talk to you and after you went he'd hardly say a word to me. You've lost it, haven't you, I spluttered, I don't know if you realise what you're saying, they've done something to you, it's like you're a different person. I'm the same as ever; you're the idiot who can't see what's going on. Sofia, Sofia, what's happened to you? You never used to be like this. Get out, just go, she said – What would you know about me?

More than a year went by before I heard any news of Sofia. One afternoon, coming out of the cinema, I ran into Nuria. We recognised each other, started talking about the movie and decided to go and have coffee. It wasn't long before we got on to Sofia. How long since you saw her? she asked me. A long time, I told her, but I also said that some mornings, when I woke up, I felt as if I had just seen her. Like you've been dreaming about her? No, I said, like I'd spent the night with her. That's weird. Something like that used to happen to Emilio too. Until she tried to kill him. Then he stopped having the nightmares.

She told me the story. It was simple. It was incomprehensible.

Six or seven months earlier, Sofia had rung up Emilio. According to what he later told Nuria, Sofia mentioned monsters, conspiracies and murders: she said the only thing that scared her more than a mad person was someone who deliberately drove others to madness. Then she arranged for him to come to her apartment, the one I'd been to a couple of times. The next day Emilio arrived exactly on time. The dark or poorly lit staircase, the bell that didn't work, the knocking at the door: up to that point it was all familiar and predictable. Sofia opened the door. She wasn't naked. She invited him in. Emilio had never been in the apartment before. The living room, according to Nuria, was pokey, but it was also in a terrible state, with filth dripping down the walls and dirty plates piled on the table. At first Emilio couldn't see a thing, the light was so dim in the room. Then he made out a man sitting in an armchair, and greeted him. The man didn't react. Sit down, said Sofia, we need to talk. Emilio sat down. A little voice inside him was saying over and over, This is not good, but he ignored it. He thought Sofia was going to ask him for a loan. Again. Although probably not with that man in the room. Sofia never asked for money in the presence of a third party, so Emilio sat down and waited.

Then Sofia said: There are one or two things about life that my husband would like to explain to you. For a moment Emilio thought that when she said 'my husband' she meant him. He thought she wanted him to say something to her new boyfriend. He smiled. He started saying there was really nothing to explain; every experience is unique . . . Suddenly Emilio understood that he was the 'you' and the 'husband' was the other man, and that something bad was about to happen, something very bad. As he tried to get to his feet, Sofia threw herself at him. What followed was rather comical. Sofia held or tried to hold Emilio's legs while her new boyfriend made a sincere but clumsy attempt to strangle him. Sofia, however, was small and so was the nameless man (somehow, in the midst of the struggle, Emilio had time and presence of mind enough to notice the resemblance between them – they were like twins) and the fight, or the caricature thereof, was soon over. Maybe it was fear that gave Emilio a taste for revenge: as soon as he got Sofia's boyfriend down on the ground he started kicking him and kept going until he was tired. He must have broken a few ribs, said Nuria, you know what Emilio's like (I didn't, but nodded all the same). Then he turned his attention to Sofia who was ineffectually trying to hold him back from behind and hitting him, although he could hardly feel it. He gave her three slaps (it was the first time he had ever laid a hand on her, according to Nuria) and left. Since then they had heard nothing about her, though Nuria still got scared at night, especially when she was coming home from work.

I'm telling you all this in case you ever feel like visiting Sofia, said Nuria. No, I said, I haven't seen her for ages and I don't have any plans to drop in on her. Then we talked about other things for a little while and said goodbye. Two days later, without really knowing what prompted me to do it, I went round to Sofia's apartment.

She opened the door. She was thinner than ever. At first she didn't recognise me. Do I look that different, Sofia? I muttered. Oh, it's you, she said. Then she sneezed and took a step back. Perhaps mistakenly, I interpreted this as an invitation to go in. She didn't stop me.

The room in which they had set up the ambush was poorly lit (the only window gave on to a gloomy, narrow air shaft) but it didn't seem dirty. In fact the first thing that struck me was how clean it was. Sofia didn't seem dirty either. I sat down in an armchair, maybe the one Emilio had sat in on the day of the ambush, and lit a cigarette. Sofia was still standing, looking at me as if she wasn't quite sure who I was. She was wearing a long, narrow skirt, more suitable for summer, a light top and sandals. She had thick socks on and for a moment I thought they were mine, but no, they couldn't have been. I asked her how she was. She didn't answer. I asked her if she was alone, if she had something to drink and how life was treating her. She just stood there so I got up and went into the kitchen. It was clean and dark; the refrigerator was empty. I looked in the cupboards. Not even a miserable tin of peas. I turned on the tap; at least she had running water, but I didn't dare drink it. I went back to the living room. Sofia was still standing quietly in the same place, expectantly or absently, I couldn't tell, in any case just like a statue. I felt a gust of cold air and thought the front door must have been open. I went to check, but no. Sofia had shut it after I came in. That was something, at least, I thought.

What happened next is confused, or perhaps that's how I prefer to remember it. I was looking at Sofia's face – was she sad or pensive or simply ill? – I was looking at her profile and I knew that if I didn't do something I was going to start crying, so I went and hugged her from behind. I remember the passage that led to the bedroom and another room, the way it narrowed. We made love slowly, desperately, like in the old days. It was cold. I didn't get undressed. But Sofia took off all her clothes. Now you're cold as ice, I thought, cold as ice and on your own.

The next day I came back to see her again. This time I stayed much longer. We talked about when we used to live together and the TV shows we used to watch till the early hours of the morning. She asked me if I had a TV in my new apartment. I said no. I miss it, she said, especially the late-night shows. The good thing about not having a TV is you have more time to read, I said. I don't read any more, she said. Not at all? Not at all – have a look, there's not a single book here. Like a sleepwalker I got up and went all round the apartment, looking in every corner, as if I had all the time in the world. I saw many things, but no books. One of the rooms was locked and I couldn't go in. I came back with an empty feeling in my chest and dropped into Emilio's armchair. Up till then I hadn't asked about her boyfriend. So I did. Sofia looked at me and smiled for the first time, I think, since we'd met again. It was a brief but perfect smile. He's gone away, she said, and he's never coming back. Then we got dressed and went out to eat at a pizzeria.

Clara

She had big breasts, slim legs and blue eyes. That's how I like to remember her. I don't know why I fell madly in love with her, but I did, and for a start, I mean for the first days, the first hours, it all went fine; then Clara returned to the city where she lived in the south of Spain (she'd been on vacation in Barcelona), and everything started to fall apart.

One night I dreamed of an angel: I walked into a huge, empty bar and saw him sitting in a corner with his elbows on the table and a cup of milky coffee in front of him. She's the love of your life, he said, looking up at me, and the force of his gaze, the fire in his eyes, threw me right across the room. I started shouting, Waiter, waiter, then opened my eyes, and escaped from that miserable dream. Other nights I didn't dream of anyone, but woke up in tears. Meanwhile, Clara and I were writing to each other. Her letters were brief. Hi, how are you, it's raining, I love you, bye. At first those letters scared me. It's all over, I thought. Nevertheless, after inspecting them more carefully, I reached the conclusion that her epistolary concision was motivated by a desire to avoid grammatical errors. Clara was proud. She couldn't write well, and she didn't want to let it show, even if it meant hurting me by seeming cold.

She was eighteen at the time. She had left high school and was studying music at a private academy and drawing with a retired landscape painter, but she wasn't all that interested in music, or in painting, really: she liked it, but couldn't get passionate about it. One day I received a letter informing me, in her usual terse fashion, that she was going to take part in a beauty contest. My response, which filled three double-sided pages, was an extravagant paean to her calm beauty, the sweetness of her eyes, the perfection of her figure, etc. The letter was a triumph of bad taste, and when I had finished it, I wondered whether or not I should send it, but in the end I did.

A few weeks went by before I heard from her. I could have called, but I didn't want to intrude and also at the time I was broke. Clara came second in the contest and was depressed for a week. Surprisingly, she sent me a telegram, which read: SECOND PLACE. STOP. GOT YOUR LETTER. STOP. COME AND SEE ME. The stops were written out.

A week later, I took a train bound for the city where she lived, the first one leaving that day. Before that, of course – I mean after the telegram – we had spoken on the phone, and I had heard the story of the beauty contest a number of times. It had made a big impact on Clara, apparently. So I packed my bags and, as soon as I could, got on a train, and very early the next morning, there I was, in that unfamiliar city. I arrived at Clara's apartment at nine-thirty, after having a coffee at the station and smoking a few cigarettes to kill some time. A fat woman with messy hair opened the door, and when I said I had come to see Clara, she looked at me as if I were a lamb on its way to the slaughterhouse. For a few minutes (which seemed extraordinarily long at the time, and thinking the whole thing over, later on, I realised that, in fact, they were), I sat in the living room and waited for her, a living room that seemed welcoming, for no special reason, overly cluttered, but welcoming and full of light. When Clara made her entrance it was like the apparition of a goddess. I know it was a stupid thing to think – and is a stupid thing to way – but that's how it was.

The following days were pleasant and unpleasant. We saw a lot of movies, almost one a day; we made love (I was the first guy Clara had slept with, which seemed incidental or anecdotal, but in the end it would cost me dearly); we walked around; I met Clara's friends; we went to two horrific parties; and I asked her to come and live with me in Barcelona. Of course, at that stage, I knew what her answer would be. A month later, I took a night train back to Barcelona; I remember it was a terrible trip.

Soon after that, Clara explained in a letter, the longest one she ever sent me, why she couldn't go on: I was putting her under intolerable pressure (by suggesting that we live together); it was all over. After that we talked three or four times on the phone. I think I also wrote her a letter containing insults and declarations of love. Once when I was traveling to Morocco, I called her from the hotel where I was staying, in Algeciras, and that time we were able to have a civilised conversation. At least she thought it was civilised. Or I did.

Years later Clara told me about the parts of her life I had missed out on. And then, years after that, both she and some of her friends told me her life story all over again, starting from the beginning or from the point where we split up – it didn't make any difference to them (I was a very minor character, after all), or to me, really, although that wasn't so easy to admit. Predictably, not long after the end of our engagement (I know 'engagement' is hyperbolic, but it's the best word I can find), Clara got married, and the lucky man was, logically enough, one of the friends I met on my first trip to her city.

But before that, she had psychological problems: she used to dream about rats; at night she would hear them in her bedroom, and for months, the months leading up to her marriage, she had to sleep on the sofa in the living room. I'm guessing those damn rats disappeared after the wedding.

So. Clara got married. And the husband, Clara's dear husband, surprised everyone, even her. After one or two years, I'm not sure exactly – Clara told me, but I've forgotten – they split up. It wasn't an amicable separation. The guy shouted, Clara shouted, she slapped him, he responded with a punch that dislocated her jaw. Sometimes, when I'm alone and can't get to sleep, but don't feel up to switching on the light, I think of Clara, who came in second in that beauty contest, with her jaw hanging out of joint, unable to get it back into place on her own, driving to the nearest hospital with one hand on the wheel, and the other supporting her jawbone. I'd like to find it funny, but I can't.

What I do find funny is her wedding night. The day before, she'd had an operation, for haemorrhoids, so I guess she was still a bit groggy. Or maybe not. I never asked her if she was able to make love with her husband. I think they'd done it before the operation. Anyway, what does it matter? All these details say more about me than they do about her.

In any case, Clara split up with her husband a year or two after the wedding, and started studying. She hadn't finished high school, so she couldn't go to a university, but she tried everything else: photography, painting (I don't know why, but she always thought she could be a good painter), music, typing, computers, all those one-year diploma courses supposedly leading to job opportunities that desperate young people keep jumping at or falling for. And although Clara was happy to have escaped from a husband who beat her, deep down she was desperate.

The rats came back, and the depression, and the mysterious illnesses. For two or three years she was treated for an ulcer, until the doctors finally realised that there was nothing wrong, at least not in her stomach. Around that time she met Luis, an executive; they became lovers, and he convinced her to study something related to business administration. According to Clara's friends, she had at last found the love of her life. Before long, they were living together; Clara got a job in an office, a legal firm or some kind of agency – a really fun job, Clara said, without a hint of irony – and her life seemed to be on track, for good this time. Luis was a sensitive guy (he never hit her), and cultured (he was, I believe, one of the two million Spaniards who bought the complete works of Mozart in instalments), and patient too (he listened, he listened to her every night and on the weekends). And although Clara didn't have much to say for herself, she never got tired of saying it. She wasn't fretting over the beauty contest any more, although she did bring it up from time to time; now it was all about her periods of depression, her mental instability, the pictures she had wanted to paint but hadn't.

I don't know why they didn't have children, maybe they didn't have time, although, according to Clara, Luis was crazy about kids. But she wasn't ready. She used her time to study, and listen to music (Mozart, but then other composers too), and take photographs, which she never showed anyone. In her own obscure and futile way, she tried to defend her freedom, tried to learn.

At the age of thirty-one, she slept with a guy from the office. It was just something that happened, not a big deal, at least for the two of them, but Clara made the mistake of telling Luis. The fight was appalling. Luis smashed a chair or a painting he had bought himself, got drunk, and didn't talk to her for a month. According to Clara, from that day on, nothing was the same, in spite of the reconciliation, in spite of their trip to a town on the coast, a rather sad and dull trip, as it turned out.

At thirty-two, her sex life was almost non-existent. Shortly before she turned thirty-three, Luis told her that he loved her, he respected her, he would never forget her, but for some months he had been seeing someone from work, who was divorced and had children, a nice, understanding woman, and he was planning to go and live with her.

On the surface, Clara took the break-up pretty well (it was the first time someone had left her). But a few months later she lapsed into depression again and had to take some time off work and undergo psychiatric treatment, which didn't help much. The medication suppressed her libido, although she did make some wilful but unsatisfactory attempts to sleep with other men, including me. She started talking about the rats again; they wouldn't leave her alone. When she got nervous she had to go to the bathroom constantly (the first night we slept together, she must have got up to pee ten times). She talked about herself in the third person; in fact, she once told me that there were three Claras in her soul: a little girl, an old crone enslaved by her family, and a young woman, the real Clara, who wanted to get out of that city for ever, and paint, and take photos, and travel, and live. For the first few days after we got back together, I feared for her life. Sometimes I wouldn't even go out shopping because I was scared of coming back and finding her dead, but as the days went by my fears gradually faded away and I realised (or perhaps conveniently convinced myself) that Clara wasn't going to take her own life; she wasn't going to throw herself off the balcony of her apartment – she wasn't going to do anything.

Soon after that, I left, but this time I decided to call her every so often, and stay in touch with one of her friends, who could fill me in (if only now and then). That's how I came to know a few things it might have been easier not to have known, stories that did nothing for my peace of mind, the kind of news an egotist should always take care to avoid. Clara went back to work (the new pills she was taking had done wonders for her outlook), but before long she was transferred to a branch in another Andalusian city – though not very far away – maybe to pay her back for such a long absence. She moved, started going to the gym (at thirty-four she was no longer the beauty I had known at seventeen), and made new friends. That's how she met Paco, who was divorced, like her.

Before long, they were married. At first, Paco would tell anyone prepared to listen what he thought of Clara's photos and paintings. And Clara thought that Paco was intelligent and had good taste. As time went by, however, Paco lost interest in Clara's aesthetic efforts and wanted to have a child. Clara was thirty-five and at first she wasn't keen on the idea, but she gave in, and they had a child. According to Clara, the child satisfied all her yearnings – that was the word she used.

According to her friends, she was getting steadily worse, whatever that meant.

On one occasion, for reasons irrelevant to this story, I had to spend a night in the city where Clara was living. I called her from the hotel, told her where I was, and we arranged to meet the following day. I would have preferred to see her that night, but after our previous encounter Clara regarded me, and perhaps with good reason, as a kind of enemy, so I didn't insist.

She was almost unrecognisable. She had put on weight and although she was wearing make-up her face looked worn, not so much by time as by frustration, which surprised me, since I'd never really thought that Clara aspired to anything. And if you don't aspire to anything, how can you be frustrated? Her smile had also undergone a transformation. Before, it had been warm and slightly dumb, the smile of a young lady from a provincial capital, but it had become a mean, hurtful smile, and it was easy to read the resentment, rage and envy behind it. We kissed each other on the cheeks like a pair of idiots and then sat down; for a while we didn't know what to say. I was the one who broke the silence. I asked about her son; she told me he was at day care, and then she asked me about mine. He's fine, I said. We both realised that unless we did something, that meeting was going to become unbearably sad. How do I look? asked Clara. It was as if she were asking me to slap her. Same as ever, I replied automatically. I remember we had a coffee, then went for a walk along an avenue lined with plane trees, which led directly to the station. My train was about to leave. We said goodbye at the door of the station, and that was the last time I saw her.

We did, however, talk on the phone before she died. I used

to call her every three or four months. I had learned from experience not to touch on personal or intimate matters (a bit like sticking to sports when chatting with strangers in bars), so we talked about her family, which, in those conversations, remained as abstract as a cubist poem, or her son's school, or her job at the office; she was still at the same place, and over the years she had got to know about all her colleagues and their lives, and all the problems the executives were having – those secrets gave her an intense and perhaps excessive pleasure. On one occasion I tried to get her to say something about her husband, but at that point Clara clammed up. You deserve the best, I told her once. That's strange, replied Clara. What's strange? I asked. It's strange that you should say that – you, of all people, said Clara. I quickly tried to change the subject, claimed I was running out of coins (I've never had a phone of my own, and never will; I always called from a phone booth), hurriedly said goodbye and hung up. I realised I couldn't face another argument with Clara; I couldn't listen to her working up another one of her endless justifications.

One night, not long ago, she told me she had cancer. Her voice was as cold as ever, the voice in which, years before, she had announced that she was going to compete in a beauty contest, the voice in which she recounted her life with the detachment of a bad storyteller, putting exclamation marks in all the wrong places, and passing over what she should have gone into, the parts where she should have cut to the quick. I remember asking her if she had already been to see a doctor, as if she had diagnosed the cancer herself (or with Paco's help). Of course, she said. At the other end of the line I heard something like a croak. She was laughing. We talked briefly about our children, and then (she must have been feeling lonely or bored) she asked me to tell her something about my life. I made something up on the spot and said I'd call her back the following week. That night I slept very badly. I had one nightmare after another, and woke up suddenly, shouting, convinced that Clara had lied to me: she didn't have cancer; something was happening to her, for sure, the way things had been happening for the last twenty years, little, fucked-up things, all full of shit and smiles, but she didn't have cancer. It was five in the morning. I got up and walked to the Paseo Marítimo, with the wind at my back, which was strange because the wind usually blows in from the sea, and hardly ever from the opposite direction. I didn't stop until I got to the phone booth next to one of the biggest cafés on the Paseo. The terrace was empty, the chairs were chained to the tables, but a little way off, right near the seaside, a homeless guy was sleeping on a bench, with his knees drawn up, and every now and then he shuddered, as if he were having nightmares.

My address book only contained one other number in Clara's city. I called it. After a long time, a woman's voice answered. I said who I was, but suddenly found I couldn't say anything more. I thought she'd hang up, but I heard the click of a lighter and smoke rushing in through lips. Are you still there? asked the woman. Yes, I said. Have you talked to Clara? Yes, I said. Did she tell you she had cancer? Yes, I said. Well, it's true.

All the years since I had met Clara suddenly came tumbling down on top of me, everything my life had been, most of it nothing to do with her. I don't know what else the woman said at the other end of the line, hundreds of miles away; I think I began to cry in spite of myself, like in the poem by Rubén Darío. I fumbled in my pockets for cigarettes, listened to fragments of stories: doctors, operations, mastectomies, discussions, different points of view, deliberations, the activities of a Clara I couldn't know or touch or help, not now. A Clara who could never save me now.

When I hung up, the homeless guy was standing about five feet away. I hadn't heard him approaching. He was very tall, too warmly dressed for the season, and he was staring at me, as if he were near-sighted or worried I might make a sudden move. I was so sad I didn't even get a fright, although afterwards, walking back through the twisting streets of the town centre, I realised that, seeing him, I had forgotten Clara for an instant, and that was just the start.

We talked on the phone quite often after that. Some weeks I called her twice a day: they were short, stupid conversations, and there was no way to say what I really wanted to say, so I talked about anything, the first thing that came into my head, some nonsense I hoped would make her smile. Once I got nostalgic and tried to summon up days gone by, but Clara put on her icy armour, and I soon got the message and gave up on nostalgia. As the date of the operation approached, my calls became more frequent. Once I talked with her son. Another time with Paco. They both seemed well, they sounded well, at least not as nervous as me. Although I'm probably wrong about that. Certainly wrong, in fact. Everyone's worried about me, said Clara one afternoon. I thought she meant her husband and her son, but 'everyone' included many more people, many more than I could imagine, everyone. The day before she was to go into the hospital, I called her in the afternoon. Paco answered. Clara wasn't there. No one had seen her or heard from her in two days. From Paco's tone of voice I sensed that he suspected she might be with me. I told him straight up: She's not here, but that night I hoped with all my heart that she would come to my place. I waited for her with the lights on, and finally fell asleep on the sofa, and dreamed of a very beautiful woman who was not Clara: a tall, slim woman, with small breasts, long legs, and deep brown eyes, who was not and never would be Clara, a woman whose presence obliterated Clara, reduced her to a poor, lost, trembling forty-something-year-old.

She didn't come to my apartment.

The next day I called Paco. And two days after that I phoned again. There was still no sign of Clara. The third time I called Paco, he talked about his son and complained about Clara's behaviour. Every night I wonder where she could be, he said. From his voice and the turn the conversation was taking, I could tell that what he needed from me, or someone, anyone, was friendship. But I was in no condition to provide him with that solace.

Joanna Silvestri

for Paula Massot

Here I am, Joanna Silvestri, thirty-seven years of age, profession: porn star, on my back in the Clinique Les Trapèzes in Nîmes, watching the afternoons go by, listening to the stories of a Chilean detective. Who is this man looking for? A ghost? I know a lot about ghosts, I told him the second afternoon, the last time he came to see me, and he smiled like an old rat, like an old rat agreeing listlessly, like an improbably polite old rat. Anyway, thank you for the flowers and the magazines, but I can barely remember the person you're looking for, I told him. Don't rack your brains, he said, I've got plenty of time. When a man says he has plenty of time, he's already snared (so how much time he has is irrelevant), and you can do whatever you like with him. But of course that isn't true. Sometimes I get to thinking about the men who've lain at my feet, and I shut my eyes and when I open them again the walls of the room are painted other colors, not the bone white I see every day, but streaky vermilion, nauseous blue, like the daubs of that awful painter, Attilio Corsini. Awful paintings I'd rather not remember, but I do, and that memory flushes out others, like an enema, other memories with a sepia tone to them, which set the afternoons wavering slightly and are hard to bear at first but in the end they can even be fun. I haven't had that many men at my feet, actually: two or three, and it didn't last, they're all behind me now – that's just the way of the world. That's what I was thinking, and I would have liked to share it with him, even though I didn't know him at all, but I didn't say any of this to the Chilean detective. And as if to make up for that lack of generosity, I called him Detective, I might have said something about solitude and intelligence, and although he hastened to say, I'm not a detective, Madame Silvestri, I could tell that he was glad I'd said it; I was looking into his eyes when I spoke, and although he didn't seem to turn a hair, I noticed the fluttering, as if a bird had flown through his head. One thing stood in for the other: I didn't say what I was thinking, but I said something that I knew he would like. I said something that I knew would bring back pleasant memories. As if someone, preferably a stranger, were to speak to me now about the Civitavecchia Adult Film Festival or the Berlin Erotic Film Fair, or the Barcelona Exhibition of Pornographic Cinema and Video, and mention my triumphs, my real and imaginary triumphs, or about 1990 – the best year of my life – when I went to Los Angeles, almost under duress, on a Milan-LA flight that I thought would be exhausting but in fact it went by like a dream, like the dream I had on the plane (it must have been somewhere over the Atlantic): I dreamed that we were heading for Los Angeles but going via Asia, with stops in Turkey, India and China, and from the window – I don't know why the plane was flying so low, but at no point were we, the passengers, at risk – I could see trains stretching away in vast caravans, a mad but precisely orchestrated railway mobilisation, like an enormous clockwork mechanism spread out over the region, not a part of the world that I know (except for a trip to India in 1987, which is better forgotten), and there were people embarking and disembarking and goods being loaded and unloaded, all of it clearly visible, as if I were looking at one of those animations that economists use to explain how things work, their origins and destinations, their movement and inertia. And when I arrived in Los Angeles, Robbie Pantoliano, Adolfo Pantoliano's brother, was waiting for me at the airport, and as soon as I saw Robbie I could tell he was a gentleman, quite the opposite of his brother Adolfo (may he rest in peace or do his time in purgatory, I wouldn't wish hell on anyone), and outside there was a limousine waiting for me, the kind you only see in Los Angeles, not even in New York, only in Beverly Hills or Orange County, and we went to the place they'd rented for me, a unit by the beach, it was small but sweet, and Robbie and his secretary Ronnie stayed to help me unpack my bags (though I said really I'd prefer to do it on my own) and explain how everything worked in the unit, as if I didn't know what a microwave oven was – Americans are like that sometimes, so nice they end up being rude – and then they put on a video so I could see the actors I'd be working with: Shane Bogart, who I knew already from a movie I'd done with Robbie's brother; Bull Edwards, I didn't know him; Darth Krecick, the name rang a bell; Jennifer Pullman, another stranger to me, and so on, three or four others, and then Robbie and Ronnie left me on my own, and I double locked the doors as they had insisted I must, and then I took a bath, wrapped myself in a black bathrobe and looked for an old movie on TV, something to relax me completely, and at some point I fell asleep there on the sofa. The next day we started shooting. It was all so different from the way I remembered it. In two weeks we made four movies in all, with more or less the same team, and working for Robbie Pantoliano was like playing and working at the same time; it was like one of those day trips that office workers and bureaucrats organise in Italy, especially in Rome: once a year they all go out to the country for a meal and leave the office and its worries behind, but this was better, the sun was better, and the apartments and the sea, and catching up with the girls I'd known before, and the atmosphere on the set: debauched but fresh, the way it should be, and I think it came up when I was talking with Shane Bogart and one of the girls, the way things had changed, and naturally, for a start, I put it down to the death of Adolfo Pantoliano, who was a thug and a crook of the worst kind, a guy who had no respect, not even for his own long-suffering whores; when a bastard like that disappears, you're bound to notice the difference, but Shane Bogart said no, it wasn't that; Pantoliano's death, which had come as a relief, even to his own brother, was just a detail in the bigger picture, the industry was undergoing major changes, he said, because of a combination of apparently unrelated factors: money, new players coming in from other sectors, the disease, the demand for a product that would be different but not too different; then they started talking about money and the way a lot of porn stars were crossing over to the regular movie industry at the time, but I wasn't listening, I was thinking back to what they'd said about the disease, and remembering Jack Holmes, who'd been California's number one porn star just a few years before, and when we finished up that day I said to Robbie and Ronnie that I'd like to find out how Jack Holmes was doing, and asked them if they had his number, if he was still living in Los Angeles. And although Robbie and Ronnie thought it was a crazy idea at first, eventually they gave me Jack's phone number and told me to call him if that's what I wanted to do, but not to expect him to be coherent, or to hear the voice I remembered from the old days. That night I had dinner with Robbie and Ronnie and Sharon Grove, who had crossed over to horror and even claimed that she was going to be in the next Carpenter or Clive Barker film, which annoyed Ronnie, hearing those two lumped together, because, for him, only a handful of directors came anywhere near Carpenter, and Danny Lo Bello was there at the dinner too – I had a thing with him when we were working together in Milan – and Patricia Page, his eighteen-year-old wife, who only worked in Danny's movies, with a contract stipulating that only her husband was allowed to penetrate her, with the other guys she just sucked their cocks, and even that she did reluctantly; the directors weren't too happy with her, and according to Robbie sooner or later she'd either have to change careers or her and Danny would have to come up with some really sensational numbers. So there I was, having dinner in one of the best restaurants in Venice Beach, looking out at the sea, exhausted after a hard day's work, not paying much attention to the lively conversation at our table – I was miles away, thinking of Jack Holmes, remembering the way he looked: a very tall, thin guy with a long nose and long, hairy arms like the arms of an ape, but what kind of ape would Jack have been? An ape in captivity, no doubt about that, a melancholy ape or maybe the ape of melancholy, which might seem like the same thing but it's not, and when dinner was over, it wasn't too late for me to call Jack at home – people have dinner early in California, sometimes they finish before it gets dark – I couldn't wait any longer, I don't know what came over me, I asked Robbie for his cell phone and took myself off to a sort of jetty, all made of wood, a kind of miniature wooden pier exclusively for tourists, with waves breaking under it, long, low, almost foamless waves that took an eternity to dissipate, and I phoned Jack Holmes. I honestly didn't expect him to answer. At first I didn't recognise his voice, it was like Robbie said, and he didn't recognise mine either. It's me, I said, Joanna Silvestri, I'm in Los Angeles. Jack was quiet for a long time and all of a sudden I realised I was shaking, the telephone was shaking, the wooden jetty was shaking, the wind had turned cold, the wind that was blowing between the jetty's pilings and ruffling the surface of those interminable, darkening waves, and then Jack said, It's been such a long time, Joanna, great to hear your voice, and I said, It's great to hear yours, Jack, and then I stopped shaking and stopped looking down and looked at the horizon, the lights of the restaurants along the beach – red, blue, yellow – which seemed sad at first but comforting too, and then Jack said, When can I see you, Joannie, and I didn't realise straightaway that he had called me Joannie, for a couple of seconds I was floating on air like I was high or weaving a chrysalis around myself, but then I realised and laughed and Jack knew why I was laughing without needing to ask or needing me to tell him anything. Whenever you like, Jack, I replied. Well, he said, I don't know if you've heard that I'm not as well as I used to be. Are you on your own, Jack? Yes, he said, I'm always on my own. Then I hung up and asked Robbie and Ronnie how to get to Jack's place, and they said I was bound to get lost, and shouldn't even think of spending the night because we were shooting early the next day, and I probably wouldn't be able to get a taxi to take me there, Jack lived near Monrovia, in a shabby old bungalow that was practically falling down, and I told them I wanted to go see Jack however hard it might be, and Robbie said, Take my Porsche, you can have it as long as you turn up on time tomorrow, and I kissed Ronnie and Robbie and got into the Porsche and started driving through the streets of Los Angeles, which had just begun to succumb to the night, the cloak of night falling, like in a song by Nicola Di Bari, or the wheels of the night rolling on, and I didn't want to put on any music, though I have to admit I was tempted by Robbie's sound system – CD or laser-disc or ultrasound or something – but I didn't need music, it was enough to step on the accelerator and feel the hum of the engine; I must have got lost at least a dozen times, and the hours went by and every time I asked someone the best way to get to Monrovia I felt freer, like I didn't care if I spent the whole night driving around in the Porsche, and twice I even caught myself singing, and finally I got to Pasadena, and from there I took Highway 210 to Monrovia, where I spent another hour looking for Jack's place, and when I found his bungalow, after midnight, I sat in the car for a while, unable and unwilling to get out, looking at myself in the mirror, with my hair in a mess and my face as well, my eyeliner had run and my lipstick was smudged and there was dust from the road on my cheeks, as if I'd run all the way and not come in Robbie Pantoliano's Porsche, or as if I'd been crying, but in fact my eyes were dry (a little bit red, maybe, but dry), and my hands were steady and I felt like laughing, as if my food at the beachside restaurant had been spiked with some kind of drug, and I'd only just realised and accepted that I was high or extremely happy.

And then I got out of the car, put on the alarm – it didn't feel like a very safe neighbourhood – and headed for the bungalow, which matched Robbie's description: a little house crying out for a coat of paint, with a rickety porch; a pile of boards that was practically falling down, but next to it there was a swimming pool, and although it was very small, the water was clean, I could see that straightaway because the pool light was on; I remember thinking that Jack had given up waiting for me or had fallen asleep, because there were no lights on in the house; the boards on the porch creaked under my feet; there was no bell, so I knocked twice on the door, first with my knuckles and then with the palm of my hand, and a light came on, I could hear someone saying something inside, and then the door opened and Jack appeared on the threshold, taller than ever, thinner than ever, and said, Joannie? as if he didn't recognise me or still hadn't completely woken up, and I said, Yes, Jack, it's me, it was hard to find you but I found you in the end, and we hugged. That night we talked until three in the morning and Jack fell asleep at least twice during the conversation. Although he looked drained and weak, he was making an effort to keep his eyes open. But in the end he was just too tired and he said he was going to bed. I don't have a spare room, Joannie, he said, so you choose: my bed or the sofa. Your bed, I said, with you. Good, he said, let's go. He took a bottle of tequila and we went to his bedroom. I hadn't seen such a messy room for years. Do you have an alarm clock? I asked him. No, Joannie, there are no clocks in this house, he said. Then he switched off the light, took off his clothes and got into bed. I stood there watching him, not moving. Then I went to the window and opened the curtains, hoping that the light of dawn would wake me up.

When I got into bed, Jack seemed to be asleep, but he wasn't, he drank another shot of tequila and then he said something I couldn't understand. I put my hand on his stomach and stroked it until he fell asleep. Then I moved my hand down a bit and touched his cock, which was big and cold like a python. A few hours later I woke up, took a shower, made breakfast, and I even had time to tidy up the living room and the kitchen a bit. We had breakfast in bed. Jack seemed happy that I was there, but all he had was coffee. I said I'd come back that evening, I told him to expect me, I wouldn't be late this time, and he said, I've got nothing to do Joannie, you can come whenever you like. It was almost like saying, It's OK if you never come back, I knew that, but I decided that Jack needed me and that I needed him too. Who are you working with? he asked. Shane Bogart, I said. He's a good kid, said Jack. We worked together once, I think it was when he was just starting out in the business; he's enthusiastic, and he doesn't like to make trouble. Yeah, he's a good kid, I said. And where are you working? In Venice? Yeah, I said, in the same old house. But you know old Adolfo got killed? Of course I know, Jack, that was years ago. I haven't been working much lately, he said. Then I gave him a kiss, a schoolgirl's kiss on his narrow, chapped lips, and I left. The trip back was much quicker; the sun was running with me, the California morning sun, which has a metallic edge to it. And from then on, after each day of shooting, I'd go to Jack's house or we'd go out together; Jack had an old station wagon and I rented a two-seater Alfa Romeo, and we'd drive off into the mountains, to Redlands, and then on Highway 10 to Palm Springs, Palm Desert, Indio, until we got to the Salton Sea, which is a lake, not a sea (and not a very pretty one either), where we ate macrobiotic food, that's what Jack was eating then, for his health, he said, and one day we stepped on the gas in my Alfa and drove to Calipatria, to the southeast of the Salton Sea, and went to see a friend of Jack's who lived in a bungalow that was even more run-down than the one Jack lived in, Graham Monroe was the guy's name, but his wife and Jack called him Mezcalito, I don't know why, maybe because he was partial to mescal, though all they drank while we were there was beer (I didn't have any – beer is fattening), and the three of them went and sunbathed behind the bungalow and hosed each other down, and I put on my bikini and watched them, I prefer not to get too much sun, my skin's very fair and I like to take care of it, but even though I stayed in the shade and didn't let them wet me with the hose, I was glad to be there, watching Jack, his legs were much thinner than I remembered, and his chest seemed to have sunken in, only his cock was the same, and his eyes too, but no, the only thing that hadn't changed was the great jackhammer, as the ads for his movies used to say, the ram that battered Marilyn Chambers' ass; the rest of him, including his eyes, was fading as fast as my Alfa Romeo flying down the Aguanga Valley or across the Desert State Park lit by the glow of a moribund Sunday. I think we made love a couple of times. Jack had lost interest. He said after so many movies he was worn out. No one's ever told me that before, I said. I like watching TV, Joannie, and reading mysteries. You mean horror stories? No, just mysteries, he said, with detectives, especially the ones where the hero dies at the end. But that never happens, I said. Of course it does, little sister, in old pulp novels you can buy by the pound. Actually, I didn't see any books in his house, except for a medical reference book and three of those pulp novels he'd mentioned, which he must have read over and over again. One night, maybe the second night I spent at his house, or the third – Jack was as slow as a snail when it came to opening up and telling secrets – while we were drinking wine by the pool, he said he probably didn't have long to live: You know how it is, Joannie, when your time's up, your time's up. I wanted to shout, Make love to me, let's get married, let's have a kid or adopt an orphan or buy a pet and a trailer and go travelling through California and Mexico – I guess I was tired and a bit drunk, it must have been a hard day on the set – but I didn't say anything, I just shifted uneasily in my deck chair, looked at the lawn that I'd mowed myself, drank some more wine, and waited for Jack to go on and say the words that had to come next, but that was all he said. We made love that night for the first time in so long. It was very hard to get Jack going, his body wasn't working anymore, only his will was still working, but he insisted on wearing a condom, a condom for that cock of his, as if any condom could hold it, at least it gave us a bit of a laugh, and in the end, we both lay on our sides, and he put his long, thick, flaccid cock between my legs, kissed me sweetly and fell asleep, but I stayed awake for ages, with the strangest ideas passing through my mind; there were moments when I felt sad and cried without making a sound so as not to wake him up or break our embrace, and there were moments when I felt happy, and I cried then too and hiccupped, not even trying to restrain myself, squeezing Jack's cock between my thighs and listening to his breathing, saying: Jack, I know you're pretending to be asleep, Jack, open your eyes and kiss me, but Jack went on sleeping or pretending to sleep, and I went on watching the thoughts race through my mind as if across a movie screen, flashing past, like a plough or a red tractor going a hundred miles an hour, leaving me almost no time to think, not that thinking was high on my list of priorities, and then there were moments when I wasn't crying or feeling sad or happy, I just felt alive and I knew that Jack was alive and although there was a kind of theatrical backdrop to everything, as if it were all some pleasant, innocent, even decorous farce, I knew it was real and worthwhile, and then I put my head in the crook of his neck and fell asleep. One day around midday Jack turned up while we were shooting. I was on all fours, sucking Bull Edwards while Shane Bogart sodomised me. At first I didn't realise that Jack had come onto the set, I was concentrating; it's not easy to groan with an eight-inch dick moving back and forth in your mouth; I know really photogenic girls who lose it as soon as they start a blow job, they look terrible, maybe because they're too into it, but I like to keep my face looking good. So my mind was on the job and, anyway, because of the position I was in, I couldn't see what was happening around me, while Bull and Shane, who were on their knees, but upright, heads raised, they saw that Jack had just come in, and their cocks got harder almost straightaway, and it wasn't just Bull and Shane who reacted, the director, Randy Cash, and Danny Lo Bello and his wife and Robbie and Ronnie and the technicians and everyone, I think, except for the cameraman, Jacinto Ventura, who was a bright, cheerful kid and a true professional, he literally couldn't take his eyes off the scene he was filming, everyone except for him reacted in some way to Jack's unexpected presence, and a silence fell over the set, not a heavy silence, not the kind that foreshadows bad news, but a luminous silence, so to speak, the silence of water falling in slow motion, and I sensed the silence and thought it must have been because I was feeling so good, because of those beautiful California days, but I also sensed something else, something indecipherable approaching, announced by the rhythmic bumping of Shane's hips on my butt, by Bull's gentle thrusting in my mouth, and then I knew that something was happening on the set, though I didn't look up, and I knew that what was happening involved and revolved around me; it was as if reality had been torn, ripped open from one end to the other, like in those operations that leave a scar from neck to groin, a broad, rough, hard scar, but I hung on and kept concentrating till Shane took his cock out of my ass and came on my butt and just after that Bull ejaculated on my face. Then they turned me over and I could see the expressions on their faces, they were very focused on what they were doing, much more than usual, and as they caressed me and said tender words, I thought, There's something going on here, there must be someone from the industry on the set, some big fish from Hollywood, and Shane and Bull have realised, they're acting for him, and I remember glancing sideways at the silhouettes surrounding us in the shadows, all still, all turned to stone – that was exactly what I thought, they've turned to stone, it must be a really important producer – but I kept quiet, I wasn't ambitious the way Shane and Bull were, I think it has something to do with being European, we have a different outlook, but I also thought, Maybe it isn't a producer, maybe an angel has come onto the set, and that was when I saw him. Jack was next to Ronnie, smiling at me. And then I saw the others: Robbie, the technicians, Danny Lo Bello and his wife, Jennifer Pullman, Margo Killer, Samantha Edge, two guys in dark suits, Jacinto Ventura, who wasn't looking into the viewfinder, and it was only then that I realised he wasn't filming anymore, and for a second or a minute we all froze, as if we'd lost the capacity to speak and move, and the only one smiling (though he was quiet too) was Jack, whose presence seemed to sanctify the set, or that's what I thought later, much later on, remembering that scene again and again: he seemed to be sanctifying our movie and our work and our lives. Then the minute came to an end, another minute began, someone said it was a wrap, someone brought bathrobes for Bull and Shane and me, Jack came over and gave me a kiss; I wasn't in the other scenes they were shooting that day, so I said let's go and have dinner in an Italian restaurant, I'd heard about one on Figueroa Street, and Robbie invited us to a party that one of his new business partners was throwing; Jack seemed reluctant but I convinced him in the end. So we went back to my place in the Alfa Romeo and talked and drank whisky for a while, and then we went out to dinner and at about eleven we turned up at the party. Everyone was there and they all knew Jack or came over to be introduced to him. And then Jack and I went to his place and watched TV in the living room – there was a silent movie on – and kissed until we fell asleep. He didn't come back to the set. I had another week's work there, but I'd already decided to stay in Los Angeles for a while after the end of the shoot. Of course I had commitments in Italy and France, but I thought I could put them off, or I thought I'd be able to convince Jack to come with me; he'd been to Italy a number of times, he'd made some movies with La Cicciolina, which had been big hits – some with just me, and some with both of us; Jack liked Italy, so one night I told him what I was thinking. But I had to give up on that idea or hope, I had to wrench it out of my head and heart, or out of my cunt, as the women say back in Torre del Greco, and although I never completely gave up, somehow I understood Jack's reluctance or his stubbornness, the luminous, fresh, honey-slow silence surrounding him and his few words, as if his tall thin figure were vanishing, and all of California along with it; in spite of my happiness, my joy, or what until shortly before I had thought of as happiness and joy, he was going, and I understood that his departure or farewell was a kind of solidification: strange, oblique, almost secret, but still a solidification, and the understanding, the certainty (if that's what it was) made me happy and yet at the same time it made me cry, it made me keep fixing my eye make-up and made me see everything differently, as if I had X-ray vision, and that power or superpower made me nervous, but I liked it too; it was like being Marvilla, the daughter of the Queen of the Amazons, although Marvilla had dark hair and mine is blonde, and one afternoon, in Jack's yard, I saw something on the horizon, I don't know what, clouds, a bird of some kind, a plane, and I felt a pain so strong I fainted and lost control of my bladder and when I woke up I was in Jack's arms and I looked into his grey eyes and began to cry and didn't stop crying for a long time. Robbie and Ronnie came to the airport to see me off along with Danny Lo Bello and his wife, who were planning to visit Italy in a few months' time. I said goodbye to Jack at his bungalow in Monrovia. Don't get up, I said, but he got up and came to the door with me. Be a good girl, Joannie, he said, and write me some time. I'll call you, I said, it's not the end of the world. He was nervous and forgot to put on his shirt. I didn't say anything; I picked up my bag and put it on the passenger seat of the Alfa Romeo. I don't know why I thought that when I turned back to look at him for the last time he'd be gone and the space he'd occupied next to the rickety little wooden gate would be empty, so fear made me delay that moment, it was the first time I'd felt afraid in Los Angeles (on that visit I mean; there'd been plenty of fear and boredom the other times) and I was annoyed to be feeling afraid, and I didn't want to turn around until I had opened the door of the Alfa Romeo and was ready to get in and drive away fast, and when I did finally open the door, I turned and Jack was there, standing by the gate, watching me, and then I knew that everything was all right, and I could go. That everything was all wrong, and I could go. That everything was sorrow, and I could go. And while the detective watches me out of the corner of his eye (he's pretending to look at the foot of the bed, but I know he's looking at my legs, my long legs underneath the sheets) and talks about a cameraman who worked with Mancuso or Marcantonio, a certain R. P. English, poor Marcantonio's second cameraman, I know that in some sense I'm still in California, on my last trip to California, although I didn't know that at the time, and Jack is still alive and looking at the sky, sitting on the edge of the pool with his feet dangling in the water, in the void, the misty synthesis of our love and our separation. And what did this man called English do? I ask the detective. He would prefer not to answer, but faced with my steady gaze, he replies: Terrible things, and then he looks at the floor, as if it were forbidden to say those words in the Clinique Les Trapèzes, in Nîmes, as if I hadn't been acquainted with some terrible things in my time. And at this point I could press him for more, but why spoil such a beautiful afternoon by obliging him to tell what would surely be a sad story. And anyway the photo he has shown me of the man presumed to be English is old and blurry, it shows a young man of twenty-something, and the English I remember was well into his thirties, maybe even over forty, a definite shadow, if you'll pardon the paradox, a broken shadow; I didn't pay much attention to him, although his features have remained in my memory: blue eyes, prominent cheekbones, full lips, small ears. But describing him like that gives a false impression. I met R. P. English on one of my many shoots around Italy, but his face receded into the shadows long ago. And the detective says, It's all right, don't worry, take your time, Madame Silvestri, at least you remember him, even that is useful, now I know for sure he's not a ghost. And I'm tempted to tell him that we are all ghosts, that all of us have gone too soon into the world of ghost movies, but he's a good man and I don't want to hurt him, so I keep it to myself. Anyway, who's to say he doesn't already know?

Prefiguration of Lalo Cura

It's hard to believe, but I was born in a neighbourhood called Los Empalados: The Impaled. The name glows like the moon. The name opens a way through the dream with its horn and man follows that path. A quaking path. Invariably harsh. The path that leads into or out of hell. That's what it all comes down to. Getting closer to hell or further away. Me, for example, I've had people killed. I've given the best birthday presents. I've backed projects of epic proportions. I've opened my eyes in the dark. Once I opened them by slow degrees in total darkness and all I saw or imagined was that name: Los Empalados, shining like the star of destiny. I'll tell you everything, naturally. My father was a renegade priest. I don't know if he was Colombian or came from some other country. But he was Latin American. He turned up one night stone broke in Medellín, preaching sermons in bars and whorehouses. Some people thought he was working for the secret police, but my mother kept him from getting killed and took him to her penthouse in the neighbourhood. They lived together for four months, I've been told, and then my father vanished into the Gospels. Latin America was calling him, and he kept slipping away into the sacrificial words until he vanished, gone without a trace. Whether he was a

Prefiguration of Lalo Cura

Catholic priest or a Protestant minister is something I'll never find out now. I know that he was alone and that he moved among the masses, fevered and loveless, full of passion and empty of hope. I was named Olegario when I was born, but people have always called me Lalo. My father was known as El Cura, the priest, and that's what my mother wrote down next to *surname* at the registry office. It's my official name. Olegario Cura. I was even baptised into the Catholic faith. She sure was a dreamer, my mother. Connie Sánchez was her name, and if you weren't so young and innocent, it would ring a bell. She was one of the stars of the Olimpo Movie Production Company. The other two stars were Doris Sánchez, my mother's younger sister, and Monica Farr, née Leticia Medina, from Valparaíso. Three good friends. The Olimpo Movie Production Company specialised in pornography, and although the business was more or less illegal and operating in a distinctly hostile environment, it didn't go under until the mid-eighties. The guy in charge was a multitalented German, Helmut Bittrich, who worked as the company's manager, director, set designer, composer, publicist and, occasionally, thug. Sometimes he even acted, under the name of Abelardo Bello. He was a weird guy, Bittrich. No one had ever seen him with an erection. He liked to do weights at the Health and Friendship Gym, but he wasn't gay. It's just that in the movies he never fucked anyone. Male or female. If you can be bothered, you'll find him playing a Peeping Tom, a schoolteacher, a spy in a seminary – always a modest, minor role. What he liked best was playing a doctor. A German doctor, of course, although most of the time he didn't even open his mouth: he was Doctor Silence. The blue-eyed doctor hidden behind a conveniently located velvet curtain. Bittrich had a house on the outskirts of town, where the neighbourhood of Los Empalados borders the wasteland, El Gran Baldío. The cottage in the movies. The house of solitude, which was later to become the house of crime, out there on its own, among clumps of trees and blackberry bushes. Connie used to take me. I'd stay in the yard playing with the dogs and the geese, which the German reared there as if they were his children. There were flowers growing wild among the weeds and the dogs' dirt holes. In the course of a regular morning ten to fifteen people would go into that house. Although the windows were shut you could hear the moans coming from inside. Sometimes there was laughter too. At lunchtime Connie and Doris would take a folding table out into the backyard, under a tree, and the employees of the Olimpo Movie Production Company would hoe into the canned food that Bittrich heated up on a gas ring. They ate directly from the cans or off cardboard plates. Once I went into the kitchen, to help, and when I opened the cupboards all I found were enema tubes, hundreds of enema tubes lined up as if for a military parade. Everything in the kitchen was fake. There were no real plates, no real knives and forks, no real pots and pans. That's what it's like in the movies, said Bittrich, watching me with those blue eyes of his – they scared me then, but thinking of them now I just feel sad. The kitchen was fake. Everything in the house was fake. Who sleeps here at night? Sometimes Uncle Helmut does, Connie replied. Uncle Helmut stays here to look after the dogs and the geese and get on with his work. Editing his homemade movies. Homemade, but the business was booming: the films went out to Germany, Holland and Switzerland. Some copies stayed in Latin America and others were sold in the United

Prefiguration of Lalo Cura

States, but most of them went to Europe, which is where Bittrich had his main client base. Maybe that's why he did a voice-over in German, narrating the various scenes. Like a travel journal for sleepwalkers. And the obsession with mother's milk, another European peculiarity. When Connie was pregnant with me, she went on working. And Bittrich made lacto-porn. Along the lines of Milch and Pregnant Fantasies, aimed at men who believe or make believe that women lactate during pregnancy. With her eight-month bulge, Connie squeezed her breasts and the milk flowed like lava. She leaned over Pajarito Gómez or Sansón Fernández or both of them and gave them a good swig of milk. That was one of the German's tricks; Connie never had milk. Or only a little bit, for two weeks, maybe three, just enough to give me a taste. But that was all. Actually the movies were like Pregnant Fantasies, not so much like Milch. There's Connie, big and blonde, with me curled up inside her, laughing as she lubricates Pajarito Gómez's asshole with Vaseline. She already has the sure, delicate movements of a mother. My moron of a father has left her and there she is, with Doris and Monica Farr, and the three of them are smiling on and off, exchanging looks and subtle signals or secrets among themselves, while Pajarito stares at her belly as if in a hypnotic trance. The mystery of life in Latin America. Like a little bird charmed by the gaze of a snake. The Force is with me, I thought, the first time I saw that movie, at the age of nineteen, crying my eyes out, grinding my teeth, pinching the sides of my head, the Force is with me. All dreams are real. I wanted to believe that when those cocks had gone as far into my mother as they could, they came up against my eyes. I often dreamed about that: my sealed, translucent eyes swimming in the black soup of life. Life? No: the dealing that imitates life. My squinting eyes, like the snake hypnotising the little bird. You get the picture: a kid's silly celluloid fantasies. All fake, as Bittrich used to say. And he was right, as he almost always was. That's why the girls adored him. They were glad to have the German around; they could always count on him for friendly advice and comfort. The girls: Connie, Doris and Monica. Three good friends lost in the mists of time. Connie tried to make it on Broadway. Even in the hardest years, I don't think she ever gave up on the possibility of happiness. There, in New York, she met Monica Farr and they shared their hardships and hopes. They cleaned hotel rooms, sold their blood, turned tricks. Always looking for a break, walking around the city hooked up to the same Walkman, typical dancers, a little bit thinner and closer together with every passing day. Chorus girls. Looking for Bob Fosse. At a party thrown by some Colombians they met Bittrich, who was passing through New York with a batch of his merchandise. They talked until dawn. No sex, just music and words. They cast their dice that night on Seventh Avenue, the Prussian artist and the Latin American whores. It was all decided then and there. In some of my nightmares I see myself resting in limbo again and then I hear, distantly at first, the sound of the dice on the pavement. I open my eyes and I scream. Something changed for ever that morning. The bond of friendship took hold, like the plague. Then Connie and Monica Farr got an acting job in Panama, where they were thoroughly exploited. The German paid for their tickets to Medellín, which was home to Connie and as good a place as any for Monica. There are photos of them descending the steps from the plane, taken by Doris, the only person

Prefiguration of Lalo Cura

who went to meet them at the airport. Connie and Monica are wearing sunglasses and tight pants. They're not very tall, but they're well proportioned. The Medellín sun is casting long shadows across an airstrip devoid of planes, except for one in the background, emerging from a hangar. There are no clouds in the sky. Connie and Monica displaying their teeth. Drinking Coca-Cola in the taxi line and striking provocative, turbulent poses. Atmospheric and terrestrial turbulence. Their attitude suggests that they have come straight from New York, surrounded by mystery. Then a very young Doris appears beside them. The three of them hugging each other, photographed by an obliging stranger leaning against the taxi's bumper, while the driver inside looks on, so old and worn it's hard to believe he's real. So begin the most passionate adventures. A month later they are already shooting the first movie: *Hecatomb*. While the world is in turmoil the German shoots *Hecatomb*. A film about the turmoil of the spirit. A saint in prison remembers nights of plenitude and fucking. Connie and Monica do it with four guys who look like shadows. Doris walks along the bank of a weakly flowing river accompanied by Bittrich's largest goose. The night is unusually starry. At dawn, Doris comes across Pajarito Gómez and they start making love in the back part of Bittrich's house. There is a great fluttering of geese. Connie and Monica at a window, clapping. The lobster-red cock of the saint shines with semen. The End. The credits appear over the image of a sleeping policeman. Bittrich's sense of humor. His movies amused drug lords and businessmen. The ordinary guys, the gunmen and the messengers, didn't understand them; they'd have been quite happy to blow the German away. Another movie: *Kundalini*. A rancher's wake. While the mourners weep and drink coffee with aguardiente, Connie enters a dark room full of farming implements. Two guys – one disguised as a bull and one as a condor – jump out of an enormous wardrobe. They proceed to force Connie's front and rear entries. Connie's lips curve into the shape of a letter. Monica and Doris touching each other up in the kitchen. Then stables full of cattle and a man approaching with difficulty, pushing his way through the cows. It's Pajarito Gómez. He never arrives: the following scene shows him stretched out in the mud, among cowpats and hooves. Monica and Doris rimming each other on a big white bed. The dead rancher opens his eyes. He sits up and climbs out of the coffin to the horror and amazement of his family and friends. Covered by the bull and the condor, Connie pronounces the word *Kundalini*. The cows escape from the stables and the credits appear over the abandoned, gradually darkening body of Pajarito Gómez. Another movie: *Impluvium*. Two genuine beggars dragging sacks along a dirt road. They reach the backyard of Bittrich's house. There they find Monica Farr, completely naked and chained in an upright position. The beggars empty the sacks: an abundant collection of sexual instruments made of steel and leather. The beggars put on masks with phallic protuberances, and, kneeling down, one in front of Monica, one behind, they penetrate her, moving their heads in a way that is, to say the least, ambiguous: it's hard to tell whether they're excited or the masks are suffocating them. Lying on an army camp bed, Pajarito Gómez smokes a cigarette. On another camp bed the conscript Sansón Fernández is jerking off. The camera pans slowly over Monica's face: she is crying. The beggars depart, dragging their sacks down a miserable, unpaved street. Still chained, Monica

Prefiguration of Lalo Cura

shuts her eyes and seems to fall asleep. She dreams of the masks, the latex noses, the pair of old carcasses who could barely hold a breath of air and yet were so enthusiastic in the performance of their task. Supernatural carcasses emptied of all the essentials. Then Monica gets dressed, walks through the centre of Medellín, and is invited to an orgy, where she meets Connie and Doris; they kiss and smile at each other, and talk about what they've been doing. Pajarito Gómez, half dressed in fatigues, has fallen asleep. When the orgy is over, before it gets dark, the owner of the house wants to show them his most prized possession. The girls follow their host to a garden covered with a metal and glass canopy. The man's bejewelled finger indicates something at the far end. The girls examine a cement swimming pool in the shape of a coffin. When they lean over the edge, they see their faces reflected in the water. Then dusk falls and the beggars come to an area where big cargo ships are docked. The music, performed by a band of kettledrummers, gets louder, more sinister and ominous, until the storm finally breaks. Bittrich adored sound effects like that. Thunder in the mountains, the sizzle of lightning, splintering trees, rain against window panes. He collected them on high quality tapes. He said it was to make his movies atmospheric, but in fact it was just because he liked the effects. The full range of sounds that rain makes in a forest. The rhythmic or random sibilance of the wind and the sea. Sounds to make you feel alone, sounds to make your hair stand on end. His great treasure was the roar of a hurricane. I heard it as a kid. The actors were drinking coffee under a tree and Bittrich was playing with an enormous German tape player, away from the others, looking pasty, the way he did when he'd been working too hard. Now you're going to hear the hurricane from inside, he said. At first I couldn't hear anything. I think I was expecting a god-almighty, ear-splitting racket, so I was disappointed when all I could hear was a kind of intermittent whirling. An intermittent ripping. Like a propeller made of meat. Then I heard voices; it wasn't the hurricane, of course, but the pilots of the plane flying in its eye. Hard voices talking in Spanish and English. Bittrich was smiling as he listened. Then I heard the hurricane again and this time I really heard it. Emptiness. A vertical bridge and emptiness, emptiness, emptiness. I'll never forget the smile on Bittrich's face. It was as if he was weeping. Is that all? I asked, not wanting to admit that I'd already had enough. That's all, said Bittrich, fascinated by the silently turning reels. Then he stopped the tape player, closed it up very carefully, went inside with the others and got back to work. Another movie: *Ferryman*. From the ruins you might think it's about life in Latin America after the Third World War. The girls wander through garbage dumps, along deserted paths. Then there's a broad, gently flowing river. Pajarito Gómez and two other guys play cards by the light of a candle. The girls come to an inn where the men are carrying guns. They make love with them all, one after another. They look out from the bushes at the river and a few pieces of wood tied clumsily together. Pajarito Gómez is the ferryman, at least that's what everyone calls him, but he doesn't budge from the table. He holds the best cards. The villains remark on how well he's playing. What a good player the ferryman is. What good luck the ferryman has. Gradually the supplies begin to run short. The cook and the kitchen hand torture Doris, penetrating her with the handles of enormous butcher's knives. Hunger reigns over the inn: some stay in bed, others wander through the bushes looking for food. While the men fall ill one by one, the girls scribble in their diaries as if possessed. Desperate pictograms. Images of the river superimposed on images of a never-ending orgy. The end is predictable. The men dress the women up as chickens, make them do their tricks, and then proceed to eat them at a feather-strewn banquet. The bones of Connie, Monica and Doris lie on the diner's patio. Pajarito Gómez plays another hand of poker. He wears his luck like a close-fitting glove. The camera is behind him and the viewer can see the cards he's holding. They are blank. The credits appear over the corpses of all the actors. Three seconds before the end of the film, the river changes colour, turning jet black. That one was especially deep, Doris used to say, it illustrates the sad fate of artists in the porn industry: first we're ruthlessly exploited, then we're devoured by thoughtless strangers. Bittrich seems to have made that movie to compete with the cannibal porn videos that were starting to cause a stir at the time. But it isn't hard to see that the film's real centre is Pajarito Gómez sitting in the gambling den. Pajarito Gómez, who could generate an inner vibration that planted his image in the viewer's eyes. A great actor wasted by life, our life, yours and mine, my friends. But the movies Bittrich made live on, unsullied. And so does Pajarito Gómez, holding those cards covered with dust, with his dirty hands and his dirty neck, his eternally half-closed eyelids, vibrating on and on. Pajarito Gómez, an emblematic figure in the pornography of the 1980s. He wasn't specially well endowed or muscular, he didn't appeal to the target audience for that kind of movie. He looked like Walter Abel. He had no experience when Bittrich dragged him from the gutter and put him in front of a camera: the rest came so naturally it's hard to believe. Pajarito had this continuous vibration, and watching him, sooner or later, depending on your powers of resistance, you'd be suddenly transfixed by the energy emanating from that scrap of a man, who looked so feeble. So unprepossessing, so undernourished. So strangely triumphant. The pre-eminent porn actor in Bittrich's Colombian cycle. The best when it came to playing dead and the best when it came to playing vacant. He was also the only member of the German's cast who survived: in 1999, the only one still alive was Pajarito Gómez, the rest had been killed or succumbed to disease. Sansón Fernández died of AIDS. Praxíteles Barrionuevo died in the Hole of Bogotá. Ernesto San Román was stabbed to death in the Areanea sauna in Medellín. Alvarito Fuentes died of AIDS in the Cartago jail. All of them young guys with supersize cocks. Frank Moreno, shot to death in Panama. Oscar Guillermo Montes, shot to death in Puerto Berrío. David Salazar, known as the Anteater, shot to death in Palmira. Victims of vendettas or fortuitous brawls. Evelio Latapia, hung in a hotel room in Popayán. Carlos José Santelices, stabbed by strangers in an alley in Maracaibo. Reinaldo Hermosilla, last seen in El Progreso, Honduras. Dionisio Aurelio Pérez, shot to death in a bar in Mexico City. Maximiliano Moret, drowned in the Marañon River. Ten- to twelve-inch cocks, sometimes so long they couldn't get them up. Young mestizos, blacks, whites, Indians, sons of Latin America, whose only assets were a pair of balls and a member tanned by exposure to the elements or miraculously pink by some weird freak of nature. The sadness of the phallus was something Bittrich understood better than anyone. I mean the sadness of those monumental members against the backdrop of this vast and

Prefiguration of Lalo Cura

desolate continent. For example, Oscar Guillermo Montes in a scene from a movie I've forgotten the rest of; he's naked from the waist down, his penis hangs flaccid and dripping. It's dark and wrinkled and the drops have a milky sheen. Behind the actor a landscape unfolds: mountains, ravines, rivers, forests, ranges, towering clouds, a city perhaps, a volcano, a desert. Oscar Guillermo Montes perched on a high ridge, an icy breeze playing with a lock of his hair. That's all. It's like a poem by Tablada, isn't it? But you've never heard of Tablada. Neither had Bittrich, and it doesn't matter, really, it's all there in that image – I must have the tape around somewhere – the loneliness I was talking about. Impossible geography, impossible anatomy. What was Bittrich aiming for with that sequence? Was he trying to justify amnesia, our amnesia? Or portray Oscar Guillermo's weary eyes? Or did he just want to show us an uncircumcised penis dripping in the continent's immensity? Or give an impression of useless grandeur: handsome young men without shame, marked out for sacrifice, fated to disappear in the immensity of chaos? Who knows? The only one who always got away was the amateur Pajarito Gómez, whose endowment extended, after plenty of work, to a maximum length of seven inches. The German flirted with death—what the hell did he care about death?—he flirted with solitude and black holes, but he never tried anything with Pajarito. Elusive and uncontrollable, Pajarito came into the camera's scope as if he just happened to be passing by and had stopped for a look. Then he began to vibrate, full on, and the viewers, whether they were solitary jerk-off artists or businessmen who used the videos to liven up the decor, barely intending to glance at them, were transfixed by that scrawny creature's moods. Pajarito Gómez gave off prostatic fluid!

And that was something different, far exceeding the German's lucubrations. And Bittrich knew it, so when Pajarito appeared in a scene there were usually no additional effects, no music or sounds of any kind, nothing to distract the viewer from what really mattered: the hieratic Pajarito Gómez, sucked or sucking, fucking or fucked, but always vibrating, as if unawares. The German's protectors were deeply suspicious of that talent; they'd have preferred to see Pajarito working in the central market unloading trucks, ruthlessly exploited until the day he disappeared. They wouldn't have been able to explain what it was they didn't like about him; they just had a vague sense that he was a guy who could attract bad luck and make people feel ill at ease. Sometimes, when I remember my childhood, I wonder how Bittrich must have felt about his protectors. He respected the drug lords; after all they put up the money, and like all good Europeans, he respected money, a point of reference in the midst of chaos. But the corrupt police and army officers, what would he have thought of them, Bittrich, a German, who read history books in his spare time? They must have seemed so ludicrous, he must have had such a good laugh at them, at night, after those unruly meetings. Monkeys in SS uniforms, that's what they were. Alone in his house, surrounded by his videos and his amazing sounds, he must have laughed and laughed. And they were the ones who wanted to get rid of Pajarito, those monkeys, with their sixth sense. Those pathetic, odious monkeys thought they could tell him, a German director in permanent exile, who he should and shouldn't be hiring. Imagine Bittrich after one of those meetings, in the dark house in Los Empalados, after everyone else has gone, drinking rum and smoking Mexican Delicados in the biggest room, the one he uses as his study and bedroom. On the table there are paper cups with dregs of whisky in them. Two or three videotapes sitting on top of the TV, the latest from the Olimpo Movie Production Company. Diaries and torn-out pages covered with figures: salaries, bribes, bonuses. Pocket money. And the words of the police commissioner, the air force lieutenant and the colonel from military intelligence still floating in the air: We don't want that jinx anywhere near the Company. When people see him in our films, their stomachs turn. It's bad taste to have that slug fucking the girls. And Bittrich let them speak, he observed them silently, and then he did what he liked. After all, they were only porn videos; it's not like there were serious profits at stake. And that was how Pajarito got to stay on with us, although the company's backers found his presence disturbing. Pajarito Gómez. A quiet and pretty reserved sort of guy, but for some mysterious reason the girls were especially fond of him. In the course of their professional duties, they all got to lay him, and it left them with a curious feeling, hard to say just what it was, but they were all ready to do it again. I guess being with Pajarito was like being nowhere. Doris even ended up living with him for a while, but it didn't work out. Doris and Pajarito: for six months they went back and forth between the Hotel Aurora, which is where he lived, and the apartment on Avenida de los Libertadores. It was too good to last, you know how it is: singular spirits can't bear so much love, so much perfection stumbled on by chance. Maybe if Doris hadn't been such a bombshell, and if she'd been mute, and if Pajarito had never vibrated ... Things finally fell apart during the shooting of *Cocaine*, one of Bittrich's worst movies. But they stayed friends until the end.

Many years later, when all the rest were dead, I tracked down Pajarito. He was living in a tiny, one-room apartment, on a street that led down to the sea, in Buenaventura. He was working as a waiter in a restaurant owned by a retired policeman: Octopus Ink, the place was called, ideal for someone who wanted to lie low. He went from home to work and back again, with a brief stop each day at a video store, where he'd usually rent a couple of movies. Walt Disney and old Colombian, Mexican or Venezuelan films. Every day, punctual as a clock. From his walk-up to Octopus Ink, and then, after dark, back to the apartment, with two videotapes under his arm. He never brought food back, only movies. He rented them on the way there or the way back, it varied, but always from the same store, a little shack, three yards by three, open eighteen hours a day. I went looking for him on a whim, just because I felt like it. I went looking and I found him in 1999; it was easy, it took less than a week. Pajarito was forty-nine then, but he looked at least ten years older. He wasn't surprised to find me sitting on his bed when he got home. I told him who I was, reminded him of the movies he'd made with my mother and my aunt. Pajarito took a chair and as he sat down the videos fell out from under his arm. You've come to kill me, Lalito, he said. He'd rented films with Ignacio López Tarso and Matt Dillon, two of his favourite actors. I reminded him of the old Pregnant Fantasies days. We both smiled. I saw your prick, it was transparent like a worm; my eyes were open, you know, watching your glass eye. Pajarito nodded, then sniffed. You always were a clever kid, he said, before you were born too, I guess, with your eyes open already, why not. I saw you, that's what matters, I said. You were pink for a start in there, then you turned transparent and you got one hell of a shock, Pajarito. Back then you weren't afraid, you moved so fast only little creatures and fetuses could see you moving. Only cockroaches, nits, lice and fetuses. Pajarito was looking at the floor. I heard him whisper: Et cetera, et cetera. Then he said: I never liked that sort of movie, one or two is OK, but it's criminal to make so many. I'm a fairly normal person, really. I was genuinely fond of Doris, I was always a friend to your mother, when you were little I never did you any harm. Do you remember? I didn't run the business, I never betrayed anyone, or killed anyone. I did a bit of dealing, a few robberies, we all did, but as you can see, it didn't set me up for retirement. Then he picked the videos up off the floor, put the one with Ignacio López Tarso in the VCR, and as the soundless images succeeded one another on the screen, he began to cry. Don't cry, Pajarito, I said, it's not worth it. His days of vibrating were over. Or maybe he was still vibrating a little, and as I sat there on the bed I was scavenging those remnants of energy with the ravenous hunger of a shipwrecked sailor. It's hard to vibrate in such a small apartment, with the smell of chicken soup permeating every cranny. It's hard to pick up a vibration when your eyes are fixed on a dumbly gesticulating Ignacio López Tarso. López Tarso's eyes in black and white: how could so much innocence and so much malice be combined? A good actor, I remarked, just to say something. One of our founding fathers, said Pajarito in agreement. He was right. Then he whispered: Et cetera, et cetera. That lousy fucking Pajarito. We sat there in silence for a long time: López Tarso went gliding through the movie's plot like a fish inside a whale; the images of Connie, Doris and Monica lit up for few seconds in my head, and Pajarito's vibration became imperceptible. I haven't come to rub you out, I said to him in the end. Back then, when I was young, I had trouble using the word *kill*. I never killed: I took people out, blew them away, put them to sleep, I topped, stiffed or wasted them, sent them to meet their maker, made them bite the dust, I iced them, snuffed them, did them in. I smoked people. But I didn't smoke Pajarito, I just wanted to see him and chat for a while. To feel his beat and remember my past. Thanks, Lalito, he said, and then he got up and filled a washbasin with water from a demijohn. With exact, artistic, resigned movements, he washed his hands and his face. When I was a kid, that's what they all called me, Connie, Monica, Doris, Bittrich, Pajarito, Sansón Fernández: they all called me Lalito. Lalito Cura playing in the garden with the dogs and the geese at the house of crime, which for me was the house of boredom and sometimes the house of dismay and happiness. These days there's no time to get bored, happiness vanished somewhere in the world, and all that's left is dismay. Perpetual dismay, composed of corpses and ordinary people, like Pajarito, who was thanking me. I was never intending to kill you, I said, I've kept all your movies, I don't watch them very often, I admit, only on special occasions, but I've looked after them. I'm a collector of your cinematic past, I said. Pajarito sat down again. He had stopped vibrating: he was watching the López Tarso movie out of the corner of his eye and his stillness suggested a mineral patience. According to the clock radio beside the bed it was two in the morning. The night before, I had dreamed of finding Pajarito: I was mounting him and shouting unintelligible words in his ear, something about a buried treasure. Or about an underground city. Or about a dead person wrapped in papers proof against putrefaction and the passage of time. But I didn't even lay my hand on his shoulder. I'll leave you some money, Pajarito, so you can live without having to work. I'll buy you whatever you like. I'll take you to a quiet place where you can spend all your time watching your favourite actors. There was no one like you in Los Empalados, I said. Ignacio López Tarso and Pajarito Gómez looked at me: stone-like patience. The pair of them gone crazily dumb. Their eyes full of humanity and fear and fetuses lost in the immensity of memory. Fetuses and other tiny wide-eyed creatures. For a moment, my friends, I felt that the whole apartment was starting to vibrate. Then I stood up very carefully and left.

Murdering Whores

for Teresa Ariño

'I saw you on television, Max, and I thought, That's my guy.'

(The guy is stubbornly jerking his head, trying to take a deep breath, but he can't.)

'I saw you with your group. Is that what you call it? Maybe you say gang, or crew, but no, I think you say group: it's a simple word and you're a simple man. You'd taken off your T-shirts and you were bare-chested, displaying your young bodies: strong pectorals and biceps, though you'd all like to have more muscle, hairless chests, mostly, but I didn't actually pay much attention to the other chests or bodies, just yours, something about you struck me, your face, your eyes gazing in the direction of the camera (though you probably didn't realise you were being filmed and beamed into our living rooms), the depthless look in your eyes, different from the way they look now, infinitely different from the way they will look soon, eyes that were fixed on glory and happiness, satisfied desire and victory, things that can only exist in the kingdom of the future, things it's better not to hope for because they never come.'

(The guy is jerking his head from left to right, still straining for breath and sweating.)

'In fact, seeing you on television was like an invitation. Imagine for a moment that I'm a princess, waiting. An impatient princess. One night I see you, and the reason I see you is that I have, in a sense, been searching, not for you personally but for the prince you are, and what that prince represents. You and your friends are dancing with your T-shirts tied around your necks or your waists. Tied or perhaps furled, a word that according to cranky old nitpickers refers to sails when they're rolled up and bound to a yard or a boom, but in my own young and cranky way, I use it to refer to garments rolled up around the neck or chest or waist. The old and I go our separate ways, as you will have guessed by now. But let's not lose sight of what really interests us. You and your group are young, and all of you are offering your hymns to the night; some of you, the leaders, are brandishing flags. The announcer, poor bastard, is impressed by the tribal dance in which you're taking part. He points it out to the other newsman. They're dancing, he says, in his loutish voice, as if we, the viewers at home, in front of our televisions, hadn't realised. Yes, they're having fun, says the other newsman. Another lout. *They* seem to be enjoying your dance, at least. It's just a conga, really. In the front line there are eight or nine. In the second there are ten. In the third there are seven or eight. In the fourth there are fifteen. United by the team colours and semi-nakedness (T-shirts tied or furled around your waists or necks, or turban-style around your heads) and the dance (if I can call it that) as it moves through the area in which you have been isolated. Your dance is like a lightning bolt in the spring night. The newsman, the newsmen, weary but still able to muster some enthusiasm, salute your initiative. You work your way across the cement steps from the right to the left, and when you reach the wire fence, you go back the other way. The guys at the head of each line are carrying flags, the team flag or the Spanish flag; the rest of you, including the ones at the ends, are waving much smaller flags, or scarves, or the T-shirts you took off earlier. It's a spring night, but it's still cold, and in the end that gives your gesture the force you wanted it to have, the force it merits, after all. Then the lines break up, you start to chant your songs, some of you raise your arms and give the Roman salute. Do you know what it means, that salute? You must, and if you don't, as you raise your arm you can guess. Under my city's night sky you salute in the direction of the television cameras, and watching at home I see you and decide to offer you my salute, in response to yours.'

(The guy shakes his head, his eyes seem to fill with tears, his shoulders tremble. Is there love in his gaze? Has his body sensed what will certainly happen, while his mind is still lagging behind? Both phenomena, the tears and the trembling, could result from the effort he is making at this moment, in vain, or from a sincere regret tearing at all his nerves.)

'So, I take off my clothes, I take off my pants, I take off my bra, I take a shower, I put on perfume, I put on clean pants, I put on a clean bra, I put on a black silk top, I put on my best pair of jeans, I put on white socks, I put on my boots, I put on a jacket, the best one I own, and I go into the garden, because to get out into the street, first I have to cross that dark garden, which you especially liked. All in less than ten minutes; normally I'm not so quick. Let's say it's your dance that is speeding up my movements. While I get dressed you're dancing. In some other dimension. Another dimension and another time, like a prince and a princess, like the eruptive call of animals coupling in springtime, I get dressed while, inside the television, you dance wildly with your eyes fixed on something that might be eternity or the key to eternity, except that your eyes as you dance are flat and empty and inexpressive.'

(The guy nods repeatedly. What were gestures of denial or desperation are transformed into gestures of affirmation, as if he'd been suddenly seized by an idea, or a *new* idea had just occurred to him.)

'Finally, even though I haven't got time to look at myself in the mirror and check that my clothes are exactly right, and in fact I probably wouldn't want to see my reflection even if I did have time (because what you and I are doing is secret), I go out, leaving just the porch light on, get onto my motorbike and drive through streets where people stranger than you or me are setting out to enjoy their Saturday night, a Saturday to match their expectations, a sad Saturday, in other words, one that will never give life to what they have dreamed and meticulously planned, a Saturday like any other, aggressive and grateful, stocky and affable, perverse and sad. Awful adjectives that aren't my style at all, they make me baulk, but, as always, in the end, I let them stand, as a farewell gesture. My motorbike and I roll on among those lights, those Christian preparations, those baseless expectations, and we come out in front of the stadium, on the Gran Avenida, which is still empty, and we stop beneath the arches of the bridges that lead to the entrance gates, and this is the really strange part: when we stop, I can feel in my legs that the world is still moving, as I suppose you know it does, the earth is moving under my feet, under the wheels of my motorbike, and for a moment, for a fraction of a second, whether or not I find you doesn't matter, you can leave with your friends, you can go and get drunk or take a bus back to the city you come from. But the feeling of abandon, as if I were being fucked by an angel, without penetration – or actually no, penetrated to the core – is brief, and just as I begin to doubt or analyse it in amazement, the gates swing open and the people start coming out of the stadium: a flock of vultures, a flock of crows.'

(The guy hangs his head. Lifts it up. His eyes try to smile. His facial muscles are seized by a spasm or a series of spasms that could mean many different things: We're meant for each other, Think of the future, Life is wonderful, Don't do anything stupid, I'm innocent, Spain rules.)

'Finding you is a problem. Will you look the same five yards away as you did on TV? Your height is a problem: I don't know if you're tall or of medium height (you're not short, I know that). Your clothes are a problem: by now it's starting to get cold, and your torso and the torsos of your companions are once again draped in T-shirts or even jackets; some are coming out of the stadium with scarves furled (like sails) around their necks and some are even using their scarves to cover their mouths and cheeks. My footsteps on the cement are lit by vertical moonlight. I search for you patiently, and yet at the same time I am anxious like the princess contemplating the empty frame in which the prince's smile should be shining. Your friends are a problem compounded: they're a temptation. I see them and am seen by them, I am desired, I know they'd pull my jeans off without a second thought; some no doubt deserve my attentions at least as much as you do, but in the end I resist, I remain faithful. Finally you appear, surrounded by conga dancers, chanting the words of a hymn that prefigures our meeting, with a serious look on your face, charged with an importance that no one but you can measure and appreciate precisely; you're tall, quite a lot taller than me, and your arms are long, just as I imagined after seeing you on TV, and when I smile at you, when I say, Hi, Max, you don't know what to say, at first you don't know what to say, you just laugh, not quite as stridently as your friends, but you laugh, my prince of the time machine, you laugh and you stop walking.'

(The guy looks at her, narrows his eyes, tries to calm his breathing, and as it becomes more regular, he seems to be thinking: breathe in, breathe out, think, breathe in, breathe out, think . . .)

'Then, instead of saying, I'm not Max, you try to catch up with your group, and for a moment I'm seized by panic, a panic that in retrospect seems closer to laughter than to fear. I follow you without a clear idea of what I am going to do next. But you and three others stop and turn and size me up with cold eyes, and I say, Max, we have to talk, and then you say, I'm not Max, that's not my name, what is this, are you joking, are you getting me mixed up with someone or what, and then I say, Sorry, you really look like Max, and I say, I want to talk with you, What about, Well, about Max, and then you smile, and you finally decide to stay behind and let your friends go off; they shout the name of the bar where you'll meet to set off home, No problem, you say, see you there, and your friends shrink away like the stadium behind us as I drive my bike at full throttle, confidently, and the Gran Avenida is almost empty at this time of night, there are only the people leaving the stadium, and you sit behind me with your arms around my waist, I feel your body against my back like a mollusc clinging to a rock, and it's true that the air on the avenue is cold and dense like the waves that push and pull at the mollusc; you cling to me so naturally, Max, like someone who senses that the sea is not only an inhospitable element but a time tunnel, you furl yourself around my waist the way your T-shirt was furled around your neck, but now the conga is danced by the air that pours like a torrent into the streaky tube that is the Gran Avenida, and you laugh or shout something, maybe you saw some friends among the people sliding past beneath the canopy of trees, maybe you're just yelling insults at strangers, oh Max, you're not shouting Goodbye or Hi or See you, you're shouting slogans that are older than blood, but surely not older than the rock to which you're clinging, happy to feel the waves, the submarine currents of the night, sure that you will not be swept away.'

(The guy murmurs something unintelligible. It looks like saliva dripping from his chin, although perhaps it's only sweat. His breathing, in any case, has settled down.)

'And so we arrive at my house on the outskirts of town, safe and sound. You take off your helmet, you touch your balls, you put your arm around my shoulders. The gesture betrays a surprising degree of tenderness and timidity. But your eyes are still not tender and timid enough. You like my house. You like my pictures. You ask me about the figures that appear in them. The Prince and the Princess, I reply. They look like the Catholic Monarchs, you say. Yes, the thought has sometimes occurred to me too, Catholic Monarchs in the confines of their kingdom, Catholic Monarchs spying on each other in a perpetual panic, a perpetual solemnity, but for me, for the person I am at least fifteen hours a day, they are a prince and a princess, a bride and groom who journey through the years, and are wounded, pierced by arrows, who lose their horses on the hunt, or never even had horses and must flee on foot, with only their eyes to guide them, and an idiotic will, which some call kindness and others good nature, as if nature could be qualified, good or bad, wild or tame, nature is nature, Max, that's a fact you have to face, and it will always be there, like an irresolvable mystery, and I'm not talking about forests catching fire but neurons and the left or the right hemisphere of the brain catching fire and blazing for centuries and centuries. But, blessed soul that you are, you think my house is pretty, and you even ask if I'm alone and then you're surprised when I laugh. Do you think I would have invited you here if I hadn't been alone? Do you think I would have ridden right across the city on my motorbike, with you pressed against my back, like a mollusc clinging to a rock, while my head (or my figurehead) plunged through time, with the sole aim of bringing you back safe and sound to this refuge, the real rock, the rock that rears magically from its foundations and breaks the surface, do you think I would have done all that if I hadn't been alone? And just on a practical level, do you think I would have taken an extra helmet, a helmet to protect your face from prying eyes, if my intention hadn't been to bring you back here, into my purest solitude?'

(The guy hangs his head and nods, his eyes scan the walls of the room down to the finest crack. His sweat begins to flow again like a fickle river – or is there a kink in time? – and droplets gather in his eyebrows and hang ominously over his eyes.)

'You don't know anything about painting, Max, but I get the feeling that you know a lot about solitude. You like my Catholic Monarchs, you like beer, you like your country, you like respect, you like your soccer team, you like your friends or buddies or pals, the gang or group or crew, the bunch that saw you stay behind to talk with some hot chick you didn't know, you don't like disorder, you don't like blacks, you don't like faggots, you don't like being treated with disrespect, you don't like getting pushed aside. There are so many things you don't like, in that way you're a lot like me. We're approaching one another, you and I, from opposite ends of the tunnel, and even though all we can see are each other's silhouettes, we keep walking resolutely towards our meeting point. In the middle of the tunnel our arms will be able to intertwine at last, and although the darkness there will be complete, making our faces invisible, I know that we will step forward without fear and touch each other's faces (the first thing you'll touch is my ass, but that too is a part of your desire to know my face), we will feel each other's eyes and perhaps pronounce one or two words of recognition. Then it will be clear (it will become clear to me) that you know nothing about painting, but you do know about solitude, which is almost the same. One day we will meet in the middle of that tunnel, Max, and I will feel your face, your nose, your mouth — which generally expresses your stupidity better than anyone else's — your empty eyes, the tiny folds that form on your cheeks when you smile, the false hardness of your face when you get serious, when you sing your hymns, those hymns you don't understand, your chin that is sometimes rock-like, but more often, I guess, like a vegetable, that chin of yours, Max, which is so typical, so archetypical that now I suspect it's your chin that brought you here, that was your downfall. And then you and I will be able to talk again, or we will talk for the first time, but before that we'll have to roll about, take off our clothes and furl them around our necks, or around the necks of the dead – those who live in the motionless scroll.'

(The guy is crying, and it looks like he's trying to speak, but in fact he's just whimpering: the movements of his cheeks and his covered lips are spasms produced by his crying).

'As the gangsters say, it's nothing personal, Max. Of course, that statement contains an element of truth and an element of falsehood. It's always something personal. We have come through a time tunnel unscathed because it's something personal. I chose you because it's something personal. Naturally I had never seen you before. You never did anything to harm me personally. I say that to put your mind at rest. You never raped me. You never raped anyone I know. It's even possible that you never raped anyone at all. It's not something personal. Maybe I'm sick. Maybe all this is a nightmare that neither you nor I is having, although it's hurting you, although the pain is real and personal. And yet I suspect that the end will not be personal. The end: extinction, the gesture that will bring all this irreparably to a close. And personally or impersonally, you and I will enter my house again, and look at my pictures (the Prince and the Princess), drink beer and get undressed, and I will feel your hands again clumsily stroking my back, my ass, my crotch, looking for my clitoris perhaps, but not knowing exactly where it is, I will undress you again, and take your cock in both hands and say, You're so big, when in fact you're not so big, Max, and that is something you ought to know by now, and I'll put it in my mouth again, and suck you like I bet you've never been sucked before, and then I'll take off all your clothes and let you take off mine, one hand busy with my buttons, a glass of whisky in the other, and I'll look you in the eyes, those eyes I saw on television (and will see again in dreams), the eyes I chose you for, and once again I'll tell you, I'll tell your sickening electric memory that it's nothing personal, and even then I'll have my doubts, I'll feel cold as I do now, I'll try to remember every word you said, even the most insignificant, but none of them will be any consolation.'

(The guy jerks his head again, nodding. What is he trying to say? Impossible to tell. His body, or rather his legs, are subject to a curious phenomenon: sometimes they are covered with a sweat as abundant as the sweat on his forehead, especially on the inner sides, sometimes the skin seems to be cold, from the groin to the knees, and takes on a bumpy texture, if not to the touch at least to the eye).

'Your words, I admit, were kind. Nevertheless, I fear that you did not give sufficient thought to what you were saying. And even less to what *I* was saying. You should always listen carefully, Max, to what women say while they're being fucked. If they don't speak, fine, there's nothing to listen to, and you'll probably have nothing to think about, but if they do, even if it's only a murmur, listen to their words and think about them, think about their meanings, think about what they express and leave unexpressed, try to understand what it is they really signify. Women are murdering whores, Max, they're monkeys stiff with cold watching the horizon from a sick tree, they're princesses searching for you in the darkness, crying, examining the words that they will never be able to say. In misunderstanding we live and plan the cycles of our life. For your friends, Max, in that stadium, which is shrinking in your memory now like a symbol of the nightmare, I was just some weird kind of hooker, a spectacle after the spectacle, reserved for a few spectators who had danced a conga with their T-shirts furled around their necks or their waists. But for you I was a princess on the Gran Avenida, shattered now by wind and fear (so that in your mind the avenue has become a time tunnel), the trophy reserved specially for you after a night of collective magic. For the police I will be a blank page. No one will ever understand my words of love. And you, Max, do you remember anything I said while you were screwing me?'

(The guy moves his head, clearly signalling assent, and his moist eyes, his tense shoulders, his stomach, his legs that jerk and jerk whenever she looks away, struggling to get free, his throbbing jugular, all say yes.)

'Do you remember I said *the wind*? Do you remember I said *the underground streets*? Do you remember I said *you are the photograph*? No, you really don't remember, do you? You were too drunk and too busy with my tits and my ass. And you had no idea, otherwise at the first opportunity you'd have been out of here like a shot. You'd like to get out of here now, wouldn't you, Max? Your image, your double, running across the garden, jumping over the fence, disappearing up the street, striding away like a middle distance runner, still half undressed, humming one of your hymns to bolster your courage, and then, after running for twenty minutes, turning up breathless in the bar where the rest of your group or club or squad or gang or whatever it's called are waiting for you, drinking a mug of beer and saying, Guys you're never going to believe what happened to me, I nearly got killed, some fucking whore from the suburbs, from the far side of the city and time, a whore from the fucking beyond who saw me on TV (we were on TV!) and took me home on her motorbike and sucked my dick and spread her legs for me and said words that were mysterious at first but then I understood them, no, I felt them, this whore said words I could feel in my liver and my balls, at first they sounded innocent or like she was hot for me or moaning because I was nailing her hard, but the thing is, guys, after a while they didn't sound so innocent, what I mean is, she didn't stop murmuring or whispering while I rode her, and that's normal, isn't it, but this wasn't normal, there was nothing normal about it, a whore who whispers while she's being fucked, OK, but then I heard what she was saying, I heard her fucking words ploughing like a boat through a sea of testosterone, and I'm telling you guys, that supernatural voice made the sea of semen shudder and shrink away, the sea disappeared, leaving the sea floor exposed and the coast all dry, just stones and mountains, cliffs, ranges, dark crevices moist with fear, the boat sailing on over that emptiness, and I saw it with my own two eyes, my own three eyes, and I said, It's all right, it's all right, honey, shitting myself, petrified, and then I stood up, trying to look normal, all jittery but trying to hide it, and said I was going to the bathroom to siphon the python or take a dump, and she looked at me like I'd recited John fucking Donne, guys, or Ovid or something, and I walked backward keeping my eyes on her, still seeing that boat sailing on imperturbably through a sea of nothingness and electricity, as if planet Earth was being reborn and I was the only witness to its birth, but who was I witnessing for, the stars I guess, and when I got to the corridor, beyond the range of her gaze and her desire, instead of opening the bathroom door, I crept to the front door and crossed the garden, saying a silent prayer, and jumped the wall and started running up the street like the last runner from Marathon, bringing news not of victory but of defeat, the runner nobody listens to or congratulates or greets with a bowl of water, but he gets there alive, guys, and learns his lesson: Don't enter that castle, Don't follow that path, Don't venture into that territory. Even if you're singled out. Even if everything is against you.'

(The guy nods his head. It's clear that he wants to express his agreement. The effort is making his face redden noticeably; his veins are swelling, his eyes are bulging.)

'But you didn't listen to my words, you couldn't distinguish them from my moaning, those last words, which might have saved you. I chose you well. Television doesn't lie, that's its only virtue (that and the old movies they show in the small hours of the morning), and the sight of your face, against the wire fence, after the conga that everyone cheered, prefigured (and hastened) the inevitable ending. I brought you home on my motorbike, I took off your clothes, I left you unconscious, I tied your hands and feet to an old chair, I put a sticking plaster over your mouth, not because I'm scared that your cries might alert someone, but because I don't want to hear you beg, I don't want to hear your pathetic stuttering apologies, your weak insistence that you're not like that, that it was all a game, that I've got it all wrong. Maybe I've got it all wrong. Maybe it's all a game. Maybe you're not like that. But the thing is, Max, no one's like that. I wasn't like that either. I'm not going to tell you about my pain, it's not as if you caused it; on the contrary, you gave me an orgasm. You were the lost prince who gave me an orgasm; you can be proud of yourself. And I gave you an opportunity to escape, but you were also the deaf prince. Now it's too late, it's getting light; your legs must be numb and cramped, your wrists are swollen; you shouldn't have struggled so much, I warned you when we started, Max, this was bound to happen. You'll have to make the best of it. Now is not the time for crying, or remembering conga lines, threats or beatings; it's time to look inside yourself and try to understand that sometimes, unexpectedly, people just walk away. You're naked in my chamber of horrors, Max, and your eyes are following my knife as it swings, as if it were the pendulum of a cuckoo clock. Close your eyes, Max, there's no need to go on looking; think of something nice, think of it as hard as you can can . . .'

(His eyes, instead of closing, open wildly, and all his muscles wrench in one last desperate effort: the shock is so violent that the chair to which he is securely tied falls over. He hits his head and his hip on the ground, he loses control of his anal sphincter and bladder; he is seized by spasms; dust and filth from the flagstones stick to his wet skin.)

'I'm not going to pick you up, Max, you're fine like that. Keep your eyes open or close them, it doesn't matter; think of something nice or don't think at all. It's getting light out but, the way things are, it might just as well be getting dark. You're the prince and you're arriving at exactly the right time. You're welcome whenever you come and wherever you come from, whether you've come on a motorbike or on foot, whether or not you know what awaits you, whether you were tricked or came knowing that you would meet your destiny here. Your face, which until recently could express only stupidity or rage or hatred, is reconfigured now and can express what can only be guessed at inside a tunnel where physical time and verbal time flow into one another and mingle. You proceed resolutely through the corridors of my palace, barely pausing for the few seconds it takes to look at the pictures of the Catholic Monarchs, to drink a glass of crystal-clear water, to touch the mirrors' quicksilver with your fingertips. The castle only seems to be quiet, Max. Sometimes you think you're alone, but deep down you know that you're not. Your hand raised in salute, your naked torso, the T-shirt furled around your waist, your warrior hymns about purity and the future, you leave all that behind. This castle is your mountain, and you will have to spend all your strength climbing and exploring it, because after that there will be nothing more; the mountain and the climbing will demand the highest price you can pay. Now think about what you're leaving, what you could and had to leave behind, and think about chance, the greatest criminal that ever walked the earth. Free yourself of fear and regret, Max, because you are already inside the castle, and here there is only the movement that will bring you ineluctably to my arms. Now you are inside the castle and you hear the doors closing behind you. Deep in the dream you walk on through passages and rooms of bare stone. What weapons do you carry, Max? Only your solitude. You know that somewhere I am waiting for you. You know that I am naked too. Sometimes you feel my tears, you see my tears flow on the dark stone and you think you have found me, but the room is empty, which distresses and yet at the same time excites you. Keep climbing, Max. The next room is dirty and doesn't seem to belong in a castle. There's an old TV that doesn't work and a folding bed with two mattresses on it. Someone is crying somewhere. You see children's drawings, old clothes covered with mold, dried blood and dust. You open another door. You call someone. You tell them not to cry. Your footsteps show in the dust on the floor of the passage. The tears sometimes seem to be dripping from the ceiling. It doesn't matter. The way things are, they might as well be spurting out the end of your dick. Sometimes all the rooms seem the same, the same room devastated by time. If you look at the ceiling you'll imagine you can see a star or a comet or a cuckoo clock sailing through the space that separates the prince's lips from those of the princess. Sometimes it all goes back to the way it used to be. The castle is dark, enormous, cold, and you are alone. But you know there is another person hidden somewhere, you feel the tears, you feel the nakedness. Peace and warmth are waiting for you in that person's arms, so you keep going, drawn on by hope, stepping around boxes full of memories that no one will ever look at again, suitcases full of old clothes that someone forgot or didn't want to throw away, and from time to time you call her, your princess – where is she? – your body stiff with cold, your teeth chattering, right in the middle of the tunnel, smiling in the darkness, free of fear for the first time perhaps, and with no intention of inspiring fear, spirited, exultant, full of life, feeling your way through the dark, opening doors, following passages that bring you closer to the tears, in the dark, guided only by your body's need for another body, falling down and getting up again, and finally you arrive at the central chamber, and finally you see me and cry out. I remain silent and cannot tell the nature of your cry. All I know is that we have finally come together, that you are the zealous prince and I am the princess without pity.'

The Return

I have good news and bad news. The good news is that there is life (of a kind) after this life. The bad news is that Jean-Claude Villeneuve is a necrophiliac.

Death caught up with me in a Paris disco at four in the morning. My doctor had warned me, but some things are stronger than reason. I was convinced, mistakenly (and even now it's something I regret), that drinking and dancing were not the most hazardous of my passions. Another reason I kept going out every night to the fashionable places in Paris was my routine as a middle manager at Fracsa; I was after what I couldn't find at work or in what people call the inner life: the buzz that you get from a certain excess.

But I'd rather not talk about that, or only as much as I have to. When my death occurred, I was recently divorced and thirty-four years old. I hardly realised what was going on. A sudden sharp pain in the chest, her face, the face of Cécile Lamballe, the woman of my dreams, imperturbable as ever, the dance floor spinning in a brutal whirl, sucking in the dancers and the shadows, and then a brief moment of darkness.

What happened next was like what you sometimes see in movies and I'd like to say a few words about that.

In life I wasn't especially intelligent. I'm still not (though

I've learned a lot). When I say intelligent, what I really mean is thoughtful. But I have a certain energy and a certain taste. What I mean is, I'm not a philistine. It couldn't be said, objectively, that I'd ever behaved like a philistine. It's true that I graduated in business studies, but that didn't stop me from reading a good book or seeing a play every now and then, or being a keener moviegoer than most. Some of the movies I was pressured to see by my ex-wife. But the others I saw for love of the seventh art.

Like just about everyone else, I went to see *Ghost*, I don't know if you remember it, a box office hit, with Demi Moore and Whoopi Goldberg, the one where Patrick Swayze gets killed and his body is left lying on a Manhattan street, or in an alley, maybe, on a dirty pavement anyway, while in a special-effects extravaganza (they were special for the time, anyway) his soul comes out of his body and stares at it in astonishment. Well, apart from the special effects, I thought it was idiotic. A typical Hollywood cop-out, inane and unbelievable.

But when my turn came, that was exactly what happened. I was stunned. First, because I had died, which always comes as a surprise, except, I guess, in some cases of suicide, and then because I was unwillingly acting out one of the worst scenes of *Ghost*. One of the many things experience has taught me is that there is sometimes more to American naiveté than meets the eye; it can hide something that we Europeans can't or don't want to understand. But once I was dead, I didn't care about that. Once I was dead, I felt like bursting out laughing.

You get used to anything in the end, but in the early hours of that morning I felt dizzy or drunk, not because I was under the influence of alcohol on the night of my death – I wasn't; on the contrary, it had been a night of pineapple juice and non-alcoholic beer – but because of the shock of being dead, the fear of being dead and not knowing what was coming next. When you die the real world *shifts* slightly and that adds to the dizziness. It's as if you'd suddenly put on a pair of glasses that don't match your prescription; they're not all that different, but not quite right. And the worst thing is you know that the glasses you've put on belong to you and nobody else. And the real world shifts slightly to the right, down a little, the distance separating you from a given object changes almost imperceptibly, but you perceive that change as an abyss, and the abyss adds to your dizziness, but in the end it doesn't matter.

It makes you want to cry or pray. The first minutes of ghosthood are minutes of imminent knockout. You're like a punch-drunk boxer staggering around the ring in the drawn-out moment of the ring's evaporation. But then you calm down and what generally happens is that you follow the people who were there when you died – your girlfriend, your friends – or you follow your own body.

I was with Cécile Lamballe, the woman of my dreams, I was with her and saw her just before I died, but when my soul came out of my body I couldn't see her anywhere. It was quite a surprise and a great disappointment, especially when I think about it now, though back then I didn't have time to be sad. There I was, looking at my body lying in a grotesque heap on the floor, as if, seized by the dance and the heart attack, I'd completely fallen apart, or as if I hadn't died of a heart attack at all but dropped from the top of a skyscraper, and while I looked on and walked around and fell over (because I was completely dizzy), a volunteer (there's always someone) gave me (or my body) mouth-to-mouth, while another one thumped my chest, then someone thought of switching off the music and a murmur of disapproval swept through the disco, which was pretty full in spite of the late hour, and the deep voice of a waiter or a security guard told them all not to touch me, to wait for the police and the magistrate, and although I was groggy I would have liked to say, Keep going, keep trying to revive me, but they were tired, and as soon as the police were mentioned they all stepped back, and my body lay there on its own at the edge of the dance floor, eyes closed, until a charitable soul put a blanket over me to cover what was now definitively dead.

Then the police turned up along with some guys who confirmed what everyone already knew, and later the magistrate arrived and only then did I realise that Cécile Lamballe had vanished from the disco, so when they picked up my body and put it in an ambulance, I followed the medics and slipped into the back of the vehicle, and off I went with them into the sad and weary Paris dawn.

What a paltry thing it seemed, my body or my ex-body (I'm not sure how to put it), confronted with the labyrinthine bureaucracy of death. First they took me to the basement of a hospital, although I couldn't swear it was a hospital, where a young woman with glasses ordered them to undress me, and when they left her on her own, she spent a few moments examining and touching me. Then they covered me with a sheet, and moved me to another room to take a complete set of fingerprints. Then they brought me back to the first room, which was empty now, and I stayed there for what seemed like a long time, though I couldn't say how many hours. Maybe it was only minutes, but I was getting more and more bored.

After a while, a black orderly came to get me and take me to another underground room, where he handed me over to a pair of young guys also dressed in white, who made me feel uneasy right from the start, I don't know why. Maybe it was their would-be sophisticated way of talking, which identified them as a pair of tenth-rate artists, maybe it was their earrings, the sort all the hipsters were wearing that season in the discos that I had frequented with an irresponsible persistence: hexagonal in shape and somehow evocative of runaways from a fantastic bestiary.

The new orderlies made some notes in a book, spoke with the black guy for a few minutes (I don't know what that was about) and then the black guy went and left us alone. So in the room there were the two young guys behind the desk, filling out forms and chatting away, there was my body on the trolley, covered from head to foot, and me standing beside it, with my left hand resting on the trolley's metal edge, trying to think with a modicum of clarity about what the days to come might hold, if there were any days to come, which was far from obvious to me right then.

Then one of the young guys approached the trolley and uncovered me, or uncovered my body, and scrutinised it for a few seconds with a thoughtful expression that didn't bode well. After a while he covered it up again, and the two of them wheeled the trolley into the next room, a sort of freezing honeycomb, which I soon discovered was a storehouse for corpses. I would never have imagined that so many people could die in the course of an ordinary night in Paris. They slid my body into a refrigerated niche and left. I didn't follow them.

I spent that whole day there in the morgue. Every so often I went to the door, which had a little glass window, and checked the time on the wall clock in the next room. The feeling of dizziness gradually abated, although at one point I got to thinking about heaven and hell, reward and punishment, and I had a panic attack, but that bout of irrational fear was soon over. And, in fact, I was starting to feel better.

Throughout the day new bodies kept arriving, but never accompanied by ghosts, and at about four in the afternoon, a near-sighted young man performed an autopsy on me and established the causes of my accidental death. I have to admit I didn't have the stomach to watch them open me up. But I went to the autopsy room and listened as the coroner and his assistant, quite a pretty girl, performed their task efficiently and quickly – if only all public servants worked like that – while I waited with my back turned, looking at the ivory-coloured tiles on the wall. Then they washed me and sewed me up and an orderly took me back to the morgue again.

I stayed there until eleven at night, sitting on the floor in front of my refrigerated niche, and although at one point I thought I was going to doze off, I was beyond the need for sleep, so what I did was just go on thinking about my past life and the enigmatic future (to give it a name of some kind) that lay before me. After ten o'clock, the comings and goings, which during the day had been like a constant but barely perceptible dripping, stopped or diminished considerably. At five past eleven the young guys with the hexagonal earrings reappeared. I was startled when they opened the door. But I was beginning to get used to my ghostly state and, having recognised them, I remained seated on the floor, thinking of the distance separating me from Cécile Lamballe, which was infinitely greater than the distance between us when I was still alive. Realisations always come too late. In life I was afraid of being a toy (or less than a toy) for Cécile, and now that I was dead, that fate, once the cause of my insomnia and pervasive insecurity, seemed sweet, and not without a certain grace and substance: the solidity of the real.

But I was talking about the hipster orderlies. I saw them come into the morgue and although I noticed something cautious in their bearing, which sat oddly with their oily, feline manner, like wannabe artists out clubbing, at first I paid no attention to their movements and their whispering until one of them opened the niche where my body was lying.

Then I got up and started watching them. Moving like seasoned professionals, they placed my body on a trolley. Then they rolled the trolley out of the morgue and along a long corridor, sloping gently upwards, which eventually led into the building's parking garage. For a moment I thought they were stealing my body. In my delirium I imagined Cécile Lamballe, the milk-white face of Cécile Lamballe; I imagined her emerging from the darkness of the parking lot to give the pseudo-artists the sum they had demanded for the rescue of my body. But there was no one in the garage – clearly, I was still a long way from recovering my powers of reasoning or even my composure.

To tell the truth I'd been really hoping for a quiet night.

For a few moments, as I followed the orderlies between the unwelcoming rows of cars with a certain trepidation and disquiet, I experienced the dizziness I had felt in my first few minutes as a ghost. They put my body in the trunk of a grey Renault, covered all over with little dents, and we emerged from the belly of that building, which I was already beginning to think of as home, into the utter freedom of the Paris night.

I can't remember now which avenues and streets we took. The orderlies were high, as I was able to ascertain from closer observation, and they were talking about people well beyond their social reach. My first impression was soon confirmed: they were pathetic losers, but there was something in their attitude, something, I thought at first, like hope, and then it seemed like innocence, which made me feel close to them somehow. Deep down, we were similar, not then and not in the moments leading up to my death, but they were similar to how I imagined myself at twenty-two or twenty-five, when I was still a student and still believed that one day the world was going to fall at my feet.

The Renault pulled up in front of a mansion in one of the most exclusive neighbourhoods of Paris. That's how it seemed to me, anyway. One of the pseudo-artists got out of the car and rang a bell. After a while, a voice from the darkness told him to move, no, *suggested* that he move a little to the right and lift his chin. The orderly did as he was told and lifted his head. The other one looked out the window of the car and waved in the direction of a television camera that was observing us from the top of the gate. The voice made a throat-clearing sound (at that point I *knew* that I would soon meet a man of the utmost reserve) and said that we could enter.

Straightaway the gate opened with a faint squeaking sound

The Return

and the car drove in along a paved drive that snaked through a garden full of trees and shrubs, with a slightly overgrown look that owed more to whim than to neglect. We stopped beside one of the wings of the house. While the orderlies were removing my body from the trunk, I looked at the building in dismay and awe. Never in all my life had I been inside a house like that. It looked old. It must have been worth a fortune. I couldn't say any more without stretching my knowledge of architecture.

We went in through one of the service entrances. We crossed the kitchen, which was spotless and cold like the kitchen in a restaurant that has been closed for many years, and then we followed a dim corridor at the end of which we took an elevator down to the basement. When the doors of the elevator opened, there was Jean-Claude Villeneuve. I recognised him immediately. The long white hair, the thick glasses, the grey gaze that seemed to belong to a helpless child, while the firm narrow lips denoted, on the contrary, a man who knew very well what he wanted. He was wearing jeans and a white, short-sleeved shirt. I was shocked, because in the photos of Villeneuve that I had seen, his clothes had always been elegant. Discreet, yes, but elegant. The Villeneuve before me now, by contrast, looked like an old rock star suffering from insomnia. His gait, however, was unmistakable; he moved with the same unsteadiness that I had seen so often on television, when he stepped up onto the catwalk at the end of his autumn-winter or spring-summer shows, almost as if it was a chore, hauled out by his favourite models to receive the public's unanimous applause.

The orderlies put my body on a dark green sofa and took a few steps back, waiting for Villeneuve's verdict. He approached my body, uncovered my face, and then without saying a word went over to a little desk made (I assume) of fine wood, from which he extracted an envelope. The orderlies took the envelope, which almost certainly contained a considerable sum of cash, though neither of them bothered to count it, and then one of them said that they would come back at seven the next morning to pick me up, and they left. Villeneuve ignored his parting words. The orderlies went out the way we'd come in; I heard the sound of the elevator and then silence. Paying no attention to my body, Villeneuve switched on a television monitor. I looked over his shoulder. The pseudo-artists were at the gate, waiting for Villeneuve to let them out. Then the car drove off into the streets of that highly exclusive neighbourhood and the metal gate shut with a brief squeaking noise.

From that moment on, everything in my new supernatural life began to change, in accelerating phases that were perfectly distinct from each other, in spite of their rapid succession. Villeneuve went over to what looked like a standard hotel minibar and took out an apple juice. He removed the cap, began to drink straight from the bottle and switched off the security monitor. As he drank, he put on some music. Music I had never heard, or maybe I had, but when I listened carefully it didn't seem familiar: electric guitars, a piano, a saxophone, a sorrowful and melancholic piece, but strong as well, as if the composer's spirit was determined not to yield. I went over to the stereo hoping to see the name on the cover of the CD but I couldn't see anything. Only Villeneuve's face, which looked strange in the semi-darkness, as if being on his own again and drinking the apple juice had given him a hot flush. I noticed a drop of sweat in the middle of his cheek. A tiny drop rolling slowly down towards his chin. I also thought I could see him trembling slightly.

Then Villeneuve put the glass down beside the CD player and approached my body. For a while he looked at me as if he didn't know what to do, though he did, or as if he was attempting to guess what hopes and desires had once agitated the contents of that plastic body bag, which were now at his disposal. He stayed like that for some time. I didn't know what his intentions were – I've always been an innocent. If I'd known, I would have been nervous. But I didn't, so I sat down in one of the comfortable leather armchairs in the room and waited.

With extreme care, Villeneuve unwrapped the parcel containing my body, rucking the bag up under my legs, and then (after two or three endless minutes) he removed it entirely and left my corpse naked on the sofa, which was upholstered with green leather. He stood up straightaway – he'd been kneeling – took off his shirt and paused, but keeping his eyes on me, and that was when I stood up too, came a little closer and saw my naked body, slightly fatter than I would have liked, but not too bad – eyes closed, an absent expression on my face – and I saw Villeneuve's torso, a sight very few people have seen, since the great designer is renowned for his discretion among many other qualities (the press, for example, has never published photos of him at the beach), and I tried to read his expression and guess what would happen next, but all I could see in his face was diffidence; he looked more diffident than in the photos, *infinitely* more diffident in fact than he looked in the photos in the fashion and gossip magazines.

Villeneuve removed his trousers and socks and lay down beside my body. Well, at that point I *did* realise what was going on, and I was dumbstruck. It's easy enough to imagine what came next, but it wasn't what you'd call bacchanalian. Villeneuve hugged me, caressed me, kissed me chastely on the lips. He massaged my penis and testicles with something of the delicacy once lavished on me by Cécile Lamballe, the woman of my dreams, and after a quarter of an hour of cuddling in the semi-darkness I noticed that he had an erection. My god, I thought, now he's going to sodomise me. But that's not what happened. To my surprise, the designer rubbed himself against one of my thighs till he came. I would have liked to shut my eyes at that point but I couldn't. My reactions were contradictory; I felt disgusted by what I was seeing, grateful for not having been sodomised, surprised to discover Villeneuve's secret, angry at the orderlies for having rented out my body, and even flattered to have served, unwillingly, as an object of desire for one of the most famous men in France.

After coming, Villeneuve closed his eyes and sighed. In that sigh I thought I could detect a hint of disgust. He sat up quickly and stayed there on the sofa with his back to my body for a few seconds, while he wiped his dripping member with his hand. You should be ashamed, I said.

It was the first time I'd spoken since my death. Villeneuve raised his head, quite unsurprised, or at any rate much less surprised than I would have been in his situation, while reaching down with one hand to feel for his glasses on the carpet.

I knew at once that he had heard me. It seemed like a miracle. Suddenly I felt so happy that I forgave him his act of depravity. And yet, like an idiot, I repeated: You should be ashamed. Who's there? said Villeneuve. It's me, I said, the ghost of the body you just raped. Villeneuve went pale, and then, almost simultaneously, a blush rose in his cheeks. I was worried that he would have a heart attack or die of fright, although to tell the truth he didn't look all that frightened.

It's not a problem, I said in a conciliatory tone, You're forgiven.

Villeneuve switched on the light and looked in all the corners of the room. I thought he'd gone crazy, because there was clearly no one else there; only a pygmy could have hidden in that room, not even a pygmy, a gnome. But then I realised that, far from being crazy, the designer was displaying nerves of steel: he wasn't looking for a person but a speaker. As I calmed down, I felt a surge of sympathy for him. There was something admirable about his methodical way of searching the room. Me, I'd have been out of there like a shot.

I'm no speaker, I said. Nor am I a video camera. Please, try to calm down; take a seat and we can talk. And most of all, don't be afraid of me. I'm not going to do anything to you. That's what I said; then I kept quiet and watched Villeneuve, who barely hesitated before continuing his search. I let him go ahead. While he messed up the room, I remained seated in one of the comfortable armchairs. Then I had an idea. I suggested that we shut ourselves in a small room (as small as a coffin were my exact words), where no speakers or cameras could possibly have been planted, and I could go on talking to him there and convince him to accept my nature, my new nature, that is. But while he was considering my proposal, it occurred to me that I hadn't expressed myself very well, since my ghostly state could not be called, in any sense, a 'nature'. My nature, however you looked at it, was still that of a living being. And yet it was clear that I was not alive. The thought crossed my mind that it might all be a dream. Summoning some ghostly courage, I told myself that if it was a dream, the best (and the only) thing I could do was to go on dreaming. From experience I know that trying to wrench yourself out of a nightmare is futile and simply adds pain to pain or terror to terror.

So I repeated my proposal, and this time Villeneuve stopped searching and froze (I examined his face, which I'd seen so often in the glossy magazines, and saw the same expression, a solitary, elegant expression, although now there were a few telltale drops of sweat rolling down his forehead and his cheeks). He left the room. I followed him. Halfway down a long corridor, he stopped and said: Are you still with me? His voice was strangely appealing, rich in tones that seemed to be converging on a genuine warmth, though perhaps it was just an illusion.

I'm here, I said.

Villeneuve moved his head in a way I couldn't interpret and continued to wander through his house, stopping in each room and on each landing to ask if I was still with him, a question to which I replied without fail, trying to make my voice sound relaxed, or at least trying to give it a singular tone (in life it was always an ordinary, run-of-the-mill sort of voice), no doubt influenced by the reedy (sometimes almost whistle-like) yet extremely distinguished voice of the designer. To each reply I also added details about the place where we happened to be, with the aim of achieving greater credibility; for example, if there was a lamp with a tobacco-coloured shade and a wrought iron stand, I said so. I'm still here, next to you, and now we're in a room where the only source of light is a lamp with a tobacco-coloured shade and a wrought iron stand. And Villeneuve said yes or corrected me – That's cast iron – but his eyes were fixed on the ground as he spoke, as if he was afraid that I might suddenly materialise, or didn't want to embarrass me, and I'd say: Sorry, I didn't notice, or: That's what I meant. And Villeneuve moved his head ambivalently, as if accepting my excuses or just getting a clearer idea of the ghost he had to deal with.

And so we went all around the house, and as we moved from place to place, Villeneuve grew or seemed to grow calmer, while I became more nervous, because I've never been much good at describing things, especially if they're not objects in everyday use, or if they happen to be paintings no doubt worth a fortune by contemporary artists I know absolutely nothing about, or sculptures that Villeneuve had collected in the course of his travels (incognito) all around the world.

And so on, until we came to a little room, covered inside with a layer of cement, in which there was nothing, not one piece of furniture, not a single light, and we shut ourselves in that room, in the dark. An embarrassing situation, on the face of it, but for me it was like a second or a third birth; that is, it was like hope beginning and with it the desperate awareness of hope. Villeneuve said: Describe the place where we are now. And I said that it was like death, not like real death but death as we imagine it when we're alive. And Villeneuve said: Describe it. Everything is dark, I said. It's like a nuclear bomb shelter. And I added that in a place like that the soul contracts, and I would have gone on spelling out what I felt, the void that had come to inhabit my soul long before I died and of which I'd been unaware until then, but Villeneuve cut me off saying, That's enough, he believed me, and suddenly he opened the door.

I followed him to the main living room, where he poured himself a whisky and proceeded, in a few well-measured sentences, to ask me to forgive him for what he had done with my body. You're forgiven, I said. I'm open-minded. To be honest, I'm not sure I know what being open-minded means, but I felt it was my duty to wipe the slate clean and clear our future relationship of any guilt or resentment.

You must be wondering why I do what I do, said Villeneuve.

I assured him that I had no intention of asking for an explanation. Nevertheless, Villeneuve insisted on giving me one. With anyone else, it would have become a very unpleasant evening, but I was listening to Jean-Claude Villeneuve, the greatest designer in France, which is to say the world, and time flew as I was given a brief account of his childhood and teenage years, his youth, his reservations about sex, his experiences with a number of men, and with a number of women, his solitary habits, his morbid dread of harming anyone which may have been a screen to hide his dread of being harmed, his artistic tastes, which I admired (and envied) unreservedly, his chronic insecurity, his conflicts with a number of famous designers, his first jobs for a fashion house, his voyages of initiation, which he declined to recount in detail, his friendships with three of Europe's finest screen actresses, his association with the pair of pseudo-artists from the morgue, who from time to time provided him with corpses, with which he spent only one night, his fragility, which he compared to an endless demolition in slow motion, and so on, until the first light of dawn began to filter through the curtains of the living room and Villeneuve brought his long exposé to a close.

We remained silent for a long time. I knew that both of us were, if not overwhelmed with joy, at least reasonably happy.

Before long the orderlies arrived. Villeneuve looked at the floor and asked me what he should do. After all, the body they had come for was mine. I thanked him for his thoughtfulness but also assured him that I was now beyond caring about such things. Do what you normally do, I said. Will you go? he asked. I had already made up my mind, and yet I pretended to think for a few seconds before saying no, I wasn't going to leave. If he didn't mind, of course. Villeneuve seemed relieved: I don't mind, on the contrary, he said. Then a bell rang, and Villeneuve switched on the monitors and opened the gates for the rent-a-corpse guys, who came in without saying a word.

Exhausted by the night's events, Villeneuve didn't get up from the sofa. The pseudo-artists greeted him, and it seemed to me that one of them was in the mood for a chat, but the other one gave him a nudge and they went down to get my body without further ado. Villeneuve had his eyes closed and seemed to be asleep. I followed the orderlies down to the basement. My body was lying there half covered by the body bag from the morgue. I watched them put it back in the bag and carry it up and place it in the trunk of the car. I imagined it waiting there, in the cold morgue, until a relative or my ex-wife came to claim it. But I mustn't give in to sentimentality, I thought, and when the orderlies' car left the garden and vanished down that elegant, tree-lined street, I didn't feel the slightest twinge of nostalgia or sadness or melancholy.

When I returned to the living room, Villeneuve was still on the sofa, with his arms crossed, shivering with cold, and he was talking to himself (though I soon realised that he thought he was talking to me). I sat on a chair in front of him, a chair of carved wood with a satin backrest, facing the window and the garden and the beautiful morning light, and I let him go on talking as long as he liked.

Buba

for Juan Villoro

The city of sanity. The city of common sense. That's what the people of Barcelona used to call their city. I liked it. It was a beautiful city and I think I felt at home there from the second day on (if I said from the very first day I'd be exaggerating) but the club wasn't doing so well, and people started going kind of sour, it always happens, I'm speaking from experience, at first the fans want your autograph, they hang around outside the hotel, they're so friendly it's exhausting, but then you have a run of bad luck, which leads to another, and soon enough they start making faces, maybe you're just lazy, they think, or partying too much, or whoring, you know what I mean, people start to take an interest in what you're getting paid, they speculate, they calculate, and there's always a wise guy who'll come out and accuse you of being a thief or something a thousand times worse. This stuff happens everywhere, I'd already been through it once, but that was back home, in my country, and this time I was a foreigner, and the press and the fans always expect something extra special from foreigners. I mean, why else would they hire us?

Me, for example, I'm a left winger, everyone knows that.

When I played in Latin America (in Chile, then in Argentina) I scored an average of ten goals per season. But my debut here was disastrous; I got injured in the third game, had to have an operation on my ligaments, and my recovery, which in theory should have been quick, was laborious and drawn-out, but I won't go into that. Suddenly I was back to feeling as lonely as a lighthouse. That's the way it was. I spent a fortune on calls to Santiago, but that only made Mom and Dad worry; they didn't understand at all. So one day I decided to go whoring. Why should I deny it? That's the way it was. Actually, I was just following some advice that Cerrone, the Argentinian goalkeeper, had given me one day. He said to me, Kid, if you can't think of anything else to do, and your problems are eating away at you, go see a whore. He was a great guy, Cerrone. I would have been nineteen at the most and I had just joined Gimnasia y Esgrima in La Plata. Cerrone was already around 35 or 40, his age was a mystery, and he was the only one of the older players who wasn't married. Some said Cerrone was queer. That made me wary of him for a start. I was a shy sort of kid and I thought that if I got to know a homosexual, he'd try and get me into bed straightaway. Anyway, maybe he was, maybe he wasn't, all I know for sure is that one afternoon, when I was lower than ever, he took me aside, it was the first time we'd talked, really, and said he was going to take me to meet some girls from Buenos Aires. I'll never forget that night. The apartment was downtown, and while Cerrone stayed in the living room drinking and watching a late show on TV, I slept with an Argentinian woman for the first time, and my depression began to lift. Going home the next morning, I knew that things would get better and that I still had plenty of glory days to look forward to in the

Argentinian League. I was bound to get depressed occasionally, I thought, but Cerrone had given me the remedy to make it bearable.

And I did the same thing at my first European club: I went whoring and it helped me to get over the injury, the recovery period and the loneliness. Did it become a habit? Maybe, maybe not; that's not something I can really judge objectively. The whores there are gorgeous, the high-class whores I mean, and most of them are pretty smart and educated too, so it really isn't difficult to develop a serious taste for them.

Anyhow, I started going out every night, even Sundays when there was a match on, and the injured players were expected to be there, in the stands, doing their bit as VIP supporters. But that doesn't help your injuries to heal, and I preferred to spend Sunday afternoons in some massage parlour with a glass of whisky and one or two lady friends on either side, discussing more serious matters. At first, of course, no one realised. I wasn't the only injured player, there must have been six or seven of us in the dry dock – bad luck seemed to be dogging the club. But of course, there's always some fucking journalist who sees you coming out of a nightclub at four in the morning, and the game's up. News travels fast in Barcelona, though it seems such a big and civilised city. Soccer news, I mean.

One morning the trainer called and said he'd found out about the life I was leading: it was inappropriate for a professional athlete and had to stop. Naturally I said, Yes, I'd just been having a bit of fun, and then I went on like before, because, come on, what else was I going to do while I was still unfit to play and the team slid down the ranking and opening the paper on a Monday morning to look at the league table was a downer week after week. Also, I was convinced that what had worked for me in Argentina was going to work for me in Spain, and the worst thing was, I was right: it did work. But then the bureaucrats got involved and told me: Listen, Acevedo, this has got to stop, you're becoming a bad example for the young and a disastrous investment for the club, we only employ hard workers here, so from now on, no more nightlife, or else. And then, before I knew it, I was liable for a fine if I broke the curfew; I could have paid it, of course, but if I was going to be throwing money away, I'd rather have sent it to someone in Chile, like my uncle Julio, so he could fix up his house.

These things happen and you have to deal with it. So I dealt with it and resolved to go out less often, once every two weeks, say, but then Buba turned up and the management decided that the best thing for me would be to move out of the hotel and share the apartment they'd rented for him right next to our training ground; it was small but kind of cozy, with two bedrooms and a terrace that was tiny but had a good view. So that was what I had to do. I packed my bags and went to the apartment with one of the club's administrators, and since Buba wasn't there, I chose the bedroom I wanted and took out my stuff and put it in the closet, and then the administrator gave me my keys and left and I lay down to take a siesta.

It was about five, and earlier that afternoon I'd put away a *fideuà*, a Barcelona speciality, which I'd already tried (I love it, but it isn't easy to digest) and as soon as I flopped onto my new bed I felt so tired it was all I could do to pull off my shoes before I fell asleep. Then I had the weirdest dream. I dreamed I was in Santiago again, in my neighborhood, La Cisterna, and I was with my father, crossing the square where there's a statue of Che Guevara, the first statue of Che in the Americas, outside Cuba, and that was what my father was telling me in the dream, the story of the statue and the various attempts to destroy it before the soldiers came and blew it away, and as we walked I was looking all around and it was like we were deep in the jungle, and my father was saying the statue should be around here somewhere, but you couldn't see anything, the grass was high and only a few feeble rays of sunlight were filtering down through the trees, just enough to see by, to show that it was daytime, and we were following a path of earth and stones, but the vegetation on either side was dense, there were even lianas, and you couldn't see anything, only shadows, until suddenly we came to a sort of clearing, with forest all around, and then my father stopped, put one hand on my shoulder and pointed with the other hand to something rearing up in the middle of the clearing, a pedestal of light-coloured cement, and on top of the pedestal there was nothing, not a trace of the statue of Che, but my father and I already knew that, Che had been removed from there a long time ago, it didn't come as a surprise, what mattered was that we were there together, my old man and me, and we had found the exact place where the statue used to stand before, but while we looked around the clearing, standing still, as if absorbed in our discovery, I noticed that there was something at the bottom of the pedestal, on the other side, something dark, which was moving, and I broke away from my father (he had been holding me by the hand) and began to walk slowly towards it.

Then I saw what it was: on the other side of the pedestal there was a black man, stark naked, drawing on the ground, and I knew straightaway that the black man was Buba, my teammate, my housemate, although to tell you the truth, like the rest of the players, I'd only ever seen Buba in a couple of photos, and when you've only glanced at someone's picture in the paper you can't have a clear idea of how they look. But it was Buba, I had no doubts about that. And then I thought: Fucking hell! I must be dreaming, I'm not in Chile, I'm not in La Cisterna, my father hasn't brought me to any square, and this jerk in his birthday suit isn't Buba, the African midfielder who just signed with our club.

Just as I came to the end of that train of thought, the black guy looked up and smiled at me, dropped the stick he'd been using to draw in the yellow earth (and it really was genuine Chilean earth), leaped to his feet and held out his hand. You're Acevedo, he said, glad to meet you, kid, that's what he said. And I thought: Maybe we're on tour? But where? In Chile? Impossible. And then we shook hands and Buba squeezed my hand hard and held on to it, and while he was squeezing my hand I looked down and saw the drawings on the earth, just scribbles, what else could they have been, but it was like I could join them up, if you see what I mean, and the scribbles made sense, that is, they weren't just scribbles, they were something more. Then I tried to bend down and get a closer look, but I couldn't because Buba's hand was gripping mine and when I tried to free myself (not so much to see the drawings anymore, but to get away from him, to put some distance between us, because I was starting to feel something like fear), I couldn't; Buba's hand and his arm seemed to be the hand and arm of a statue, a freshly cast statue, and my hand was embedded in that material, which felt like mud and then like molten lava.

I think that was when I woke up. I heard noises in the kitchen and then steps going from the living room to the other bedroom, and my arm was numb (I'd fallen asleep in an awkward position, which happened quite often back then, while I was recovering from the injury), and I stayed in my bedroom waiting; the door was open, so he must have seen me; I waited and waited but he didn't come to the door. I heard his footsteps, I cleared my throat, coughed, stood up; then I heard someone opening the front door and shutting it again, very quietly. I spent the rest of the day alone, sitting in front of the TV, getting more and more nervous. I had a look in his room (I'm not a busybody but I couldn't help myself); he'd put his clothes in the closet drawers: track suits, some formal wear and some African robes that looked like fancy dress to me but actually they were beautiful. He'd laid out his toiletries in the bathroom: a straight-edge razor (I use disposable razors and hadn't seen a straight-edge for a while), lotion, English aftershave (or bought in England anyway), and a very large, earth-coloured sponge in the bathtub.

Buba returned to our new home at nine o'clock that night. My eyes were hurting from watching so much TV, and he told me he'd come back from a session with the city's sportswriters. We didn't really hit it off at the start and it took us a while to become friends, though sometimes, thinking back, I come to the melancholy conclusion that we were never what you would really call friends. Other times, though, right now for example, I think we were pretty good friends, and one thing's for sure, anyway: if Buba had a friend in that club, it was me.

It's not like our life together was difficult. A woman came in twice a week to clean the apartment and we tidied up after ourselves, washed our own dishes, made our beds, you know, the usual deal. Sometimes I went out at night with Herrera, a local kid who'd come up through the ranks and ended up securing a place on the national team, and sometimes Buba came with us, but not very often, because he didn't really like going out. When I stayed home I'd watch TV and Buba would shut himself in his room and put on music. African music. At first I didn't like Buba's cassettes at all. In fact, the first time I heard them, the day after he moved in, I got a fright. I was watching a documentary about the Amazon, waiting for a Van Damme movie to begin, and all of a sudden it was like someone was being killed in Buba's room. Put yourself in my place. It's not every day you face something like that; it would have rattled anyone. What did I do? Well, I stood up, I had my back to Buba's door, and naturally I braced myself, but then I realised it was a tape, the shouts were coming from the cassette player. Then the noises died away, all you could hear was something like a drum, and then someone groaning, or weeping, gradually getting louder. I could only take so much. I remember walking to the door, rapping on it with my knuckles: no response. At that point I thought it was Buba weeping and groaning, not the cassette. But then I heard Buba's voice asking what I wanted and I didn't know what to say. It was all quite embarrassing. I asked him to turn it down. I tried as hard as I possibly could to make my voice sound normal. Buba was quiet for a while. Then the music stopped (by then it was just a drum beat really, with maybe some kind of flute as well) and Buba said he was going to sleep. Good night, I said and returned to the armchair, where I sat for a while watching the documentary about Amazon Indians with the sound off.

Buba

Otherwise, everyday life, as they say, was easy enough. Buba had just arrived and he still hadn't played a game with the first team. The club had a surplus of players at the time but there's no point going into that. In addition to the Spaniards, including four players from the national team, there was Antoine García the French sweeper, Delève the Belgian forward, Neuhuys the Dutch centre-back, Jovanovic the Yugoslavian forward, plus the Argentinian Percutti and the Uruguayan Buzatti, who were midfielders. But things were going badly for us: after ten disastrous matches we were in the middle of the rankings and it looked like we were heading down. To tell the truth, I don't know why they signed Buba. I guess they did it to appease the fans, who were complaining more and more bitterly, but on the face of it, at least, they'd screwed up completely. Everyone was hoping they'd sign an emergency replacement for me, a winger, that is, not a midfielder, because we already had Percutti, but managers everywhere tend to be pretty stupid: they jumped at the first opportunity and that's how Buba ended up with us. Lots of people thought the plan was to get him to do a stint with the second team, which was way down in the second division B at the time, but Buba's agent said no way, the contract was perfectly clear: either Buba played with the first team or he didn't play at all. So there we were, the two of us, in our apartment near the training ground, him on the bench every Sunday, and me still recovering from the injury and sunk in that awful depression. And we were the two youngest players, like I told you already, and if I didn't I'm telling you now, although there was some speculation about that too for a while. I was twenty-two at the time, no doubt there. People said Buba was nineteen, though he looked more like he was twenty-nine, and naturally some smartass journalist claimed that our managers had been duped: in Buba's country birth certificates were issued à la carte, he said; Buba not only looked older but was older; in short, the deal had been a rip-off.

I didn't know what to think, really. In any case, living with Buba day by day wasn't hard at all. Sometimes he shut himself in his bedroom at night and put on his shouting and groaning music, but you get used to anything. Anyway I liked to watch TV with the sound up loud till the early hours of the morning, and as far as I know Buba never complained about that. At the start we had trouble communicating, because we didn't share a language, so we talked mainly with gestures. But then Buba learned some Spanish and some mornings at breakfast we even talked about movies, always a favourite topic of mine, though to tell the truth Buba wasn't very talkative, or very interested in movies, for that matter. In fact, now that I think of it, Buba was pretty quiet. It's not that he was shy or scared of putting his foot in it; Herrera, who could speak English, once told me it was just that he didn't have anything to say. Crazy Herrera. He was such a great guy. A good friend, too. We used to go out a lot, Herrera, Pepito Vila, who had come up from the juniors too, Buba and me. But Buba was always quiet, watching it all as if he was only half there, and although Herrera sometimes went out of his way to speak to him in English, and he spoke fluent English, Herrera, Buba would always go off on a tangent, as if he couldn't be bothered explaining stuff about his childhood and his country, and especially not about his family, to the point where Herrera was convinced that something bad must have happened to him when he was a kid, because he kept refusing to give away anything personal at all; it's like his village was razed, said Herrera, who was left-wing and still is, it's like he saw his parents and brothers and sisters killed right in front of him, and he's been trying to erase it from his mind all these years, which would have made sense if Herrera's assumptions had been correct, but in fact, and this is something I always knew or sensed, Herrera was wrong; the reason Buba didn't talk much was just that he wasn't very talkative, irrespective of whether his childhood and teenage years had been happy or traumatic: Buba's life was surrounded by mystery because that's how Buba was, simple as that.

But there was one thing we knew for sure: the team was in a bad way. Herrera and Buba looked like they'd be stuck on the bench till the end of the season, I was injured, and any provincial team could come and beat us on our home ground. Then, when it seemed like we'd hit rock bottom and nothing more could go wrong, Percutti got injured and the boss had no choice but to select Buba. I remember it like it was yesterday. We had to play on a Saturday, and at the Thursday training session, Percutti fucked up his knee in an accidental collision with the centre-back, Palau. So our trainer got Buba to take his place at Friday training and it was obvious to Herrera and me that he'd be selected for the Saturday match.

When we told him that afternoon, in the hotel where they were keeping us together (although we were playing at home against a theoretically weak opponent, the club had decided that every match was vital), Buba looked at us as if he was sizing us up for the first time, and then he came up with some excuse and went and shut himself in the bathroom. Herrera and I watched TV for a while and worked out when we'd go join the card game that Buzatti was organizing in his room. Naturally we weren't expecting Buba to come.

After a little while we heard this wild music coming from the bathroom. I'd already told Herrera about Buba's taste in music and the way he shut himself in his bedroom with that damned cassette player, but he'd never heard it for himself. We sat there listening to the groans and drums for a while, then Herrera, who knew a lot about music and the arts and stuff, said it was by Mango something or other, from Sierra Leone or Liberia, one of the stars of world music anyway, and we left it at that. Then the door opened and Buba came out of the bathroom, sat down beside us, quietly, as if he was interested in the TV show too, and I noticed a slightly odd smell, like the smell of sweat, but it wasn't sweat, a rancid smell, but not exactly rancid either. He smelled of moisture, of mushrooms or toadstools. He smelled strange. It made me nervous, I have to admit, and I know it made Herrera nervous too, both of us were nervous, we both wanted to get out of there, to run to Buzatti's room, where we were sure to find six or seven friends playing cards, stud poker or eleven, a civilised game. But the fact is that neither of us moved, as if Buba's odour and his presence beside us had robbed us of all initiative. It wasn't fear. It had nothing to do with fear. It was something much faster. As if the air surrounding us had condensed and we had turned to liquid. Well, that's what I felt, anyway. And then Buba started talking and told us he needed blood. Herrera's blood and mine.

I think Herrera laughed, not a lot, just a bit. Then one of us switched the TV off, I can't remember who, maybe Herrera, maybe me. And Buba said he could do it, as long as we gave him the drops of blood and kept our mouths shut. What can you do? asked Herrera. Make sure we win the match, I said. I don't know how I knew, but the fact is I had known from the very first moment. Yes, make sure we win the match, said Buba. And then Herrera and I laughed and maybe we looked at each other; Herrera was sitting in an armchair, I was sitting at the foot of my bed, and Buba was sitting at the head of his, waiting deferentially. I think Herrera asked some questions. I asked a question too. Buba replied with numbers. He raised his left hand and showed us his middle, ring and little fingers. He said we had nothing to lose. His thumb and index finger were crossed as if they were forming a lasso or a noose in which a tiny animal was choking. He predicted that Herrera would play. He talked about responsibility to the colours of the shirt and about opportunity. His Spanish was still shaky.

The next thing I remember is that Buba went back into the bathroom and when he came out he was carrying a glass and his straight-edge razor. We're not cutting ourselves with that, said Herrera. The razor is good, said Buba. Not with your razor, said Herrera. Why not? said Buba. Because we don't fucking feel like it, said Herrera. Am I right? He was looking at me. Yes, I said: I'll cut myself with my own razor. I remember that when I got up to go to the bathroom, my legs were shaking. I couldn't find my little razor, I'd probably left it at the apartment, so I grabbed the one provided by the hotel. When I came back in, Herrera was still gone and Buba seemed to be asleep, sitting at the head of his bed, though when I closed the door behind me, he raised his head and looked at me, without saying a word. We said nothing until someone knocked at the door. I went to open it. It was Herrera. The two of us sat down on my bed, Buba sat opposite on his and held the glass between the two beds. Then, with a rapid movement, he lifted one of the fingers on the hand that was holding the glass and made a clean cut in it. Now you, he said to Herrera, who performed the task with a little tiepin, the only sharp thing he'd been able to find. Then it was my turn. When we tried to go to the bathroom to wash our hands, Buba beat us to it. Let me in, Buba, I shouted through the door. All we got by way of reply was the music that Herrera had described a few minutes earlier, somewhat hastily (or that's what I was thinking at least), as world music.

I stayed up late that night. I spent a while in Buzatti's room, then I went to the hotel bar, but there weren't any players left there. I ordered a whisky and drank it at a table with a good, clear view of the city lights. After a while I sensed that someone was sitting down beside me. I started. It was the trainer, who couldn't sleep either. He asked me what I was doing awake at that hour of the night. I told him I was nervous. But you're not even playing tomorrow, Acevedo, he said. That makes it worse, I said. The trainer looked out at the city, nodding, and rubbed his hands. What are you drinking? he asked. The same as you, I said. Well, he said, it's good for the nerves. Then he started talking about his son and his family, who lived in England, but mostly about his son, and finally we both got up and put our empty glasses on the bar. When I got back to the room, Buba was sleeping quietly in his bed. Normally I wouldn't have switched on the light, but this time I did. Buba didn't even move. I went to the bathroom: all clean and tidy. I put on my pyjamas and got into bed and switched off the light. I listened to Buba's regular breathing for a few minutes. I can't remember how long it took me to fall asleep.

The next day we won three-nil. Herrera scored the first goal. That was his first for the season. Buba scored the other two. The journalists made some cautious remarks about a substantial change in our game and highlighted Buba's excellent performance. I watched the match. I know what really happened. Actually, Buba didn't play well. Herrera did, and Delève and Buzatti. The backbone of the team. Actually, for quite a lot of the match, it was like Buba was somewhere else. But he scored two goals and that was enough.

Maybe I should say something about his goals. The first (which was the second goal of the match) came after a corner kick from Palau. In the confusion, Buba swung his leg, connected, and scored. The second one was strange: the other team had already accepted defeat, we were in the 85th minute, all the players were tired, ours especially I think, they were clearly playing it safe, and then someone passed the ball to Buba, expecting him to pass it back, I guess, or just slow the game down, but Buba went running down the sideline, fast, moving much faster than he had all match, and when he got to about four metres from the penalty area, and everyone was expecting him to send it back to the centre, he took a shot that surprised the two defenders in front of him and the goalkeeper, a shot with a spin on it like I'd never seen before, the sort of diabolical shot the Brazilians seem to have a monopoly on, which snuck into the top right-hand corner of the goal mouth and sent the crowd wild.

That night, after celebrating the victory, I talked with him. I asked him about the magic, the spell, the blood in the glass. Buba looked at me and went all serious. Bring your ear closer, he said. We were in a disco and we could barely hear one another. He whispered some words that I couldn't understand at first. By that stage I was probably drunk. Then he took his mouth away from my ear and smiled at me. What he had said was: You soon will score better goals. OK, great, I said.

From then on everything went great. We won the next match four-two, even though we were playing away. Herrera scored a goal with a header, Delève put away a penalty kick, and Buba scored the other two, which were completely weird, or that's how they seemed to me, with my inside knowledge; before the trip (I didn't go), I'd taken part in the ceremony of the cut fingers and the glass and the blood.

Three weeks later they summoned me and I made my reappearance in the second half, in the 75th minute. We were playing the top-ranked team on their home ground and we won one-nil. I scored the goal in the 88th minute. I took the pass from Buba or that's what everyone thought, but I have my doubts. All I know is that Buba took off down the right-hand side of the field, and I started running down the left-hand side. There were four defenders, one chasing Buba, two in the middle, and one about three yards away from me. I still can't explain what happened next. The defenders in the middle seemed to freeze on the spot. I kept running with the right wingback on my heels. Buba came up to the penalty area with the left wingback close behind him too. Then he dummied and centred. I went into the penalty area with no hope of receiving the pass, but what with the centre-backs in a daze or dizzy all of a sudden and the weird swing of the ball, the fact is I found myself miraculously in possession inside the area, with their goalkeeper coming forward and the right wingback coming up behind my left shoulder, not knowing whether to foul me or not, so I just took a shot and scored and we won.

I had a safe place on the team for the following Sunday.

Buba

And from then on I began to score more goals than I'd ever scored in my life. Herrera was on a roll as well. Everyone loved Buba. And they loved Herrera and me too. From one day to the next we became the kings of the city. It was all working out for us. The club began an unstoppable climb. We were winning matches and hearts.

And our blood ritual was repeated without fail before every match. In fact, after the first time, Herrera and I bought ourselves straight-edge razors like Buba's; every time we played away, the first thing we put in our bags was the straight-edge, and when we played at home, we got together the night before at our apartment (they'd stopped keeping us together in a hotel) and performed the ceremony: Buba collected his blood and ours in a glass and then shut himself in the bathroom, and while we heard the music coming out of there, Herrera would talk about books he'd read or plays he'd seen and I just listened and agreed with everything he said, until Buba reappeared and we looked at him as if to ask if everything was all right, and Buba would smile at us and go to the kitchen to fetch a sponge and a bucket before returning to the bathroom, where he'd spend at least fifteen minutes cleaning and tidying up, and when we went into the bathroom, everything was exactly the same as before. Sometimes, when I went to a disco with Herrera and Buba stayed home (because he didn't like discos much) Herrera and I would get talking and he'd ask me what I thought Buba did with our blood in the bathroom, because you couldn't tell — when Buba was finished there wasn't a trace of blood anywhere, the glass we used was sparkling, the floor was spotless, it was like the cleaning lady had just left — and I said to Herrera I didn't know, I had no idea what Buba did when he shut himself in there, and Herrera looked at me and said: If I was living with him I'd be scared, and I looked at Herrera thinking: Are you serious? but Herrera said, I'm just kidding, Buba's our friend; it's thanks to him I'm on the team and the club is going to win the championship; it's thanks to him we're tasting sweet success, and that was the truth.

Besides, I was never scared of Buba. Sometimes, when we were watching TV in our apartment before going to bed, I'd glance at him out of the corner of my eye and think how strange it all was. But I didn't think about it for long. Soccer is strange.

In the end, after starting the year so disastrously, we won the League Championship and paraded through the centre of Barcelona in the midst of a jubilant crowd and spoke from the town hall balcony to another jubilant crowd, which chanted our names, and we dedicated our victory to the Virgin of Montserrat, in the monastery of Montserrat, a virgin as black as Buba, strange as it may seem, and we gave interviews until we were hoarse. I spent my vacation in Chile. Buba went to Africa. Herrera and his girlfriend took off to the Caribbean.

We met up again at preseason training, in a sports center in the east of Holland, near an ugly, grey city that made me feel extremely apprehensive.

Everyone was there, except for Buba. He'd had some kind of problem back in his country. Herrera seemed exhausted, though he was sporting a celebrity tan. He told me he'd considered getting married. I told him about my vacation in Chile, but as you know, when it's summer in Europe, it's winter in Chile, so my vacation hadn't been especially exciting. The family was well. That was about it. We were worried about Buba and the holdup. We didn't want to admit it, but we were worried. Herrera and I were soon convinced that without him we were lost. Our trainer, on the other hand, tried to play down Buba's lack of punctuality.

One morning Buba arrived on a flight that had come via Rome and Frankfurt and took his place on the team again. The preseason matches, however, were disastrous. We were beaten by a team from the Dutch third division. We tied with a team of amateurs from the city where we were staying. Neither Herrera nor I dared to ask Buba to do the blood ritual, although we had our razors ready. In fact, and it took me a while to realise this, it was like we were afraid to ask Buba for a bit of his magic. Of course we went on being friends, and one night the three of us went out to a Dutch disco, but instead of talking about blood, we talked about the rumours that always circulate before the season starts, the players who were changing teams, the new signings, the Champions League, in which we'd be playing that year, the contracts that were expiring or had to be renegotiated. We also talked about movies and the vacation that had just come to an end, and Herrera talked about books, but he was on his own there, mainly because he was the only one of us who read.

Then we went back to Barcelona, and Buba and I went back to our routine, just the two of us in that apartment opposite the training ground, and the Champions League began, and the night before the first match, Herrera turned up at our place and bit the bullet. He asked Buba what was happening. Isn't there going to be any magic this year? And Buba smiled and said it wasn't magic. And Herrera said, What the fuck is it then? And Buba shrugged his shoulders and said it was something only he understood. And then he made a face like he was saying, It's no big deal. And Herrera said he wanted to keep on going, he believed in Buba, whatever it was he'd been doing. And Buba said he was tired, and when he said that I looked at his face: he didn't look nineteen or twenty at all, he looked at least ten years older, like a player who had worn his body out. And, to my surprise, Herrera accepted what Buba had said, calmly, just like that. He said, OK, let's drop it. What about dinner? My treat. That's the way he was, Herrera. A great guy.

So we went out to dinner at one of the best restaurants in the city, and a press photographer who was there took a picture of us, the one I've got hanging in the dining room: Herrera, Buba and me, dressed up and smiling, with a lavish meal (if you'll pardon the cliché) spread out in front of us (it really was lavish); we look like we're ready to take on the world, although deep down we weren't at all sure (especially Herrera and me) that we could take on anyone at all. And nothing was said about magic or blood while we were there: we talked about movies and travel (for pleasure not work), and that was about all. When we left the restaurant, after having signed autographs for the waiters and the cook and the kitchen hands, we went walking through the empty streets of the city, such a beautiful city, the city of sanity and common sense, as some devotees call it, but also the city of splendour, where you could feel at ease with yourself, and for me, looking back, it's the city of my youth – anyway, as I was saying, we went walking through the streets of Barcelona, because, as every athlete knows, the best thing to do after a heavy meal is stretch your legs, and when we'd been walking around for a while, looking at the floodlit buildings (Herrera named the great architects who'd designed them like they were people he'd met), Buba said with a rather sad smile that, if we wanted to, we could repeat last year's experiment.

That was the word he used. Experiment. Herrera and I kept quiet. Then we went back to my car and drove to the apartment without saying a single word. I cut myself with my razor. Herrera used a knife from the kitchen. When Buba came out of the bathroom, he looked at us, and, for the first time he didn't shut the door behind him when he went to get the sponge and a bucket of water from the kitchen. I remember Herrera stood up but then sat down again straightaway. Then Buba shut himself in the bathroom and when he came out it was all like before. I suggested we celebrate with one last whisky. Herrera accepted. Buba shook his head. I guess none of us felt like talking; the only one who spoke was Buba. He said: This isn't necessary, we're already rich. That was all. Then Herrera and I downed our whiskies and we all went to bed. The next day we started off in the League with a six-zero victory. Buba scored three goals, Herrera scored one and I scored two. It was a glorious season, people still remember it, which is amazing, considering how long ago it was, although if I really think about it, if I exercise my memory, it seems right and proper (though I say so myself) that my second and final season playing with Buba in Europe should have been saved from oblivion. You saw the matches on TV. If you'd been in Barcelona you'd have gone crazy. We won the national League by more than fifteen points and were European Champions without having lost a single match, just two draws: with Milan at San Siro and with Bayern on their home ground. Every other game we won.

Buba became the man of the moment, top goal scorer in the Spanish League and the Champions League, and his value soared. Halfway through the season, his agent tried to renegotiate the contract and more than triple the annual payment, and the club had no choice but to sell him to Juventus at the beginning of the following preseason. There were lots of clubs vying for Herrera too, but since he'd come up through the ranks and been virtually raised in the junior teams, he didn't want to leave, though I know for sure he had offers from Manchester, where he would have got more money. I had a string of offers too, but after letting Buba go, the club couldn't afford to lose me, so they upped my fee and I stayed.

By then I'd met a Catalan woman who would soon become my wife and I think that influenced my decision not to leave. I don't regret it. That season we were champions in the Spanish League again, but in the Champions League we came up against Buba's team in the semifinals and we were eliminated. They beat us three-zero in Italy and Buba scored one of the goals, one of the most beautiful goals I've ever seen, from a foul, or a free kick, as you guys say, more than twenty yards from the goal, what the Brazilians would call a dead leaf, an autumn leaf, when the ball looks like it's heading over the top and then suddenly it drops like a falling leaf, Didí could pull it off, so they say, but I'd never seen Buba do it, and after that goal I remember Herrera looked at me – I was in the wall and Herrera was behind me, marking an Italian player – and when our goalkeeper went to get the ball from the net, Herrera looked at me and smiled as if to say, Well, what do you know, and I smiled too. It was the first goal for the Italians and after that Buba virtually disappeared from the game. They took him off in the fiftieth minute. Before leaving the field he hugged Herrera and me. After the match we spent some time with him in the passage to the locker rooms.

Buba

In the return match on our home ground we tied with the Italians zero-zero. It was one of the strangest games I've ever played. Everything seemed to be happening in slow motion and in the end the Italians eliminated us. But overall it was a memorable season. We won the Spanish League again, Herrera and I were both selected for our national teams for the World Cup, and Buba went from strength to strength. His team won the Italian League (the famous *Scudetto*) and the Champions League. He was *the* star player. Sometimes we'd call him and chat for a while. Not long before we left for summer vacation (it was going to be shorter than usual because that year the international players had to start preparing for the World Cup almost right away) the news hit the front page of the sports papers: Buba had been killed in a car accident on the way to the Turin airport.

We were stunned. What more can I say? Honestly, we were just stunned. The World Cup was terrible. Chile was eliminated in the quarterfinals, without having won a single match. Spain didn't even get to the quarterfinals, although they did win once. My performance was appalling as I'm sure you remember. The less said the better. Buba's team? No, they were eliminated in the qualifying round by Cameroon or Nigeria, I can't remember which. Even if he'd been alive, Buba wouldn't have been able to go to the World Cup. As a player I mean.

The seasons went by and there were other championships and World Cups and other friends. I was in Barcelona for another six years. And four more years in Spain after that. Throughout that time, I had other days and nights of glory, of course, but it was never the same. I finished my soccer career with Colo-Colo, playing as a midfielder, not a left winger (left wingers have an expiration date). Then I set up my sports store. I could have been a trainer, I did the course, but by then I was tired of it, to tell you the truth. Herrera played for a couple more years. Then he retired at the height of his fame. He played more than a hundred international matches (I only played forty) and when he quit, the Barcelona fans paid him a really exceptional tribute. Now he has I don't know how many businesses there, and he's doing well, as you'd expect.

We didn't see each other for many years. Until recently, when they made a TV programme, a nostalgic kind of show, about the team who won the first Champions League. I got the invitation, and although I don't like travelling any more, I accepted, because it was an opportunity to meet up with old friends. What can I say? The city's just as beautiful as ever. They put us up in a first-class hotel and my wife went straight off to see her family and friends. I decided to lie down on the bed and take a nap, but after a quarter of an hour I realised I wouldn't be able to sleep. Then a kid from the production company came to get me and took me to the TV studios. I ran into Pepito Vila in the make-up room. He was completely bald and I almost didn't recognise him. Then Delève turned up and that was the killer. They were all so old. But my spirits rose a bit when I saw Herrera, before going onto the set. Him I would have recognised anywhere. We hugged and exchanged a few words, enough to make it clear that we'd be having dinner together that night, whatever else happened.

The programme was long and detailed. There was stuff about the Cup, what it had meant for the club, about Buba and his first year in Europe, but there was also stuff about Buzatti and Delève, Palau and Pepito Vila, and me, and especially about Herrera and his long sports career, an example for the young. There were six ex-players, three journalists and two celebrity fans: a movie actor and a Brazilian singer who turned out to be the most fanatical supporter I've ever come across. She was called Liza Do Elisa, though I don't think that was her real name, and when the interviews were finished (I said hardly anything, a few dumb remarks, my stomach was all in knots) she came to dinner with us, with Herrera and me and Pepito Vila and one of the journalists, maybe she was a friend of the journalist's, I don't know, anyhow, suddenly I found myself in a dimly lit restaurant with all these people, and then in a disco, which was even darker, except for the dance floor, where I danced, sometimes on my own, sometimes with Liza Do Elisa, and then, some time after midnight, I ended up in a bar near the port, sitting at a grimy table, drinking coffee with a shot, along with Herrera and the Brazilian singer – the others had gone.

I don't remember which of them brought it up. Maybe Liza Do Elisa was talking about magic, she could've been, or maybe it was Herrera who got her on to it, I think she mentioned black magic and white magic, and then she started telling stories, true stories, things that had happened to her as a child, or when she was young and making her way in the world of show business. I remember looking at her and thinking she was a formidable woman: she was speaking in the same forceful, vehement way as she'd spoken in front of the TV cameras. She'd had to struggle to make it and she was permanently on guard, as if she could be attacked at any moment. She was a pretty woman, about thirty-five, with a nice rack. You could tell her life hadn't been easy. But Herrera wasn't interested in her life story, I realised that straightaway. Herrera wanted to talk about magic, voodoo, Candomblé rituals, black people's business, in short. And Liza Do Elisa was happy to oblige.

So I finished my coffee and let them talk, and since, to be honest, I wasn't all that interested in the topic of their conversation, I ordered a whisky and then another, and when daylight was already beginning to shine in through the windows of the bar, Herrera said he had a story a bit like the ones Liza Do Elisa had been telling, and he was going to tell it and see what she thought. Then I shut my eyes, like I was sleepy, although I wasn't sleepy at all, and listened to Herrera telling Buba's story, our story, but without saying that Buba was Buba and pretending that he and I were some French players he'd met a while back, and Liza Do Elisa went quiet (I think it was the first time she'd been quiet all night) until Herrera came to the end, to Buba's death, and only then did she speak up and say yes, it was possible, and Herrera asked about the blood that the three players spilled into the glass, and Liza Do Elisa said it was part of the ceremony, and Herrera asked about the music that came from the bathroom when the black guy shut himself in there, and Liza Do Elisa said it was part of the ceremony, and then Herrera asked about what happened to the blood when the black guy took it into the bathroom, and about the sponge and the bucket of water with bleach, and he also wanted to know what Liza Do Elisa thought the guy did in the bathroom, and the Brazilian singer replied to all his questions by saying that it was part of the ceremony, until Herrera started getting annoyed and said obviously it was part of the ceremony but he wanted to know what the ceremony was. And then Liza Do Elisa said, Nobody raises his voice to me, especially not – and I quote – if he wants to fuck me, to which Herrera replied with a laugh that reminded me of the good old days – the Herrera of the Champions League and the two Spanish Leagues we won together, I mean, the two we won with Buba and the five we won overall – and then he said he hadn't meant to offend her (Liza Do Elisa took offence at the slightest little thing), and repeated his question.

The singer seemed to be deep in thought for a while, then she looked at Herrera and me (but she looked much more intensely at Herrera) and said she didn't know for sure. Maybe he drank the blood, maybe he poured it down the toilet, maybe he pissed or shat on it, maybe he didn't do any of those things, maybe he took his clothes off and smeared himself with blood and then took a shower, but it was all speculation. Then the three of us sat there in silence until Liza Do Elisa said that whatever he did, one thing was for sure: the guy had suffered and loved deeply.

And then Herrera asked her what she thought about this black guy who had played in the French team: did his magic work? No, said Liza Do Elisa. He was crazy. How could it work? And Herrera asked, How come his teammates started playing better? Because they were good players, said the singer. And then I weighed in and asked what she meant when she said he'd suffered deeply, how do you mean? And she replied, With his whole body, but more than that, with his whole mind.

"What do you mean, Liza?" I insisted.

"That he was crazy," said the singer.

The bar's metal gates had been pulled down. On a wall I noticed various photos of our team. The singer asked us (not just Herrera, me too) if we'd been talking about Buba. Not one muscle in Herrera's face moved. I might have nodded. Liza Do Elisa crossed herself. I got up and went to take a look at the photos. There we were, the eleven of us: Herrera standing with his arms crossed next to Miquel Serra, the goalkeeper, and Palau, and, in front of them, squatting down, Buba and me. I was smiling, as if I didn't have a care in the world, and Buba was serious, looking straight at the camera.

I went to the bathroom and when I came back Herrera was paying at the bar, and the singer was standing beside the table, smoothing her close-fitting, deep red dress. Before we left, the bartender, or maybe he was the owner, the guy who'd put up with us until dawn, anyway, asked me to sign another one of the photos decorating the wall. It was a photo of me on my own, taken just after I arrived in the city. I asked him his name. He said he was called Narcis. To Narcis, I signed it, affectionately.

It was already getting light when we left. We walked through the streets of Barcelona, like in the old days. I wasn't surprised to notice that Herrera had his arm around the singer's waist. Then we hailed a taxi and they accompanied me back to my hotel.

Photos

When it comes to poets, give me the French, thinks Arturo Belano, lost in Africa, leafing through a sort of photo album in which Francophone poetry celebrates itself, sons of bitches, he thinks, sitting on the ground, a ground of red clay, or something like that, but it's not clay, not even clayey, though it is red, or rather coppery in colour, or reddish, except at midday when it's yellow, the book lying between his legs, a fat book, nine hundred and thirty pages, so close enough to a thousand pages long, a hardback, *La poésie contemporaine de langue française depuis 1945*, edited by Serge Brindeau, published by Bordas, a compendium of little texts about all the poets writing in French around the world, be it in France or Belgium, Canada or North Africa, sub-Saharan Africa or the Middle East, so it's not such a miracle to find the book here, thinks Belano, because if it includes African poets, some copies would have come to Africa, obviously, in the luggage of the poets themselves or the luggage of some tragically naïve bookseller committed to the Francophone cause, though it's still a miracle that one of those copies should happen to turn up just here, in this village, forsaken by god and abandoned by the human race, where there's no one left but me and the ghosts of the contributors and not much else except the book and the changing colours of the earth, it's weird, but the earth does actually change colour every so often, dark yellow in the morning, yellow at midday, with watery streaks, like crystallised, dirty water, and who'd want to look at it after that, thinks Belano, looking up at the sky through which three clouds are floating, like three signs in a blue field, the field of conjectures or the field of mystical doctrines, amazed by the elegance of the clouds and their unspeakably slow procession, then looking at the photos, his nose almost touching the page, examining those faces with all their contortions, which isn't the word exactly, yes it is, Jean Pérol, for example, who looks like he's listening to a joke, or Gérald Neveu (whom Belano has read), who looks like he's dazzled by the sun or living in a month that's a monstrous coupling of July and August, something that only Africans can stand or the poets of Germany and France, or Vera Feyder, who is holding and stroking a cat, as if holding and stroking were one and the same, and they are, thinks Belano, or Jean-Philippe Salabreuil (whom he has read), so young, so handsome, he looks like a movie star, looking at me from the far side of death with a half smile, telling me or the African reader to whom this book belonged that it's all right, that the constant motion of the spirit is futile and it's all right, and Belano shuts his eyes without lowering his head, then he opens them again and turns the page and here we have Patrice Cauda, who looks like he hits his wife – what am I saying, his wife, I mean his girl-friend – and Jean Dubacq, who looks like he works in a bank, like a sad bank clerk with little hope left, a Catholic, and Jacques Arnold, who looks like the manager of the bank that employs the unfortunate Dubacq, and Janine Mitaud, large mouth, sparkling eyes, a middle-aged woman with short hair, a slim neck and, to judge from her expression, a subtle sense of humour, and Philippe Jaccottet (whom he has read), who's thin and has a kind-looking face, though maybe, thinks Belano, it's one of those kind-looking faces you should never trust, and Claude de Burine, the incarnation of Little Orphan Annie – even her dress, or what the photo shows of her dress, is identical to Little Orphan Annie's – but who is this Claude de Burine, Belano asks himself aloud, alone in an African village whose inhabitants have all fled or been killed, sitting on the ground with his knees up, while his fingers flick with a singular rapidity through the pages of *La poésie contemporaine* in search of information about this poet, which he eventually finds: Claude de Burine, he reads, was born in Saint-Léger-des-Vignes (Nièvre), in 1931, and she is the author of *Lettres à l'enfance* (Rougerie, 1957), *La Gardienne* (Le soleil dans la tête – good name for a publishing house – 1960), *L'allumeur de réverbères* (Rougerie, 1963) and *Hanches* (Librairie Saint-Germain-des-Prés, 1969), and that's all the biographical information there is, as if at the age of thirty-eight, after the publication of *Hanches*, Little Orphan Annie had disappeared, although the author of the introductory note says: *Claude de Burine, avant toute autre chose, dit l'amour, l'amour inépuisable*, and when Belano reads that, it all makes sense in his overheated brain: someone who *dit l'amour* could perfectly well disappear at the age of thirty-eight, especially, *especially* if that person is the double of Little Orphan Annie, with the same round eyes, the same hair, the eyebrows of someone who has seen the inside of a foundling hospital, an expression of perplexity and pain, a pain alleviated to some degree by caricature, but it's pain all the same, and then Belano says to himself, I'm going to find a lot of pain here, and turns back to the photos and discovers, under the photo of Claude de Burine, between the photo of Philippe Jaccottet and the photo of Jacques Réda, Marc Alyn and Dominique Tron sharing the same snapshot, a lighter moment, Dominique Tron who's so different from Claude de Burine, on the one hand, the existentialist, the beatnik, the rocker, and on the other, meekness incarnate, a woman forsaken and banished, thinks Belano, as if Dominique lived in a whirlwind while the all-suffering Claude looked on from a metaphysical distance, and again Belano's curiosity is piqued and he consults the index and then after reading *né à Bin el Ouidane (Maroc) le 11 décembre 1950*, he realises that Dominique Tron is a man, and he thinks as he brushes a (completely imaginary) mosquito away from his ear, I must be suffering from sunstroke, and reads Tron's list of publications: *Stéréophonies* (Seghers, 1965, that is, at the age of fifteen), *Kamikaze Galapagos* (Seghers, 1967, that is, at the age of seventeen), *La Souffrance est inutile* (Seghers, 1968, that is, at the age of eighteen), *D'Épuisement en épuisement jusqu'à l'aurore, Elisabeth*, an autobiographical oratorio, followed by a mystery, *Boucles de feu* (Seghers, 1968, that is, again, at the age of eighteen), and *De la Science-fiction c'est nous à l'interprétation des corps* (Eric Losfeld, 1972, that is, at the age of twenty-two), and that's all there is, largely because *La poésie contemporaine* was published in 1973, had it been published in 1974 there surely would have been more titles, and then Belano thinks about his own youth, when he used to churn it out like Tron, and was perhaps even better looking than Tron, he thinks, squinting at the photo, but to publish a poem, in Mexico, all those years ago when he lived in Mexico City, he'd had to sweat blood, because Mexico is Mexico, he reflects, and France is France, and then he shuts his eyes and sees a torrent of ghostly, emblematic Mexicans flowing like a grey breath of air along a dry river bed, and before opening his eyes, holding the book firmly in both hands, he sees Claude de Burine again, the photo-portrait of Claude de Burine, in her lonely poet's tower, watching the adolescent cyclone that is Dominique Tron, who wrote *La souffrance est inutile*, and perhaps he wrote it for her, for Claude, a book that is a burning bridge, which Dominique himself will not cross, but Claude will, oblivious to the bridge, oblivious to everything, she will cross it and be burnt in the attempt, thinks Belano, as all poets are burnt, even the bad ones, on those burning bridges that are so enticing, so fascinating when you're eighteen, or twenty-one, but then so dull, so monotonous, beginning and ending so predictably, those bridges that he crossed like Ulysses on his way home, theorised and conjured up before his eyes like fantastic Ouija boards, enormous burning structures repeated over and over into the depths of the screen, which may stop poets at eighteen or twenty-one, but twenty-three-year-old poets can cross them with their eyes closed, like sleepwalking warriors, thinks Belano as he imagines the helpless, the fragile, the terribly fragile Claude de Burine running towards the arms of Dominique Tron, on a course he chooses to imagine as erratic, although there is something in Claude's eyes, and in Dominique's, and in the eyes of the burning bridge, that strikes him as familiar, something that – like the changing colours all around the empty village – speaks in a down-to-earth way of the arid, sad and terrible end to come, and then Belano shuts his eyes and keeps still, and opens his eyes again and turns to another page, although this time he's determined to look at the photos and nothing else, and that's how he finds Pierre Morency, a good-looking kid, Jean-Guy Pilon, a difficult character, not photogenic, Fernand Ouellette, a man who's going bald (and remembering that the book was published in 1973, all things considered, it's pretty safe to assume that he's completely bald by now), and Nicole Brossard, a girl with straight hair, with a part in the middle, big eyes, a square jaw, pretty, Belano finds her pretty, but he doesn't want to know how old Nicole is or what books she has written so he turns the page, and suddenly enters (though in the village where he happens to be stranded there is no such thing as a sudden entry) the kingdom of the thousand and one nights of literature and memory, because he has come to the photos of Mohammed Khaïr-Eddine and Kateb Yacine and Anna Gréki and Malek Haddad and Abdellatif Laabi and Ridha Zili, Arab poets who write in French, and he remembers having seen some of those poets already, many years ago, maybe in 1972, before the publication of the book he is holding, or in 1971, or perhaps he's mistaken and is seeing them for the first time, with a persistent and as yet unexplained feeling, somewhere between perplexity – a singularly sweet perplexity – and envy, wishing he had belonged to that group, it was 1973 or '74, he remembers now, in a book on Arab poets or North African poets that a Uruguayan woman carried around with her for a couple of days everywhere she went in Mexico City, a book with an ochre or yellow cover, the colour of desert sands, and then Belano turns the page and more photos appear, Kamal Ibrahim (whom he has read), Salah Stétié, Marwan Hoss, Fouad Gabriel Naffah (a diabolically ugly poet), and Nadia Tuéni, Andrée Chedid and Vénus Khoury, and Belano cranes forward, his face almost touching the page, to see the women poets in more detail, and Nadia and Vénus seem truly beautiful, with Nadia he'd fuck until dawn, he thinks (assuming that night will fall again sometime, since where he is, the evenings drag on as if the village were following the sun in its westward march, Belano thinks, with a certain disquiet) and with Vénus he'd fuck until three in the morning, and then I'd get up, light a cigarette and go out for a walk along the esplanade in Malgrat de Mar, but with Nadia he'd go on till dawn, and the things he'd do with Vénus he'd do with Nadia too, but he'd do things with Nadia that he wouldn't do with anyone else, thinks Belano as he stares without blinking at Nadia's smile, his nose almost touching the page, and Nadia's lively eyes, her dark shining abundant hair, a protective cowl of shadow, and then Belano looks up and can no longer see the three solitary clouds in the African sky over the village where he has washed up, a village the sun is dragging westward – the clouds have disappeared, as if they were superfluous now that he has seen the smile of the Arab poet of the thousand and one nights, and then Belano breaks his promise, looks up the name Tuéni in the index and turns intrepidly to the pages in the critical section where he knows he will find her biographical note, a note that says that Nadia was born in Beirut in 1935, which means that when the book was published she was thirty-eight, although the photo is earlier, and the note also says that she has published a number of books, including *Les Textes blonds* (Beyrouth, Éd. An-Nahar, 1963), *L'Age d'écume* (Seghers, 1966), *Juin et les mécréantes* (Seghers, 1968), and *Poèmes pour une histoire* (Seghers, 1972), and in the paragraphs about her, Belano reads *habituée aux chimères*, and he reads *chez ce poète des marées, des ouragans, des naufrages*, and he reads *fille elle-même d'un père druze et d'une mère française*, and he reads *mariée à un*

Chrétien orthodoxe, and he reads *Nadia Tuéni (née Nadia Mohammed Ali Hamadé)*, and he reads *Timidir la Chrétienne, Sabba la Musulmane, Dâhoun la Juive, Sioun la Druze*, and he stops reading and looks up because he thinks he heard something, the cry of a vulture or a turkey buzzard, even though he knows there are no turkey buzzards here, but that can be fixed, given time, not necessarily years of time, hours or even minutes would do, at some point you stop knowing what you used to know, it's as simple and as hard as that, even a Mexican turkey buzzard could turn up in this lousy village, thinks Belano with tears in his eyes, and it's not the sound of the turkey buzzards making him cry but the physical presence of Nadia Tuéni's image looking at him from a page in the book with a petrified smile that seems to open out like blown glass in the landscape surrounding Belano, which is also made of glass, and then he thinks he hears words, the words he has just read but cannot read now because he is crying, *l'air torride, habituée aux chimères*, and a story about Druses, Jews, Muslims and Christians, from which Nadia emerges at the age of thirty-eight (the same age as Claude de Burine) with the hair of an Arab princess, immaculate, perfectly serene, like the accidental muse of certain poets, or their provisional muse, the one who says, Don't worry, or who says, Worry, but not too much, the one who doesn't speak in dry and definite words but whispers, whose parting gift is a kind look, and then Belano thinks of the age the real Nadia Tuéni must be, in 1996, and he realises that now she is sixty-one, and he stops crying, *l'air torride* has dried his tears once again, and he starts turning the pages, he returns to the mug shots of the Francophone poets with an obstinacy worthy of a higher enterprise, like a scavenging bird he returns to the face of Tchicaya U

Tam'si, born in Mpili in 1931, the face of Matala Mukadi, born in Luiska in 1942, the face of Samuel-Martin Eno Belinga, born in Ebolowa in 1935, the face of Elologué Epanya Yondo, born in Douala in 1930, and so many other faces, faces of poets who write in French, photogenic or not, the face of Michel Van Schendel, born in Asnières in 1929, the face of Raoul Duguay (whom he has read), born in Val d'Or in 1939, the face of Suzanne Paradis, born in Beaumont in 1936, the face of Daniel Biga (whom he has read), born in Saint-Sylvestre in 1940, the face of Denise Jallais, born in Saint-Nazaire in 1932 and almost as pretty as Nadia, Belano thinks with a kind of comprehensive tremor, while evening keeps dragging the village westward, and turkey buzzards start to appear in the tops of some small trees, except that Denise is blonde and Nadia is dark, both very beautiful, sixty-one and sixty-four respectively, I hope they're alive, he thinks, his gaze fixed not on the photos in the book but on the line of the treetops against the sky where the birds are teetering, crows or vultures or turkey buzzards, and then Belano remembers a poem by Gregory Corso, in which the hapless North American poet spoke of his one true love, an Egyptian woman dead two thousand five hundred years ago, and Belano remembers Corso's street-kid face and a figure from Egyptian art that he saw a long time ago on a matchbox, a girl getting out of a bath or a river or a swimming pool, and the beat poet (the enthusiastic, hapless Corso) is watching her from the other side of time, and the Egyptian girl with long legs senses that she is being watched, and that's all, her flirting with Corso is as brief as a sigh in the immensity of time, but time itself and its remote sovereignty can also pass like a sigh, thinks Belano as he watches the birds up in the branches, silhouettes on the horizon, an electrocardiogram agitated by the ruffling or spreading of wings as it waits for death, my death, thinks Belano, and then he shuts his eyes for a long time, as if he were thinking or crying with his eyes shut, and when he opens them again the crows are there, the electroencephalogram trembling on the African horizon, and then Belano shuts the book and stands up, still holding it, grateful, and begins to walk westward, towards the coast, with the book of Francophone poets under his arm, grateful, and his thought speeds ahead of his steps through the jungles and deserts of Liberia, as it did when he was an adolescent in Mexico, and soon his steps lead him away from the village.

Meeting with Enrique Lihn

for Celina Manzoni

In 1999, after returning from Venezuela, I dreamed that I was being taken to Enrique Lihn's apartment, in a country that could well have been Chile, in a city that could well have been Santiago, bearing in mind that Chile and Santiago once resembled Hell, a resemblance that, in some subterranean layer of the real city and the imaginary city, will forever remain. Of course I knew that Lihn was dead, but when they offered to take me to meet him I accepted without hesitation. Maybe I thought that the people I was with were playing a joke, or that a miracle might be possible. But probably I just wasn't thinking, or had misunderstood the invitation. In any case we came to a seven-storey building, with a façade painted a faded yellow and a bar on the ground floor, a bar of considerable dimensions, with a long counter and several booths, and my friends (although it seems odd to describe them like that; let's just say the enthusiasts who had offered to take me to meet the poet) led me to a booth, and there was Lihn. At first I could hardly recognise him, it wasn't the face I had seen on his books; he'd grown thinner and younger, he'd become more handsome, and his eyes looked much brighter than the black-and-white eyes in the back-cover photographs. In fact,

Lihn didn't look like Lihn at all, he looked like a Hollywood actor, a B-list actor, the kind who stars in TV movies or films that are never shown in European cinemas and go straight to video. But at the same time he was Lihn, although he no longer looked like him; I was in no doubt about that. The enthusiasts greeted him, calling him Enrique with a fake-sounding familiarity and asked him questions I couldn't understand, and then they introduced us, although to tell the truth I didn't need to be introduced, because for a time, a short time, I had corresponded with him, and his letters had, in a way, kept me going; I'm talking about 1981 or 1982, when I was living like a recluse in a house outside Gerona with practically no money and no prospects of ever getting any, and literature was a vast minefield occupied by enemies, except for a few classic authors (just a few), and every day I had to walk through that minefield, with only the poems of Archilocus to guide me, and any false move could have been fatal. It's like that for all young writers. There comes a time when you have no support, not even from friends, forget about mentors, and there's no one to give you a hand; publication, prizes and grants are reserved for the others, the ones who said 'Yes, sir,' over and over, or those who praised the literary mandarins, a never-ending horde distinguished only by their aptitude for discipline and punishment – nothing escapes them and they forgive nothing. Anyway, as I was saying, all young writers feel like that at some point or other in their lives. But at the time I was twenty-eight years old and in no sense could I consider myself a young writer. I was adrift. I wasn't the typical Latin American writer living in Europe thanks to some government sinecure. I was a nobody and not inclined to show any mercy or beg for it. Then I started corresponding with Enrique Lihn. Naturally I was the one who initiated the correspondence. I didn't have to wait long for his reply. A long, crotchety letter, as we might say in Chile: gloomy and irritable. In my reply I told him about my life, my house in the country, on one of the hills outside Gerona, the medieval city before it, the countryside or the void behind. I also told him about my dog, Laika, and said that in my opinion Chilean literature, with one or two exceptions, was shit. It was evident from his next letter that we were already friends. What followed was what typically happens when a famous poet befriends an unknown. He read my poems and included some of them in a kind of reading he organised to present the work of the younger generation at the Chilean-North American Institute of Culture. In his letter he identified a set of hopefuls destined, so he thought, to be the six tigers of Chilean poetry in the year 2000. The six tigers were Bertoni, Maquieira, Gonzalo Muñoz, Martínez, Rodrigo Lira and myself. I think. Maybe there were seven tigers. But I think there were only six. And it would have been hard for the six of us to be anything much in 2000, because by then Rodrigo Lira, the best of the lot, had killed himself and what was left of him had been rotting for years in some cemetery, or else was ash, blowing around the streets mingled with the filth of Santiago. Cats would have been more appropriate than tigers. Bertoni, as far as I know, is a kind of hippie who lives by the sea, collecting shells and seaweed. Maquieira made a careful study of Cardenal and Coronel Urtecho's anthology of North American poetry, published two books and then settled down to drinking. Gonzalo Muñoz went to Mexico, so I heard, where he disappeared, not into ethylic oblivion like Lowry's consul, but into the advertising industry. Martínez made a careful study of *Duchamp du signe* and then died. As for Rodrigo Lira, well, I already explained what became of him. Not so much tigers as cats, whichever way you look at it. The kittens of a far-flung province. Anyway, what I wanted to say is that I knew Lihn, so no introduction was necessary. Nevertheless the enthusiasts proceeded to introduce me and neither I nor Lihn objected. So there we were, in a booth, and voices were saying, This is Roberto Bolaño, and I held out my hand, my arm was enveloped by the darkness of the booth, and I grasped Lihn's hand, a slightly cold hand, which squeezed mine for a few seconds – the hand of a sad person, I thought, a hand and a handshake that corresponded perfectly to the face that was scrutinising me without showing any sign of recognition. The correspondence was gestural, bodily, and opened onto an opaque eloquence that had nothing to say, or at least not to me. Once that moment was past, the enthusiasts started talking again and the silence receded; they were all asking Lihn for his opinions on the most disparate issues and events, and at that point my disdain evaporated at once, because I realised that they were just like I had once been: young poets with no support, kids who'd been shut out by the new centre-left Chilean government and didn't have any backing or patronage, all they had was Lihn, a Lihn who looked much more handsome and prepossessing than the real Enrique Lihn as he appeared in the author photos, a Lihn who resembled his poems, who had adopted their age, who lived in a building similar to his poems, and who could disappear, as his poems sometimes did, with a characteristic elegance and poise. When I realised this, I remember I felt better. I mean I began to make sense of the situation and find it amusing. I had nothing to fear: I was at home, with friends, with a writer I had always admired. It wasn't a horror movie. Or not an out-and-out horror movie, but a horror movie leavened with large doses of black humour. And just as I thought of black humour, Lihn extracted a little bottle of pills from his pocket. I have to take one every three hours, he said. The enthusiasts fell silent once again. A waiter brought a glass of water. The pill was big. That's what I thought when I saw it fall into the glass of water. But in fact it wasn't big. It was dense. Lihn began to break it up with a spoon and I realised that the pill looked like an onion with countless layers. I leaned forward and peered into the glass. For a moment I was quite sure that it was an infinite pill. The curved glass had a magnifying effect, like a lens: inside, the pale pink pill was disintegrating as if giving birth to a galaxy or the universe. But galaxies are born or die (I forget which) suddenly, and what I could see through the curved side of that glass was unfolding in slow motion, each incomprehensible stage drawn out as I watched, every retraction and shudder. Then, feeling exhausted, I sat back, and my gaze, detached from the medicinal solution, rose to meet Lihn's eyes, which seemed to be saying: No comment, it's bad enough having to swallow this concoction every three hours, don't go looking for symbolic meanings – the water, the onion, the slow march of the stars. The enthusiasts had moved away from our table. Some were at the bar. I couldn't see the others. But when I looked at Lihn again, there was an enthusiast with him, whispering something in his ear, before leaving the booth to find his friends, who were scattered around the establishment. And at that moment I knew that Lihn knew he was dead. My heart's given up on me, he said. It doesn't exist any more.

Something's not right here, I thought. Lihn died of cancer, not a heart attack. An enormous heaviness was coming over me. So I got up and went to stretch my legs, but not in the bar; I went out into the street. The sidewalks were grey and uneven and the sky looked like a mirror without a tain, the place where everything should have been reflected but where, in the end, nothing was. Nevertheless a feeling of normality prevailed and pervaded all vision. When I felt I'd had enough fresh air and it was time to get back to the bar, as I was climbing the three steps up to the door (stone steps, single blocks of a stone that had a granite-like consistency and the sheen of a gem), I ran into a guy who was shorter than me and dressed like a fifties gangster, a guy who had something of the caricature about him, the classic affable killer, who got me mixed up with someone he knew and greeted me, and I replied to his greeting although from the start I was sure that I didn't know him and that he was mistaken, but I behaved as if I knew him, as if I, too, had mixed him up with someone else, so the two of us greeted each other as we attempted ineffectively to climb those shining (yet lowly) stone steps, but the hit man's confusion lasted no more than a few seconds, he soon realised that he was mistaken, and then he looked at me in a different way, as if he were asking himself if I was confused too or if, on the contrary, I had been pulling his leg from the start, and since he was thick and suspicious (though sharp in his own paradoxical way), he asked me who I was, I remember, he asked me with a malicious smile on his lips, and I said, Shit, Jara, it's me, Bolaño, and it would have been clear to anyone from his smile that he wasn't Jara, but he played the game, as if suddenly, struck by a lightning bolt (and no, I'm not quoting one of Lihn's poems, much less one of mine), he fancied the idea of living the life of that unknown Jara for a minute or two, the Jara he would never be, except right there, stalled on the highest of those radiant steps, and he asked me about my life, he asked me (thick as a plank) who I was, admitting de facto that he was Jara, but a Jara who had forgotten the very existence of Bolaño, which is perfectly understandable after all, so I explained to him who I was, and, while I was at it, who he was too, thereby creating a Jara to suit me and him, that is, to suit that moment – an improbable, intelligent, courageous, rich, generous, daring Jara, in love with a beautiful woman and loved by her in return – and then the gangster smiled, more and more deeply convinced that I was making fun of him but unable to bring the episode to a close and proceed to teach me a lesson, as if he had suddenly fallen in love with the image I was constructing for him, encouraging me to go on telling him not just about Jara but also about Jara's friends and finally the world, a world which seemed too wide even for Jara, a world in which even the great Jara was an ant whose death on a shining step would not have mattered at all to anyone, and then, at last, his friends appeared, two taller hit men wearing light-coloured double-breasted suits, who looked at me and at the false Jara as if to ask him who I was, and he had no choice but to say it's Bolaño, and the two hit men greeted me, I shook their hands (rings, expensive watches, gold bracelets), and when they invited me to have a drink with them, I said, I can't, I'm with a friend, and pushed past Jara through the door and disappeared inside. Lihn was still in the booth. But now there were no enthusiasts to be seen in his vicinity. The glass was empty. He had taken the medicine and was waiting. Without saying a word we went up to his apartment. He lived on the seventh floor and we took the elevator, a very large elevator into which more than thirty people could have fitted. His apartment was rather small, especially for a Chilean writer, and there were no books. To a question from me he replied that he hardly needed to read any more. But there are always books, he added. You could see the bar from his apartment. As if the floor were made of glass. I spent a while on my knees, watching the people down there, looking for the enthusiasts, or the three gangsters, but I could see only unfamiliar people, eating or drinking, but mostly moving from one table or booth to another, or up and down the bar, all seized by a feverish excitement, like characters in an early twentieth-century novel. After a while I reached the conclusion that something was wrong. If the floor of Lihn's apartment was glass and so was the roof of the bar, what about all the storeys from the second to the sixth? Were they made of glass too? Then I looked down again and realised that between the first floor and the seventh floor there was nothing but empty space. This discovery distressed me. Jesus, Lihn, where have you brought me, I thought, though soon I was thinking, Jesus, Lihn, where have they brought you? I got to my feet carefully, because I knew that in that place, as opposed to the normal world, objects were more fragile than people, and I went looking for Lihn (who had disappeared) in the various rooms of the apartment, which didn't seem small any more, like a European writer's apartment, but spacious, enormous, like a writer's apartment in Chile, in the Third World, with cheap domestic help, and expensive, fragile objects, an apartment full of shifting shadows and rooms in semidarkness, in which I found two books, one a classic, like a smooth stone, the other modern, timeless, like shit, and gradually, as I looked for Lihn, I too began to grow cold, increasingly manic and cold, I started feeling ill, as if the apartment were turning on an imaginary axis, but then a door opened and I saw a swimming pool, and there was Lihn, swimming, and before I could open my mouth and say something about entropy, Lihn said that the bad thing about his medicine, the medicine he was taking to keep him alive, was that in a way it was turning him into a guinea pig for the drug company, words that I somehow expected to hear, as if the whole thing were a play and I had suddenly remembered my lines and the lines of my fellow actors, and then Lihn got out of the swimming pool and we went down to the ground floor, and we made our way through the crowded bar, and Lihn said: The tigers are finished, and: It was sweet while it lasted, and: You're not going to believe this, Bolaño, but in this neighborhood, only the dead go out for a walk. And by then we had reached the front of the bar and were standing at a window, looking at the streets and the façades of the buildings in that peculiar neighbourhood where the only people out walking were dead. And we looked and looked, and the façades were clearly the façades of another time, like the sidewalks covered with parked cars, which also belonged to another time, a time that was silent yet mobile (Lihn was watching it move), a terrible time that endured for no reason other than sheer inertia.

Part III
The Insufferable Gaucho

Jim

Many years ago I had a friend named Jim, and he was the saddest North American I've ever come across. I've seen a lot of desperate men. But never one as sad as Jim. Once he went to Peru – supposedly for more than six months, but it wasn't long before I saw him again. The Mexican street kids used to ask him, what's poetry made of, Jim? Listening to them, Jim would stare at the clouds and then he'd start throwing up. Vocabulary, eloquence, the search for truth. Epiphany. Like when you have a vision of the Virgin. He was mugged several times in Central America, which is surprising, because he'd been a Marine and fought in Vietnam. No more fighting, Jim used to say. I'm a poet now, searching for the extraordinary, trying to express it in ordinary, everyday words. So you think there are ordinary, everyday words? I think there are, Jim used to say. His wife was a Chicana poet; every so often she'd threaten to leave him. He showed me a photo of her. She wasn't especially pretty. Her face betrayed suffering, and under that suffering, simmering rage. I imagined her in an apartment in San Francisco or a house in Los Angeles, with the windows shut and the curtains open, sitting at a table, eating sliced bread and a bowl of green soup. Jim liked dark women, apparently, history's secret women, he would say, without elaborating. As for me, I liked blondes. Once I saw him watching fire-eaters on a street in Mexico City. I saw him from behind, and I didn't say hello, but it was obviously Jim. The badly cut hair, the dirty white shirt and the stoop, as if he were still weighed down by his pack. Somehow his neck, his red neck, summoned up the image of a lynching in the country – a landscape in black and white, without billboards or gas station lights – the country as it is or ought to be: one expanse of idle land blurring into the next, brick-walled rooms or bunkers from which we have escaped, standing there, awaiting our return. Jim had his hands in his pockets. The fire-eater was waving his torch and laughing fiercely. His blackened face was ageless: he could have been thirty-five or fifteen. He wasn't wearing a shirt and there was a vertical scar from his navel to his breastbone. Every so often he'd fill his mouth with flammable liquid and spit out a long snake of fire. The people in the street would watch him for a while, admire his skill, and continue on their way, except for Jim, who remained there on the edge of the sidewalk, stock-still, as if he expected something more from the fire-eater, a tenth signal (having deciphered the usual nine), or as if he'd seen in that discoloured face the features of an old friend or of someone he'd killed. I watched him for a good long while. I was eighteen or nineteen at the time and believed I was immortal. If I'd realised that I wasn't, I would have turned around and walked away. After a while I got tired of looking at Jim's back and the fire-eater's grimaces. So I went over and called his name. Jim didn't seem to hear me. When he turned around I noticed that his face was covered with sweat. He seemed to be feverish, and it took him a while to work out who I was; he greeted me with a nod and then turned back to

Jim

the fire-eater. Standing beside him, I noticed he was crying. He probably had a fever as well. I also discovered something that surprised me less at the time than it does now, writing this: the fire-eater was performing exclusively for Jim, as if all the other passersby on that corner in Mexico City simply didn't exist. Sometimes the flames came within a yard of where we were standing. What are you waiting for, I said, you want to get barbecued in the street? It was a stupid wisecrack, I said it without thinking, but then it hit me: that's exactly what Jim's waiting for. That year, I seem to remember, there was a song they kept playing in some of the funkier places with a refrain that went, *Chingado, hechizado (Fucked up, spellbound)*. That was Jim: fucked up and spellbound. Mexico's spell had bound him and now he was looking his demons right in the face. Let's get out of here, I said. I also asked him if he was high, or feeling ill. He shook his head. The fire-eater was staring at us. Then, with his cheeks puffed out like Aeolus, the god of the winds, he began to approach us. In a fraction of a second I realised that it wasn't a gust of wind we'd be getting. Let's go, I said, and yanked Jim away from the fatal edge of that sidewalk. We took ourselves off down the street towards Reforma, and after a while we went our separate ways. Jim didn't say a word in all that time. I never saw him again.

The Insufferable Gaucho

for Rodrigo Fresán

In the opinion of those who knew him well, Manuel Pereda had two outstanding virtues: he was a caring and affectionate father, and an irreproachable lawyer with a record of honesty, in a time and place that were hardly conducive to such rectitude. As a result of the first virtue, his son and daughter, Bebe and Cuca, whose childhood and adolescent years had been happy, later accused him of having sheltered them from the hard realities of life, focusing their attack particularly on his handling of practical matters. Of his work as a lawyer, there is little to be said. He prospered and made more friends than enemies, which was no mean feat, and when he had the choice between becoming a judge or a candidate for a political party, he chose the bench without hesitation, although it obviously meant giving up the opportunities for greater financial gain that would have been open to him in politics.

After three years, however, disappointed by his judicial career, he gave up public life and spent some time, perhaps even years, reading and travelling. Naturally there was also a Mrs Pereda, née Hirschman, with whom the lawyer was, so they say, madly in love. There are photos from the time to prove it: in one of them, Pereda, in a black suit, is dancing a tango with a blonde, almost platinum blonde, woman, who is looking at the camera and smiling, while the lawyer's eyes remain fixed on her, like the eyes of a sleepwalker or a sheep. Unfortunately, Mrs Pereda died suddenly, when Cuca was five and Bebe was seven. The young widower never remarried, although there were various women in his social circle with whom he was known to maintain friendly (though never intimate) relations, and who had, moreover, all the qualities required to become the new Mrs Pereda.

When the lawyer's two or three close friends asked him why he remained single, his response was always that he didn't want to impose the unbearable burden (as he put it) of a stepmother on his offspring. In Pereda's opinion, most of Argentina's recent problems could be traced back to the figure of the stepmother. As a nation, we never had a mother, he would say, or she was never there, or she left us on the doorstep of the orphanage. But we've had plenty of stepmothers, of all sorts, starting with the great Peronist stepmother. And he would conclude: In Latin America, when it comes to stepmothers, we're the experts.

In spite of everything, his life was happy. It's hard not to be happy, he used to say, in Buenos Aires, which is a perfect blend of Paris and Berlin, although if you look closely it's more like a perfect blend of Lyon and Prague. Every day he got up at the same time as his children, had breakfast with them, and dropped them off at school. He spent the rest of the morning reading at least two newspapers; and, after a snack at eleven (consisting basically of cold cuts and sausage on buttered French bread and two or three little glasses of Argentine or Chilean wine, except on special occasions, when the wine was, naturally, French), he took a siesta until one.

His lunch, which he ate on his own in an enormous, empty dining room while reading a book under the absent-minded gaze of the elderly maid, and watched by the black-and-white eyes of his deceased wife, looking out from photographs in ornate silver frames, was light: soup, a small portion of fish and mashed potato, some of which he would leave to go cold. In the afternoon, he helped his children with their homework, or sat through Cuca's piano lessons in silence, or Bebe's English and French classes, given by two teachers with Italian surnames, who came to the house. Sometimes, when Cuca had learned to play a piece right through, the maid and the cook would come to listen, and the lawyer, filled with pride, would hear them murmur words of praise, which struck him at first as excessive, but then, on reflection, seemed perfectly apt. After saying goodnight to his children and reminding his domestic staff for the umpteenth time not to open the door to anyone, he would go to his favourite café, on Corrientes, where he would stay until one at the very latest, listening to his friends or friends of theirs discussing issues that he would have found supremely boring, he suspected, had he known anything about them, after which he would go home, where everyone, by that time, was asleep.

Eventually the children grew up. First Cuca got married and went to live in Rio de Janeiro; then Bebe started writing and indeed became a highly successful writer, which was a source of great pride for Pereda, who read each and every page his son published. Bebe went on living at home for a few more years (where else could he have had it so good?), after which, like his sister, he flew the coop.

At first the lawyer tried to resign himself to solitude. He had an affair with a widow, went on a long trip through

France and Italy, met a girl called Rebeca, and finally contented himself with organising his huge, chaotic library. When Bebe came back from the United States, where he had spent a year teaching at a university, Pereda had aged prematurely. Bebe was worried and tried to spend as much time as he could with his father, so sometimes they went to the movies or the theatre, where the lawyer would usually fall into a deep sleep, and sometimes Bebe dragged him along (though he only had to drag him at first) to the literary gatherings held in a café called El Lapiz Negro, where authors basking in the glory of some municipal prize held forth at length about the nation's destiny. Pereda, who never opened his mouth at those gatherings, began to take an interest in what his son's colleagues had to say. When they talked about literature, he was completely bored. In his opinion, the best Argentine writers were Borges and his son; any further commentary on that subject was superfluous. But when they talked about national and international politics, the lawyer's body grew tense, as if under the effect of an electric current. From then on, his daily habits changed. He began to get up early and look through the old books in his library, searching for something, though he couldn't have said what. He spent his mornings reading. He decided to give up wine and heavy meals, because he realised they were dulling his intellect. His personal hygiene also underwent a change. He no longer spruced himself up when he was going out. He soon stopped taking a daily shower. One day he went to read the paper in a park without putting on a tie. His old friends barely recognised this new Pereda as the lawyer they had known, who had been irreproachable in every respect. One day he woke up feeling more agitated than usual. He had lunch with a retired judge and a retired journalist, and laughed all the way through the meal. Afterward, while they were drinking cognac, the judge asked him what he found so funny. Buenos Aires is sinking, Pereda replied. The ex-journalist thought that the lawyer had gone crazy and recommended some time by the seaside: the beach, that invigorating air. The judge, less given to speculation, simply thought that Pereda had gone off on a tangent.

A few days later, however, the Argentine economy collapsed. Accounts in American dollars were frozen, and those who hadn't moved their capital (or their savings) offshore suddenly discovered that they had nothing left, except perhaps a few bonds and bank bills – just looking at them was enough to give you goosebumps – vague promises inspired in equal parts by some forgotten tango and the words of the national anthem. I told you so, said the lawyer to anyone who would listen. Then, accompanied by his cook and maid, he stood in long lines, like many other inhabitants of Buenos Aires, and entered into long conversations with strangers (who struck him as utterly charming) in streets thronged with people swindled by the government or the banks, or some other culprit.

When the President resigned, Pereda was there among the protestors as they banged their pots and pans. It wasn't the only demonstration. Sometimes it seemed that the elderly had taken control of the streets, old people of all social classes, and he liked that, although he didn't know why; it seemed like a sign that something was changing, that something was moving in the darkness, although he was also happy to join in the wildcat strikes and blockades that soon degenerated into brawling. In the space of a few days, Argentina had three different Presidents. It didn't occur to anyone to start a revolution, or mount a military coup. That was when Pereda decided to go back to the country.

Before leaving, he explained his plan to the maid and the cook. Buenos Aires is falling apart; I'm going to the ranch, he said. They talked for hours, sitting at the kitchen table. The cook had been to the ranch as often as Pereda, who in the past had always said that the country was no place for a man like him, a cultivated family man, who wanted to make sure that his children got a good education. His mental images of the ranch had blurred and faded, leaving only a house with a hole in the middle, an enormous, threatening tree, and a barn whose dim interior flickered with shadows that might have been rats. Nevertheless, that night, as he drank tea in the kitchen, he told his employees that he had hardly any money left for their wages (it was all frozen in the bank – in other words, as good as lost), and the only solution he could think of was to take them to the country, where at least they wouldn't be short of food, or so he liked to think.

The maid and the cook listened to him compassionately. At one point the lawyer burst into tears. Trying to console him, they told him not to worry about the money; they were prepared to go on working even if he couldn't pay them. The lawyer definitively rejected any such arrangement. I'm too old to become a pimp, he said with an apologetic smile. The next morning, he packed a suitcase and took a taxi to the station. The women waved goodbye from the sidewalk.

The long, monotonous train trip gave him ample time for reflection. At first, the carriage was full. He observed that there were basically two topics of conversation: the country's state of bankruptcy and how the Argentine team was shaping up for the World Cup in Korea and Japan. The press of passengers reminded him of the trains departing from Moscow in the film *Doctor Zhivago,* which he had seen some time before, except that in the Russian carriages as filmed by that English director, the talk was not about ice hockey or skiing. What hope have we got, he thought, although he had to agree that on paper the Argentine selection looked unbeatable. When night fell, the conversations petered out, and the lawyer thought of his children, Cuca and Bebe, both of them abroad; he was also surprised to find himself remembering a number of women with whom he had been intimately acquainted; quietly they emerged from oblivion, their skin covered with perspiration, infusing his restless spirit with a kind of serenity, although it wasn't altogether serene, perhaps not exactly a sense of adventure, but something like that.

Then the train began to advance across the pampas, and the lawyer leaned his head against the cold glass of the window and fell asleep.

When he woke, the carriage was half empty and there was a man who looked part Indian sitting beside him, reading a Batman comic. Where are we? asked Pereda. In Coronel Gutiérrez, said the man. Ah, that's all right, thought the lawyer, I'm going to Capitán Jourdan. Then he got up, stretched his legs, and sat down again. Out on the dry plain he saw a rabbit that seemed to be racing the train. There were five other rabbits running behind it. The first rabbit, running just outside the window, had wide-open eyes, as if the race against the train required a superhuman effort (super-leporine, actually, thought the lawyer). The rabbits in pursuit, on the other hand, seemed to be running in tandem, like cyclists in the Tour de France. With a couple of big leaps, the rabbit bringing up the rear relieved the front-runner, who dropped back to last position, while the third rabbit moved up to second place, and the fourth moved up to third; and all the while the group was closing in on the solitary rabbit running beside the lawyer's window. Rabbits, he thought, how wonderful! On the plains there was nothing else to be seen: a vast, boundless expanse of scanty grass under massive, low clouds, and no indication that a town might be near. Are you going to Capitán Jourdan? Pereda asked the Batman reader, who seemed to be examining every panel with extreme care, scrutinising every detail, as if he were visiting a portable museum. No, he replied, I'm getting off at El Apeadero. Pereda tried to remember a station of that name but couldn't. And what's that, a station or a factory? The guy with the Indian look stared back at him fixedly: A station, he replied. He seems annoyed, thought Pereda. It wasn't the sort of question he would normally have asked, given his habitual discretion. The pampas had made him enquire in that frank, manly, and down-to-earth way, he thought.

When he rested his forehead against the window again, he saw that the rabbits in pursuit had caught up with the lone racing rabbit, and were attacking it ferociously, tearing at its body with their claws and teeth, those long rodents' teeth, thought Pereda with a horrified frisson. He looked back and saw a bundle of tawny fur thrashing about beside the rails.

The only passengers who got off at the station in Capitán Jourdan were Pereda and a woman with two children. The platform was half wood, half cement, and in spite of his best efforts Pereda couldn't find a railway employee anywhere. The woman and the children set off walking on a cart track, and although they were clearly moving away and their figures were visibly shrinking, it took more than three quarters of an hour, according to the lawyer's reckoning, for them to disappear over the horizon. Is the earth round? Pereda wondered. Of course it is, he told himself, as he settled down for a lengthy wait on an old wooden bench against the wall of the station offices. Inevitably, he remembered Borges's story 'The South', and when he thought of the store mentioned in the final paragraphs, tears brimmed in his eyes. Then he remembered the plot of Bebe's last novel, and imagined his son writing on a computer, in an austere office at a Midwestern university. When Bebe comes back and finds out I've gone to the ranch . . . , he thought in enthusiastic anticipation. The glare and the warm breeze blowing off the plain made him drowsy; he fell asleep. A hand shook him awake. A man as old as he was, wearing a worn-out railway uniform, asked him what he was doing there. Pereda said he was the owner of the Alamo Negro ranch. The man stood there looking at him for a while, then said: The judge. That's right, replied Pereda, there was a time when I was a judge. Don't you remember me, Mister Judge? Pereda scrutinised the man: he needed a new uniform and a haircut, urgently. Pereda shook his head. I'm Severo Infante, said the man. We used to play together when we were kids. But, *che,* that's ages ago – how could I remember, Pereda retorted, and the sound of his voice, not to mention the words he had used, sounded odd, as if the air of Capitán Jourdan had invigorated his vocal chords or his throat.

Of course, you're right, Mister Judge, said Severo Infante, but I feel like celebrating anyway. Bouncing like a kangaroo, the station employee disappeared into the ticket office, then came out with a bottle and a glass. Your health, he said, handing Pereda the glass, which he half filled with a clear liquid that seemed to be pure alcohol. Pereda took a sip – it tasted of scorched earth and stones – and left the glass on the bench. He said he had given up drinking. Then he got up and asked the way to his ranch. They went out the back door. Capitán Jourdan is over there, said Severo, just beyond the dry pond. Alamo Negro is the other way, a bit further, but you can't get lost in the daylight. You look after yourself, said Pereda, and set off in the direction of his ranch.

The main house was almost in ruins. That night it was cold, and Pereda tried to gather some sticks and light a campfire, but he couldn't find anything to burn, and in the end he wrapped himself up in his overcoat, rested his head on his suitcase, and told himself, as he fell asleep, that tomorrow would be another day. He woke with the first light of dawn. There was still water in the well, although the bucket had disappeared and the rope was rotten. I need to buy a rope and a bucket, he thought. For breakfast he ate what was left of a packet of peanuts he had bought on the train. He inspected the multitudinous low-ceilinged rooms of the ranch house. Then he set off for Capitán Jourdan, and was surprised to see rabbits but no cattle on the way. He observed them uneasily. Occasionally they would hop towards him, but he only had to wave his arms to make them disappear. Although he had never been particularly keen on guns, he would have been glad of one then. Apart from that, the walk was pleasant: the air was fresh, the sky was clear; it was neither hot nor cold. From time to time he spotted a tree all alone out on the plain, and the vision struck him as poetic, as if the tree and the austere scenery of the deserted countryside had been arranged just for him, and had been awaiting his arrival with an imperturbable patience.

None of the roads in Capitán Jourdan were paved and the housefronts were thickly coated with dust. As he entered the town, he saw a man asleep beside some flowerpots containing plastic flowers. My god, it's so shabby! he thought. The main square was broad, and the town hall, built of brick, gave the collection of squat, derelict buildings a vague air of civilisation. He asked a gardener who was sitting in the square smoking a cigarette where he could find a hardware store. The gardener looked at him curiously, then accompanied him to the door of the only hardware store in town. The owner, an Indian, sold him all the rope he had in stock: forty yards of braided hemp, which Pereda examined at length, as if looking for loose threads. Put it on my account, he said when he had decided what to buy. The Indian looked at him nonplussed. Whose account? he asked. Manuel Pereda's, said Pereda, as he piled up his new possessions in a corner of the store. Then he asked the Indian where he could buy a horse. There are no horses left here, he said, only rabbits. Pereda thought it was a joke and responded with a quick, dry laugh. The gardener, who was looking in from the threshold, said there might be a strawberry roan to be had at Don Dulce's ranch. Pereda asked him how he could get there, and the gardener walked a couple of blocks with him, to a vacant lot full of rubble. Beyond lay open country.

The ranch was called Mi Paraíso and it didn't seem to be as run down as Alamo Negro. A few chickens were pecking around in the yard. The door to the shed had been pulled off its hinges and someone had propped it against a wall nearby. Some Indian-looking kids were playing with bolas. A woman came out of the main house and said good afternoon. Pereda asked her for a glass of water. Between mouthfuls he asked if there was a horse for sale. You'll have to wait for the boss, said the woman, and went back into the house. Pereda sat down beside the well and kept himself busy brushing away the flies that were buzzing around everywhere, as if the yard were used for pickling meat, thought Pereda, although the only pickles he knew were the ones he used to buy many years ago at a store that imported them directly from England. After an hour, he heard the sound of a jeep and stood up.

Don Dulce was a little pink-faced guy, with blue eyes, wearing a short-sleeved shirt, even though, by the time he arrived, it was starting to get cold. From the jeep emerged an even shorter guy: a gaucho attired in baggy *bombachas* and a diaper-like *chiripá,* who threw Pereda a sidelong glance and started carrying rabbit skins into the shed. Pereda introduced himself. He said he was the owner of Alamo Negro and that he was planning to do some work on the ranch and needed to buy a horse. Don Dulce invited him to dinner. Around the table sat the host, the woman who had appeared earlier, the children, the gaucho, and Pereda. There was a fire in the hearth, not to heat the room but for grilling meat. The bread was hard and unleavened, the way the Jews make it, thought Pereda, remembering his Jewish wife with a twinge of nostalgia. But no one at Mi Paraíso seemed to be Jewish. Don Dulce spoke like a local, although Pereda did notice a few expressions that were typical of the Buenos Aires loud mouth, as if his host had grown up in Villa Luro and hadn't been living on the pampas all that long.

When it came to buying the horse, everything went smoothly. Choosing was not a problem, because there was only one horse for sale. When Pereda said he might need a month to pay, Don Dulce didn't object, although the gaucho, who hadn't said a word all through the meal, stared at the newcomer warily. They saddled the horse, showed the guest his way home, and said goodbye.

How long has it been since I rode a horse? Pereda wondered. For a few seconds he worried that his bones, accustomed to the comfort of Buenos Aires and its armchairs, might break under the strain. The night was dark as pitch or coal. Stupid expressions, thought Pereda. European nights might be pitch-dark or coal-black, but not American nights, which are dark like a void, where there's nothing to hold on to, no shelter from the elements, just empty, storm-whipped space, above and below. May the rain fall soft on you, he heard Don Dulce shout. God willing, he replied from the darkness.

On the way back to his ranch, he dozed off a couple of times. The first time he saw armchairs raining down over a city, which he eventually recognised as Buenos Aires. Suddenly the armchairs burst into flames, lighting up the city sky as they burned. The other time he saw himself on horseback, with his father, riding away from Alamo Negro. His father seemed to be sad. When will we come back? asked the young Pereda. Never again, Manuelito, said his father. He woke up from this second nap in one of the streets of Capitán Jourdan. He saw a corner store that was open. He heard voices, and someone strumming a guitar, tuning it but never settling on a particular song to play, just as he had read in Borges. For a moment he thought that his destiny, his screwed-up American destiny, would be to meet his death like Dahlman in 'The South', and it seemed wrong, partly because he now had debts to repay, and partly because he wasn't ready to die, although Pereda was aware that no one is ever ready for death. Seized by a sudden inspiration, he entered the store on horseback. Inside he found an old gaucho strumming the guitar, the barman, and three younger guys sitting at a table, who started when they saw the horse come in. Pereda was inwardly satisfied by the thought that the scene was like something from a story by di Benedetto. Nevertheless, he set his face and approached the zinc-topped bar. He ordered a glass of eau-de-vie, which he drank with one hand, while in the other he held his riding crop discreetly out of view, since he hadn't yet acquired the traditional sheath knife. He asked the barman to put the drink on his account, and on his way out, as he passed the young gauchos, he told them to move aside because he was going to spit. It was meant as a reaffirmation of authority, but before the gauchos could grasp what was happening, the virulent gob of phlegm had flown from his lips; they barely had time to jump. May the rain fall soft on you, he said, before disappearing into the darkness of Capitán Jourdan.

From then on, Pereda went into town each day on his horse, which he named José Bianco. He often went to buy tools with which to repair the ranch house, but he also passed the time of day chatting with the gardener, or with the keepers of the general store and the hardware store, whose livelihoods he diminished day by day, as he added to the accounts he had with each of them. Other gauchos and storekeepers soon joined in these conversations, and sometimes even children came to hear the stories Pereda told. The stories, of course, portrayed the teller in a favourable light, although they weren't exactly cheerful. For example he told them how he had once owned a horse very like José Bianco, which had been killed in a confrontation with the police. Luckily I was a judge, he said, and when the police come up against a judge or an ex-judge, they usually back off.

Police work's about order, he said, while judges defend justice. Do you see the difference, boys? The gauchos would usually nod, although not all of them were sure just what he was talking about.

Sometimes he went to the station, where his friend Severo would reminisce at length about their childhood pranks. Although Pereda was privately convinced that he couldn't have been as silly as he came across in those stories, he let Severo talk until he was tired or fell asleep, then walked out onto the platform to wait for the train and the letter it should have been bringing.

Finally the letter arrived. In it, his cook explained that life was hard in Buenos Aires, but that he shouldn't worry, because both she and the maid were going to the house every two days, and it was in perfect order. With the crisis, some apartments in the neighbourhood suddenly seemed to have given way to entropy, but his was as clean, as stately and as comfortable as ever, perhaps even more so, since the usual wear and tear had slowed down to a standstill. Then she went on to relate various pieces of news about the neighbours, gossip tinged with fatalism, since they all felt cheated and no one could see a light at the end of the tunnel. The cook said it was all down to the Peronists, that pack of thieves, while the maid was more sweeping: she blamed all the politicians, and the Argentine people in general; they'd been as docile as sheep, and now they were getting what they deserved. As to sending him money, both of them were looking into it, she assured him; the problem was, they still hadn't figured out how to make sure it wouldn't be filched by some racketeer on the way.

In the evening, as he was returning to Alamo Negro at a gallop, the lawyer could sometimes see a far-off village in ruins that didn't seem to have been there before. Sometimes a slender column of smoke rose from the village and dissipated in the vast sky over the plains. Occasionally he encountered the vehicle in which Don Dulce and his gaucho got around. They would stop to talk and smoke for a while, Don Dulce and the gaucho sitting in their jeep, the lawyer still mounted on José Bianco. Don Dulce was out after rabbits. Pereda once asked him how he hunted them, and Don Dulce told his gaucho to show the lawyer one of the traps, which was halfway between a bird cage and a rat trap. In any case, Pereda never saw a single rabbit in the jeep, only the skins, because the gaucho skinned them on the spot, beside the traps. After those chats, Pereda always felt that Don Dulce was somehow debasing the nation. Rabbit hunting! What sort of job is that for a gaucho? he asked himself. Then he would give his horse an affectionate pat, Come on, *che,* José Bianco, let's go, he'd say, and head back to the ranch.

One day the cook turned up. She had brought money for him. She rode behind him on José Bianco half way from the station to the ranch, then they walked the rest of the way, in silence, contemplating the plains. By this stage the ranch house was more comfortable than it had been when Pereda arrived; they ate rabbit stew, and then, by the light of an oil lamp, the cook handed over the money she had brought, and explained where it had come from, which objects from the house she had been forced to sell off at a fraction of their value. Pereda didn't even bother to count the bills. The next morning, when he woke up, he saw that the cook had worked all night cleaning up some of the rooms. He reproached her gently. Don Manuel, she said, it's like a pigsty here.

Two days later, in spite of the lawyer's entreaties, she took the train back to Buenos Aires. When I'm away from Buenos Aires I feel like another person, she explained to him as they waited on the platform, just the two of them. And I'm too old to become someone else. Women, they're all the same, thought Pereda. Everything is changing, the cook explained to him. The city was full of beggars, and respectable people were organising neighbourhood soup kitchens just to have something to put in their stomachs. There must have been ten different kinds of currency, not counting the official money. No one was bored. People were desperate, but not bored. As she spoke, Pereda was watching the rabbits that had appeared on the other side of the tracks. The rabbits looked at them, then bounded away across the plain. Sometimes it's as if the country round here were crawling with lice or fleas, thought the lawyer. With the money the cook had brought, he paid his debts and hired a pair of gauchos to repair the roof of the ranch house, which was falling in. The problem was that he knew next to nothing about carpentry, and the gauchos knew even less.

One was called José and must have been around seventy. He didn't have a horse. The other was called Campodónico and was probably younger, though maybe not. Both wore the traditional baggy *bombachas*, but their headgear consisted of caps they had made themselves from rabbit skins. Neither had a family, so after a while they both came to live at Alamo Negro. At night, by the light of a fire out in the open, Pereda whiled away the time recounting adventures that had taken

The Insufferable Gaucho

place exclusively in his imagination. He spoke to them of Argentina, Buenos Aires, and the pampas, and he asked them which one of the three they would choose. Argentina's like a novel, he said, a lie, or make-believe at best. Buenos Aires is full of crooks and loudmouths, a hellish place, with nothing to recommend it except the women, and some of the writers, but only a few. Ah, but the pampas – the pampas are eternal. A limitless cemetery, that's what they're like. Can you imagine that, boys, a limitless cemetery? The gauchos smiled and confessed that it was pretty hard to imagine something like that, since cemeteries are for humans, and although the number of humans is big, there's a limit to it. Ah, but the cemetery I'm talking about, said Pereda, is an exact copy of eternity.

With the money he had left, he went to Coronel Gutiérrez and bought himself a mare and a colt. The mare would let itself be ridden, but the colt was not much use for anything and had to be treated with extreme caution. Sometimes, in the evening, when he was sick of working or sitting around, Pereda went into Capitán Jourdan with his gauchos. He rode José Bianco; the gauchos rode the mare. When he entered the store a respectful hush would fall over the clients, some playing cards, others playing draughts. When the mayor, who was prone to depression, turned up, there would always be four brave volunteers for a game of Monopoly that lasted until dawn. The habit of playing games (not to speak of Monopoly) seemed ill bred and dishonourable to Pereda. A store is a place where people converse or listen in silence to the conversations of others, he thought. A store is like an empty classroom. A store is a smoky church.

Some nights, especially when gauchos from out of town or

some disoriented travelling salesman turned up, Pereda felt a powerful desire to start a fight. Nothing serious, just a scrap, but with real knives, not chalked sticks. Other nights he would fall asleep between his two gauchos and dream that his wife was leading their children by the hand and scolding him for the way he had let himself lapse into brutishness. And what about the rest of the country? replied the lawyer. But that's no excuse, *che*, rejoined Mrs Pereda, née Hirschman. At which point the lawyer was obliged to agree, with tears welling up in his eyes.

In general, however, his dreams were peaceful, and when he woke up in the morning he was in good spirits and keen to start work. Although, to tell the truth, not a lot of work was done at Alamo Negro. The repairing of the ranch house roof was a disaster. In order to start a kitchen garden, the lawyer and Campodónico bought seeds in Coronel Guttiérez, but the earth, it seemed, would accept no foreign seed. For a time, the lawyer tried to get the colt, which he called 'my stud horse', to cover the mare. If the mare had a filly, all the better. That way, he imagined, he could soon build up a breeding stock that would lead the recovery; but the colt didn't seem to be interested in covering the mare, and although he searched for miles around, Pereda couldn't find a sire, since the gauchos had sold their horses to the slaughterhouse, and now got around on foot, or on bicycles, or hitched rides on the endless dirt tracks of the pampas.

We have fallen, we're down, Pereda would say to his audience, but we can still pick ourselves up and go to our deaths like men. He too had to set rabbit traps to survive. In the evenings, when he left the house with his men, he would often let José and Campodónico empty the traps, along with a new recruit known as The Old Guy, while he set off alone for the ruined village. There he found some young people, younger than his gauchos, but so nervous and disinclined to converse that it wasn't even worth inviting them for a meal. The wire fences were still standing in some places. Occasionally he would go to the railway line and stay there a long time, without dismounting, he and José Bianco both chewing grass stalks, waiting for the train to pass. And often it didn't, as if that part of Argentina had been erased from memory as well as from the map.

One afternoon, as he was vainly attempting to get his colt to mount the mare, he saw a car driving over the plain, coming directly towards Alamo Negro. The car pulled up in the yard and four men got out. At first he didn't recognise his son. Nor did Bebe realise that the old guy in *bombachas* with a beard, long tangled hair, and a bare chest tanned by the sun was his father. Son of my soul, said Pereda, hugging him, blood of my blood, vindication of my days, and he could have gone on like that if Bebe hadn't stopped him to introduce his friends, two writers from Buenos Aires and the publisher Ibarrola, who loved books and nature, and had financed the trip. In honour of his son's guests, that night the lawyer had a big bonfire built in the yard and sent for the foremost of Capitán Jourdan's guitar-strumming gauchos, warning him beforehand that he was to do strictly that: strum, without playing any song in particular, in accordance with the country way.

Campodónico and José were dispatched to fetch ten litres of wine and a litre of eau-de-vie, which they brought back from Capitán Jourdan in the mayor's van. A good supply of rabbits was laid in, and one was roasted for each person present, although the the meat didn't seem to find much favour with the visitors from the city. That night there were more than thirty people gathered around the fire, besides Pereda's gauchos and his guests from Buenos Aires. Before the party began, Pereda announced that he didn't want any fighting or unruly behaviour, which was quite unnecessary, since the locals were peace-loving people who had to steel themselves to kill rabbits. All the same, the lawyer considered setting aside one of the multitudinous rooms so that people could lay down their knives, large and small, before taking part in the festivities, but on reflection he decided that such a measure really would be a little excessive.

By three in the morning the elders had set off back to Capitán Jourdan, and there were just a few young men left at the ranch, wondering what to do, since the food and drink had run out, and the guys from the city had already turned in. The next morning Bebe tried to convince his father to return to Buenos Aires with him. Things are gradually settling down, he said; personally he was doing all right. He gave his father a book, one of the many gifts he had brought, and told him that it had been published in Spain. Now I'm known throughout Latin America, he explained. But the lawyer had no idea what his son was talking about. He asked if he was married yet, and when Bebe said no, suggested he find himself an Indian woman and come to live at Alamo Negro.

An Indian woman, Bebe repeated in a tone of voice that struck the lawyer as wistful.

Among the gifts his son had brought was a Beretta 92 pistol with two clips and a box of ammunition. The lawyer looked at the pistol in amazement. Do you honestly think I'm going to need it? he asked. You never know. You're really on your own here, said Bebe. Later that morning they saddled up the mare for Ibarrola, who wanted to take a look at the countryside; Pereda accompanied him on José Bianco. For two hours, the publisher held forth in praise of the idyllic, unspoiled life, as he saw it, enjoyed by the inhabitants of Capitán Jourdan. When he spotted the first of the ruined houses, he broke into a gallop, but it was much further away than he had thought, and before he got there, a rabbit leaped up and bit him on the neck. The publisher's cry vanished at once into the vast open space.

From where he was, all Pereda saw was a dark shape springing from the ground, tracing an arc towards the publisher's head, and then disappearing. Dumb-ass Basque, he thought. He spurred José Bianco, and, approaching Ibarrola, saw that he was holding his neck with one hand and covering his face with the other. Without saying a word, Pereda removed the hand from Ibarrola's neck. There was a bleeding scratch under his ear. Pereda asked him if he had a handkerchief. The publisher replied in the affirmative, and only then did Pereda realise that he was crying. Put the handkerchief on the wound, he said. Then he took the mare's reins and they made their way to the ruined house. There was no one there; they didn't dismount. As they returned to the ranch, the handkerchief that Ibarrola was holding against the wound gradually turned red. They said nothing. When they got back, Pereda ordered his gauchos to strip the publisher to the waist, and they flung him onto a table in the yard. Pereda washed the wound, which he proceeded to cauterise with a knife heated until the blade was red-hot, then made a dressing with another handkerchief, held in place with a makeshift bandage: one of his old shirts, which he soaked in eau-de-vie, what little was left, more as a ritual than a sanitary measure, but it couldn't do any harm.

When Bebe and the two writers came back from a walk around Capitán Jourdan, they found Ibarrola still unconscious on the table, and Pereda sitting beside him in a chair, observing him intently like a medical student. Behind Pereda, equally absorbed by the sight of the wounded man, stood the ranch's three gauchos.

The sun was beating down mercilessly in the yard. Son of a bitch! shouted one of Bebe's friends, your dad's gone and killed our publisher. But the publisher wasn't dead, and made a full recovery, except for the scar, which he would later display with pride, explaining that it had been caused by the bite of a jumping snake and the subsequent cauterisation; he even said he felt better than ever, although he did return to Buenos Aires that night with the writers.

From then on, there were often visitors from the city. Sometimes Bebe came on his own, with his riding clothes and his notebooks, in which he wrote vaguely melancholic stories with vaguely crime-related plots. Sometimes he would come with Buenos Aires luminaries, usually writers, but quite often a painter, which pleased Pereda, since painters, for some reason, seemed to know much more about carpentry and bricklaying than the bunch of gauchos who hung around Alamo Negro all day like a bad smell.

On one occasion Bebe came with a psychiatrist. The psychiatrist was blonde and had steely blue eyes and high cheekbones, like an extra from the Ring cycle. The only problem with her, according to Pereda, was that she talked a lot. One morning he invited her to go for a ride. The psychiatrist accepted. He saddled up the mare, mounted José

Bianco, and they headed west. As they rode, the psychiatrist talked about her job in a Buenos Aires mental hospital. She told him (and the rabbits that surreptitiously accompanied them for parts of the way) that people were becoming more and more unbalanced – studies had proven it – which led the psychiatrist to conjecture that perhaps mental instability was not so much a disease as a stratum of normality, just below the surface of normality as it was commonly conceived. All this sounded like Chinese to Pereda, but intimidated as he was by the beauty of his son's guest, he refrained from saying so. At midday they stopped for a lunch of rabbit jerky and wine. The wine and the meat, a dark meat that shone like alabaster when touched by light and seemed to be literally seething with protein, fuelled the psychiatrist's poetic streak, and, as Pereda noticed out of the corner of his eye, prompted her to let her hair down.

She began quoting lines from Hernández and Lugones in a well-modulated voice. She wondered aloud where Sarmiento had gone wrong. She ran through lists of books and deeds while the horses trotted imperturbably westward, to places Pereda himself had never reached on previous excursions but was glad to visit in such fine although occasionally tiresome company. At about five in the afternoon, they spotted the shell of a ranch house on the horizon. Enthused, they spurred their mounts in that direction, but at six they were still not there, which led the psychiatrist to remark on how deceptive distances could be. When they finally arrived, five or six malnourished children came out to greet them, and a woman wearing a very wide skirt that bulged voluminously, as if there were some kind of animal under it, coiled around her legs. The children kept their eyes fixed on the psychiatrist, who adopted a maternal attitude, though not for long, since she soon noticed, as she later explained to Pereda, a malevolent intention in their gaze, a mischievous plan formulated, so she felt, in a language full of consonants, yelps, and grudges.

Pereda, who was coming to the conclusion that the psychiatrist was not entirely in her right mind, accepted the skirted woman's hospitality, and during the meal, which they ate in a room full of old photographs, he learned that the owners of the ranch had gone off to the city a long time ago (she couldn't say which city), and the labourers having ceased to receive their monthly pay-packet, had gradually drifted away too. The woman also told them about a river and flooding, although Pereda had no idea where the river could be, and no one in Capitán Jourdan had mentioned any kind of flooding. Predictably, they ate rabbit stew, which their hostess had prepared with an expert hand. As they were getting ready to go, Pereda pointed out the way to Alamo Negro, his ranch, in case they ever got tired of living out there. I don't pay much, but at least there's company, he said seriously, as if explaining that death came after life. Then he gathered the children around him and proceeded to dispense advice. When he had finished speaking, he saw that the psychiatrist and the skirted woman had fallen asleep on their chairs. Day was about to break when they left. The light of a full moon shimmered on the plain, and from time to time they saw a rabbit jump, but Pereda paid no attention, and after a long spell of silence he softly began to sing a song in French that his late wife had liked.

The song was about a pier and mist, and faithless lovers (as all lovers are in the end, he thought indulgently), and places that remain steadfastly faithful.

Sometimes, as he walked or rode José Bianco around the dubious boundaries of his ranch, Pereda thought that nothing would ever be the same unless the cattle returned. Cows, he shouted, where are you?

In winter, the skirted woman turned up at Alamo Negro with the children in tow, and things changed. She was known to some people in Capitán Jourdan and they were pleased to see her again. The woman didn't talk much but there could be no doubt that she worked harder than the six gauchos Pereda had on the payroll at the time, loosely speaking, since he often went for months without paying them. In any case, some of the gauchos had what could be called an idiosyncratic conception of time. They could adapt to a forty-day month without any major headaches. Or to a four-hundred-and-forty day year. None of them, in fact, Pereda included, wanted to think about time. By the fireside, some of the gauchos talked about electroshock therapy, while others spoke like professional sports commentators, except that they were commenting on a match played long ago, when they were twenty or thirty and belonged to some gang of hooligans. Sons of bitches, thought Pereda tenderly, with a manly sort of tenderness, of course.

One night, sick of hearing the old guys rambling on about psychiatric hospitals and slums where parents made their children go without milk so they could travel to support their soccer team in some historic match, he asked them about their political opinions. At first the gauchos were reluctant to talk about politics, but when he finally got them to open up, it turned out that, in one way or another, they were all nostalgic for General Perón.

This is where we part company, said Pereda, and pulled out his knife. For a few seconds he thought that the gauchos would do the same and his destiny would be sealed that night, but the old guys recoiled in fear and asked what he was doing, for God's sake. What had they done? What had got into him? The flickering fire threw tiger-like stripes of light across their faces, but, gripping his knife and trembling, Pereda felt that the shame of the nation or the continent had turned them into tame cats. That's why the cattle have been replaced by rabbits, he thought as he turned and walked back to his room.

I'd slaughter the lot of you if you weren't so pathetic, he shouted.

The next morning he was worried that the gauchos might have gone back to Capitán Jourdan, but they were all still there, working in the yard or drinking mate by the fire, as if nothing had happened. A few days later the skirted woman arrived from the ranch out west and Alamo Negro began to change for the better, starting with the food, because the woman knew ten different ways to cook a rabbit, and where to find herbs, and how to start a kitchen garden and grow some fresh vegetables.

One night the woman walked along the veranda and went into Pereda's room. She was wearing only a petticoat; the lawyer made space for her in the bed, and spent the rest of the night looking up at the ceiling and feeling that warm and unfamiliar body against his ribs. Day was breaking by the time he fell asleep, and when he woke up, the woman was gone. Got yourself shacked up, said Bebe when his father informed him. Only technically, the lawyer pointed out. By that stage, with money borrowed here and there, he had been able to enlarge the stables and acquire four cows. When he was bored of an afternoon, he would saddle up José Bianco and take the cows out for a walk. The rabbits, who had never seen a cow in their lives, stared in amazement.

Pereda and the cows looked like they were bound for the ends of the earth, but they had just gone out for a walk.

One morning a doctor and a nurse appeared at Alamo Negro. Having lost their jobs in Buenos Aires, they were working for a Spanish NGO, providing a mobile medical service. The doctor wanted to test the gauchos for hepatitis. When the pair came back a week later, Pereda did his best to put on a feast: rice and rabbit casserole. The doctor said it tasted better than *paella valenciana*, then proceeded to vaccinate all the gauchos free of charge. She gave the cook a bottle of pills and told her to make sure each child took one every morning. Before they left, Pereda asked how his folks were doing health-wise. They're anemic, said the doctor, but no one has Hepatitis B or C. That's a relief, said Pereda. Yes, I guess it is, said the doctor.

As they were getting ready to go, Pereda took a look inside their van. The back was a mess: sleeping bags and boxes full of first-aid supplies: medicines and disinfectants. Where are you going now? he asked. South, said the doctor. Her eyes were red and the lawyer couldn't tell if it was due to lack of sleep or to crying. As the van drove away raising a cloud of dust, he thought he would miss them.

That night he spoke to the gauchos gathered in the general store. I believe we are losing our memory, he said. And just as well too. For once, the gauchos looked at him as if they had a better grasp of what he was saying than he did himself. Shortly afterward, he received a letter from Bebe summoning him to Buenos Aires: he had to sign some papers so that his house could be sold. Should I take the train, Pereda wondered, or ride? That night he could hardly sleep. He imagined people thronging the sidewalks as he made his entry mounted on José Bianco. Cars stopping, dumbstruck policemen, a newspaper vendor smiling, his compatriots playing soccer in vacant lots with the parsimonious movements of the malnourished. Pereda's entry into Buenos Aires, as he imagined the scene, had the ambiance of Christ's entry into Jerusalem or Brussels as depicted by Ensor. All of us enter Jerusalem sooner or later, he thought as he tossed and turned. Every single one of us. And some never leave. But most do. And then we are seized and crucified. Especially the poor gauchos.

He also imagined a downtown street, the quintessential Buenos Aires street, with all the charms of the capital; he was riding along it on his trusty José Bianco, while from the windows above white flowers began to rain down. Who was throwing the flowers? He couldn't tell, since, like the street itself, the windows of the buildings remained empty. It must be the dead, Pereda supposed drowsily. The dead of Jerusalem and the dead of Buenos Aires.

The next morning he spoke with the skirted woman and the gauchos and told them he would be away for a while. None of them said anything, although that night, at dinner, the woman asked if he was going to Buenos Aires. Pereda nodded. Then take care and may the rain fall soft on you, said the woman.

Two days later, he took the train and went back the way he had come more than three years earlier. When he arrived at

The Insufferable Gaucho

Constitución station, a few people stared as if he were wearing fancy dress, but most were not particularly perturbed by an old man attired like a cross between a gaucho and a rabbit trapper. The taxi driver who took him to his apartment enquired where he was from, and when Pereda, lost in his own ruminations, failed to answer, asked if he spoke Spanish. By way of reply, Pereda pulled out his knife and proceeded to trim his nails, which were as long as a wild cat's.

No one answered the door. The keys were under the mat; he went in. The apartment seemed clean, perhaps even too clean – it smelled of mothballs. Feeling exhausted, Pereda trudged to his bedroom and flopped onto the bed without taking off his boots. When he woke up it was dark. He went into the living room without switching on any lights, and called his cook. First he spoke to her husband, who wanted to know who was calling, and didn't sound very convinced when he identified himself. Then the cook came on. I'm in Buenos Aires, Estela, he said. She didn't seem surprised. When asked if she was happy to know that he was back home, she said: There's always something unexpected happening here. Then he tried to call his maid, but an impersonal, female voice informed him that the number he had dialled was not in service. Feeling dispirited and perhaps hungry, he tried to remember the faces of his employees, but the images he could summon were vague: shadows moving in the corridor, a commotion of clean laundry, murmurs and hushed voices.

The amazing thing is that I can remember their phone numbers, thought Pereda, sitting in the dark living room of his apartment. A little later on he went out. Wandering aimlessly, or so he thought, he ended up at the cafe where Bebe used to meet his artistic and literary friends. From the street he looked into the spacious, well-lit, bustling interior. Bebe and an old man (an old man like me! thought Pereda) were presiding over one of the most animated tables. At another, closer to the window through which Pereda was spying, he noticed a group of writers who looked more like advertising executives. One of them, with an adolescent air, although he was at least fifty and maybe even over sixty, kept putting a white powder up his nose and holding forth about world literature. Suddenly, the eyes of the pseudo-adolescent met Pereda's. For a moment their gazes locked, as if, for each of them, the presence of the other were a gash in the ambient reality. Resolutely and with surprising agility, the writer with the adolescent air sprang to his feet and rushed out into the street. Before Pereda knew what was going on, the writer was upon him.

What are you staring at? he demanded, brushing remnants of white powder from his nose. Pereda looked him up and down. The writer was taller and slimmer and possibly stronger than he was. What are you staring at, you rude old fool? What are you staring at? The pseudo-adolescent's gang was looking on, following the scene as if something similar happened every night.

Pereda realised that he had grasped his knife, and let himself go. He took a step forward and, without anyone noticing that he was armed, planted the point of the blade, though not deeply, in his opponent's groin. Later, he would remember the look of surprise on the writer's face, in which terror was blended with something like reproof, and the words with which he groped for an explanation (Hey, what are you doing, you asshole?), as if there were any way to explain fever and revulsion.

I think you need a napkin, Pereda remarked in a clear strong voice, pointing at his adversary's blood-stained crotch. Mother, said the coke-head, looking down. When he looked up again, he was surrounded by friends and colleagues, but Pereda was gone.

What should I do, the lawyer wondered as he roamed through his beloved city, finding it strange and familiar, marvellous and pathetic. Do I stay in Buenos Aires and become a champion of justice, or go back to the pampas, where I don't belong, and try to do something useful . . . I don't know, something with the rabbits, maybe, or the locals, those poor gauchos who accept me and put up with me and never complain? The shadows of the city declined to provide an answer. Keeping quiet, as usual, Pereda thought reproachfully. But when the day began to dawn, he decided to go back.

Police Rat

for Robert Amutio and Chris Andrews

My name is José, though people call me Pepe, and some, usually those who don't know me well, or with whom I'm not on familiar terms, call me Pepe the Cop. Pepe is a benign, well-meaning, genial diminutive, neither scornful nor flattering, and yet the appellation does imply, if I can put it this way, a certain affection, something more than detached respect. Then there's the other name, the alias, the tail or the hump that I lug around cheerfully, without taking offence, partly because it's never or almost never used in my presence. Pepe the Cop: it's like tossing affection and fear, desire and abuse into the same dark bag. Where does the word *cop* come from? It comes from *copper,* he who cops or caps, that is captures, takes hold of, nabs, in other words, he who has the authority to arrest and hold, who doesn't have to answer to anyone, who has *impunity*. And they call me Pepe the Cop because that's exactly what I am; it's a job like any other, but few people are prepared to take it on. If I'd known what I know now when I joined the force, I wouldn't have been prepared to take it on either. What made me join the police force? That's a question I've often asked myself, especially lately, and I can't come up with a convincing answer.

Police Rat

I was probably dimmer than most in my youth. Maybe I was disappointed in love (though I can't actually recall being in love at the time), or maybe it was fate; maybe I realised I was different, and looked for a solitary job, a job that would allow me to spend hour after hour in the most absolute solitude, but would, at the same time, be of some practical use, so I wouldn't be a burden on anyone.

In any case, there was a vacancy for a police officer and I applied and the bosses took a look at me, and in less than half a minute the job was mine. One of them at least, and maybe the others as well, already knew that I was one of Josephine the Singer's nephews, although they were careful not to go spreading it around. My brothers and cousins – the other nephews – were normal in every way, and happy. I was happy too in my way, but it was obvious that I was related to Josephine, that I belonged to her line. Maybe that influenced the bosses' decision to give me the job. Or not – maybe I was just the first to apply. Maybe they thought no one else would, and if they made me wait, I'd change my mind. I really can't say. All I know for sure is that I joined the force and from the very first day I spent my time wandering through the sewers, sometimes the main ones, where the water flows, sometimes the branch sewers, where we are constantly digging tunnels to gain access to new food sources or provide escape routes or link up with labyrinths that seem, at first glance, to serve no purpose, and yet all those byways go to make up the network in which our people circulate and survive.

Sometimes, partly because it was one of my duties and partly because I was bored, I'd leave the main sewers and the branch ones too and go into the dead sewers, conduits frequented only by our explorers and traders, usually on their own, but occasionally accompanied by their spouses and obedient offspring. There was nothing in there, as a rule, just terrifying noises, but sometimes, as I made my way cautiously through that hostile territory, I would come across the body of an explorer or the bodies of a trader and his young children. In the early days, when I was still raw, those discoveries terrified me; I would be so disturbed it was as if I became someone else. What I would do was carry the body out from the dead sewer to the police outpost, which was always deserted, and there I'd try to determine the cause of death as well as I could with the means at my disposal. Then I would go to fetch the coroner and, if he was in the mood, he'd get dressed or change his clothes, grab his bag and accompany me to the outpost. Once we were there, I'd leave him alone with the corpse or the corpses and go out again. When our police officers discover a body, instead of returning to the scene of the crime, they generally make a vain effort to mix with civilians, working alongside them and participating in their conversations, but I'm different, I don't mind going back to inspect the crime scene and look for details that might have escaped my notice, and retrace the poor victims' steps or sniff my way, cautiously of course, back up the tunnel from which the attack had been launched.

After a few hours I'd return to the outpost and find the coroner's note tacked to the wall. Causes of death: slit throats, loss of blood, broken necks; and there were often lacerations to the paws – our kind never give in without a fight, we struggle to the last. The killer was usually some carnivore that had strayed into the sewers, a snake, sometimes even a blind alligator. There was no point pursuing them; most died of hunger before long anyway.

When I took a break I'd seek out the company of other

police officers. I met one who was very old and withered by age and work; he had known my aunt and liked to talk about her. Nobody understood Josephine, he said, but everyone loved her or pretended to, and she was happy – or pretended to be. Those words were Chinese to me, like a lot of what that old officer said. I've never understood music; it's not an art that we practise, except on rare occasions. In fact, we don't practise (and therefore don't understand) any of the arts, really. Every now and then a rat who paints, for example, will appear in our midst, or a rat who writes poems and takes it into his head to recite them. As a general rule, we don't make fun of those individuals. On the contrary, we pity them, because we know that they're condemned to solitude. Why? Well, because creating works of art and contemplating them are activities in which our people as a rule are unable to take part, and the exceptions, the *mavericks*, are very few, so if, for example, a poet or even just a reciter of poetry comes along, it's most unlikely that another poet or reciter will be born in the same generation, which means that the poet may never encounter the only individual capable of appreciating his efforts. Which is not to say that we won't interrupt our daily occupations to listen to the poet or applaud him, or even move that the reciter be granted a pension. On the contrary, we do everything in our power – or rather what little we can – to provide the *maverick* with a simulation of understanding and affection, since we know that, fundamentally, affection is what he or she requires. Any simulation, however, collapses eventually, like a house of cards. We live in a collective, and what the collective depends on is, above all, the daily labour, the ceaseless activity of each of its members, working towards a goal that transcends our individual aspirations but is nevertheless the only guarantee of our existence as individuals.

Of all the artists we have known, or at least of those who remain in our memories like skeletal question marks, the greatest was, without a doubt, my aunt Josephine. Great in the sense that she made exceptional demands on us; incommensurably great in the sense that our community acquiesced or pretended to acquiesce to her whims.

The old police officer liked to talk about her, but his memories, I soon realised, were as flimsy as a cigarette paper. Sometimes he said that Josephine was fat and tyrannical, and that dealing with her required enormous patience or an enormous sense of sacrifice, two not unrelated virtues, both quite common among us. Sometimes, however, by contrast, he said that all he had glimpsed of Josephine – he'd have been an adolescent, just starting out in the force – was a shadow, a tremulous shadow, trailing a range of odd squeaking noises, which constituted, at the time, the entirety of her repertoire, yet could, if not transport her listeners, certainly plunge some of those in the front row into a state of extreme sadness. Those rats and mice, of whom we have no record now, are perhaps the only ones to have glimpsed something in my aunt's musical art. But what? They probably didn't know themselves. Something indefinite, a lake of emptiness. Something resembling the desire to eat, perhaps, or the need to fuck, or the longing for sleep that sometimes overtakes us, since those who work without respite must at least sleep from time to time, especially in winter, when the temperature falls, as they say the leaves fall from the trees in the outside world, and our chilled bodies yearn for a warm corner to share with our kind, a burrow full of hot fur and the familiar movements and sounds – such as they are, neither coarse nor gracious – of our everyday nocturnal life, or the life that we call nocturnal for the sake of convenience.

The difficulty of finding warm places to sleep is one of the main disadvantages of being a police officer. We generally sleep alone, in makeshift holes, sometimes in unfamiliar territory, although of course, whenever possible, we try to find an alternative. Sometimes, but not very often, we curl up in holes that we share with other police, all eyes shut, ears and noses on alert. And sometimes we go to the sleeping quarters of those who, for one reason or another, live along the perimeter. As you would expect, they are quite unperturbed by our presence. Sometimes we say goodnight before falling exhausted into a warm and restorative sleep. Sometimes we simply mumble our names; our hosts know who we are and know they have nothing to fear from us. They treat us well. They don't make a fuss or show any sign of joy, but they don't throw us out of their burrows. Occasionally someone will say, in a voice still thick with sleep, Pepe the Cop, and I will reply, Yes, yes, good night. After a few hours, however, while all the others are still sleeping, I get up and start again, because police work is never done, and our hours of sleep have to be fitted in around the incessant demands of the job. Patrolling the sewers is a task that requires the utmost concentration. Generally we don't see or meet with anyone; we can do the rounds of the main and branch sewers, and go into the disused tunnels originally dug by our people, all without coming across a single living being.

We do, however, glimpse shadows, and hear noises – objects falling into the water, distant squeaking. At the begining, when you're new to the job, you're hypersensitive to those noises and you live in a state of perpetual fright. As time goes by, however, you grow accustomed to them, and although you try to stay alert, you lose the fear, or build it into the daily routine, which is the same as losing it, in the end. There are even police officers who have slept in the dead sewers. I have never met one personally, but the old guys often tell stories in which an officer, back in the old days, of course, overtaken by fatigue, would curl up and go to sleep in a dead sewer. How seriously should we take those stories? I don't know. No police officer today would dare to do such a thing. The dead sewers are places that have been forgotten for one reason or another. When the tunnel-diggers reach a dead sewer, they block the tunnel. The water in them barely flows at all, so the putrefaction is almost unbearable. It is safe to say that our people only use the dead sewers to flee from one zone to another. The quickest way to get into them is by swimming, but swimming in such places involves greater risks than we are usually prepared to take.

It was in a dead sewer that my investigation began. A group of our pioneers who, over time, had multiplied and settled just beyond the perimeter came and told me that the daughter of one of the older rats had disappeared. While half the group worked, the other half went looking for this girl, who was called Elisa, and who, according to her relatives and friends, was very beautiful and strong, as well as possessing a lively intelligence. I wasn't sure exactly what possessing a lively intelligence meant. I associated it vaguely with cheerfulness, but not curiosity. I was tired that day, and after examining the area in the company of one of the missing girl's relatives, I conjectured that the unfortunate Elisa had been the victim of some predator roaming in the vicinity of the new colony. I looked for traces of the predator. All I found were old tracks, which showed that other creatures had passed that way, before the arrival of our pioneers.

Finally I discovered a trail of fresh blood. I told Elisa's relative to go back to the burrow and I continued on my own. The trail of blood was curious: it kept stopping at the edge of a canal, but then reappearing a few yards further on (and sometimes *many* yards further), always on the same side, not the far side, as one might have expected. Whatever had left that trail clearly wasn't trying to cross the canal, so why had it kept getting into the water? In any case, the trail itself was barely detectable, so the precautions taken by the predator, whatever it was, seemed, at first, to be excessive. After a while I came to a dead sewer.

I got into the water there, and swam towards a bank of accumulated rotting trash, and when I reached it I had to climb up a beach of filth. Beyond the bank, above water level, I could see the thick bars at the top of the sewer's entrance. For a moment I was afraid I might find the predator huddled in some corner, feasting on the body of the hapless Elisa. But I could hear nothing, so I kept going.

A few minutes later, among cardboard boxes and old food cans, I found the girl's body left in one of the few relatively dry parts of the sewer.

Elisa's neck was torn open. Apart from that, I couldn't see any other wound. In one of the cans I found the remains of a baby rat. I examined them: dead for at least a month. I searched the surroundings but couldn't detect the slightest trace of the predator. The baby's corpse was complete. The only wound on poor Elisa's body was the one that had killed her. I began to think that perhaps it hadn't been a predator.

Then I put the girl on my back and picked up the baby in my mouth, trying not to damage his skin with my sharp teeth. I retreated from the dead sewer and returned to the pioneers' burrow. Elisa's mother was large and strong, one of those specimens who can face up to a cat, but when she saw the body of her daughter, she burst into long sobs that made her companions blush. I showed them the body of the baby and asked them if they knew anything about him. No one knew anything, no child had been lost. I said that I had to take both bodies to the station. I asked for help. The mother carried Elisa's body. I carried the baby. When we left, the pioneers returned to work, digging tunnels, looking for food.

This time I went to fetch the coroner and stayed with him until he finished examining both bodies. Elisa's mother, asleep beside us, was seized from time to time by dreams, which wrested incomprehensible and incoherent words from her. After three hours the coroner had decided what he was going to tell me; it was what I had been afraid to imagine. The baby had died of hunger; Elisa had died from the wound to her throat. I asked him if that wound could have been inflicted by a snake. I don't think so, said the coroner, unless it's a new kind of snake. I asked him if the wound could have been inflicted by a blind alligator. Impossible, said the coroner. Maybe a weasel, he said. Weasels have been seen in the sewers recently. Scared to death, I said. That's true, replied the coroner. Most of them die of hunger. They get lost, they drown, they're eaten by alligators. We can forget the weasels, said the coroner. Then I asked him if Elisa had struggled with her killer. The coroner looked at the girl's corpse for a long time. No, he concluded. That's what I thought, I said. While we were talking, another police officer appeared. His rounds, as opposed to mine, had been quite uneventful. We woke Elisa's mother. The coroner said goodbye. Is it all over? asked the mother. It's all over, I replied. She thanked us and left. I asked my colleague to help me get rid of Elisa's corpse.

The two of us took it to a canal where the current was strong and threw it in. Why don't you throw out the baby's body too? asked my colleague. I don't know, I said, I want to examine it, maybe we missed something. Then he went back to his beat and I went back to mine. I asked every rat I met the same question: Have you heard anything about a missing baby? I got all sorts of answers, but in general our people look after their young, and what they told me was all second-hand. My rounds took me back to the perimeter. The pioneers were working on a tunnel, all of them, including Elisa's mother, whose bulky, greasy body could barely squeeze through the crack, but her teeth and claws were still the best for digging.

I decided to go back to the dead sewer and try to see what it was that I had missed. I looked for tracks but couldn't find any. Signs of violence. Signs of life. The baby hadn't made its own way into the sewer, that much was obvious. I looked for food scraps, traces of dried shit, a burrow, all in vain.

Suddenly I heard a faint splashing. I hid. After a while I saw a white snake break the surface of the water. It was thick and must have been a yard long. I saw it dive and resurface a couple of times. Then it emerged cautiously from the water and scaled the bank, making a hissing sound like a leaking gas pipe. For our people, that snake was as lethal as gas. It approached my hiding place. Coming from that direction, it couldn't attack directly, which meant, in principle, that I had time to escape (but once in the water I would be easy prey) or sink my teeth into its neck. It was only when the snake went away without any sign of having seen me that I realised it was blind, a descendant of those pet snakes that humans flush down the toilet when they get tired of them. For a moment I felt sorry for it. And I celebrated my good luck in an indirect way. I imagined the snake's parents or great-great-grandparents descending through the infinite network of sewer pipes; I imagined their bewilderment in the darkness of the sewers, not knowing what to do, resigned to death or suffering, and I imagined the few that survived, adapting themselves to an infernal diet, exercising their power, sleeping and dying in that endless winter.

Fear stimulates the imagination, it seems. When the snake was gone, I resumed my methodical search of the dead sewer. I didn't find anything out of the ordinary. The next day I talked with the coroner again. I asked him to take another look at the baby's corpse. At first he looked at me as if I'd gone insane. Haven't you got rid of it? he asked. No, I said, I want you to check it over one more time. Eventually he promised he would, as long as he didn't have too much work that day. As I did my rounds, waiting for the coroner's final report, I kept looking for a family that had lost a baby in the previous month. Unfortunately, the work we do, especially those who live near the perimeter, keeps us constantly on the move, and by then the mother of the dead baby could well have been digging tunnels or searching for food several miles away. Unsurprisingly, my enquiries didn't yield any promising leads.

When I returned to the station I found a note from the coroner – and another from my commanding officer, asking me why I still hadn't got rid of the baby's corpse. The coroner's note confirmed his earlier conclusion: there were no wounds; the cause of death had been hunger and possibly also exposure to the cold. The little ones are particularly vulnerable to harsh environmental conditions. I thought about it long and hard. The baby must have cried itself hoarse, as any baby would in a situation like that. Surely his cries would have attracted a predator? Why hadn't they? The killer must have snatched the baby, then used back ways to reach the dead sewer. And there, he had left the baby alone and waited for him to die, of natural causes, as it were. Could it have been the baby-snatcher who later killed Elisa? Yes, that was the most likely scenario.

Then a question occurred to me, something I hadn't asked the coroner, so I got up and went looking for him. On the way, I saw many rats who seemed carefree or playful or preoccupied with their own problems, scurrying in one direction or the other. Some of them greeted me warmly. Someone said, Look, there goes Pepe the Cop. The only thing I could feel was the sweat beginning to soak all through my fur, as if I'd just crawled out of the stagnant waters of a dead sewer.

I found the coroner sleeping alongside five or six other rats, all of them, to judge from their weariness, doctors or medical students. When I roused him from his sleep he looked at me as if he didn't know who I was. How many days did he take to die? I asked him. José, is that you? asked the coroner. What do you want? How many days does it take a baby to die of hunger? We left the burrow. Why did I ever become a pathologist? said the coroner. Then he thought for a while. It depends on the baby's constitution. Two days or less in some cases, but a plump, well-nourished baby could last five days or more. And without drinking? I asked. A bit less, said the coroner. Then he added: I don't know what you're trying to get at. Did he die of hunger or thirst? I asked. Hunger. Are you sure? As sure as you can be in a case like this, said the coroner.

Back at the station I got to thinking: the baby had been taken a month ago and probably took three or four days to die. He must have been crying all that time. And yet the noise hadn't attracted any predators. I returned to the dead sewer once again. This time I knew what I was looking for and it didn't take me long to find it: a gag. All the time he was dying, the baby had been gagged. No, not *all* the time. Every now and then the killer had taken off the gag and given the baby a drink, or maybe left it on, but soaked the cloth with water. I picked up what was left of the gag and got out of that dead sewer.

The coroner was waiting for me at the station. What did you find there, Pepe? he asked when he saw me. The gag, I said, handing him the scrap of dirty cloth. The coroner examined it for a few seconds, without touching it. Is the baby's body still here? he asked me. Get rid of it, he said, people are starting to talk about the way you're behaving. Talk about or criticise? I asked. It comes to the same thing, said the coroner before he left. I didn't feel up to working, but I pulled myself together and went out. Apart from the usual accidents, which can be relied upon to blight everything we undertake, it was a routine beat like any other. When I returned to the station, after hours of exhausting work, I got rid of the baby's body. For days there were no new developments. There were attacks by predators, accidents, old tunnels collapsed, several of our number were killed by a poison before we could find a way to neutralise it. Our history consists of the various ways we find to elude the traps that open endlessly before us. Routine and mettle. Recovering bodies and recording incidents. Identical, calm days. Until I found the bodies of two young rats, a female and a male.

I had heard they were missing on my rounds of the tunnels. The parents weren't worried; they thought the young couple had probably decided to go and live together in a different burrow. But as I was leaving, not overly preoccupied by the double disappearance, someone who had been friends with them both told me that neither the young Eustaquio nor the young Marisa had ever expressed any such wish. They're just friends, good friends, which is remarkable given Eustaquio's peculiarity. And what kind of peculiarity is that? I asked. He composes and declaims verse, said the friend (so he was obviously unfit for work). And what about Marisa? Not her, said the friend. What do you mean, not her? I asked. She doesn't have any peculiarity like that. To another police officer, these details would have seemed irrelevant. But my instincts were alerted. I asked if there was a dead sewer anywhere near the burrow. They told me that the closest one was a mile away, at a lower level. I set off in that direction. Along the way I came across an old rat followed by a group of youngsters. The old guy was warning them about weasels. We said hello. He was a teacher leading an excursion. The youngsters weren't ready yet for work, but nearly. I asked them if they'd noticed anything strange in the course of their outing. Everything is strange, shouted the old guy, as we went off in opposite directions, strange is normal, fever is health, poison is food. Then he burst into cheerful laughter, which went on ringing in my ears, even when I turned into another passage.

After a while I came to the dead sewer. Sewers in which

the water is stagnant are all pretty much the same, but I can usually tell, with a fair degree of certainty, whether or not I've been in a particular dead sewer before. That one was unfamiliar. I examined the entrance for a while, looking for a dry way in. Then I jumped into the water and swam. As I drew closer I thought I could see waves coming from an island of detritus. Naturally, I was worried about running into a snake, and I swam towards the island as quickly as I could. The ground there was soft; I sunk into a whitish mud up to my knees. The smell was the same as in all the dead sewers, not decomposing matter so much as the inner essence of decomposition. I made my way slowly from island to island. Occasionally I had the impression that something was clutching at my feet, but it was only trash. On the last island I found the bodies. There was only one wound on young Eustaquio's body: his throat was torn open. It was clear that young Marisa, however, had put up a fight. Her skin was covered with bites. I found blood on her teeth and claws, from which it was simple to deduce that the killer had been wounded. I struggled with the bodies one at a time, and finally got them out of the sewer. Then I tried to transport them to the nearest settlement, carrying one for fifty yards, putting it down, going back for the other. At one point, as I was going back for young Marisa's body, I saw a white snake that had come out of the canal and was heading towards her. I froze. The snake wrapped itself twice around her body, then crushed it. When it began to swallow her, I turned and ran to where I'd left Eustaquio. I wanted to scream. But I didn't even let out a whimper.

From that day on, I intensified my investigations. I was no longer satisfied with routine police work: patrolling the perimeter and dealing with problems that anyone with a modicum of common sense could solve. Every day I went out to the furthest burrows. I engaged their inhabitants in the most trivial conversations. I discovered a colony of rat-moles living among us, performing the lowliest tasks. I met an old white mouse, a white mouse who couldn't remember his age. In his youth he had been inoculated with a contagious disease, along with many of his kind, white mice who had been imprisoned and then released into the sewers in the hope of killing us all. Many died, said the white mouse, who could barely move, but the black rats and the white mice interbred, we fucked like crazy (as only those who are close to death can fuck) and in the end not only did the black rats become immune, but a new species also emerged: brown rats, resistant to any infection, any alien virus.

I liked that old white mouse who was born, so he said, in a laboratory on the surface. The light is blinding up there, he said, so bright that the surface dwellers don't even appreciate it. Have you been to the sewer mouths, Pepe? Yes, once or twice, I replied. So you've seen the river that the sewers all flow into, you've seen the reeds, the pale sand? Yes, but always at night, I replied. So you've seen the moonlight shimmering on the river? I didn't really notice the moonlight. What did you notice, then, Pepe? The barking of the dogs, the packs of dogs that live by the river. The moonlight too, I admitted, but I couldn't really enjoy the view. The moon is exquisite, said the white mouse; if someone were to ask me where I'd like to live, I would reply without hesitation: the moon.

Like a moon-dweller I patrolled the sewers and underground drains. After a while I found another victim. As before, the killer had left the body in a dead sewer. I picked it up and carried it to the station. That night I spoke with the coroner again. I pointed out the similarity between the tear in the throat and the other victims' wounds. It could be a coincidence, he said. And whatever's doing this doesn't eat them, I said. The coroner examined the body. Look at the wound, I said. Tell me what kind of teeth rip the skin like that. Any kind, any kind, said the coroner. No, not any kind, look carefully. What do you want me to say? said the coroner. The truth, I said. And what is the truth, in your opinion? I think these wounds were made by a rat, I said. But rats don't kill rats, said the coroner, looking at the body again. This one does, I said. Then I went to work and when I returned to the station I found the coroner and the chief commissioner waiting for me. The commissioner didn't beat around the bush. He asked me where I'd got the crazy idea that a rat had been responsible for the crimes. He wanted to know if I had shared my suspicions with anyone else. He warned me not to. Stop fantasising, Pepe, he said, and concentrate on doing your job. Real life is complicated enough without inventing unreal things that are bound to throw it out of joint. I was dead tired; I asked him what he meant by *out of joint*. I mean, said the commissioner, looking at the coroner as if to seek his approval and adopting a deep and gentle tone of voice, that in life, especially if it's short, as our lives unfortunately are, we should strive for order, not disorder, and especially not an imaginary disorder. The coroner looked at me gravely and nodded. I nodded too.

But I remained alert. For several days the killer seemed to have disappeared. Every time I went to the perimeter and made contact with a new colony, I asked about the first victim, the baby who had died of hunger. Finally an old explorer told me about a mother who had lost her baby. They thought it had fallen into the canal or been taken by a predator. But since there were many children in that group and only a few adults, they didn't spend a long time looking for the baby. Shortly afterward, they moved to the northern sewers, near a big well, and the explorer lost touch with them. When I had some time to spare, I went looking for that group. I knew they would have multiplied since the baby's disappearance; the children would have grown up, and perhaps they would have forgotten. But if I was lucky enough to find the baby's mother, she would still be able to tell me something. The killer, meanwhile, was on the loose. One night I found a body in the morgue with the killer's signature wound: the throat was torn open, almost neatly. I spoke with the police officer who had found the body. I asked him if he thought it had been a predator. What else could it be? he said. You think it was an accident, do you, Pepe? An accident, I thought. A permanent accident. I asked him where he had found the body. In a dead sewer down south, he replied. I suggested that he keep an eye on the dead sewers in that sector. Why? he wanted to know. Because you never know what you'll find there. He looked at me as if I were crazy. You're tired, he said, let's get some sleep. We went to the station's sleeping room. The air was warm. Another police rat was snoring in there. Good night, said my colleague. Good night, I said, but I couldn't sleep. I started thinking about the killer's movements, the way he sometimes struck in the north and sometimes in the south. After tossing and turning for a while I got up.

I headed north, stumbling along. On the way I came across some rats who were setting off to work in the dim tunnels;

they were confident and resolute. I heard some youngsters saying, Pepe the Cop, Pepe the Cop, then laughing, as if my nickname were the funniest joke in the world. Or maybe they were laughing for some other reason. In any case I didn't stop.

Gradually the tunnels were all deserted. Only now and then did I encounter a pair of rats or hear them going about their business down other tunnels, or glimpse their shadows huddled around something that could have been food, or poison. After a while, the noises stopped and I could hear only the sound of my heart and the dripping that never ceases in our world. When I came to the big well, the reek of death made me tread even more warily. Half consumed by maggots, the carcasses of two average-size dogs lay there, rigid, paws sticking up.

The colony of rats I'd been looking for was also exploiting the canine remains, a little further on. They were living near the sewer mouth, with all the dangers that entails, but also the advantage of extra food, which is never scarce on the frontier. I found them gathered in a small open space. They were big and fat and their coats were glossy. They had the serious expression of those who live in constant danger. When I told them I was a police officer, a suspicious look came into their eyes. When I told them I was looking for a rat who had lost her baby, no one answered, but from their expressions I could tell straightaway that my search, or that part of it at least, was over. Then I described the baby, his age, the dead sewer where I had found him, the way he had died. One of the rats said that the baby was her son. What do you want? asked the others.

Justice, I said. I'm looking for the killer.

The oldest rat, with a scar-covered hide, asked me, puffing

like a bellows, if I thought the killer was one of them. It could be, I said. A rat? she asked. It could be. The mother said her baby used to go out alone. But he couldn't have got into a dead sewer alone, I replied. Maybe he was taken by a predator, said a young rat. A predator would have eaten the body. This baby was killed for pleasure, not food.

As I'd expected, they all shook their heads. It's unthinkable, they said. There's no way one of us, however crazy, could be capable of something like that. Still smarting from the police commissioner's words, I judged it wiser not to contradict them. I nudged the mother to an out-of-the-way place and tried to console her, although the truth is that after three months – that was how long it had been – the pain of the loss had considerably diminished. She told me that she had other children, some grown up and hard for her to recognise, and some younger than the one who had died, who were already working and foraging successfully on their own. Nevertheless, I tried to get her to remember the day when the baby had disappeared. At first she was confused. She got the days mixed up; she even mixed up her babies. Alarmed by this, I asked her if she had lost more than one, but she reassured me, saying, No, babies do get lost, though usually only for a few hours, and they either come back to the burrow on their own, or are found when a member of the group hears them crying. Your son cried too, I said, slightly annoyed by her self-satisfied expression, but the killer kept him gagged most of the time.

She didn't seem moved, so I went back to the day of the baby's disappearance. We weren't living here, she said, we were in a drain in the interior. A group of explorers was living nearby; they had been the first to settle in the area, and then another group came, a bigger one, and we decided to move; we had no alternative really, apart from wandering around the tunnels. I pointed out that in spite of all this, the children were well nourished. There wasn't a shortage of food, but we had to go and search for it outside. The explorers had dug tunnels that led directly to the upper regions, and no poison or traps could stop us. All the groups went up to the surface twice a day, at least; there were rats who spent whole days up there, wandering through the old half-ruined buildings, using the cavities in the walls to get around, and there were some who never came back.

I asked her if they were outside the day her baby disappeared. We were working in the tunnels, some were sleeping, and there were probably some outside as well, she replied. I asked her if she'd noticed anything strange about anyone in the group. Strange? Abnormal behavior or attitudes; long, unexplained absences. No, she said, as you should know, the way we behave depends on the situation; we try to adapt to it as quickly and as fully as possible. Shortly after the baby's disappearance, in any case, the group set off to find a safer area. I could tell I wouldn't get anything more out of that simple, hard-working rat. I said goodbye to the group and left the drain they were using as their burrow.

But I didn't return to the station that day. Halfway there, when I was sure no one had followed me, I doubled back and went looking for a dead sewer near the drain. After a while I found one. It was small and the stench wasn't overpowering. I examined it thoroughly. The rat I was looking for didn't seem to have used that place. Nor did I find signs of predators. Although there wasn't a dry place anywhere, I decided to stay. In order to make myself a little more comfortable, I gathered what pieces of damp cardboard and plastic I could find and settled myself on them. I imagined the warmth of my fur against the damp materials producing little clouds of steam. The steam began to make me feel drowsy; then it seemed to be forming a dome within which I was invulnerable. I'd almost fallen asleep when I heard voices.

Before long they appeared in the distance: two young male rats, talking animatedly. I recognised one of them straightaway – he was from the group that I had just visited. The other one was completely unfamiliar; maybe he'd been working at the time of my visit, maybe he belonged to another group. The discussion they were having was heated, but without overstepping the bounds of civility. Their arguments were incomprehensible, partly because they were still a way off (though, splashing through the shallow water on their little paws, they were heading straight for my refuge), and partly because they were using words that belonged to another language, a language that rang false, that was alien to me, and instantly revolting: words like pictograms or ciphers, words that crawl on the underside of the word *freedom*, as fire is said to crawl into the tunnels, turning them into ovens.

I would have liked to scurry away discreetly. But my police instincts were telling me that unless I intervened, another murder was about to be committed. I jumped off the pile of cardboard. The two rats froze. Good evening, I said. I asked them if they belonged to the same group. They shook their heads.

You, I said, pointing to the rat I didn't know with my paw, out of here. The young rat seemed to have a reputation to defend; he hesitated. Out of here, I'm a police officer, I said. I'm Pepe the Cop, I shouted. Then he glanced at his friend, turned and left. Watch out for predators, I said to him before he disappeared behind a mound of trash, there's no one to help you if you get attacked by a predator in the dead sewers.

The other rat didn't even bother to say goodbye to his friend. He stayed there with me, quietly, waiting until we were alone, with his thoughtful little eyes fixed on me, as I guess mine were studying him. I've got you, finally, I said when we were alone. He didn't answer. What's your name? I asked. Hector, he said. Now that he was speaking to me, his voice was no different from thousands I had heard. Why did you kill the baby? I asked softly. He didn't answer. For a moment I was scared. Hector was strong, and probably bigger than me, and younger too, but I was a police officer.

Now I'm going to tie your paws and your snout and take you to the police station, I said. I think he smiled, but I'm not sure. You're more scared than I am, he said, and I'm pretty scared. I don't think so, I replied, you're not scared – you're sick, you're a disgusting predatory bastard. Hector laughed. *You're* scared, though, aren't you, he said, much more than your aunt Josephine was. You've heard of Josephine? I asked. I've heard of her, he said, Who hasn't? My aunt wasn't scared, I said, she might have been a poor crazy dreamer, but she wasn't scared.

You're wrong there; she was scared to death, he said, glancing sideways distractedly, as if we were surrounded by ghostly presences and he were discreetly seeking their approval. The members of her audience were scared to death as well, although they didn't know it. But she didn't die once and for all: she died every day at the centre of fear, and in fear she came back to life. Words, I spat. Now lie face down while

I tie your snout, I said, taking out the cord I had brought for that purpose. Hector snorted.

You've got no idea, he said. Do you think the crimes will stop if you arrest me? Do you think your bosses will give me a fair trial? They'll probably tear me to pieces in secret and dump my remains where predators will take them. You're a damn predator, I said. I'm a free rat, he replied impudently. I'm at home in fear and I know perfectly well where our people are headed. His words were so presumptuous I chose not to dignify them with an answer. Instead I said, You're young. Maybe there's a way to cure you. We don't kill our own kind. And who's going to cure you, Pepe? he asked. And your bosses? Where are the doctors to cure them? Lie face down, I said. Hector stared at me; I dropped the cord. Our bodies locked in a fight to the death.

After ten eternal-seeming minutes, he lay beside me, lifeless, his neck crushed by a bite. As for me, my back was covered with wounds, my snout was torn open and I couldn't see anything out of my left eye. I took his body back to the station. The few rats I encountered no doubt supposed that Hector had been the victim of a predator. I left his body in the morgue and went to find the coroner. It's all solved now, were the first words I could articulate. Then I slumped to the ground and waited. The coroner examined my wounds and sewed up my snout and my eyelid. As he was attending to me, he asked how it had happened. I found the killer, I said. I stopped him; we fought. The coroner said he had to call the commissioner. He clicked his tongue and a thin, sleepy-looking adolescent emerged from the darkness. I assumed he was a medical student. The coroner told him to go to the commissioner's place and tell him that the coroner and Pepe the Cop were waiting for him at the station. The adolescent nodded and disappeared. Then the coroner and I went to the morgue.

Hector's body was lying there and his coat was beginning to lose its gloss. It was just another body now, one among many. While the coroner was examining it, I took a nap in a corner. I was woken by the commissioner's voice and a couple of shoves. Get up, Pepe, said the coroner. I followed them. The commissioner and the coroner scurried down tunnels that were unfamiliar to me. I followed them, half asleep, watching their tails, with an intense burning pain in my back. Soon we came to an empty burrow. There, on a kind of throne, or maybe it was a cradle, I saw a seething shadow. The commissioner and the coroner told me to go forward.

Tell me the story, said a voice that was many voices, emerging from the darkness. At first I was terrified and shrank away, but then I realised that it was a very old queen rat – several rats, that is, whose tails had become knotted in early childhood, which rendered them unfit for work, but endowed them, instead, with the requisite wisdom to advise our people in critical situations. So I told the story from beginning to end, and tried to make my words dispassionate and objective, as if I were writing a report. When I finished, the voice that was many voices emerging from the darkness asked me if I was the nephew of Josephine the Singer. That's correct, I said. We were born when Josephine was still alive, said the queen rat, shifting herselves laboriously. I could just make out a huge dark ball dotted with little eyes dimmed by age. The queen rat, I conjectured, was fat, and a build-up of filth had immobilised her hind paws. An anomaly, she said. It took me a while to realise that she was referring to Hector. A poison that shall not spell the end of life for us, she said: a kind of lunatic, an individualist. There's something I don't understand, I said. The commissioner touched me on the shoulder with his paw, as if to stop me from speaking, but the queen rat asked me to explain what it was that I didn't understand. Why did he let the baby die of hunger, instead of ripping his throat open, as he did with the other victims? For a few seconds all I could hear from the seething shadow was a sound of sighing.

Maybe, she said after a while, he wanted to witness the process of death from beginning to end, without intervening or intervening as little as possible. And, after another interminable silence, she added: We must remember that he was insane, that we are in the realm of the monstrous – rats do not kill rats.

I hung my head and stayed there, I don't know for how long. I might even have fallen asleep. Suddenly I felt the commissioner's paw on my shoulder again, and heard his voice ordering me to follow him. We went back the way we had come, in silence. Just as I had feared, Hector's body had disappeared from the morgue. I asked where it was. In the belly of some predator, I hope, said the commissioner. Then I was told what I had already guessed. It was strictly forbidden to talk about Hector with anyone. The case was closed, and the best thing for me to do was to forget about him and get on with my life and my work.

I didn't feel like sleeping at the station that night, so I found myself a place in a burrow full of tough, grimy rats, and when I woke up I was alone. That night I dreamed that an unknown virus had infected our people. Rats are capable of killing rats. The sentence echoed in my cranial cavity until I woke. I knew that nothing would ever be the same again. I knew it was only a question of time. Our capacity to adapt to the environment, our hard-working nature, our long collective march towards a happiness that, deep down, we knew to be illusory, but which had served as a pretext, a setting, a backdrop for our daily acts of heroism, all these were condemned to disappear, which meant that we, as a people, were condemned to disappear as well.

I went back to my daily rounds; there was nothing else I could do. A police officer was killed and torn to pieces by a predator; there were several fatalities as a result of more poisoning from the outside; a number of tunnels were flooded. One night, however, I yielded to the fever that was consuming my body and returned to the dead sewers.

I'm not sure whether that sewer was one of those in which I'd found a victim, or even if I'd been there before. All dead sewers are the same, in the end. I spent a long time in there, hiding, waiting. Nothing. Only distant noises, splashes: I couldn't say what caused them. When I returned to the station, with red eyes from my long vigil, I found some rats who swore they'd seen a pair of weasels in the tunnels nearby. There was a new police officer with them. He looked at me, waiting for some kind of sign. The weasels had cornered three rats and several young in the end of a tunnel. If we wait for backup it'll be too late, said the new officer.

Too late for what? I asked, yawning. For the young and their guardians, he replied. It's already too late, I thought, for everything. I also thought: When did it become too late? Was it in the time of my aunt Josephine? Or a hundred years before that? Or a thousand, three thousand years before? Weren't we damned right from the origin of our species? The officer was watching me, waiting for a cue. He was young and he couldn't have been on the job for more than a week. Some of the rats around us were whispering, others were pressing their ears to the walls of the tunnel; most of them, it was all they could do to stop themselves from shaking and running away. What do you suggest? I asked. We do it by the book, replied the officer, we go into the tunnel and rescue the young.

Have you ever taken on a weasel? Are you ready to be torn apart by a weasel? I asked. I know how to fight, Pepe, he replied. There was nothing much left to say, so I got up and told him to stay behind me. The tunnel was black and stank of weasel, but I know how to move in the dark. Two rats came forward as volunteers and followed us.

Álvaro Rousselot's Journey

for Carmen Pérez de Vega

Although it may not warrant an eminent place in the annals of literary mystery, the curious case of Álvaro Rousselot is worthy of attention, for a few minutes at least.

Keen readers of mid-twentieth-century Argentine literature, who do exist, albeit not in great numbers, will no doubt remember that Rousselot was a skilled narrator and an abundant inventor of original plots, a sound stylist in literary Spanish, but not averse to the use of Buenos Aires slang or *lunfardo*, when the story required it (as was often the case), though never in a mannered way, at least not for those of us who count ourselves among his faithful readers.

The action of that sinister and eminently sardonic character Time has, however, prompted a reconsideration of Rousselot's apparent simplicity. Perhaps he was complicated. By which I mean *much* more complicated than we had imagined. But there is an alternative explanation: perhaps he was simply another victim of chance.

Such cases are not unusual among lovers of literature. In fact, they are not unusual among lovers of anything. In the end we all fall victim to the object of our adoration, perhaps because passion runs its course more swiftly than other human emotions, perhaps as a result of excessive familiarity with the object of desire.

In any case, Rousselot loved literature as much as any Argentine writer of his generation, or of the preceding and following generations, which is to say that his love was somewhat disillusioned. What I mean is that he was not especially different from the others, his peers – he knew the same torments and moments of joy – yet nothing even remotely similar happened to any of them.

At this point it could be objected, quite reasonably, that the others were destined for hells or singularities of their own. Angela Caputo, for example, killed herself in an unimaginable manner: no one who had read her poems, with their ambivalently childish atmosphere, could have predicted such an atrocious death, stage-managed down to the finest detail to maximise the terrifying effect. Or Sánchez Brady, whose texts were hermetic and whose life was cut short by the military regime in the seventies, when he had passed the age of fifty and lost interest in literature and the world in general.

Paradoxical deaths and destinies, yet they do not eclipse the case of Rousselot, the enigma that imperceptibly enveloped his life, the sense that his work, his writing, stood near or on the edge or the brink of something he knew almost nothing about.

His story can be recounted simply, perhaps because, in the final analysis, it is a simple story. In 1950, at the age of thirty, Rousselot published his first book, a novel about daily life in a remote Patagonian penitentiary, under the rather laconic title *Solitude*. Not surprisingly, the book relates numerous confessions about past lives and fleeting moments of happiness; it also relates numerous acts of violence. Halfway through, it becomes apparent that most of the characters are dead. With only thirty pages left to go, it is suddenly obvious that they are *all* dead, except for one, but the identity of that single living character is never revealed. The book was not much of a success in Buenos Aires, selling less than a thousand copies, but, thanks to some friends, Rousselot had the pleasure of seeing a well-respected publisher bring out a French edition in 1954. *Solitude* became *Nights on the Pampas* in the land of Victor Hugo, where it made little impact, except on two critics, one of whom reviewed it warmly, while the other was perhaps excessively enthusiastic; then it vanished into the limbo of remote shelves and overloaded tables in second-hand bookstores.

At the end of 1957, however, a film entitled *Lost Voices* was released; it was directed by a Frenchman named Guy Morini, and for anyone who had read *Solitude*, it was clearly a clever adaptation of Rousselot's book. Morini's film began and ended altogether differently, but its stem or middle section corresponded exactly to the novel. It would, I think, be impossible to recapture Rousselot's feeling of stunned amazement in the dark, half-empty Buenos Aires cinema where he first saw the Frenchman's film. Naturally, he considered himself a victim of plagiarism. As the days went by, other explanations occurred to him, but he kept coming back to the idea that his work had been plagiarised. Of the friends who were informed and went to see the film, half were in favour of suing the production company, while the others were inclined to think, more or less resignedly, that these things happen – think of Brahms. By that time, Rousselot had already published a second novel, *The Archives of the Calle*

Peru, a detective story, with a plot that revolved around the appearance of three bodies in three different places in Buenos Aires: the first two victims had been killed by the third, the victim in turn of an unknown assailant.

This second novel was not what one might have expected from the author of *Solitude*, but the critics received it well, although it is perhaps the least successful of Rousselot's works. When Morini's film came out in Buenos Aires, *The Archives of the Calle Peru* had already been kicking around the city's bookshops for almost a year, and Rousselot had married María Eugenia Carrasco, a young woman who moved in the capital's literary circles, and he had recently taken a job with the law firm Zimmerman & Gurruchaga.

Rousselot's life was orderly: he got up at six in the morning and wrote or tried to write until eight, at which time he interrupted his commerce with the muses, took a shower and rushed off to the office, where he arrived at around ten to nine. He spent most mornings in court or going through files. At two in the afternoon, he returned home, had lunch with his wife, and then went back to the office for the afternoon. At seven, he would have a drink with some of his legal colleagues, and by eight, at the latest, he was back home, where Mrs Rousselot, as she now was, had his dinner ready, after which Rousselot would read, while María Eugenia listened to the radio. On Saturdays and Sundays he wrote for a little longer, and went out at night, unaccompanied by his wife, to see his literary friends.

The release of *Lost Voices* brought him a degree of notoriety beyond his circle of associates. His best friend at the law firm, who was not particularly interested in literature, advised him to sue Morini for breach of copyright. Having thought it over carefully, Rousselot decided not to do anything. After *The Archives of the Calle Peru*, he published a slim volume of stories, and then, almost immediately, his third novel, *Life of a Newlywed*, in which, as the title suggests, he recounted a man's first months of married life, and how, as the days go by, the man comes to realise that he has made a terrible mistake: not only is the woman he thought he knew a stranger, she is also a kind of monster who threatens his mental balance and even his physical safety. And yet the guy loves her (or rather discovers that he is physically attracted to her in a way that he hadn't been before), so he holds on for as long as he can before fleeing.

The book was, obviously, meant to be humorous, and was taken as such by the reading public, to the surprise of Rousselot and his publisher. It had to be reprinted after three months, and within a year more than fifteen thousand copies had been sold. From one day to the next, Rousselot's name soared from comfortable semi-obscurity to provisional stardom. He took it in stride. With the windfall earnings, he treated himself, his wife, and his sister-in-law to a vacation in Punta del Este, which he spent surreptitiously reading *In Search of Lost Time*, a book he had always pretended to have read. While María Eugenia and her sister lolled about on the seashore, he strove to redeem that lie, but above all to fill the gap left by his ignorance of France's most celebrated novelist.

He would have been better off reading the Cabbalists. Seven months after his vacation in Punta del Este, before *Life of a Newlywed* had come out in French, Morini's new film, *The Shape of the Day*, opened in Buenos Aires. It was exactly like *Life of a Newlywed* but better, that is, revised and considerably extended, much as Morini had done with *Lost Voices*, compressing the novel's plot into the central part of the film, while the beginning and the end served as commentaries on the main story (or ways into and out of it, or digressions leading nowhere, or simply – and here lay the charm of the procedure – delicately filmed scenes from the lives of the minor characters).

This time, Rousselot was extremely aggrieved. His case against Morini was the talk of the Argentinian literary world for a week or so. And yet, when everyone presumed that he would take swift legal action for breach of copyright, he decided, to the dismay of those who had expected him to adopt a stronger and more decisive stance, that he would do nothing. Few could really understand his reaction. He did not protest, or appeal to the honour and integrity of the artist. After his initial surprise and indignation, Rousselot simply opted not to act, at least not legally. He waited. Something inside him, which could perhaps, without too great a risk of error, be called the writer's spirit, trapped him in a limbo of apparent passivity, and began to harden or change him, or prepare him for future surprises.

In other respects his life as a writer and as a man had already changed as much as he could reasonably have hoped, or more: his books were well reviewed and widely read, they even supplemented his income, and his family life was suddenly enriched by the news that María Eugenia was going to be a mother. When Morini's third film came to Buenos Aires, Rousselot stayed home for a week, resisting the temptation to rush to the cinema like a man possessed. He also instructed his friends not to tell him the plot. At first he thought he would not go to see the film. But after a week it was too much for him, and one night, having kissed his baby son and entrusted him to the nanny's care as if he were leaving for a war and would never return, he stepped out, resignedly, arm in arm with his wife, and went to the cinema.

Morini's film was called *The Vanished Woman*, and had nothing in common with any of Rousselot's works, or with either of Morini's previous films. As they left the cinema, María Eugenia said she thought it was bad and boring. Álvaro Rousselot kept his opinion to himself, but he agreed. A few months later, he published his next novel, the longest yet (206 pages), entitled *The Juggler's Family*, in which he departed from the style that had characterised his work up till then, with its elements of fantasy and crime fiction, and experimented with what, at a stretch, could be called the choral or polyphonic novel. It wasn't a form that came naturally to him, and seemed rather forced, but the book was redeemed by other features: the decency and simplicity of the characters, a naturalism that elegantly avoided the clichés of the naturalist novel, and the stories themselves, which were slight and resolute, joyful and pointless, and captured the indomitable Argentine spirit.

The Juggler's Family was, without doubt, Rousselot's greatest success, the book that brought all the others back into print, and his triumph was consummated by the Municipal Literary Award, presented at a ceremony in the course of which he was described as one of the five rising stars among the nation's younger writers. But that is another story. It is common knowledge that the rising stars of any literary world are like flowers that bloom and fade in a day; and whether the day is literal and brief or stretches out over ten or twenty years, it must eventually come to an end.

The French, who distrust our municipal literary awards on principle, were slow to translate and publish *The Juggler's Family*. By then, fashions in Latin American fiction had shifted north to more tropical climes. When the novel came out in Paris, Morini had already made his fourth and fifth films, a conventional but engaging French detective story and a turkey about a supposedly amusing family vacation in Saint-Tropez.

Both films were released in Argentina, and Rousselot was relieved to discover that neither bore the slightest resemblance to anything he had written. It was as if Morini had distanced himself from Rousselot, or, under pressure from creditors and swept up in the whirlwind of the movie business, had neglected the relationship. After relief came sadness. For a few days Rousselot was even preoccupied by the thought that he had lost his best reader, the reader for whom he had really been writing, the only one who was capable of fully responding to his work. He tried to get in touch with his translators, but they were busy with other books and other authors, and replied to his letters with polite and evasive phrases. One of them had never seen any of Morini's films. The other had seen one of the films in question but hadn't translated the corresponding book (or even read it, to judge from his letter).

When Rousselot asked his publishers in Paris if Morini might have had access to the manuscript of *Life of a Newlywed* before its publication, they weren't even surprised. They replied indifferently that many people had access to a manuscript at various stages prior to printing. Feeling embarrassed, Rousselot decided to stop annoying people with his letters and suspend his investigations until such time as he could finally go to Paris himself. A year later he was invited to a literary festival in Frankfurt.

The Argentine delegation was sizeable and the journey was pleasant. Rousselot got to know two old Buenos Aires writers whom he considered his masters. He tried to help them in any way he could, offering to render the sort of little services one might expect from a secretary or a valet rather than a colleague. This behaviour was condemned by a writer of his own generation, who called him obsequious and servile, but Rousselot was happy and paid no attention. The stay in Frankfurt was enjoyable, in spite of the weather, and Rousselot spent all his time with the pair of old writers.

The atmosphere of slightly artificial happiness was, in fact, largely Rousselot's own creation. He knew that when the festival was over, he would go on to Paris, while the others would return to Buenos Aires or take a short vacation somewhere in Europe. When the day of departure came and he went to the airport to see off the members of the delegation who were returning to Argentina, his eyes filled with tears. One of the old writers noticed and told him not to worry, they would see each other again soon, and the door of his house in Buenos Aires would always be open. But Rousselot couldn't understand what anyone was saying to him. He was on the brink of tears because he was afraid of being left on his own, and, above all, afraid of going to Paris and confronting the mystery awaiting him there.

The first thing he did, as soon as he had settled into a little hotel in Saint-Germain-des-Prés, was to call the translator of *Solitude (Nights on the Pampas)*, unsuccessfully. The phone rang, but no one picked up, and when Rousselot went to the publisher's offices, they had no idea where the translator might be. To tell the truth, they had no idea who Rousselot was either, although he pointed out that they had published two of his books, *Nights on the Pampas* and *Life of a Newlywed*. Finally, a guy who must have been about fifty, and whose role in the company Rousselot never managed to ascertain, identified the visitor, and, abruptly changing the topic, proceeded to inform him, in an absurdly serious tone, that the sales of his books had been very poor.

Rousselot then visited the publishers of *The Juggler's Family* (which Morini, it seemed, had never read) and made a half-hearted attempt to obtain the address of the translator they had employed, hoping that he would be able to put him in touch with the translators of *Nights on the Pampas* and *Life of a Newlywed*. This second publishing house was significantly smaller and seemed to be run by just two people: the woman who received Rousselot, whom he guessed was a secretary, and the publisher, a young guy, who greeted him with a smile and a hug, and insisted on speaking Spanish, although it was soon clear that his grasp of the language was tenuous. When asked why he wanted to speak with the translator of *The Juggler's Family*, Rousselot was at a loss for words, because he had just realised how absurd it was to think that any of his translators would be able to lead him to Morini. Nevertheless, encouraged by the publisher's warm welcome (and his readiness to listen, since he didn't seem to have anything better to do that morning), Rousselot decided to tell him the whole Morini story, from A to Z.

When he had finished, the publisher lit a cigarette, and paced up and down the office for a long time in silence, from one wall to the other and back, a distance of barely three yards. Rousselot waited, becoming increasingly nervous.

Finally the publisher stopped in front of a glass-fronted bookcase full of manuscripts and asked Rousselot if it was his first time in Paris. Rather taken aback, Rousselot admitted that it was. Parisians are cannibals, said the publisher. Rousselot hastened to point out that he was not intending to take any kind of legal action against Morini; he only wanted to meet him and perhaps ask him how he'd come up with the plots of the two films in which he, Rousselot, had, so to speak, a particular interest. The publisher burst into uproarious laughter. It's all about money here, he said, ever since Camus. Rousselot looked at him, bewildered. He didn't know whether the publisher meant that idealism had died with Camus, and money was now the prime concern, or that Camus had established the law of supply and demand among artists and intellectuals.

I'm not interested in money, said Rousselot quietly. Nor am I, my poor friend, said the publisher, and look where it's got me.

They parted with the understanding that Rousselot would call the publisher and arrange to have dinner one night. He spent the rest of the day sightseeing. He went to the Louvre and the Eiffel Tower; he ate in a restaurant in the Latin Quarter, and visited a couple of second-hand bookshops. That night, from his hotel, he called an Argentine writer he had known back in Buenos Aires and who now lived in Paris. They weren't exactly friends, but Rousselot admired his work and had been instrumental in getting a number of his pieces published in a Buenos Aires magazine.

The Argentine writer was called Riquelme and he was happy to hear from Rousselot. Rousselot wanted to arrange to meet up some time during the week, perhaps for lunch or dinner, but Riquelme wouldn't hear of it and asked him where he was calling from. Rousselot told him the name of his hotel and mentioned that he was thinking of going to bed. Riquelme said, Don't even think of getting into your pyjamas, I'll be right there; it's my treat tonight. Rousselot was overwhelmed, powerless to resist. He hadn't seen Riquelme for years, and, waiting in the hotel lobby, tried to remember what he looked like. He had blond hair and a round, broad, face with a ruddy complexion; he was short. It had been a while since Rousselot had read any of his work.

When Riquelme finally appeared, Rousselot hardly recognised him: he seemed taller, not so blond, and he was wearing glasses. The night was rich in confessions and revelations. Rousselot told his friend what he had told his French publisher that morning, and Riquelme told Rousselot that he was writing the great Argentine novel of the twentieth century. He had passed the 800-page mark, and hoped to finish it in less than three years. Although Rousselot prudently refrained from asking about the plot, Riquelme explained several sections of his book in detail. They visited various bars and clubs. At some point during the night, Rousselot realised that both he and Riquelme were behaving like adolescents. At first this embarrassed him, but then he surrendered to the situation, happy to know that his hotel was there at the end of the night, his hotel room and the word 'hotel', which in that instant seemed a miraculous (that is to say instantaneous) incarnation of risk and freedom.

He drank a lot. On waking, he discovered a woman beside him. The woman's name was Simone and she was a prostitute. They had breakfast together in a café near the hotel. Simone liked to talk, so Rousselot discovered that she didn't have a pimp, because a pimp will always rip you off, that she had just turned twenty-eight, and that she liked watching movies. Since he wasn't interested in the world of Parisian pimps and Simone's age didn't seem a fruitful topic of conversation, they started talking about movies. She liked French cinema, and before long they got on to Morini. His first films were very good, in Simone's opinion. Rousselot could have kissed her when she said that.

At two in the afternoon they returned to the hotel and didn't re-emerge until dinner time. It would probably be true to say that Rousselot had never felt so good in his life. He wanted to write, and eat, and go out dancing with Simone, and wander aimlessly through the streets of the Left Bank. In fact, he felt so good that during the meal, shortly before they ordered dessert, he explained the reason for his trip to Paris. To Rousselot's surprise, Simone was not at all surprised by the revelation that he was a writer or that Morini had plagiarised or copied his work, or freely adapted two of his novels to make his two best films.

Things like that do happen, was her laconic response, and even stranger things. Then, point blank, she asked him if he was married. The answer was implicit in the question, and with a resigned gesture Rousselot showed her the gold ring constricting his finger in that moment as it never had before. And do you have children? asked Simone. A little boy, said Rousselot with a tenderness engendered by the mental image of his offspring. And he added, He looks just like me. Then Simone asked him to keep her company on the way home. In the taxi, neither of them said a word; both looked out of their windows at the unpredictable spills of bright and dark, which made the City of Light seem like a medieval Russian city, or at least like the images of such cities that Soviet directors used to offer for public consumption every now and then in their films. Finally the taxi pulled up in front of a four-storey building and Simone invited him to come in. Rousselot wondered whether he should, and then he remembered that he hadn't paid her. Shamefaced, he got out of the taxi without worrying about how he would get back to his hotel (there didn't seem to be many taxis in that neighbourhood). Before going into the building, he held out a bunch of uncounted bills, which Simone put into her handbag, without counting them either.

The building didn't have an elevator. By the time they reached the fourth floor, Rousselot was out of breath. In the dimly lit living room an old woman was drinking a whitish-coloured liqueur. In response to a sign from Simone, Rousselot sat down next to the old woman, who produced a glass and filled it with that appalling liquid, while Simone vanished through one of the doors, then reappeared after a while and summoned him with a gesture. What now? thought Rousselot.

The room was small; it contained a bed in which a child was sleeping. My son, said Simone. He's lovely, said Rousselot. And he was a pretty child, but perhaps that was only because he was sleeping. He had blond hair, which was rather too long, and resembled his mother, although Rousselot noted that there was already something thoroughly manly about his childish features. When he went back to the living room, Simone was paying the old woman, who then took her leave of Madame, and even wished her visitor an effusive good night, calling him *Sir*. Rousselot was thinking that the day had been eventful enough and that it was time to leave when Simone said he could spend the night with her, if he liked. But you can't sleep in my bed, she said; she didn't want her son to see her in bed with a stranger. So they made love in Simone's room, and then Rousselot went out into the living room, lay down on the couch and fell asleep.

He spent the next day *en famille*, so to speak. The little boy's name was Marc; Rousselot found him to be very bright (as well as speaking better French than he did). The novelist spared no expense: they had breakfast in the centre of Paris, went to a park, had lunch in a restaurant on the Rue de Verneuil, which he had been told about in Buenos Aires, then they went rowing on a lake, and finally they visited a supermarket where Simone bought all the ingredients for a proper French meal. They took taxis everywhere. As they waited for ice-creams on a café terrace on the Boulevard Saint-Germain, Rousselot recognised a pair of famous writers. He admired them from a distance. Simone asked him if he knew them. He said no, but he was a passionate reader of their books. Then go and ask them for an autograph, she said.

At first it seemed a perfectly reasonable idea, the natural thing to do, but at the last moment Rousselot decided that he didn't have the right to annoy anyone, least of all people he'd always admired. That night he slept in Simone's bed; they covered each other's mouths to stop their moans waking the child, and made love for hours, violently at times, as if loving each other were the only thing they knew how to do. The next day he returned to his hotel before the child woke up.

His suitcase had not been put out in the street as he had feared, and no one was surprised to see him appear out of nowhere, like a ghost. At reception there were two messages from Riquelme. The first was to say he had found out how to

Álvaro Rousselot's Journey

locate Morini. The second was to ask if Rousselot was still interested in meeting him.

He showered, shaved, brushed his teeth (a horrifying experience), put on clean clothes and called Riquelme. They talked for a long time. Riquelme told him that a friend of his, a Spanish journalist, knew another journalist, a Frenchman, who was a freelance movie, theatre and music critic. The French journalist had been a friend of Morini's and still had his telephone number. When the Spaniard had asked for the number, the Frenchman had given it to him without a second thought. Then Riquelme and the Spanish journalist had called Morini's number without getting their hopes up, and were amazed when the woman who answered told them that they had indeed reached the director's residence.

Now all they had to do was set up a meeting (at which Riquelme and the Spanish journalist wanted to be present) on some pretext — anything, for example an interview for an Argentinian newspaper . . . with a surprise ending. What do you mean a surprise ending? shouted Rousselot. That's when the bogus journalist reveals his true identity and confronts the plagiarist, Riquelme replied.

That night, as Rousselot was taking photographs more or less at random on the banks of the Seine, a bum came up and asked him for some change. Rousselot offered him a bill if he would consent to be photographed. The bum agreed, and for a while they walked along together in silence, stopping every now and then to allow the Argentine writer to move off to an appropriate distance and take a photo. On the third occasion the bum suggested a pose, which Rousselot accepted without demur. The writer took eight photos in all: the bum on his knees with his arms stretched out to the sides, and in other poses, such as pretending to sleep on a bench, thoughtfully watching the river flow by, or smiling and waving his hand. When the photo session was over, Rousselot gave him two bills and all the coins in his pocket, and then the pair of them stood there together, as if there were something more to be said but neither of them dared say it. Where are you from? the bum asked. Buenos Aires, Argentina, replied Rousselot. What a coincidence, said the bum in Spanish, I'm Argentine too. Rousselot was not at all surprised by this revelation. The bum began to hum a tango, then told him that in Europe, where he'd been living for more than fifteen years, he had found happiness and even some wisdom now and then. Rousselot realised that the bum had started using the familiar form of address, which he hadn't done when they were speaking in French. Even his voice, the tone of his voice, seemed to have changed. Rousselot felt a deep sadness overwhelming him, as if he knew that, come the end of the day, he would have to look into an abyss. The bum noticed and asked him what he was worried about.

Nothing, a girl, said Rousselot, trying to adopt the same tone as his compatriot. Then he said a rather hurried goodbye and, as he was climbing the stairs, he heard the bum's voice telling him that death was the only sure thing. My name is Enzo Cherubini and I'm telling you, death is the only sure thing there is. When Rousselot turned around, the bum was walking off in the opposite direction.

That night he called Simone but she wasn't home. He talked for a while with the old woman who looked after the child, then hung up. At ten, Riquelme came visiting. Reluctant to go out, Rousselot said he felt feverish and nauseous, but his excuses were futile. Sadly, he came to the realisation that Paris had transformed his colleague into a force of nature it was futile to resist. That night they dined in a little restaurant with a charcoal grill in the Rue Racine, where they were joined by the Spanish journalist, named Paco Morral, who liked to imitate the Buenos Aires accent, very badly, and believed that Spanish cinema was far better than French cinema, much denser, an opinion shared by Riquelme.

The meal went on and on, and Rousselot began to feel ill. When he returned to his hotel at four in the morning, he was running a fever and began to vomit. He woke shortly before midday with the feeling that he had lived in Paris for many years. He went through the pockets of his jacket looking for the cell-phone number that he had managed to extract from Riquelme, and called Morini. A woman, the one who had previously spoken to Riquelme, he supposed, picked up the receiver and told him that Monsieur Morini had left that morning to spend a few days with his parents. Rousselot's first thought was that she was lying, or that before his hurried departure, the director had lied to her. He said he was an Argentine journalist who wanted to interview Morini for a well-known magazine with a big circulation, widely read all over Latin America, from Argentina to Mexico. The only problem, he alleged, was that he had limited time, since he had to fly home in a couple of days. Humbly he asked for the address of Morini's parents. He didn't have to insist. The woman listened politely, then gave him the name of a village in Normandy, followed by a street and a number.

Rousselot thanked her, then called Simone. No one was home. Suddenly he realised that he didn't even know what day it was. He thought of asking one of the hotel staff but felt embarrassed. He called Riquelme. A hoarse voice answered on the other end of the line. Rousselot asked him about the village where Morini's parents lived: did he know where it was? Who's Morini? asked Riquelme. Rousselot had to remind him and explain part of the story again. No idea, said Riquelme, and hung up. After feeling annoyed for a while, Rousselot told himself it was better that way, if Riquelme lost interest in the whole business. Then he packed his suitcase and went to the train station.

The trip to Normandy gave him time to go back over what he had done since arriving in Paris. An absolute zero lit up in his mind, then delicately disappeared for ever. The train stopped in Rouen. Other Argentines, and Rousselot himself in other circumstances, would have set off at once to explore the town, like bloodhounds following the scent of Flaubert. But he didn't even leave the station; he waited twenty minutes for the train to Caen, thinking of Simone, who personified the grace of French women, and of Riquelme and his odd journalist friend: in the end, both of them were more interested in rummaging through their own failures than in discovering someone else's story, however singular it might be, and perhaps that wasn't so unusual. People are only interested in themselves, he concluded gravely.

From Caen, he took a taxi to Le Hamel. He was surprised to find that the address he had been given in Paris corresponded to a hotel. The hotel had four storeys and was not without a certain charm, but it was shut until the beginning of the season. For half an hour Rousselot walked around in the vicinity, wondering if the woman who lived with Morini had sent him on a wild goose chase, until eventually he began to feel tired and headed for the port. In a bar he was told that he'd be very lucky to find a hotel open in Le Hamel. The patron, a cadaverously pale guy with red hair, suggested he go to Arromanches, unless he wanted to sleep in one of the *auberges* that stayed open all year round. Rousselot thanked him and went looking for a taxi.

He booked into the best hotel he could find in Arromanches, a pile made of brick, stone and wood, which creaked in the gusting wind. Tonight I will dream of Proust, he thought. Then he called Simone's place and talked to the old lady who looked after her child. Madame won't be home until after four; she has an orgy tonight, said the woman. A what? asked Rousselot. The woman repeated the sentence. My God, thought Rousselot, and hung up without saying goodbye. To make things worse, that night he didn't dream of Proust but of Buenos Aires, where thousands of Riquelmes had taken up residence in the Argentine PEN Club, all armed with tickets to Paris, all shouting, all cursing a name, the name of someone or something, but Rousselot couldn't hear it properly; it was like a tongue-twister or a password they were trying to keep secret although it was gnawing their insides away.

The next morning, at breakfast, he was stunned to discover that he had no money left. Le Hamel was three or four kilometres from Arromanches; he decided to walk. To lift his spirits, he told himself that on D-Day the English soldiers had landed on those beaches. But his spirits remained as low as could be, and although he had thought it might take half an hour, in the end it took him more than twice that time to reach Le Hamel. On the way he started doing sums, remembering how much money he had brought with him to Europe, how much he'd had left when he arrived in Paris, how much he had spent on meals, on Simone (quite a lot, he thought, melancholically), on Riquelme, on taxis (they've been ripping me off the whole time!), and wondering whether he could have been robbed at some point without realising. The only people who could have done that, he concluded gallantly, were the Spanish journalist and Riquelme. And the idea didn't seem preposterous in those surroundings where so many lives had been lost.

He observed Morini's hotel from the beach. By that stage, anyone else would have given up. For anyone else, circling around that hotel would have been as good as admitting to idiocy, or to a sort of degradation that Rousselot thought of as Parisian, or cinematic, or even literary, although for him the word 'literary' retained all its original lustre, or some of it, at least. In his situation, anyone else would have been calling the Argentine embassy, inventing a credible lie and borrowing some money to pay for the hotel. But, instead of gritting his teeth and making the phone calls, Rousselot rang the hotel's doorbell and was not surprised to hear the voice of an old woman who, leaning out of one of the windows on the second floor, asked him what he wanted and was not surprised by his reply: I need to see your son. Then the old woman disappeared, and Rousselot waited by the door for what seemed like an eternity.

He kept checking his pulse and touching his forehead to see if he had a fever. When the door finally opened, he saw a lean, rather swarthy face, with large bags under the eyes; it was, he judged, the face of a degenerate, and it was vaguely familiar. Morini invited him in. My parents, he said, have been working as caretakers of this hotel for more than thirty years. They sat down in the lobby, where the armchairs were protected from dust by enormous sheets embroidered with

Álvaro Rousselot's Journey

the hotel's monogram. On one wall Rousselot saw an oil painting of the beaches of Le Hamel, with bathers in *belle époque* costumes, while opposite, a collection of portraits of famous guests (or so he supposed) observed them from a zone infiltrated by mist. He shivered. I am Álvaro Rousselot, he said, the author of *Solitude* – I mean, the author of *Nights on the Pampas*.

It took a few seconds for Morini to react, but then he leapt to his feet, let out a cry of terror, and disappeared down a corridor. Such a spectacular response was the last thing Rousselot had been expecting. He remained seated, lit a cigarette (the ash dropped progressively onto the carpet), and thought sadly of Simone and her son, and a café in Paris that served the best croissants he had ever tasted in his life. Then he stood up and started calling Morini. Guy, he called, rather hesitantly, Guy, Guy, Guy.

Rousselot found him in an attic where the hotel's cleaning equipment was piled. Morini had opened the window and seemed to be hypnotised by the garden that surrounded the building, and by the neighbouring garden, which belonged to a private residence, and was visible, in part, through dark lattice-work. Rousselot walked over and patted him on the back. Morini seemed smaller and more fragile than before. For a while they both stood there looking at one garden, then the other. Then Rousselot wrote the address of his hotel in Paris and the address of the hotel where he was currently staying on a piece of paper and slipped it into the director's trouser pocket. He felt he had committed a reprehensible act, executed a reprehensible gesture, but then, as he was walking back to Arromanches, everything he had done in Paris, every gesture and action, seemed reprehensible, futile, senseless, and even ridiculous. I should kill myself, he thought as he walked along the seashore.

Back in Arromanches, he did what any sensible man would have done as soon as he realised that his money had run out. He rang Simone, explained the situation, and asked her for a loan. The first thing Simone said was that she didn't want a pimp, to which Rousselot replied that he was asking for a *loan*, and that he was planning to repay it with thirty-per-cent interest, but then they both started laughing and Simone told him not to do anything, just stay put in the hotel, and in a few hours, as soon as she could borrow a car from one of her friends, she'd come and get him. She also called him *chéri* a few times, to which he responded by using the word *chérie*, which had never seemed so tender. For the rest of the day Rousselot felt that he really was an Argentine writer, something he had begun to doubt over the previous days, or perhaps the previous years, partly because he was unsure of himself, but also because he was unsure about the possibility of an Argentine literature.

Two Catholic Tales

I. The Vocation

1. I was seventeen years old and my days, and I mean all of them, were a continual shuddering. I had no distractions; nothing could dissipate the anxiety that kept building up inside me. I was living like an interloping extra in scenes from the passion of St Vincent. St Vincent – deacon to Bishop Valero, tortured by the governor Dacian in the year 304 – have pity on me! **2.** Sometimes I talked with Juanito. Not just sometimes. Often. We sat in armchairs at his place and talked about movies. Juanito liked Gary Cooper. Elegance, temperance, integrity, courage, he used to say. Temperance? Courage? I knew what lay behind his certitudes, and would have liked to spit them back in his face, but instead I dug my fingernails into the armrests and bit my lip when he wasn't looking and even closed my eyes and pretended to be meditating on his words. But I wasn't meditating. Not at all: images of the martyrdom of St Vincent were flashing in my mind like magic lantern slides. **3.** First he is tied to an X-shaped wooden cross and they tear at his flesh with hooks and dislocate his limbs. Then he is subjected to torture by fire, roasted on a grill over hot coals. And then he's a captive in a dungeon where the ground is covered with shards of glass and pottery. And then a crow keeps watch over the martyr's corpse, abandoned in a wasteland, and fends off a ravening wolf. And then the saint's body is cast into the sea from a boat, a millstone tied around his neck. And then the waves wash the body up on the coast, and there it is piously buried by a matron and other Christians. **4.** Sometimes I used to feel dizzy. Nauseous. Juanito would talk about the last film we had seen and I would nod and realise that I was drowning, as if the armchairs were at the bottom of a very deep lake. I could remember the movie theatre, I could remember buying the tickets, but I simply couldn't remember the scenes that my friend (my one and only friend!) was talking about, as if the lake-floor darkness had infiltrated everything. If I open my mouth, water will come in. If I breathe, water will come in. If I stay alive, water will come in and flood my lungs for ever and ever. **5.** Sometimes Juanito's mother would come into the room and ask me personal questions. How my studies were going, what book I was reading, if I'd been to the circus that had just set up on the outskirts of the city. Juanito's mother was always very elegantly dressed, and, like us, she was addicted to the movies. **6.** Once I dreamed of her, once I opened the door of her bedroom, and instead of seeing a bed, a dresser and a closet, I saw an empty room with a red brick floor, and that was just the antechamber of a very, very long corridor, like the highway tunnel that goes through the mountains and then on towards France, except that in this case the tunnel wasn't on a mountain highway but in the bedroom of my best friend's mother. I have to keep reminding myself: Juanito's my best friend. And, as opposed to a normal tunnel, this one seemed to be suspended in a very fragile kind of silence, like the silence of the second half of January or the first half of February. **7.** Unspeakable acts, fateful nights. I recited the formula to Juanito. Unspeakable acts? Fateful nights? Is the act unspeakable because the night is fateful, or is the night fateful because the act is unspeakable? What sort of question is that? I asked, on the brink of tears. You're crazy. You don't understand anything, I said, looking out of the window. **8.** Juanito's father isn't tall but he cuts a dashing figure. He was in the army and during the war he was wounded a number of times. His medals are displayed on the wall of his study, in a glass-fronted case. He didn't know anyone when he first came to the city, Juanito says, and people were either afraid of him or jealous. After a few months here, he met my mother, Juanito says. They were engaged for five years. Then my father tied the knot. Sometimes my aunt talks about Juanito's father. According to her, he was a good, honest police chief. That's what people said, at least. If a maid was caught stealing from her employers, Juanito's father locked her up for three days without so much as a crust of bread. On the fourth day he would question her personally, and the maid would be quick to confess her sin, giving him the precise location of the jewels or the name of the labourer who had stolen them. Then the guards would arrest the man and lock him up, and Juanito's father would put the maid on a train and advise her not to come back. **9.** The whole village applauded this procedure, as if it were a sign of the police chief's intellectual distinction. **10.** When Juanito's father first arrived, the only people he knew socially were the regulars at the casino. Juanito's mother was seventeen years old and she was very blonde, to judge from a number of photos hanging unobtrusively around the house, much blonder than she is now, and she had been educated at the Heart of Mary, a school run by nuns in the northern part of the old fort. Juanito's father must have been about thirty. He still goes to the casino every afternoon, although he's retired now, and drinks a glass of cognac or coffee with a shot, and usually plays dice with the regulars. New regulars, not the regulars from the old days, but it's not so different, because of course they're all in awe of him. Juanito's older brother lives in Madrid, where he's a well-known lawyer. Juanito's sister is married and she lives in Madrid too. I'm the only one left in this damn house, Juanito says. And me! And me! **11.** Our city is shrinking every day. Sometimes I get the feeling that everyone is either leaving or shut up inside packing a suitcase. If I left, I wouldn't take a suitcase. Not even a few belongings wrapped up in a little bundle. Sometimes I put my head in my hands and listen to the rats running in the walls. St Vincent, grant me strength. St Vincent, grant me temperance. **12.** Do you want to be a saint? Juanito's mother asked me two years ago. Yes, Ma'am. I think that's a very good idea, but you have to be very good. Are you? I try to be, Ma'am. And a year ago, as I was walking along Avenida General Mola, Juanito's father said hello and then he stopped and asked if I was Encarnación's nephew. Yes, Sir, I said. You're the one who wants to become a priest? I nodded and smiled. **13.** Why did I do that? What was that stupid, apologetic smile for? Why did I look away smiling like a moron? **14.** Humility. **15.** That's excellent, said Juanito's father. Fantastic. You have to study hard, don't you? I nodded and smiled. And cut down on the movies? Yes, Sir, but I don't go to the movies much. **16.** I watched Juanito's father receding into the distance: old but still vigorous, he held himself straight and looked as if he were walking on tiptoes. I watched him go down the stairs that lead to the Calle de los Vidrieros; I watched him as he walked away without a moment's unsteadiness or hesitation, without looking into a single shop. Not like Juanito's mother, who was always looking in storefront windows, and sometimes she would go into the stores, and if you stayed outside, waiting for her, you could sometimes hear her laugh. If I open my mouth, water will come in. If I breathe, water will come in. If I stay alive, water will come in and flood my lungs for ever and ever. **17.** And what are you going to be, dickhead? Juanito asked me. Be or do? I asked him back. Be, dickhead. Whatever God wants, I said. God puts us all in our rightful places, said my aunt. Our forefathers were good people. There were no soldiers in our family, but there were priests. Like who? I asked as I nodded off to sleep. My aunt grunted. I saw a square blanketed with snow, and I saw the farmers come with their produce, sweep the snow away and wearily set up their market stalls. St Vincent, for example, my aunt burst out. Deacon to the bishop of Zaragoza, who, in the year 304, *anno domini*, though it might well have been 305, 306, 307 or 303, was arrested and taken to Valencia, where Dacian, the governor, submitted him to cruel tortures, as a result of which he died. **18.** Why do you think St Vincent is dressed in red? I asked Juanito. No idea. Because all the Catholic martyrs wear a red garment, to identify them as martyrs. This boy's clever, said Father Zubieta. We were alone and Father Zubieta's study was bone-chillingly cold, and Father Zubieta or rather Father Zubieta's clothes smelled of a combination of dark tobacco and sour milk. If you decide to enter the seminary, the door is open. The vocation, the call, when it comes, can make you tremble, but let's not get carried away.

Did I tremble? Did I feel the earth move? Did I experience the rapture of divine union? **19.** Let's not get carried away. Let's not get carried away. It's what the reds wear, said Juanito. The reds wear khaki, I said, green, with camouflage patterns. No, said Juanito, those red faggots wear red. Like whores. That piqued my curiosity. Like whores? Which whores, where? Well, here, for a start, said Juanito, and I guess in Madrid too. Here, in this city? Yes, said Juanito, and then he tried to change the subject. You mean there are whores even here, in this little city or town or godforsaken backwater? Well, yes, said Juanito. I thought your father had reformed them all. Reformed? Do you think my father's a priest or something? My father was a war hero and then a police commissioner. My father doesn't reform. He solves crimes. That's all. And where have you seen these whores? On Cerro del Moro, where they've always been, said Juanito. Good God. **20.** My aunt says that St Vincent – Enough about your aunt and St Vincent, your aunt is raving mad. How can you trace your family back to the year 300? Who's got a family that old? Not even the House of Alba. But after a while, he added: Your aunt's not a bad person; she's got a good heart, but her mind's not right. Shall we go to the movies this afternoon? They're showing a Clark Gable film. And Juanito's mother: Go on, go, I went two days ago and it's very entertaining. And Juanito: The thing is, he doesn't have any money. Juanito's mother: Well, you'll just have to lend him some. **21.** God have mercy on my soul. Sometimes I wish they'd all just die. My friend and his mother and his father and my aunt and all the neighbours and passers-by and drivers who leave their cars parked by the river and even the poor innocent children who run around in the park beside the river. God have pity on my soul and make me better. Or unmake me. **22.** Anyway, if they all died, what would I do with so many bodies? How could I go on living in this city, or sub-city? Would I try to bury them all? Would I throw their bodies into the river? How much time would I have before their flesh began to rot and the stench became unbearable? Ah, snow. **23.** Snow covered the streets of our city. Before going into the cinema we bought roasted chestnuts and sugared almonds. We had our scarves up around our noses and Juanito was laughing and talking about adventures in the old Dutch East Indies. They didn't let anyone in with chestnuts – it was a question of basic hygiene – but they made an exception for Juanito. Gary Cooper would have been better in this role, said Juanito. Asia. The Chinese. Leper colonies. Mosquitoes. **24.** When we came out we went our separate ways in the Calle de los Cuchillos. I stood still in the falling snow and Juanito went running off home. Poor kid, I thought, but Juanito was only a year younger than me. When he disappeared from sight, I went up the Calle de los Toneleros to the Plaza del Sordo, and then I turned and followed the walls of the old fort, headed for Cerro del Moro. The snow reflected the light of the streetlamps, and, in a fleeting but also natural and even serene way, the old house-fronts gathered the glamour of the past. I peered through a gap in the whitewash on a window and saw a tidy room, with the Sacred Heart of Jesus presiding on one of the walls. But I was blind and deaf and continued up the hill, on the dark side of the street so I wouldn't be recognised. When I reached the Plazuela del Cadalso, and only then, I realised that throughout the climb I hadn't come across a single person. In this weather, I thought, who would exchange the warmth of home for the freezing streets? It was already dark, and from the square you could see the lights of some of the neighbourhoods and the bridges beyond the Plaza de Don Rodrigo and the river bending around and then continuing eastward. The stars were shining in the sky. I thought they looked like snowflakes. Suspended snowflakes, picked out by God to remain still in the firmament, but snowflakes all the same. **25.** I was starting to freeze. I decided to go back to my aunt's house and drink some hot chocolate or soup beside the heater. I felt weary and my head was spinning. I went back the way I'd come. Then I saw him. Just a shadow at first. **26.** But it wasn't a shadow, it was a monk. He could have been a Franciscan, judging from his habit. His thoughtful face was almost entirely obscured by a large hood. Why do I say thoughtful? Because he was looking at the ground. **27.** Where was he from? How'd he get there? I didn't know. Maybe he'd been administering the last rites to someone who was dying. Maybe he'd been visiting a sick child. Maybe he'd been supplying a destitute person with a frugal meal. In any case, he was walking without making the slightest sound. For a moment I thought it was an apparition. But soon I realised that the snow was muffling my own footfalls as well. **28.** He was barefoot. Noticing that was like being struck by lightning. We came down Cerro del Moro. When we passed the church of Santa Barbara, I saw him make the sign of the cross. His immaculate footprints shone in the snow like a message from God. I started crying. I would gladly have knelt down and kissed those crystalline prints – the answer for which I had waited so long – but I didn't, for fear he might disappear down some alley. We left the centre. We crossed the Plaza Mayor, and then we crossed a bridge. The monk was walking at a steady pace, neither slowly nor quickly, as the Church herself should proceed. **29.** We followed the Avenida Sanjurjo, lined with plane trees, until we reached the train station. It was stifling inside. The monk went to the bathroom and then bought a ticket. When he came out of the bathroom, I noticed that he had put on a pair of shoes. His ankles were as slender as sticks. He went out onto the platform. I saw him sitting there, hanging his head, waiting and praying. I remained standing on the platform, shivering with cold, hidden by a pillar. When the train arrived, the monk jumped with surprising agility into one of the carriages. **30.** When I left, on my own, I looked for his prints in the snow, the footprints of his bare feet, but I could find no trace of them.

II. Chance

1. I asked him how old he thought I was. He said sixty, although he knew I wasn't that old. Do I look that bad? I asked. Worse, he said. And you think you're in better shape? I said. How come you're shaking, then? Are you cold? Have you gone crazy? And why are you telling me about Commissioner Damian Valle anyway? Is he still the commissioner? Is he still the same? The old guy said Valle had changed a bit, but he was still a prize son of a bitch. Is he still the commissioner? He might as well be, he said. If he wants to do you harm, he will, even if he's retired or dying in hospital. I thought for a few minutes and then asked him again why he was shaking. I'm cold, he said (the liar), and my teeth hurt. I don't want to hear any more about Don Damian, I said. Do you think I'm friends with that pig? Do you think I associate with thugs? No, he said. Well I don't want to hear any more about him. **2.** He reflected for a while. What about, I really don't know. Then he gave me a crust of bread. It was hard and I said if he ate food like that it wasn't surprising his teeth hurt. We eat better in the asylum, I said, and that's saying something. Get out of here, Vicente, said the old guy. Does anyone know you're here? Well, good for you. Make yourself scarce before they realise. Don't say hello to anyone. Keep your eyes on the ground and get out of here as fast as you can. **3.** But I didn't leave right away. I squatted down in front of him and tried to remember the good times. My mind was blank. It felt like something was burning in my head. The old guy pulled his blanket tighter around him and moved his jaws as if he was chewing, but there was nothing in his mouth. I remembered the years in the asylum: the injections, the hosing-down, the ropes they used for tying us up at night, many of us anyway. I saw those funny beds again, the ones with a clever system of pulleys that can be used to hoist them into an upright position. It took me five years to work out what they were for. The patients called them American beds. **4.** Can a human being who is used to sleeping horizontally fall asleep in an upright position? Yes. It's difficult at first. But if the person is properly tied, it's possible. That's what the American beds were for, sleeping vertically as well as horizontally. Not, as I originally thought, to punish the patients, but to prevent them from choking on their own vomit and dying. **5.** Naturally, there were patients who spoke to the American beds. They addressed them politely. They confided in them. Some patients were also afraid of them. Some claimed to have been winked at by a certain bed. One patient said that another bed had raped him. A bed fucked you up the ass? You've really lost it, pal! The American beds were said to walk along the corridors at night, straight and tall, and gather to chat in the refectory — they spoke English — and all of them attended those meetings, the beds that were empty and the ones that weren't, and naturally these stories were told by the patients who for one reason or another happened to be tied to the beds on meeting nights. **6.** Otherwise, life in the asylum was very quiet. Shouts could be heard coming from certain restricted areas. But no one approached those areas or opened the door or put their ear to the keyhole. The house was quiet, and the park — tended by gardeners who were crazy too and not allowed to leave, but not as crazy as the others — was quiet as well, and the road you could see through the pines and the poplars was quiet, and even our thoughts, as they occurred to us, were enveloped in a frightening silence. **7.** In certain respects, the living was easy. Sometimes we'd look at each other and feel privileged. We're crazy, we're innocent. The only thing that spoiled that feeling was anticipation, when there was something to anticipate. But most of the patients had a remedy for that: ass-fucking the weaker ones or getting assfucked. Did I do that? we used to say. Did I really do that? And then we'd smile and change the subject. The doctors, the lofty physicians, had no idea, and as long as we didn't bother the nurses and the aides, they turned a blind eye. We did get carried away a few times. Man is an animal. **8.** That's what I used to think sometimes. The thought formed in the centre of my brain. And I concentrated on that thought until my mind went blank. Sometimes, at the beginning, I could hear something like tangling cables. Electrical cables or snakes. But as a rule, especially as those scenes receded into the past, my mind would go blank: no noises, no images, no words, no breakwaters of words. **9.** Anyway, I've never assumed that I'm smarter than anybody else. I've never been an intellectual show-off. If I'd been to school, I'd be a lawyer or a judge now. Or the inventor of a new, improved American bed! I have words, that much I humbly admit. But I don't make a big deal about it. And just as I have words, I have silence. You're as silent as a cat, the old guy told me when I was still a kid, though he was old already then. **10.** I wasn't born here. According to the old guy, I was born in Zaragoza and my mother had no choice but to come and live in this city. One city or another, it makes no difference to me. If I hadn't been poor, I would have been able to study here. It doesn't matter! I learned to read. That's enough! Best not to dwell on that subject. I could have got married here too. I met a girl who was called, I forget, she had a typical girl's name, and at one point I could have married her. Then I met another girl, older than me, a foreigner like me, from somewhere in the south, Andalusia or Murcia, a slut who was always in a bad mood. I could have started a family with her too, made a home, but I was destined for other things, and so was the slut. **11.** Sometimes I found the city stifling. Too small. I felt as if I was locked in a crossword puzzle. **12.** Around that time I made up my mind to start begging at church doors. I would arrive at ten and take up my position on the cathedral steps or go to the church of San Jeremías, in the Calle José Antonio, or the church of Santa Barbara, which was my favourite, in the Calle Salamanca, and sometimes, before settling down on the steps of Santa Barbara to begin my day's work, I would go to the ten o'clock mass and pray with all my might – it was like laughing silently, laughing, laughing, happy to be alive, and the more

I prayed, the more I laughed — that was my way of opening myself to divine penetration, and my laughter was not a sign of disrespect or the laughter of an unbeliever: on the contrary, it was the clamorous laughter of a lamb trembling before its Creator. **13.** After that, I would go to Confession, recount my mishaps and misfortunes, take Communion and finally, before returning to the steps, I would stop for a few moments in front of the picture of St Barbara. Why was she always depicted with a peacock and a tower? A peacock and a tower. What did it mean? **14.** One afternoon I asked the priest. Why are you interested in such things? he asked me in turn. I don't know, Father, curiosity, I replied. You know it's a bad habit, don't you, curiosity? he said. I know, Father, but my curiosity is pure, I always pray to St Barbara. That's good, my son, said the priest, St Barbara is kind to the poor, you keep praying to her. But I want to know about the peacock and the tower, I said. The peacock, said the priest, is the symbol of immortality. As for the tower, did you notice it has three windows? The windows are there to illustrate the saint's words; she said that light poured into her cell and her soul through the windows of the Father, the Son and the Holy Spirit. Do you understand? **15.** I didn't get an education, Father, but I have common sense and I can work things out, I replied. **16.** Then I went to take my place, the place that was rightfully mine, and I begged until the church doors were closed. I always kept one coin in the palm of my hand. The others in my pocket. And I endured hunger, while people ate bread and pieces of sausage or cheese in front of me. I thought. I thought and studied without moving from those steps. **17.** And so I learned that the father of St Barbara, a powerful man named Dioscurus, shut her up in a tower, imprisoned her because she was being pursued by suitors. And I learned that, before entering that tower, St Barbara baptised herself with water from a tank or a trough or a pond in which farmers stored rainwater. And I learned that she escaped from the tower, the tower with three windows to let the light in, but was arrested and brought before a judge. And the judge condemned her to death. **18.** All the teachings of the priests are cold. Cold soup. Cold tea. Blankets that don't keep you warm in the depths of winter. **19.** Get out of here, Vicente, said the old guy, his jaws working all the while. As if he was chewing sunflower seeds. Get some clothes to make you blend in and go, before the commissioner finds out. **20.** I put my hand in my pocket and counted the coins. It had begun to snow. I said goodbye to the old guy and went out into the street. **21.** I walked aimlessly. With no destination. Standing in the Calle Corona, I looked at the Church of Santa Barbara. I prayed a bit. St Barbara, have pity on me, I said. My left arm had gone to sleep. I was hungry. I wanted to die. But not for good. Maybe I just wanted to sleep. My teeth were chattering. St Barbara, have pity on your servant. **22.** When they decapitated her, I mean when they cut St Barbara's head off, her executioners were struck by a bolt of lightning. And what about the judge who sentenced her? And her father who locked her up? The lightning struck, but first there was a clap of thunder. Or the other way around. Great. My God, my God, my God. **23.** I didn't go any closer. I was happy to look at the church from a distance and then I walked on, heading for a bar where in my day you used to be able to get a cheap meal. I couldn't find it. I went into a bakery and got a baguette. Then I jumped a wall and ate it, out of sight of prying eyes. I know it's forbidden to jump over walls and eat in abandoned gardens or derelict houses, because it isn't safe. A beam could fall on you, Commissioner Damian Valle told me. Also, it's private property. It might be a shit-heap, crawling with spiders and rats, but it will go on being private property until the end of time. And a beam could fall on your head and destroy that exceptional skull of yours, said Commissioner Damian Valle. **24.** When I'd finished eating, I jumped back over the wall into the street. Suddenly I felt sad. I don't know if it was the snow or what. Recently, eating gets me down. I'm not sad when I'm actually eating, but afterward, sitting on a brick, watching snowflakes fall into the abandoned garden – I don't know. Despair and anguish. So I slapped my legs and got walking. The streets started to empty out. I spent some time looking in store windows. But I was pretending. What I was really doing was looking for my reflection in each pane of glass. Then the windows came to an end and there were only stairways. I hung my head and climbed. A street. Then the parish church of the Conception. Then the church of San Bernardo. Then the walls and, after that, the fort. There wasn't a soul to be seen. I was on Cerro del Moro. I remembered the old man's words: Go, go, don't let them catch you again, you poor bastard. All the bad things I did. St Barbara, have pity on me, have pity on your poor son. I remembered there was a woman who lived in one of those alleys. I decided to visit her and ask for a bowl of soup, an old sweater she didn't need any more, and a bit of money to buy a train ticket. Where did that woman live? The alleys kept getting narrower. I saw a big door and knocked. No one answered. I pushed the door open and walked in: a patio. Someone had forgotten to take in the washing and now the snow was falling on those yellowish clothes. I made my way through the shirts and underpants to a door with a bronze knocker that looked like a handle. I stroked the knocker, but I didn't knock. I pushed the door open. Outside, night was falling hurriedly. My mind was blank. The snowflakes made a sizzling sound. I kept going. I couldn't remember that corridor, I couldn't remember the name of the woman – she was a slut, but kind-hearted; she did wrong but she felt bad about it – I couldn't remember that darkness, that windowless tower. But then I saw a door ajar and slipped through the opening. I'd come to a kind of granary, with sacks piled up to the roof. There was a bed in one corner. I saw a child stretched out on the bed. He was naked and shivering. I took the knife out of my pocket. I saw a friar sitting at a table. His face was covered by a hood; he was leaning forward, intently reading a missal. Why was the child naked? Wasn't there even a blanket in that room? Why was the friar reading his missal instead of kneeling down and asking for forgiveness. Everything goes haywire at some point. The friar looked at me, said something; I replied. Don't come near me, I said. Then I stabbed him with the knife. Both of us groaned for a while until he fell silent. But I had to be sure, so I stabbed him again. Then I killed the child. Quickly, for God's sake! Then I sat down on the bed and shivered for a while. Enough. I had to go. My clothes were spattered with blood. I looked through the friar's pockets and found some money. There were some sweet potatoes on the table. I ate one. Good and sweet. While I was eating the sweet potato, I opened a closet. Sacks of onions and potatoes. But there was also a clean habit on a hanger. I got undressed. It was so cold. After checking each pocket, so as not to leave any incriminating evidence, I put my clothes and my shoes in a bag, and tied it to my belt. Fuck you, Damian Valle. That was when I realised I was leaving my footprints all around the room. The soles of my feet were covered with blood. While continuing to move around, I carefully examined the prints. Suddenly I felt like laughing. They were dance steps. The footprints of St Vitus. Footprints leading nowhere. But I knew where to go. **25.** Everything was dark, except for the snow. I started going down Cerro del Moro. **26.** I was barefoot and it was cold. My feet sank into the snow, and with every step I took, some blood came off my skin. When I'd gone a few yards I realised that someone was following me. A policeman? I didn't care. They rule the earth, but right then, as I walked through the luminous snow, I knew that I was in charge. **27.** I left Cerro del Moro behind. On the level ground the snow was deeper still; I crossed a bridge, hanging my head. Out of the corner of my eye, I glimpsed the shadow of an equestrian statue. My pursuer was a fat, ugly adolescent. Who was I? That didn't matter at all. **28.** As I walked, I said goodbye to everything I saw. It was poignant. I quickened my pace to warm myself up. I crossed the bridge, and it was as if I had passed through a time tunnel. **29.** I could have killed the boy, made him follow me down an alley and stuck it to him till he croaked. But why bother? He was bound to be some whore's kid from Cerro del Moro; he'd never talk. **30.** I washed my old shoes in the bathroom at the station, I wet them and scrubbed away the bloodstains. My feet had gone to sleep. Wake up. Then I bought a ticket for the next train. Whichever, I didn't care where it was going.

Literature + Illness = Illness

for my friend the hepatologist Dr Victor Vargas

Illness and Public Speaking

No one should be surprised if the speaker loses his thread. Let us imagine the following scenario. The speaker is going to speak about illness. Ten people spread themselves around the auditorium. The buzz of anticipation in the air is worthy of a better reward. The talk is scheduled to begin at seven in the evening or eight at night. No one in the audience has had dinner. By seven (or eight, or nine), they are all present and seated, with their cell phones switched off. It's a pleasure to speak to such a well-mannered group of people. But the speaker fails to appear, and finally one of the organisers of the event announces that he will not be coming because, at the last minute, he has fallen gravely ill.

Illness and Freedom

Writing about illness, especially if one is gravely ill, can be torture. Writing about illness if one is not only gravely ill but also a hypochondriac is an act of masochism or desperation. But it can also be a liberating act. It's tempting — I know it's an evil temptation — but all the same it *is* tempting to exercise the tyranny of the ill for a few minutes, like those little old ladies you meet in hospital waiting rooms, who launch into an explanation of the clinical or medical or pharmacological aspects of their life, instead of explaining the political or sexual or work-related aspects. Little old ladies who give the impression that they have transcended good and evil, and look for all the world like they know their Nietzsche, and not just Nietzsche, but Kant and Hegel and Schelling too, not to mention their closest philosophical relative: Ortega y Gasset. They could be his sisters, or rather his cronies, although actually they're more like the philosopher's clones. The resemblance is so striking that sometimes (as I reach the limits of my desperation) it occurs to me that Ortega y Gasset's paradise, or his hell — depending on the gaze but above all the sensibility of the observer — is to be found in hospital waiting rooms: a paradise in which thousands of duplicates of Ortega y Gasset live out the various episodes of our lives. But I mustn't wander too far from what I really wanted to talk about, which, in fact, was freedom, a kind of liberation: writing badly, speaking badly, holding forth about plate tectonics in the middle of a reptiles' dinner party — it's so liberating and so richly deserved — offering myself up to the compassion of strangers and then dishing out insults at random, spitting as I talk, passing out indiscriminately, becoming a nightmare for the friends I don't deserve, *milking a cow and pouring the milk over its head,* as Nicanor Parra says in a magnificent and mysterious line.

Illness and Height

But let's if not get to the point at least approach it briefly, where it lies like a seed deposited by the wind or pure chance bang in the middle of a vast bare tabletop. Not long ago, as I was leaving the consulting rooms of my specialist Victor Vargas, among the patients waiting to go in I found a woman waiting for me to come out. She was a small woman, by which I mean short; her head barely came up to my chest – the top of it would have been about an inch above my nipples – even though, as I soon realised, she was wearing spectacularly high heels. Needless to say, the consultation had not been reassuring, at all; the news my doctor had for me was unequivocally bad. I felt – I don't know – not exactly dizzy, which would have been understandable after all, but more as if everyone else had been stricken with dizziness, while I was the only one keeping reasonably calm and standing up straight, more or less. I had the impression that they were crawling on all fours, while I was upright or seated with my legs crossed, which to all intents and purposes is as good as standing or walking or maintaining a vertical position. I wouldn't, however, go so far as to say that I felt well, because it's one thing to remain upright while everyone else is on their hands and knees, and another thing entirely to watch, with a feeling I shall, for want of a better word, call *tenderness* or curiosity or morbid curiosity, while those around you are suddenly reduced, one and all, to crawling. Tenderness, melancholy, nostalgia: feelings befitting the sentimental lover, but hardly appropriate in the outpatients' ward of a Barcelona hospital. Of course, had that hospital been a mental asylum, such a vision would not have disturbed me at all, since from a tender age I have been familiar with – though never obeyed – the proverbial injunction, When in Rome, do as the Romans do, and the best way to behave in an asylum, apart from maintaining a dignified silence, is to crawl or observe the crawling of one's partners in misfortune. But I wasn't in an asylum; I was in one of the best public hospitals in Barcelona, a hospital that I know well, because I've been a patient there five or six times, and until that occasion I had never seen anyone on all fours, although I had seen some patients turn canary yellow, and others suddenly stop breathing – they were dying, which is not unusual in such a place, but crawling, I'd never seen anyone do that, which made me think that the doctor's news must have been much worse than I had initially realised, in other words, I was in *seriously* bad condition. And when I came out of the consulting rooms and saw everyone crawling, this sense of my own illness intensified, and I was about to succumb to fear and start crawling too. But I didn't, because of that little woman: she stepped forward and said her name, Dr X, and then pronounced the name of my specialist, my dear Dr Vargas – my relationship with him is like the marriage of a Greek shipping magnate who loves his wife but prefers to see her as rarely as he can—and Dr X went on to say that she knew about my illness or the progress of my illness and that she would like me to participate in a study she was conducting. I asked her politely about the nature of the study. Her reply was vague. She explained that it would only take half an hour of my time, if that; she had a series of tests for me. I don't know why, but I ended up saying yes, and then she led me away from the consulting rooms to an elevator of impressive proportions, in which there was a gurney, with no one to push it, and no one on it, of course, a gurney that lived in the elevator, going up and down, like a normal-sized girl alongside – or inside – her oversized boyfriend. It really was very large, that elevator, large enough to accommodate not just one gurney but two, plus a wheelchair, all with their respective occupants, and the strangest thing was that we were alone in there, the tiny doctor and myself, and at that point, having calmed down or become more excited, I'm not sure which, I realised that the tiny doctor was not at all bad-looking. No sooner had I come to that realisation than I found myself wondering what would happen if I suggested that we make love in the elevator, since we had a bed at our disposal. And then, inevitably, I remembered Susan Sarandon, dressed up as a nun, asking Sean Penn how he could think about fucking when he had only a few days left to live. In a censorious tone of voice, of course. And, unsurprisingly, I've forgotten the name of the film, but it was a good film, I think it was directed by Tim Robbins, who's a good actor and maybe a good director too, but he's never been on death row. When people are about to die, all they want to do is fuck. People in jails and hospitals, all they want to do is fuck. The helpless, the impotent, the castrated, all they want to do is fuck. The seriously injured, the suicidal, the impenitent disciples of Heidegger. Even Wittgenstein, the greatest philosopher of the twentieth century, all he wanted to do was fuck. Even the dead, I read somewhere, all they want to do is fuck. Sad to say and hard to admit, but that's the way it is.

Literature + Illness = Illness

Illness and Dionysus

To tell the truth, the honest truth, cross my heart and hope to die, it's something I find very hard to admit. That seminal explosion, those cumulus and cirrus clouds that blanket our imaginary geography are enough to sadden anyone. Fucking when you don't have the strength to fuck can be beautiful, even epic. Then it turns into a nightmare. But what can you do? That's how it is. Consider, for instance, a Mexican jail. A new prisoner arrives. Not what you'd call handsome: squat, greasy, pot-bellied, cross-eyed, malevolent and smelly into the bargain. Before long, this guy, whose shadow creeps over the prison walls or the walls of the corridors at an exasperating, slug-like pace, becomes the lover of another guy, who is just as ugly, but stronger. It's not a long, drawn-out romance, proceeding by tentative steps and hesitations. It's not a case of elective affinity, as Goethe understood it. It's love at first sight; primitive, if you like, but their objective is not so different from that of many normal couples or couples we consider to be normal. They are sweethearts. Their flirting and their swooning are like X-ray images. They fuck every night. Sometimes they hit each other. Sometimes they tell the stories of their lives, as if they were friends, but they're not really friends, they're lovers. And on Sundays, their respective wives, who are every bit as ugly as they are, come to visit. Obviously, neither of these men is what we would normally call a homosexual. If someone called them homosexuals to their faces, they'd probably get so angry and be so offended, they'd brutally rape the offender, then kill him.

That's how it is. Victor Hugo, who, according to Daudet, was capable of eating a whole orange in one mouthful – a supreme test of good health, according to Daudet, and a sign of pig-like manners, according to my wife – set down the following reflection in *Les Misérables*: sinister people, malicious people know a sinister and malicious happiness. Or that's what I seem to remember, because *Les Misérables* is a book I read in Mexico many years ago and left behind in Mexico when I left Mexico for good, and I'm not planning to buy it or reread it, because there's no point reading, much less rereading, books that have been made into movies, and I think *Les Misérables* has even been turned into a musical. Anyway, the malicious people in question, with their malicious happiness, are the horrible family who adopt Cosette when she is a little girl, and not only are they the perfect incarnations of evil and a certain *petit bourgeois* meanness or rather the meanness of those who aspire to join the *petit bourgeoisie*, they are also, at this point in history, thanks to technological progress, emblematic of the middle class in its entirety, or almost, be it left- or right-wing, educated or illiterate, corrupt or apparently upstanding: healthy individuals, busily maintaining their good health; they may be less violent, less courageous, more prudent and more discreet, but basically they're just the same as the two Mexican gunmen living out their idyll in the confines of a penitentiary. There's no stopping Dionysus. He has infiltrated the churches and the NGOs, the governments and the royal families, the offices and the shantytowns. Dionysus is to blame for everything. Dionysus rules. And his antagonist or counterpart is not even Apollo but Mr Uppity or Mrs Toplofty, Mr Prissy or

Mrs Lonely Neuron — bodyguards who are ready to cross over to the enemy camp at the first suspicious bang.

Illness and Apollo

Where has that faggot Apollo got to? Apollo is ill, seriously ill.

Illness and French Poetry

As the French are well aware, the finest poetry of the nineteenth century was written in France, and in some sense the pages and the lines of that poetry prefigured the major and still unresolved problems that Europe and Western culture were to face in the twentieth century. A short list of the key themes would include revolution, death, boredom and escape. That great poetry is the work of a handful of poets, and its point of departure is not Lamartine, or Hugo or Nerval, but Baudelaire. Let's say that it begins with Baudelaire, reaches its highest volatility with Lautréamont and Rimbaud and comes to an end with Mallarmé. Of course there are other remarkable poets, like Corbière or Verlaine, and others of considerable talent, like Laforgue or Catulle Mendès or Charles Cros, and even a few who are not entirely insignificant, like Banville. But, really, with Baudelaire, Lautréamont, Rimbaud, and Mallarmé, there's plenty to be going on with. Let's begin with the last of the four. I don't mean the youngest, but the last one to die, Mallarmé, who missed out on the twentieth century by two years. He wrote in *Brise marine*:

> The flesh is sad – and I've read every book.
> O to escape – to get away. Birds look
> as though they're drunk for unknown spray and skies.
> No ancient gardens mirrored in the eyes,
> nothing can hold this heart steeped in the sea –
> not my lamp's desolate luminosity
> nor the blank paper guarded by its white
> nor the young wife feeding her child, O night!
> I'm off! You steamer with your swaying helm,
> raise anchor for some more exotic realm!
> Ennui, crushed down by cruel hopes, still relies
> on handkerchief's definitive goodbyes!
> Is this the kind of squall-inviting mast
> the storm winds buckle above shipwrecks cast
> away – no mast, no islets flourishing? . . .
> Still, my soul, listen to the sailors sing!

A charming poem. Although Nabokov would have advised the translators, E.H. and A.M. Blackmore, to abandon the rhyme scheme, to use free verse, to produce a deliberately ugly version, and if he'd known Alfonso Reyes, who translated the poem into Spanish, with rhymes, he'd have given him the same advice. Now Reyes might not mean a lot to Western culture as a whole, but he does (or should) mean a great deal to that part of Western culture that is Latin America. What did Mallarmé mean when he said that the flesh was sad and that he'd read all the books? That he'd had his fill of reading and of fucking? That beyond a certain point, every book we read and every act of carnal knowledge is a repetition? And after that there is only travel? That fucking and reading are boring in the end, and that travel is the only way out? I think Mallarmé is talking about

Literature + Illness = Illness

illness, about the battle between illness and health: two totalitarian states, or powers if you prefer. I think he's talking about illness tricked out in the rags of boredom. And yet he presents an image of illness that has a certain originality; he speaks of illness as *resignation*, resignation to living, or to whatever. In other words, he's talking about defeat. And in order to counter that defeat, he vainly invokes sex and reading, which, I suspect, in Mallarmé's case — to his greater glory and the bemusement of his good wife — were interchangeable, because how else could anyone in their right mind say that the flesh is sad, period, in that emphatic way? How could anyone declare that the flesh is *essentially* sad, that *la petite mort*, which doesn't even last a minute, casts a pall over all lovemaking, which, it is widely known, can last for hours and hours, and go on interminably? If the line had been written by a Spanish poet like Campoamor, it might have meant something like that, but such a reading is quite at odds with the work and life of Mallarmé, which are indissolubly linked, except in this poem, this encoded manifesto, which Paul Gauguin, and he alone, followed to the letter (as far as we know, Mallarmé himself never listened to the sailors singing, or if he did, it certainly wasn't on board a ship bound for an unknown destination). And the claim to have read all the books makes even less sense, because although books themselves may come to an end, no one ever finishes reading them all, and Mallarmé was well aware of that. Books are finite, sexual encounters are finite, but the desire to read and to fuck is infinite; it surpasses our own deaths, our fears, our hopes for peace. And what is left for Mallarmé, in this famous poem, when the desire to read and the desire to fuck, so he says, are all used up? Well, what is left is travel, the desire to go travelling. And maybe that's the key to the crime. Because if

Mallarmé had concluded that the only thing left to do was pray or cry or go crazy, maybe he'd have come up with the perfect alibi. But no, what Mallarmé says is that the only thing left to do is travel – which is like saying 'to sail is necessary, to live is not necessary', a sentence I used to be able to quote in Latin, but that's just one of the many things I've forgotten with the help of my liver's travelling toxins – in other words he sides with the bare-chested traveller, with Freedom (who's bare-chested too), with the simple existence of the sailor and the explorer, which isn't so simple when you get right down to it: an affirmation of life, but also a constant game with death, and the first rung on the ladder, the first step in a certain kind of poetic apprenticeship. The second step is sex, and the third, books. Which means that the Mallarmean choice is paradoxical or regressive, a starting over. And at this point, before we return to the elevator, I can't help recalling a poem by Baudelaire, the father of them all, in which he speaks of travel, the voyage, the naïve enthusiasm of setting out, and the bitterness that every voyage bequeaths to the voyager when all is said and done, and it occurs to me that perhaps Mallarmé's sonnet is a reply to Baudelaire's poem, one of the most terrible poems I have read, an *ill poem,* a poem that offers no way out, but perhaps the most clear-eyed poem of the entire nineteenth century.

Illness and Travel

Travelling makes you ill. In the old days, doctors used to recommend travel, especially for patients suffering from nervous illnesses. The patients, who were generally wealthy,

Literature + Illness = Illness

complied and set off on long trips that lasted months and sometimes years. Poor people who had nervous illnesses didn't get to travel. Some, presumably, went crazy. But the travelling patients also went crazy, or, worse still, acquired new illnesses as they moved from one city or climate or culinary culture to another. Really, it's healthier not to travel; it's healthier not to budge and never leave home, warmly wrapped up in winter, only removing your scarf in summertime; it's healthier not to open your mouth or blink; it's healthier not to breathe. But the fact is, we breathe and travel. Myself, for example, I began travelling very young, at the age of seven or eight. First in my father's truck, on lonely Chilean highways that had a post-nuclear feel to them and made my hair bristle, then in trains and buses, until at the age of fifteen, I boarded a plane for the first time and went to live in Mexico. From that moment on, I was constantly travelling. Consequence: multiple illnesses. In childhood: major headaches, which made my parents wonder if I had a nervous illness, and whether it might be advisable for me to undertake, as soon as possible, a long therapeutic voyage. In adolescence: insomnia and problems of a sexual nature. As a young man: the loss of my teeth, which I left here and there on my way from country to country, like Hansel and Gretel's breadcrumbs; a bad diet, which gave me heartburn and then gastritis; excessive reading, which weakened my eyes, so I had to wear glasses; calluses on my feet from long, aimless walks; and an endless string of lingering colds and flus. I was poor, lived rough, and thought myself lucky because, after all, I was free of life-threatening illnesses. My sex-life was immoderate but I never caught a venereal disease. I read immoderately, but I never wanted to be a successful author. I even regarded the loss of my teeth as a kind of homage to Gary Snyder, whose life of Zen wandering had led him to neglect dental care. But it all catches up with you. Children. Books. Illness. The voyage comes to an end.

Illness and Dead Ends

Baudelaire's poem is called 'The Voyage'. It is a long and delirious poem, possessed of the delirium that results from extreme lucidity, and this is not the moment to read it all the way through. Here are the first lines in Richard Howard's translation:

> The child enthralled by lithographs and maps
> can satisfy his hunger for the world

The poem, then, begins with a child. *Naturally* the poem of adventure and horror begins with the pure gaze of a child. Then it goes on:

> One morning we set out. Our heart is full,
> our mind ablaze with rancour and disgust,
> we yield it all to the rhythm of the waves,
> our infinite self awash on the finite sea:
>
> some are escaping from their country's shame,
> some from the horror of life at home, and some
> – astrologers blinded by a woman's stare –
> are fugitives from Circe's tyranny;
> rather than be turned to swine they drug

Literature + Illness = Illness

> themselves on wind and sea and glowing skies;
> rain and snow and incinerating suns
> gradually erase her kisses' scars.
>
> But only those who leave for leaving's sake
> are travellers; hearts tugging like balloons,
> they never balk at what they call their fate
> and, not knowing why, keep muttering 'away' . . .

In a way, the voyage undertaken by the crew in Baudelaire's poem is similar to the voyage of a convict ship. I shall set off, I shall venture into unknown territory, and see what I find, see what happens. But first I shall give up everything. Or to put it another way: genuine travel requires travellers who have nothing to lose. The voyage, this long and hazardous nineteenth-century voyage, resembles the patient's voyage on a gurney, from his room to the operating theatre, where masked men and women await him, like bandits from the sect of the Hashishin. It's true that the early stages of the voyage are not devoid of paradisiacal visions, which owe more to the travellers' desires or cultural background than to reality:

> Awesome travellers! What noble chronicles
> we read in your unfathomable eyes!
> Open the sea-chests of your memories

The poem also says: Tell us what you've seen! And the traveller, or the ghost that represents the traveller and his companions, replies by listing the circles of Hell. Baudelaire's traveller clearly isn't saying that the flesh is sad or that he has read all the books, although he just as clearly knows that entropy's gem and trophy, the flesh, is more than merely sad, and that once a single book has been read, all the others have been read as well. Baudelaire's traveller has a full heart and a mind ablaze with rancour and disgust, which means that he's probably a radical, modern traveller, although of course he's someone who, understandably, wants to come through; he wants to *see*, but he also wants to come through it alive. The voyage, as it unfolds in the poem, is like a ship or an unruly caravan heading straight for the abyss, but the traveller, to judge from his disgust, desperation, and scorn, wants to come through it alive. And what he finds in the end, like Ulysses or the patient travelling on his gurney who confuses the ceiling with the abyss, is his own image:

> It is a bitter truth our travels teach!
> Tiny and monotonous, the world
> has shown – will always show us – what we are:
> oases of fear in the wasteland of ennui!

In that line alone there is more than enough. In the middle of a desert of ennui, an oasis of fear, or horror. There is no more lucid diagnosis of the illness of modern humanity. To break out of ennui, to escape from boredom, all we have at our disposal – and it's not even automatically at our disposal, again we have to make an effort – is horror, in other words, evil. Either we live like zombies, like slaves fed on soma, or we become slave drivers, malignant individuals, like that guy who, after killing his wife and three children, said, as the sweat poured off him, that he felt strange, possessed by something he'd never known: freedom, and then he said that the victims had deserved it, although a few hours later, when he'd calmed down a bit, he also said that no one deserved to die so horribly, and added that he'd probably gone crazy and told the police not to listen to him. An oasis is always an oasis, especially if you come to it from a desert of boredom. In an oasis you can drink, eat, tend to your wounds, and rest, but if it's an oasis of horror, if that's the only sort there is, the traveller will be able to confirm, and this time irrefutably, that the flesh is sad, that a day comes when all the books have indeed been read, and that travel is the pursuit of a mirage. All the indications are that every oasis in existence has either attained or is drifting towards the condition of horror.

Illness and The Documentary

One of the most vivid images of illness I can recall is of a guy whose name I've forgotten, a New York artist who worked in the space between begging and the avant-garde, between the adepts of fist-fucking and the modern-day mendicants. One night, years ago, very late, when the TV audience had dwindled to me, I saw him in a documentary. He was an extreme masochist, and extracted the raw materials of his art from his proclivity or fate or incurable vice. Half actor, half painter. As I remember, he wasn't very tall and he was going bald. He filmed his experiments: scenes or dramatisations of pain. Pain that grew more and more intense, and sometimes brought the artist to the brink of death. One day, after a routine visit to the hospital, they tell him he has a fatal illness. At first he is surprised. But the surprise doesn't last long. Almost straightaway, the guy begins to film his final performance, which, as opposed to the earlier ones, turns out to be admirably restrained, at least at the start. He seems calm and, above all, subdued, as if he had ceased to believe in the effectiveness of wild gestures and overacting. We see him, for example, on a bicycle, pedalling along a kind of seaside boulevard – it must be Coney Island – then sitting on a breakwater, reminiscing about unrelated scenes from his childhood and adolescence while he looks at the ocean and occasionally throws a sidelong glance at the camera. His voice and expression are neither cold nor warm. He doesn't sound like an alien, or a man desperately hiding under his bed with his eyes shut tight. Perhaps he has the voice, and the expression, of a blind man, but if so, it is clearly the voice of a blind man addressing himself to the blind. I wouldn't say that he has serenely accepted his fate or resolved to resist it with all his strength, what I would say is that he is a man who is utterly indifferent to his fate. The final scenes take place in the hospital. The guy knows he won't be getting out of there alive; he knows that death is the only thing left, but he still looks at the camera, whose function is to document this final performance. And only at this point does the sleepless viewer realise that there are in fact two cameras, and two films: the documentary that he is watching on television, a French or German production, and the documentary recording the performance, which will follow the artist whose name I've forgotten or never knew right up to the moment of his death, the documentary that he is directing, with an iron hand or an iron gaze, from his procrustean bed. That's how it is. A voice, the voice of the French or German narrator, says goodbye to the New Yorker, and then, when the screen has faded to black, pronounces the date of his death, a few weeks later. The pain artist's documentary, however, follows the dying step by step, but we don't see that, we can only imagine it, or let the image fade to black and read the clinical date of his death, because if we watched, if we saw, it would be unbearable.

Illness and Poetry

Between the vast deserts of boredom and the not-so-scarce oases of horror, there is, however, a third option, or perhaps a delusion, which Baudelaire indicates in the following lines:

> Once we have burned our brains out, we can plunge
> to Hell or Heaven – any abyss will do –
> deep in the Unknown to find the *new*!

That final line, deep in the Unknown to find the new, is art's paltry flag pitting itself against the horror that adds to horror without making a substantial difference, just as one infinity added to another produces an infinite sum. A losing battle from the start, like all the battles poets fight. This is something that Lautréamont seems to contradict, because his voyage takes him from the periphery to the metropolis, and his way of travelling and seeing remains cloaked in the most impenetrable mystery, so that we can't tell if we're dealing with a militant nihilist or an outrageous optimist or the secret mastermind of the imminent Commune; and it's something that Rimbaud clearly understood, since he plunged with equal fervour into reading, sex, and travel, only to discover and accept, with a diamond-like lucidity, that writing doesn't matter at all (writing is obviously the same as reading, and sometimes it's quite similar to travelling, and it can even, on special occasions, resemble sex, but all that, Rimbaud tells us, is a mirage: there is only the desert and from time to time the remote, degrading lights of an oasis). And then along comes Mallarmé, the least innocent of all the great poets, who says that we must travel, we must set off travelling again. At this point, even the most naïve reader has to wonder: What's got into Mallarmé? Why is he so enthusiastic? Is he trying to sell us a trip or sending us to our deaths with our hands and feet tied? Is this an elaborate joke or simply a pattern of sounds? It would be utterly absurd to suppose that Mallarmé had not read Baudelaire. So what is he trying to do? The answer, I think, is perfectly simple. Mallarmé wants to start all over again, even though he knows that the voyage and the voyagers are doomed. In other words, for the author of *Igitur*, the illness afflicts not only our actions, but also language itself. But while we are looking for the antidote or the medicine to cure us, that is, the *new*, which can only be found by plunging deep into the Unknown, we have to go on exploring sex, books, and travel, although we know that they lead us to the abyss, which, as it happens, is the only place where the antidote can be found.

Illness and Tests

And now it is time to return to that enormous elevator, the biggest I've ever seen, an elevator in which there was space enough for a shepherd to pen a smallish flock of sheep, or a farmer to stable two mad cows, or a nurse to fit two empty gurneys, and in which I was torn between asking the tiny doctor — almost as small as a Japanese doll — if she would make love with me, or at least give it a try, and (this was the likelier option) bursting into tears, like Alice in Wonderland, and flooding the elevator not with blood, as in Kubrick's *The Shining*, but with salt water. This was one of those situations in which good manners, which are never redundant, and rarely a hindrance, did in fact hinder me, and soon the Japanese doctor and I were shut in a cubicle, with a window from which you could see the back part of the hospital, doing some very odd tests, which seemed to me exactly like the tests you find on the puzzle page of the Sunday paper. I was careful to do them as well as I could, as if I wanted to prove to her that my specialist was mistaken — a futile enterprise, because however perfectly I did the tests, the little Japanese doctor remained impassive: not even a tiny smile of encouragement. Between tests, while she was getting the next one ready, we talked. I asked her about the chances of success with a liver transplant. Vely good, she said. What percent? I asked. Sixty per cent, she said. Jesus, I said, that's not much. In politics it's absolute majority, she said. One of the tests, maybe the simplest, made a big impression on me. It consisted of holding my hands out in a vertical position for a few seconds, that is, with the fingers pointing up, the palms facing her and the backs to me. I asked her what the hell that test was about. Her reply was that at a more advanced stage of my illness, I wouldn't be able to hold my fingers in that position. They would, inevitably, curve towards her. I think I said: Christ almighty. Maybe I laughed. In any case, every day since then, wherever I happen to be, I take that test. I hold my hands out, palms facing away, and for a few seconds I examine my knuckles, my nails, the wrinkles that form on each phalange. The day when my fingers can't hold themselves up straight, I don't really know what I'll do, although I do know what I *won't* do. Mallarmé wrote that a roll of the dice will never abolish chance. And yet every day the dice have to be rolled, just as the vertical-fingers test has to be taken every day.

Illness and Kafka

Elias Canetti, in his book on the twentieth century's greatest writer, says that Kafka understood that the dice had been rolled and that nothing could come between him and writing the day he spat blood for the first time. What do I mean when I say that nothing could come between him and his writing? To be honest, I don't really know. I guess I mean that Kafka understood that travel, sex, and books are paths that lead nowhere except to the loss of the self, and yet they must be followed and the self must be lost, in order to find it again, or to find something, whatever it may be – a book, an expression, a misplaced object – in order to find anything at all, a method, perhaps, and, with a bit of luck, the *new*, which has been there all along.

The Myths of Cthulhu

for Alan Pauls

These are dark times we live in, but let me begin with a buoyant declaration. Literature in Spanish is in excellent condition! Magnificent, superlative condition!

In fact, if it was any better I'd be worried.

But let's not get too carried away. It's good, but it's not going to give anyone a heart attack. There's nothing to suggest any kind of great leap forward.

According to a critic by the name of Conte, Pérez Reverte is Spain's perfect novelist. I don't have a copy of the article in which he makes that claim, so I can't cite it exactly. As I recall, he said that Pérez Reverte was the *most* perfect novelist in contemporary Spanish literature, as if it were possible to go on perfecting oneself after having achieved perfection. His principal quality, but I don't know if it was Conte who said this or the novelist Juan Marsé, is readability. A readability that makes him not only the most perfect novelist but also the most read. That is: the one who sells the most books.

★

But if we adopt that point of view, Spanish fiction's perfect novelist could just as well be Vázquez Figueroa, who spends his spare time inventing desalination machines or desalination plants: contraptions that will soon be turning sea water into fresh water, suitable for irrigation, showers, and probably even for drinking. Vázquez Figueroa might not be the *most* perfect, but he certainly is perfect in his way. He's readable. He's enjoyable. He sells a lot. His stories, like those of Pérez Reverte, are full of adventures.

I really wish I had a copy of Conte's review. It's a pity I don't collect press clippings, like that character in Cela's *The Beehive,* who keeps an article that he wrote for a provincial newspaper, probably one of the Workers' Movement papers, in the pocket of his shabby jacket – a likable character, by the way; in the movie, he was played by José Sacristán, and that's how I always see him in my mind's eye, with that pale helpless face, the incongruous face of a beaten dog, carrying that crumpled clipping around in his pocket as he wanders over the impossible tablelands of Spain. At this point I hope you'll allow me to indulge in a pair of elucidatory digressions or sighs: José Sacristán, what a fine actor! His performances are so enjoyable, so readable. And Camilo José Cela, what an odd phenomenon! More and more he reminds me of a Chilean estate-holder or a Mexican rancher; his illegitimate children (as Latin Americans would politely say) or his bastards keep springing up like weeds: vulgar, reluctant, but tenacious and gruff, like candid lilacs out of the dead land, as the candid Eliot put it.

★

By attaching Cela's incredibly fat corpse to a horse, we could produce the new El Cid of Spanish letters, and we have!

Statement of principles:

In principle, I have nothing against clear, enjoyable writing. In practice, it depends.

It's always a good idea to state this principle when venturing into the world of literature: a sort of Club Med cunningly disguised as a swamp, a desert, a working-class suburb, or a novel-as-mirror reflecting itself.

Here's a rhetorical question that I'd like someone to answer for me: Why does Pérez Reverte or Vázquez Figueroa or any other bestselling author, for example Muñoz Molina or that young man who goes by the resonant name of De Prada, sell so much? Is it just because their books are enjoyable and easy to follow? Is it just because they tell stories that keep the reader in suspense? Won't anyone give me an answer? Where is the man who will dare to answer? It's all right, you can keep quiet. I hate to see people lose their friends. I'll answer the question myself. The answer is no. It's not just that. They sell and they are popular because their stories can be *understood*. That is, because the readers, who are never wrong – I don't mean as readers, obviously, but as consumers, of books in this case – understand their novels or stories perfectly. This is something that the critic Conte knows, or perhaps, given his youth, intuits. It's something that the novelist Marsé, who is old, has learned from experience. The public, the public, as García Lorca said to a hustler while they hid in an entrance hall, is never, never,

never wrong. And why is the public never wrong? Because the public *understands*.

It is, of course, only reasonable to accept and indeed to demand that a novel should be clear and entertaining, since the novel, as an art form, is at best tenuously related to the great forces that shape public history and our private stories, namely science and television; nevertheless, when the rule of clarity and entertainment-value is extended to serious non-fiction and philosophy, the results can be catastrophic, at least at first glance, although the idea, the ideal, remains compelling, a goal to be desired and aspired to in the longer term. 'Weak thought', for example. Honestly, I have no idea what weak thought was or is supposed to be. Its promoter, I seem to remember, was a 20th-century Italian philosopher. I never read any of his books or any book about him. One reason – this is a fact, not an excuse – is that I had no money to buy books. So I must have learned of his existence in the pages of some newspaper. That's how I discovered that there was such a thing as weak thought. The philosopher is probably still alive. But in the end he's immaterial. Maybe I completely misunderstood what he meant by weak thought. Probably. But what matters is the *title* of his book. Just as when we talk about *Don Quixote*, what we're usually referring to is not so much the book itself as the title and a couple of windmills. And when we talk about Kafka (may God forgive me), it's less about Kafka and the fire than a lady or a gentleman at a window. (This is known as encapsulation, an image retained and metabolised by the body, fixed in historical memory, the solidification of chance and fate.) The strength of weak thought – this intuition came to me in a fit of dizziness, brought on by hunger – sprang from the way it presented itself as a philosophical method for people unfamiliar with philosophical systems. Weak thought for the weak classes. With a bit of well-targeted marketing, a construction worker in Gerona, who has never sat down on the scaffolding, thirty yards above street level, with his copy of the *Tractatus logico-philosophicus*, or reread it while chewing through his *chope* roll, might be prompted to read the Italian philosopher instead or one of his disciples, whose clear, enjoyable, intelligible style is bound to go straight to his heart.

At that moment, in spite of the dizziness, I felt like Nietzsche when he had his Eternal Return epiphany. An inexorable succession of nanoseconds, each one blessed by eternity.

What is *chope*? What does a *chope* roll consist of? Is the bread rubbed with tomato and a few drops of olive oil, or is it just plain bread that is wrapped in aluminium foil, also known by its brand name as *albal*? And what does the *chope* consist of? Mortadella cheese, maybe? Or a mixture of mortadella and boiled ham? Or salami and mortadella? Does it contain chorizo or sausage? And how did the foil come to have the brand name *albal*? Is it a family name, the name of Mr Nemesio Albal? Or is it an allusion to *el alba*, the dawn, the bright dawn of lovers and workers who, before setting off for their daily labour, put a pound of bread and the corresponding ration of sliced *chope* into their lunch boxes?

Dawn with a slight metallic sheen. Bright dawn over the shithole. That was the title of a poem I wrote with Bruno Montané centuries ago. The other day I came across the title and the poem attributed to another poet. Honestly, honestly, what are these people thinking? The lengths they go to, tracking, poaching, harassing. And the worst thing is, it's an appalling title.

But let us return to weak thought, which goes down like a treat on the scaffolding. It's pleasant to read, you can't deny that. It isn't short on clarity either. And the socially weak or powerless understand the message perfectly. Hitler, to take another example, there was an essayist or philosopher – take your pick – who specialised in weak thought. He's always understandable! Self-help books are in fact books of practical philosophy, enjoyable down-to-earth philosophy that the woman and the man in the street can understand. That Spanish philosopher, who analyses and interprets the ups and downs of Big Brother, is a readable and clear philosopher, although in his case the revelation came a couple of decades late. I can't recall his name for the moment, because, as many of you will have guessed, I am writing this speech on the fly a few days before delivering it. All I can remember is that the philosopher in question lived for many years in a Latin American country; I imagine him there feeling thoroughly sick of his tropical exile, and the mosquitoes, and the ghastly exuberance of the flowers of evil. Now the old philosopher lives in a Spanish city, somewhere north of Andalusia, enduring endless winters, muffled in a scarf and a woollen cap, watching the competitors in Big Brother and taking notes in a notebook with pages white and cold as snow.

For books about theology, there's no one to match Sánchez Dragó. For books about popular science, there's no one to match some guy whose name escapes me for the moment, a specialist in UFOs. For books about intertextuality, there's no one to match Lucía Extebarría. For books about multiculturalism, there's no one to match Sánchez Dragó. For political books, there's no one to match Juan Goytisolo. For books about history and mythology, there's no one to match Sánchez Dragó. For a book about the ill-treatment of women today, there's no one to match that lovely talk-show host Ana Rosa Quintana. For books about travel, there's no one to match Sánchez Dragó. I just love Sánchez Dragó. He doesn't look his age. I wonder if he dyes his hair with henna or ordinary dye from the hairdresser. Maybe his hair hasn't gone grey. And if he hasn't gone grey, how come he hasn't gone bald, which is what usually happens to men whose hair doesn't lose its original colour?

And now for the question that has been tormenting me: Why hasn't Sánchez Dragó invited me to appear on his TV show? What is he waiting for? Does he want me to get down on my knees and grovel at his feet like a sinner before the burning bush? Is he waiting for my health to deteriorate even further? Or for me to get a recommendation from Pitita Ridruejo? Well, you watch out, Víctor Sánchez Dragó! There's a limit to my patience and I was a gangster in a former life! Don't say you weren't warned, Gregorio Sánchez Dragó!

Hear this. To the right hand side of the routine signpost (coming – of course – from north-northwest), right where a bored skeleton yawns, you can already see Comala, the city of death. This speech is bound for that city, mounted on an ass, as all of us in our various more or less premeditated ways are bound for the city of Comala. But before we get there, I would like to relate a story told by Nicanor Parra, whom I would consider my master if I was worthy to be his disciple, which I'm not. One day, not so long ago, Nicanor Parra received an honorary doctorate from the University of Concepción. The honour might have been conferred by the University of Santa Barbara or Mulchén or Coigüe; I've been told that in the '90s all you needed to start up a private university in Chile was to have finished primary school and secured the use of a reasonable sized house; it's one of the boons of the free-market system. The University of Concepción, however, has a certain prestige; it's a big university and still a state-run institution as far as I know, and a tribute to Nicanor Parra was organised there and they gave him an honorary doctorate and invited him to conduct a master class. So Nicanor Parra turns up and the first thing he explains is that when he was a kid or a teenager, he went to that university – not to study, but to sell sandwiches (sometimes called *sánguches* in Chile), which the students used to wolf down between classes. Sometimes Nicanor Parra went there with his uncle, sometimes he went with his mother, and occasionally he went on his own, with a bag full of sandwiches, wrapped not in *albal* foil but in newspaper or brown paper, and perhaps he didn't carry them in a bag but in a basket, covered with a dish cloth, for hygienic and aesthetic and even practical reasons. And addressing that roomful of smiling southern professors, Nicanor Parra evoked the old University of Concepción, which was probably disappearing into the void, and continues to disappear, even now, into the void's inertia or our perception of it; and he remembered his younger self: badly dressed, we can assume, wearing sandals and the ill-fitting clothes of a poor adolescent, and everything – even the smell of that time, a smell of Chilean colds and southern flus – was trapped like a butterfly by the question that Wittgenstein asks himself and us, speaking from another time, from faraway Europe, a question to which there is no answer: Is *this* hand a hand or isn't it?

Latin America was Europe's mental asylum just as North America was its factory. The foremen have taken over the factory now and the labour force is made up of escapees from the asylum. For over sixty years, the asylum has been burning in its own oil, its own fat.

Today I read an interview with a famous and shrewd Latin American author. They ask him to name three people he admires. He replies: Nelson Mandela, Gabriel García Márquez and Mario Vargas Llosa. With that answer as a starting point, you could write a whole thesis about the current state of Latin American literature. The casual reader might wonder what links those three figures. There is something that links two of them: the Nobel Prize. And there is something more that links all three: years ago they were all left wing. They probably all admire the voice of Miriam Makeba. All three have probably danced to her catchy hit song 'Pata Pata', García Márquez and Vargas Llosa in colourful Latin American apartments, Mandela in the solitude of his prison cell. All three have made way for deplorable heirs: the clear and entertaining epigones of García Márquez and Vargas Llosa, and, in the case of Mandela, the indescribable Thabo Mbeki, the current president of South Africa, who denies the existence of AIDS. How could anyone name those three, without batting an eyelid, as the figures he most admires? Why not Bush, Putin and Castro? Why not Mullah Omar, Haider and Berlusconi? Why not Sánchez Dragó, Sánchez Dragó and Sánchez Dragó, disguised as the Holy Trinity?

Declarations like that are a sign of the times. Of course, I'm prepared to do whatever's necessary (though that sounds unnecessarily melodramatic) to ensure that the shrewd writer in question remains free to make that declaration or any other, according to his taste and inclinations – to ensure that everyone can say what they want to say and write what they want to write and publish it as well. I'm against censorship and self-censorship. But on one condition, as Alcaeus of Mytilene said: if you're going to say what you want to say, you're going to hear what you don't want to hear.

The fact is, Latin American literature isn't Borges or Macedonio Fernández or Onetti or Bioy or Cortázar or Rulfo or Revueltas or even that pair of old bucks García Márquez and Vargas Llosa. Latin American literature is Isabel Allende, Luís Sepúlveda, Ángeles Mastretta, Sergio Ramírez, Tomás Eloy Martínez, a certain Aguilar Camín or Comín and many other illustrious names that escape me for the moment.

The work of Reinaldo Arenas is already lost. And the work of Puig, Copi, Roberto Arlt. No one reads Ibargüengoitia any more. Monterroso, who might well have included Mandela, García Márquez and Vargas Llosa in his list of unforgettable figures (though maybe he would have replaced Vargas Llosa with Bryce Echenique), will soon be swallowed up by the mechanism of oblivion. This is the age of the writer as civil servant, the writer as thug, the writer as gym rat, the writer who goes to Houston or the Mayo Clinic in New York for medical treatment. Vargas Llosa never gave a better lesson in literature than when he went jogging at the crack of dawn. And García Márquez never taught us more than when he welcomed the Pope in Havana, wearing patent leather boots – García, not the Pope, who I guess would have been wearing sandals—along with Castro, who was booted too. I can still remember the smile that García Márquez was not quite able to contain on that grand occasion. Half-closed eyes, taut skin as if he'd just had a face-lift, slightly puckered lips, Saracen lips, as Amado Nervo would have said, green with envy.

What can Sergio Pitol, Fernando Vallejo, and Ricardo Piglia do to counter the avalanche of glamour? Not much. They can write. But writing and literature are worthless if they aren't accompanied by something more imposing than mere survival. Literature, especially in Latin America, and I suspect in Spain as well, means success, by which, of course, I mean social success: massive print runs; translations into more than thirty languages (I can name twenty languages, but beyond twenty-five I run into trouble, not because I doubt that language number twenty-six exists, but because it's hard for me to imagine the Burmese publishing industry or Burmese readers quivering with emotion at the magical-realist escapades of Eva Luna); a house in New York or Los Angeles; dinners with the rich and famous (as a result of which we learn that Bill Clinton can recite whole paragraphs of *Huckleberry Finn* by heart, or that President Aznar reads Cernuda); making the cover of *Newsweek* and landing six-figure advances.

Writers today, as Pere Gimferrer would be quick to point out, are no longer young men of means unafraid to inveigh against the norms of respectable society, much less a bunch of misfits, but products of the middle and working classes determined to scale the Everest of respectability, hungry for respectability. Blond- and dark-haired children of Madrid, born into the lower-middle class and hoping to end their days on the next rung up. They don't reject respectability. They pursue it desperately. And in order to attain it they really have to sweat. They have to sign books, smile, travel to unfamiliar places, smile, make fools of themselves on celebrity talk shows, keep on smiling, never, never bite the hand that feeds them, participate in literary festivals and reply good-humouredly to the most moronic questions, smile in the most appalling situations, look intelligent, control population growth, and always say thank you.

It's hardly surprising that they are prone to sudden fatigue. The struggle for respectability is exhausting. But the new writers had and in some cases still have parents (may God preserve them for many years to come), parents who exhausted themselves, who wore themselves out for a manual labourer's paltry wages, and as a result the new writers know that there are things in life far more exhausting than smiling incessantly and saying yes to the powerful. Of course there are far more exhausting things. And there's something touching about their efforts to secure a place in the pastures of respectability, although it means elbowing others aside. There are no more heroes like Aldana, who said, Now it is time to die, but there are professional pundits and talk show guests, there are members of the academy and political party animals (on the left and the right), there are cunning plagiarists, seasoned social climbers, Machiavellian cowards, figures who would not be out of place in earlier ages of literary history, and who, in the face of numerous obstacles, play their parts, often with a certain elegance – and they are precisely the writers that we, the readers or the viewers or the public (the public, the public, as Margarita Xirgu whispered into García Lorca's ear) deserve.

God bless Hernán Rivera Letelier, God bless his schmaltz, his sentimentality, his politically correct opinions, his clumsy formal tricks, since I am partly responsible. God bless the idiot children of García Márquez and the idiot children of Octavio Paz, since I am to blame for them seeing the light. God bless Fidel Castro's concentration camps for homosexuals and the twenty thousand who disappeared in Argentina and Videla's puzzled mug and Perón's old macho grin projected into the sky and the child-killers of Rio de Janeiro and Hugo Chávez's Spanish which smells of shit and is shit, since I created it.

Everything is folklore in the end. We're good at fighting and lousy in bed. Or was it the other way round, Maquicira? I can't remember any more. Fuguet is right: you have to land those fellowships and massive advances. You have to sell yourself before the buyers (whoever they are) lose interest. The last Latin Americans who knew who Jacques Vaché was were Julio Cortázar and Mario Santiago, and both of them are dead. The story of Penelope Cruz in India is worthy of our most illustrious stylists. Pe arrives in India. Since she likes local colour or authenticity she goes to eat in one of the worst restaurants in Calcutta or Bombay. Pe's own words. One of the worst or one of the cheapest or one of the most down-market places. She sees a hungry little boy at the door who stares back at her fixedly. Pe gets up, goes out and asks the boy what's wrong. The boy asks her for a glass of milk. Which is odd, because Pe isn't drinking milk. Nevertheless, the actress gets a glass of milk and takes it to the boy, who is waiting patiently at the door. He gulps the glass of milk straight down, under Pe's benevolent gaze. When the boy finishes the glass, Pe tells us, his grateful happy smile makes her think of all the things she has but doesn't need, although Pe is wrong there, because in fact she needs everything she has, absolutely everything. A few days later, Pe has a long philosophical but also practical conversation with Mother Teresa of Calcutta. At one point she tells the story of the boy. She talks about the necessary and the superfluous, about being and not-being, about being-in-relation-to and not-being-in-relation-with . . . what? How does it work? And in the end what does it mean 'to be'? To be oneself? Pe gets confused. Meanwhile Mother Teresa keeps moving like a rheumatic weasel around the room or the porch where they're talking, while the Calcutta sun, the balmy sun, but also the sun of the living dead, scatters its dying rays, as it sinks away in the west. Yes, yes, says Mother Teresa and then she murmurs something that Pe doesn't understand. What? asks Pe in English. Be yourself. Don't worry about fixing the world, says Mother Teresa: help, help, help one person, give a glass of milk to one child, and that will be enough, sponsor one child, just one, and that will be enough, says Mother Teresa in Italian, clearly in a bad mood. When night falls, Pe returns to her hotel. She takes a shower, changes her clothes, dabs herself with perfume, all the while unable to forget Mother Teresa's words. When dessert is served: suddenly – illumination! It's all a matter of taking a tiny pinch out of your savings. It's all a matter of not getting distressed. Give an Indian child twelve thousand pesetas a year and you're already doing something. And don't get distressed and don't feel guilty. Don't smoke, eat dried fruit, and don't feel guilty. Thrift and goodness are indissolubly linked.

A number of enigmas are still floating in the air like ectoplasm. If Pe went to eat in a cheap restaurant, why didn't she end up with a case of gastroenteritis? And why did Pe, who isn't short of money, go to a cheap restaurant in the first place? To save money?

We're lousy in bed, lousy at braving the elements, but good at saving. We hoard everything. As if we knew the asylum was going to burn down. We hide everything. The treasures that Pizarro will return to rob over and over again, but also utterly useless things: junk, loose threads, letters, buttons, which we stash in places that are then wiped from our memories, because our memories are weak. And yet we like to keep, to hoard, to save. If we could, we'd save ourselves for better times. We're lost without mom and dad. Although we suspect that mom and dad made us ugly and stupid and bad so they could shine by contrast in the eyes of posterity. Saving, for mom and dad, meant permanence, work and a pantheon, while for us, saving is about success, money and respectability. We're only interested in success, money and respectability. We are the middle-class generation.

Permanence has been swept aside by the rapidity of empty images. The pantheon, we discover to our astonishment, is the doghouse of the burning asylum.

If we could crucify Borges, we would. We are the fearful killers, the careful killers. We think our brain is a marble mausoleum, when in fact it's a house made of cardboard boxes, a shack stranded between an empty field and an endless dusk. (And, anyway, who's to say that we didn't crucify Borges? Borges said as much by dying in Geneva.)

And so let us do as García Márquez bids and read Alexandre Dumas. Let us follow the advice of Pérez Dragó or García Conte and read Pérez Reverte. The reader (and by the same token the publishing industry) will find salvation in the bestseller. Who would have thought. All that carrying on about Proust, all those hours spent examining pages of Joyce suspended on a wire, and the answer was there all along, in the bestseller. Ah, the bestseller. But we're lousy in bed and we'll probably put our foot in it again. Everything suggests that there is no way out of this.

Part IV
Posthumous Stories

Colonia Lindavista

When we arrived in Mexico, in 1968, a friend of my mother's put us up for the first few days, after which we rented an apartment in Colonia Lindavista. I've forgotten the name of the street; sometimes I think it was called Aurora, but maybe I'm getting mixed up. In Blanes I lived for a few years in an apartment on a Calle Aurora, so it seems unlikely that I lived on another Calle Aurora in Mexico, although the name's not all that unusual: quite a few cities have a street with that name. The Calle Aurora in Blanes, by the way, is no more than twenty yards long, and more like an alley than a street. The one in Colonia Lindavista, if it really was called Calle Aurora, was narrow but long, four blocks at least, and we lived there for the first year of our long residence in Mexico.

The woman we rented the apartment from was called Eulalia Martínez. She was a widow and she had three daughters and a son. She lived on the first floor of the building, a building that seemed normal to me at the time, but thinking back now, I see it as a conglomerate of oddities and blunders, because the second floor, which you got to by climbing an outdoor staircase, and the third floor, to which there was a metal ladder, had been added much later on and possibly without permits. The differences were striking: the apartment on the first floor had high ceilings and a certain dignity; it was ugly but it had been built according to an architect's plans. The second and third floors were the fruit of ad hoc interactions between Doña Eulalia's aesthetic sense and the skills of a builder friend. The reasoning behind this architectonic corpulence was not entirely mercenary. The owner of our apartment had four children, and the four apartments on the two additional floors had been built for them, so that they would stay close to their mother when they got married.

When we arrived, however, the only apartment that was occupied was the one directly above ours. Doña Eulalia's three daughters were unmarried and lived with their mother downstairs. The son, Pepe, who was the youngest, was the only one who had married, and he lived above us with his wife, Lupita. They were our closest neighbours during that time.

There's not much more I can say about Doña Eulalia. She was a strong-willed woman who'd been lucky in life, and she may not have been a very nice person. I scarcely knew her daughters. They were what used to be known, in those long-gone years, as old maids, and they endured their fate with all the grace they could muster, which is to say not very much; at best they gave off a dingy kind of resignation, which stained the things around them or the way I remember those things now that they've all disappeared. The daughters were rarely to be seen, or at least I didn't see them much; they watched soap operas and gossiped spitefully about the other women in the neighbourhood, whom they saw at the grocer's or in the dark entrance way where a skeletal Indian woman sold *nixtamal* tortillas.

Colonia Lindavista

Pepe and his wife, Lupita, were different.

My mother and father, who were three or four years younger than I am now, made friends with them almost right away. I was interested in Pepe. In the neighbourhood all the boys my age called him 'The Pilot' because he flew for the Mexican Air Force. Lupita was a housewife. Before getting married she had worked as a secretary or a clerk in a government office. Both of them were friendly and hospitable, or tried to be. Sometimes my parents would go up to their apartment and stay there a while, listening to records and drinking. My parents were older than Pepe and Lupita, but they were Chilean, and at the time Chileans saw themselves as the acme of modernity, at least in Latin America. The age gap was offset by the markedly youthful spirit of my progenitors.

On a few occasions I went up to their apartment too. The living room (which we called a *living*) was relatively modern, and Pepe had a record player that seemed to be a recent acquisition. On the walls and the sideboards in the dining room there were photos of him and Lupita, and photos of the airplanes he flew, which were what interested me the most; but he preferred not to talk about his work, as if he were always protecting some military secret. Classified information, as they said in the North American TV shows. The secrets of the Mexican Air Force, which, frankly, no one was losing any sleep over, except for Pepe with his somewhat extravagant sense of duty and responsibility.

Little by little, from conversations at the dinner table or overheard while I was studying, I began to get a sense of what our neighbours' life was really like. They'd been married for five years and still didn't have any children. There were frequent visits to the gynaecologist. According to the doctors,

Lupita was perfectly capable of having children. And the tests showed that Pepe was the same. The problem was mental, the doctors said. As the years went by, Pepe's mother began to resent the fact that Lupita hadn't provided her with grandchildren. Lupita once confessed to my mother that the problem was the apartment, and being so close to her mother-in-law. If they went somewhere else, she said, she'd probably be able to get pregnant right away.

I think Lupita was right.

Another thing: Pepe and Lupita were short. I was taller than Pepe and I was seventeen at the time. So I guess Pepe can't have been more than five foot nine, and Lupita would have been about five foot two at the most. Pepe was dark, with very black hair, and a thoughtful expression, as if there was always something on his mind. Every morning he went to work wearing his air force officer's uniform. He was always impeccably turned out, except on the weekend, when he put on a sweatshirt and jeans and didn't shave. Lupita had fair skin, dyed-blonde hair, and a more or less permanent perm, which she used to get done at the hairdresser's, or did herself, using a little kit containing all a woman's hair needs, which Pepe brought back from the United States. She used to smile when she said hello. Sometimes from my room I could hear them having sex. This was around the time I started getting serious about writing and I used to stay up very late. My life seemed pretty dull to me. In fact I was dissatisfied with everything about it. I used to write until two or three in the morning, and that was when the groans would suddenly begin in the apartment upstairs.

At first it all seemed normal. If Pepe and Lupita wanted to have a child they had to fuck. But then I asked myself,

Colonia Lindavista

Why were they starting so late at night? Why couldn't I hear any voices *before* the groans began? Needless to say, my knowledge of sex at the time was limited to what I'd been able to glean from movies and porn magazines. In other words, it was minimal. But I knew enough to sense that something strange was happening in the apartment upstairs. In my imagination, I began to embellish Pepe and Lupita's sex life with incomprehensible gestures, as if sadomasochistic scenes were being played out upstairs, scenes that I couldn't completely visualise, that weren't built around actions intended to produce pain or pleasure, but around dramatised movements that Pepe and Lupita were executing in spite of themselves, movements that were gradually unhinging them.

None of this was obvious from the outside. And in fact I soon reached the smug conclusion that nobody else had noticed. My mother, who was, in a way, Lupita's friend and confidante, thought that all the couple's problems would be solved by moving away. My father had no opinion on the matter. Freshly arrived in Mexico, we were too busy taking in all the new things that dazzled us every day to puzzle over the secret life of our neighbours. When I think back to that time, I see my parents and my sister, and then I see myself, and the little group we compose looks overwhelmingly desolate.

Six blocks from our house there was a Gigante supermarket where we went on Saturdays to shop for the whole week. That's something I can remember in elaborate detail. I also remember that I was sent to an Opus Dei high school, although in defence of my parents I should point out that they had never heard of Opus Dei. It took me more than a year myself to realise what a diabolical place it was. My Ethics teacher was a self-confessed Nazi, which was weird, because he was a little guy from Chiapas with indigenous features, who'd studied in Italy on a scholarship – a nice, dumb guy, basically, who would have been gassed by the real Nazis without a second thought – and my Logic teacher believed in the heroic will of José Antonio (many years later, in Spain, I ended up living on an avenue named after José Antonio). But, at the beginning, like my parents, I had no idea what was going on at that school.

Pepe and Lupita were the only people who interested me. And a friend of Pepe's, his only friend, actually, a fair-haired guy, the best pilot in his year at the academy, a tall thin guy who'd been injured in an accident when his fighter crashed and would never be able to fly again. He turned up at the house almost every weekend, and after saying hello to Pepe's mother and his sisters, who adored him, he went up to his friend's apartment and stayed there drinking and watching TV while Lupita made dinner. Sometimes he came during the week, and then he would be wearing his uniform, a uniform I have trouble visualising now; I would have said it was blue, but I could be wrong, and if I shut my eyes and try to conjure up the image of Pepe and his fair-haired friend, I see them wearing green uniforms, light green, a dashing pair of pilots, alongside Lupita, who's wearing a white blouse and a blue skirt (she's the one wearing blue).

Sometimes the fair-haired guy stayed for dinner. My parents would go to bed while the music went on playing upstairs. I'd be the only one awake in our apartment, because that's when I used to start writing. And in a way the noise from the apartment upstairs kept me company. At about two in the morning, the voices and the music would stop and a strange silence would fill the whole building: not just Pepe's apartment but ours as well and the apartment where Pepe's mother lived, which was holding up the extensions and seemed to creak at that time of night, as if the weight of the extra storeys was too much to bear. And then I could only hear the wind, the night wind of Mexico City, and the steps of the fair-haired guy as he walked to the door, accompanied by Pepe's steps, then the sound of footsteps on the stairs, and on our landing, and then going down the next flight of stairs to the ground floor, and the iron gate opening, and the steps fading away down Calle Aurora. Then I'd stop writing (I can't remember what I was writing, something awful, probably, but something long that kept me absorbed) and listen for the sounds that didn't come from Pepe's apartment, as if after the fair-haired guy had left, everything in there, including Pepe and Lupita, had suddenly frozen.

The Secret of Evil

This story is very simple, although it could have been very complicated. Also, it's incomplete, because stories like this don't have an ending. It's night in Paris, and a North American journalist is sleeping. Suddenly the telephone rings, and someone asks in English, with an unidentifiable accent, for Joe A. Kelso. Speaking, says the journalist and then looks at his watch. It's four in the morning; he's only had about three hours sleep and he's tired. The voice on the other end of the line says, I have to see you, to pass on some information. The journalist asks him what it's about. As usual with calls like this, the voice gives nothing away. The journalist asks for some indication, at least. In impeccable English, far more correct than Kelso's, the voice expresses a preference for a face-to-face meeting. Then, straight away, it adds, There is no time to lose. Where? Kelso asks. The voice mentions one of the bridges over the Seine. And adds: You can get there in twenty minutes on foot. The journalist, who has had hundreds of meetings like this, says that he'll be there in half an hour. Getting dressed, he thinks it's a pretty stupid way to waste the night, and yet he realises, with a slight shock of surprise, that he's no longer sleepy, that the call, in spite of its predictability, has left him wide awake. When he reaches the bridge, five minutes after the appointed time, he can see nothing but cars. For a while he stands still at one end, waiting. Then he walks across the bridge, which is still deserted, and after waiting for a few minutes at the other end, finally crosses back again and decides to give up and go home to bed. While he's walking home, he thinks about the voice: it definitely wasn't a North American voice and it probably wasn't British either, though he's not so sure about that now. It could have been a South African or an Australian, he thinks, or a Dutchman, maybe, or someone from northern Europe who learned English at school and has since perfected his command of the language in various Anglophone countries. As he crosses the street he hears someone call his name: Mr Kelso. He realises straightaway that it's the man who arranged to meet him on the bridge, speaking from a dark entranceway. Kelso is about to stop, but the voice instructs him to keep walking. When he reaches the next corner, he turns around and sees that no one is following him. He's tempted to retrace his steps, but after a moment's hesitation he decides that it's best to continue on his way. Suddenly the man appears from a side street and greets him. Kelso returns his greeting. The man holds out his hand. Sacha Pinsky, he says. Kelso shakes his hand and introduces himself in turn. Pinsky pats him on the back and asks if he'd like a whisky. A little whisky, is what he actually says. He asks Kelso if he's hungry. He assures the journalist that he knows a bar where they can get hot croissants, freshly baked. Kelso looks at his face. Although Pinsky is wearing a hat, his face is a pasty white, as if he'd been locked away for years and years. But where? Kelso wonders. In a prison or an institution for the mentally ill. In any case, it's too late to pull out now, and Kelso wouldn't mind a hot croissant. The place is called Chez Pain, and in spite of the fact that it's in his neighbourhood (in a narrow side street, admittedly), this is the first time he's set foot inside, and perhaps the first time he's even seen it. Mostly he frequents establishments in Montparnasse with a dubious air of legend about them: the place where Scott Fitzgerald once ate, the place where Joyce and Beckett drank Irish whiskey, the bars favoured by Hemingway and Dos Passos, Truman Capote and Tennessee Williams. Pinsky was right about the croissants at Chez Pain: they're good, they're freshly baked, and the coffee isn't bad at all. Which makes Kelso think – and it's a chilling thought – that this guy could well be a local, a neighbour. As he considers this possibility, Kelso is seized by a shudder. A bore, a paranoiac, a madman, a watcher with no one to watch him in turn, someone it's going be hard to get rid of. Well, he eventually says, I'm listening. The pale man, who is sipping his coffee but not eating, looks at him and smiles. There is something intensely sad about his smile, and tired as well, as if it were the only way in which he could allow himself to express his tiredness, his exhaustion and lack of sleep. But as soon as he stops smiling, his features recover their iciness.

The Old Man of the Mountain

Things are always happening by chance. One day Belano meets Lima, and they become friends. Both live in Mexico City and their friendship, like those of many young poets, is sealed by a common rejection of certain social norms and by the literary affinities they share. As I said, they're young. They're very young, in fact, and full of energy, in their own way, and they believe in literature's analgesic powers. They recite Homer and Frank O'Hara, Archilochus and John Giorno, and although they don't know it, their lives are running along the brink of the abyss.

One day – this is in 1975 – Belano says that William Burroughs is dead, and when Lima hears the news he goes very pale and says, He can't be, Burroughs is alive. Belano doesn't insist; he says he thinks that Burroughs is dead, but maybe he's mistaken. When did he die? asks Lima. Not long ago, I think, says Belano, feeling less and less sure, I read it somewhere. What intervenes at this point in the story is something that might be called a silence. Or a gap. A very short gap, in any case, and yet, for Belano, it opens up and will last, mysteriously, until the century's final years.

Two days later, Lima turns up with proof, and it's indisputable, that Burroughs is alive.

Years go by. Occasionally, just occasionally, and without knowing why, Belano remembers the day on which he arbitrarily announced the death of Burroughs. It was a clear day; he was walking with Lima on Calle Sullivan; they'd left a friend's place and the rest of the day was free. They might have been talking about the Beats. Then he said that Burroughs was dead, and Lima went pale and said, He can't be. Sometimes Belano thinks he can remember Lima shouting: He can't be! It's impossible. Unjust. Or something like that. He also remembers Lima's grief, as if he'd been told of the death of a very dear relative, a grief (although Belano knows that *grief* is not the right word) that persisted through the following days, until Lima was able to confirm that the information was incorrect. Something about that day, however, something indefinable, leaves a trace of uneasiness in Belano. Uneasiness and joy. The uneasiness is actually fear in disguise. And the joy? Belano generally thinks, or wants to believe, that what lies hidden behind the joy is nostalgia for his own youth, but what lies hidden is really ferocity: a dark, enclosed space busy with blurry figures, adhering to one another or superimposed, and constantly on the move. Figures that feed on a violence they can barely control (or can only control by means of a very strange economy). Although it seems counterintuitive, there is an airy quality to the uneasiness provoked by the memory of that day. And the joy is subterranean, like a geometric ship, perfectly rectangular in shape, gliding along a groove.

Sometimes Belano examines the groove.

He leans forward, he bends over, his spinal column curves like the trunk of a tree in a storm and he examines the groove: a deep, clean trace, parting a strange kind of skin, the mere sight of which makes him feel nauseous. The years go by. And they rewind. In 1975 Belano and Lima are friends, and every day they walk, unknowingly, along the brink of the abyss. Until one day they leave Mexico. Lima sets off for France and Belano for Spain. From now on, their lives, which have been joined, will follow different paths. Lima travels through Europe and the Middle East. Belano travels through Europe and Africa. Both fall in love, both try in vain to find happiness or to get themselves killed. Eventually, years later, Belano settles down in a village by the Mediterranean. Lima returns to Mexico. He returns to Mexico City.

But things have happened in the meantime. In 1975, Mexico City is a radiant place. Belano and Lima publish their poems, usually together, in the same magazines, and participate in readings at the Casa del Lago. By 1976, both are known to, and above all feared by, a literary establishment that simply cannot stand them. Two wild, suicidal ants. Belano and Lima lead a group of adolescent poets who have no respect for anyone. Anyone at all. An unforgivable offence for the literary powers that be; Belano and Lima are blackballed. This is in 1976. At the end of the year, Lima, who is Mexican, leaves the country. Shortly afterward, in January 1977, Belano, who is Chilean, follows him.

That's how it goes. 1975. 1976. Two young men sentenced to life. Europe. A new phase beginning and as it begins – pulling them back from the brink of the abyss. And separation, because although it's true that Belano and Lima meet in Paris and then in Barcelona and then in a railway station in Roussillon, their destinies eventually diverge and their bodies move apart, like two arrows suddenly, inevitably, veering off on separate trajectories.

So that's how it goes. 1977. 1978. 1979. And then 1980, and the '80s, a black decade for Latin America.

All the same, every now and then, Belano and Lima hear news of each other. Belano, especially, hears about Lima. One day, for instance, he hears that his old friend has been hit by a bus, and miraculously survived. The accident leaves Lima with a limp for the rest of his life. It also converts him into a legend. Or that's what Belano thinks, anyway, far away from Mexico City. From time to time, a friend who lives in Barcelona has visitors from Mexico, who bring news of Lima, which the friend then passes on to Belano.

The Colonel's Son

You're not going to believe this, but last night, at about four a.m., I saw a movie on TV that could have been my biography or my autobiography or a summary of my days on this bitch of a planet. It scared me so fucking shitless I tell you I just about fell off my chair.

I was stunned. I could tell right away the film was bad, or the sort we call bad – poor fools that we are – because the actors aren't much good and the director's not much good and the cretinous special effects guys are pretty hopeless too. But really it was just a very low-budget film, pure B-grade schlock. What I mean, just to be perfectly clear, is a film that cost about four euros or five dollars. I don't know who they conned to raise the money, but I can tell you that all the producer shelled out was a bit of small change, and they had to make do with that.

I can't even remember the title, really I can't, but I'll go to my grave calling it *The Colonel's Son*, and I swear it was the most democratic, the most revolutionary film I'd seen in ages, and I don't say that because the film in itself revolutionised anything, not at all, it was pathetic really, full of clichés and tired devices, prejudice and stereotypes, and yet at the same time every frame was infused with and gave off a revolutionary atmosphere, or rather an atmosphere in which you could sense the revolution, not in its totality, but a fragment, a minuscule, microscopic fragment of the revolution, as if you were watching *Jurassic Park,* say, except the dinosaurs never showed, no, I mean as if it was *Jurassic Park* and no one ever even *mentioned* the fucking reptiles, but their presence was inescapable and unbearably oppressive.

Do you see what I'm getting at? I've never read any of Osvaldo Lamborghini's *Proletarian Chamber Theatre,* but I'm certain that Lamborghini, with his masochistic streak, would have been happy to watch *The Colonel's Son* at three or four in the morning. What was it about? Well, don't laugh, it was about zombies. No kidding, like George Romero's movies, more or less; it had to be a kind of homage to Romero's two great zombie flicks. But if the political background to Romero is Karl Marx, the political background to the movie last night was Arthur Rimbaud and Alfred Jarry. Pure French insanity.

Don't laugh. Romero is straightforward and tragic: he talks about communities sinking into the mire and about survivors. He also has a sense of humour. You remember his second film, the one where the zombies wander around the mall because that's the only place they can vaguely remember from their previous lives? Well, last night's film was different. It didn't have much of a sense of humour, although I laughed like a madman, and it wasn't about a communal tragedy either. The protagonist was a boy who – I'm guessing, because I didn't see the start – turns up one day with his girlfriend at the place where his father works. I didn't see the start, like I said, so I can't be sure. Maybe the boy goes to visit his father and that's where he meets the girl. Her name is Julie and she's pretty and young, and she wants to be – or seem to be – up to date, the way young people do. The boy is the son of Colonel Reynolds. The colonel is a widower and loves his son – that's obvious right from the start – but he's also a soldier, so the relationship that he has with his son is one in which there's no place for displays of affection.

What is Julie doing at the base? We don't know. Maybe she went to deliver some pizzas and got lost. Maybe she's the sister of one of the guinea pigs that Colonel Reynolds is using, although that seems unlikely. Maybe she met the colonel's son when she was hitching a ride out of the city. What we do know is that Julie is there and that at some point she gets lost in an underground labyrinth and innocently walks through a door that she never should have opened. On the other side is a zombie, and it starts chasing her. Julie flees, of course, but the zombie manages to corner her and scratch her; at one point he even bites her arm and her legs. The scene is suggestive of a rape. Then the colonel's son, who's been searching for her, appears, and between them they manage to overpower and kill the zombie, if such a thing is possible. Then they flee down increasingly narrow and tortuous underground passages, until they finally make their way out through the sewers to the surface. As they're escaping, Julie begins to feel the first symptoms of the illness. She's tired and hungry and begs the colonel's son to leave her or forget her. His resolve, however, is unshakeable. He has fallen in love with Julie, or perhaps he was already in love (which suggests that he has known her for some time); in any case, armed with the generosity of the very young, he has no intention, come what may, of leaving her to face her fate alone.

When they reach the surface, Julie's hunger is uncontrollable. The streets have a desolate look. The film was probably shot on the outskirts of some North American city: deserted neighbourhoods, the sort of half-derelict buildings that directors who have no budget use for shooting after midnight. That's where they end up, the colonel's son and Julie, who's hungry; she's been complaining all the time they were running away. It hurts, I'm hungry: but the colonel's son doesn't seem to hear; all he cares about is saving her, getting away from the military base, and never seeing his father again.

The relationship between father and son is odd. It's clear from the start that the colonel puts his son before his duties as a soldier, but of course his love isn't reciprocated; the son has a long way to go before he'll be able to understand his father, or solitude, or the sad fate to which all beings are condemned. Young Reynolds is, after all, an adolescent, and he's in love and nothing else matters to him. But careful, don't be misled by appearances. The son appears to be a young fool, a young hothead, rash and thoughtless, just like we were, except that he speaks English, and his particular desert is a devastated neighbourhood in a North American megalopolis, while we spoke Spanish (of a kind) and lived, stifled, on desolate avenues in the cities of Latin America.

When the two of them emerge from the maze of underground passages, the landscape is somehow familiar to us. The lighting is poor; the windows of the buildings are smashed; there are hardly any cars on the streets.

The colonel's son drags Julie to a food store. One of those stores that stays open till three or four in the morning. A filthy store where tins of food are stacked up next to chocolate bars and bags of potato chips. There's only one guy working there. Naturally, he's an immigrant, and to judge from his age and the look of anxiety and annoyance that comes over his face, he must be the owner. The colonel's son leads Julie to the counter where the doughnuts and the sweets are, but Julie goes straight to the fridge and starts eating a raw hamburger. The storekeeper is watching them through the one-way mirror, and when he sees her throw up he comes out and asks if they're trying to eat without paying. The colonel's son reaches into the pocket of his jeans and throws him some bills.

At this point four people come in. They're Mexicans. It's not hard to imagine them taking classes at a drama school, or, for that matter, dealing drugs on the corners of their neighbourhood, or picking tomatoes with John Steinbeck's farmhands. Three guys and a girl, in their twenties, mindless and prepared to die in any old alleyway. The Mexicans show an interest in Julie's vomit too. The storekeeper says the money's not enough. The colonel's son says it is. Who's going to pay for the damage? Who's going to pay for this filth? says the storekeeper, pointing at the vomit, which is a nuclear shade of green. While they're arguing, one of the Mexicans has slipped in behind the till and is emptying it. Meanwhile the other three are staring at the vomit as if it concealed the secret of the universe.

When the storekeeper realises he's being robbed, he pulls out a pistol and threatens the Mexicans. This gives the colonel's son a chance to grab a few sweets from the counter and beg Julie to get out of there with him, but Julie has gone back to the raw meat, and as she tears into a steak, she begins to cry and says she doesn't understand and implores young Reynolds to do something. The Mexicans start brawling with the storekeeper. They pull out their knives and flash them in the bluish light of the food store. They manage to get hold of the storekeeper's pistol and shoot him. He drops to the floor. One of the Mexicans goes to the counter where the alcoholic drinks are kept and grabs some bottles without bothering to see what kind of liquor they contain. As he passes Julie, she bites him on the arm. The Mexican howls. Julie sinks her teeth in and won't let go, despite the pleas of the colonel's son. Another gunshot.

Someone shouts, C'mon, let's go. The Mexican manages to pull his arm free and catches up with his companions, crying out in pain. Young Reynolds examines the storekeeper's body lying on the floor. He's alive, he says, we have to get him to a hospital. No, says Julie, leave him, the police will take care of him. Their steps, as they walk out of the store, are quick but unsteady. They see a black van parked outside and break into it. Just as young Reynolds manages to get it going, the storekeeper appears and begs them to take him to a hospital. Julie looks at him but doesn't say a word. The storekeeper's white shirt is stained with blood. The colonel's son tells him to get in. When he's in the van and they're about to go, they hear the siren of a police car. Then the storekeeper says he wants to get out. Can't do that, says the colonel's son, and tears away.

The chase begins. It doesn't take long for the police to start shooting. The storekeeper opens the van's back door and shouts, That's enough. He's cut down by a hail of bullets. Julie, who's sitting in the back seat, turns and peers into the darkness. She hears him crying. The storekeeper is crying for the life that's slipping away from him, a life of ceaseless work

The Colonel's Son

and struggling in a foreign land to give his family a better future. And now it's all over.

Then Julie gets out of her seat and goes into the back part of the van. And while the colonel's son shakes off the police, Julie starts eating the storekeeper's chest. With a radiant smile on his face, young Reynolds turns to Julie and says, We've lost the cops, but she is crouched on all fours in the back, as if she were a tiger or were making love, and her only reaction is to breathe a satisfied sigh, because she's assuaged her appetite; momentarily, as we shall soon discover. All the colonel's son can do, of course, is cry out in terror. Then he says: What've you done, Julie? How could you do that? It's clear from his tone of voice, however, that he's in love, and that although his girl's a cannibal, she is, in spite of everything, his girl. Julie's reply is simple: she was hungry.

At this point, while young Reynolds is mutely venting his exasperation, the police car appears again and the young pair resume their flight through dark, deserted streets. There's still a surprise in store for us: when the police open fire on the fugitives, the back door of the van opens, and the storekeeper appears, but he's become a ravenous zombie. First he tears open a cop's throat, then sets on the guy's partner, who empties the magazine of his gun at him, in vain, then freezes in horror, before being devoured in turn. Just then two cars from the military base close off the alley, and using two rather strange weapons, like laser guns, neutralise first the storekeeper and then the two zombie policemen. Colonel Reynolds gets out of one of the cars and asks his soldiers if they've seen his son. The soldiers reply in the negative. Another car appears in the alley and a woman,

Colonel Landovski, gets out. She informs Reynolds that from now on, she'll be in charge of the operation. Reynolds says he doesn't give a damn who's in charge, all he wants is to find his son safe and sound. Your son's probably been infected by now, says Colonel Landovski. It's an odd scene: Landovski takes on the role of 'father', prepared to sacrifice the boy, while Reynolds takes on the role of 'mother', prepared to do anything to ensure the survival of his son. A fifth or sixth car pulls up at the corner, but no one gets out. It's the Mexicans.

They recognise the van from the food store, the van in which the young lovers fled. One of the Mexicans, the one Julie bit, is pretty sick. He's running a fever and raving incoherently. He wants to eat. I'm hungry, he keeps telling his friends. He asks them to take him to a hospital. The Mexican girl backs him up. We have to take him to a hospital, she says sensibly. The other two agree, but first they want to find the bitch who bit Chucho and teach her a lesson she'll never forget.

Since we forget everything in the end, I'm only guessing that they talk about killing her. They're spurring each other on to vengeance. They speak of honour, respect, principles, the right thing. Then they start the car and drive off. At no point do the soldiers show any sign of having noticed them, as if this ghostly street were a busy thoroughfare.

In the following scene Julie and young Reynolds are walking over a bridge. Where can we find a taxi? the boy wonders. Julie announces that she can't walk any further. On the other side of the bridge is a phone booth. Wait for me here, says young Reynolds, and runs off towards the booth, only to find that there's no phonebook and that the receiver has been ripped out. Looking back, he sees that Julie has climbed onto the balustrade of the bridge. He shouts, Julie, don't! and starts running. But Julie jumps and her body disappears into the water, although it soon floats to the surface and is swept away by the current, face down. The colonel's son goes down a stairway to the river. The water is very shallow: a foot, three feet at the deepest. The river has man-made banks and even the bed has been paved. A homeless black man, hidden among some concrete pillars down the river, is watching young Reynolds. The boy's search brings him near this man, who tells him to give up, the girl is dead. No, says the colonel's son, no, and goes on searching, closely followed by the black guy.

When young Reynolds finds her, the girl is floating in a pool. Julie, Julie, calls her young lover, and the girl, who has been face down in the water for who knows how many minutes, coughs and calls his name. All my fucking life I've never seen anything like that, says the black guy.

Just then, the Mexicans appear (the verb *to appear* will appear often in this story), fifty yards away. They've got out of their car and are looking on; one is sitting on the hood, another leaning against a fender, and the girl is up on the roof; only the wounded guy is still inside, watching or trying to watch them through the window. The Mexicans make menacing gestures and threaten them with a litany of punishments, tortures and humiliations. This is getting nasty, says the black guy. Follow me. They enter the city's system of sewers. The Mexicans follow them. But the labyrinth of tunnels is sufficiently complicated for the black guy and the young couple to lose their pursuers. Finally they reach a refuge that's almost as welcoming as a nightclub. This is my place, says the black guy. Then he tells them the story of his life. The jobs he's had to do. The constant presence of the police. The hardbitten life of a North American working man in the twentieth or twenty-first century. My muscles couldn't take any more, says the black guy.

His place isn't bad. He has a bed, where they lay Julie down, and books, which, so he says, he's picked up over the years in the sewers. Self-help books and books about the revolution and books on technical subjects, like how to repair a lawn mower. There's also a kind of bathroom, with a primitive shower. This water's always clean, says the black guy. A stream of crystal-clear water falls continually from a hole in the ceiling. We all build our places with whatever we can find, he explains. Then he picks up an iron bar and says that they can rest; he'll go out and keep watch.

It's always night in the sewers, but that night, the last night of peace, is particularly strange. The boy falls asleep in a shabby armchair after making love with Julie. The black guy falls asleep too, mumbling incomprehensibly. The girl is the only one who doesn't feel sleepy, and she goes into other rooms, because her appetite has begun to rage again. But with a difference: now Julie knows that self-inflicted pain can be a substitute for food. So we see her sticking needles in her face and piercing her nipples with wires.

At this point the Mexicans reappear and easily overpower first the black guy, then the son of Colonel Reynolds. They look for the girl. They shout threats. If she doesn't come out of her hiding place, they'll kill the black guy and her boyfriend. Then a door opens and Julie appears. She has changed a lot. She has become the indisputable queen of piercing. The leader of the Mexicans (the biggest guy) finds her attractive.

The Colonel's Son

The sick Mexican is lying on the ground, begging them to take him to a hospital. The Mexican girl is comforting him, but her eyes are fixed on the new Julie. The other Mexican is holding the colonel's son, who is screaming like a man possessed; the possibility (or the strong probability) that Julie will be raped is more than he can bear. The black guy is lying unconscious on the ground.

Julie and the Mexican go into in a room and shut the door. No, Julie, no, no, no, sobs young Reynolds. The Mexican's voice can be heard through the door: That's it, baby. C'mon, let's get that off. Holy shit! You really do like those hooks, don't you? Kneel down baby, yeah, that's it, that's it. Lift up your ass, perfect, oh yeah. And more stuff like that until suddenly he starts yelling, and there are blows, as if someone was getting kicked, or thrown against a wall, then picked up and thrown against the opposite wall, and then the yelling stops and there's only the sound of biting and chewing, until the door opens and Julie appears again with her lips (and in fact the whole of her face) smeared with blood, holding the Mexican's head in one hand.

Which makes the other Mexican go crazy; he pulls out a pistol, goes up to Julie and empties it into her, but of course the bullets don't harm her at all, and she laughs contentedly before grabbing the guy's shirt, pulling him towards her and tearing his throat open with a single bite. Young Reynolds and the black guy, who has recovered consciousness, are gaping at the scene. The Mexican girl, however, has the presence of mind to try to escape, but Julie catches her as she's climbing a metal stairway that leads to the mouth of the upper sewer. The girl kicks and curses furiously, but then, yielding to Julie's greater strength, she lets go and falls. Don't do it, Julie, the colonel's son has just enough time to say, before his sweetheart's teeth destroy the face of the Mexican girl. Then Julie extracts her victim's heart and eats it.

At this point, a voice says: So you think you've won, you whore. Julie turns around and what we see is the last Mexican, now fully transformed into a zombie. The two of them begin to fight. Julie is helped by the black guy and her boyfriend and for a few seconds it looks like she's going to win. But Julie's victims pick themselves up and join in the fight, and zombies, it seems, are ten times stronger than normal humans, which means that the fight inevitably begins to go the Mexicans' way. So our three heroes flee. The black guy takes them to a room. They barricade the door. The black guy tells them to go; he'll try, God knows how, to stop the zombies. Julie and young Reynolds don't have to be told twice, and go off to another room. At one point in their flight, Julie looks her boyfriend in the eye and asks him, just with her gaze or maybe with words, I can't remember now, how he can still love her. Young Reynolds replies by kissing her on the cheek, then he wipes his lips and kisses her on the mouth. I love you, he says, I love you more than ever.

Then they hear a yell and they know that the black guy is gone. There's no way out of the room where they've taken refuge; it's full of old furniture piled up chaotically, but with passages between; it's like a labyrinth of the transient, of things without the will to last. I have to leave you, says Julie. Young Reynolds doesn't know what she means. Only when Julie uses her extraordinary strength to throw him under some armchairs and broken-down washing machines and faulty or obsolete television sets does he understand that the girl is prepared to sacrifice herself for him. He hardly has time to react. Julie goes out and fights and loses and the Mexican zombies are coming for him. With tears streaming down his face, young Reynolds tries to make himself invisible, curling up into a ball of flesh under the pile of junk.

The Mexican zombies, however, find him and try to drag him out of there. Young Reynolds sees their hungry faces, then the hungry face of the black guy and Julie's face, watching him, showing no sign of emotion. At this point, Colonel Reynolds, escorted by three of his men, kicks down the door and starts blowing away all the zombies with the special gun. All the time he's firing, the colonel is calling his son's name. Here I am, Dad, says young Reynolds.

The nightmare is over.

The next scene shows the colonel comfortably seated in his office proposing to his son that they go to Alaska for a vacation together. Young Reynolds says he'll think it over. There's no rush, son, says the colonel. Then the colonel's on his own and he begins to smile to himself, as if he can't quite believe how incredibly lucky he's been. His son is alive. Meanwhile, young Reynolds has left his father's office and started walking through the underground passageways at the base. There's a look of deep uneasiness on his face. Gradually, however, distant noises begin to penetrate his self-absorption. He can hear shouts and howls, the cries of people for whom pain has become a way of life. Barely aware of what he's doing, he starts walking towards the source of the cries. He doesn't have to go far. The passage turns a corner and there is a door; it opens onto an enormous laboratory, stretching away before him.

He is warmly greeted by some military scientists who have

known him since he was a boy. He continues on his way. He discovers a series of glass cells. The Mexicans have been placed in them, each in a separate cell. He keeps walking. He finds Julie's cell. Julie recognises him. The colonel's son puts his hand on the glass and Julie puts her hand up to his, as if she were touching it. In a larger cell some scientists are working on the black guy. He could become a great warrior, they say. They are sending electric shocks through his brain. The black guy is full of hatred and resentment. He howls. The colonel's son hides in a corner. When the scientists go for their coffee break, he gets up and asks the black guy if he recognises him. Vaguely, says the black guy. All my memories are vague. And fucking strange, too.

We were friends, says the colonel's son. We met by the river. I remember an apartment on 30th Street, says the black guy, and a woman laughing, but I don't know what I was doing there. The boy frees the black guy from his chains. Freed, he walks like a kind of robocop. A zombie robocop. Don't attack me, says the colonel's son, I'm your friend. I understand, says the black guy, who goes to a shelf and takes down an assault rifle. When the scientists come back, the black guy greets them with a volley of fire. Meanwhile the boy frees Julie and tells her that they have to flee again. They kiss. The soldiers try to take out the black guy. As Julie and her boyfriend are sneaking away, she frees the Mexicans. More soldiers arrive. The bullets destroy some containers where body parts are kept. Viscera and spinal columns crawl over the floor of the laboratory. A siren begins to shriek. In this pitched battle it isn't clear which side has the advantage, or even if there really are sides, not just individuals fighting

The Colonel's Son

for their own lives and for the deaths of the others. Over the PA a voice is repeating: Block the passages on level five. My son! shouts Colonel Reynolds and rushes down to level five like a madman.

Colonel Landovski shoots the black guy to bits and is devoured in turn by the Mexican girl. The soldiers repel an attack mounted by bloody pieces of human flesh. The second attack, however, breaks through their lines of defence and they're devoured by tiny scraps of raw meat. There are more and more zombies. The battle becomes totally chaotic. The colonel reaches level five. Through a window he sees his son and Julie, and gestures to show that the passage is still open, there is still an escape route. The colonel's son takes Julie by the hand and they head in the direction that his father indicated. I'm hurting all over, says Julie. Don't start that again, says the boy, when we get away from here you'll feel better. Do you believe me? I believe you, says Julie.

In the passage that hasn't yet been blocked, Colonel Reynolds appears, unarmed, his shirt drenched with sweat, not only because he hasn't stopped running but also because the temperature on level five has increased dramatically. Colonel Reynolds' face has been transfigured. It could be said that his expression resembles that of Abraham. With every cell in his body he calls out his son's name and repeats how dearly he loves him. His military career, his scientific research, duty, honour and his country are all swept away by the force of love. Here, through here. Follow me. Hurry up. Soon the doors will shut automatically. Come with me and you'll be able to escape. All he gets in response is the sad gaze of his son, who at this moment, and perhaps for the first time, *knows* more than his father. The father at one end of the passage. The son at the other end. And suddenly the doors shut and they're separated for ever.

Behind the son there's a kind of furnace. It isn't clear whether the furnace was there already or whether the fire caused by the zombie rebellion has spread. It's some blaze. Julie and the boy hold hands. Come on, Julie, says the boy, don't be afraid, nothing will separate us now. Meanwhile, on the other side, the colonel is trying to break down the door, in vain. His son and Julie walk towards the fire. On the other side, the colonel beats at the door with his fists. His knuckles go red with blood. I'm not afraid, says Julie. I love you, says young Reynolds. On the other side, the colonel is trying to break down the door, in vain. The young lovers walk towards the fire and disappear. The screen goes an intense red. The only sound is a machine gun hammering. Then an explosion, screams, groans, electrical sparking. On the other side, shut off from all this, the colonel is trying to break down the door, in vain.

Scholars of Sodom

for Celina Manzoni

I.

It's 1972 and I can see V. S. Naipaul strolling through the streets of Buenos Aires. Well, sometimes he's strolling, but sometimes, when he's on his way to meetings or keeping appointments, his gait is quick and his eyes take in only what he needs to see in order to reach his destination with a minimum of bother, whether it's a private dwelling or, more often, a restaurant or a café, since many of those who've agreed to meet him have chosen a public place, as if they were intimidated by this peculiar Englishman, or as if they'd been disconcerted by the author of *Miguel Street* and *A House for Mr Biswas* when they met him in the flesh and had thought: Well, I didn't think it would be like this, or: This isn't the man I'd imagined, or: Nobody told me. So there he is, Naipaul, and it seems that all he can notice are outward movements, but in fact he's noticing inward movements too, although he interprets them in his own way, sometimes arbitrarily, and he's moving through Buenos Aires in the year 1972 and writing as he moves or perhaps only wanting to write as his legs move through that strange city, and he's still young, forty years old, but he already has a considerable body of work behind him, a body of work that doesn't weigh him down or prevent him from moving briskly through Buenos Aires when he has an appointment to keep – the weight of the work, that's something to which we shall have to return, the weight and the pride that he takes in his work, the weight and the responsibility, which don't prevent his legs from moving nimbly or his hand from rising to hail a taxi, as he acts in character, like the man he is, a man who keeps his appointments punctually – but he *is* weighed down by the work when he goes strolling through Buenos Aires without appointments to exercise his British punctuality, without any pressing obligations, just walking along those strange avenues and streets, through that city in the southern hemisphere, so like the cities of the northern hemisphere, and yet nothing like them at all, a hole, a void that someone has suddenly inflated, a show that is strictly for local consumption; that's when he feels the weight of the work, and it's tiring to carry that weight as he walks, it exhausts him, it's irritating and shameful.

II.

Many years ago, before V. S. Naipaul – a writer whom I hold in high regard, by the way – won the Nobel Prize, I tried to write a story about him, with the title 'Scholars of Sodom'. The story began in Buenos Aires, where Naipaul had gone to write the long article on Eva Perón that was later included in a book published in Spain by Seix Barral in 1983. In the story, Naipaul arrived in Buenos Aires, I think it was his second visit to the city, and took a cab – and that's where I got stuck, which doesn't say much for my powers of imagination. I had some other scenes in mind that I didn't get around to writing. Mainly meetings and visits. Naipaul at newspaper offices. Naipaul at the home of a writer and political activist. Naipaul at the home of an upper-class literary lady. Naipaul making phone calls, returning to his hotel late at night, staying up and diligently making notes. Naipaul observing people. Sitting at a table in a famous café trying not to miss a single word. Naipaul visiting Borges. Naipaul returning to England and going through his notes. A brief but engaging account of the following series of events: the election of Perón's candidate, Perón's return, the election of Perón, the first symptoms of conflict within the Peronist camp, the right-wing armed groups, the Montoneros, the death of Perón, his widow's presidency, the indescribable López Rega, the army's position, violence flaring up again between right- and left-wing Peronists, the coup, the dirty war, the killings. But I might be getting all mixed up. Maybe Naipaul's article stopped before the coup; it probably came out before it was known how many had disappeared, before the scale of the atrocities was confirmed. In my story, Naipaul simply walked through the streets of Buenos Aires and somehow had a presentiment of the hell that would soon engulf the city. In that respect his article was prophetic, a modest, minor prophecy, nothing to match Sábato's *Abaddon the Exterminator*, but with a modicum of good will it could be seen as a member of the same family, a family of nihilist works paralysed by horror. When I say 'paralysed', I mean it literally, not as a criticism. I'm thinking of the way some small boys freeze when suddenly confronted by an unforeseen horror, unable even to shut their eyes. I'm thinking of the way some girls have been known to die from a heart attack before the rapist has finished with them. Some literary artists are like those boys and girls. And that's how Naipaul was in my story, in spite of himself. He kept his eyes open and maintained his customary lucidity. He had what the Spanish call *bad milk*, a kind of spleen that immunised him against appeals to vulgar sentimentality. But in his nights of wandering around Buenos Aires, he, or his antennae, also picked up the static of hell. The problem was that he didn't know how to extract the messages from that noise, a predicament that certain writers, certain literary artists, find particularly unsettling. Naipaul's vision of Argentina could hardly have been less flattering. As the days went by, he came to find not only the city but the country as a whole insufferably aggravating. His uneasy feeling about the place seemed to be intensified by every visit, every new acquaintance he made. If I remember rightly, in my story Naipaul had arranged to meet Bioy Casares at a tennis club. Bioy didn't play any more, but he still went there to drink vermouth and chat with his friends and sit in the sun. The writer and his friends at the tennis club struck Naipaul as monuments to feeblemindedness, living illustrations of how a whole country could sink into imbecility. His meetings with journalists and politicians and union leaders left him with the same impression. After those exhausting days, Naipaul dreamed of Buenos Aires and the pampas, of Argentina as a whole, and his dreams invariably turned into nightmares. Argentinians are not especially popular in the rest of Latin America, but I can assure you that no Latin American has written a critique as devastating as Naipaul's. Not even a Chilean. Once, in a conversation with Rodrigo Fresán, I asked him what he thought of Naipaul's essay. Fresán, whose knowledge of literature in English is encyclopedic, barely remembered it, even though Naipaul is one of his favourite authors. But to get back to the story: Naipaul listens and notes down his impressions but mostly he walks around Buenos Aires. And suddenly, without giving the reader any sort of warning, he starts talking about sodomy. Sodomy as an Argentinian custom. Not just among homosexuals – in fact, now that I come to think of it, I can't remember Naipaul mentioning homosexuality at all. He is talking about heterosexual relationships. You can imagine Naipaul, inconspicuously positioned in a bar (or a corner store – why not, since we're imagining), listening to the conversations of journalists, who start off by talking about politics, how the country has merrily set its course towards the abyss, and then, to cheer themselves up, they move on to amorous encounters, sexual conquests and lovers. All of their faceless lovers have at some point, Naipaul reminds himself, been sodomised. I took her up the ass, he writes. It's an act that in Europe, he reflects, would be regarded as shameful, or at least passed over in silence, but in the bars of Buenos Aires it's something to brag about, a sign of virility, of ultimate possession, since if you haven't fucked your lover or your girlfriend or your wife up the ass, you haven't really taken possession of her. And just as Naipaul is appalled by violence and thoughtlessness in politics, the sexual custom of 'taking her up the ass', which he sees as a kind of violation, fills him ineluctably with disgust and contempt: a contempt of Argentinians that intensifies as the article proceeds. No one, it seems, is exempt from this pernicious custom. Well, no, there is one person quoted in the essay who rejects sodomy, though not with Naipaul's vehemence. The others, to a greater or lesser degree, accept and *practise* it, or have done so at some point, which leads Naipaul to conclude that Argentina is an unrepentantly macho country (whose machismo is thinly disguised by a dramaturgy of death and blood) and that in this hell of unfettered masculinity, Perón is the supermacho and Evita is the woman possessed, *totally* possessed. Any civilised society, thinks Naipaul, would condemn this sexual practice as aberrant and degrading, but not Argentina. In the article or perhaps in my story, Naipaul is seized by an escalating vertigo. His strolls become the endless wanderings of a sleepwalker. He begins to feel queasy. It's as if, by their mere physical presence, the Argentinians he's visiting and talking to are causing a feeling of nausea that threatens to overwhelm him. He tries to find an explanation for their pernicious habit. And it's only logical, he thinks, to trace it back to the origins of the Argentinian people, descended from impoverished Spanish and Italian peasants. When those barbaric immigrants arrived on the pampas they brought their sexual practices along with their poverty. He seems to be satisfied with this explanation. In fact, it's so obvious that he accepts it as valid without further consideration. I remember that when I read the paragraph in which Naipaul explains what he takes to be the origin of the Argentinian habit of sodomy, I was somewhat taken aback. As well as being logically flawed, the explanation has no basis in historical or social facts. What did Naipaul know about the sexual customs of Spanish and Italian rural labourers from 1850 to 1925? Maybe, while touring the bars on Corrientes late one night, he heard a sportswriter recounting the sexual exploits of his grandfather or great-grandfather, who, when night fell over Sicily or Asturias, used to go fuck the sheep. Maybe. In my story, Naipaul closes his eyes and imagines a Mediterranean shepherd boy fucking a sheep or a goat. Then the shepherd boy caresses the goat and falls asleep. The shepherd boy dreams in the moonlight: he sees himself many years later, many pounds heavier, many inches taller, in possession of a large moustache, married, with numerous children, the boys working on the farm, tending the flock that has multiplied (or dwindled), the girls busy in the house or the garden, subjected to his molestations or to those of their brothers, and finally his wife, queen and slave, sodomised nightly, taken up the ass – a picturesque vignette that owes more to the erotico-bucolic desires of a nineteenth-century French pornographer than to harsh reality, which has the face of a castrated dog. I'm not saying that the good peasant couples of Sicily and Valencia *never* practiced sodomy, but surely not with the regularity of a custom destined to flourish beyond the seas. Now if Naipaul's immigrants had come from Greece, maybe the idea would merit consideration. Argentina might have been better off with a General Peronidis. Not much better off perhaps, but even so. Ah, if the Argentinians spoke Demotic. A Buenos Aires Demotic, combining the slangs of Piraeus and Salonica. With a gaucho Fierrescopulos, a faithful copy of Ulysses, and a Macedonio Hernandikis hammering the bed of Procrustes into shape. But, for better or for worse, Argentina is what it is and has the origins it has, which is to say, of this you may be sure, that it comes from everywhere but Paris.

The Room Next Door

I was once, if I remember rightly, present at a gathering of madmen. Most of them were suffering from auditory hallucinations. A guy came up and asked if he could have a few words with me in private. We went to another room. The guy said that his medication was unhinging him. I'm getting more nervous every day, he said, And sometimes I have weird thoughts. That often happens, I told him. The guy said it was the first time it had happened to him. Then he rolled up the sleeves of his sweater and scratched his navel. He had a hand gun pushed into the top of his trousers. What's that? I asked him. It's my fucking belly button, said the guy: It itches and itches and what can I do? I'm scratching it all day long. Sure enough the skin around his navel was red and raw. I told him I didn't mean his navel, but what was below it. Is that a gun? I asked. Yes, it's a gun, said the guy, and he pulled it out and aimed it at the only window in the room. I considered asking if it was a fake, but I didn't. It looked real to me. I asked if I could have a look. Weapons aren't for loan, the guy said. It's like with cars and women. If you steal a car, you can lend it. Not something I'd recommend, but you can. The same if you're with a hooker. I wouldn't do it myself, I'd never lend any woman, but, you know, you could. When it comes to weapons, though, no way. And what if they're stolen or fakes? I asked him. Not even then. Once your fingerprints are on a weapon, you can't lend it. You understand? Sort of, I said. You have a commitment to the weapon, said the guy. In other words, you have to take care of it for the rest of your life, I said. Exactly, said the guy, you're married and that's all there is to it. You've got it pregnant with your fucking prints and that's all there is to it. Responsibility, said the guy. Then he raised his arm and aimed the gun straight at my head. I don't know if it was then or later that I thought of Moreau's *belle inertie,* or maybe I remembered having thought about it earlier, in a feverish and futile sort of way: beautiful inertia, the compositional procedure by which Moreau was able, in his canvases, to freeze, suspend and fix any scene, however hectic. I shut my eyes. I heard him asking me why I'd shut my eyes. Moreau's tranquillity, some critics call it. Moreau's fear, say others who are less drawn to his work. Terror bedecked with jewels. I remembered his transparent pictures, his 'unfinished' pictures, his gigantic, shadowy men, and his women, small in comparison to the masculine figures and inexpressibly beautiful. J. K. Huysmans wrote of his pictures: 'An identical impression was created by these different scenes: that of a spiritual onanism, repeated in a chaste body.' Spiritual onanism? Onanism period. All Moreau's giants and women, all the jewels, all the geometrical poise and splendour drop like paratroopers into the zone of chastity or responsibility. One night, when I was a sensitive young man of twenty, I overheard, in a boarding house in Guatemala, two men talking in the room next door. One of the voices was deep, the other was what you might call gravelly. At first, of course, I paid no attention to what they were saying. Both were Central Americans, though perhaps not from the same country, to judge from their intonation and turns of phrase. The guy with the gravelly voice started talking about a woman. He weighed up her beauty, the way she dressed and carried herself, her culinary skills. The guy with the deep voice agreed with everything he said. I imagined him lying on his bed, smoking, while the guy with the gravelly voice sat at the foot of the other bed, or maybe in the middle, with his shoes off, but still wearing his shirt and trousers. I didn't get the feeling they were friends; maybe they were sharing the room because they had no choice, or to save some money. They might have had dinner and some drinks together; that was probably as far as it went. But that was more than enough in Central America back then. I fell asleep several times while listening to them. Why didn't I sleep right through till the next morning? I don't know. Maybe I was too nervous. Maybe the voices from the other room got louder every now and then, and that was enough to wake me up. At one point the guy with the deep voice laughed. The guy with the gravelly voice said, or repeated, that he had killed his wife. I assumed that it was the woman he'd been praising before I fell asleep. I killed her, he said, and then he waited for the other guy to respond. It was a load off my mind. I did what was right. Nobody laughs at me. The guy with the deep voice shifted in his bed and said nothing. I imagined him with dark skin, with Indian and African blood, more African than Indian, a guy from Panama on his way home, maybe, or heading north to Mexico and the US border. After a long silence, during which all I could hear were strange noises, he asked the other guy if he was serious, if he'd really killed her. The guy with the gravelly voice said nothing; maybe he nodded. Then the black guy asked if he wanted a smoke. Why not, said the guy with the gravelly voice, one more before we go to sleep. I didn't hear any more from them. The guy with the gravelly voice might have got up to switch off the light, while the black guy watched from his bed. I imagined a bedside table with an ashtray. A dark room, like mine, with a minuscule window that looked on to a dirt road. The guy with the gravelly voice was skinny and white, for sure. A nervous type. The other guy was black, big and solidly built, the sort of guy who doesn't often lose his cool. I stayed awake for a long time. When I reckoned they'd gone to sleep, I got up, trying not to make any noise, and switched on the light. I lit a cigarette and began to read. Dawn was infinitely distant. When I eventually started to feel sleepy again and switched off the light and stretched out on the bed, I heard something in the room next door. A woman's voice – it sounded like she had her lips to the wall – said Good night. Then I looked at my room, which, like the room next door, contained three beds, and I was afraid, and a scream rose in my throat, but I stifled it because I knew I had to.

Labyrinth

They're seated. They're looking at the camera. They are, from left to right: J. Henric, J.-J. Goux, Ph. Sollers, J. Kristeva, M.-Th. Réveillé, P. Guyotat, C. Devade and M. Devade.

There's no photo credit.

They're sitting around a table. It's an ordinary table, made of wood, perhaps, or plastic, it could even be a marble table on metal legs, but nothing could be less germane to my purpose than to give an exhaustive description of it. The table is a table that is large enough to seat the above-mentioned individuals and it's in a café. Or appears to be. Let's suppose, for the moment, that it's in a café.

The eight people who appear in the photo, who are *posing* for the photo, are fanned out around one side of the table in a crescent or a kind of bent-open horseshoe, so that each of them can be seen clearly and completely. In other words, no one is facing away from the camera and no one is shown in profile. In front of them, or rather between them and the photographer (and this is slightly strange), there are three plants – a rhododendron, a ficus and an immortelle – rising from a planter, which may serve, but this is speculation, as a barrier between two quite distinct sections of the café.

The photo was probably taken in 1977 or thereabouts.

Labyrinth

But let us return to the figures. On the left-hand side we have, as I said, J. Henric, that is, the writer Jacques Henric, born in 1938 and the author of *Archées, Artaud traversé par la Chine*, and *Chasses*. Henric is a solidly built man, broad-shouldered, muscular-looking, probably not very tall. He's wearing a checked shirt with the sleeves rolled halfway up his forearms. He's not what you would call a handsome man; he has the square face of a farmer or a construction worker, thick eyebrows and a dark chin, one of those chins that needs to be shaved twice a day (or so some people claim). His legs are crossed and his hands are clasped over his knee.

Next to him is J.-J. Goux. About J.-J. Goux I know nothing. He's probably called Jean-Jacques, but in this story, for the sake of convenience, I'll continue to use his initials. J.-J. Goux is young and blond. He's wearing glasses. There's nothing especially attractive about his features (although, compared to Henric, he looks not only more handsome but also more intelligent). The line of his jaw is symmetrical and his lips are full, the lower lip slightly thicker than the upper. He's wearing a turtleneck sweater and a dark leather jacket.

Beside J.-J. is Ph. Sollers, Philippe Sollers, born in 1936, the editor of *Tel Quel,* author of *Drame, Nombres,* and *Paradis,* a public figure familiar to everyone. Sollers has his arms crossed, the left arm resting on the surface of the table, the right arm resting on the left (and his right hand indolently cupping the elbow of his left arm). His face is round. It would be a gross exaggeration to say that it's the face of a fat man, but it probably will be in a few years' time: it's the face of a man who enjoys a good meal. An ironic, intelligent smile is hovering about his lips. His eyes, which are much livelier than those of Henric or J.-J., and smaller too, remain fixed on the camera, and the bags underneath them help to give his round face a look that is at once preoccupied, perky and playful. Like J.-J., he's wearing a turtleneck sweater, though the sweater that Sollers is wearing is white, dazzlingly white, while J.-J.'s is probably yellow or light green. Over the sweater Sollers is wearing a garment that appears at first glance to be a dark-coloured leather jacket, though it could be made of a lighter material, possibly suede. He's the only one who's smoking.

Beside Sollers is J. Kristeva, Julia Kristeva, the Bulgarian semiologist, his wife. She is the author of *La traversée des signes, Pouvoirs de l'horreur,* and *Le langage, cet inconnu*. She's slim, with prominent cheekbones, black hair parted in the middle and gathered into a bun at the back. Her eyes are dark and lively, as lively as those of Sollers, although there are differences: as well as being larger, they transmit a certain hospitable warmth (that is, a certain serenity) which is absent from her husband's eyes. She's wearing just a turtleneck sweater, which is very close-fitting but the neck is loose, and a long V-shaped necklace that accentuates the form of her torso. At first glance she could almost be Vietnamese. Except that her breasts, it seems, are larger than those of the average Vietnamese woman. Hers is the only smile that allows us a glimpse of teeth.

Beside la Kristeva is M.-Th. Réveillé. About her too I know nothing. She's probably called Marie-Thérèse. Let's suppose that she is. Marie-Thérèse, then, is the first person so far not to be wearing a turtleneck sweater. Henric isn't either, actually, but his neck is short (he barely has a neck at all) while Marie-Thérèse Réveillé, by contrast, has a neck that is long and entirely revealed by the dark garment she is wearing. Her hair is straight and long, with a centre part, light brown in colour, or perhaps honey blonde. Thanks to the slight leftward turn of her face, a pearl can be seen suspended from her ear, like a stray satellite.

Next to Marie-Thérèse Réveillé is P. Guyotat, that is, Pierre Guyotat, born in 1940, the author of *Tombeau pour cinq cent mille soldats, Eden, Eden, Eden,* and *Prostitution*. Guyotat is bald. That's his most striking characteristic. He's also the most handsome man in the group. His bald head is radiant, his skull capacious and the black hair on his temples resembles nothing so much as the bay leaves that used to wreathe the heads of victorious Roman generals. Neither shrinking away nor striking a pose, he has the expression of a man who travels by night. He's wearing a leather jacket, a shirt and a T-shirt. The T-shirt (but here there must be some mistake) is white with black horizontal stripes and a thicker black stripe around the neck, like something a child might wear, or a Soviet parachutist. His eyebrows are narrow and definite. They mark the border between his immense forehead and a face that is wavering between concentration and indifference. The eyes are inquisitive, but perhaps they give a false impression. His lips are pressed together in a way that may not be deliberate.

Next to Guyotat is C. Devade. Caroline? Carole? Carla? Colette? Claudine? We'll never know. Let's say, for the sake of convenience, that she's called Carla Devade. She could well be the youngest member of the group. Her hair is short, without a fringe, and, although the photo is in black and white, it's reasonable to suppose that her skin has an olive tone, suggesting a Mediterranean background. Maybe Carla Devade is from the south of France, or Catalonia, or Italy. Only Julia Kristeva is as dark, but Kristeva's skin – although perhaps it's a trick of the light – has a metallic, bronze-like quality, while Carla Devade's is silky and yielding. She is wearing a dark sweater with a round neck, and a blouse. Her lips and her eyes betray more than a hint of a smile: a sign of recognition, perhaps.

Next to Carla Devade is M. Devade. This is presumably the writer Marc Devade, who was still a member of *Tel Quel*'s editorial committee in 1972. His relationship with Carla Devade is obvious: man and wife. Could they be brother and sister? Possibly, but the physical dissimilarities are numerous. Marc Devade (I find it hard to call him Marc, I would have preferred to translate that M into Marcel or Max) is blond, chubby-cheeked and has very light eyes. So it makes more sense to presume that they are man and wife. Just to be different, Devade is wearing a turtleneck sweater, like J.-J. Goux, Sollers and Kristeva, and a dark jacket. His eyes are large and beautiful, and his mouth is decisive. His hair, as I said, is blond; it's long (longer than that of the other men) and elegantly combed back. His forehead is broad and perhaps slightly bulging. And he has, although this may be an illusion produced by the graininess of the image, a dimple in his chin.

How many of them are looking directly at the photographer? Only half of the group: Henric, J.-J. Goux, Sollers and Marc Devade. Marie-Thérèse Réveillé and Carla Devade are looking away to the left, past Henric. Guyotat's gaze is angled slightly to the right, fixed on a point a yard or two from where the photographer is standing. And Kristeva, whose gaze is the strangest of all, appears to be looking straight at the camera, but in fact she's looking at the photographer's stomach, or to be more precise, into the empty space beside his hip.

The photo was taken in winter or autumn, or maybe at the beginning of spring, but certainly not in summer. Who are

Labyrinth

the most warmly dressed? J.-J. Goux, Sollers and Marc Devade, without question: they're wearing jackets over their turtleneck sweaters, and thick jackets too from the look of them, especially J.-J. and Devade's. Kristeva is a case apart: her turtleneck sweater is light, more elegant than practical, and she's not wearing anything over it. Then we have Guyotat. He might be as warmly dressed as the four I've already mentioned. He doesn't seem to be, but it's true that he's the only one wearing three layers: the black leather jacket, the shirt and the striped T-shirt. You could imagine him wearing those clothes even if the photo had been taken in summer. It's quite possible. All we can say for sure is that Guyotat is dressed as if he were on his way to somewhere else. As for Carla Devade, she's in between. Her blouse, whose collar is showing over the top of her sweater, looks soft and warm; the sweater itself is casual, but of good quality, neither very heavy nor very light. Finally we have Jacques Henric and Marie Thérèse Réveillé. Henric is clearly not a man who feels the cold, although his Canadian lumberjack's shirt looks warm enough. And the least warmly dressed of all is Marie-Thérèse Réveillé. Under her light, knitted, open-necked sweater there are only her breasts, cupped by a black or white bra.

All of them, more or less warmly dressed, captured by the camera at that moment in 1977 or thereabouts, are friends, and some of them are lovers too. For a start, Sollers and Kristeva, obviously, and the two Devades, Marc and Carla. Those, we might say, are the stable couples. And yet there are certain features of the photo (something about the arrangement of the objects, the petrified, musical rhododendron, two of its leaves invading the space of the ficus like clouds within a cloud, the grass growing in the planter, which looks more like fire than grass, the immortelle leaning whimsically to the left, the glasses in the centre of the table, well away from the edges, except for Kristeva's, as if the other members of the group were worried they might fall) which suggest that there is a more complex and subtle web of relations among these men and women.

Let's imagine J.-J. Goux, for example, who is looking out at us through his thick submarine spectacles.

His space in the photo is momentarily vacant and we see him walking along Rue de l'École de Médecine, with books under his arm, of course, two books, till he comes out onto the Boulevard Saint-Germain. There he turns his steps towards the Mabillon metro station, but first he stops in front of a bar, checks the time, goes in and orders a cognac. After a while J.-J. moves away from the bar and sits down at a table near the window. What does he do? He opens a book. We can't tell what book it is, but we do know that he's finding it difficult to concentrate. Every twenty seconds or so he lifts his head and looks out onto the Boulevard Saint-Germain, his gaze a little more gloomy each time. It's raining and people are walking hurriedly under their open umbrellas. J.-J.'s blond hair isn't wet, from which we can deduce that it began to rain after he entered the bar. It's getting dark. J.-J. remains seated in the same place, and now there are two cognacs and two coffees on his tab. Coming closer we can see that the dark rings under his eyes have the look of a war zone. At no point has he taken off his glasses. He's a pitiful sight. After a very long wait, he goes back out onto the street where he is gripped by a shiver, perhaps because of the cold. For a moment he stands still on the sidewalk and looks both ways, then he starts

Labyrinth

walking in the direction of the Mabillon metro station. When he reaches the entrance, he runs his hand through his hair several times, as if he'd suddenly realised that his hair was a mess, although it's not. Then he goes down the steps and the story ends or freezes in an empty space where appearances gradually fade away. Who was J.-J. Goux waiting for? Someone he's in love with? Someone he was hoping to sleep with that night? And how was his delicate sensibility affected by that person's failure to show up?

Let's suppose that the person who didn't come was Jacques Henric. While J.-J. was waiting for him, Henric was riding a 250-cc Honda motorbike to the entrance of the apartment building where the Devades live. But no. That's impossible. Let's imagine that Henric simply climbed onto his Honda and rode away into a vaguely literary, vaguely unstable Paris, and that his absence on this occasion is strategic, as amorous absences nearly always are.

So let's set up the couples again. Carla Devade and Marc Devade. Sollers and Kristeva. J.-J. Goux and Jacques Henric. Marie-Thérèse Réveillé and Pierre Guyotat. And let's set up the night. J.-J. Goux is sitting and reading a book whose title is immaterial, in a bar on the Boulevard Saint-Germain; his turtleneck sweater won't let his skin breathe, but he doesn't yet feel entirely ill at ease. Henric is stretched out on his bed, half undressed, smoking and looking at the ceiling. Sollers is shut up in his study, writing (pinkly snug and warm inside his turtleneck sweater). Julia Kristeva is at the university. Marie-Thérèse Réveillé is walking along Avenue de Friedland near the intersection with Rue Balzac, and the headlights of cars are shining in her face. Guyotat is in a bar on Rue Lacépède, near the Jardin des Plantes, drinking with some friends. Carla

Devade is in her apartment, sitting on a chair in the kitchen, doing nothing. Marc Devade is at the *Tel Quel* office, speaking politely on the phone to one of the poets he most admires and hates. Soon Sollers and Kristeva will be together, reading after dinner. They will not make love tonight. Soon Marie-Thérèse Réveillé and Guyotat will be together in bed, and he will sodomise her. They will fall asleep at five in the morning, after exchanging a few words in the bathroom. Soon Carla Devade and Marc Devade will be together, and she will shout, and he will shout, and she will go to the bedroom and pick up a novel, any one of the many that are lying on her bedside table, and he will sit at his desk and try to write but he won't be able to. Carla will fall asleep at one in the morning, Marc at half-past two, and they will try not to touch each other. Soon Jacques Henric will go down to the underground parking lot and climb onto his Honda and venture out into the cold streets of Paris, becoming cold himself, a man who shapes his own destiny, and knows, or at least believes, that he is lucky. He will be the only member of the group to see the day dawning, with the disastrous retreat of the last night wanderers, each an enigmatic letter in an imaginary alphabet. Soon J.-J. Goux, who was the first to fall asleep, will have a dream in which a photo will appear, and he'll hear a voice warning him of the devil's presence and of hapless death. He'll wake with a start from this dream or auditory nightmare and won't be able to get back to sleep for the rest of the night.

Day breaks and the photo is illuminated once again. Marie-Thérèse Réveillé and Carla Devade look off to the left, at an object beyond Henric's muscular shoulders. There is recognition or acceptance in Carla's gaze: that much is clear from her half-smile and gentle eyes. Marie-Thérèse, however, has a penetrating gaze: her lips are slightly open, as if she were having difficulty breathing, and her eyes are trying to fix on (trying, unsuccessfully, to *nail*) the object of her attention, which is presumably moving. Both women are looking in the same direction, but it's clear that they have quite different emotional reactions to whatever it is they are seeing. Carla's gentleness may be conditioned by ignorance. Marie-Thérèse's insecurity, her defensive yet inquisitorial glare, may result from the sudden stripping away of various layers of experience.

Any moment now, J.-J. Goux might start to cry. The voice that warned him of the devil's presence is still ringing, though faintly, in his ears. He is not, however, looking to the left, at the object that has attracted the women's attention, but directly at the camera, and an infinitesimal smile is creeping over his lips, a would-be ironic smile confined, for the moment, to the safer domain of placidity.

When night falls over the photograph again, J.-J. Goux will head straight for his apartment, make himself a sandwich, watch television for exactly fifteen minutes, not one more, then sit in an armchair in the living room and call Philippe Sollers. The phone will ring five times and J.-J. will hang up slowly, holding the receiver in his right hand, raising his left hand to his lips, and touching them with two fingers, as if to check that he's still there, that the person there is *him*, in a living room that's not too big, not too small, crowded with books, and dark.

As for Carla Devade, having lost her acquiescent smile, she'll call Marie-Thérèse Réveillé, who will pick up the phone after three rings. In a roundabout way, they'll talk about things they don't really want to talk about at all, and arrange to meet in three days' time at a café on Rue Galande. Tonight Marie-Thérèse will go out on her own, with nowhere in particular to go, and Carla will shut herself in her room as soon as she hears the sound of Marc Devade's key sliding into the lock. But for now nothing tragic will happen. Marc Devade will read an essay by a Bulgarian linguist; Guyotat will go to see a film by Jacques Rivette; Julia Kristeva will stay up late reading; Philippe Sollers will stay up late writing, and he and his wife will barely exchange a few words, shut away in their respective studies; Jacques Henric will sit down at his typewriter but nothing will occur to him, so after twenty minutes he'll put on his leather jacket and his boots and go down to the underground parking garage and look for his Honda in the dark; for some reason the lights in the parking lot don't seem to be working, but Henric can remember where he left his bike, so he walks in the dark, in the belly of that whalelike parking lot, without fear or apprehension of any kind, until about halfway there he hears an unusual noise (not a knocking in the pipes or the noise of a car door opening or closing) and he stops, without really understanding why, and listens, but the noise is not repeated, and now the silence is absolute.

And then the night ends (or a small part of the night, at least, a manageable part) and light wraps the photo like a bandage on fire, and there he is again, Pierre Guyotat, almost a familiar presence now, with his powerful, shiny bald head and his leather jacket, the jacket of an anarchist or a commissar from the Spanish Civil War, and his sidelong gaze, veering off to the right, as if into the space behind the photographer, as if directed at someone near or at the bar, perhaps, standing or sitting on a stool, someone whose back is turned to Guyotat and whose face would be invisible to him unless, and this is not unlikely, there is a mirror behind the bar. It may be a woman. A young woman, maybe. Guyotat looks at her reflection in the mirror and looks at the back of her neck. Guyotat's gaze, however, is far less intense than the gaze of this woman, which is plumbing an abyss. Here we can reasonably conclude that, while Guyotat is looking at a stranger, Marie-Thérèse and Carla are looking at a man they know, although, as is usually (or, in fact, inevitably) the case, their perceptions of him are entirely different.

Let's call these two beyond the frame X and Z. X is the woman at the bar. Z is the man who is known to Marie-Thérèse and Carla. They don't know him very well, of course. From Carla's gaze (which is not only gentle but protective) it could be inferred that he is young, although from Marie-Thérèse's gaze it could also be inferred that he is a potentially dangerous individual. Who else knows Z? No one, or at least there is nothing to suggest that his presence is of any concern to the others. Maybe he's a young writer who at some stage has tried to get his work published in *Tel Quel*; maybe he's a young journalist from South America – no, from Central America – who at some point tried to write an article about the group. He may well be an ambitious young man. If he's a Central American in Paris, as well as ambitious, he may well be bitter. Of the people sitting around the table, he knows only Marie-Thérèse, Carla, Sollers and Marc Devade. Let's say he once visited the *Tel Quel* office and was introduced to those four (he also once shook hands with Marcelin Pleynet, but Pleynet's not in the photo). He has never seen the others in his life, or only (in the cases of

Guyotat and Jacques Henric) in author photos. So we can imagine the young Central American, hungry and bitter, in the *Tel Quel* office, and we can imagine Philippe Sollers and Marc Devade, wavering between puzzlement and indifference as they listen to him, and we can even imagine that Carla Devade is there by pure chance; she has come to meet her husband, she has brought some papers that Marc left behind on his desk, she's there because she couldn't stand being alone in the apartment a minute longer, etc. What we can't imagine (or justify) in any way at all is Marie-Thérèse's presence in the office. She is Guyotat's partner, she doesn't work for *Tel Quel* and she has no reason to be there. And yet there she is and that is where she meets the young Central American. Is she there on that day because of Carla Devade? Has Carla arranged to meet Marie-Thérèse at the office because she knows that Marc will not be coming home with her? Or has Marie-Thérèse come to meet someone else? Let's return, discreetly, to the afternoon when the Central American came to the office on Rue Jacob to pay his respects.

It's the end of the working day. The secretary has already gone home, and when the bell rings it's Marc Devade who opens the door and lets the visitor in without meeting his eye. The Central American crosses the threshold and follows Marc Devade to an office at the end of the corridor. He leaves a trail of drops on the wooden floor behind him, although it stopped raining quite some time ago. Devade is, of course, oblivious to this detail; he walks ahead talking about something or other – the weather, money, chores – with that elegance that only certain Frenchmen seem to possess. In the office, which is spacious, and contains a desk, several chairs, two armchairs, and shelves full of books and magazines,

Labyrinth

Sollers is waiting, and as soon as the introductions are over the Central American hails him as a genius, one of the century's most brilliant minds, a compliment that would be par for the course in certain tropical nations on the far side of the Atlantic but which, in the *Tel Quel* office and the ears of Philippe Sollers, verges on the preposterous. In fact, as soon as the Central American makes his declaration, Sollers catches Devade's eye and both of them are wondering whether they've let a madman in. Deep down, however, Sollers is eighty per cent in agreement with the Central American's appraisal, so once he has set aside the idea that the visitor might be mocking him, the conversation proceeds in an amicable fashion, at least for a start. The Central American speaks of Julia Kristeva (and winks at Sollers as he mentions that eminent Bulgarian), he speaks of Marcelin Pleynet (whom he has already met), and of Denis Roche (whose work he claims to be translating). Devade listens to him with a slightly wry smile. Sollers listens, nodding from time to time, his boredom increasing with every passing second. Suddenly, a sound of steps in the corridor. The door opens. Carla Devade appears, wearing tight corduroy trousers, flat shoes and a disconsolate smile on her pretty Mediterranean face. Marc Devade gets up from his chair; for a moment the couple whisper questions and answers. The Central American has fallen silent; Sollers is mechanically flipping through an English magazine. Then Carla and Marc walk across the room (Carla taking tentative little steps, holding her husband's arm), the Central American stands up, is introduced, and obsequiously greets the newcomer. The conversation is immediately resumed, but the Central American's chatter veers off in a new direction, unfortunately for him (he changes the subject from literature to the matchless beauty and grace of French women), at which point Sollers completely loses interest. Shortly afterward, the visit is brought to a close: Sollers looks at his watch, says it's late; Devade shows the Central American to the door, shakes his hand, and the visitor, instead of waiting for the elevator, rushes down the stairs. On the second-floor landing he runs into Marie-Thérèse Réveillé. The Central American is talking to himself in Spanish, not under his breath but out loud. As their paths cross, Marie-Thérèse notices a fierce look in his eyes. They bump into each other. Both apologise. They look at each other again (and this is surprising, the way their eyes meet again *after* the apology), and what she sees, beneath the expedient mask of bitterness, is a well of unbearable horror and fear.

So the Central American, Z, is there in the café when the photo is taken, and Carla and Marie-Thérèse have recognised him, they've remembered him; perhaps he has just arrived, perhaps he walked past the table at which the group is sitting and greeted them, but except for the two women, they had no idea who he was; this happens quite often, of course, but it's something that the Central American still can't accept with equanimity. There he is, to the left of the group, with some Central American friends, or waiting for them, maybe, and deep within him – nourished by affronts and grudges, fuelled by bitterness and the chill of the City of Light – there's a seething. His appearance, however, is equivocal: it makes Carla Devade feel like a protective older sister or a missionary nun in Africa, but it catches at Marie-Thérèse Réveillé like barbed wire and triggers a vague erotic longing.

And then night falls again and the photo empties out or

disappears under a scribble of lines entirely traced by the night's mechanism, and Sollers is writing in his study, and Kristeva is writing in the study next door, soundproofed studies so they can't hear each other typing, for example, or getting up to consult a book, or coughing or talking to themselves, and Carla and Marc Devade are leaving a cinema (they've been to a film by Rivette), not talking to each other, although, a couple of times, Marc and then Carla, who's more distracted, greet people they know, and J.-J. Goux is preparing his dinner, a frugal dinner consisting of bread, pâté, cheese and a glass of wine, and Guyotat is undressing Marie-Thérèse Réveillé and throwing her onto the sofa with a violent thrust that Marie-Thérèse intercepts in midair as if she were catching a butterfly of lucidity in a net of lucidity, and Henric is leaving his apartment, going down to the parking lot and he stops again as the lights go out, first the ones near the metal roller gate that opens onto the street, and then the others, till there is only the light down at the back, flickering helplessly, illuminating his multicoloured Honda, and then it fails as well. And it occurs to Henric that his motorbike is like an Assyrian god, but for the moment his legs refuse to walk on into the darkness, and Marie-Thérèse shuts her eyes and opens her legs, one foot on the sofa, the other on the carpet, while Guyotat pushes into her, the panties still around her thighs, and calls her his little whore, his little bitch, and asks her what she did all day, what happened to her, what streets she wandered down, and J.-J. Goux is sitting at the table and spreading pâté on a piece of bread and lifting it to his mouth and chewing, first on the right side, then on the left, unhurriedly, with a book by Robert Pinget open beside him at page two and the television switched off but the screen reflecting his image, a man on his own with his mouth closed and his cheeks full, looking thoughtful and absent, and Carla Devade and Marc Devade are making love, Carla on top, illuminated only by the light in the corridor, a light they usually leave on, and Carla is groaning and trying not to look at her husband's face, his blond hair in a mess now, his light eyes, his broad and placid face, his delicate, elegant hands, devoid of the fire she's longing for, ineffectually holding her hips, as if he were trying to keep her there with him, but he has no real sense of what she might be fleeing from or what her flight might mean, a flight that goes on and on like torture, and Kristeva and Sollers are going to bed, first her, she has to lecture early the next day, then him, and both of them take books that they will leave on their bedside tables when sleep comes to close their eyes, and Philippe Sollers will dream that he is walking along a beach in Brittany with a scientist who has discovered a way to destroy the world; they will be walking westward along this long, deserted beach, bounded by rocks and black cliffs, and suddenly Sollers will realise that the scientist (who is talking and explaining) is himself and that the man walking beside him is a murderer; this will dawn on him when he looks down at the wet sand (with its soup-like consistency) and the crabs skittering away to hide and the prints the two of them are leaving on the beach (there is a certain logic to this: identifying the murderer by his footprints), and Julia Kristeva will dream of a little village in Germany where years ago she participated in a seminar, and she'll see the streets of the village, clean and empty, and sit down in a square that's tiny but full of plants and trees, and close her eyes and listen to the distant cheeping of a single bird and wonder if the bird is in a cage or free, and she'll feel

Labyrinth

a breeze on her neck and her face, neither cold nor warm, a perfect breeze, perfumed with lavender and orange blossom, and then she'll remember her seminar and look at her watch, but it will have stopped.

So the Central American is outside the frame of the photograph, sharing that pristine and deceptive territory with the object of Guyotat's gaze: an unknown woman armed only, for the moment, with her beauty. Their eyes will not meet. They will pass each other by like shadows, briefly sharing the same hazardous ambit: the itinerant theatre of Paris. The Central American could quite easily become a murderer. Perhaps, back in his country, he will, but not here, where the only blood he could possibly shed is his own. This Pol Pot won't kill anyone in Paris. And actually, back in Tegucigalpa or San Salvador, he'll probably end up teaching in a university. As for the unknown woman, she will not be captured by Guyotat's asbestos nets. She's at the bar, waiting for the boyfriend she'll marry before long (him or the next one), and their marriage will be disastrous, though not without its moments of comfort. Literature brushes past these literary creatures and kisses them on the lips, but they don't even notice.

The section of restaurant or café that contains the photo's nest of smoke continues imperturbably on its voyage through nothingness. Behind Sollers, for instance, we can make out the fragmentary figures of three men. None of the faces can be seen in its entirety. The man on the left, in profile: a forehead, one eyebrow, the back part of his ear, the top of his head. The man on the right: a little piece of his forehead, his cheekbone, strands of dark hair. The man in the middle, who seems to be calling the tune: most of his forehead, traversed by two clearly visible wrinkles, his eyebrows, the bridge of his nose, and a discreet quiff. Behind them, there is a pane of glass and behind the glass many people walking about curiously among stalls or exhibition stands, bookstands perhaps, mostly facing away from our characters (who have their backs to them in turn), except for a child with a round face and straight bangs, wearing a jacket that may be too small for him, looking sideways towards the café, as if from that distance he could observe everything going on inside, which, on the face of it, seems rather unlikely.

And in a corner, to the right: the waiting man, the listening man. His face appears just above Marc Devade's blond hair. His hair is dark and abundant, his eyebrows are thick, he is thin. In one hand (a hand resting listlessly against his right temple), he is holding a cigarette. A spiral of smoke is rising from the cigarette towards the ceiling, and the camera has captured it almost as if it were the image of a ghost. Telekinesis. An expert could identify the brand of cigarette that he's smoking in half a second just by the solid look of that smoke. Gauloises, no doubt. He's gazing off towards the photo's right-hand side – that is, he's pretending not to know that the photo is being taken, but in a way he too is posing.

And there is yet another person: careful examination reveals something protruding from Guyotat's neck like a cancerous growth, which turns out to be made up of a nose, a withered forehead, the outline of an upper lip, the profile of a man who is looking, with a certain gravity, in the same direction as the smoking man, although their gazes could not be more different.

And then the photo is occluded and all that is left is the smoke of a Gauloise floating in the air, as if the viewfinder had suddenly swung to the right, towards the black hole of chance, and Sollers comes to a sudden halt in the street, a street near the Place Wagram, and feels in his pockets as if he had left his address book behind or lost it, and Marie-Thérèse Réveillé is driving on the Boulevard Malesherbes, near the Place Wagram, and J.-J. Goux is talking on the phone with Marc Devade (J.-J.'s voice is unsteady, Devade isn't saying a word), and Guyotat and Henric are walking on Rue Saint-André des Arts, heading for Rue Dauphine, and by chance they run into Carla Devade who says hello and joins them, and Julia Kristeva is coming out of class surrounded by a retinue of students, quite a few of whom are foreign (two Spaniards, a Mexican, an Italian, two Germans), and once more the photo dissolves into nothingness.

Aurora borealis. Terrible dawn. As they open their eyes, they are almost transparent. Marc Devade, alone in bed, snug in grey pyjamas, dreaming of the Académie Goncourt. J.-J. Goux at his window, watching clouds float through the sky over Paris and comparing them unfavourably to certain clouds in paintings by Pisarro or the clouds in his nightmare. Julia Kristeva is sleeping and her calm face seems an Assyrian mask until, with a very slight wince of discomfort, she wakes. Philippe Sollers is in the kitchen, leaning on the edge of the sink, and blood is dripping from his right index finger. Carla Devade is climbing the stairs to her apartment after having spent the night with Guyotat. Marie-Thérèse Réveillé is making coffee and reading a book.

Jacques Henric is walking through a dark parking garage, which echoes to the sound of his boots on the cement.

A world of forms is unfolding before his eyes, a world of distant noises. The possibility of fear is approaching the way wind approaches a provincial capital. Henric stops, his heart speeds up, he tries to orient himself. Before, he could at least glimpse shadows and silhouettes at the far end of the parking lot; now it seems hermetically black, like the darkness in an empty coffin at the bottom of a crypt. So he decides to keep still. In that stillness, his heartbeat gradually slows and memory brings back images of the day. He remembers Guyotat, whom he secretly admires, openly pursuing little Carla. Once again, he sees them smiling and then he sees them walking away down a street where yellow lights scatter and regroup sporadically, without any obvious pattern, although Henric knows deep down that everything is determined in some way, everything is causally linked to something else, and human nature leaves very little room for the truly gratuitous. He touches his crotch. He is startled by this movement, the first he has made for some time. He has an erection and yet he doesn't feel sexually aroused in any way.

The Vagaries of
The Literature of Doom

It's odd that it was bourgeois writers who transported José Hernández's *Martín Fierro* to the centre of the Argentine canon. The point is debatable, of course, but the truth is that Fierro, the gaucho, paradigm of the dispossessed, of the brave man (but also of the thug), presides over a canon, the Argentine canon, that only keeps getting stranger. As a poem, *Martín Fierro* is nothing out of this world. As a novel, however, it's alive, full of meanings to explore, which means that the wind still gusts (or blasts) through it, it still smells of the out-of-doors, it still cheerfully accepts the blows of fate. Nevertheless, it's a novel of freedom and squalor, not of good breeding and manners. It's a novel about bravery rather than intelligence, let alone morality.

If *Martín Fierro* dominates Argentine literature and its place is in the centre of the canon, the work of Borges, probably the greatest writer born in Latin America, is only a footnote.

It's odd that Borges wrote so much and so well about *Martín Fierro*. Not just the young Borges, who can be nationalistic at times, if only on the page, but also the adult Borges, who is occasionally thrown into ecstasies (strange ecstasies, as if he were contemplating the gestures of the Sphinx) by the four most memorable scenes in Hernández's work, and who sometimes even writes perfect, listless stories with plots imitative of Hernández's. When Borges recalls Hernández, it's not with the affection and admiration with which he refers to Güiraldes, or with the surprise and resignation evoked by Evaristo Carriego, that familiar bogeyman. With Hernández, or with *Martín Fierro,* Borges seems to be acting, acting to perfection, in fact, but in a play that strikes him from the beginning as not so much odious as wrongheaded. And yet, odious or wrongheaded, it also seems to him inevitable. In this sense, his silent death in Geneva is highly eloquent. More than eloquent. In fact, his death in Geneva talks a blue streak.

With Borges alive, Argentine literature becomes what most readers think of as Argentine literature. That is: there's Macedonio Fernández, who at times resembles the Valéry of Buenos Aires; there's Güiraldes, who's rich and ailing; there's Ezequiel Martínez Estrada; there's Marechal, who later turns Peronist; there's Mujica Láinez; there's Bioy Casares, who writes Latin America's first and best fantastic novel, though all the writers of Latin America rush to deny it; there's Bianco; there's Mallea, the pedant; there's Silvina Ocampo; there's Sábato; there's Cortázar, best of them all; there's Roberto Arlt, most hard done by. When Borges dies, everything suddenly comes to an end. It's as if Merlin had died, though Buenos Aires' literary circles aren't exactly Camelot. Gone, most of all, is the reign of balance. Apollonian intelligence gives way to Dionysian desperation. Sleep, an often hypocritical, false, accommodating, cowardly sleep, becomes nightmare, a nightmare that's often honest, loyal, brave, a nightmare that operates without a safety net, but a nightmare in the end, and, what's worse, a literary nightmare, literary suicide, a literary dead end.

And yet with the passage of the years it's fair to ask whether the nightmare, or the skin of the nightmare, is really as radical as its exponents proclaimed. Many of them live much better than I do. In this sense, I can say that I'm an Apollonian rat and they're starting to look more and more like angora or Siamese cats neatly defleaed by a collar labeled Acme or Dionysius, which at this point in history amounts to the same thing.

Regrettably, Argentine literature today has three reference points. Two are public. The third is secret. All three are in some sense reactions against Borges. All three ultimately represent a step backward and are conservative, not revolutionary, although all three, or at least two of them, have set themselves up as leftist alternatives.

The first is the fiefdom of Osvaldo Soriano, who was a good minor novelist. When it comes to Soriano, you have to have a brain full of fecal matter to see him as someone around whom a literary movement can be built. I don't mean he's bad. As I've said: he's good, he's fun, he's essentially an author of crime novels or something vaguely like crime novels, whose main virtue – praised at length by the always perceptive Spanish critical establishment – is his sparing use of adjectives, a restraint lost, in any case, after his fourth or fifth book. Hardly the basis for a school. Apart from Soriano's kindness and generosity, which are said to be great, I suspect that his sway is due to sales, to his accessibility, his mass readership, although to speak of a mass readership when we're really talking about twenty thousand people is clearly an exaggeration. What Argentine writers have learned from

Soriano is that they, too, can make money. No need to write original books, like Cortázar or Bioy, or total novels, like Cortázar or Marechal, or perfect stories, like Cortázar or Bioy, and no need, especially, to squander your time and health in a lousy library when you're never going to win a Nobel Prize anyway. All you have to do is write like Soriano. A little bit of humour, lots of Buenos Aires solidarity and camaraderie, a dash of tango, a worn-out boxer or two, an old but solid Marlowe. But, sobbing, I ask myself on my knees, solid where? Solid in heaven, solid in the toilet of your literary agent? What kind of nobody are you, anyway? You have an agent? And an Argentine agent, no less?

If the Argentine writer answers this last question in the affirmative, we can be sure that he won't write like Soriano but like Thomas Mann, like the Thomas Mann of *Faust*. Or, dizzied by the vastness of the pampa, like Goethe himself.

The second line of descent is more complex. It begins with Roberto Arlt, though it's likely that Arlt is totally innocent of this mess. Let's say, to put it modestly, that Arlt is Jesus Christ. Argentina is Israel, of course, and Buenos Aires is Jerusalem. Arlt is born and lives a rather short life, dying at forty-two, if I'm not mistaken. He's a contemporary of Borges. Borges is born in 1899 and Arlt in 1900. But unlike Borges, Arlt grows up poor, and as an adolescent he goes to work instead of to Geneva. Arlt's most frequently held job was as a reporter, and it's in the light of the newspaper trade that one views many of his virtues, as well as his defects. Arlt is quick, bold, malleable, a born survivor, but he's also an autodidact, though not an autodidact in the sense that Borges was: Arlt's apprenticeship proceeds in disorder and chaos, through the reading of terrible translations, in the gutter rather than the library. Arlt is a Russian, a character out of Dostoyevsky, whereas Borges is an Englishman, a character out of Chesterton or Shaw or Stevenson. Sometimes, despite himself, Borges even seems like a character out of Kipling. In the war between the literary factions of Boedo and Florida, Arlt is with Boedo, although my impression is that his thirst for battle was never excessive. His oeuvre consists of two story collections and three novels, though in fact he wrote four novels, and his uncollected stories, stories that appeared in newspapers and magazines and that Arlt could write while he talked about women with his fellow reporters, would fill at least two more books. He's also the author of a volume of newspaper columns called *Aguafuertes porteñas* [Etchings from Buenos Aires], in the best French impressionist tradition, and *Aguafuertes españolas* [Etchings from Spain], sketches of daily life in Spain in the 1930s, which are full of gypsies, the poor, and the benevolent. He tried to get rich through deals that had nothing to do with the Argentine literature of the day, though they did have something to do with science fiction, and they were always categorical failures. Then he died and, as he would have said, that was the end of everything.

But it wasn't the end of everything, because like Jesus Christ, Arlt had his St Paul. Arlt's St Paul, the founder of his church, is Ricardo Piglia. I often ask myself: What would have happened if Piglia, instead of falling in love with Arlt, had fallen in love with Gombrowicz? Why didn't Piglia devote himself to spreading the Gombrowiczian good news, or specialise in Juan Emar, the Chilean writer who bears a marked resemblance to the monument to the unknown soldier? A mystery. In any case, it's Piglia who raises up Arlt in his own coffin soaring over Buenos Aires, in a very Piglian or Arltian scene, though one that takes place only in Piglia's imagination, not in reality. It wasn't a crane that lowered Arlt's coffin. The stairs were wide enough for the job. The body in the box wasn't a heavyweight champion's.

By this I don't mean to say that Arlt is a bad writer, because in fact he's an excellent writer, nor do I mean to say that Piglia is a bad writer, because I think Piglia is one of the best Latin American novelists writing today. The problem is, I find it hard to stand the nonsense – thuggish nonsense, doomy nonsense – that Piglia knits around Arlt, who's probably the only innocent person in this whole business. I can in no way condone bad translators of Russian, as Nabokov said to Edmund Wilson while mixing his third martini, and I can't accept plagiarism as one of the arts. Seen as a closet or a basement, Arlt's work is fine. Seen as the main room of the house, it's a macabre joke. Seen as the kitchen, it promises food poisoning. Seen as the bathroom, it'll end up giving us scabies. Seen as the library, it's a guarantee of the destruction of literature.

Or in other words: the literature of doom has to exist, but if nothing else exists, it's the end of literature.

Like solipsistic literature – so in vogue in Europe now that the young Henry James is again roaming about at will – a literature of the I, of extreme subjectivity, of course must and should exist. But if all writers were solipsists, literature would turn into the obligatory military service of the mini-me or into a river of autobiographies, memoirs, journals that would soon become a cesspit, and then, again, literature would cease to exist. Because who really cares about the sentimental meanderings of a professor? Who can say, without lying through

The Vagaries of The Literature of Doom

his teeth, that the daily routine of a dreary professor in Madrid, no matter how distinguished, is more interesting than the nightmares and dreams and ambitions of the celebrated and ridiculous Carlos Argentino Daneri? No one with half a brain. Listen: I don't have anything against autobiographies, so long as the writer has a penis that's twelve inches long when erect. So long as the writer is a woman who was once a whore and is moderately wealthy in her old age. So long as the author of the tome in question has lived a remarkable life. It goes without saying that if I had to choose between the solipsists and the bad boys of the literature of doom I'd take the latter. But only as a lesser evil.

The third lineage in play in contemporary or post-Borgesian Argentine literature is the one that begins with Osvaldo Lamborghini. This is the secret current. It's as secret as the life of Lamborghini, who died in Barcelona in 1985, if I'm not mistaken, and who left as literary executor his most beloved disciple, César Aira, which is like a rat naming a hungry cat as executor.

If Arlt, who as a writer is the best of the three, is the basement of the house that is Argentine literature, and Soriano is a vase in the guest room, Lamborghini is a little box on a shelf in the basement. A little cardboard box, covered in dust. And if you open the box, what you find inside is hell. Forgive me for being so melodramatic. I always have the same problem with Lamborghini. There's no way to describe his work without falling into hyperbole. The word *cruelty* fits it like a glove. *Harshness* does too, but especially *cruelty*. The unsuspecting reader may glimpse the sort of sadomasochistic game of writing workshops that charitable souls with pedagogical inclinations organise in insane asylums. Perhaps, but that doesn't go far enough. Lamborghini is always two steps ahead of (or behind) his pursuers.

It's strange to think about Lamborghini now. He died at forty-five, which means that I'm four years older than he was then. Sometimes I pick up one of his two books, edited by Aira – which is only a figure of speech, since they might just as well have been edited by the linotypist or by the doorman at his publishing house in Barcelona, Serbal – and I can hardly read it, not because I think it's bad but because it scares me, especially all of *Tadeys,* an excruciating novel, which I read (two or three pages at a time, not a page more) only when I feel especially brave. Few books can be said to smell of blood, spilled guts, bodily fluids, unpardonable acts.

Today, when it's so fashionable to talk about nihilists (although what's usually meant by this is Islamic terrorists, who aren't nihilists at all), it isn't a bad idea to take a look at the work of a real nihilist. The problem with Lamborghini is that he ended up in the wrong profession. He should have gone to work as a hit man, or a prostitute, or a gravedigger, which are less complicated jobs than trying to destroy literature. Literature is an armour-plated machine. It doesn't care about writers. Sometimes it doesn't even notice they exist. Literature's enemy is something else, something much bigger and more powerful, that in the end will conquer it. But that's another story.

Lamborghini's friends are fated to plagiarise him ad nauseam, something that might – if he could see them vomit – make Lamborghini himself happy. They're also fated to write badly, horribly, except for Aira, who maintains a grey, uniform prose that, sometimes, when he's faithful to

The Vagaries of The Literature of Doom

Lamborghini, crystallises into memorable works, like the story 'Cecil Taylor' or the novella *How I Became a Nun*, but that in its neo-avant-garde and Rousselian (and utterly acritical) drift, is mostly just boring. Prose that devours itself without finding a way to move forward. A criticism that translates into the acceptance — qualified, of course — of that tropical figure, the professional Latin American writer, who always has a word of praise for anyone who asks for it.

Of these three lineages — the three strongest in Argentine literature, the three departure points of the literature of doom — I'm afraid that the one which will triumph is the one that most faithfully represents the sentimental rabble, in the words of Borges. The sentimental rabble is no longer the Right (largely because the Right busies itself with publicity and the joys of cocaine and the plotting of currency devaluations and starvation, and in literary matters is functionally illiterate or settles for reciting lines from *Martín Fierro*) but the Left, and what the Left demands of its intellectuals is soma, which is exactly what it receives from its masters. Soma, soma, soma Soriano, forgive me, yours is the kingdom.

Arlt and Piglia are another story. Let's call theirs a love affair and leave them in peace. Both of them — Arlt without a doubt — are an important part of Argentine and Latin American literature, and their fate is to ride alone across the ghost-ridden pampa. But that's no basis for a school.

Corollary. One must reread Borges.

NATASHA WIMMER

Crimes

She's sleeping with two men. She's had other lovers before and now she has two. That's the way it is. They don't know about each other. One says he's in love with her. The other one says nothing. She doesn't care much what either of them says. Declarations of love, declarations of hate. Words. She's sleeping with two men; that's just the way it is.

She's a journalist. Now she's sitting in a bar near the newspaper office with a book open in front of her, but she can't read. She tries, but she can't. She's distracted by what's happening outside, although there's nothing special to see. She shuts the book and stands up. The man behind the bar sees her coming and smiles. She asks what she owes him. The man names a sum. She opens her purse and hands him a note. How's things? asks the man. She looks him in the eye and says: So so. The man asks her if she'd like something more. On the house. She shakes her head, No, I'm fine, thanks. She stands there for a while, waiting for something. Then almost inaudibly she takes her leave and walks out of the bar.

She returns unhurriedly to the office. Waiting for the elevator, she notices a young man, about twenty-five, wearing an old suit and a tie whose design intrigues her: identical sky-blue faces screwed up in surprise against a background of watery green. Beside the young man, on the floor, is a suitcase of considerable dimensions. They say hello. The doors of the elevator open and both of them get in. Having examined her, the young man says that he sells socks, and that if she's interested he can offer her a good deal. She says she's not interested and then she thinks that it's strange to find a sock salesman inside the building, especially at a time when most of the offices are closed. The sock salesman gets out first, at the third floor, where there's an architect's studio and the office of a legal firm. As he's stepping out of the elevator, he raises his left hand and touches his forehead with the tips of his fingers. A salute, she thinks, and smiles at him. As the doors of the elevator close, he returns her smile.

When she gets back to the newspaper office, the only person there is a woman, sitting on a chair next to the window, smoking. The journalist goes to her desk, switches on her computer, and then walks over to the window. At this point the woman who's smoking realises she's there and looks at her. The journalist sits on the windowsill and looks down into the street, which, unusually, makes her feel dizzy. Both of them are quiet for a few seconds. The woman who's smoking asks the journalist if she's OK. Fine, she says, I came back to finish the article about Calama. The smoking woman turns and looks out of the window at the river of cars flowing away from the city centre, then half closes her eyes and laughs. I read something about it, she says. Complete shit, says the journalist. It was kind of funny, says the woman who's smoking. I don't get you, says the journalist. After thinking for a moment, the smoking woman says, Actually, it wasn't funny at all, and looks out of the window at the traffic again. Then the journalist gets up and walks over to her desk. She has stories to file and she's running late. She takes a walkman from a drawer and puts the headphones on. She gets to work. But after a while she takes the headphones off and turns on her chair. There's something weird about all this, she says. The woman who's smoking looks at her and asks her what she's talking about. About the woman in Calama, she says. At that moment the silence in the newspaper office is absolute. Or so it seems. Not even the hum of the elevator.

She was twenty-seven and she was stabbed twenty-seven times. Too much of a coincidence. Why? says the smoking woman, stuff like that happens. It's a lot of stab wounds, the journalist replies, but without much conviction. I've seen stranger things than that, says the woman who's smoking. After a moment of silence she adds: And maybe that's just a typo anyway. It could be, thinks the journalist. Is something bothering you? asks the smoking woman. The victim, the journalist replies. It could have been any of us. The woman who's smoking looks at her with a raised eyebrow. It could have been me, says the journalist. No way – you're nothing like her, says the smoking woman. I'm sleeping with two men like she was, says the journalist. The woman who's smoking smiles and repeats: No way. Everyone's against her, one way or another. Against who? The victim, of course. The smoking woman shrugs her shoulders. The reporters who cover stories like this are no better than the killers. Not all of them, says the woman who's smoking, there are some really good ones. Most of them are useless barflies, murmurs the journalist. Not all of them, says the smoking woman. Twenty-seven years old, twenty-seven stab wounds, I'm not convinced. Anyhow, they might have got the victim's age mixed up with the number of stab wounds. She had a nine-year-old kid, says the journalist, holding the headphones in her left hand and stroking them. The woman who's smoking stubs out the cigarette in the ashtray beside the window and stands up. Let's go, she says. No, I'm going to stay for a bit, says the journalist, and puts the headphones back on.

She's listening to Delalande. Her back is hurting, but otherwise she feels fine and she's keen to keep working. Out of the corner of her eye she watches the woman who was smoking lean over her desk and put something into her handbag. Soon she feels her colleague's hand gently pressing her shoulder to say goodbye. She goes on working. After half an hour she gets up and goes to the newspaper's archives (which are hardly ever consulted any more) and that's when she sees him.

He's standing there, just outside the open door, not daring to cross the threshold, looking at her with a half-smile on his face. She stifles a cry and asks him what he wants. It's me, he says, the sock salesman. The suitcase is sitting at his feet. I know, she says, I don't want to buy anything. I just wanted to have a little look around, he says. She examines him for a few seconds; she's not frightened now but angry, and she senses that the presence of the young salesman is a sign of something important, but what that something is eludes her grasp. All she knows is that it's important (or has some degree of importance) and that she's no longer afraid. Haven't you ever been in a newspaper office? she asks. I haven't, actually, he says. Come in, she says. He hesitates or pretends to hesitate and then he picks up the suitcase and walks in. Are you a journalist? She nods. And what are you writing? She tells him she's writing an article about a murder. The salesman puts the suitcase down again and his gaze wanders from table to table.

Can I tell you something? She looks at him and her mind is blank. In the elevator, he says, it seemed to me that you were suffering for some reason. Me? she says. Yes, I thought you were suffering, although of course I don't know why. Everyone suffers, she says, as if they were talking in general terms. Neither of them has taken a seat. He's standing with his back to the door. She has retreated and is standing near the window. Both of them are frozen now, tensely upright, waiting. But when they speak, their voices have a false tone of familiarity.

What murder are you working on? he asks. The murder of a woman, she says. He smiles. He has a nice smile, she thinks, although it makes him look older (he's probably no more than twenty-five). It's always women who get killed, he says, and gestures with his right hand in a way that she can't interpret. As if she'd suddenly woken up, she realises that she's alone in the office with a stranger, at a time when the building is almost empty. A slight shudder sweeps through her body. He notices, and looks for a place to sit down, as if to reassure her. Seated, he looks even taller than he is. Tell me about it, he says. The request exasperates her. Wait till the issue comes out. No, tell me now, maybe I can make a suggestion, he says. You're an expert on the subject, are you? she says. He looks at her without replying. She realises she's made a mistake and tries to correct it, but before she can say anything more, he tells her that he's not an expert on murder. And why should I tell you about it? she says. Maybe you need to talk to someone. You could be right, she says. He smiles again. It was a woman who'd broken up with her husband, she says. Did the husband kill her? No. The husband has nothing to do with the crime. How come you're so sure? Because they arrested the killer the same day, she says. Ah, I see, he says. She was twenty-seven, she broke up with her husband, then she had a boyfriend, she lived with him, a younger guy, twenty-four, then she split with this boyfriend and starting going out with another guy. Boyfriend A and boyfriend B, he says. If you like, she says, and suddenly she feels calm, tired and calm, as if a part of the imaginary struggle (whose rules remain opaque to her) was already over and done.

I'm guessing, says the sock salesman, that this woman was good-looking. Yes, she was a beautiful woman, and very young too. Well, not all that young, he says. So you think a twenty-seven-year-old woman isn't young? Come on, let's be objective: young, sure, but not *very* young, he says. How old are you? Twenty-nine. I would have guessed twenty-five, she says. No, twenty-nine. He doesn't ask her age. Did she work or did she live off her boyfriends? She was a secretary. This woman never lived off anyone. And she had a nine-year-old son. And who killed her, boyfriend A or boyfriend B? he asks. Who would you say? Boyfriend A, of course. She nods. Because he was jealous. Yes, she says. But do you think it was just because he was jealous? No, she says. Ah, so you see, we have the same theory, you and I, he says. She chooses not to reply and moves away from the window. I should switch on a light, he says. No, leave it, she says, pulling out a chair and sitting down. After a while, he says: And it's getting you down, this story about a murder that happened a couple of months ago, I think it was. She looks at him and says nothing. Maybe you identify with the victim? Are you married? No, she says, but I've thought about her quite a bit. Are you married? No, me neither, he says, but I've lived with a few women. Do you think men have a problem with women who like sex? he asks. She looks away: beyond the windowpane night is enfolding the buildings. What she feels is a kind of claustrophobia. She got killed because she liked it, the journalist says without looking at him. She hears him say, Ah, and the tone of that ah is somewhere between irony and agony. She used to get up early, at a quarter past six every morning. She worked for a mining company in Calama, she was a secretary, and the stories in the papers say that her love life was a continual source of conflict. A continual source, he repeats, how poetic. Men kept falling in love with her, although she wasn't classically beautiful, she says. Beauty's relative, he says: There's a kind of beauty for everyone. Do you think? she asks, and looks at him again, steadily. Yes I do, says the sock salesman, everyone: the ugly, the not-so-ugly, the average-looking and the beautiful. But just because the not-so-ugly seem desirable to the ugly, that doesn't make them beautiful. So you get what I mean, he says. Yes, I get what you mean, she says ironically, but I don't agree; beauty's the same for everyone, like justice. Justice is the same for everyone? Don't make me laugh, he says. In theory, at least. It's all different in theory, he sighs, but let's not argue; tell me more about your murdered secretary. Did you see the body? The body? No, I didn't see it. I didn't cover the story, I just wrote an article about the crime. So you didn't go to the morgue in Calama? You didn't see the victim or talk with the killer? She looks at him and smiles mysteriously. The killer, yeah, I talked with him, she says.

Well, that's something, at least, he says. And? Nothing, she says, we talked, he told me he was sorry for what he'd done, he said he was crazy about the victim. Well put, he says. They met at the airport in Calama; he was a security guard, and she worked there for a while, as a receptionist. Before getting the job at the mine, says the sock salesman. In a mining company, she says. Same thing, he says. Well, not exactly. And how did he kill her? he asks. With a knife, she says. He stabbed her twenty-seven times. Don't you think that's strange? He looks down at the toes of his shoes for a few seconds. Then he looks at her again and says, What am I supposed to think is strange? The fact that she was twenty-seven and got stabbed twenty-seven times? Then a fury seizes her and she says, I'm in pretty much the same situation, so I guess I'm going to get killed one day too. She's on the point of saying, And you're the sad bastard who's going to kill me, but she checks herself just in time. She's shaking. But he can't tell from where he's sitting. To sum up: it's her ex who kills her. The night of the murder she sleeps with the current boyfriend. The ex knows what's going on. She's told him and he's been informed by others. Jealousy is eating him. He badgers and threatens her. But she pays him no attention; she's decided to get on with her life. She's met another man. They sleep together. That's the key to the crime: by refusing to give anything up she signs her death warrant. Yes, says the sock salesman, now I understand. No, you don't understand at all.

I Can't Read

This story is about four people. Two children, Lautaro and Pascual, a woman, Andrea, and another child, named Carlos. It's also about Chile, and, in a way, about Latin America in general.

When my son Lautaro was eight years old, he made friends with Pascual, who was four at the time. A friendship between children of such different ages is unusual, and maybe it was entirely due to the fact that when they met, in November 1998, Lautaro hadn't seen or played with another child for days on end, because Carolina and I had been trundling him around all over the place, much to his disgruntlement. It was Carolina's first trip to Chile and my first trip back since leaving in January 1974.

So when Lautaro met Pascual they immediately became friends.

I think it was when we went to have dinner with Pascual's parents. The second time they met was when Alexandra, Pascual's mother, took Carolina and Lautaro to a swimming pool. I didn't go. And the boys might have seen each other again later on. So twice, or three times at the most.

The swimming pool was in the foothills of the Cordillera and, according to Carolina, the water was icy cold and

I Can't Read

neither she nor Alexandra went in. But Pascual and Lautaro did, and they had a great time.

A strange thing happened (one of the many strange things that will happen in this story and carry it and perhaps turn out to be what it's really about): when they got to the swimming pool, Lautaro asked Carolina if he could have a pee. She, of course, said yes, and then Lautaro went to the edge of the pool, pulled down his trunks a bit and peed into the water. That night, Carolina said that she'd been embarrassed, not for Lautaro, but because of what Alexandra might have thought. The fact is Lautaro had never done anything like that before. The swimming pool wasn't really busy, but there were a few people, and my son is not some wild boy who pees wherever he feels like it. It was very strange, Carolina said that night: the enormous Cordillera looming behind the swimming pool as if it were *waiting,* the laughter and the muted voices of the adults, oblivious to Lautaro's surprising urination, and Lautaro himself, wearing only his swimming trunks, peeing onto the blue surface of the water. What happened next? I asked. Well, she got up from where she was sunbathing, walked over to our son, and took him to the bathroom. It was like he was under hypnosis, said Carolina. Then he felt ashamed and didn't want to get into the pool, where Pascual was already splashing around, though after a while he forgot all about it and went in. But Carolina didn't. Alexandra asked if it was because of the pee, and Carolina said it was because of the cold, which was the truth.

I'd met Alexandra at the airport, a few minutes after stepping off the plane. It was almost a quarter of a century since I'd been in Chile. I'd been invited by *Paula* magazine, as one of the judges for their short story competition, and when we got through customs and immigration, Alexandra was there waiting for us, along with some people I didn't know. When she said her name, Alexandra Edwards, I asked her if she was the daughter of Jorge Edwards, the writer, and she looked at me, frowned slightly, as if considering how to reply, then said no. I'm the daughter of the photographer, she explained a little while later. By that stage I was already one of her admirers. I have to say it's not hard to admire her, because she's very pretty. But it wasn't her physical beauty that impressed me; it was something else, a side of her that I've gradually come to know and will probably never know completely, and yet I know it well enough to be sure that we'll always be friends. We'd arrived in the morning, and that afternoon, I remember, I had lunch with the rest of the judges, and I had to make a speech, and Alexandra was there, on the other side of the table, laughing with her eyes, which is something that Chilean women often do, or that's how it seemed to me at the time, a mistaken impression that must have been due to finding myself back in the country after so many years away; women everywhere laugh with their eyes, all the time, and men do too occasionally, and sometimes it's actually happening, and sometimes we only think it is, that silent laughter, which reminds me of Andrea, who is one of the main characters in this story, Andrea and Lautaro and Pascual and Carlitos, but I still hadn't met Andrea, or Pascual, and I'd never even heard of Carlitos, although the fortunate day was drawing near, as someone might have said – myself, perhaps, in January 1974.

Anyway, in spite of the age difference, Lautaro and Pascual became friends, and maybe it was there at the swimming pool perched in the foothills of the Cordillera that their friendship was cemented, after the peeing incident. When Carolina told me, I couldn't believe it: Lautaro urinating, not *in* the pool, underwater, as almost all kids do, but from the edge, for everyone to see.

That night, however, I fell asleep and dreamed of my son in that landscape, which had once been mine, the landscape of my twentieth year, and I came to understand a part of what he must have felt. If I'd been killed in Chile, at the end of 1973 or the beginning of 1974, he wouldn't have been born, I thought, and the act of urinating from the edge of the swimming pool – as if he were asleep or had suddenly been overtaken by a dream – was a physical way of acknowledging that fact and its shadow: having been born and being in a world that might have existed without him.

In the dream I understood that when Lautaro peed in the pool, he was dreaming too, and I understood that although I would never be able to approach his dream, I would always be there beside him. And when I woke up I remembered that one night, when I was a boy, I got out of bed and urinated abundantly in my sister's closet. But I was a sleepwalker, and Lautaro, fortunately, is not.

During that trip, which took up almost all of November 1998, I didn't see Andrea. Well, I did, but without really seeing her.

I met Alexandra and Alexandra's partner, Marcial, both of whom became friends, and whatever I say about them will be conditioned by the friendship that binds us, so perhaps it's better that I don't say too much.

But I didn't see Andrea. If I think back, all I can remember is a smile, like the smile of the Cheshire Cat, in the corridor of Alexandra and Marcial's apartment, a voice emerging from the shadows, a pair of dark and very deep eyes that were laughing as Alexandra's eyes had laughed when I made my first speech, just after arriving in Chile, but with a significant difference: Andrea, unlike Alexandra, was an invisible woman. I mean, she was invisible for me; at some point I saw her without really seeing her; I heard her, but I couldn't tell where her voice was coming from.

One of the things that Lautaro did around that time was to invent a method for approaching automatic doors without making them open. So in a way – I don't know if it was before or after our first trip to Chile (shortly before, I think) – he too began to play at being invisible, and quite successfully too.

The first time I saw him demonstrate this skill was in Blanes, at a bakery in Blanes, before that trip to Chile. I can't remember which writer said that if God was omnipresent, automatic doors should always be open. And since they're not, God doesn't exist. As well as being remarkable in itself, my son's method put paid to that argument. Lautaro didn't approach from the sides. Sometimes the sensors are placed in such a way that they don't register a sidelong approach and the doors remain closed. That's the easy or tricky way (though there's really not much of a trick to it), but my son chose the hard way; that is, he confronted the doors head on, refusing to stack the odds in his favour, adopting a direct approach, which the sensors are bound to detect and react to, opening the doors to let you in or out.

The originality of his technique lay in the movements that he made as he came towards the automatic doors. He would start off slowly, as if measuring the sensor's range, tapping his feet intermittently, as if the sensor could pick up vibrations in the ground, and moving his arms like the slowly turning sails of a windmill. Then the door would open, allowing him to gauge the critical distance. He would step back immediately and the door would close again, and then the real approach would begin. Each movement was slowed down as far as possible. His feet, for instance, didn't leave the ground; he slid them imperceptibly. His arms, held away from his torso, moved very slightly, like insects or auxiliary craft, as if unattached, as if this approach were being made not by a single body but by a shadow and two phantom shadows, two pilot shadows, and even his face was transformed; it seemed to blur but also to be concentrating on invisibility, on stasis and movement, on insubstantiality and paradox.

Once, in a big department store in Barcelona, I tried, in vain, to imitate him; the sensor kept detecting me, the doors opened every time. Lautaro, however, could go right up and touch the glass, reinforced or not, with the tip of his nose, unnoticed by the electronic eye, and this couldn't be explained, as I thought at first, by his height, because at eight my son was relatively tall, or by his slimness, since he's quite solidly built, but only by his aptitude, determination and skill.

Something else that I remember vividly from our first trip to Chile, and which enters unexpectedly into this story, is a bird. This bird was not invisible, but when it appeared one afternoon, I'm sure that I was the only one to see it.

We were staying in a serviced apartment in Providencia, on the eighth or the ninth storey, and one afternoon when I had nothing to do I noticed a bird perched on one of the balconies of a neighbouring building. For a while the bird sat still and seemed to be surveying the city as I was from the balcony of my apartment, except that the bird was looking at the city and I was looking at it. I'm myopic, my distance vision is poor, but at some point I reached the conclusion that this strange and solitary bird was a raptor, a falcon or something like that (I'm an ornithological ignoramus, except when it comes to parrots). Very soon after that, the falcon or whatever it was went plummeting down, which dispelled any doubts I might have still had. But then came the really surprising part: the bird began to fly towards my balcony. I was afraid but I didn't move. It came to rest on the flat roof of a building right next to ours, and for a while we examined each other. Until I couldn't bear it any longer and went back inside.

The day this happened was also the day when Lautaro showed Pascual his knack of approaching automatic doors without making them open, and Pascual gave Lautaro an airplane. Lautaro loved the airplane; it had been one of Pascual's favourite toys, and maybe it was because of that gift that Lautaro showed him how to make like the invisible man, or, in Pascual's low-tech version, like an Indian.

I saw the boys from a café terrace where I was sitting with Alexandra, Carolina and Marcial. The others didn't see. I can't remember what we were talking about; all I remember is that Pascual and Lautaro approached a clothing store, unsuccessfully at first, because the door kept opening, and a woman with dyed blonde hair, wearing grey trousers and a black jacket, came out and said something to them, something I couldn't hear, partly because I was listening to what my wife and friends were saying, and partly because the store was a fair way off, on the far side of that covered square, and

I Can't Read

I remember Lautaro and Pascual running away at first, then I remember them standing, looking up, listening to that slim bottle blonde, who was probably telling them off, but then, when the woman disappeared back into the store, Lautaro resumed the operation while Pascual observed him from a predetermined spot, and at some point – I wasn't watching them all the time – my son succeeded in touching the glass of the closed door with his nose, and it was only then, two days before our flight back to Europe, that I knew I'd arrived in Chile and that everything would be all right. It was an apocalyptic thought.

In 1999, the following year, I went back to Chile at the invitation of the Book Fair. Almost all the Chilean writers decided to attack me *en patota,* as they say in Chile: that is, in a gang. I guess it was their way of congratulating me for winning the Rómulo Gallegos Prize. I counterattacked. A woman of a certain age, who all her life had relied on the alms distributed to artists by a charitable state, called me a toady. Since I've never been a cultural attaché or held a sinecure, I was surprised by this accusation. I was also called a *patero,* which is not the same as a *patota.* A *patero* doesn't necessarily belong to a *patota,* as you might be forgiven for supposing, although there are always *pateros* in a *patota.* A *patero* is a sycophant, a flatterer, a brown-nose, an asslicker. The amazing thing about these accusations is that they were made by left- as well as right-wing Chileans who were busy licking ass nonstop to hang on to their scraps of fame, while everything that I'd accomplished (not that it amounts to much) was down to me and no one else. What was it that they didn't like about me? Well, someone said it was my teeth. Fair enough; I can't argue with that.

Beach

I gave up heroin and went home and began the methadone treatment administered at the outpatient clinic and I didn't have much else to do except get up each morning and watch TV and try to sleep at night, but I couldn't, something made me unable to close my eyes and rest, and that was my routine until one day I couldn't stand it anymore and I bought myself a pair of black swim trunks at a store in the centre of town and I went to the beach, wearing the trunks and with a towel and a magazine, and I spread my towel not too far from the sea and then I lay down and spent a while trying to decide whether to go into the sea or not, I could think of lots of reasons to go in but also some not to (the children playing at the water's edge, for example), until at last it was too late and I went home, and the next morning I bought some sunscreen and I went to the beach again, and at around twelve I headed to the clinic and got my dose of methadone and said hello to some familiar faces, no friends, just familiar faces from the methadone line who were surprised to see me in swim trunks, but I acted as if there was nothing strange about it, and then I walked back to the beach and this time I went for a dip and tried to swim, though I couldn't, and that was enough for me, and the next day I went back to the beach and put on sunscreen all over and then I fell asleep on the sand, and when I woke up I felt very well-rested, and I hadn't burned my back or anything, and this went on for a week or maybe two, I can't remember, the only thing I'm sure of is that each day I got more tan and though I didn't talk to anyone each day I felt better, or different, which isn't the same thing but in my case it seemed like it, and one day an old couple turned up on the beach, I remember it clearly, it looked like they'd been together for a long time, she was fat, or round, and must have been about seventy, and he was thin, or more than thin, a walking skeleton, I think that was why I noticed him, because usually I didn't take much notice of the people on the beach, but I did notice them, and it was because the guy was so skinny, I saw him and got scared, fuck, it's death coming for me, I thought, but nothing was coming for me, it was just two old people, the man maybe seventy-five and the woman about seventy, or the other way around, and she seemed to be in good health, but he looked as if he were going to breathe his last breath any time now or as if this were his last summer, and at first, once I was over my initial fright, it was hard for me to look away from the old man's face, from his skull barely covered by a thin layer of skin, but then I got used to watching the two of them surreptitiously, lying on the sand, on my stomach, with my face hidden in my arms, or from the boardwalk, sitting on a bench facing the beach, as I pretended to brush sand off myself, and I remember that the old woman always came to the beach with an umbrella, under which she quickly ducked, and she didn't wear a swimsuit, although sometimes I saw her in a swimsuit, but usually she was in a very loose summer dress that made her look fatter than she was, and under that umbrella the old woman sat reading, she had a very thick book, while the skeleton that was her husband lay on the sand in nothing but a tiny swimsuit, almost a thong, and drank in the sun with a voracity that brought me distant memories of junkies frozen in blissful immobility, of junkies focused on what they were doing, on the only thing they could do, and then my head ached and I left the beach, I had something to eat on the Paseo Marítimo, a little dish of anchovies and a beer, and then I smoked a cigarette and watched the beach through the window of the bar, and then I went back and the old man and the old woman were still there, she under her umbrella, he exposed to the sun's rays, and then, suddenly, for no reason, I felt like crying and I got in the water and swam and when I was a long way from the shore I looked at the sun and it seemed strange to me that it was there, that big thing so unlike us, and then I started to swim towards the beach (twice I almost drowned) and when I got back I dropped down next to my towel and sat there panting for quite a while, but without losing sight of the old couple, and then I may have fallen asleep on the sand, and when I woke up the beach was beginning to empty, but the old man and the old woman were still there, she with her novel under the umbrella and he on his back in the sun with his eyes closed and a strange expression on his skull-like face, as if he could feel each second passing and he was savouring it, though the sun's rays were weak, though the sun had already dipped behind the buildings along the beach, behind the hills, but that didn't seem to bother him, and then I watched him and I watched the sun, and sometimes my back stung a little, as if that afternoon I'd burned myself, and I looked at them and then I got up, I slung my towel over my shoulders like a cape and went to sit on one of the benches of the Paseo Marítimo, where I pretended to brush nonexistent sand off my legs, and from up there I had a different vision of the couple, and I said to myself that maybe he wasn't about to die, I said to myself that maybe time didn't exist in the way I'd always thought it existed, I reflected on time as the sun's distance lengthened the shadows of the buildings, and then I went home and took a shower and examined my red back, a back that didn't seem to belong to me but to someone else, someone I wouldn't get to know for years and then I turned on the TV and watched shows that I didn't understand at all, until I fell asleep in my chair, and the next day it was back to the same old thing, the beach, the clinic, the beach again, a routine that was sometimes interrupted by new people on the beach, a woman, for example, who was always standing, who never lay down in the sand, who wore a bikini bottom and a blue T-shirt, and who only went into the water up to the knees, and who was reading a book, like the old woman, but this woman read it standing up, and sometimes she knelt down, though in a very odd way, and picked up a big bottle of Pepsi and drank, standing up, of course, and then put the bottle back down on the towel, which I don't know why she'd brought since she never lay down on it or went swimming, and sometimes this woman scared me, she seemed too strange, but most of the time I just felt sorry for her, and I saw other strange things too, all kinds of things happen at the beach, maybe because it's the only place where we're all half-naked, though nothing too important ever happened, once as I was walking along the shore I thought I saw an ex-junkie like me, sitting on a mound of sand with a baby on his lap, and another time I saw some Russian girls, three Russian girls, who were probably hookers and who were talking on cell phones and laughing, all three of them, but what really interested me most was the old couple, partly because I had the feeling that the old man might die at any moment, and when I thought this, or when I realised I was thinking this, crazy ideas would come into my head, like the thought that after the old man's death there would be a tsunami and the town would be destroyed by a giant wave, or that the earth would begin to shake and a massive earthquake would swallow up the whole town in a wave of dust, and when I thought about all this, I hid my head in my hands and began to weep, and while I was weeping I dreamed (or imagined) that it was nighttime, say three in the morning, and I'd left my house and gone to the beach, and on the beach I found the old man lying on the sand, and in the sky, up near the stars, but closer to Earth than the other stars, there shone a black sun, an enormous sun, silent and black, and I went down to the beach and lay on the sand too, the only two people on the beach were the old man and me, and when I opened my eyes again I realised that the Russian hookers and the girl who was always standing and the ex-junkie with the baby were watching me curiously, maybe wondering who that weird guy was, the guy with the sunburned shoulders and back, and even the old woman was gazing at me from under her umbrella, interrupting the reading of her interminable book for a few seconds, maybe wondering who that young man was, that man with silent tears running down his face, a man of thirty-five who had nothing at all but who was recovering his will and his courage and who knew that he would live a while longer.

NATASHA WIMMER

Muscles

I.

I don't know if my brother was a cultured or civilised person, though some nights I think that he probably was and that being civilised is probably what saved him from suicide.

His favorite books were *Kabyle Customs* by John Hodge and all the volumes of Professor Ramiro Lira's *Works of the Pre-Socratic Philosophers* (which are more like pamphlets, really, but my brother explained that this was because the works of those poor philosophers had been swallowed by the black hole of time, which is what will happen to all of us). And others.

'No hole's going to swallow me,' I'd say to him.

'It's going to happen to both of us, Marta, there's no avoiding it,' he'd say, without a hint of sadness.

But I think it's a very sad thought.

It was usually over breakfast that we talked about the Pre-Socratic philosophers. The one he liked best was Empedocles. That Empedocles, he used to say, he's like Spiderman. My favourite was Heraclitus. We almost never talked about the philosophers at night, I don't know why. It must have been because at night we had much more to talk about, or because sometimes we were both too tired when we got back from work – you need to be sharp if you're going to talk about philosophy – though little by little, and especially after the death of our parents, that began to change as well, and our nighttime conversations gradually became more grown-up; we started talking more seriously, as if our words were venturing into much more open and hazardous territory, now that our parents were no longer there to anchor them. But in the mornings, both before their death and after, our favourite topic was the Pre-Socratics, as if the start of a new day (though, if you think about it, the day begins long before that, at midnight) had restored the energy we had as kids and made everything different, better, refreshed. I remember our breakfasts: a cup of coffee with milk, bread with tomato and olive oil, a steak, a bowl of cereal or two tubs of yogurt with honey and muesli, Super Egg (100% egg protein), Fuel Tank (with megacalorie protein: 3000 calories per dose), Super Mega Mass, Victory Mega Aminos (in capsules), Fat Burner (lipotropes to help dissolve fat), and an orange, a banana or an apple, depending on the season. That was for Enric. I don't eat much: I'd have maybe half a biscuit, the kind my brother used to buy, made with whole wheat flour and enriched with some kind of vitamins, and a cup of black coffee.

There could be something invigorating about that table, seen from the kitchen, at seven-thirty or eight in the morning. The plates and the mugs and the bowls and the packets that looked like NASA rations seemed to be saying: 'Go out into the street. The day is full of promise. The world is young and so are you.' My brother would sit at that table and open a pamphlet containing the complete works of some Pre-Socratic philosopher, or a magazine, and while his right hand was busy with a spoon or a fork, his left hand would turn the pages.

'Listen to what this son of a bitch Diogenes of Apollonia says.'

I'd keep quiet and wait for him to speak, doing my best to look attentive.

' "When beginning any account, it seems to me that one should make the starting point incontrovertible and the style simple and dignified." How do you like that?'

'It sounds reasonable.'

'It's fucking *reasonable* all right!'

After breakfast my brother helped me to take the dishes to the kitchen and then he went to work. From the age of sixteen he'd been working at Fonollosa Brothers Auto Repairs, near Plaza Molina, in a neighbourhood where people have expensive, complicated cars to fix. I'd stay home a while longer, watching TV or reading one of the Pre-Socratics (we did the dishes at night) and then I'd go to work, that is to the Academía Malú; the name makes it sound like a school (a school for whores, my brother used to say), though in fact it's a hairdressing salon.

Why was my brother so rude about the Academía Malú? The answer's simple but it's a sore point. My friend or ex-friend Montse García worked there; Enric went out with her for a month or so, two at the most, till Montse decided that they weren't right for each other. At least that's how she explained it to me when they split up. My brother just mumbled something incomprehensible and from then on, whenever the

Academía came up, he always made some snide or obscene remark.

'But what happened with you and Montse?' I asked him one night.

'Nothing,' said my brother. 'We were incompatible. It's none of your business.'

My brother was like that, and the death of our parents just made it worse. Sometimes, from my room, I could hear him talking to himself: We're orphans, that's an irrefutable fact, and we have to get used it, he'd say. And then he'd repeat it, over and over, obsessively, like someone who's forgotten the real words to a song: We're orphans, we're orphans, etc. At times like that I wanted to hug him, or get up and take him a mug of hot milk, but that would've only made it worse; my brother would've broken down crying for sure, and after a while I'd have started crying too. So I never got out of bed, and he'd go on talking to himself until he was finally overtaken by sleep.

But in the morning I'd sometimes try to reason with him: 'We're not the only orphans in the world. And anyway, to be an orphan, I mean a real orphan, I think you have to be a minor, and we're not minors any more.'

'You are, Marta,' he'd say, 'and it's my duty to look after you.'

According to Montse García, my brother was immature. I only went out with them twice when they were together, both times because my brother asked me to, and on both occasions I was able to confirm the accuracy of my friend's or ex-friend's judgement. The first time we went to see a movie by Almodóvar. Enric suggested a Van Damme movie, but Montse and I refused. We were late because of the argument, and when we arrived the cinema was dark, the film had started, and my brother decided, absurdly, not to sit with us. The second time we went to the gym, the Rosales gym in Calle Bonaventura, right near our place, where my brother works out every day. It wasn't that he didn't make an effort; this time, he was trying too hard. He wanted us to see him inserted into all the gym's contraptions, and in the end one of them nearly decapitated him. I'm fond of my brother, but there are limits, like the doors of the Rosales gym. I've never been able to stand bodybuilders; my idea of handsome may keep shifting unreliably, as my brother says, but it has never taken the form of a hulk. I should say that Montse García was with me on this, although at the time she was interested in my brother, and he'd been bodybuilding since he was sixteen (he started just after he got the job at the auto repair shop). I think it was one of the guys from his work, by the name of Paco Contreras, who got him into it. This Paco competed in various bodybuilding championships in Catalonia and then he moved to Dos Hermanas in Andalusia, where he died. Sometimes my brother would get a letter from him and read one or two sentences to me. Then he'd put the letters in a little chest that he kept under his bed, the only place in the house where things could be kept under lock and key. According to Montse, this Paco had perverted my brother. I told her the story myself and regretted it immediately. My brother may be many things but he isn't stupid, and certainly not simple (who is, really?), and yet the story, the way I told it, badly or partially, did made him look stupid. I never met Paco Contreras. According to my brother, he was an amazing guy, the best friend he'd ever have, etc., etc. So when Montse said that this Paco had perverted my brother, I told her she was wrong, Enric was a serious, responsible, clean-living person, the best brother I'd ever have.

'Well, what else could you say, you poor thing?'

Sometimes I wanted to kill her. But I did everything I could to make things work out between her and Enric. I preferred them to go out on their own, of course, though if it had been up to my brother, I've have gone along every time. A week after they started going out, Montse and I went to the bathroom at the Academía Malú and she asked me if my brother was sick.

'He's super-fit,' I said.

'Well, something's not right,' she said, and declined to elaborate, although I knew what she was referring to.

This happened a few months after the death of our parents. Montse was the first girl my brother had been out with. And there haven't been any others since. Sometimes I think that he must have been feeling alone and a bit lost in the world. Our parents died in a bus accident, on the way from Barcelona to Benidorm, setting off for their first vacation on their own. My brother was very close to them. So was I, but in a different way. The official who met us at the morgue in Benidorm (he was dressed like a pathologist, though I don't think he actually was one) told us that our parents' bodies had been found holding hands, and that it had been quite a job to separate them.

'It made an impression on us all, and I thought you'd like to know,' he said.

'They must have been asleep at the time of the crash,' said my brother. 'They liked to sleep holding hands.'

'And how do you know that?' I asked.

Muscles

'It's the kind of thing an older brother knows,' said the official or the pathologist.

'I saw them, lots of times,' said my brother with tears brimming in his eyes.

Later, when we were in the hospital cafeteria, waiting for the papers so we could take our parents back to Barcelona, he said that it was all because of the calcination. He said that the crash must have caused an explosion, and the explosion would have produced a fireball hot enough to fuse the hands of our deceased progenitors.

'They would have had to use a saw to separate them.'

He said this in a cold, offhand way, but I knew that my brother was suffering as he had never suffered before. So when he started going out with Montse García a few months later, I think one night I even prayed that he'd sleep with her and that they'd form some kind of lasting relationship. But what happened is that Montse, who had seemed keen before she went out with him, gradually cooled off and then she got bitter, and by the time they broke up sixty days later, she was treating me as an enemy, as if I were to blame for the disappointments of her short-lived romance. When she finally decided to break it off, our relationship improved markedly for a few days, and I even thought that we could go back to being good friends like before. But Enric's shadow kept coming between us whenever I tried to get close to her again.

'It can't be healthy to spend all day at the gym. Why would a guy want muscles like that, anyway? It isn't normal,' she said to me one day.

'He also reads the Pre-Socratic philosophers,' I replied.

'Like I said, your brother's not right in the head. You be

careful. One night you might find him in your room with a knife, about to cut your throat.'

'My brother is a kind person; he wouldn't hurt anyone.'

'You're an idiot, Marta,' she said, and that was the end of our friendship.

From then on, we only spoke to each other when it was strictly necessary for work: Pass me some clips, can I have the dryer, can you get that colour down?

What a pity.

II.

One night my brother turned up with Tomé and Florencio. He'd never invited anyone home: not when our parents were alive, and not in the months since they died. At first I thought they were two friends from the gym but I only had to take a second look to realise that these guys didn't work out.

'They'll be staying here tonight,' my brother said in the kitchen. We were getting dinner ready, and Florencio and Tomé were channel-surfing in the living room.

'Where?' I said. It's a small flat, and there's no guest room.

'In Mom and Dad's bedroom,' he said, looking away.

He must have been expecting me to protest, but I thought it was a good idea, though maybe I was a bit surprised that I hadn't come up with it myself. Of course: our parents' empty bedroom. That was fine by me. I asked him who they were, where he'd met them, what they did.

'At the gym. They're South Americans.'

We had salad and grilled steak for dinner.

Florencio and Tomé looked like they were nearly thirty, but I knew they'd look like that until they were fifty. They were hungry and they sampled every concoction my brother laid out on the table. I don't know if they were aware of the immense honour he was doing them, putting his stock of supplements at their disposal. I asked them if they were bodybuilders too.

'We do fitness training,' said Tomé.

'Do you know what that is?' asked Florencio.

I don't like people thinking I'm stupid. Or ignorant, which is worse.

'Of course I know what it is; my brother's been going to the gym since he was sixteen,' I said, and immediately wished I'd kept my mouth shut.

Florencio and Tomé laughed in unison, and then my brother laughed as well. I asked them what was so funny. My brother looked at me, lost for words, with an expression of utter bewilderment, but also of happiness, on his face.

'Feisty, aren't you?' said Florencio.

'Very feisty,' said Tomé.

'She's always had a strong character, my sister,' said Enric.

'And you've worked all this out from what I said about fitness training?'

'From the way you said it. Looking me in the eye. Sure of yourself,' said Florencio.

'If I had my tarot pack here, I'd do a reading for you,' said Tomé.

'So you do fitness training and tarot readings?'

'And a few other things as well,' said Tomé.

Florencio and my brother laughed again. But in my brother's case it was, I realised, nervous rather than happy laughter. He was worried, although he was trying to hide it. The two South Americans, however, seemed relaxed, as if they were used to sleeping in a different house every night.

I finished eating before they did and went off to my bedroom and shut the door. My brother came to tell me there was a good movie on, but I said I had to get up early. I wasn't sleepy. I took off my shoes and flopped onto the bed, still dressed, with the complete works of Xenophanes of Colophon ('For all things are from earth and in earth all things end'), until I heard them get up from the table. First they went to the kitchen, washed the dishes, laughed again (what was there in the kitchen that could have made them laugh?) and then they came back to the living room and started watching something on TV. I can't remember falling asleep. But I do remember this: a sentence from Xenophanes ('He sees as a whole, he thinks as a whole, he hears as a whole') which for some reason I found unsettling. I was woken by noises from my brother's room. At first, although the light was still on in my room, I didn't know where I was. Then I heard the shouting and the moaning. It was my brother moaning, I was absolutely sure of that. And one of the South Americans was shouting (in an urgent, imperious, affectionate way), but I couldn't tell which one of them it was. I got undressed, put on my nightie, and for a while I just lay there listening and thinking. I tried to read Xenophanes, but I couldn't get past the following sentence or fragment: 'wild cherry.' It made me feel very sad. Then I got up and tried to hear what the South American was saying. With my ear to the wall I could hear the odd word or sentence (in a way it was like reading the fragments of Xenophanes): 'that's the way', 'nice and tight', 'careful', 'slowly'. Then I went back to bed and fell asleep. In the morning, for the first time in I don't know how many years, my brother didn't have breakfast with me.

Muscles

I thought they'd done something to him; I knocked on his door. After a while he said to come in. The room smelt of the hair-removal cream my brother uses. I asked him if he was sick. He said no, he was fine, but he thought he'd go to work a bit later.

'And the South Americans?'

'In Mom and Dad's room, sleeping. We stayed up late last night.'

'I heard you,' I said. 'You went to bed with one of them.'

My brother surprised me by laughing.

'Did we wake you up?'

'No, I woke up anyway, I was feeling restless, then I heard you. By chance. I wasn't spying on you.'

'Well, it's no big deal. Let me get a bit more sleep.'

I stood there, frozen, watching him, not knowing what to do or say, until I heard voices in Mom and Dad's room and then I turned around and walked out of the apartment without having breakfast. I worked all morning in a daze, as if I was the one who hadn't got any sleep. At midday I went to have lunch at a Chinese restaurant where some of the other girls from the Academía Malú used to go and then I went walking in the streets around Plaza de España. I thought about when I was seven and my brother was sixteen and he was the person I loved most in the world. One time he told me that his dream was to play Maciste when he grew up. I had no idea who Maciste was, so he showed me a picture of him in a movie magazine. I didn't like him. You're much better looking, I said, and he looked pleased and smiled. Then, for some reason, as I was walking around, I remembered him hugging Mom and Dad, giving them all his pay, taking me to the movies (though we never went to see a

Maciste film), and doing little poses in front of the mirror in the elevator.

I must have been feeling terrible that afternoon – though I can't really remember; I know I was thinking about my brother and our apartment, and my mental images of him and of it seemed to be shackled, sunken, black and white, irreparable – and it must have been obvious because even Montse García came over to ask if there was something wrong.

'What could possibly be wrong?' I said. I guess I must have said it in a way that sounded aggressive, although I didn't mean to.

'Maybe that brother of yours has been horrible to you,' said Montse.

'Enric is going through a rough patch, but he's gradually getting it together,' I replied. 'He's trying to find his way, which is more than you can say for some.'

From the way Montse looked at me I guessed that she still felt something for him.

'Your brother's a bad person, seriously,' she said. 'He's never satisfied with anything, but he doesn't know what he wants. He'll screw things up for everyone else just to make himself happy, but the thing is he doesn't know how to be happy. Am I making myself clear?'

'I could kill you sometimes,' I said.

'I know it's not easy to hear this stuff. But you're alone in the world, Marta, and you have to watch out for yourself. I like you. You're a good person and that's why I'm saying this, although I know you're not going to listen.'

For a moment I was tempted to tell her about what had

happened the night before, but I decided that it was better to keep my mouth shut.

That night, when I got home, Enric, Florencio and Tomé were already in the living room watching TV. I made a coffee and sat as far away from them as I could, at the end of the table, near the window, where my father used to sit. Enric and Tomé were sprawled on the sofa and Florencio was in the armchair, which is where I normally sit to watch TV. There were containers of high-calorie, high-protein food scattered over the table, the kind my brother eats, but these were new. I also saw a baguette, ham, cheese, and several bottles of beer.

'The guys brought some supplies,' said my brother.

I didn't respond. The containers of food, the pills, the Fuel Tank and the Super Egg (vanilla and chocolate flavoured, respectively) were expensive, more than five thousand pesetas a tub, and I couldn't imagine that scruffy pair having so much money. It would have cost them more than fifty thousand pesetas all together.

'Where did you steal it from?'

'I like your sister,' said Florencio.

My brother looked at me and then at them with a half-amused, half-incredulous expression on his face.

'We went to get some stuff from our place,' said Florencio. 'And we decided to pick up some food on the way.'

'I brought my tarot cards as well,' said Tomé.

'If you have a place of your own, why do you want to move in here?'

'That was just a manner of speaking,' said Florencio. 'Actually, it's a boarding house. When you don't have a place of your own, you end up calling any place home, even a shithole like that boarding house. Enric invited us to stay here for a few days, till we see how things work out.'

'In other words, you're broke.'

'You could say our finances are tight.'

At that moment, for some reason, they looked handsome to me. Both of them had just taken a shower. Tomé's hair was still wet, and his manner was unassuming but self-assured. Everything seemed to be much simpler and clearer for them than it was for my brother and me.

'So you stole that food.'

'Well, yeah, that's right, we did,' said Florencio.

'We thought it would be rude to turn up empty-handed, and Enric likes that stuff; he spends a fortune on it.'

'It isn't cheap, that's for sure,' said my brother.

'We went to a store on Avenida Roma, near the Modelo Prison, a store that specialises in bodybuilding supplements, and we took whatever we could.'

'You shouldn't have done that, guys,' my brother said.

'Hey, it was the least we could do,' said Tomé.

My brother smiled happily: 'Now I have supplies for like five months.'

'What if you'd been caught?' I said.

'We never get caught,' said Florencio.

'We bought a packet of soy cookies,' said Tomé.

Suddenly I ran out of arguments. I would have liked to ask them how many days they were planning to stay at our place, but I didn't want to go too far. It's one thing to be frank and another to be rude. It's one thing to be aggressive and another to be hospitable. So I kept quiet, sitting on my father's chair, staring at the bottom of my coffee cup and occasionally glancing up at the game show they were watching on TV

(Florencio and Tomé knew all the answers) until it was time to eat.

'The guys made dinner tonight,' said my brother.

Poor fool, I thought, without getting up. That night we ate rice and vegetables. My brother, who always eats meat, didn't complain; on the contrary, he praised the flavour of the meal and went back for seconds and thirds. Florencio set the table, and Tomé served the food. They opened a bottle of expensive wine ('You stole this too?' I asked – 'Naturally,' replied Florencio) and we all had some.

'Let's drink a toast to Marta and Enric,' said Tomé. 'Two very special people. There's no one else like you two.'

I could feel myself blushing. I'm not used to drinking wine (my parents were teetotalers, my brother too, until yesterday, anyway) and I'm even less used to public compliments.

TRANSLATOR'S NOTE: The quotations from Diogenes of Apollonia and Xenophanes of Colophon in 'Muscles' are given in Jonathan Barnes's translation, from *Early Greek Philosophy* (London: Penguin, 1987).

The Tour

My idea was to interview John Malone, the musician who'd disappeared. Five years earlier, Malone had already slipped out of the dark zone where the legends live, and he wasn't really newsworthy any more, although the fans hadn't forgotten his name. In the seventh decade of the twentieth century, along with Jacob Morley and Dan Endycott, he'd been a founding member of Broken Zoo, one of the most successful rock groups of the time. Broken Zoo recorded their first LP in 1966. It was a magnificent record, up there with the best stuff coming out of England – and this is the mid-sixties I'm talking about, with the Beatles and the Rolling Stones in top form. The second LP came out soon after and, to everyone's surprise, it was even better than the first. Broken Zoo did a tour of Europe and then a tour of the States. The North American tour went on for months. As they travelled from city to city, the record climbed up the charts and finally reached number one. When they got back to London, they took a few days off to rest. Morley shut himself up in a house that he'd recently bought on the outskirts of London, where he had a private recording studio. Endycott kept himself busy getting off with all the pretty groupies who came swarming around the band, till one of them got off with him, and they bought a house in Belgravia and got married. As for Malone, he seemed more lethargic. According to some of the books about Broken Zoo, he attended 'weird parties', though what the authors meant by *weird* is not exactly clear. I'm guessing it's what they said back then to indicate a mix of sex and drugs. Shortly afterward, Malone disappeared. And after sensibly allowing a month or two to elapse, Broken Zoo's manager called a press conference, at which he admitted what everyone already knew: John Malone had quit the group without a word of explanation. Not long after that, Morley and Endycott, along with the drummer Ronnie Palmer, and another band member called Corrigan, came out with their own versions of the events. Malone hadn't been in touch with anyone except Palmer. He called him three weeks after his disappearance, just to say that he was fine, and to tell them not to wait for him because he wasn't planning to come back. Many people thought that this would be the end of the group. Malone was the best of the lot, and it was hard to imagine Broken Zoo going on without him. But then Morley shut himself up for a month or so in his mansion, and Endycott went there too and worked ten hours a day, and they put together the group's third LP. Contrary to the expectations of the critics, Broken Zoo's third record was better than the first and the second. Seventy per cent of the material on the first record was written by Malone: lyrics as well as music. On the second record, it was seventy-five per cent. The rest was provided by Morley and Endycott, except for one track, which is something of an anomaly, with lyrics co-written by Morley and Palmer. For the third record, however, Morley and Endycott wrote ninety per cent of the material, and the remaining ten per cent was contributed by Palmer, Morley, Endycott and a new member, Venable, who'd joined the group when it was clear that Malone wouldn't be coming back. One of the songs is dedicated to Malone. There's no bitterness in it. Just friendship and admiration. The title is 'When are You Going to Come Back?' It was released as a single and in less than two weeks it went to the top of the charts in London. Malone, of course, didn't come back, and although, at the time, various journalists went searching for him, all their efforts were fruitless. There was even a rumour that he had died in a city in France and been buried in a pauper's grave. Broken Zoo's third album was followed by a fourth, which was greeted with unanimous praise, and after the fourth came a fifth and then a sixth, a flawless double album, the group's apotheosis, and after that they didn't play for while, but then they brought out a seventh LP, which was pretty good, and then an eighth, and in the middle of the eighties they made their ninth album, another double, and Morley and Endycott must have signed a pact with the devil, because this record swept the world, from Japan to Holland, from New Zealand to Canada, tearing through Thailand like a tornado, which is really saying something. Then the group broke up, though every now and then, on a special occasion, they'd get back together to play their old songs at a select venue. In 1995 a journalist from *Rolling Stone* found out where Malone was living. His article stunned the die-hard fans of Broken Zoo, who cherished the group's first vinyl LPs. But most of the magazine's readers didn't really care what had happened to a guy who was widely assumed to be dead. In a way, Malone's life during all those years had been a living death. When he left London, he had simply gone back to his parents' house. That was all. He stayed there for two years, doing nothing, while the members of his old band set out to take the universe by storm.

Daniela

My name is Daniela de Montecristo and I am a citizen of the universe, although I was born in Buenos Aires, the capital of Argentina, in the year 1915, the youngest of three sisters. Later my father remarried and had a little son, but the child died before his first birthday, and Papa had to be happy with what he had, that is, with my sisters and me. I don't know why I'm explaining all this. It's ancient history, or children's stories if you like, of no interest to anyone now. I lost my virginity at the age of thirteen. That might interest someone. I was deflowered by one of the ranch hands. I can't remember his name, all I know is that he was a ranch hand and must have been somewhere between twenty-five and forty-five. He didn't rape me, I do remember that. At least I never thought of it as rape, afterward I mean, when it was over, and I was getting dressed behind an ombu tree, and the ranch hand, around the other side, was pensively rolling a cigarette, which he then lit and gave me for a couple of puffs on it, my first ever puffs of smoke. I remember that vividly. The bitter taste of the tobacco and the plains stretching away endlessly and my legs trembling. What was really trembling, though, were my thoughts. I could have gone and told on him. All that night I kept turning the idea over in my mind, and the next two nights as well. But I didn't do it. Partly because I wanted to repeat the experience. Partly because it wasn't my father's ranch; it belonged to one of his friends, so the punishment wouldn't have been administered by my blood relations, it would have fallen outside what I took to be the ambit of real justice, the justice of the blood. My father never had a ranch. My older sister married a lawyer, a pathetic shyster who never tired of declaring his inordinate love for my father. My other sister married the son of a ranch owner, a crazy kid who within a few years managed to gamble away a small fortune and get himself cut out of the will. To sum up: my family was always middle class, and whatever efforts we made, from our various starting points, in our various and often contradictory ways, to climb up a rung and enter the rigid, immutable upper crust, official guardian of justice and morality, the fact is we never moved out of our social compartment, which, although comfortable, condemned the livelier minds in the clan (myself, for example) to a restlessness that even then, at the age of thirteen, on that ranch, which wasn't our property, I could glimpse like a dizzying mirage, a space in time where time itself was cancelled, time as we know it, and that was why I began by saying that I am a citizen of the universe and not, as the saying goes, of the world, because I may be old but it should be quite clear that I'm not stupid, and the world cannot contain a dizzying mirage like that, although perhaps the universe can. But I was talking about restlessness. I was talking about the night when I thought about telling on the ranch hand who had deflowered me. I didn't, and I didn't have sex with him again. Restlessness, my first apprehension of restlessness, declared itself as a fever, so my father sent me back to Buenos Aires, where I was entrusted to the care of a physician, Dr Guarini.

Suntan

The previous summer I'd been a temporary foster parent to a child from the Third World. It was a terrible experience. When I took her to the airport I was a wreck, and Olga (that was her name), she was a wreck as well. We cried all the way, we didn't stop for a minute. She kept sobbing that she wanted to stay with me, the poor thing. Just as well there were no photographers. Even so, I stayed in the car for a while, fixing my makeup, before we got out. The man from the NGO who was there to take the children back was waiting by the information counter. He looked at me and realised right away that I was taking it hard. It's normal, the first time, he said. There was another girl there with her foster family. In spite of the dark glasses, they recognised me immediately. The mother came over and said: It gives us such a boost to know that you're taking part in the programme too, Lucía. I had no idea what she meant, but I smiled and said I was just another volunteer. Half an hour later the children and the man from the NGO boarded the plane and disappeared, leaving the foster parents in the departure lounge. One of them suggested that we go for a drink. I declined. I shook hands with all of them (no kisses) and left. In the car I cried all the way back to my apartment, but two days later I had to go to

Milan, for work, and I spent August in Marbella and Mallorca. Eventually the summer came to an end and work began again in earnest.

And all sorts of things happened after that.

Eight months later the same NGO wrote to me to see if I wanted to foster a child again in July. I thought about it all that day, carrying the letter around in my handbag, and eventually decided to repeat the experience. I called them and said I'd participate again, as long as they did whatever they could to make sure it was Olga. They said they'd try, but the organisation had a rule, or something – I didn't understand. Call me, I said. A month later they called and said they were doing their best to get Olga. At that time I was acting in a play, a wonderful English production, a musical about the poor people of London, or maybe it was Manchester, set at the beginning of the century, a play in which I had to sing and dance as well as act. For some reason, talking with the people from the NGO helped me with my work. It was just after the première and the reviews hadn't been very good. Especially the comments about me. Well, not just me; some of the other actors came off badly too. After that phone call my performances improved; they were stronger, more convincing, and the others were inspired by my energy on stage.

Then I was offered a television show. I said yes without a second thought.

Then I met a doctor in Madrid called Gorka (his family came from the Basque country) and we fell in love.

To be completely honest, for a while I forgot all about the girl and the NGO. I was living at a frantic pace: interviews, TV appearances, a small but gratifying part in a film, and my own talk show with celebrity guests (actresses, models, athletes, heart-throbs).

One morning they called and said that Olga wouldn't be able to spend her vacation month with me. Why not? I asked, although for a moment I had no idea who Olga was, what vacation month they were talking about, or who had called to tell me this and was now replying to my question in a condescending tone of voice that I didn't like at all, explaining something about regulations, which left me even more confused. When I finally realised what it was about, I said I didn't have time to talk right then and told them to call me back the following night, insisting that I wanted Olga. We completely understand, said the voice: It's human, it's normal.

Having reached this point in my story, there's something I think I should clarify. There are show-business personalities who'll stop at nothing to appear on TV and in the magazines. Generalising broadly, they belong to one of two kinds: those who are working and those who aren't. Those who are working might go to a leper colony in India to promote their new record or TV show. The others can't afford to fly to India, but they might visit an orphanage in Tangiers or a prison in Rabat to keep themselves visible and boost their chances of getting some work soon. Not that either kind of personality necessarily goes to India or Morocco – those are just examples I'm using to make a general point: fame is measured in exclusives, calibrated by the size of the splash you can make with a scandal or a spectacular act of charity. But there was no such design behind my decision to foster a child for the month of July. No one knew anything about it, I mean no one who works for the glossy magazines. Olga's stay at my apartment was a secret, and during the days we spent on Mallorca with my family we kept well out of the public eye. I play the bimbo sometimes, if it's in the script, but I went to college and I earned my degree in art history.

So let me make it perfectly clear that I didn't want the girl for self-promotion. I have nothing against publicity as such, but there's a line between vulgar and sophisticated publicity. And that line should never be crossed, or so I was taught as a child, because there's no going back.

The next day I got a call from the NGO. They said they'd done everything humanly possible, but it wasn't going to be Olga. Instead they talked to me about Mariam, or María, a twelve-year-old Saharan girl who had lost her father in the war, a lovely girl, they said, and very clever for her age. Olga was twelve as well, I thought, and then I remembered her birthday and realised that I hadn't even sent her a card, and before I knew it I was crying, while the guy from the NGO went on giving me information about Mariam; she'd seen all sorts of atrocities, he said, and yet had somehow preserved her innocence. What do you mean? I asked. That's she's still a girl, in spite of everything she's been through. But she's twelve, I said. You haven't seen what I've seen, Lucía, he said in a velvety voice. The guy was trying to hit on me! He started telling me stories, not about the children, but about things that had happened to him. You have to travel a lot in this job. I travel a lot too, I said. I know, he said. For a while we talked about our respective travels. Then I agreed to foster Mariam and we said goodbye and hung up.

The only people I told were my parents and my sister. I didn't say anything to Gorka. Partly because he wasn't in Madrid (he'd gone to Mallorca for a sailing regatta), partly because I'm an independent woman and it was my decision and mine alone. Naturally, Gorka had plans for the summer, vague plans to go to an island in the Caribbean, and then to find a place in Mallorca, near his sailing friends, where we could stay till the beginning of September. I adore the sea. And I enjoy the regattas. I'm actually a better sailor than Gorka, who took it up quite recently (I've been sailing since I was a child), but like the rest of us, he's entitled to waste his time however he sees fit.

Death of Ulises

Belano, our dear Arturo Belano, returns to Mexico City. More than twenty years have passed since the last time he was there. The plane is flying over the city, and he wakes with a start. The uneasiness he has felt throughout the trip intensifies. At the airport in Mexico City he has to catch a connecting flight to Guadalajara, for the Book Fair, to which he's been invited. Belano is now a fairly well-known author and is often invited to international events, although he doesn't travel much. This is his first trip to Mexico in more than twenty years. Last year he had two invitations and he pulled out at the last minute. The year before last he had four and he pulled out at the last minute. I can't remember how many invitations he had three years ago, but he pulled out at the last minute. Still, here he is in Mexico, in the Mexico City airport, following a group of perfect strangers who are heading towards the transit zone to catch the plane to Guadalajara. The corridor leads through a labyrinth of glass. Belano is the last in line. His steps are increasingly slow and hesitant. In a waiting room he spots a young Argentine writer who is also going to Guadalajara. Belano immediately takes cover behind a pillar. The Argentine is reading the paper, whose cultural supplement — maybe that's what he's reading — is

Death of Ulises

entirely devoted to the Book Fair. After a few moments, he looks up and glances around, as if he knew he was being observed, but he doesn't see Belano, and his gaze returns to the paper. After a while a very beautiful woman approaches the Argentine and kisses him from behind. Belano knows her. She's a Mexican, born in Guadalajara. The Argentine man and the Mexican woman both live in Barcelona, together, and Belano is a friend of theirs. The Mexican woman and the Argentine man exchange a few words. Somehow both of them have sensed that they are being watched. Belano tries to read their lips, but he can't work out what they're saying. He doesn't leave his hiding place until their backs are turned. By the time he can finally escape from that corridor, the line of passengers heading for the connecting flight to Guadalajara has disappeared, and Belano realises, with a deepening sense of relief, that he has no desire to go to Guadalajara and take part in the Book Fair; what he wants to do is to stay in Mexico City. And that is what he does. He heads for the exit. His passport is examined, and soon he's outside, looking for a taxi.

Back in Mexico, he thinks.

The taxi driver looks at him as if he were an old acquaintance. Belano has heard stories about the taxi drivers of Mexico City and muggings in the vicinity of the airport. But all those stories vanish now. Where are we going, young man? asks the driver, who is younger than Belano. Belano gives him the most recent address that he has for Ulises Lima. OK, says the driver, and the taxi pulls away and plunges into the city. Belano shuts his eyes, the way he used to when he lived there, but now he's so tired that he opens them almost immediately, and his old city, the city of his adolescence, displays itself to him for free. Nothing has changed, he thinks, although he knows that everything has changed.

It's a cemetery morning. The sky's a dirty yellow. The clouds, moving slowly from south to north, look like graveyards adrift; sometimes they part to reveal scraps of grey sky, sometimes they come together with a dry, earthy grinding that no one, not even Belano, can hear, but it gives him a headache, the way it did when he was an adolescent and lived in Colonia Lindavista or Colonia Guadalupe-Tepeyac.

The people walking on the sidewalks, however, are the same; they're younger, they probably hadn't even been born when he left, but basically these are the faces he saw in 1968, in 1974, in 1976. The taxi driver tries to engage him in conversation, but Belano doesn't feel like talking. When he can finally close his eyes again, he sees his taxi driving at full speed down a busy avenue, while robbers hold up other taxis and the passengers die with terrified expressions on their faces. Vaguely familiar gestures and words. Fear. Then he sees nothing and falls asleep the way a stone falls down a well.

Here we are, says the taxi driver.

Belano looks out of the window. They're in the street where Ulises Lima used to live. He pays and gets out. Is this your first time in Mexico? asks the driver. No, I used to live here. Are you Mexican? the driver asks as he gives him the change. More or less, says Belano.

Then he's standing alone on the sidewalk, looking at the façade of the building.

Belano's hair is short. A bald patch like a tonsure reveals the top of his scalp. He's no longer the long-haired youth who once roamed these streets. Now he's wearing a black leather jacket and grey trousers and a white shirt and a pair of

Death of Ulises

Martinelli shoes. He's been invited to Mexico to participate in a conference that will gather a group of Latin American writers. At least two of his friends have also been invited. His books are read (a bit) in Spain and Latin America, and all of them have been translated into various languages. What am I doing here? he wonders.

He walks towards the entrance of the building. He takes out his address book. He presses the buzzer of the apartment where Ulises Lima used to live. Three long buzzes. No one answers. He buzzes another apartment. A woman's voice asks who it is. I'm a friend of Ulises Lima, says Belano. She hangs up abruptly. He buzzes another apartment. A man's voice shouts, Who is it? A friend of Ulises Lima, says Belano, feeling more and more ridiculous. The door opens with an electric click, and Belano starts climbing the stairs to the third floor. By the time he reaches the landing, the effort is making him sweat. There are three doors and a long, dimly lit corridor. This is where Ulises Lima spent the last days of his life, he thinks, but when he rings the doorbell he finds himself irrationally hoping to hear his friend's approaching steps and then to see his smiling face appear at the crack in the door.

Nobody answers.

Belano goes back down the stairs. He finds a hotel nearby, without having to leave Colonia Cuauhtémoc. He sits on the bed for a long time, watching Mexican television and letting his mind go blank. Not a single show is familiar, but somehow the old shows infiltrate the new ones, and Belano has the impression that he can see the face of El Loco Valdés on the screen or hear his voice. Later, channel surfing, he comes across a Tin-Tan movie and watches to the end. Tin-Tan was El Loco's elder brother. He was already dead when

Belano came to live in Mexico. El Loco Valdés might be dead now too.

When the movie's over, Belano takes a shower and then, without even drying himself, he calls a friend. No one's home. Just the answering machine, but Belano doesn't want to leave a message.

He hangs up. He gets dressed. He goes to the window and looks out at Calle Río Panuco. He doesn't see people or cars or trees, only the grey pavement and a calm that has something timeless about it. Then a boy appears, walking down the opposite sidewalk with a young woman who might be his big sister or his mother. Belano shuts his eyes.

He isn't hungry, he isn't sleepy, he doesn't feel like going out. So he sits down on the bed again and goes on watching television, smoking one cigarette after another, until he finishes the pack. Then he puts on his black leather jacket and goes out into the street.

Irresistibly, the way a hit song keeps playing in your head, he finds himself returning to Ulises Lima's apartment.

The sun is beginning to set over Mexico City when, after a series of fruitless attempts, Belano succeeds in getting someone in the building to buzz him through the street door. I must be going crazy, he thinks, as he climbs the stairs two by two. Nothing's affecting me: the altitude, not having eaten, being alone in Mexico City. For a few interminable and, in their way, happy seconds, he stands in front of Ulises's door without ringing. Then he presses the button three times. As he is turning to go, about to leave the building (though not for the last time, he knows that), the door of the adjacent apartment opens and an enormous, hairless, coppery head, on which slashes of red can be dimly made out (as if the

Death of Ulises

possessor of the head had been painting a wall or a ceiling), emerges and asks him who he's looking for.

At first, Belano doesn't know what to say. There's no point saying he's looking for Ulises Lima, and he can't be bothered making something up, so he keeps quiet and looks at his interlocutor: the head belongs to a young man, he wouldn't be more than twenty-five, and from his expression Belano guesses that he's annoyed or lives in a permanent state of annoyance. It's empty, that place, says the young man. I know, says Belano. So what are you ringing for, idiot? says the young man. Belano looks him in the eye and says nothing. The door opens and the hairless young man comes out into the corridor. He's fat, and all he's wearing is a pair of baggy jeans held up by an old belt. The buckle, partly hidden by the young man's belly, is large and made of metal. Is he coming out to hit me? wonders Belano. For a moment they examine each other. Our hero Arturo Belano, dear readers, is forty-six by this stage, and as you all know, or should know, his liver, his pancreas and even his colon are in a bad way, but he still knows how to box, and he's sizing up the voluminous figure in front of him. When he lived in Mexico he got into plenty of fights and never lost, though it's hard to credit now. Schoolyard scraps and barroom brawls. Belano looks at the fat guy, trying to figure out when to attack, when to hit him and where. But the fat guy just stares at Belano and looks back into his apartment, and then another young man appears, wearing a brown sweatshirt with a transfer on it that shows three men striking defiant poses in the middle of a street full of trash, and 'Los Amos del Barrio' written in red letters at the top.

Belano is momentarily hypnotised by the design. Those

pathetic-looking guys on the sweatshirt seem familiar. Or maybe not. Maybe it's the street that seems familiar. I've been there, years ago, he thinks, years ago I walked down that street, with time on my hands, just looking around.

The guy in the sweatshirt, who's almost as fat as the other one, asks Belano something in a voice that sounds like water boiling. Belano doesn't understand. But it wasn't an aggressive question, he's sure of that. What? he asks. Are you a fan of Los Amos del Barrio? repeats the fat guy in the sweatshirt.

Belano smiles. No, I'm not from here, he says.

Then the second fat guy is pushed aside and a third fat guy appears; he's very dark, an Aztec kind of fat guy with a little moustache, and he asks his roommates what's going on. Three against one, thinks Belano, time to go. The fat guy with the little moustache looks at him and asks what he wants. This jerk was ringing the bell at Ulises Lima's place, says the first fat guy. Did you know Ulises Lima? asks the fat guy with the little moustache. Yes, says Belano, I was a friend of his. And what's your name, jerk? asks the fat guy in the sweatshirt. Arturo Belano says his name and then adds that he'll be on his way, he's sorry to have bothered them, but now the three fat guys are looking at him with real interest, as if they were seeing him from a different point of view, and the fat guy in the sweatshirt smiles and says, Cut the bullshit, your name can't be Arturo Belano, though from the way he says it, Belano can tell that although he's unconvinced, he'd like to believe it's true.

Then he sees himself – and it's as if he's watching a movie, a movie so sad he'd never go to see it – in the fat guys' apartment, and they're offering their guest a beer. No thanks, I

Death of Ulises

don't drink any more, he says, sitting in a rickety armchair, its cloth cover printed with wilting flowers, holding a glass of water he can't bring himself to drink from, because the water in Mexico City, so he's been warned, though in fact he's always known this, can give you gastroenteritis, while the fat guys settle down in the surrounding armchairs, except for the one without a shirt, who sits on the floor, as if he's afraid the other chair might break under his weight or afraid of how his friends might react if it did.

The fat guy without a shirt is behaving a bit like a slave, Belano thinks.

What happens next is chaotic and sentimental: the fat guys inform him that they were the last disciples of Ulises Lima (that's the word they use: *disciples*). They tell Belano about his death, how he was run down by a mysterious car, a black Impala, and they talk about his life, a succession of legendary drinking bouts, as if the bars and rooms where Ulises Lima got sick and threw up were the successive volumes of his complete works. But mainly they talk about themselves: they have a rock group called El Ojete de Morelos and they perform in discos in the suburbs of Mexico City. They've made a record, which the official radio stations won't touch because of the lyrics. But the little stations play their songs all day long. We're getting famous, they say, but we're still rebels. The way of Ulises Lima, they say, Ulises Lima's tracer fire, the poetry of Mexico's greatest poet.

As good as their word, they put on a CD of their songs, and Belano sits there motionless, listening, with his hand clamped around the glass of water he still hasn't sipped from, looking at the dirty floor and the walls covered with posters for Los Amos del Barrio and El Ojete de Morelos and other bands he's never heard of, maybe they're earlier groups, whose members went on to form Los Amos and El Ojete: Mexican kids staring out at him from photos or from hell, holding their electric guitars as if they were brandishing weapons or freezing to death.

The Troublemaker

Some of his works were shown in 2003, during the European protests against the war in Iraq, at an exhibition organised by the poet Ponç Altés: mere sketches, as the artist pointed out himself, trials, private exercises done in some anonymous and dingy room. About Vallirana, there is little to be said: he was young, just twenty-one, unemployed, and he came from a family that was relatively poor (but loving: they supported him). His literary tastes were still developing, although he had, by then, read the complete works of Alfred Jarry, his favourite writer, whose radiance the passing days could do nothing to dim. As to Vallirana's personality at that time, the accounts diverge. Generally speaking, it could be said that he was a somewhat (though not excessively) reserved young man and somewhat shy (although his shyness was not excessive either). He believed only in art and science. For him, the union of art and science was a matter of *work*. In that sense it could be said that he was deeply Catalonian. God and chance belonged to art, eternity and labyrinths to science. When the protests against the war in Iraq began, he spent three days shut up in his room, like those young men in Japan who retreat to a tiny bedroom in the family home and refuse to come out again to look for work or go shopping or see a movie or take a walk in the park. Being an only child and living in El Masnou, not Tokyo, Vallirana had a larger bedroom, and he spent only three days in there, watching television almost nonstop (there was a set at the foot of his bed), barely sleeping, following the protests, and thinking. When the three days were over, he went up onto the roof and made a little sign. The sign said: 'NO WAR – LONG LIVE SADDAM HUSSEIN'. He wrote it in Roman square capitals – the result was rather stylish – on a modest-sized sheet of white cardboard, which he stapled onto a wooden stick about four feet long. In a moment of malicious inspiration, he illustrated both sides of the sign with little flowers that looked more like four-leafed clovers. The next day he took the train to Barcelona and participated in an anti-war demonstration in Hospitalet, which was poorly attended, but that night he joined the crowd banging pots and pans in Plaza San Jaume, and held his sign up high. No one said anything to him in Hospitalet. Or in Plaza San Jaume, where Vallirana contributed powerfully to the racket with an umpire's whistle. He missed the last train back to El Masnou and slept on a bench in the subway along with the homeless. The next day he took part in a march with students from the Universidad Autónoma, who chanted antiwar and anti-US slogans as they walked from the campus to Sarrià, stopping the traffic on numerous occasions. A girl who was studying journalism came up to him as they crossed one of the ring roads and said that she was against the war but that didn't mean she supported Saddam Hussein. The girl was called Dolors, and Vallirana told her that his name was Enric de Montherlant. When the demonstration was over, they went to have coffee on Plaza de Sarrià, and agreed to meet the following day and join the big march from the Rambla de Catalunya to Plaza Catalunya. Then Vallirana went back to El Masnou, where he took a shower and changed his clothes, vaguely suspecting that he had picked up fleas the previous night. His whole body was, as it turned out, covered with tiny, bright red bites. Before going to sleep, Vallirana made a great many notes. He asked himself questions. And he didn't choose the lazy solution of leaving them all unanswered. When he'd finished writing, he went up to the rooftop terrace and made another sign. This one said: 'NO WAR – LONG LIVE THE IRAQI PEOPLE – DEATH TO THE JEWS'. The first phrase, NO WAR, was written in big letters, the second in smaller ones, and the third in letters that were smaller again. The characters had curves and twists that were vaguely reminiscent of Arabic script. Comic-book Arabic script. On both sides of the sign he drew peace symbols. When he had finished he said to himself: Now let's see what happens. Then he dined on a ham sandwich and tomato bread, and shut himself in his room and masturbated, thinking about Dolors, until he fell asleep, the TV on with the volume turned down so as not to bother his parents. First thing the next morning he caught a train. In his carriage there were labourers and students, but mainly commuters on the way to the office, men wearing ties and women in respectable, ugly suits, although, here and there, he could see a few people dressed with a little more taste, who didn't seem completely resigned to leading failed lives. These individuals seemed to have staked everything on sex and seduction, on attracting and being attracted, which wasn't much, thought Vallirana, but at least it was something. The others made a pitiful showing: women with glasses and too much fat on their hips and thighs, men who could only inspire disgust if they stripped off in a bedroom. As for the labourers, who were easily identifiable by their blue or yellow overalls and their lunch boxes or foil-wrapped sandwiches, they seemed to be in another world; and to a large extent they were, since most of them were immigrants from Africa or South America, who didn't care what the Spanish were doing. The students were dozing or going over their notes. When the train went into the tunnel in Barcelona, before reaching the Arco del Triunfo station, Vallirana shouted, 'No war!' Some of the passengers, it seemed, were woken by the shout, and others were scared, but after the initial moment of surprise, almost everyone in the carriage responded by taking up the cry: 'No war!'

Sevilla Kills Me

1. *The title*. In theory, and with no input from me whatsoever, the title of my talk was supposed to be 'Where does the new Latin American novel come from?' If I stay on topic, my answer will be about three minutes long. We come from the middle classes or from a more or less settled proletariat or from families of low-level drug traffickers who're tired of gunshots and want respectability instead. As Pere Gimferrer says: in the old days, writers came from the upper classes or the aristocracy, and by choosing literature they chose – at least for a certain period that might be a lifetime or four or five years – social censure, the destruction of learned values, mockery and constant criticism. Now, on the other hand, especially in Latin America, writers come from the lower middle classes or from the ranks of the proletariat and what they want, at the end of the day, is a light veneer of respectability. That is, writers today seek recognition, though not the recognition of their peers but of what are often called 'political authorities', the usurpers of power, whatever century it is (the young writers don't care!), and thereby the recognition of the public, or book sales, which makes publishers happy but makes writers even happier, because these are writers who, as children at home, saw how

hard it is to work eight hours a day, or nine or ten, which was how long their parents worked, and this was when there was work, because the only thing worse than working ten hours a day is not being able to work at all and having to drag oneself around looking for a job (paid, of course) in the labyrinth, or worse, in the hideous crossword puzzle of Latin America. So young writers have been burned, as they say, and they devote themselves body and soul to selling. Some rely more on their bodies, others on their souls, but in the end it's all about selling. What doesn't sell? Ah, that's an important consideration. Disruption doesn't sell. Writing that plumbs the depths with open eyes doesn't sell. For example: Macedonio Fernández doesn't sell. Macedonio may have been one of Borges's three great teachers (and Borges is or should be at the centre of our canon) but never mind that. Everything says that we should read him, but Macedonio doesn't sell, so forget him. If Lamborghini doesn't sell, so much for Lamborghini. Wilcock is only known in Argentina and only by a few lucky readers. Forget Wilcock, then. Where does the new Latin American literature come from? The answer is very simple. It comes from fear. It comes from the terrible (and in a certain way fairly understandable) fear of working in an office and selling cheap trash on the Paseo Ahumada. It comes from the desire for respectability, which is simply a cover for fear. To those who don't know any better, we might seem like extras from a New York gangster movie, always talking about respect. Frankly, at first glance we're a pitiful group of writers in our thirties and forties, along with the occasional fifty-year-old, waiting for Godot, which in this case is the Nobel, the Rulfo, the Cervantes, the Príncipe de Asturias, the Rómulo Gallegos.

Sevilla Kills Me

2. *The lecture must go on.* I hope no one takes what I just said the wrong way. I was kidding. I didn't mean what I wrote, or what I said. At this stage in my life I don't want to make any more unnecessary enemies. I'm here because I want to teach you to be men. Not true. Just kidding. Actually, it makes me insanely envious to look at you. Not just you but all young Latin American writers. You have a future, I promise you. Sorry. Kidding again. Your future is as grey as the dictatorship of Castro, of Stroessner, of Pinochet, as the countless corrupt governments that follow one after the other on our continent. I hope no one tries to challenge me to a fight. I can't fight without medical authorisation. In fact, when this talk is over I plan to lock myself in my room to watch pornography. You want me to visit the Cartuja? Fuck that. You want me to go see some flamenco? Wrong again. The only thing I'll see is a rodeo, Mexican or Chilean or Argentine. And once I'm there, amid the smell of fresh horse shit and flowering Chile-bells, I'll fall asleep and dream.

3. *The lecture must plant its feet firmly on the ground.* That's right. Let's plant our feet firmly on the ground. Some of the writers here are people I call friends. From them I expect nothing but perfect consideration. The rest of you I don't know, but I've read some of you and heard excellent things about others. Of course, certain writers are missing, writers without whom there's no understanding this entelechy that we call new Latin American literature. It's only fair to list them. I'll begin with the most difficult, a radical writer if there ever was one: Daniel Sada. And then I should mention César Aira, Juan Villoro, Alan Pauls, Rodrigo Rey Rosa, Ibsen Martínez,

Carmen Boullosa, the very young Antonio Ungar, the Chileans Gonzalo Contreras, Pedro Lemebel, Jaime Collyer, Alberto Fuguet, and María Moreno, and Mario Bellatin, who has the fortune or misfortune of being considered Mexican by the Mexicans and Peruvian by the Peruvians, and I could go on like this for at least another minute. It's a promising scene, especially if viewed from a bridge. The river is wide and mighty and its surface is broken by the heads of at least twenty-five writers under fifty, under forty, under thirty. How many will drown? I'd say all of them.

4. *The inheritance.* The treasure left to us by our parents, or by those we thought were our putative parents, is pitiful. In fact, we're like children trapped in the mansion of a paedophile. Some of you will say that it's better to be at the mercy of a paedophile than a killer. You're right. But our paedophiles are also killers.

NATASHA WIMMER

The Days of Chaos

Just when Arturo Belano thought that all his adventures were over and done with, his wife, the woman who had been his wife and still was and probably would be until the end of his days (legally speaking, at least), came to see him in his apartment by the sea and announced that their son, the handsome young Gerónimo, had disappeared in Berlin during the Days of Chaos.

This was in the year 2005.

Arturo packed his bags and that night he boarded a plane bound for Berlin. He arrived at three in the morning. From the window of the taxi he observed that the city was at least outwardly calm, although he glimpsed the vehicles of the riot police and fires burning here and there in the streets. But in general everything seemed calm; the city was under sedation.

This was in the year 2005.

Arturo Belano was over fifty and Gerónimo was fifteen. Géronimo had gone to Berlin with a group of friends; it was the first time he'd travelled without one of his parents. The morning Arturo's wife came over, the group had just returned, minus Gerónimo and another boy called Félix, whom Arturo remembered as very tall and thin and pimply. Arturo had known Félix since the kid was five years old. Sometimes, when he went to pick up his son from school, Félix and Gerónimo would stay and play in the park for a while. In fact, they might even have met one another for the first time in preschool, before either of them was three, though Arturo couldn't remember having seen Félix's face back then. Félix wasn't his son's best friend, but there was a kind of familiarity between them.

This was in the year 2005.

Gerónimo Belano was fifteen. Arturo Belano was over fifty, and sometimes he could barely believe that he was still alive. Arturo had set off on his first long trip at the age of fifteen too. His parents had decided to leave Chile and start a new life in Mexico.

Permissions

Last Evenings on Earth

This work was originally published with a subsidy from the Directorate-General of Books, Archives and Libraries of the Spanish Ministry of Culture.

The Return

Grateful acknowledgement is made to the magazines where some of these stories originally appeared: *Harper's*, the *New Yorker* and *Playboy*.

The Insufferable Gaucho

The translation of 'Brise Marine' ('Sea Breeze') by Stéphane Mallarmé in 'Literature + Illness = Illness' is by E. H. and A. M. Blackmore, and is quoted from *Six French Poets of the Nineteenth Century* (Oxford, Oxford University Press, 2000). The translation of 'Le Voyage' ('Travellers') by Charles Baudelaire in 'Literature + Illness = Illness' is by Richard Howard, and is quoted from *Les Fleurs du mal: The Complete Text of The Flowers of Evil* (London, Picador, 1987). In 'The Myths of Cthulhu', 'Hear this. To the right hand side of the routine signpost (coming – of course from north-northwest), right where a bored skeleton yawns' is a slightly modified version of Andrew Hurley's translation of some lines of poetry in Jorge Luis Borges's story 'The Aleph' (in *Collected Fictions*, Viking, New York, 1998).

Grateful acknowledgment is made to *Harper's*, the *New Yorker* and *Zoetrope*, where some of this material first appeared.

Posthumous Stories

Grateful acknowledgement is made to the magazines where some of these stories originally appeared: *Granta*, *Harper's* and the *New Yorker*.

Three pieces, 'Vagaries of the Literature of Doom', 'Beach' and 'Sevilla Kills Me', appeared in Roberto Bolaño's *Between Parentheses* (Picador, 2012), and are included here in Natasha Wimmer's translations. These pieces appeared in the original Spanish editions of both *El secreto del mal* and *Entre paréntesis*.